THE LAST GHOSTRIDER

Quillquest Books

USA

PRAISE FOR THE LAST GHOSTRIDER

"When I thought it couldn't get any funnier it did and I laughed till I cried, then it hit me like a freight train with the reality of the war, reminding me we are just kids in uniform putting our lives on the line. This is a soldier's book expressed through a soldier's eyes, not a career officer's self serving after action report."

~ Sgt. John Maynard
442nd Infantry, U.S. Army

"...The Last Ghostrider, while a fictionalized account of Sgt Fusco's personal view of his life in the Army and the war he chose to participate in, is set in real places and recounts real events that actually happened. As a result it is a very compelling journey, riveting in its ability to grasp the reader's attention and hold it, making him wonder what is the next adventure our Remington Raider will encounter. Fusco encounters a myriad of situations that will make the reader feel the emotion and intensity of the situation, visualize the hazardous terrain of II Corps, and understand those emotions that can only be experienced by the individual soldier in combat. The Last Ghostrider accurately captures the esprit of the unit, their commitment to mission and their fellow Ghostriders."

~ Capt. John Salonich, (Ghostrider 19)
U.S. Army, Ret.

"Reading this book was an honest and humorous journey from civilian life to the Army and the Vietnam War from the perspective of a middle class American Caucasion male who was trying to do the right thing at the wrong time, just like me."

~ Capt. Daniel White, (Ghostrider 26)
U.S. Army, Ret.

Quillquest Books

A division of the Quillquest Publishing Co.

Quillquest Books, Quillquest Junior Books, Quillquest Classic Books,
and the sailing quill are the exclusive trademarks of the Quillquest
Publishing Co., Quillquest Enterprises, Virginia, USA.
For information or comment regarding this book contact:
Quillquestbooks@msn.com

This book is a work of fiction. Names, characters,
businesses, organizations, places, events, and incidents
are either the product of the author's imagination or are
used fictitiously.

ISBN-10: 0-940075-09-1

ISBN-13: 978-0-940075-09-2

Also by Frank Mosco

Fiction_____

The Whitemoon Crisis
Monkey
Cane's Gate

Nonfiction_____

Adventures in Black & White, Vol 1
People, Places & Things

Adventures in Black & White, Vol 2
Native American Dancers

Cybersafe
What you need to know to safely navigate the Internet

Film Scripts_____

The Last Jazz
Cane's Gate
A Monkey Tale

A SPECIAL THANKS...

Were this book a run of the mill non-fiction combat chronicle I would probably have relied on the interviews, reports, and memories of dozens of my former fellow Ghostriders, but being it is fiction I needed only enough reality to make the story work, which was already abundantly available from personal experience and written accounts. Most all of the combat segments of the book are based on actual events, still there were memories to be sparked and blanks to be filled in to compensate for my sometimes inadequate research and to camouflage my auctorial shortcomings. For this I turned to a few fellow Ghostriders to which I would like to express my sincere gratitude.

189th AHC pilot Captain John Salonich, Ghostrider 19, (Spoon 6), U.S. Army retired, who is an encyclopedia of our time and place in the highlands of Vietnam and was always willing to fill in the blanks of my rusty 38-year-old memories.

189th AHC pilot, Captain Daniel White, Ghostrider 26, (Hickory Grove), U.S. Army retired, another of those magnificent men in their Ghostrider flying machines who laid it all on the line and shared a few experiences.

And in addition - a special thanks and tribute to the late Colonel David H. Hackworth, whose example and pen showed me that a little uninhibited truth can travel far and influence people, even in fiction.

THIS BOOK IS DEDICATED TO MY HEROES...

My late father

Francis Ralph Mosco,
SSG, 2nd Armored Division,
U.S. Army service from 1939-1945
North Africa, Sicily, Europe, WWII

My son

Daniel Vincent Mosco,
SP4, 1st Infantry Division,
U.S. Army service 2003-2006
Samara, Iraq, 2004-05

And to

All of my fellow Ghostriders
who wore this patch
from 1966 to 1971, Vietnam.
(even the *beaucoup dien cai dau*)

PREFACE

In the year of my birth, 1949, two things happened that would come together to determine an important part of my life. One was the communist somehow obtained the atomic bomb, which instantly permiated the halls of the world's democracies with fear and paranoia, and the other was a hit song called *Ghostriders In The Sky*.

I tried three times over the years to write a book about Vietnam, not because I felt it was a book that needed to be written - there were probably hundreds already on the shelves and a thousand more on the way - but because it was a book I promised I would write. I said it to a few fellow Ghostriders back in 1970 and when they asked me what kind of book it would be, I simply shrugged my shoulders and told them I wasn't sure because at the time I wasn't sure what the hell the Vietnam War was about. "But," I said, "it will probably be a little different than most because this damn war sure as hell is different." Not that I had any firsthand knowledge of other wars. I was young and stupid and we were all inebriated at the time, but a promise is a promise, and after 38 years it's a promise I finally managed to keep.

On each attempt to write a book about the Ghostriders I reached a deadend after only a few chapters when I came to realize I wasn't writing anything that seemed original and was taking the same approach as a hundred other writers. Most importantly, I felt I simply didn't know enough or felt I really wasn't qualified to write something with any degree of authority that would do justice to the subject. Then finally with the help of a young new generation soldier soon to be deployed to Iraq, I realized that not knowing enough was exactly what the story was about. When laughing about the crazy characters and the often general irrational lunacy of military life, my young soldier son and I came to realize that some things in the Army never change and hadn't changed since my time in Vietnam or even my father's service during WWII. He then suggested with all clarity that that's exactly what the Ghostrider book should be. "It's been over thirty years," he said. "I think people are more than ready to laugh at the war, at least some of it anyway. Just be honest and have fun with it." Whether he was right or not, only time and the readers will testify.

For some this book might be a real hoot and for others it might bring back a few bad memories. All I know is, the book, like my tour in Vietnam, was a hell of a ride. So let me begin by saying there is absolutely nothing funny about war unless you happen to be in one, then the intensity and seriousness of it all somehow manages to accentuate those moments of humor and irony. As for not making the story a total fiction but more a *faction*, I think the following explanation should suffice.

In 1980 I was invited as a keynote speaker along with retired General William Westmoreland to address a gathering of congressional members and a few hundred upper echelon members of national veteran organizations, as well as an assortment of other dignitaries from around the country. The breakfast event was hosted by and took place at Cypress Gardens, Florida, and was for the noble purpose of promoting the acceptance and creation of the Vietnam Memorial in Washington, DC. In preparation I had written what I thought was an appropriate speech fitting the occasion and the audience in question. As I reviewed the speech however, I became increasingly uneasy and dissatisfied with its lack of sincerity and frankness. I then spent the entire night prior to the event rethinking, writing, and rewriting until finally trashing it altogether just an hour before I was to speak. I felt it lacked any real and honest impact and decided to just tell the truth as I knew it.

Apprehensive about whether my views of the war would conflict with those of General Westmoreland's, and thinking I would be facing an audience of skeptics and a generation of veterans who to date were noted for turning away and dismissing the contributions of those with whom I had served, I decided to bare all and simply speak frankly about the citizen soldiers of my generation and their Vietnam experience. Pulling no punches, I spoke of their personal sacrifices, political and moral conflicts and dilemma, and of their difficult domestic plight as unappreciated returning warriors. I compared them to those who had gone before in America's previous wars and spoke of the value to them, if to no one else, of the proposed Vietnam Memorial as an avenue of closure. As I spoke I looked into the eyes of that large silent audience and began to feel I was being negatively received as just another Vietnam vet crying in his beer. At the end of my brief twenty minute speech the audience simply sat and stared for what seemed an uncomfortable eternity until, to my surprise, they all rose and erupted in applause. Then observing more closely, I began to see not only acceptance but also understanding and surprisingly, tears, realizing that what had just taken place was a soldier had delivered an honest and sincere message to other soldiers, an unencumbered universal message which had not been filtered through some desk bound media talking head, liberal peacenik, bean counting bureaucrat, or weak-kneed politician - and the message had hit its mark. Also to my surprise the subsequent speech of General Westmoreland, the former Commander in Vietnam and Army Chief of Staff, followed in spirit and word along the lines of my own with similarly expressed resentment and political disillusionment.

At the conclusion of the event and after the media flurry, I was invited by the General to join him on a personal tour of the gardens and a private lunch. In doing so I found him to be, like many accomplished high-ranking officers, a well-read philosopher of sorts and a gentleman. I was, however, surprised and a bit taken back at his reaction when he learned my service in Vietnam was in 1970 and 71, of which he seemed to dismiss its importance by stating, *"Oh, well then, you were in an entirely different war."*

An entirely different war? Is this how the famous General regarded the nearly 100 men of my battalion who died after my arrival?

I would later realize Westmoreland was most likely speaking politically if not strategically and that perhaps from his lofty point of view he was correct, at least in some respects, some of which he may not even have been aware at the time. He was correct in that I wasn't in *his* war for he had left the country before I arrived. And let's face it, considering his potential to influence its outcome, 'Westy', for whatever reasons, didn't have the best track record when it came to Vietnam. In fact it could be said that he and his cronies quite often didn't have a clue about how to manage the war. For various reasons, however, in truth it *was* a different war in '70 and '71 and beyond, not because the enemy had changed its character or those who served were less dedicated, less willing, or less capable, or because some at home and serving in Vietnam thought the war couldn't be won. Not even because of the politics and the peaceniks, though all of that contributed. It was primarily because of the personal and collective frustration and perception by those of us who were there, of an overall effort without purpose or direction in an atmosphere of constant lethal fear, without any sense of cause or goal, noble or otherwise. In a nutshell, in the eyes and spirit of many of the enlisted men and officers alike, the latter half of the Vietnam War was the equivalent of a prison term measured in time on the calendar in anticipation of release and freedom. Though some of us went to Vietnam for career advancement, some for beer and bonuses, some unwillingly, and still others just for shits and giggles, it became for most of us a time of the indentured soldier, on average far younger than those who had served there previously, becoming shackled to a mission of self preservation, confusion and ignorance. A situation that became somehow, remarkably, and to the credit of those who endured, truly *the best of times and the worst of times*, times dedicated not to an ambiguous cause but to each other. Times of our young lives we shall never forget.

The Last Ghostrider is a fictional story told through the narrative of an enlisted soldier relating his brief happenstance Army career, most all of which was inspired by or taken from actual characters, events, and of course, my own experiences. The Ghostriders of the 189th Assault Helicopter Company were part of the 52nd Combat Aviation Battalion, based at the Camp Holloway Army Air Field in the II Corps area of operations and the Central Highlands of the Republic of South Vietnam. Though the book is inclusive of actual events based on mine or other Gostriders' and 52nd CAB Flying Dragons' eyewitness accounts, they have been rearranged or altered to maintain a continuity of story. They served as an inspiration and to incorporate the experience of military life and the war, and were sometimes included just for the hell of it. The characters names have been changed to protect the innocent, the crazies, the criminally insane and the blatantly inept, not to mention the guilty. And some characters are obviously fictitious or exaggerated.

Though it will spark many memories for those who were there, this book is not intended to be a chronological document of historic accuracy and certainly not what today is referred to as *politically correct*. In fact, had such a concept as political correctness or even such a phrase existed in Vietnam at that time in our lives it would have been the most laughably dismissed hypothesis since that put forth by the Flat Earth Society. In addition it should be noted that in many life experiences, and most assuredly in war, there can always be found extreme degrees of humor, irony, cruelty, kindness, tragedy, insensitivity, and insanity; all of those wonderful attributes of the human element that manifest themselves in times of extreme stress and conflict, and lend themselves easily to literature. Our military and the Vietnam War experience was no exception.

It is my hope *The Last Ghostrider* will be viewed as what it is, an unconventional, insightful, and irreverent journey through the perils of Army life and war, tempered with the affection of time, maturity, and hopefully a damn good resilient sense of humor. And I sincerely hope that readers will understand that the liberties taken in this book through its frankness and humor were in no way intended to belittle the true dedication, valor, achievements and sacrifices of the members of the 189th Assault Helicopter Company or any others who served honorably in the Vietnam War. The 189th AHC Ghostriders & Avengers, and other members of the 52nd Combat Aviation Battalion Flying Dragons have an indisputably long established proven valiant and respected history in the Vietnam War, and will be forever remembered and appreciated by those for which they served, supported, saved, and died.

Finally, for those of us who returned, it goes without saying we will always be humbled by the memories of others in our ranks that made the ultimate sacrifice, wherever they may be.

So lock and load, damn the rockets, screw the politicians, pop a cork or a rusty can, role another one, and tighten your Jesus nut, because like it or not this book is for…

…the *Ghostriders in the sky.*

And if they can't take a joke …

Frank Mosco

A NOVEL OF THE VIETNAM WAR BY

FRANK MOSCO

THE LAST GHOSTRIDER

A NOTE *from the author*

    Everything in this book is true except everything in this book that isn't, but probably is, or could be, and if not should be. And only those of us who were there know for sure.
    'Nuff said.

PROLOGUE

1971 – KONTUM PROVINCE, VIETNAM

~~~~/N~H/ It was dark, damn dark, black as the Devil's own soul and not a star in the sky - not that I could even see any sky. Then I heard it, then only silence, and then it came again. Closer. Voices. NVA voices. I'm dead, I thought to myself as I crouched alone in my dark hole. Sure as shit I'm a dead man. Stupid and dead, and I probably deserve it because I'm a damn fool.

"Think of it as a woman," Coma told me back at the hooch. "Ease right into her until you're ready to get your rocks off. Then you know you're in control, that you own the night and it's working for you."

A woman? Shit!

He warned me. He said it would be freaky, to not dwell on it, to just embrace it, but I honestly didn't think the night could get so dark and I sure as hell didn't think something as harmless as the absence of light could be so damn unnerving. I put my hand in front of my face and brought it in until it touched my nose, and I still couldn't see it. Okay Fusco, so it's dark, so what? You spent nights alone in the woods and hills hunting and messing around when you were a kid and it was no big deal. Yeah, that's what I told myself, but it wasn't comforting because this was different, these hills and mountains were full of death. So maybe I was a little hypersensitive. Who the hell wouldn't be?

But… embrace it? Shit!

I could imagine him over there, crouched in his camouflaged hole, laughing to himself as he visualized me quivering alone in the dark, wide eyed and scared shitless, experiencing some kind of life revealing epiphany. Hell, I didn't want that crap. I was just a pencil, a damn clerk and de facto door gunner. Sure I'd seen my share of shit and I had to deal with it like everybody else, but for some reason this gun-baring guru thought I needed an introspective adjustment, a spiritual tune-up. The weird thing is he was probably right. With all the recent events of my life I had reached a point to where I didn't know if I was coming or going. There in the pitch-black night of the central highlands of Vietnam, my mind had no problem at all wondering or wandering or even running wild, racing in every direction, including the past. Racing so damn fast I could hardly keep up. It was like the household cat parked its ass on the control button of the family slide projector, sending a hundred flashing memories into non-stop auto. And above it all I could hear things, all kinds of things. I could hear the NVA and the bastards were getting closer, and I could hear other things that weren't even there. It was damn spooky. And I could even hear my own blood rushing through my brain right along side the hundred family slides flashing from the past. It was a hell of a reality rush; bizarre, fast, and furious, yet slow, surreal, and frightening, like running back a sixty-yard punt return in front of a screaming crowd that you can't hear for the sound of your own heartbeat and heavy breathing. Suddenly each second seemed like a minute and each minute like an hour. Yeah, frightening yet exhilarating, affording me some kind of sick twisted satisfaction in knowing I was going against every natural instinct of well-being, self preservation, and survival, defying fate and a violent death. It was a rush.

Shit! Sure as hell, we're dead.

So there I huddled hidden in a dirty little hole, wrapped in 40 pounds of explosives, hugging an M-16, embracing the harsh whore of darkness, and wondering just how the hell I had gotten there in the first place. Not there in a dark covered hole scoping out an LZ but there in that damn country, in that life, in that dark hole of my soul. Suddenly I was thinking about who I was, what I was, and where I was, not to mention just how much longer I would survive to be whomever or whatever or wherever I was. And it all somehow seemed unfair, like I hadn't lived long enough to experience or know any of these things in the first place, as though I was somehow too unqualified to die. And I knew I shouldn't be thinking that shit because it wasn't the time and certainly wasn't the place. Maybe Coma was right. Maybe I did need a reality fix if for no other reason than to learn to turn everything on and off at will

and live in the moment, focusing on nothing but life and death…
on survival.

What was it he said; "You either can or you can't - so fuck the
rest and move on."

Then, just as suddenly, I remembered Leroy. For me Vietnam
began with Leroy. How was Leroy? Where was Leroy? Had there
ever even been a Leroy? Shit, I was losing it and I didn't even
know what it was I was losing.

Typical. Just fuckin' typical.

1967 – LEROY'S DILEMMA

"You're dead."

"No, I'm not dead."

"Yes."

"No."

"Yes."

"No."

"Yes. Says right here, see? Says you were killed in action," explained the Veterans Administration clerk as he toyed with his prized Hawaiian hula girl snow globe souvenir paperweight that said Waikiki Beach on the front, then moved it to the other side of his desk. He brushed back a portion of what little remaining orange-red hair he possessed that managed to hang down over his heavily freckled pale-skinned forehead, then turned the file around so Leroy could read it and pointed to the entry on the first page.

Leroy noticed a slight trembling in the man's hand and quickly deduced it wasn't nerves but more a natural thing, some form of character trait like that of an overly nervous Mexican Chihuahua dog. Oddly, the only time the trembling subsided was when the little man fondled the Hawaiian hula girl snow globe.

"See there," said the clerk. "Says, *Smith, Leroy Benjamin, Lance Corporal, United States Marine Corps, killed in action.* See? Killed... in action. Okay?"

"No, that's wrong. I'm Leroy Smith and I'm here, right here in front of you, see? See? I'm sitting right here. I'm breathing, my eyes are open, I have a pulse, I can shit, fart, piss, get a hard-on, and I want my fuckin' money and meds."

"Your G.I. insurance was paid to your mother."

"Not that money you dumb ass. You damn government people scared my mother half way to Havana when she got that. She thought I died again."

"So you admit you were dead?"

"No, I don't admit I was dead. I wasn't dead. I'm not dead. Look man, here's my DD-214. See here, says Smith, Leroy Benjamin, United States Marine Corps, separated June 12, 1967, honorably discharged. Ya see? Ya see all that?"

"Then what about the money?"

"What money?"

"The life insurance money. The dead money."

"Who said anything about dead money?"

"You did. You said, 'You wanted your money', and I said, 'It was paid to your mother', and you said, 'She took it to Havana', and I said..."

"No, I didn't say that."

"Yes. You said..."

"No."

"Yes."

"No, I didn't say that. You said that."

"I didn't say that. I mean, I did say that but I said that you said that not that I said that."

"Okay. But what about my money? And my meds?"

"What money?"

"My money. My disability money... and my meds."

"I thought you said you didn't say anything about money."

"I didn't. I said, look at my DD-214 because it says I'm not dead because I'm not dead, I'm right here."

"How do you know that isn't a mistake?"

"How the hell can it be a mistake?"

"People make mistakes you know," said the VA clerk as he again reflectively fiddled with the Hawaiian hula girl snow globe, remembering the only time in his life he ever got a blowjob. It was during the only time in his life he ever took a real vacation and went to Hawaii via some half-ass fly-by-night travel agency five-day package deal. The encounter took place at a luau after he had consumed a few drinks in the form of three tall Mai Tais and a Blue Hawaii. He was a 31-year-old virgin and she was a 62-year-old retired medical therapist from Missouri. The 19-second experience changed his life, leaving him to believe he had become an empowered man of the world and one of the beautiful people he had always heard about and seen on TV and in the movies, so he purchased the snow globe to commemorate the occasion.

"I know people make mistakes," said Leroy. "You VA people make mistakes, lots of mistakes, and you're turning my whole life into a fuckin' mistake."

Leroy touched his hand to his head anticipating yet another of his recurring migraines, a stress headache being brought on by yet another day of frustration resulting from yet another trip through the looking glass of the VA bureaucracy in an effort to obtain his disability payments, medications to combat the residual pain of his combat wounds, and the subsequent medications he needed to combat the migraine headaches resulting from his visits to the VA. It seemed to be a never-ending vicious cycle of having, each month, to convince the VA he was still alive and still in need of medical treatment. Each month a different clerk, each month a different doctor, each month a new migraine that seemed to last all month.

"You don't have to get ugly," said the clerk.

"Ugly? How the hell can I get ugly? According to you I'm dead. I can't get ugly if I'm dead can I?"

"Then you admit it's a mistake."

"What's a mistake?"

"Your status."

"What status?"

"Your status as a dead soldier."

"That's right, exactly. My status as a dead soldier is a mistake because I'm not dead."

"Not that status. Your other status."

"What other status?"

"You're L.B. Smith status. L.B. Smith is deceased."

"Yes I know. What's the difference?" asked Leroy.

"What do you mean?"

"Deceased. What's the fuckin' difference?"

"It means you're dead."

"No, that was another L.B. Smith. He's dead. I'm alive."

"No, says here he's MIA."

"No, he's not MIA. He was a black guy from Detroit and he went home in a box. He's dead. I'm a white guy from Virginia, and I'm alive."

"Says here, disposition unknown. MIA."

"MIA my ass. I saw him get his head blown off."

"Well, if he didn't have a head then how do you know it was him?"

"Because it wasn't me."

"So, L.B. Smith is dead?"

"Yes."

"Then how can you be L.B. Smith?"

"Because I was born L.B. Smith, you stupid shit. Who the hell were you when you were born?"

"I don't remember. I was too young at the time. I don't remember any of it," replied the VA clerk as he once again admired and slid the Hawaiian hula girl snow globe to the opposite side of his desk.

"Then you believe your mother?" asked Leroy.

"Of course I believe my mother. Why shouldn't I believe my mother? She wouldn't lie about a thing like that."

"Well, I believe my mother too and she says I'm L.B. Smith, her son, and she says I'm alive."

"How can you believe your mother if she ran off to Havana with your dead money? I wouldn't believe someone who ran off to Havana with my dead money. Is she a communist?" the clerk asked suspiciously as he again moved the Hawaiian hula girl snow globe back across the desk.

"No, God damnit. She's not a fuckin' communist and she didn't run off to Havana with my dead money. She sent it back but they wouldn't take it. And if you're dead then what's the fuckin' point of believing anything anyway?" reasoned Leroy as he stared curiously at the little man's Hawaiian hula girl snow globe paperweight with Waikiki Beach embossed on the front, wondering who the hell would put a hula dancer and a palm tree in a snow globe, much less buy one. The thought was as confusing to him as their conversation.

"But I'm not dead. You are," said the little man.

"I didn't say *you* were dead."

"Yes, you said…"

"No, I said…" Leroy paused in frustration, seriously considering some form of violence that would drive home his point but decided against it. "Shit man, listen," he continued. "If I'm dead, then why am I here?"

"Because you're MIA."

"No, L.B. Smith is MIA, the other L.B. Smith. But he's really not MIA because he's dead."

"So, what's the problem?"

"What's the problem?'

"The problem. What's the problem?" asked the VA clerk as he fondly stroked and again contemplated moving the Hawaiian hula girl snow globe to the other side of his desk.

"What's the problem?"

"Yes. What's the problem?"

"What do you mean, what's the problem?"

"I mean, what's the problem?"

"What's the problem?"

"Yes, the problem. What's the problem?"

"The problem is I'm gonna' frag your fuckin' ass if you don't grow a fuckin' brain in the next ten fuckin' seconds! And if you move that fuckin' snow thing again I'm gonna' take it and shove it down your fuckin' throat. Jesus Christ man, where do they find you fuckin' people anyway?"

"I'm a fully qualified civil servant Mr. Smith. An official functionary of the federal government, and as such I am not required to take verbal abuse."

"What did you call me?"

"Mr. Smith."

"Ah hah! So you admit it!"

"Admit what?"

"That I'm him, I'm Smith, L.B. Smith. You called me, *Mr. Smith*. You admit it. I'm alive."

"I'm afraid I'm not qualified to make that distinction."

Leroy sat there for a long silent moment of serious deliberation until he finally said with low slow intent, "You know, if I'm dead they can't really convict me for killing someone can they? Not even if I kill a fully qualified civil servant and functionary of the government. Can they?"

"Um... would... would you... like to speak to my supervisor?"

"Before or after I break your fuckin' neck?" smiled Leroy.

"What...what... Are you trying to be humorous?"

"Humorous? Humorous? No. Hell no. Oh hell no! There's nothing fuckin' humorous about gettin' fuckin' killed! And I should fuckin' know! Don't you fuckin' think I should fuckin' know? Because according to you I'm already dead so I should fuckin' know, right? Right?"

Leroy reached out and wrapped his large ex-Marine Corps hands around the feeble little Veterans Administration bureaucrat's neck and yanked him over the top of the desk, sending all the desktop paraphernalia crashing to the floor, including the VA clerk's precious little commemorative Hawaiian blow job hula girl glass snow globe that said Waikiki Beach on the front. It shattered sending the snowy liquid spilling out in all directions with the little hula girl's head popping off and shooting across the floor.

The man began desperately calling for help through Leroy's chokehold but with little success, being his garbled cries were hardly audible. It was a useless effort anyway since the little bureaucrat's fellow workers barely noticed, most of them with their heads down, pretending to be awake or hypnotically focused on assorted papers and files, nearly unconscious in their own little foggy world of routinization. One small middle-aged woman, however, who wore her graying hair up in adolescent pig tales with green bows that said *Age Of Aquarius* on them, did look up to discover Leroy easily handling and twisting the little man back and forth like a long experienced janitor would work a heavy, wet, limp, well seasoned mop. She stared a moment, twirled one of her pigtails around her finger with concern, then looked about the room to gauge the response of her thirty-seven fellow Veterans Administration employees, and seeing no response whatsoever from any of them, she nervously returned to her own pretense of work.

Leroy finally dropped the little bureaucrat on top of the desk.

"I'm... I'm..." choked the desperate little man. "I'm going to have you arrested."

Leroy leaned in nose-to-nose with the whimpering little man, his broad trademark shit-eating smile growing wide.

"You sorry little bastard, you don't have the balls to call the pigs on me," he said, knowing that to be arrested and prosecuted he first had to be alive and identified as such.

Unfortunately a few hours later, after a great deal of debate and confusion, the responding police officers departed with the following advice to the babbling traumatized Veterans Administration desk jockey.

"Listen buddy, thirty-eight people here say they didn't see a thing," offered the reasonably intelligent cop. "And besides, you can't charge a dead man with a crime and according to you this man is dead. Maybe you should take a vacation or get some therapy or something."

When the cop turned to leave he winked at Leroy with a salute and a, "Semper Fi, bro."

Though well intentioned, Leroy wasn't impressed by the favor of this fellow ex-Marine. While he observed the little VA man's supervisor curiously inspecting the now headless little hula girl, he again wondered to himself just how much more of this he could tolerate before he'd finally toss in the towel. Although Leroy may have appeared triumphant in his minor divergence involving the little Veterans Administration bureaucrat with the contradictory Hawaiian hula girl snow globe, from his point of view it was just another set back, another defeat, one of many. The reality was Leroy Benjamin Smith had once again lost. He once again lost the opportunity to be identified as Leroy Benjamin Smith. He once again lost the opportunity to be officially identified as a living breathing functional ex-Marine. And he had once again lost the opportunity to obtain his disability money and medications without a hassle equal to or greater than a catastrophic act of God. So went my friend Leroy's dilemma nearly every day of his post combat life. He was perhaps the most frustrated dead man I had ever known and as far as I know he remains dead and frustrated to this day, unable as they say, to even get arrested.

Leroy was a friend of mine and was pretty much my personal introduction to the Vietnam War. He had become a Marine after being expelled from a South Georgia parochial boarding school for the unforgivably sinful offense of shooting a moon at a passing high strung air-headed red headed coed from the second floor dormitory window. And it wasn't just your normal moon, it was a full fruit basket that caused her to become so upset and traumatized that she went directly to the dean of students in tears. I know this because I was there, and I know she was a high-strung airhead because I married her a few years later.

I'd known Leroy since we were kids. We met at a church sponsored summer camp in Virginia named Camp Mawava where one day while playing a pick-up game of football we caught the eye of the camp athletic director, who by chance, was also the football coach at a Jesus boarding school seven-hundred miles away in South Georgia. Seeing diamonds in the rough, the coach immediately went into a recruiting mode, spinning our heads with visions of gridiron glory and telling us that going to his Jesus school was so much fun it was just like going to Camp Mawava all year long. It sounded so appealing that a half dozen of us bought into his sales pitch and headed south, discovering after our arrival that the coach who recruited us had now deserted us, moving on to greener pastures and bigger and better things, like a paycheck that didn't bounce. So there we were, left with a part time preacher teacher coach who had never played football and with a team that had never won a game but had in fact gained national fame in its inaugural season the previous year when it made the news and the pages of Sports Illustrated by being shut out with a high school record score of 129 to 0. The only reason the score wasn't any higher was because someone was merciful enough to let the clock run continuously during the fourth quarter.

Leroy, two years ahead of me in school, had a dry but great sense of humor, a broad shit-eating smile, was physically capable, confident, and intelligent. Well, I now have my reservations about the intelligent part, after all, Leroy did join the Marine Corps, and fate and the Marines being what they are, it led to his demise. For not long after enlisting in the Marines, Leroy ended up getting blown away in some oddly named dank jungle on the other side of the planet. But that was just the beginning of Leroy's dilemma. In typical military fashion Leroy's parents were respectfully notified of his death and the pending delivery of his remains for burial. Accordingly we all mourned and waited the morbid moment of his arrival. Someone in the bureaucratic military system, however, failed to inform Leroy that *he* was required to attend the funeral as well.

At first Leroy's lack of participation was puzzling but naturally understandable. Let's face it; nobody really wants to attend his or her own funeral. And then there was the confusion and fog of war, and the logistics of transportation, and all the other excuses the Marine Corps could conjure, creating a situation not unlike lost luggage at the airport or a special-order sofa from Sears where everybody knows it's coming but who the hell actually knows when, and for that matter, if it will even be the correct color, a true mystery indeed. In time when it became obvious Leroy wasn't going to show, the situation inevitably evolved into a traumatic experience for his family. This required that serious inquiries be made, inquiries that resulted in the conclusion that Leroy's loss was, well, truly a loss, and neither L.B. Smith nor L.B. Smith ever showed up for L.B. Smith's funeral.

Then one afternoon as Leroy's mother sat in quiet bereavement in a dark corner of her home pondering the tragic loss of her only son, another government organization, the United States Post Office, showed up with a letter that inquired as to why Leroy had not lately received any mail and stating that some correspondence from home was much needed and would be more than appreciated. The letter was from Leroy of course, whom it seems had been all shot up, laid up, and a little down and out in a hospital somewhere in the Philippines. As it turned out, Leroy's entire squad had been wiped out in an ambush, including, according to the Marine Corps, L.B. Smith, and not having the identifiable body of the other L.B. Smith, declared him, L.B. Smith, to be MIA. You have to wonder as to what the odds could have been of having two Leroy Benjamin Smiths in the same squad, but more incredibly you have to wonder what over-striped genius could have maintained that situation long enough to create such a confusing post mortem state of affairs in the first place. It just goes to prove how difficult it really is to remove a square peg from a round hole once it's been forced in, at least in the military.

As we all know, the Marines are famous for extracting recruits brains and identities while in boot camp and replacing them with a cookie cutter mentality, a mentality that instills the ability to kill and die on command without question or hesitation, leaving the rest to be sorted out by God and historians - and hopefully the Corps. As for what they do with those brains and identities until the point of an individual's discharge and return to the civilian world is a mystery. Considering Leroy was a little more independent than most, as demonstrated by his willingness and ability to hang his bare ass out a window while attending a Jesus school, it's entirely possible he failed to learn this and as such failed to realize he was, by Marine Corps decree, supposed to be dead. And military paperwork being what it is, with an emphasis on quantity rather than quality, and being unable to match the correct tag with the correct toe, some future McDonald's burger bagger passing as a graves registration specialist in Vietnam decided one L.B. Smith was just as good as another L.B. Smith, the result being a KIA notice going in one direction, an MIA notice going in another direction, and a headless body going who the hell knows where but certainly not to Newport News, Virginia, or Detroit.

Okay, so war doesn't always come wrapped in proficiency. I'll be the first to admit that, especially when those performing forces involved are comprised mostly of unwilling conscript talent. Fortunately however the *Hey, why isn't anybody writing me?* letter was the ultimate responsibility of the U.S. Postal Service, not the U.S. military service, and was correctly delivered to Leroy's mother, resulting in things finally working out for the best, or at least offering up some clarification. For when Leroy did finally come home, he arrived a mental mess destined to eventually end up in hiding as a post-traumatically stressed out hermit in some old growth high altitude wilderness in Oregon. Honestly speaking, I can't say I wouldn't have done the same. After all, how long can you fight the bureaucratic fog of the Veterans Administration for much needed meds and benefits, especially when you're dead and no one wants to listen to you? Only Leroy's congressman offered a sympathetic ear, because as we all know, politicians have long appreciated votes from the netherworld. Unfortunately for Leroy, however, the joyful anticipation and belief that his congressman would right all wrongs was short lived because soon after their meeting in the great halls of Washington, Leroy's Capital Hill hopes were shattered when that same congressman was caught in an illicit affair with a young congressional page of the same gender. This not surprisingly resulted in the congressman's loss of all credibility and clout necessary to intimidate bureaucracies into admitting and correcting mistakes such as the defunct Marine Leroy Smith. After the *Page Petting* debacle no one inside or even outside the beltway would take the congressman's calls, not even Leroy. After all, he *was* a Marine.

And so it went for years until Leroy finally decided to check out altogether and move to another planet, leaving behind his

money, his meds, and many unanswered questions, including who
the hell actually ended up with an occupied body bag labeled
Lance Corporal L.B. SMITH, MEMBERS MISSING. That's the
MIA Lance Corporal L.B. Smith who was but wasn't actually the
KIA Lance Corporal L.B. Smith, not the KIA Lance Corporal L.B.
Smith who was convinced he was still alive and kicking and now
voluntarily MIA somewhere in the Northwest mountains of
Oregon with a case of Jack Daniels and a lifetime supply of
medical cannabis, and bending the ear of a smelly sympathetic
Sasquach who most assuredly knows, understands, and appreciates
what it means to be overlooked, forgotten, rejected, neglected, and
completely misunderstood.

～✦～

Now, I only mention Leroy because Leroy's dilemma was my
first real exposure to the inner workings of the military and, of
course, that *non-declared non-war* war in Southeast Asia, or the
Vietnam Conflict or *Police Action*, as some politicians in
Washington referred to it in a Pontius Pilate sort of way. The entire
L.B. Smith circus of events should have given me a heads-up of
things to come, as well as an insight as to how the world and the
U.S. Military could mess with your destiny. Like most young
American boys of the time, however, and I suppose most prior
times, I was ignorantly and excessively trusting of all my elders
and my government.

My father, a decorated Army combat veteran of World War II,
told me as I left to join the green machine, "Son, there's nothing
wrong with the Army, just most of the people in it". As I would
realize later in life, my father was usually right about most
everything and this time was no exception. He was a very
pragmatic individual who rightfully believed in the theory; *a
lesson earned is better than a lesson learned as long as it doesn't
kill you.* Later, when I was leaving for Vietnam, he volunteered an
additional quip of wisdom. "Remember," he said, "there's no such
thing as a dead hero, just some dumb son of a bitch who was in the
wrong place at the wrong time."

Quite natually I took these practical words to heart, being they
were coming from a well decorated veteran who survived some
serious combat and near death on multiple occasions with the 2nd
Armored Division in North Africa, Sicily, and Europe, and in

addition, had the guts to tell General George Patton that in a combat zone it was a stupid-ass idea to polish tanks and combat vehicles to a high sheen just for the sake of looking *spiffy*. Tanks, my father argued, that were originally and intentionally painted a subdued olive drab for obvious reasons. Naturally, being only a Sergeant, he lost the argument with Patton and everyone had to polish their tanks anyway, but they subsequently won a moral victory by bathing them in dull mud at the first opportunity. The only dumb ass in the unit who didn't mud-up his clean shiny tank was the first one to be blown away in the very next engagement. Apparently his Sherman was shining in the wrong place at the wrong time. The Army made him a hero, of course, and gave him a medal, posthumously, which my father was quick to point out didn't mean a damn thing and didn't do anybody any good except maybe the undertaker who would have gotten the business sooner or later anyway. As I said, a very practical man.

My father and his four Dago brothers all survived some intense combat with every branch of the military in both theatres of the war, the youngest again with the Marines in Korea. And they all seemingly took it in stride. But then why not, it was their duty, their generational legacy, and in their minority first-generation kick-ass immigrant nature to do so. So who was I to argue with their advice and my legacy?

I on the other hand, was the product of a whole new generation and a whole new generational mindset. Part of a generation that actually had the audacity to believe that people in their own country should take care of their own problems, or at least try. In addition, I thought someone should at least clearly define what those problems might be before they put *my* ass on the line on their behalf. Hell, was that asking too much? It's not that I was unpatriotic and I was no coward, and certainly more than willing to defend my right to pay taxes, listen to imported British-American rock and roll, drive little foreign cars made by our former enemies, and defend democracy and my country in general. The key phrase being of course, *my country*. And as I would later learn, one does tend to acquire a few doubts defending and/or dying for people with which one can't communicate, who don't seem to really give a shit, and who's only apparent purpose in life is to hustle or steal whatever isn't tattooed or super glued to my body.

So I eventually found myself heading for Asia on a government chartered commercial airliner, consuming a bag lunch and watching, but paying little attention to, the in-flight flick *Butch Cassidy and the Sundance Kid,* in which two famous Hollywood non-violent peacenik actors ran around killing people. I was soon to be stepping onto a searing tarmac in a hot confusing unventilated country I'd hardly ever heard of, and to which I had paid little or no attention while attending that live-in parochial Jesus school where there was no TV and a general attitude that all is in God's hands and right with the world as long as you can't hear it, see it, or smell it, and it doesn't dump in your own front yard. And that pretty much held true - until Leroy Smith that is. Now I found myself wondering if I was destined to share a similar fate.

CHAPTER 2

1968 – PROMISES PROMISES

The flight on the commercial airliner from Tacoma, Washington to Vietnam was the most solemn flight I would ever experience. No one spoke, no one slept, no one breathed, and the anxiety was so thick you could cut it with a banana. However, a brief interruption came in the form of a stopover in Hawaii where they actually turned us loose and let us wander around the airport for a while. There we were in boonie fatigues, strolling through this open-air beautiful palm ridden tropical airport, politely ogling the girls in hip-huggers and being politely but totally ignored by the airport patrons as though we were invisible. I felt as though I were walking naked yet somehow unnoticed, as in one of those dreams often had by insecure pubescents where butt and balls are dangling right there in the middle of the hall in front of God and the entire student body. It's not that I expected to be stared at, even though a plane load of soldiers wasn't typical in an airport, it's that I wasn't expecting to be completely ignored. It was as though the Baltimore Colts had just run out of the locker room and on to the field at Memorial Stadium and the fans didn't even notice. We were the home team all right, but we were being treated like we just got off the special bus for a tour through the zoo.

Surprisingly, considering the attitude of the times and the fact most of my fellow passengers were draftees, no one of our group hotfooted it to freedom. I have to admit the possibility certainly crossed my mind and I'm sure it must have flashed through everyone else's as well, especially the draftees. As for me, it wasn't so much a thought of patriotic desertion but more the fact that this was Hawaii. Hell, it was Hawaii! Paradise! The South Pacific! It was the place where Elvis did the rockahula. It was TV's Hawaiian Eye, Michener's Adventures In Paradise, and the home of hula girl souvenir snow globes. I had visions of Fletcher Christian and the gang groovin' at a pig roast with beautiful topless women, John Wayne bar fights over spilled coconut drinks, and high times and romantic music at places with exotic names like Bali Hai and Boola Boola. But all we were getting to see now was the damn airport and some beautiful but snobby young longhaired long legged lovelies in hip huggers and skimpy halter tops. We were like starving men walking past a bakery full of aromatic delights just out of the oven, or a pack of horny hound dogs looking at an in-heat sexy French Poodle in a pet shop window. It was having a ten million dollar lottery ticket with all the right numbers except the last, which was just one digit short. For us, this paradise just wasn't going to happen.

In reality, however, it was also more than that. I suppose you could say it was the first phase of some sort of out of country psychological desperation coming over us. Hawaii was the last vestige of English speaking civilization as we knew it, even though we didn't know it at the time, and somewhere inside me as we lifted off the runway and continued on our journey, I was mentally and emotionally clawing, digging my fingernails into the seat and reaching out to that isolated chunk of American paradise in the middle of the ocean, saying to myself, *Hey, wait a minute! I'd like to reconsider. I think I was temporarily insane when I volunteered for Vietnam, and besides, my wife can't cook anything but tuna casserole and Kool-Aid and I don't want my kid to grow up anemic.* The gods of appeal weren't listening, however, and the hip huggers and pristine palm gardens shrunk to a small spot in the Pacific Ocean only to be replaced by anxious concocted visions of places, faces, and horrors yet to be realized. I couldn't pretend I was somewhere else nor could I pretend I was going somewhere else. Reality, as usual, was a real bitch.

Another brief break was a stop on Wake Island, which was nothing more than an airstrip somehow squeezed onto a small peace of desolate horseshoe shaped coral surrounding an emerald lagoon. Here we off-loaded into a cracker box terminal and out the other side where we had a few minutes to walk around and view partially buried rusted remnants of WWII along the beach. It was hard to believe so many men fought and died on that little atoll back in the forties. Hell, it was hard to believe that many men even had room to live on that barren piece of shell rock moreover build an airstrip there. And it hadn't been too many years ago that President Truman and the noted military philosophical blowhard General MacArthur met there to measure their penises over another non-war war back when many of us were in diapers.

Newer generations and I didn't know much about this place and older generations were fast forgetting it. It was like stepping into the past and I wondered if I would soon have anything in common with the Americans who served and died there. Would I be forgotten like them?

How our Boeing 707 managed to even land on Wake Island was a mystery. The short runway ran pretty much from water's edge to water's edge and at the end of it, just off the beach and sticking out of the water, was another large aircraft from who knows what era, 1940's or yesterday. However old the plane might have been, it was an unnerving reminder of what could be and an unnerving experience seeing it when we landed and while taking off. Rocketing down the runway, that unfortunate aircraft in the water, now serving as a marine habitat, touted and warned us that there, but for the grace of aerospace technology and a damn good pilot, go we.

Once again airborne and for lack of any other thought, I tried to remember and make sense of the whirlwind of circumstances that brought me to this point in time and space. It all seemed like a million years ago yet only yesterday, with the emotions as conflicting as the memories of ironies, lunacy, hilarity, and unpredictable decision outcomes taking place in the person of someone other than myself. I felt as though I were an outside observer or frozen in a dream from which there was no escape, being forced to watch the entire feature from start to finish with no input and no will of my own. Some may call it destiny, others may call it fate, in the enlisted man's Army it was called a great many things, most of which boiled down to intentionally or unintentionally getting shafted. With me, Specialist Fourth Class Vincent E. Fusco of Annapolis, Maryland, like millions of others, the journey began in 1968 with the infamous Army recruiter.

Most everyone was getting drafted so why should I be any different? After all, I wasn't going to join the clergy and I wasn't going right off to college because I felt after twelve years of education I deserved a brain break. I didn't have the money for it anyway and was too stupid to know, and had never been informed by the educational system, that the government had a host of loans and grant programs for people with half a brain who wanted to continue to improve the other half in an institution of higher learning. In addition, I was too proud and unconnected to fake a deferring ailment, permanent disability, or even retardation, not that I would even try, and I sure as hell wasn't gay or about to claim I was. Complicating the situation was the fact that good jobs were scarce if you were of draft age and likely to be or yet to be drafted, or for that matter, had already been drafted, served and returned home and as a result were not employable because you were considered to be a drug crazed baby killer - thank you Hollywood. So thinking I would soon be drafted and getting pressured by my father to *do something productive,* I thought – at his insistence - that I would enlist and in doing so, was determined to become something other than a run of the mill grunt, one of those unfortunates who ate, drank, crapped, fought, and died in the mud at the whim and guidance of the commissioned who, being anointed by an act of Congress, may or may not know shit from combat Shinola. As my father once said, "There's nothing more dangerous than a 2nd Lieutenant."

Getting drafted was a crapshoot no matter how you looked at it. So okay, I thought, I'll do my duty but come out of the experience with a skill that would not only uphold the family fighting tradition and make the home folks proud but also help get chicks and money. I would be, I decided proudly, *a fly guy.* Hell, it's no big deal. After all the military was just a longer ball game with a bigger locker room. At the time I even considered, though briefly, a military career. And so, while my father waited in his truck, I ventured into the downtown post office/federal building where there could be found the most talented used car salesmen on the planet, better known as military recruiters.

They were all there on the second floor, each recruiting office next to the other, lined up like little cubby boxes in my grandmother's chicken coup. First in line, and my first stop, was the Air Force where I was eagerly greeted with a blue suited smile. By the way, recruiters are the only people in the military who always smile on the job. This is due to a number of reasons, the most prominent of which being recruiters are *short*, meaning they're most likely serving out their last duty tour and will soon be making lots of money growing aloe plants or selling aluminum siding to other veterans who bought funky old used houses with their G.I. Bill. Another reason is they are sadistic bastards who are hell bent on insuring that as many young dumb asses as possible get screwed as badly as they had been screwed when they were young dumb asses who walked into a recruiter's office. Then finally, there's the best reason of all, they're actually getting paid to do this and know that if and when the gullible recruit somehow survives and comes home to seek revenge, they will by that time be living on a houseboat in some warm obscure place thousands of miles from the scene of the crime, safely sucking beer and drawing a military pension.

"Ready to join the Air Force, son?" smiled the Air Force recruiter.

"Well that depends, sir. Can I be a pilot?"

"Sure you can. Got college? What kind of degree?"

"No sir, just high school. But I can learn anything and do anything."

"I'm sure you can but sorry, you gotta' have a college degree to fly. Got lots of other good jobs in the Air Force though."

"Well, I really want to learn to fly."

His smile quickly diminished to a forced grin. "Sorry. Why don't you try the Navy? They'll take anybody."

Try the Navy, he said. The Navy? Sure why not the Navy, I thought. I grew up on the water near the Academy at Annapolis, surrounded by Navy. And those midshipmen guys were pretty damn neat, and I hear the Navy has the best food anyway, and I could go swimming or fishing whenever I wanted, and what the hell, wings are wings. Not to mention there was that great football game each year. Rah, rah, go Navy, beat Army. So I went to the next office where I found a white suited Navy smile.

"Now there's a Navy man if ever I saw one", said the spider to the fly.

"I'm interested in learning to fly, sir. I'd like to fly."

"Sure, no problem. What kind of college degree do you have?"

"Don't have one, sir, just high school."

"Sorry, can't help you. Gotta' have some kind of college degree. But how 'bout…"

"No thanks. I want to fly."

"Well then, why don't you try the jar heads?"

"The what?"

"Marines."

"The Marines?"

"Marines. They'll take anybody. Just down the hall there."

I walked down the hall wondering why someone with a Liberal Arts Degree in basket weaving or bongo drums was better qualified to learn to fly than was I but quickly lost the thought when I entered the next office which housed both the Marine Corps recruiter and the Army recruiter. I guess it's true when they say misery loves company. The Marine guy was strategically situated immediately adjacent to the door, sitting at attention like some obedient pit bull on Prozac. I don't know if his strategy was to snatch potential recruits as soon as they passed over the threshold or to prevent them from leaving. He did, however, have an interesting and simple approach to recruiting. I looked at him and he looked at me. He kind of half-ass smiled, then said with a clear degree of skepticism, "You don't want to talk to me."

Ah ha, I thought, both a test and a challenge. Then, remembering the plight of my living dead friend Leroy, I smiled and replied, "You're right", and passed on through to the Army recruiter, one amiable Staff Sergeant Finkel.

"I want to fly," I said.

"No problem," smiled Staff Sergeant Finkel.

"I don't have any college, just high school," I said, waiting for the hammer to fall.

"No problem," smiled Staff Sergeant Finkel.

"No problem?" I said.

"Nope. No problem at all," said Staff Sergeant Finkel.

My little red warning light should have gone on at that moment but after so much rejection I was simply overwhelmed.

"What do you want to fly?" asked Staff Sergeant Finkel.

"Planes."

I wanted to request NASA but thought that might be just a little too ambitious.

"Planes?"

"Yes sir. Airplanes."

"Okay, let's see what we got here."

I glanced back at the Marine recruiter who returned my glance with the devious look of a Mexican border town hustler who just sold somebody his sister all the while claiming and swearing she was a three time virgin. I don't know why but I started to get the feeling these guys were a tag team.

The Army recruiter pulled out a volume of military opportunity the size of a New York City phone book, flipped through the pages and fingered a fixed wing program. As he did he tossed out a few qualifying questions like how old are you, are you from planet earth and, "What's your name son?"

"Fusco. Vincent Fusco," I replied.

"Well Vince, you'll have to pass the officers exam and the FAST test," warned Staff Sergeant Finkel

"Yes sir. What's a *fast* test?" I asked, thinking I'd have to run a mile under four minutes.

"Flight aptitude test. It's a brain drainer. Think you can handle it?"

"Yes sir."

"Good man. I'm counting on you son."

The Marine guy chuckled.

And so went my first encounter with my personal and attentive recruiter. I told him I knew I was likely to be drafted and was more than willing to serve my country and not afraid to fight and thought I would get a leg up on the whole draft thing. He offered a broad smile of acceptance, not because he thought I was an all-American patriotic young man, but because due to the existing political and civil climate regarding the war and the military in general, he assumed I must have been some idiotic dim-witted throwback pudfucker right off the farm and ripe for the pickin'. I'm not so sure he was wrong.

I completed a shit-pot full of paper work and was sent to Fort Holabird near Baltimore the very next morning where I spent hours filling out what seemed to me to be the very same shit-pot full of paper work I had filled out previously at Staff Sergeant Finkel's office the day before. It was as though they didn't believe me the first time and required confirmation, or perhaps it was just another standard military retention test, redundancy being a favorite military concept. My experience on the way to Holabird, however, was far more interesting than the drudgery of writing on endless government forms and stationary my name, date of birth, and every other numerical combination that had ever applied to my life and body in any way shape or form.

It happened to be in April, just after civil rights leader Martin Luther King had been assassinated, and much of the nation was in an uproar. Riots were taking place all over the country and in response martial law had been declared in many major cities. Here the Maryland National Guard was out in full force and had pretty much taken over the city of Baltimore where everything was closed and the only vehicles on the road were military and law enforcement. Along our path of travel we could see shattered store windows on nearly every street as well as a few smoldering fires and wrecked cars. Each corner sported a gun toting, locked and loaded Guardsman, while jeeps, tanks, and other OD green machines zipped around the city like Pac Man in a maze.

As we cruised along one street we caught sight of a black activist opportunist running around the corner with a contraband TV. When our bus rounded the same corner we saw him again, this time he was face down and bloodied on the sidewalk being subdued by two Guardsmen and handcuffed by a policeman. Apparently upon turning the corner he had an encounter with a patrol car, of which now had the TV protruding out of its broken windshield. Turning onto another street we came upon two jeeps and a half dozen Guardsmen who were securing a four-door sedan that had smashed headlong into the side of a building. Two of the Guardsmen were drawn down on three black men spread-eagled on the sidewalk while other Guardsmen were unloading and sorting on the ground a trunk full of serious weapons, ammo and accessories.

And all this time I thought the war was in Vietnam. Go figure.

Being just an average white kid who had pretty much minded his own business most all of his life, I had not developed any prejudices other than that awareness imposed on me by Hollywood and television, being mostly that Apache Indians were bad and would tie you to a wagon wheel and skin you alive, that the Japs were bad and would tie you to bamboo trees and skin you alive, that the Nazis had a propensity to be extremely nasty and were fond of wholesale slaughter, and that the Russians were supposedly going to bury all of us with Nikita Kruschev's nuclear shoe. Other than that there was only Howard Sweeny, the junior high school bully and resident dip-shit with the deductive powers of a potted plant, who pushed and threatened to beat the shit out of me nearly every day in the halls between classes until one day I decided he shoved me one time too many and I finally just whacked him upside the head with my oversized hardback copy of *Science For Our New Age*. It was one of those defining moments but not so much so that it afforded me the wisdom of the world. So, needless to say, all this domestic upheaval made an impression and kind of played with my naïve psyche, raising questions such as; if I join the Army will I fight over there or over here, and how can I fight over there if there's a fight over here, and who will fight over here if there's a fight over there, and who the hell are the bad guys over there and over here anyway? Hell, I still hadn't figured out North Korea and China who wasted very little time trying to kill us after we liberated their countries from Japan, or the Russians, our former allies, with their Iron Curtin and world domination routine.

Life could be confusing and unless one is being groomed to be king, just reaching the age of 19 doesn't automatically instill a world of wisdom and understanding of global affairs and cultures. Though I wasn't totally naïve, I still had residual childish and simplistic Christian beliefs, enough to lead me to trust in such basic concepts as, if you don't want to step in and smell like shit then stay the hell out of the cow pasture. What can I say, it's a genetically inherent insight. They were silly little questions but they certainly seemed important to me at the time. Just the same, I was committed now and this was my induction into the world of worldly affairs, and in spite of all this personal confusion, I somehow managed to survive my traumatic first encounter with combat on the streets of Baltimore and went on to take the officer's test, which my recruiter affectionately referred to as *The Liar's Test*, all the while keeping in mind his coaching and advice.

"Remember," he told me. "Give the answers you think they want to hear, not the answers you think and probably know are correct."

Though that sounded more like political science than military advice, I took it. I did. It worked. I passed. Gaining great insight into the underlying philosophy of the war and military leadership in general - no pun intended.

Then there came the FAST test, which was anything but fast. A five part five hour exam that would have been much easier and gone a lot faster had the Army Specialist administering the test had any decent workable knowledge of the English language. For all I knew that guy could have been an imported mix of Bulgarian, Puerto Rican and Eskimo. Before each one-hour section of the five-part test he would read the two pages of instructions with unbelievable speed then say, "You have one hour. Begin." That was the only part of his oratory I actually understood, *you have one hour, begin*, forcing me to spend the first ten minutes of my precious one hour re-reading the instructions that for some reason were more complicated than the test itself. You have one hour, begin. Yeah, right.

So there I was, left all alone in a big room with this one hour test timer, one of those kitchen gadgets that was the noisiest most irritating damn thing I had ever heard. I finally came to the conclusion the timer must have been part of the program, some tricky psychological deal of some kind designed to measure my patience, endurance, and potential under stress as an officer candidate, or to trigger my reaction as a potentially crazed maniac serial killer. With that understanding in mind, I stepped up to the challenge and somehow managed to keep my sanity and complete the test, all five one hour sections, the graded results of which were placed in a big brown sealed envelope and given to me for hand delivery to my recruiter the next day.

As instructed, promptly the next day I hand delivered the large brown envelope to Staff Sergeant Finkel who opened it with great surprise.

"I'll be damned, Fusco, you passed!" said an excited Staff Sergeant Finkel. "You know you're the first one I've had to pass that thing in six months. I'll be damned. You passed. You actually passed."

The Marine recruiter chuckled.

Now I had never considered myself to be a genius so I concluded there must have been a lot of stupid wannabe recruits out there somewhere. It never dawned on me that the really smart ones had escaped to a foreign country like Canada or Mexico or Berkeley, or mysteriously contracted some exotic draft exempting physical deformity, or that perhaps after the Bulgarian Puerto Rican Eskimo linguistic experience decided to trash the brown envelope altogether, change their name and join the Peace Corps. But pass I did, and as a result of my passing the FAST test the recruiter awarded me with a colorful certificate of guarantee for fixed wing training in the United States Army. It was impressive, looking much like some classy stock certificate, complete with the picture of an airplane. And he gave me another paper showing a date to report for induction, of which I quickly asked to be extended in order to squeeze in as much pre-military free spiriting as possible. I had heard of the delayed entry program and summer was just around the corncr. Hell, I had a lot of fishing to do. Of course he wasn't pleased with this request because it screwed up his monthly quota, but then I was after all the first recruit in six months to pass the dreaded FAST test administered by the trilingual foreign SP4 and I suppose the recruiter wasn't about to lose such a talented pudfucker fresh off the farm chump like me, so he agreed.

The Marine guy chuckled.

Half the summer came and went and the entire time that Marine Recruiter's chuckle haunted me. I heard it on the beach, I heard it in my sleep, it floated across the still waters at dawn when I cast my fishing line, and I somehow even felt it under my skin. What the hell did he know that I didn't? Why did he find pleasure in the Army's successful recruitment of a talented FAST test passer? Oh well, I thought, the Marines' loss was the Army's gain and I'm going to be a fly guy, a real John Wayne Flying Tiger hero with wings on his chest and a post-service future full of stewardesses and exotic destinations, and I wouldn't even have to park my brain in a jar for the duration. Thank you Uncle Sam.

For induction I returned to Fort Holabird where I once again filled out the same shit-pot full of paperwork and took another shit-pot full of tests, as though my life had somehow change during the last eight weeks. I also endured the rigors of a high speed high anxiety group physical and came to eventually find myself sitting in a large gymnasium size room with another hundred or so inductees waiting for transportation to places unknown. Until then, I decided to pretty much keep to myself through the entire ordeal, after all, what kind of conversation do you strike up with a bunch of strange guys standing around in their underwear. Now, being fully clothed, having been sworn in, and having consumed an Army brown bag lunch, I was chatting and just about to get to know the guy next to me when he suddenly disappeared in a puff of military smoke. To this day I'm not sure I understand how it happened. There we were on an *Army* base, a hundred plus *Army* volunteers and draftees obediently sitting and playing with the remnants of our *Army* lunch when in walks a Marine Corps sergeant with a clipboard. A *Marine* sergeant!

"Alright, eyes front and listen up," he demanded.

We looked up, none of us seriously concerned with anything he had to say. He was after all a Marine.

He pointed to the man on the end of the first row of seats in front of him and began, "As I count you off I want you to raise your right hand," he ordered. "That's your right hand. The one that you jerk off with."

Funny, I thought, seeing the humor and not the sarcasm. Then he began counting and the right hands, along with a few lefts, went up.

"One, two, three, four, five, six…"

He went through the entire first row then the second and was counting down the third to finally stop at the man sitting to my immediate left.

"…thirty-seven, thirty-eight, thirty-nine, forty."

The forty men sat there with their arms raised, probably thinking this was some form of military body odor exam. The Marine sergeant wrote something down on his clipboard then looked up sharply and stated, "Congratulations gentlemen. You forty with your hands raised are all now in the United States Marine Corps. Get up and proceed through that door and get on bus number twenty-two."

Everyone sat in shock and stared for a long silent moment then started to mumble thinking this guy was confused and somehow managed to be in the wrong room and the wrong building. This was after all an Army base.

"Let's go people! Move it! I'm not talking just to hear my own fuckin' voice! Get on that Goddamn bus! Move it! Move it!"

The mumbles quickly turned into protest and in one case even tears. The guy next to me was, like me, I had learned in our brief encounter, a volunteer. He had enlisted - *enlisted* - in the Army. *The Army*. When he informed the Marine sergeant they must have made a mistake he was quickly informed that *"the Marines don't make fuckin' mistakes and that he could take it up with his fuckin' congressman when he got back from fuckin' Vietnam."* All forty men quickly disappeared out of the building, leaving me to sit there staring at forty empty seats and empty little brown paper bags, suddenly feeling like Pinocchio and waiting for my donkey ears and tail to begin growing. What the hell just happened and what the hell would I have done, I thought, had that Marine sergeant been able to count to forty-one? I once again recalled and heard that Marine recruiter's chuckle, except this time it was clear as a bell. The bastard knew, I thought, the bastard knew all the time.

Fortunately for me the next bus was destined for Fort Bragg, not Paris Island, which meant I was still in the Army.

By the way, what my agreeable recruiter didn't bother to inform me of was that though I had two half-brothers I was my father's only son and being the only son who could carry on the family name, I was exempt from the draft altogether. Nor did he inform me there was such a thing as a two-year voluntary draft; he stuck me with three years and during those years in the military I would eventually discover that one could fill volumes with what the Army doesn't tell you, regardless of whether or not it's important and necessary for you to know. I assumed that the Pentagon assumed that the best way to guarantee good morale within the ranks was to keep everyone in the dark about most everything; this *village idiot* theory of benevolent neglect being based on that old axiom that ignorance is bliss. Be ignorant. Die ignorant. Die happy.

CHAPTER 3

A NAKED NUT &
A MAD MEXICAN MIDGET

"I'll give you sorry fuckin' bunch of maggots ten fuckin' seconds to get off this fuckin' bus before I start kickin' ass and takin' fuckin' names! Now grab your gear and get the hell off this God damn bus and line up on that fuckin' yellow line, and I mean NOW! NOW! NOW! WHAT THE HELL ARE YOU WAITIN' FOR? MOVE IT PEOPLE! MOVE IT! MOVE IT! MOVE IT! MOVE IT! MOVE IT! GET OFF THIS FUCKIN' BUS AND LINE UP ON THE YELLOW LINE. ARE YOU FUCKIN' DEAF? I SAID MOVE IT! MOVE IT!"

Okay, I had heard the stories and seen the movies, especially that movie "The D.I.", you know, the one with that guy from the TV show called Dragnet playing the Marine drill instructor, and I knew what to expect, but still the reception we got when our bus pulled into Fort Bragg made an impression. Obviously these guys weren't recruiters. They just weren't that cordial. I suppose the one inside the bus screaming at us would have been comical had it not been for the four waiting drill sergeants outside the bus emphasizing his crude verbosity with a good deal of hands on physical encouragement. It was kind of like the first day back at the Jesus school after summer vacation, except the most touchy feeling part of that experience was all the hugs and kisses from all those preachers' daughters. Or like the family's annual pilgrimage up to Pennsylvania to visit Grandma, the worst of that reception being when her enthusiastic embrace shoved my face right into her Mount Rushmore size tits. If anything, this was more like your older brothers pushing and slapping you around, gagging you, and then locking you in the closet because they didn't want you tagging along to the movie theater where they were going to see something forbidden. Hell, I'd had kinder receptions at the line of scrimmage in a serious rival football game. My here-to-for short life of experience didn't offer much else to reference for comparison. Though I had never really lost a fight and relished the full contact of football, I had always managed to avoid most physical squabbles and lived as a civilized young man. These guys, however, were just down right mean and there was no avoiding them because they were running the program, and the program was in your face. Maybe our Army reception would have left a different impression or been more tolerable and less shocking had it not taken place at three o'clock in the morning, crudely yanking us from a highway white line sleep after a seven-hour trip. And maybe they were a little grumpy because they were forced to be up late as well. Hell, I thought, even the meanest dog has its moments, as would these overbearing monsters once they discovered our finer qualities and accepted us as human, and I was right, they did - but it took eight weeks.

Army basic training at Fort Bragg, though physically challenging, wasn't actually much of a mental challenge, so I won't get into it too deeply other than to say it was an intensive cultural experience with some very interesting highlights. We were a diverse group, the bulk of which were draftees originating from the Philadelphia, Washington DC, and Baltimore areas, and my being of a kind of ethnic alphabet soup with an Italian name that was often misperceived to be Mexican or Puerto Rican, and somehow even Russian or Jewish, afforded me automatic acceptance with most minority whites, and as a consequence of being perceived as a minority, gained favor with most all of the black guys as well. And the Italian guys new right off the mark I was of their ilk, which also proved helpful by somehow putting me in an urban category, as in; *tread softly with this dude 'cause he might have an uncle named Guido*. This was, of course, purely a media influenced perception but when faced with group survival in situations like the military or prison, few of us Dagos will bother to rectify it or claim otherwise. As for the rest, my mother was a mix of Scotch-Irish, Pennsylvania Dutch, Johnny Bull and Native American, which pretty much held up in most all other company. Also an added benefit was that I had a lifetime of peripheral exposure and interaction with the WASPY self serving sophisticate socialites and yacht club types of Annapolis, which set me up to roll with the best of them, not that any of those folks would ever be caught dead or alive in a uniform. For the most part, those were the movers and shakers and clowns that liked to start wars not fight them, then sit back and say, *"Tiss tiss, that war is so nasty. Isn't it sad how our boys have to suffer so? By the way, how are my defense stocks doing?"* This social exposure plus the teachings of a very proper and dutiful mother helped stand me well with a lot of lofty pretentious officers like the ones on my officer candidate acceptance interview board. Mother's poise, the example of numerous Midshipmen from the Naval Academy, and recruiter Staff Sergeant Finkel's principals of the officer liar's test got me through the interview ordeal with flying colors, destined to be an officer and a gentleman. So I was off and running. But first came basic at Bragg.

In the beginning of our basic training cycle there was what was called a dead week or zero week. Supposedly it was a period of adjustment and processing where we were rudely herded off the busses and into the barn, separated into platoons according to the alphabet, and told to hurry up and wait. The processing part consisted of being issued a new ill-fitting wardrobe, getting relieved of our personal belongings, our hair, our identity, our dignity, and yes, filling out that same shit-pot full of paperwork we had filled out twice already before ever being sworn in and leaving home - and then again being told to hurry up and wait.

The adjustment part was a little more difficult. It meant adjusting to getting up at OH!-430 in the morning and bumping into walls and each other while trying to figure out just what the hell O430 was in the first place. It also meant adjusting to eating three regularly scheduled well-balanced hearty meals each day, great food, all you could eat, - in five minutes. And it also meant listening to all the bullshit from the guys in the barracks who thought they knew everything there was to know about the Army, including what 0430 was. Ironically, those same *know-it-alls* would be the first to fall to the wayside during training. My father warned me about them. He called them *shit house lawyers.* In addition, and most importantly, the dead week process meant learning that come hell or high water, war or peace, chocolate or vanilla, each and every swinging dick in the enlisted man's military had to stand in line to do just about everything and/or nothing at all, and absolutely nothing demonstrated this stand in line protocol more than the *Zero-Week-Third-Day-Anal-Rush.*

You would think that introducing all this healthy regimentation to the average American human body would be a good thing, and you would be right. A better sleep routine, hygiene improvement, new clothes, a hair cut that allowed oxygen to reach the brain, and actually seeing the sunrise are things that fill a man's soul with a sense of well being and a desire to achieve, especially after figuring out what the hell 0430 is. Did I mention the food? It was great, and there was lots of it, and it was balanced, and healthy, and yummy, and for some reason nobody took a shit for days while adjusting to the shock of all that wonderful healthy indulgence. That is until day three.

Now in all those dull beige circa 1942 wood-framed barracks at Fort Bragg there existed what we dead-week still partial civilians called a bathroom or a restroom, one for each platoon. The Army called it a latrine and it seems only in the military is it ever called that. The latrine itself was a marvel of government planning, consisting of only half a dozen sinks to accommodate a platoon of more than forty rushed soldiers wanting to shave, and only half a dozen showers to accommodate a platoon of more than forty rushed soldiers wanting to shower, and only three, as in ONLY THREE, toilets. Not only were there only three toilets but also these *only three toilets* were, like the sinks and showers, side-by-side and open-aired so that taking a shit in the barracks latrine was not simply a natural calling but a community event. I'm sure all of us took notice of the toilet situation but none of us really considered it to be of any consequence because for some odd reason none of us ever had to make use of them - that is until day three of our dead week. It was on that day that the will and magnitude of the influence of the military over our lives made its most profound impression, for it was on that day and at the very same moment that every damn recruit in the entire dead-week company had to take a dump. For me it was a genuine revelation and the word regimentation would never hold the same meaning again, and like many new experiences in the Army it was an incredible thing to behold. There in the isolated world of Fort Bragg, North Carolina, nearly two hundred identically dressed identically bald individuals were moved to be moved in an identical way at an identical time on only twelve identical commodes, and it was a true symphony of desperation.

Some of us managed to keep our poise through the entire experience but there were also those of lesser constitutions who saw the entire situation as more than desperate. Those were the ones who wondered aimlessly from barracks to barracks in the naïve belief there may by chance be an available commode. Yeah right. The even more truly desperate of those few dared to even extend their search into the neighboring barracks of the seasoned 82nd Airborne troops. Rudely rejected, they somehow managed to return with their lives and bodies still in tact, yet still fully loaded, and were forced to wait at the end of the line. The lucky ones, and I was fortunate to be one of those, managed to be in front of the line thinking relief was imminent and all would soon be well. At least that's what we thought. But stepping up and dropping your drawers and mounting the throne only to look up with great embarrassment into the faces of nearly forty tap dancing, gut wrenched, desperate, impatient individuals who could only be compared to a blood thirsty lynching party in some cheesy old B-western was not exactly conducive to a relaxed release, especially the release of what was probably the foremost, if not the most painfully all-inclusive serious crap of each of our entire young lives. The phrase *grin and bear it* comes to mind and the rest I'll just leave to your imagination other than to say the newly introduced concept of hurry up and wait was poorly practiced during the event of the zero week third day anal rush, a day when all the stars in the universe aligned themselves with all the Army meat and potatoes backed up in our still adjusting dead week systems to cause a group experience that will never be flushed from our collective memory.

Though the dead-week and the acceptance of shitting in public put us all on an equal personal plain, it was still easy enough to notice our diversity within the group. Aside from the usual All-American G.I. mix there was in our basic training platoon the proverbial fat guy who couldn't do anything right, causing all of us grief with the gods in the Smokey Bear hats, an attempted suicide by a guy named Waddle who climbed under the barracks before breakfast one morning and sliced his wrist, an exchange student who ran around buck ass naked claiming he shouldn't have been drafted because he wasn't an American citizen, and an exceptionally short Chicano Airborne Special Forces Drill Sergeant who came in drunk one night at 0230 hours and forced all of us to stand out in the rain in our skivvies while he declared that none of us were capable of kicking his ass, even with the aid of an entrenching tool, which he was willing to provide. Tossing the entrenching tool on the ground in front of us, he then challenged any one of us to try. After enduring his ballsy flap for what seemed half the night, three of us, guessing or hoping he was bluffing and that he was just a little guy with a short-man complex and too much tequila, and also hoping he wasn't as lethal as he professed to be and we knew he could be, finally stepped up to accept the challenge and the entrenching tool at which time he dismissed the platoon and instructed the three of us to join him in his quarters. As we stood there in his room dripping like used up fish bait, he proceeded to shower us with praise and inform us we were the only real men in the entire platoon, then he offered up drinks all around which was worse than if we had actually taken him on with the entrenching tool. Worse because while our comrades were now dry, warm, and snug in their bunks we were forced to stand there and listen to him rationalize all of his combat inner demons until the cows came home with the sunrise, half of which we didn't understand because it emerged as a mix of south of the border Spanish and marginal English interpreted through the liquid slur and influence of a bottle of Johnnie Walker.

The short troubled drill sergeant quickly and mysteriously disappeared the next day, but the paramount oddity of the entire affair was that he wasn't even our drill sergeant. In his drunken state he had haphazardly wandered into the wrong barracks, our barracks, choosing us as the targets of his challenging inebriated affections and attempts to delineate the conflicts of his war torn soul. The next day after news of the incident reached the higher ups someone somewhere ordered a formal apology be made to the offended troops involved, meaning those of us who stood in the rain and endured the little man's ranting. Orders being orders, the apology was made but it was made to the now correct but incorrect platoon of soldiers, his platoon of soldiers, none of which had the slightest damn idea why the hell they were receiving an apology or what the hell had happened to their drill sergeant. Just the same, as that bewildered platoon of men had done all through the basic training program, they blindly and graciously accepted the apologetic rhetoric without question, which ended the episode leaving everyone in the Army happy except those of us who had actually been forced to stand in the rain for half the night enduring that short little bastard's Napoleonic delusions of grandeur. But then as my father would say, "Hell boy, it didn't kill ya so don't sweat it."

As for Waddle's attempted suicide, the reasons and rumors were abundant, claiming it was the result of everything from a Dear John letter to penis paranoia contracted while being forced to take showers with forty otherwise ethnically well endowed guys. The latter growing from the fact that Waddle was not that well endowed and had lived a cushy life as the only and youngest boy in a family of five sisters.

The naked exchange student however was something else altogether. His name was Jorge Numas and he claimed to be from some European Caribbean island. Jorge, being the dutiful type who always followed directions in an effort to stay under the radar, registered for the draft when he was eighteen simply because someone told him that in America you're supposed to register for the draft when you're eighteen. Then being a bit of a playboy who hardly ever attended classes resulted in his getting failing grades that inexorably lead to a vulnerable draft status of 1-A and his eventual induction into the Army.

A few of us tried to console Jorge by reasoning that his getting drafted would make him a shoe-in for U.S. citizenship of which he had no interest whatsoever because he much preferred being a live foreigner to being a dead U.S. citizen. In addition, he was stinking rich, didn't want to pay U.S. taxes, and according to Jorge, had gotten two American girls pregnant and couldn't marry either one, both of which he loved dearly. He couldn't marry them because his family had prearranged a marriage to his cousin who, to his displeasure, had big ears, big feet and small tits. Jorge, it seemed, was stuck between Uncle Sam and a hard place, floundering in a sea of dilemma, and just wanting to get the hell out of the country. Now being that no one in the system would listen to poor old Jorge because they all assumed that, like a few million other American boys, he was trying to dodge his military obligation, he decided to gain their attention in a more direct manner. He did this by showing up for our morning formation buck ass naked. When our platoon drill Sergeant, company First Sergeant, and Commanding Officer tried to deal with him they found themselves facing a highly animated distraught Jorge who would simply collapse in a bare ass heap of uncontrollable jelly and begin to roll and rant and rave and cry in his native tongue, which no one understood.

For the rest of us, Jorge's desperate tearful gibberish faded in the distance as we were marched off into the sunrise, returning later that day to discover that, like the little Chicano drill sergeant with the big ideas, and the paranoid suicidal homesick Waddle, the unfortunate naked nut Jorge had been hauled away to points unknown - never to be heard from again.

"I wonder where they took him?" asked a Private E-Nothing Trainee Sigmund Q. Minaburge.

"Nut house," someone answered.

"No, really. I wonder where they took him?" repeated Private E-Nothing Trainee Sigmund Q. Minaburge.

"Yo man, who give a fuck what happen ta dat crazy fucker? Any place be better'n this fuckin' place. Who give a fuck," repeated a black draftee from DC as he scratched his balls and leaned against a tree. "You aks me, he one lucky mofucka."

"But where'd they take him?" repeated a sincere Private E-Nothing Trainee Sigmund Q. Minaburge.

"Boy wha'chew care wha day do wit dat crazy mofucka anyway?" said DC.

"What if they sent him home?" ask Private E-Nothing Trainee Sigmund Q. Minaburge.

"Or decided he's too damn crazy to kill people and they gave him some cushy dick-job like emptying trash cans at the Pentagon," offered another thoughtful Private E-Nothing Trainee.

"Yeah," echoed another of the group.

The clouds seemed to part and take on a golden glow and silvery streaks of sunlight shined down on our platoon through the branches of our *take five and smoke 'em if you got 'em tree* like some sort of religious episode right out of the Old Testament. Nearly every formerly dull-minded draftee grew suddenly inspired by Jorge's antics. If Jorge could do it then why couldn't I, they all thought in unison for the first time since our training began. I could almost hear Arlo Guthry crooning Alice's Restaurant in the background and visualize a morning formation of forty naked Private E-Nothing trainees pissing and moaning and gyrating around on the ground like a bunch of overzealous holy-rollers high on joy juice and Jesus. The biblical moment was shattered, however, when the voice of another trainee explored yet another possibility.

"Probably give him a lobotomy," speculated one of the more intelligent or at least more eloquent Private E-Nothings.

"A what?" asked Private E-Nothing Trainee Sigmund Q. Minaburge?

"A lobotomy."

"What duh fuck's a lobotomy?" came DC.

"A neutralization treatment," clarified Private E-Nothing Trainee Einstein the eloquent one.

"Oh man dats some funky shit, man," said an angrily animated DC. "Dey can't do dat. Dey can't do dat, right? I mean, shit man, dey can't just cut yo nuts off just cause yo a crazy mofucka?"

"No. Electricity. They zap your brain with electricity," clarified Einstein. "It's like a permanent fix. Like smokin' four joints and drinking a case of Boone's Farm Apple Wine…forever," revealed the all-knowing articulate shit-house lawyer Private E-Nothing trainee Einstein.

A collective "Wow" reverberated from the less illuminated.

"Don't sound too bad," said Private E-Nothing trainee Sigmund Q. Minaburge. "Better than over there in the jungle."

The collective minds of the draftees fell back into cloudy subdued disarray as their mental wonderings began returning to reality.

What I was observing for the first time was the phenomenon of *groupthink* and not just any groupthink but *enlisted ranks military groupthink*. One would think that groupthink is a process where all members of the group think the same way at the same time, a kind of you-think-I-think-we-think thing where all thoughts cruise along like a school of fish who don't know they're wet, which for military purposes would be ideal, and in fact is the generally accepted definition and concept. The kind of think process that lines men up by the thousands and marches them across an empty field into certain death. But this particular type of military groupthink was contrary to all the rules, a social condition which could only exist in the military, especially in an American conscript military where all men and their opinions are created equal - kind of - with each thought flying around freely through space among the group like so many ping pong balls bouncing around in a clear plastic bingo drawing machine waiting to be plucked out at just the right moment. It was an amazing thing to behold.

The only place where military groupthink could possibly be more profound, I thought, would have to be in the French Foreign Legion where there is not only extreme social and intellectual diversity but multiple language challenges as well, and probably one of the best explanations as to why the U.S. and not the French were now fighting in Vietnam in the first place. After all, you can only go so far on a croissant, a bottle of wine, and a smile, backed by a bullet. I tried to imagine a group think conversation about the circumstances of a crazed naked Hungarian recruit who had second thoughts regarding his enlistment in the French Foreign Legion, but then I quickly dismissed the vision with the simple deduction that he would most likely be shot on the spot, unlike our American system where G.I.s are required to face a bureaucratic military justice fiasco first - then be shot.

This, my initial exposure to an enlisted military groupthink occurrence, was interesting to say the least and something of which I would study and make mental note as well as occasionally even participate throughout my Army career. I quickly concluded that this form of groupthink was not an easy thing to achieve. It depended entirely on the mental and cultural mix of the major and marginal intellects brought together to participate, destined to think together separately while remaining separately together, a diversity that if it could be expressed in graphic form would be equal only to a Picasso painting. Observing the process over the years led me to believe that military groupthink is a witch's brew of fact, speculation, bullshit, conjecture, misperception, misinformation, rumor, wishful thinking, lies, assumption, fantasy, hearsay, stupidity, genius, supposition, and a myriad of possible mental maladies and influences, all gurgling together over a fire of stress, strain, boredom, and the occasional excess of alcohol or other substances. Briefly stated, this type of military groupthink is not exactly an Oxford round table but more a real culturally influenced intellectual hootenanny. Even more simply put it is pretty much equal to our American news media without the glitz or the naked politics of Washington. It was also something that would churn uncomfortably in the back of my mind as I occasionally wondered just how far up the chain of command the groupthink process functioned... or tried to function... or failed to function, and possibly even mutated into something even more complicated and difficult to understand.

"You mean dey gonna' take out dat crazy mofucka's brain?" asked DC.

"No," clarified Private E-Nothing Trainee Einstein. "They're going to arrest his brain."

"How the hell you gonna' arrest somebody's fuckin' brain?" inquired a deep voice from behind the tree. He was taking an extended piss that seemed to last forever as though it was pouring heavily out of a Clydesdale horse in a pasture. "I been busted 'nuff to know you can't jus' arrest somebody's body parts, man. 'Specially somebody's fuckin' brain. How you comin' up wit dis bizarre shit?"

"I'm talking about a degree of arrestment, a medical process restricting his mind so he doesn't freak out all the time," responded Einstein.

"My old man's a doctor. He just gives my mother Darvon. Does the same thing," offered a fore-to-now quiet Private E-Nothing trainee observer.

"I heard about lobotomies. Heard that's what they're doing to those crazy ass flower children in California who are freakin' out on LSD and jumpin' off freeway overpasses and shit 'cause they think they can fly," said another.

More of the group was participating in the groupthink process now, contributing eagerly. It was freedom of speech, democracy in practice, mental expansion, and a personal coming of age and maturity, citizens evolving and intellectually sharing right there before my eyes. I just sat there in silent amazement.

"LSD? I tried that shit once," said someone else. "Talk about arresting your brain. That shit will arrest your brain and send it to places where there ain't even places."

"I heard the CIA invented that shit, tested it on prisoners and even some G.I.s like they did with the bomb back in the fifties. S'posed to be a truth serum or something."

"Yeah, you got that right. Weirdest truth you ever seen, man."

"You can always tell when the government invents shit like that," offered another formerly quiet olive drab expert.

"How come?"

"Initials. They always give stuff initials like they don't want anybody to know what it is. They never name anything. They always just give shit initials," said the normally quiet little Private E-Nothing sprawled on the grass at the edge of the group. Somehow he managed to pick his nose and talk at the same time.

"Wha da fuck you talkin' 'bout?" came DC.

"You know, FBI, CIA, IRS, LSD, and all this Army stuff they're always dumpin' on us like PT and OD. I figure if its only got initials it must be bad," said the nose picking Private Quiet. "Did you know that the CIA owns all the McDonalds hamburger joints in America so they can put drugs and stuff in our food and make us do whatever the government wants us to do? How do you think Nixon got elected?"

"Yeah, like the Army puttin' salt peter in our food at the mess hall so we can't get horny and shit."

"Well I gots some news fo da Army, man. Dat shit ain't workin' so all you mofuckas better not be bendin' over in da shower or dis brotha gonna' have him some good time," declared Private E-Nothing Trainee Big Howard Moore who had finally finished pissing behind the tree. He buttoned up then swooped up his crotch with one hand and smiled. We could all see with amazement the outline of his currently hardened huge organ that had apparently just been inspired by sheer mention.

At first there was a group chuckle then all fell silent as they contemplated the frightening possibility of Big Howard being a man of his word, among other things, and recalling that he was there courtesy of the Philadelphia judicial system, not to mention the fact we had all seen Big Howard in the shower and if we had our druthers we would most likely prefer an encounter with a horny rouge elephant. Big Howard's declaration pretty much ended that particular groupthink, being no one really wanted to spin the conversation off in that direction. And for some reason, from that day forward Big Howard always had the shower to himself. As for the subject of Jorge, well, as a result of the groupthink process he was now somehow associated with Big Howard's idea of fun and became a subject no one had any desire to explore further, not even Private E-Nothing Trainee Sigmund Q. Minaburge.

The entire Jorge incident left me to contemplate just how easy it would be for spies and insurgents from an enemy state to infiltrate our military simply by registering for the draft. I labeled this the *Jorge Loophole* and came to think such a concept would have been even more practicable in our particular basic training company due to the fact we had a colorful First Sergeant who considered everyone in the company, if not the entire United States Army, to be a foreigner. He made this perfectly clear when he addressed us during our first week of training, which was, except for the time he helped haul away Jorge the naked exchange student, the only time we ever saw him.

"My name is First Sergeant Grayhawk and you will always address me as First Sergeant or First Sergeant Grayhawk. You will never ever address me as Sir because I am not an officer and I am not some pussy Marine Corps toy soldier. I am a First Sergeant in the United States Army and, unlike the previously mentioned, I actually work for a living. You may call my father Sir but to do that I will first have to kill you because he has passed on to the happy hunting ground and you must go there to speak with him. If any of you dumb ass maggots ever call me Sir, I will personally demonstrate how remarkably well my outstanding highly polished size eleven U.S. government Army issue boot will fit up your fuckin' ass. DO YOU UNDERSTAND ME?"

A full company of voices rang out in unified agreement, "YES FIRST SERGEANT!"

"But that will never happen," continued First Sergeant Grayhawk, "because none of you fuckin' foreigners will ever talk to me. You will not talk to me because I do not like talking to stupid ignorant fuckin' foreigners and you Spics, Splivs, Greaseballs, Niggers, Coons, Chicanos, Guineas, Wops, Dagos, Meatballs, Greasers, Nazis Krauts, Pollok's, Limies, Chinks, Dinks, Gooks, Japs, Nips, red nosed Mics, camel fuckers, fagots, Kikes, and dykes are all God damn foreigners. The only people who can talk to me are my Commanding Officer and my mother. I say my mother because my mother is an American Indian and I am an American Indian and this is *my fuckin' country,* and you God damn maggots are all visitors in *my fuckin' country!* You are visitors in *my* country because I and I alone permit you to be visitors in *my* country and I am giving you the privilege and opportunity of defending *my* country and *my* flag by being in *my* Army where, if it becomes necessary, you will fight and die for *my* country and *my* flag and *my mother*. If you do not fight and die bravely, and with great enthusiasm and dignity, I will take that as an insult to my mother and I will personally find you and kill you again. I will do this without hesitation because in my previous life as a warrior I personally killed and scalped General George Armstrong Custer at the Battle of Little Big Horn, and if I can kill and scalp a fuckin' General you can bet your ugly ass girl friend's virginity that I will not hesitate to kill a lowlife fuckin' foreigner like you. IS THAT UNDERSTOOD?"

"YES FIRST SERGEANT!"

First Sergeant Grayhawk went on to explain how we not only had an obligation to serve *his country* honorably but also had an obligation to live up to our company's tradition and historic fame as Buffalo Soldiers, gained in the previous century while fighting *his* people. Our company, A-Company of the 9th Battalion of the 2nd Brigade, the former Buffalo Solders, explained First Sergeant Grayhawk, was the only company worthy of the honor of *his* guidance and leadership and none of us *limp-dick numb-nuts sons-a-bitchin' foreigners* had better disappoint him or bring dishonor to *his* country or *his* Army or *his* company! It was an enlightening lesson in history, social, and military protocol, which we all took to heart if for no other reason than the fear of his size eleven outstandingly well polished boot, not to mention the fact that none of us were fond of the idea of dying twice in the same war, especially with the possibility of being scalped the second time around.

The reason we never saw First Sergeant Grayhawk again was because a few weeks later while visiting another company at the rifle range he was shot accidentally on purpose by an emotionally unstable drafted foreigner from Pittsburgh, PA. It was an embarrassing moment for the Buffalo Soldiers and especially First Sergeant Grayhawk who was only there to escort a reporter and photographer from The Army Times newspaper. Unfortunately for First Sergeant Grayhawk the reporter was eager and more than willing to outshine his competing journalist comrades in Vietnam by featuring the entire incident, complete with graphic photos of First Sergeant Grayhawk gripping his painful bloody injury.

Among us foreigners in the ranks of the Buffalo Soldier Company the affair became known as *Custer's Revenge* but for First Sergeant Grayhawk the embarrassment and injury was far more serious, forcing him to spend a great deal of time laying in the hospital recuperating and contemplating *his* future in *his* company and *his* Army without... *his testicles.*

And so went our life in basic training at Fort Bragg. Eight weeks of enduring the physical and psychological demands of military life, and the social demands of a potluck stew of ethnically diverse individuals; all the while ignorant of what was happening in the outside world such as the Soviet Union invading Czechoslovakia, thousands of anti-war protesters invading the Democratic Convention in Chicago, and polyester slowly and covertly invading the universe of fashion. Had I known of these I'm not sure I could have determined which was worse.

CHAPTER 4

PET MONKEY REJECT

We completed basic training and received our orders immediately after a graduation ceremony, a ceremony that consisted mostly of marching to audibly offensive John Philip Sousa noise and listening to a few short speeches including one by our battalion commander who we were seeing for the first time. After the ceremony the orders handed out were our first introduction to the true nature of military reasoning and wisdom, or possibly some quirky upper echelon group think. The majority of our platoon, which consisted mostly of draftees, went on to advance infantry training at Fort Polk, Louisiana, which we all knew was a guaranteed ticket to Vietnam. And then there were the few exceptions such as Roger Herlacher who had a Bachelor's Degree in engineering. He was assigned to Germany for the duration of his enlistment to teach music at a U.S. military base grade school. He received this assignment because somewhere in his massive shit pot full of paper work he mentioned he could play the flute, which as we all know, is far more important to the Army than being able to build a bridge. Another college graduate who majored in chemistry went to cook school, probably because he majored in chemistry and could mix stuff like flour and water. Sigmund Q. Minaburge, who never finished high school because he had no deductive reasoning whatsoever, was ordered into Army intelligence, and another high school drop out and borderline total moron was sent off for EOD (Explosive Ordnance Disposal) training where he would be allowed to play with explosives and defuse land mines. Of the few of us who were regular Army, one guy went to OCS (Officer Candidate School) and I was on my way to Warrant Officer Candidate School at Fort Rucker, Alabama, that to my surprise, turned out to be for helicopter pilots, as in - *helicopter* pilots?

As warned on our first day of flight school, more than half the WOCs (Warrant Officer Candidates) would not complete or, should I say, survive the course. Like a mass of sea turtle hatchlings being picked off by sea gulls on their way to the safety of the surf, the Army went out of it's way to pick us off one by one. Many never even had a chance to reach the water to prove they could swim, or in this case reach the sky to fly. Like many of that unfortunate half, my flight school career was to be short lived. Though I got a little further in the program than others, I was pretty much doomed and my flying career nipped in the bud when I received my mid-program warm and fuzzy evaluation and interview by the Company Commander, Major Ellingsworth.

Major Ellingsworth was a nice enough guy I suppose. He was a bit lanky with thin blond hair and a sorry half-ass undecided blond see-through mustache. His forte and ticket to his command position seemed, to me at least, to be his eyes. They were piercing, intense and commanding, and no matter in what direction Major Ellingsworth was actually looking, his eyes always seemed to be focused on whatever person was observing or looking at him. It was uncanny. He was like one of those Mexican fuzzy felt paintings of Elvis or Marilyn Monroe whose eyes always seemed to follow you around the room. It made for perpetual obedience by all subordinates if for no other reason than putting them in a constant state of paranoia.

Major Elingsworth had a huge class ring on his finger that I first assumed indicated he was a West Pointer but later discovered was from some mail-order Jesus School in Lubbock, Texas. This meant he could not only kill you but he could save your soul in the process. It was the same mail-order Jesus School that Major Ellingsworth's sister, brother and cousin, who was now an Army chaplain stationed at Fort Bliss, had graduated from because his father, a local undertaker and minister, was founder, President, and Dean of Students. The entire school fit in the top right hand drawer of his father's desk at the mortuary where he kept the graduate packages consisting of a diploma, a class ring, and a custom made imitation leather bound fully illustrated Bible. It was all yours for the low low price of $497 – plus postage and handling. The college of divinity wasn't exactly a gold mine but it did manage to buy the old man a new yellow Cadillac convertible and an annual heathanistic vacation in Rio de Janeiro. Major Ellingsworth also sported an ever so slight twitch in his left nostril that complimented a condescending forced smile that would warm the heart of a hermit crab - just before he stepped on it. They say he developed the twitch when he was a flight instructor.

"Sir, Candidate Fusco reporting as ordered, sir." It was the standard manner in which we addressed our superiors and I was exceptionally proud of my delivery.

"Well Candidate Foo... Fuzz...Fuzzgo, I see here you're doing real well," said Major Ellingsworth as he perused my report card from behind his desk. "Uh huh, yeah, doing real well."

I began to feel as though I was being examined by a dentist. Should I respond or just stand there and drool?

"Sir, Um, that's candidate Fusco, Sir. As in Foos-ko."

That was screw-up number one. Never correct a superior officer in a way that he knows he's being corrected even if he's a dumb dick, but then that was only screw-up number one and he got over it with just a slight wince and twitch.

"How do you like the Army so far, Candidate Fuzz... go?"

"Sir, candidate Fusco, I like it fine, sir," I said, trying not to expose my conditioned uncomfortable anxiety derived from past life experiences of being called to the principal's office.

"You can drop the standard candidate response, candidate. I'm not a TAC and I don't want this interview to last all damn day. Now, how'd you say things were goin?"

"Um, fine sir. Just fine."

"Good. Good. Keep up the good work. And how do you feel about the flight program so far?"

"It's fine, sir."

"Have any questions?"

I've learned since then when an Army training officer or superior asks if you have any questions, you should never ask any questions, even if you have questions that need to be asked. The reasoning being they instinctively and automatically assume you are stupid, which is an impression you want to avoid, or they might think that you might think they're stupid, which is an impression you want to avoid, or as occurred in my case as I committed screw-up number two, they assume you have not fully and willingly accepted the Army doctrine and have an exceptionally shitty attitude, which is an impression you definitely want to avoid. My question was simple, "I was wondering, sir, when will I get my fixed wing training?"

"What? Get what?" A slight twitch.

"Fixed wing training, sir. I'm supposed to get fixed wing training. Airplanes."

"I know what the hell fixed wing training is, candidate. You think I don't know what the hell fixed wing training is? Who the hell said you'd get fixed wing training?"

"My recruiter, sir. I enlisted for fixed wing training. I have a certificate of guarantee for fixed wing training."

His expression did a total Lon Chaney. I had broken the law, violated the code, raped his damn sister, insulted his grandmother's apple pie, and seemingly called into question all the honor that had ever existed in the United States military since General George Washington got false teeth.

"What the hell do you want fixed wing training for, Fuzzgot?"

"It's candidate *Fusco*, sir."

"I know you're a candidate."

"It's why I enlisted, sir. I have a written guarantee for fixed wing training."

"A guarantee?"

"Yes sir, a written guarantee… for fixed wing training. With a picture of an airplane on it."

"Fixed wing is for pussies, Fuzzgo. You some kind of a pussy?"

"No sir. I just thought I'd have a career in fixed wing aircraft, sir," I lied.

"A career?"

"Yes sir," I lied.

"You one of those opportunistic dick heads who thinks he's going back in the world and fly some damn commercial cocktail lounge after Uncle Sam puts out good military blood, sweat, and money to make you a highly proficient pilot and instrument of warfare?"

"Uh, no sir", I lied. "It's just I have this guarantee and…"

He laughed. Not your normal laugh laugh kind of laugh, but one of those, *Here we go again with one of those dumb shits who actually believed his recruiter,* kind of laughs.

"There aren't any guarantees in this man's Army, son. We serve to fight and we fight to serve. Do you believe that, candidate Foozkum?"

"Yes sir," I lied.

"You're here to become a chopper pilot. If the Army didn't need you here they wouldn't have sent you here. Isn't that correct, candidate Foozkum?"

"Uh, yes sir," I lied. "But... That's Fusco, sir. But I enlisted for..."

"I'm beginning to think you have an attitude problem, candidate Fuzzgo." Twitch. "Do you have an attitude problem, candidate Fuzzgo?"

"No sir. But I have a guarantee for..."

"It sounds like a personal problem to me, candidate Fuzzgo." Twitch. "I don't like personal problems, candidate Fuzzgo." Twitch. "Personal problems fuck up my day." Twitch. "Do you have a personal problem, candidate Fuzzgo?" He leaned across his desk - twitching. "Are you trying to fuck up my day?"

"Uh, no sir."

"Good. Then what the hell's the problem, candidate Fuzzgo?"

"Fixed wing, sir." That was screw-up and strike number three. Never be persistently insistent with a superior officer. It causes a brain overload that can backfire in your direction.

He looked at me for a long moment as though he were waiting for me to grow a visible brain like some kind of Chia Pet, or at least let some light shine into the one I had.

"Okay," he exhaled in exhausted defeat, "Here's the deal. You complete your rotary wing qualification, get your wings and Warrant commission, then you go to Vietnam, and if you don't get your ass killed in Vietnam, which you will because you have an attitude problem, then you serve out your three year enlistment and re-up for a direct commission, a *hard commission* as a Lieutenant and fixed wing training."

"Re-up, sir? A hard commission, sir? I'd already be a Chief Warrant Officer, sir. Wouldn't that be a demotion?"

"That's correct candidate Fuzzgo, but with a hard commission as a career officer, a leader of men. You need a hard commission for fixed wing. A real officer, not some flaky Warrant Officer with a fixed wing future flying some socialite General and his God damn golf clubs around in some God damned pussy ass fixed wing aircraft that was never meant to see the honor and dignity of combat. Is that what you want candidate Fuzzgo? Or droppin' a bunch of airborne wienies out of some aerodynamically misguided fat jack ugly ass mud hog C-130. Is that what you want, candidate Fuzzgot? Rotary wing, son. Rotary wing. That's where it's at. Can't beat the prestige and combat dignity of choppers."

Be it Fuzzgo, Fooskum, or Fucko, it didn't matter because somewhere during our conversation Major Ellingsworth's piercing empty wondering stationary eyes somehow seared the words BAD ATTITUDE or NATIONAL TRAITOR across my forehead making me a marked WOC, and from that day forward every instructor and TAC officer at Fort Rucker went out of his way to make my life miserable.

In flight school, if you receive five disciplinary pink slips, which are actually yellow slips, from instructors or TACs for any reason at all then you are history, shit-canned with all the status and dignity of an old Army mule who was somehow mistakenly admitted into the astronaut program at NASA then unceremoniously stolen away in the middle of the night to save bureaucratic face and embarrassment.

The disciplinary yellow pink slips came easily and quickly. The first was for a low but passing score on a navigation test, the second for missing a hair, just one damn hair, on my lower neck when I shaved one morning. The third was for trying to exit the mess hall with a banana stashed in one of the many unused pockets of my flight suit. The banana incident was the result of the discipline of the then traditional military academy style square meals that left little time for actual food consumption. "Sir - permission to sit, permission to bite, permission to chew, permission to fart, permission to do it all again." Over the centuries this tradition must have cost our country billions in wasted food at West Point, Annapolis, and officer training programs everywhere, but a better weight loss program has yet to be invented. People are often under the impression that the first thing officer candidates do when they finally get some free time is embark on a quest for the company of the opposite sex – wrong. What they do is hustle on down to the nearest fast food joint, the faster the better, for a pig out and then it's beer all around. After that, well who knows? When my smuggled contraband banana was discovered it was promptly squashed in place in my pocket while a TAC officer had me braced against the wall then wrote me up for being out of uniform, banana goo being an unauthorized addition to the flight suit of course.

The fourth yellow pink slip was probably the most entertaining and I must admit, enjoyable. While returning from a few beers one weekend evening, five WOCs, including myself and an oversized former Marine Recon named Stenzil who used to eat bugs and perform other *in the bush* psycho shit to impress the ladies and bar maids, were walking into the barracks when we were confronted by a harassing TAC officer named Churchof. Churchof was in an exceptionally bad mood because he had the weekend duty and also hadn't been laid in twelve weeks because his wife was pregnant and his mother-in-law was visiting. Now TACs are officers of the sadistic drill sergeant persuasion and this particular TAC had a particularly bad rep for being particularly excessive when it came to harassing WOCs. On this occasion he had us brace the wall at attention while he proceeded with a full array of insults and harassment, which included his assurance that he was going to see to it that each of us were dropped from the program. And since we weren't going to be around long enough to become pilots because, in his opinion, we were all queers and pussies, he added that we could all play at being choppers and he instructed us to twirl our arm around in the air like a main rotor blade and make the sound WHOP WHOP WHOP. So there we were, four Warrant Officer Candidates WHOP WHOPPING around the hallway being forced to agree with all of asshole Churchof's insults and harassment when he decided to break former psycho Marine Recon Stenzil's swagger stick, an honor Stenzil was awarded during his previous service with the U.S. Marine Corps and was legitimately authorized to carry. This blatant act of disrespect by TAC Churchof toward the swagger honor prompted Stenzil to quickly return the gesture by breaking TAC Churchof - literally. He broke his nose, he broke his arm, and he broke two of the TAC's ribs, and we, for having voluntarily stood by at the scene of the exchange as witnesses, all received the award of another yellow pink slip; an honor we proudly and readily accepted without question because none of us could deny what we witnessed and none of us really liked that particular son of a bitch Churchof anyway. As for Stenzil, like the naked nut and the mad midget

Drill Sergeant back at Fort Braggg, he quickly disappeared to parts unknown.

My final yellow pink slip came with great excitement, and if I may say so, a great deal of flair. With the brand of national traitor across my forehead and the accumulation of four yellow pink slips, it was more than obvious by now this Warrant Officer Candidate was inevitably doomed to the ranks of the Sad Sacks. During a flight exercise requiring me to hover over the tarmac at the tail end of a daisychain formation of a number of other OH-13 training choppers, I was being assaulted with an unbelievable barrage of verbal abuse and threats by the flight training officer. It was then I decided to give in to temptation and live up to the cordial Major Ellingsworth's expectations.

"Hold your position, Candidate! Watch your pedals! Pedals! Watch your pedals! What the hell's wrong with you?! You're a total fuck up Fusco, you know that?! I'm gonna' kick your ass out of the program! Easy stick! Easy stick there! Can't you see the aircraft in front of you? God damnit Fusco, my fuckin' pet monkey can fly better than this, you stupid shit!"

The line of aircraft in front of us was all over the map, making it impossible to stay in formation. The reason, I assumed, was because they were having as much fun as I was with their flight instructors. He was so personable I could hardly stand it, especially when he emphasized nearly every other statement with a slap on the helmet, my helmet. The harassment we incurred as WOCs was no big deal. It was just a mind game and as long as you didn't take it personally and didn't let it bug you it could be tolerated with some semblance of dignity. I knew all this was just part of the training, learning to fly under stress and all that. No real man however would even begin to tolerate getting bitch slapped upside the helmet and certainly no real combat pilot would expect to be continuously whacked upside the head while bobbing and weaving and buzzing along just above a hostile jungle canopy at a hundred miles per hour. Therefore my natural and desired instincts dictated that the officer and gentleman next to me receive a well placed elbow somewhere between his upper lip and his over-priced tear drop hot pilot sun shades, or what you might call the Stenzil response. Military decorum and fear of a court martial however called for a more deliberate and calculated reaction. I would appeal to his logic.

"I'm doing the best I can, sir."

"Well that's not fuckin' good enough is it you damn idiot?" he responded - with another whack on my head.

"But they're all over the place up there, sir."

"I'm not interested in your fuckin' excuses, candidate." Slap!

The last slap was the last slap I was willing to accept, and though it wouldn't make my mother very proud, I quickly utilized part of my newfound military vocabulary to respond.

"Yes sir. Well then sir, you and your fuckin' pet monkey can fly this fuckin' thing because I just fuckin' quit your fuckin' program... sir!"

With that patent declaration of independence I let go of the controls and judging from his response this was something that had never happened to this particular instructor on any prior occasion. My declaration and turning lose of the cyclic seemed to blow the cushion right out from under us, and being only a few meters off the ground, and his surprised and tardy reaction being a bit off the mark, the result was an excessively hard meeting of tarmac and aircraft. The skids slammed and spread to a near pancake state almost as wide as the instructor's eyes and the new stain in the ass of his nomex flight suit, and was probably heard all over Knox Field clear to Major Ellingsworth's office.

My actions were a spur of the moment calculated risk reinforcing my status as an attitude waiting to happen. A risk resulting in an incident that somehow got swept under the carpet, most likely in an effort to save Major Ellingsworth embarrassment and supporting the basic philosophy of the officer liar's test. The slaphappy instructor salvaged his flight career, although with a slight twitch, simply by pointing a big finger at me the lowly warrant officer candidate, and I was hastily flunked out of the program and sentenced to the ranks for the duration to ponder and solve my so-called *personal problem*. So like the suicidal Waddle, Jorge the happenstance naked nut case, the drunken Airborne Special Forces Mexican midget drill sergeant, and my bug eating Marine friend Stenzil I was now destined for military obscurity, just another soldier in possession of just another squashed banana and useless written Army guarantee. I had been duped by a uniformed used car salesman and was on my way, though indirectly, to that circus of a war in Vietnam, all the while hearing the echoes of that Marine Corps recruiter's subtle chuckle and wishing I were sharing a makeshift lean-to with Leroy and Bigfoot somewhere in the tranquil Oregon high country.

As for the TAC's pet monkey... Who the hell knows? Maybe it graduated.

CHAPTER 5

SEX, QUACKS &
THE WAZOO

As would be expect, I wasn't bee-lined to Vietnam directly from my disappointing failure in flight school. In the Army every soldier has to have an officially designated reason for living before he's afforded the opportunity to die for his country in someone else's country. The Army, being considerate and also probably remembering I still had possession of my fixed wing written guarantee, which could be a possible legal ticket out because it would prove a breach of contract by Uncle Sam, and possibly fearing there might be a lawyer in the family bright enough to figure that out, gave me counseling and a choice of a new MOS (Military Occupational Specialty). This choice meaning they politely encouraged me to choose a new Army profession, which was a nice way of saying *you can go anywhere but here dumb ass*. So I mulled over the phone book size volume of opportunity until I found a training program that was many months long with a name of equal character. The course description talked of exotic things like electronics and computers and futuristically advanced technology - a brilliant work of enticing fiction. The course was titled *Continuous Wave Acquisition Radar Technician Surface To Air Hawk Missile System Air Defense*. Now there was a handle that would impress just about anybody's mother, I thought. Not only that, the course was six months long and when serving an Army hitch, time and timing are everything. Once I made my choice they wasted no time putting me on a westbound hop out of Alabama. It was near midnight when they did it, making me feel like some top-secret high priority package, or as I admitted to myself later, a low priority failure. Midnight, an Army red eye flight on a C-130 and I was the only passenger. That meant I was special, I thought, or maybe they were just going to fly out over the Gulf and shove me out. Is that what they do to incorrigible failures with five yellow pink slips?

The Air Defense School was located at Fort Bliss, Texas, a place that at that time in no way whatsoever came close to resembling its name. The only good thing about Fort Bliss is that it sat next to El Paso, which sat on the U.S. and Mexican border next to Juarez, or the Wazoo, as we affectionately came to call it. It was the quintessential Mexican border town offering every vice known to man and except for the addition of low voltage electricity and a few sidewalks, probably hadn't changed since Poncho Villa and General "Black Jack" Pershing faced off over tequila shooters. Historically and in reality, Juarez and El Paso were the same city separated only by language and a drainage ditch called the Rio Grand. Oh, and of course a national border. They were a single city just the same, kind of like a Royal family where there are sons and there are bastard sons representing both shining privilege and stark dark secrets. The Mexican side, the dark bastardly side, was the only place I'd ever been other than Vietnam where one could be ripped off, grossed out, and totally screwed over all at the same time without even realizing it. El Paso, on the other hand, was, well… it was El Paso, where sage brush tumble weeds rolled freely down an empty Main Street at midnight, anemic skinny-ass jack rabbits were the principal wildlife thriving in an anemic weedy treeless environment, men wore guns and hats in restaurants, and nobody cut their grass because, well, there was no grass growing in El Paso for all those cactus cowboys to cut. In fact, it was not uncommon for houses in the suburbs to sport front lawns consisting only of colored gravel. The pink, blue, green, red, and assorted variations made for a truly alien experience for someone like myself who came from a planet where green things grew everywhere right next to cool deep water.

But then hell, I thought, just how bad could it be? In six months the war could be over, and even if it wasn't there was all the fun and games to be had in Wazoo. At least that's what I thought. But Army luck being what it was, nonexistent, my hopefully time consuming six month course of study was circumvented shortly before I arrived when some overly ambitious efficiency expert genius in OD fatigues came up with the idea that what could be taught to a group of soldiers in six months could just as easily be taught in three. The idea being to cut out much of the tedious but essential elements of education, those same elements necessary for the proficient tender loving care, maintenance, and operation of the highly technical and exceptionally expensive surface to air Hawk missile radar system. For example, the existing six-month program included and began with a one-month basic electronics course followed by five months of learning the intricacies and details of thousands of volts of complicated high tech confusion and lethal radiation. For some reason they decided to cut the basic electronics course out completely and abbreviated the rest of the training to the point where the entire course ran a brief three months. To me that was tantamount to taking a kid right out of biology class after cutting up a frog and telling him to do brain surgery on a human. For those of us without mental telepathy and the deductive powers of Albert Einstein, it made for a bit of a challenge, not to mention the inner doubts aroused when we toyed with the fact that the aircraft and pilots we were supposed to shoot down with the Hawk missile system received millions of dollars worth of training over a period of years. It may have been a good idea at the time, but from our unenlightened point of view it was like asking a slightly retarded shade tree mechanic to jazz up and maintain mission control for an Apollo space shot.

In spite of our uncanny insight and valuable opinion, and our inability to protest, a hand picked dozen of us were chosen to be the test guinea pigs of the newly designed Continuous Wave Acquisition Radar Technician Surface To Air Hawk Missile System Prototype Test Course; a course destined to succeed because as we all know, the Army does not like to fail when it comes to pet prototype adventures, even if it has to rig the outcome. For all I knew success might have meant saving the military money, which was never really a concern or concept easily grasped by the average military mind. Or success may have meant producing more proficient technicians because, as we all know, learning less in less time always advances proficiency. My guess, however, is that shortening and mangling the program boiled down to some overly ambitious career dickhead looking for a way to get out of a dead end job by reinventing the wheel and gaining favor while earning a ribbon and bragging rights in doing so. Personally I would have liked learning basic electronics since I had no damn idea what the instructor was talking about through most of the condensed program, which boiled down to a crash course on how not to fry your nuts or your brain while testing and chassis changing forty-thousand volt circuit boards on multimillion dollar equipment that the government most assuredly paid millions too much for in the first place. To complicate the situation our particular class instructor was probably one of the most boring and semi-inarticulate people ever to grace a high tech environment. This presented us with the biggest challenge of all, just staying awake, which was usually accomplished by recalling to memory the bullfight or donkey show visited the night before in the Wazoo. Such disgusting memories often have a tendency to keep one awake.

As a result, I never did learn the difference between an oscilloscope and a Pezz dispenser and fortunately for both the Army and myself, I never had to put any of my unlearned confusion to practice. In the end, however, a shortened course of study, or even a longer one, really didn't matter much because like most Army enlisted men's training programs, we simply weren't expected to learn anything, only to pass the course. It was a fact of military life and strategic philosophy, as every officer who has ever served in the military knows or is taught, each and every enlisted man below the NCO ranks is so stupid, inept, incompetent, and ham-fisted that if it weren't for the officer corps they wouldn't be able to tell the difference between daylight and dog shit, or be able to take a piss without drooling all over their leg. On the other hand, no enlisted man ever made a decision that got 25,000 men killed in the short period between breakfast and lunch, a decision seemingly repeated throughout history by senior officers and academy savants everywhere.

Just the same, the three months were eventfully filled with the fun and games of the Wazoo where many of us young just off the farm pudfuckers gained an uncanny insight of the international flavor of society and life in general. It was also a lesson in survival with an array of unwritten rules and laws. For example, each company maintained what was called a Hearts & Flowers Fund to which everyone would contribute a buck each payday. In reality, it was a ransom fund to be used for rescuing G.I.s who were incarcerated by the local Wazoo Federallies. It was necessary due to a neat little trick the Mexicans pulled on a regular basis, and if you weren't forewarned or briefed on it you could end up forever lost in the black hole of the corrupt and heavy-handed south of the border penal system.

A number of bars and establishments in the Wazoo were participants in this particular ruse and their game was simple; arrest an innocent G.I. for what appeared to be legitimate reasons, (in the Wazoo, to the Mexican police anything qualified as a legitimate reason), then let him rot in a jail cell until somebody came to rescue him baring money and goodwill. In most cases it involved a few Mexican ladies, and I use the term sparingly, meandering up to and sitting at the table of a few unsuspecting weekenders who were quietly and happily partaking of the local cervasa and cuisine. The ladies would order themselves some drinks which appeared to be high priced cocktails, then make like the Juarez welcome wagon or garden club with the young credulous soldiers. When the waiter eventually came to collect the tab, it inevitably would include the over-inflated price of the watered drinks of the uninvited ladies, so over-inflated that most guys in their right mind would protest as most did, especially since it included what appeared to be every drink those ladies had consumed in the last five weeks. In many cases the G.I.s would pay only their fare share of the tab and attempt to exit at which time they would come face to face with members of the local uniformed head knockers who just happened to be nearby conveniently witnessing the entire affair.

"Policia!" said the bartender. "They won pay for de ladies drinks!"

"Senors, chu deed not pay for de ladies drinks?" asked one of the two Wazoo Policia who just happen to be standing by.

"You're right," a young soldier would say. "This place is a rip off. You should do something about it."

"But Senors, chu deed not pay for de ladies drinks," smiled the other short Wazoo Policia, proudly exposing his gold tooth, the one that replaced the one that was knocked out by an angry G.I. who refused to pay for some ladies drinks.

"That's right. Because we didn't order their drinks."

"But Senors, chu deed not pay for de ladies drinks."

"But we didn't order the ladies drinks so why should we pay for the ladies drinks?"

"But Senors, chu deed not pay for de ladies drinks," echoed the taller Policia with the potbelly and a collection of burrito drip stains on his shirt. The same Policia who was the big brother of one of the ladies whose drinks didn't get paid for.

"No, you don't understand," the G.I. would say. "It was a rip off. We didn't invite those girls to our table and we didn't order their drinks. We even told them to leave. And even if we did order the drinks we wouldn't pay because they were just water."

"Agua? Agua! Bull de shit, Gringo! Bull de shit!" objected the bartender who was so unconvincing that he wouldn't pass an audition to play the part of a turnip in a food commercial.

"G.I. Gringos," smiled the short gold-toothed Policia, "chu need to pay for de ladies drinks."

"Agua! Chu lie! Bull de shit, Gringo. Chu tell lie!"

"Yeah, well, bull dee sheet to you too, Pedro. 'Cause you're a damn crook and I ain't payin' for your whore's water."

Naturally, this was always the wrong thing to say being the bartender was married to the table whore who was also the sister of the pot bellied Policia with the burrito stains. Needless to say one thing would lead to another, sometimes through dialogue, sometimes violence, but most of the time would end up with the G.I.s taking the happy trail to a rat farm the Wazoo Policia called a jail. There they would joyfully and permanently relieve you of everything and anything of value, and if you were dumb enough to bring your automobile you could count on that becoming the latest permanent edition to the police motor pool as well unless it was an exceptionally sweet ride. If so, it would then be auctioned off for the cause or offered to a local official for favor. Either way you could count on never seeing your sweet hard-earned V-8 baby again.

This was just one of many methods the Wazoo police used to gain revenue. There were others just a slick and some that were just plain blatant but they got away with it because basically the Mexicans knew that the authorities at Fort Bliss knew that the G.I.s were usually as innocent as newborn babes. Well, kind of. This was obvious because had a G.I. done something seriously bad he most likely would have been stabbed or shot or beaten to death. The unfortunate alternative was for the known innocent incarcerated Americans to choose the long and grueling Mexican gauntlet legal route in an effort to seek and gain justice. Mexican justice, should it be found at all, meant this most likely would result in the poor G.I.s ending up disappearing or, if they were lucky, so far lost in the Mexican penal system they would forget their nationality, native language, and the fact they were ever even in the U.S. Army to begin with, which may have been a blessing as well because the Army justice system in itself was a conflicting concept and would consider each and every day spent behind bars, innocent or guilty, as *bad time,* for which the G.I. would be court-martialed. "Damned if you do and fucked if you don't," we would warn each other.

Regardless of all this and other negative border town attributes, the Wazoo was never put off limits and attracted many thousands of American G.I.s over the years, including the *Continuous Wave Acquisition Radar Technician Surface To Air Hawk Missile System Air Defense Prototype Test Class of 1969.* The adventures and distractions were well worth the risk and to be duped into the rat farm over the weekend and return broke, busted, and disgusted on a Monday morning was for some G.I.s more a badge of honor than a career killer. No one actually held it against you and it was just one of those things the Army pretty much winked at and wrote off to the price of international relations or simply tolerated because no one wanted to suffer the embarrassment. In addition, most Commanding Officers, including Post Commanders, were very reluctant to admit that such problems existed under their command. Out of sight, out of mind, and out of my damn career file was the commanding lifer's creed. "Viva la Wazoo and Viva la Mexico!" was ours.

As our shortened prototype class progressed and life continued, I received an accelerated promotion to Specialist 4th Class, which was highly appreciated, especially since I had already been made a SP4 when I flunked out of flight school where I was getting paid as a WOC E-5. I also discovered the taco, underground music, a German bar in El Paso where they served real German dark beer in a glass boot to under-aged G.I.s, Texans who didn't say howdy, purchased a real Italian Fiat 600 from a real Italian, actually saw it snow on the desert, and was treated to a cross-country visit from my high school high-strung air-headed redheaded sweetheart at which time, due to too much dark beer from the boot, resulted in an accelerated wedding for which I surprisingly discovered the Army also had a program. Unofficial as it was.

After making arrangements to get married off base and thinking all my matrimonial ducks were in a row, my presence was requested, or should I say demanded, by a Chaplain Captain who had somehow gotten word of our intended joining from an impatient future mother-in-law. The chaplain was a tall but frail, spongy, disjointed, academic type with intense anxious insecure round eyes that were somehow both hidden and exaggerated behind Government Issue black horn-rimmed glasses. His constant expression of near panic left the impression that if he were ever to have to change lanes on a freeway he would probably experience an instant aneurysm, or that he could easily panic and get lost in his own house providing he could find it in the first place. I could imagine his wife probably matched and laid out his clothes for him each morning even though it was a uniform providing little or no challenge or confusion. Intellectually the Chaplain Captain was a marvel of religious, social, and biblical edification who had read and could regurgitate just about everything from the Quran to the Dead Sea Scrolls, but when it came to the demands and utilization of original thought he was about as inept as an upside down turtle in the Daytona 500. I knew there were people like this on the planet but managed to avoid them whenever possible, all the while fascinated by their ability to somehow survive and even thrive and multiply.

It was evident the Chaplain Captain was enthusiastically dedicated to his calling, however, and obviously determined to somehow justify his existence in the United States Army by treating my situation as though it were a national crisis. Mustering all his wavering frailty behind his *hard commission,* he immediately proceeded to ream my ass for not consulting with him and baring my soul before I ventured into a lifetime commitment of matrimony, and nearly convinced me that my nuptials were in a real bind. That is until my instincts dismissed all accepted military standards of rank, assuring me that my first impression of him would correctly also be my last.

"I hear you're getting married," he said in a near panic.

"Yes sir."

"How are you getting married?"

Knowing we both existed in the same society, I thought the question was a little naïve but then I usually faired well at pop quizzes and played along.

"In a church, sir."

"Oh no. You can't do that!"

"I can't?"

"Hell, no."

He actually said that, 'Hell no', and he was a chaplain, leading me to assume Army chaplains have to maintain a certain degree of military decorum, either that or it was his lame-ass way of demonstrating he was just one of the troops.

"Why didn't you come to me first?" he asked, as though I had violated some previous sacred agreement of trust.

"It's not really a problem, sir. We're just getting married, that's all."

"That's all?" he said. "How do you know it's not a problem? You haven't talked to me yet. Do you really know this girl?"

"You mean in the biblical sense, sir?"

"Um…Uh huh. I think we need to talk… um, what's your name again?"

"Fusco, sir," I stated, pointing to the name stenciled in big fat letters over the pocket of my fatigue blouse.

"I think we need to talk, Lieutenant Fusco."

"Specialist, sir," I stated, pointing to the SP4 rank pin on my collar.

"What?"

"Specialist Fourth Class Fusco, sir."

"Yes, we need to talk Lieutenant Specialist Fusco."

"Just Specialist, sir."

"Uh huh. Well, I want you and your… um…"

"Fiancé?"

"Fiancé… to come to my office tomorrow at three o'clock."

"Yes sir. Fifteen hundred hours."

"No, three o'clock."

I gathered chaplains didn't utilize military time, probably because they don't go through basic training. But then if they did go through basic training they probably would never have become chaplains, especially after extensive exposure to the highly colorful vocabulary of drill sergeants, having to take group showers with multi-racial incorrigibles forced to enlist by the judicial system, and suffering the indignity and embarrassment of shitting in public, not to mention the indecency and humiliation of the bend over and spread'em flash light up your ass line-up during the induction center physicals. Like many military lawyers and doctors, they were just thrown into the mix and afforded automatic *hard commissions* on the assumption they were natural born gentlemen who were intelligent enough to appreciate it, know the difference between daylight and dog shit, and would never actually have to use their rank for anything other than to receive a bigger pay check and legally pass over the threshold of the Officer's Club.

"But we're getting married tomorrow, sir."

"No you're not."

"I'm not?"

"Not until I have a chance to counsel you. And you shouldn't get married in a church. You need to get married in my chapel."

"Isn't that the same thing, sir?"

"No, it's not. It's *my* chapel. It's an Army chapel. You should have come to me first."

"But I'm just getting married, sir. I'm marrying my girl friend."

"No you're not. Not until you talk to me. That's why I'm here. I'll decide if you're getting married."

He seemed so upset as to nearly come to tears and I almost felt sympathy for him though I can't imagine why. Needless to say, I was at a loss for words. Being relatively new to the Army and on my way to becoming a highly disciplined tool of destruction, I was aware that some self control, discipline, and sacrifice was expected but I surely didn't recall any training, indoctrination, or information regarding the Army's ability to determine matters of matrimony except maybe between two people of the same gender. I therefore concluded this Chaplain Captain was pissed off because, like Staff Sergeant Finkel the recruiter car salesman, he had some kind of quota to fulfill, had to answer to some senior God dude at the Pentagon, and was expected to perform X amount of baptisms, X amount of confessions, X amount of funerals, X amount of exorcisms, and X amount of derailed marriages, all achieved within the confines and demanding schedule of the front nine, back nine, and cocktails at the O-club, of course.

The next day, three o'clock, not 1500 hours, rolled around and my lady and I strolled into the Chaplain Captain's office in the rear of the Chaplain Captain's chapel. It was a windowless and relatively small office, though maneuverable, very neat, and very dimly lit, consisting of a desk facing two chairs and a wall of books and assorted printed literature to the side. The dim light made the room seem even smaller than it actually was and when the Chaplain Captain closed the door behind us the room seemed to lessen in size even more. Why he closed the door was a mystery to me considering the office was part of his small chapel and aside from the three of us there was no one else in the building. When he settled nervously behind his desk I noticed an eight by ten picture of a blond haired blue eyed Jesus that hung neatly just above a crossed missiles insignia of the Army Air Defense. A match made in Heaven, I thought, and about as contradictory as a minister in a military uniform.

"So this is the young lady," he observed.

I wasn't sure how to read the comment. It was so clinical I didn't know if it was an accusation, a declaration of guilt, or a warm welcome. I wanted to say something like, "No, you dumb shit, it's just some Wazoo whore I brought by to rattle your roller coaster," but I couldn't say that, of course, because the Chaplain Captain sported an automatic *hard commission* meaning he not only had God on his side but Army regulations as well and sooner or later someone somewhere, possibly at the O-club or on the seventh green, might inform him that such comments were inappropriate when addressed to a Captain by a lowly enlisted man. And he might actually believe them.

"Yes, sir. This is Stacie, my fiancé."

"How do you do, Stacie? I'm Chaplain Keuwac."

Chaplain *Quack*, I thought to myself. Yeah, you got that right.

"So, you two want to get married," he stated, as though we were considering the purchase of some linoleum or a new washing machine. "May I ask why?"

Stacie looked at me and I could see in her eyes she had just figured out that though all three of us were members of the same species, one of us was a little askew but I knew better. I knew two of us were a little askew and one of them wasn't me.

The room got smaller.

"Because we love each other, Chaplain Quack," she replied.

"Keuwac. That's *Captain Ku-wak*," Chaplain Captain Quack corrected.

"But I thought you were a Chaplain?"

"That's correct."

"But you said, Captain."

"That's correct."

"Captains kill people. I thought Army Captains kill people. Do you kill people?"

"Well, not really. I save people. Figuratively speaking"

"Oh, that's sweet," said Stacie, turning to me. "You didn't tell me that you saved people after you shoot them. That's sweet. Honey, don't you think that's sweet?"

"I didn't tell you I shoot people."

"Doesn't everybody in the Army shoot people? You know, those poor little yellow people on TV over there in Japan."

"No," I answered. "That's just in the movies."

"They just shoot them in the movies?"

"Um… I think we're kind of loosing direction here," Chaplain Captain Quack interrupted uncomfortably. "Now, about your marriage."

"Oh, we're not married," Stacie informed Chaplain Quack.

"Yes, I know. But you want to get married, correct?"

"Yes."

"Uh huh."

"We've known each other since high school you know," said Stacie.

"Uh huh."

"And we've been engaged for six months."

"Uh huh."

Having regained direction, it seemed all Chaplain Captain Quack could say was, 'uh huh, uh huh,' leading me to wonder in what direction we were supposed to be going in the first place. Then he looked at me accusingly and said, "And you're pregnant."

"No," I replied. "She is."

"Uh huh."

"It's really alright," said Stacie. "We've only had to move the wedding up a few months."

"Uh huh, uh huh. Yes, well… uh, before we begin I'd like you to fill out these questionnaires for me."

He handed us each a one-page survey of multiple-choice questions. As he did I noticed a ring on his finger that looked familiar but dismissed it. We completed the surveys with reserve and caution, resisting the desire to cheat, then handed them back. He mulled over the papers for what seemed a silent eternity, that is except for a few uh huhs, then blurted out brusquely, "By all accounts, and according to these surveys, you two should not be compatible. No, not compatible at all. Do you realize this?"

Actually, I thought our compatibility had already manifested itself, which was why we were getting married ahead of schedule in the first place. Since I didn't agree with him I felt a defensive response of some kind was warranted, perhaps some form of diplomatic statement that would avoid challenging his highly regarded status and unearned hard commission and justify the mysterious bonding that had evolved between Stacie and me. In other words, I didn't know what the hell to say so I came up with the best answer I could.

"Actually sir, I was never into astrology much."

"Uhhhhh huh."

Due to his spiritual programming, intense focus on the mission at hand, and an inability to think outside the parameters of his own social ignorance and limited universe, Captain Chaplain Quack was unflappable, and with his demonstrating no evident appreciative sense of humor or ability to recognize the same, I saw no real challenge or opportunity for continued efforts in that regard. I decided to just let the two mental giants have at it in hopes that somehow it would all come out in the wash.

Stacie grew uneasy and her hands went to her stomach. I wasn't sure if she was going to barf or just boogie on out of the building in a panic.

"What…what do you mean… What do you mean 'not compatible'?" she asked nervously, probably thinking I had failed to tell her I had some incurable disease or was an adopted space alien.

"Well, you see, certain types of personalities just aren't compatible with other types of personalities and according to this survey… Well, you know, actually, at this juncture it's really not important."

"Why not?" asked Stacie.

"Well, because you're…"

"What?"

"…with child."

"Oh no," she corrected quickly. "I'm with him."

Chaplain Captain Quack just stared. He had finally come up against his equal and it was a fascinating thing to behold. They were pushing the intellectual envelope and I could hardly wait to see where it went.

"I think we need to talk about… um, sex," suggested Captain Quack.

The room got smaller.

"Why?" asked Stacie. "I'm not going to have sex with you. Do Chaplains even have sex?"

"Well, um… not if they're Catholic. At least they're not suppose… um, well."

"Are you Catholic?"

"No, I'm a Protestant."

"Well then, I couldn't have sex with you anyway. I'm a Southern Baptist."

"No. Yes… I mean, technically we could… I mean you could but obviously you… I mean we wouldn't…"

"Then I guess we don't have to talk about it. Sex, I mean," Stacie stated with complete clarity.

"Well, you do want to get married, don't you?"

"Yes, but not to you. And what's that got to do with sex?"

"Exactly," he replied.

"Oh," she said. "I see."

And I'm sure she did or at least thought she did.

Chaplain Captain Quack reached across his desk and handed each of us a short stack of pamphlets and booklets about sex and the moral implications of intercourse, both pre-marital and post-marital, which at this point in our relationship was the equivalent of enrolling a fish in a swimming class. He then began offering up the most incredible revelations.

"You know one of the great joys of marriage is that it affords two people the opportunity to have intercourse," said Chaplain

Captain Quack as though he had exclusively discovered the concept and was revealing it for the first time in front of an intellectual audience of shrinks at a world social science convention somewhere in Sweden. I'm sure he thought we should have felt privileged and honored to learn this secret but there are some things in life that are just plain understood by even the most intellectually challenged individuals. The majority of people, at least the one's I knew, were able to easily determine the purpose and potential of the various sexual mechanics of the human body, I thought, so I really couldn't disagree with Chaplain Captain Quack's statement and therefore had no response. I simply waited for the punch line.

"But you must realize this is an opportunity which should never be taken for granted," he continued. "And keep in mind that all good things should be practiced in moderation."

Practice, I thought. Who the hell needs practice?

"For example," he clarified further. "Do you know there are some married couples who actually have intercourse as often as once a month?"

Boom!

Now, Stacie had this thing where when she got flustered, nervous, or was at a loss for words, she would burst into an uncontrollable nervous, boisterous laughter and sure enough this had evolved into one of those occasions. Stacie cracked up, setting Chaplain Captain Quack back in his seat without a clue as to why. As for me, having heard the Chaplain's revelation regarding the properly accepted frequency of copulation, my first instinct and concern was an honest to God hope and desire that Stacie wasn't taking mental notes, not that she was capable. My second thought was that somewhere at Fort Bliss, Texas, was a Mrs. Chaplain Captain Quack who had to be either the most sexually frustrated woman in the solar system or bopping every swinging dick *hard* commissioned officer that walked through the hallowed doors of the O-Club. Other than that the room seemed to implode altogether and my brain instinctively shut down and went numb and all I actually remember was an order to report to the chapel at one o'clock, not 1300 hours, on a certain day, which happened to be my birthday, and to bring two witnesses for legal purposes. I brought the entire guinea pig Continuous Wave Acquisition Radar

Technician Surface To Air Hawk Missile System Air Defense Prototype Class of 1969 and immediately following Chaplain Captain Quack's long, long, long, long grueling sermon and ceremony, we all changed into civvies and went to the Wazoo where some people actually have sexual intercourse as often as twenty times a day and not necessarily always with the same species.

We celebrated our marriage and my birthday by getting stinking drunk in some junky juke joint with the entire Continuous Wave Acquisition Radar Technician Surface To Air Hawk Missile System Air Defense Prototype Class of 1969 taking turns dancing with my new bride and fending off the advances of indigenous dangerous looking horny predator Mexican caballeros who wanted to do the same. It was a good time for all except for one member of our class named Morris Shoelacker from Texarkana, Arkansas, who came back the next day married to a Mexican girl with which he could neither communicate nor remember marrying. Six months later while he was in Korea, and after gaining her U.S. citizenship, she gave him a no-strings no-fault divorce and five hundred dollars as per their agreement made that night in Wazoo, which he also could not remember but readily accepted. This afforded his freedom and the newly divorced US citizen Mrs. Shoelacker the opportunity to bring into her newly adopted homeland her mother and father, her six children supposedly conceived during previous marriages, and about five thousand brothers and sisters. Not bad for an eighteen year old going on sixteen.

All in all, for Stacie and I, it was a wedding and honeymoon only an under-paid Army enlisted man could appreciate, culminating with two young inebriated lovers driving off through the tumbleweeds into a prickly Texas sunset and a prickly future that only the war time sixties could spawn.

CHAPTER 6

HURRY UP & COORS

Weeks later, after the class at Fort Bliss had ended and we were all highly qualified to short circuit millions of dollars worth of critical national defense radar equipment, we eagerly awaited our orders with the anticipation that each of us would receive one of the warm and sunny assignments we had entered on our dream sheets. A dream sheet is a form where they let you choose your three most preferred locations for assignment depending on your particular specialty. The choice is from a list of approved duty stations requiring your particular MOS. I, for example, had put down the Hawk missile site at Homestead, Florida, for my first choice. For my second choice I entered the Hawk missile site at Homestead, Florida, and for my third choice, with the hopes of taking up scuba diving and keeping up a great tan, I wrote in the Hawk missile site at Homestead, Florida.

Dream sheets are a long and honored military tradition, meaning they are a long shot as in *not a hope in hell*, and honored only for a select few senior officers and occasional Command Sergeant Majors. Therefore, needless to say, our hopeful selections were an exercise in futility, kind of like jerking off at an execution as they'd say in the barracks, because all of us received orders for the icy cold regions of Korea, a place not even one of us had any desire to visit in our lifetime or selected on our dream sheet. Then, on the day before we were to depart the bliss of Fort Bliss, out of the clear blue sky, or the dark hole of the Pentagon, someone had a brain fart and decided to reroute three of us to Fort Sill, Oklahoma - as in *Oklahoma?* And to make it even more challenging we had only two days to get there.

Our orders dictated a unit of destination with special orders for top-secret intensive training. What kind of top-secret intensive training we weren't told simply because it was top-secret. Either that or the Army simply didn't seem to think it was necessary for us to know, after all, we were only enlisted men who didn't know the difference between daylight and dog shit. We were further instructed that due to the seriousness and intensity of this training that we knew nothing about, we would be required to live on and be restricted to the base, meaning no dependants were permitted. So off to the airport went Stacie and off to the land of Custer and Sitting Bull went we three, all crammed in my newly acquired little blue used Fiat 600 that sported suicide doors that opened the wrong way and an *ITALIA* sticker across the back window.

The Fiat was a great little go-kart of a car, fantastic on gas, which I had purchased for $400 from an Italian exchange officer who happened to be heading back to his blessed Italia. I'm sure my only reason for finding such a great deal was that the Italian officer probably didn't feel like sticking the little blue bugger in his luggage, which is most likely how he brought it into the country to begin with. An added benefit was that the little car still sported an officer's base window sticker. This meant we could whiz on through the base main gate at all hours of the day and night with only a hasty salute, never being challenged for required passes. A great asset until the sticker expired.

We reported to Fort Sill as directed and to the unit specified in our orders which, surprisingly, turned out to be an artillery company. Naturally this shouldn't have been surprising being Fort Sill is the Army's primary artillery base and training center. Just the same, we surrendered our orders to the resident company clerk who after reading them pulled a total blank.

"Says here, you guys are supposed to report for intensive training," observed the astute clerk.

"That's what it says," we all agreed.

"Why?"

"For intensive training," we answered.

"Yep, says, you're supposed to report here... for intensive training," he repeated while exploring the multiple copies of the orders.

"That's what it says," we again agreed.

He continued to muse over the orders until he decided they were beyond his comprehension then rose and walked across the room and passed them on to his First Sergeant.

"Says, they're supposed to report here for intensive training," he informed his First Sergeant.

"Here?"

"Yep. For intensive training."

The First Sergeant looked at the orders, then looked at us, then looked at the orders, then looked at us again.

"You guys are supposed to report here?" asked the First Sergeant.

"Yes, First Sergeant," we replied in unison.

"For intensive training?"

"Yes, First Sergeant."

"What kind of intensive training?"

We looked to each other for an answer, which we didn't really have, and having none I stated, "Top-secret, Top."

"What kind of top-secret?"

"The kind that requires intensive training, Top."

"What kind of intensive training?"

"The top-secret kind, Top."

I could tell this First Sergeant had a sincere desire to decipher our perplexing orders if for no other reason than simple curiosity. Admittedly, the desire was just as sincere among the three of us as well who had exhausted all avenues of imagination during the trip from Texas. We toyed with the possibility that we had been selected to work on some top-secret missile project but dismissed the idea deciding that the Army had to realize we didn't really know anything about missiles other than the quickest way to short circuit a missile system. We also considered the possibility we had been targeted for some form of undercover work of the 007 nature but dismissed that over a lunch of chilly dogs at a roadside Dairy Doodle, on the grounds we were enlisted men who could only afford lunch at a Dairy Doodle and weren't officially smart enough to delve into such challenging activities. We finally decided that whatever it was we were about to learn, or try to learn, or pretend to learn, or try to pretend to learn, it was a hell of a lot better than freezing our asses off in Korea.

The First Sergeant mused over the orders until he decided they were beyond his comprehension then passed them on to his Commanding Officer, a Captain Goable, who called us into his office. We stood silent for a long moment until he finally said, "First Sergeant says you have orders to report here."

"Yes sir," we confirmed in unison.

"Says here, you're supposed to report here for intensive training," said Captain Goable.

"Yes sir."

"Why?" asked Captain Goable.

"For intensive training, sir."

"Yeah okay. Why?" asked Captain Goable.

"Because that's what it says, sir."

"Intensive training?"

"Yes sir."

"Here?"

"Yes sir."

"What kind of intensive training?" asked Captain Goable.

"The top-secret kind, sir."

"Top-secret?" asked Captain Goable.

"Yes sir. Top-secret intensive training."

"But you guys are Air Defense," observed Captain Goable.

"Yes sir."

"You know this is an artillery unit?" asked Captain Goable.

"No sir."

"Well this is an artillery unit," said Captain Goable.

"Yes sir."

Captain Goable looked intensely at the orders, nodded his head yes a few times, then posed, "What kind of top-secret intensive training?"

"The kind they didn't tell us about, sir."

After gazing at the orders for an additional long silent moment he instructed us to wait in the First Sergeant's office during which time he made a phone call. Following the call he informed us that no one in his chain of command had the slightest damn idea why we were there. He then instructed the First Sergeant who then instructed the company clerk who then instructed us to pass the time, hurry up and wait as they say, until things could be sorted out to his satisfaction, which they soon were by way of a phone call to Fort Bliss, Texas, from where he was informed we were the top ten percent of our class and had been sent there for top-secret intensive training. This shed little light at all on our situation resulting in Captain Goable and the First Sergeant washing their hands of us altogether by having us escorted to the empty top floor of a nearby three story big modern empty barracks building where we occupied the entire south wing. Out of sight, out of mind, as they say.

The next day we were assigned a Staff Sergeant Lipscomb as a baby sitter who was also just passing the time, his last 30 days until his retirement. Like the company clerk, the First Sergeant, and Captain Goable of the artillery unit for which we were ordered to report, Staff Sergeant Lipscomb knew nothing of our situation, which was a lot more than we knew, therefore, according to his instructions we did nothing, which as far as we surmised was more than Staff Sergeant Lipscomb ever did.

After doing nothing for a few days we were joined by others of a similar fate until by the end of the week we eventually numbered about twenty souls, all with the same orders and lack of knowledge regarding our intended intensive top-secret training. As we grew to know each other and compared notes we discovered that some of us were there because we were in the top ten percent of our particular MOS classes, others because they had failed their particular MOS classes, and still others, and these guys I bonded with immediately, were there because they were former flight school Warrant Officer Candidates who somehow managed to get on the bad attitude national traitor shit list and accumulate five prestigious yellow pink slips, joining me in Major Elingsworth's hall of infamy.

Finally, after a week of sleeping in, playing cards and grab-ass, and waiting as fast as we could, our rarely seen good natured Sergeant Lipscomb strolled in with two cases of Coors beer and some news. He usually only delivered two cases of Coors.

"Well boys, I finally got some news for you. There's good news and bad news. Which one do you want first?"

In unison we all said, "Coors!" which won out the day and was a fitting prep for the news, both good and bad.

"I've got some orders for you."

Staff Sergeant Lipscomb was a good natured gentleman with a sense of humor, leading him to pause for affect before stating, "You've all been promoted to Specialist Fourth Class."

This took us all by surprise being that some of us were already SP4s and the rest were only Private E-2s as yet to be promoted to PFC. In addition, most didn't have the time in service or filling the active slots required for promotion eligibility. I was especially honored since the Army thought so much of me as to promote me to SP4 a third time. At this rate, I thought, I could make Specialist

Fourth Class in no time and then be on the fast track for promotion to Specialist Fourth Class or maybe even Specialist Fourth Class. But being the forgiving and good-natured lot that we were, we all graciously accepted our promotions with poise and dignity and Army PX 3.2 Coors beer, then we braced for Sergeant Lipscomb's bad next bombshell.

"The other news is…" he paused again, "…nobody on this entire base knows why the hell you guys are here."

We all stared in disbelief. Someone in the Army had actually screwed up or come to work with a hangover and given us freedom and late accelerated early promotions all in one day. And to think this was in the days before computers. In the face of our dilemma, and through the connections and good will of Sergeant Lipscomb, plus the fact we didn't belong to any given unit in the United States Army, we were all given permanent off post passes and instructed to not get caught doing whatever it was we decided to do and to be sure we were in our bunks each morning when nobody checked to see if we were in our bunks each morning. That, of course, led to the exploration and exploitation of each and every topless go-go bar and questionable establishment in the city of Lawton, the honing of party and drinking skills, and the ability to find and enter the main gate of Fort Sill while inebriated without the aid of radar. Then, weeks later, Sergeant Lipscomb appeared with more good news.

"Since we don't know what to do with you guys we're going to put you in some classes."

Naturally we moaned and groaned a bit, having enjoyed the freedom of unlimited access to the city and thinking we were destined to some long and boring training experience, until we heard what those classes were. It turned out the first class consisted of how to choose, evaluate, and set up a Sergeant Missile launch site, which was a total waste of time being the big cumbersome Sergeant Missile was obsolete. We knew it was obsolete because we were told it was obsolete by the instructor before we started the class. Following the successful completion of that program we were taught the computer launcher system of the Pershing Missile, another soon to be discarded obsolete system. We were told that as well. The toughest part of the courses was trying to find out why these big obsolete missiles were hiding out on an artillery base anyway, a question no one seemed to be able to answer. Then things became a little more exciting when we were taught how to blow shit up, becoming whiz-bangs at destroying those same perfectly good obsolete missiles, and artillery pieces, and vehicles of all ilks. Take my word for it, det-cord, thermal devices, and C-4 can be lots of fun but blasting caps are tricky little bastards.

To further fill our agenda we were then trained, qualified, and licensed to drive every size wheeled vehicle in the Fort Sill arsenal. The latter took only one day as taught by the Army, actually half a day with us spending the other half hiding and asleep in a semi-truck trailer. We popped in and out of a few other classes as well, being so brief and uninteresting I can't even recall what they were except that most all of the courses taken, with the exception of the driving school, demolition, and EOD, required top secret and crypto clearances.

So there we were, a small group of enlisted failures and phenoms who had, for some reason and by some twist of fate, become professional military students; a privilege usually reserved only for anointed higher up *hard commissioned* career officers who have been chosen to rule the universe. We became convinced that had we somehow been mistakenly slipped into and completed the courses at the Army's Command School it was a cinch we would have figured out how to end the war with victory in less than two weeks, but then fate and unique military groupthink only goes so far and we were denied the privilege. All of the higher knowledge we did accumulate, however, took place over the period of about a month and a half, after which we were once again left to our own devices and once again forced to wait as fast as we could for our orders. The days ran into weeks and the weeks extended into a lot of Coors and Go Go bars until eventually one night while we were up on the roof of the barracks telling lies, sharing a bottle, and laying on our backs counting UFOs, a Marine Captain called Jiggy strolled into our lives and asked if we would like to volunteer for a special project. The unwritten rule of never ever volunteering for anything in the Army surfaced quickly in our collective mind and, confidentially, seeing a Marine I immediately had flashes of my friend Leroy Smith as well. But then somehow my first impression led me to think this Marine seemed to be anything but your average die-hard jarhead and that first impression was correct. It seems he had just returned from Vietnam and was here to supervise the construction of a prototypical honest to God Vietnam in-country outpost in the boonies of Fort Sill and he was in need of assistance.

Now, by this time we were all pretty much bored out of our skulls and, in fact, one trooper took an unofficial week's vacation and went home to Boston while another of our small company decided the Army was a waste of his life entirely and flew the coop altogether. Was he ever caught or even missed I have no idea because we never had any morning formations or roll calls to signal the release of the hounds. And being we had somehow fallen into this huge accommodating military crack, we didn't really want to make waves or set off any alarms. So with the shrug of a shoulder or two we indolently but eagerly accepted Captain Jiggy's challenge and for two weeks each day we trucked out to the hills and dug trenches and bunkers and filled sand bags and generally got all messed up playing solder in the dirt and the mud. I can honestly say it was a good uncomplicated time and the good Marine Captain Jiggy, who would never reveal how he came by that moniker, and having been baptized by fire in Vietnam, was now a born again cordial dude who had no qualms about keeping us in beer and hot lunches. As we labored the running joke became how many top-secret-crypto-high-tech-intensively-trained soldiers did it take to fill a sand bag? The answer being; eighteen - one to lean on the shovel and seventeen to hold the beer.

We finally completed the construction of the genuine authentic imitation Vietnam outpost after two weeks, at which time Captain Jiggy was quick to inform us we were a collection of fine outstanding troops who had done an outstanding job and had we not been misguided into the Army would have made outstanding Marines.

"In the Nam, however," stated Captain Jiggy, "this entire outpost would have been built in one or two days."

In our defense we argued that in the Nam there would not have been a steady supply of day time Coors and night time Go Go bars to hinder the progress. Captain Jiggy conceded and joined us in a final overindulgence of Coors while we compared our Wazoo adventures to his war stories and ended the day appreciating a tranquil, though inebriated, Oklahoma sunset.

With Sergeant Lipscomb becoming a civilian, the outpost completed and the Marine laying us off, we were once again at the mercy of our own devices and the great black hole of the military bureaucracy. Our freedom led to becoming so adventuresome and starved for anti-boredom remedies to fill our time that a few of us started to spend time in the hills of the nearby Wichita Wildlife Refuge skinny dipping, rock climbing, and chasing and getting treed by angry buffalo. Some of us even went to the local Fort Sill jump club where, for fifteen bucks, you got a crash course in departing perfectly good airplanes with perfectly old obsolete T-10 steerable military parachutes; three jumps, two static and one free fall. On one occasion, ex-WOCs Mike Sims, Cowboy Colby, and myself made a jump over General Custer's old parade grounds and got caught in a persuasive wind that sent us hellbent for a nearby interstate highway. Mike and Cowboy managed to hit the ground a safe distance from where the rubber met the big and busy road but a combination of wind and my un-cooperative steerable steered me just over the top of an oncoming eighteen-wheeler and into a very surprised group of indigenous black angus beef cows on the other side of the freeway. It was on that day the phrase OH SHIT became a permanent and integral part of my vocabulary, a two word phrase that now has a tendency to almost always erupt during times of stress, high emotions, and good sex.

To this day I'm not sure who was more unnerved, the damn cows or myself, including one of the cows that became shrouded in my chute and tried to drag my ass through every freshly plunked pile of sweet smelling dung in the pasture. To make things even more embarrassing I was rescued by a former airborne Captain who had pulled his pick-up truck over on the interstate, hopped the fence, shoed off the cows, freed me from my T-10, then went into uncontrollable laughter. He gave me a lift back to the base but insisted, due to the lingering and poignant aromatic cow paddy residue on my clothing, that I ride in the rear of his new Chevy truck.

It took a while to live the experience down, all the while having to endure names such as, Cow Jumper, Shit Skidder, and Paddy Fucker. My fellow deviates even went so far as to forge an official Army document declaring I was on the priority list of airborne troops to be utilized for any possible upcoming operations for the purpose of combatting a communist insurrection among domestic cattle and/or indigenous buffalo. Okay, so the Army really is one huge locker room. It was all lots of fun but like all good things our intellectual pursuits and exploits were quelled when finally, and not too soon, a message came from the black hole of Army reasoning.

"Gentlemen, I know you've all been waiting for orders, but apparently they're not going to come so the base commander has decided that we are to give all of you a full tour of Fort Sill and let you choose whatever company or assignment you want."

This, of course, was unprecedented in any man's Army and immediately made all of us exceptionally nervous. Giving an enlisted man a choice went against all existing military doctrine and reasoning. Personally I wasn't sure if this opportunity, if indeed it was an opportunity, was heaven sent or hell incognito, but I was sure of one thing, Fort Sill was located on American soil next to an American town complete with all the amenities including paved roads, Go Go bars, and a Pizza Hut. In addition, it afforded me the opportunity to actually have sex at least once a month as directed by Chaplain Captain Quack and hopefully get invited to the premier of my first-born. It was on this occasion I truly learned to appreciate the phrase, *a bird in hand...* Or so I thought at the time.

CHAPTER 7

THE GREAT OKLAHOMA
CRAPPER REBELLION

The three of us, Cowboy Colby from Texas, Mike Sims of Utah, and myself, all national traitors and warrant officer flight school rejects, decided to stick together without even bothering to tour the base. We had already scoped out the 17th Ordinance Company just next door knowing our choice of units wasn't so much a matter of what we wanted but more a matter of what we didn't want. We didn't want to blow shit up and we didn't want to piss around with obsolete missiles and we sure as hell didn't want to be cooks, MPs, artillery cadre, or work in some boring ass office all day. After all, we were highly trained top-secret crypto tech types who wanted to prove our worth in a worthwhile job. What we didn't know, however, was just how difficult it is to do that in a stateside Army unit that didn't have anything to do.

The 17th Ordinance Company sounded and appeared to be technical and challenging, possibly holding a lot of promise. At least that's what we thought when we made our choice and reported to the First Sergeant for duty, who after close scrutiny of our 201 files that were full of top secret red flags and mysterious sealed envelopes as well as a long list of critical MOS's, looked up and asked,

"Can any of you guys type?"

Trained to respond quickly and positively to any and all inquires of a Top Sergeant we unanimously replied, "Yes," which we just as quickly discovered was the equivalent of pleading guilty in front of a criminal court judge.

He tossed the 201 files to the company clerk and without the least bit of hesitation or consideration whatsoever for our highly trained critical MOS top-secret crypto could almost fly asses, said, "Change their primary MOS to Clerk Typist."

Right there, in a matter of seconds and at the whim of a First Sergeant, hundreds of thousands of taxpayer training dollars went down the tubes. And in just minutes, with only a few strokes on the company clerk's obsolete Remington manual typewriter, totally devaluated were months, if not nearly a full year of training, as well as our mysterious and enviable black hole high value status at the Pentagon. It was one of those whimsical little decisions that would evolve into a critical turning point in our military careers and our lives, of which we hadn't a clue at the time. Immediately we had a collective visual rush of sitting behind a dull gray steel desk in some dull office filling out dull paperwork in quadruple-triplicate for the next two years and it was a vision of unprecedented horror. Suddenly I found myself envying that college graduate engineer from basic training who was teaching the flute to spoiled snotty little military brats in Germany. We didn't protest; we couldn't and wouldn't because, as anyone who knows anything about the Army understands, only God and the President can counterman the decision of a First Sergeant, and no President is that stupid or that brave.

Checked over, checked in, and chumped, we were shown to our quarters then escorted to our workstations. Cowboy ended up in the armory in the basement. Why they needed a clerk typist in the armory I don't know, but he eventually resolved himself to his sentence and settled in just the same, which was altogether well because Cowboy couldn't really type anyway. Sims and I envied him, however, because he at least was down in the basement, out of sight and out of mind. I on the other hand, drew a high profile slot being assigned to the orderly room and slated to be the next company clerk working right there in front of God, Company Commander, and the First Sergeant all day, each and every day. Needless to say, I was a bit anxious and didn't sleep too well that first night, repeating the prayer of astronaut Alan Shepard, *"Oh Lord, please don't let me fuck up."* But then, fate stepped in once again the very next day when, due to a review of our high clearances, an assignment change sent Sims and I on a daily 15 minute commute to a mysterious place they simply called the Tech Area, or unofficially called *Lala Land*. It seems the 17th Ordinance Company was a STRAC unit, whatever that meant, and the ordinance in question was the nasty, but also delicate kind, which included, but wasn't limited to, special warheads for special weapons, some of which were the spooky things that go boom, grow mushrooms, and make everything glow in the dark -

permanently. According to my previously learned military decorum, STRAC simply meant a soldier who has his shit together. In the new Army, however, it now meant Strategic Army Corps, translating to a possible bug-out to any place at any time. Pack and scoot at the drop of a hat and sorry but that's just tough shit soldier.

The tech area was a square compound of just a few acres surrounded by a ten foot high barbed wire topped chain link fence, surrounded even further by open grassy rolling hills as far as the eye could see. At the front gate, parked like a souvenir or trophy, sat one of the original 1940's atomic bombs, the big fat one about the size of a Volkswagen. I always wondered if it was still loaded and lethal. Knowing it really wasn't, I had a screaming desire to whack it right on the nose in front of a crowd just for shits and giggles, but then the tech area wasn't exactly a stand up comedy club and I knew such a stunt probably wouldn't be appreciated. The seriousness of the place was clearly demonstrated by the process of checking into work there each day. At the gate we had to surrender our military IDs and our watches and our cigarette lighters and anything else that could possible house a camera or micro electronic spy device, or tool of destruction, in exchange for a special clip-on pass. We then walked across the compound to our particular building and surrendered that clip-on pass for a different clip-on pass of a different color. That pass was again surrendered when entering our particular work area inside the building. It seemed ridiculously redundant, but then this was the U.S. military where redundancy is a force in the universe to be religiously admired and practiced. It is redundant procedures such as these that affords senior NCOs and officers the ability to deny and disclaim all responsibility for all things screwed up that may reflect negatively on the nation, the corps, their unit, their ability, their intelligence, their career, their permanent record, their mother, or the weather on planet Mars.

Our job, as we soon discovered, was to sit in a small twelve by twelve foot room with no windows and a Dutch door, the bottom half of which was always closed and locked while occupied, a security feature, we speculated, designed to repel attacking pigmies, very short spies, or emotionally disturbed Chicano Drill Sergeants. The room housed a few dozen technical manuals used by the technical people who worked in the technical area, a society of which we were no longer a part thanks to an unappreciative Top Sergeant who just mangled our careers with the brief stroke of the company clerk's outdated Remington typewriter. It was not exactly a demanding job nor was it a two-man job but then there was this redundancy thing going on and, of course, it was always nice to have someone to talk to while pretending to seriously perform a function that could be achieved by a half stoned trained monkey.

As important as it was, the job was quite simple being, when the technical people checked out the technical manuals to work in the technical areas we checked out the technical people, counted all the pages in the technical manuals, entered the count in a log, and had them sign their John Hancocks. We never questioned anyone's legitimate right to check out and play with our technical manuals because we knew whoever got as far as the half Dutch door had to be the real deal, otherwise they would never have passed through all those ID checkpoints and special pass exchanges to arrive at our destination in the first place. We grew to have absolute faith in the redundancy program, which logically is why the redundancy program was created. If the wrong person, say a spy or subversive, ever did get hold of the technical manuals, there was no way we would accept the responsibility because of the redundant security system. On the other hand, due to all that redundancy, the only two parties who could possibly be charged with the responsibility for such a breach would be us or the President of the United States, and it wasn't hard to guess who would end up being crushed under the heavy anvil of military justice.

"It wasn't our fault," we would probably tell the third redundant investigators for the fourth or fifth time. "It was a breakdown in the redundant security system. Go blame a private."

When the technical people returned the technical manuals at the end of the day we went through the same process of verifying they were who they said they were by asking for a cigarette and a signature, and then counting all the pages to make sure none had been lost or confiscated as substitute toilet paper. Fortunately for us, no pages ever came up missing. I say fortunately because no one ever told us what to do if they had. We discussed this among ourselves at great length and came to the conclusion that we would simply have to shoot whoever it was that came up short. We had one .45 automatic pistol between us for what we assumed was that purpose, but in the Army's wisdom we were not issued any ammunition. Probably because someone was concerned we may become so intensely bored as to revert to playing Russian roulette for relief but then this was ridiculous, of course, because the weapon in question was not a revolver which eliminated that possibility altogether. Sure, the weapons situation made us feel slighted, insulted to say the least. After all, even Barney Fife had one bullet.

The manuals were checked out in the morning, checked back in for the lunch break, checked back out after the lunch break, and checked back in at the end of the day. The time between the issuance and return of the manuals was torture of the highest degree, true boredom to the tenth power and then some. If we were lucky someone would sneak in a comic book or a Playboy magazine that helped pass the time, and since there were no radios or electronic devices permitted in the area it was about the best anyone could hope for. This sometimes made for a long day, a very, very, very long, long day.

The entire tech area seemed to be in the same mode, being a kind of torturous form of slow motion existence. Hell, if someone would have somehow smuggled in one of those electric vibrating football games it would have been like Christmas in July, or quite possibly resulted in multiple cardiac failures due to over stimulation and excitement. Sims and I once fantasized about actually sneaking in one of those games but just couldn't deal with the multiple and emotional possibilities, not to mention the difficulty of sneaking it out again. We then thought of sneaking in a lower tech Battleship game and realized there was actually something to the idea, but rather than jam plastic grid charts up our asses and little metal ships in other assorted orifices, we thought of a different approach altogether, and you might say we succeeded. I imagine to this day if someone ever decided to actually open, use, or read one of those technical manuals it would result in a great deal of confusion if not some form of intelligence maelstrom, for written and mixed in with what are supposed to be highly classified special weapons schematics are our homemade battleship game position grid charts filled with sunken Naval ships of all kinds, not to mention the few games which included the Kon Tiki and a submersible nuclear banana.

As for all those the tech guys, let's face it, there wasn't a lot of tinkering they could do with weird stuff like that and experimentation or creative modification for career enhancement was certainly out of the question. For the most part, they looked like a collection of Stepford Soldiers trying their best to casually and authoritatively look fast while standing still. The ridiculous point of the entire operation was that everybody knew that everybody knew that everybody didn't do shit but wouldn't admit it. Such group denial only fed the entire redundancy routine and led to an ever-present state of paranoia. No one wanted to be caught doing nothing while everyone was actually doing... nothing.

There was one element that gave Sims and I some advantage and popularity, however. Not being allowed to bring in matches or lighters but allowed to have cigarettes, a previous occupant of our little secured documents cubby hole had the genius to wire in and mount on the wall a porcelain light socket rigged with a heat coil that acted as a cigarette lighter. Pull the little chain and you're lit. That device made us popular because everyone in the building had to come to us for a light, which required some social exchange and occasional offerings. Soft drinks were permitted if we could get someone to bring us one because under no circumstances were we allowed to leave our little twelve foot cubby hole without first securing each and every manual and locking it up. This had to be witnessed and verified by a nearby security guard who had no idea what he was looking at in the first place. All national security or paranoid redundancy aside, when nature calls, nature calls, and it was a great deal easier to just jump the Dutch door, give the guard a high sign, and go for the pisser.

The real torture, however, wasn't the isolation or the boredom, it was - THE DRUM. Across from our little cubbyhole was a very large room in the middle of which sat only one item, a white fifty-gallon drum. Appropriately it was simply referred to as *the drum* because no one seemed to know what the hell it contained and, truth be told, no one actually wanted to know. It just sat there all alone, totally ignored like a dull beige four door Nash Rambler in a world full of colorful shiny candy apple red Corvettes. It didn't exist officially or otherwise and no one, either because they couldn't or wouldn't, would acknowledge it's presence or talk about it, or even look at it. The closest I ever got to an answer regarding its contents was that, *"It was none of my business but if only one teaspoon of that shit ever got out you can kiss all of Fort Sill, Lawton, Oklahoma, and your ass goodbye."*

Following that response I never asked again, never wanted to talk about it, and never even looked at it. Although I certainly was conscience of the fact it was there, and there was nothing more uncomfortable than working across the hall from - THE DRUM!

An additional fun thing about the 17th Ordinance Company was the fact it was undermanned. Apparently the redundancy factor failed in this regard. Supposedly the company was to consist of about 200 individuals with an additional attachment of Military Police for security. However the company consisted of less than 150 troops and no security attachment at all, which as it turned out, was a bitch for us top-secret types. It seemed only personnel with top-secret or higher clearances could pull guard duty at the tech area after hours. Ironically, it didn't seem to matter that the guys pulling the regular security duty during the day didn't require the same clearances. The clearance requirement was also questionable being the after-hours guards were stationed outside the fence and not inside. We top secret types available for extra duty numbered only 16, which meant pulling all night guard duty in rotated shifts about twice, sometimes three times a week. We were also the only guards on the base toting loaded pump-action riot guns and while walking the perimeter late at night were constantly being tested and observed by higher up base brass and sneaky security types. While foot patrolling the outside perimeter, it was required that the two guards on duty stay on opposite sides of the square tech area and walk in the same direction so that we maintained a visual command of the entire area at all times. That, of course, was physically impossible so naturally we didn't. Instead, by walking in opposite directions we passed each other twice each round and stopped for a cigarette and some good ole boy conversation that helped pass the time and fight the cold and boredom. And it did get very cold and extremely boring.

As far as actual security went, a great many high ranking officers may never know just how close they came to becoming

Swiss cheese by quietly strolling or driving up to the fat A-bomb in front of Lala Land in the wee hours of the night just to strut their stuff and find out if a guard on duty was awake and knew his three special orders. We knew the three special orders but we also knew there were millions of tricky communist, radicals, anti-war enthusiast, and other degenerates out there impersonating higher up base brass, not to mention ambitious CID, CIA, and multiple undercover types. This meant we didn't know if any of these guys were the real deal or some commie kook imposter out for a smidgen of the contents of *the drum*, not to mention all of the other weird stuff inside the fence. Unknown to them and even the Sergeant of the Guard was our agreed rule of thumb being one of us would talk, deal with the guard duty chicken shit, and play the dutiful soldier with the Mickey Mouse brass, while the other stayed back in the dark shadows at a distance, locked, cocked, and beaded.

The only serious incident that ever took place while I was part of the company was when some kid named Garfield Jones lost his cool and drew down and emptied his full load on a skunk that had crept up behind him, scared him out of his socks, and dumped it's own full load all over his neatly pressed winter wool fatigues. He had to go to the hospital to be de-fumed, but then there is nothing more permanent than skunk stink. He smelled so bad in fact, that the investigating officers refused to investigate, defaulting to the reasoning that any event smelling that bad could not have been intentional. In addition, Garfield was kicked out of his apartment by his wife then banned from the barracks by the First Sergeant. Though he stunk to high heaven, Garfield actually looked on the situation as a blessing, being he didn't have to go to work or pull any duty of any kind for at least two weeks while the stink wore off. He just lived alone in an empty barracks with meals delivered, away from his wife and the Army. His only requirement was to take at least three thorough showers a day which were to be verified by his platoon sergeant who refused to do so, allowing Garfield, who by now was used to the stink, the opportunity to stretch the two weeks into four by taking as few showers as possible.

A big bonus of our elite top secret guard status and the shortage of personnel was that, unlike most companies that gave troops a day off after night duty, we were required to be at work bright and early the next day. This some how affected my state of mind and on many freezing cold nights while walking Lala Land's perimeter, talking to the fat bomb, dodging the skunks, and watching the elk drift down from the hills, I fantasized and contemplated the many ways I was going to *do in* that Army recruiter, the amiable Staff Sergeant Finkel, as well as his buddy that damn chuckling Marine.

As though things couldn't get worse, the three of us were also assigned to the Headquarters platoon under a Staff Sergeant Polk, whose only apparent military function was to show up for reveille, make sure everyone cleaned house, show up again for the morning formation, then show up again for the final formation of the day at 1700 hours. Like many lifer NCOs in support units or functions, his time between formations was usually spent sucking beer and bull shitting at the NCO club. Polk was a quintessential example of this type of NCO.

Now there are a lot of uptight assholes in the Army, but Staff Sergeant Polk was exceptional. For the most part, he was a fair man who enthusiastically hated everyone in the platoon without exception, regardless of race, color, or credo. There were, however, a few exceptions in that he obviously hated some more than others. Ironically that became a badge of honor for those of us in that category; an obvious oversight on his part being we select few became celebrities or unsung heroes of a sort. It was as though the rest of the platoon were watching a NASCAR race and waiting for a crash. The entire situation was a mystery to us. We weren't sure if his attitude was because he was black and had a chip on his shoulder or because he was stupid with no people skills and had to constantly struggle to compensate to avoid making that impression. I do know for a fact the fault wasn't ours for we hadn't been there long and hardly knew the man. We all respected his rank and his person and position, and had no axes to grind, which didn't seem to make a difference. For whatever reason, Staff Sergeant Polk was a first class jerk who seemed to be forever stuck in the *buckfuck* mode. For those unknowing; buckfuck is that state of mind or disease which occurs when an enlisted man has gained the rank and authority of buck sergeant then suddenly thinks he is bigger, badder, wiser, and more powerful than God and all other things in the universe, recognizing no law other than his own and no man of a lower rank to be any more intelligent than a bicycle horn. As honest Abe Lincoln once said "…if you want to test a man's character, give him power." Unfortunately the Army didn't test NCO character and didn't issue people skills along with their stripes.

Staff Sergeant Polk's major beef, as he often reminded us, was that it took him fifteen years to make at least E-5 buck sergeant. Now that he had finally gained one additional rocker under those sergeant's chevrons he was forced to baby sit a platoon of young draftees and regulars who were E-4s and E-5s with less than two or three years in service. He saw no justice or value in our positions and ranks, nor did he seem to take into account he had only an eighth grade education as opposed to our contemporary Army's average 14 years. It was as though he lived in a constant state of menopause and was blind to all things positive about this new generation of soldiers. Neither did he have to live with the skunks outside Lala Land or that damn drum inside, which from our point of view was in itself worth a full commission. And where that drum was concerned, our point of view came all too damn close, all too damn often.

As I stood at attention during one morning company formation soon after our arrival, Staff Sergeant Polk walked right up to my face expressing contemptuously, "You think you're too God damn good to be in this man's Army don't you, Fusco?"

I have to admit he caught me completely off guard. I had long since left such formation harassment back in basic training and flight school and having pretty much kept to myself, I cringed, confused, and offered up the only answer I thought appropriate being, "What?"

"What? What the fuck does that mean, Fusco?"

"What?" I repeated.

"Yeah, that's it. You think you're better than the rest of us don't you… Fusco?"

"What?"

"You're not even going to answer me are you, Fusco? You think you're just too God damn good to even answer me don't you, Fusco?"

"What?"

"What!"

"What?"

"WHAT! Is that all you can say?"

"What?"

"WHAT! WHAT THE FUCK, FUSCO!"

If it were possible for a black man's face to turn red with anger I could swear that Staff Sergeant Polk's face did exactly that, flashing like a beacon atop a speeding multi-ladder fire truck at midnight.

He was partially correct, however, at least at that moment because "what" was pretty much all I could think of, especially after his morning whisky breath permeated my entire brain. In addition, it was just too damn early to be playing mind games so I simply settled for "what", which to me was all I needed to say. I was certain the rest of the platoon had no problem deciphering my *what*, evident I could tell by the heads turning and looking at him and at each other as though Staff Sergeant Polk had lost his marbles. To them and to me my *what* was as clear as a bell. My *what* was a statement. My *what* was sheer poetry. My *what* was Clair De Lune, Jail House Rock, and the National Anthem all in one. My *what* was simple. My *what* meant, what the hell are you talking about? My *what* meant, where in hell did you get that idea? My *what* meant, why are you making a complete dick of yourself in front of all these men. My *what* meant, what the hell crawled up your ass and made you jump on mine? My *what* meant, who the hell in this man's Army decided you had enough brains and people skills to wear sergeant stripes? And, my *what* meant, yes you reprehensible insecure power hungry small-minded ass-wipe, I am not going to dignify your dumb damn dead from the neck up question with an answer. And apparently my *what* was an effective response because for lack of a better, or should I say, more intelligent response to my *what*, Staff Sergeant Polk dismissed the platoon and returned, I assume, to wherever he stowed his morning joy juice. But as the song says, "the beat goes on" and Staff Sergeant Polk soon exacted his misguided justice for the embarrassment my *what* rained down on him.

Cowboy and I were both married and as soon as possible linked up with our wives and moved off base. This seemed to irk Staff Sergeant Polk to the max, who had an obvious and exceptional hatred for all three of us newly arrived high tech top secret crypto could almost fly non-typing typist, so he informed us in his own direct unsubtle way that though we lived off base we weren't anybody special and we still had to make morning reveille each day. In addition, while everyone else in his headquarters platoon was at morning chow we were given the privilege of cleaning the floors in the barracks and halls, and as if that weren't enough of a privilege, to also clean the latrines and shitters. Naturally, this was a little tough to swallow and we quickly came to learn that other off-post personnel in the company weren't required to perform such privileged duties, or to even show up until the morning work formation hours later.

Now being an average prideful American and not fond of cleaning shitters, and especially not being much of a morning person, this naturally led to rebellion when one dreary Monday morning Cowboy and I simply refused to do the job; inspired to revolt on that particular day by the sight of a number of disgusting, stopped up, overflowing toilets. Staff Sergeant Polk threatened to have us busted then repeated the order, but motivated by the sight of those seriously shitty shitters we again refused and requested an audience with the CO. Polk refused. We again refused. He again refused. We then again refused, leaving him no alternative but to march us down to face the First Sergeant who in turn got downright nasty with both of us about the entire affair, his old Army and old school theory being that if your platoon sergeant tells you to eat shit and die, then you eat shit and die. To us however, eating shit, taking shit, and cleaning shit were three totally different social and military concepts, therefore we stood our ground, which was about to lead us to the gallows when fortunately, being it was a wet and dreary day, the company commander, Captain Sears, had yet to disappear from our company billet to the post officers' tactical training area, better known as the golf course, and he just happened to be sitting in his office where he overheard our discussion.

"What's the problem out there, Top?" asked Captain Sears.

"Nothing I can't handle, sir."

"It doesn't sound like it to me. Send those three into my office."

Now except for spreading the skids on a training chopper, this was my first true act of rebellion in the military and though it was a very uncomfortable situation, I thought it to be a critical juncture in my career, if not my entire young adult life. After all, Cowboy and I were literally standing up for our right of separate and independent consideration to not be included in Army shit which inevitably flows down hill, or even out of commodes and that, I thought, had to be a precedent setting all time first.

"Now, what the hell's the problem, Specialist Fusco?" asked Captain Sears.

"Well sir. We don't want to clean shitters we don't use," I answered cautiously.

"You mean, the latrine," Captain Sears corrected.

"Yes sir, the latrine," I corrected. Ah, I thought, an officer and a gentleman.

"Everybody gets the shitter duty sometime, Fusco?"

"You mean, latrine, sir."

Captain Sears tilted his head as though to say, *let's not go there smart ass*, and I quickly got the message then continued making my case.

"Sir, we have to clean the latrine, showers and barracks floors in the upstairs headquarters platoon area every day while everyone else goes to morning chow."

"Who is *we*, Fusco?"

"Specialist Colby and myself, sir."

"Just the two of you?" asked Captain Sears.

"Yes sir."

"Is that true Sergeant Polk?"

Polk hemmed and mumbled then stated with great authority, "Yes sir".

"Are these two men being punished for something, Sergeant Polk?" asked Captain Sears with a raised eyebrow.

"Well, no sir," answered Staff Sergeant Polk.

"I don't understand. You two men are being denied breakfast. These two men don't get to eat breakfast?" he asked, looking at Staff Sergeant Polk.

"No sir," spoke up Colby. "We don't have time. We have to make reveille."

"You're the one they call Cowboy, right?"

"Um… Yes sir."

"Why?"

"Because we have to make reveille, sir."

"No, I mean why do they call you Cowboy?"

"Because I'm from Texas, sir."

"You a cowboy?"

"No sir. My family is in the food business. They own a Dairy Queen."

"Then you're a soda jerk."

"I guess so, sir. But you can't make ice cream without cows, sir."

"Good point."

Cowboy seemed to be making an impression and I thought the good-natured conversation between he and Captain Sears might possibly tilt the case in our favor.

"You work in the armory, right?" asked Captain Sears.

"Yes sir."

"So you like guns and know your weapons."

"No sir."

Captain Sears was beginning to get a bit confused. He had a soda jerk cowboy who didn't know anything about cows except they made ice cream and a Texas armorer who didn't like guns.

"Then why are you in the armory, Specialist Cowboy?"

"Because I can type, sir."

"You can type?"

"No, sir. I mean a little bit, sir. Kind of."

Captain Sears had to think about that one and I could see he didn't make the connection. I could imagine his mind scanning all four years at the United States Military Academy at West Point and then pulling a blank. Four years and absolutely no training to prepare an officer for a conversation with a misplaced over-qualified over-trained top secret non-typist typist under-qualified ice cream cowboy armory clerk who knew little or nothing about guns.

"I'm from Texas," Captain Sears stated proudly.

Cowboy perked up, thinking he had made a breakthrough, "Really sir? Where from?"

"Waco."

"A cowboy, sir?"

"Hell no. I'm a soldier."

Cowboy's hopes dwindled and Captain Sears got back to the business at hand.

"Everybody has to make reveille, Specialist Cowboy, even soda jerks from Texas. Why should you be any different?"

"Well sir, because I..."

"Where?" interrupted Captain Sears.

"Sir?"

"Texas. Where are you from in Texas?"

"Oh, um, Corpus Christi, sir."

Captain Sears offered a slight nod of approval, "Nice in Corpus Christi. Got water. I like water."

"Yes sir," agreed Cowboy.

"You ever clean the shitters at your father's Diary Queen in Corpus Christy, Cowboy?"

"Yes, sir."

Staff Sergeant Polk let slip a bit of satisfaction in the form of a slight grin and light sarcastic chuckle that didn't go un-noticed by Captain Sears.

"Sergeant Polk, why are these men being denied breakfast?" asked Captain Sears.

"They're not, sir."

I could see we were sinking fast as a result of implied semantics. Staff Sergeant Polk was going to win and we were going to end up cleaning the shitters. THE SHITTERS! Those fetid slimy-ass shitters sitting there upstairs, overstuffed, stopped up, stinking putrid Monday morning, haven't been touched for two days, disgusting squalid God-awful shitters! NO FUCKIN' WAY! Okay Fusco, be cool, I thought. Think, do what Perry Mason would do in a case like this and, of course, I didn't.

"Damnit, sir!" I exclaimed. "We live off post and..."

"What? You live off post?" interrupted Captain Sears.

Go for it Fusco. You and Perry Mason just got Polk's balls in a sling, I thought. Now yank it!

"Um, yes sir. We live off post, sir, and we have to leave home at 0500 in the morning to be here for reveille then clean the floors and the showers and the shitters upstairs while everybody else, the guys who dirty the damn things in the first place, go hang out for coffee, eggs, and bacon in the mess hall. We don't live upstairs, sir, and we never even go up there except to clean those damn shitters. And every damn Monday morning those damn shitters are stopped up and jammed up and overflowed and... well it's a hell of a mess, sir, and it smells like... um, shit... sir."

I didn't know if what I spewed out would help our case or get us busted down to Private E-nothings but it sure as hell felt good. Now, looking at Captain Sears, I could see the worm turning but didn't expect him to be so sympathetic or empathetic as he would prove to be. Must be the West Pointer in him, I thought, remembering all the crap and harassment he had to take from upper classman.

"Well, you're not going to clean the shitters any more Specialists Fusco and Specialist Cowboy. And from now on you don't show up here until 0730 hours for morning formation. Got that?"

"Yes sir," we acknowledged in unison.

"Did you clean the shitters this morning?"

Polk jumped in with an *I gotcha'* attitude, "No sir, they sure as hell ain't and they're runnin' out of time."

Captain Sears looked at Staff Sergeant Polk with a raised eyebrow, then to his office door, "Top!"

Like all good First Sergeants do when summoned by their company commander, Top popped into the office with all the sharp humility of a hyper Mahatma Gandhi.

"Yes sir," reported Top.

"Top, I don't want any of my off-post personnel showing up for reveille unless it's on my orders. Is that understood?"

"Yes sir, no off-post personnel at reveille," Top repeated.

Captain Sears looked to us with a bit of a smile, "Why don't you two go over to the mess hall and grab yourselves some breakfast."

"Yes sir", we snapped in unison.

As we exited the office, Polk quickly turned to follow but was called back by Captain Sears. We lingered by the orderly room door and overheard him ream Polk's ass with expressed concerns regarding how people like him were the reason the Army couldn't keep good troops and how he expects his NCOs to set an example of leadership in a fair and unprejudiced manner, he then finished up with instructions to Top.

"Top, Sergeant Polk here is going to go upstairs and clean the shitters. I want you to keep everybody downstairs until he's finished then I want you to go upstairs and inspect those shitters. And I mean they better be pretty Goddamn clean or he's going to clean those shitters again."

"Yes sir, pretty Goddamn clean, sir," Top echoed obediently."

"Got that Sergeant Polk?" Captain Sears inquired of Staff Sergeant Polk.

Staff Sergeant Polk choked up so badly he couldn't speak. Hearing the shuffle of boots coming out of the office, we bee-lined it for the mess hall. We had won the first and only battle of *The Great Oklahoma Crapper Rebellion* and we were elated.

As we stood in the chow line, Cowboy looked at me, bubbling over with joy, smiled and said, "And they say there's no justice in this man's Army."

"Yeah," I agreed, "But payback is a real bitch. Something tells me we're going to be pulling guard duty for the rest of our natural Army lives."

"Oh shit," stated Cowboy as he sank into depression, nearly coming to tears. "Oh shit."

We won the battle, I thought to myself, but did we win the war?

The Great Oklahoma Crapper Rebellion was actually our first encounter with Captain Sears whom we only saw occasionally at the morning formations. It was rumored he spent the rest of his time on the Officer's golf course, but if that's what made him diplomatically agreeable that was fine with us.

Polk cleaned the shitters and during the next company formation didn't hesitate to cancel all off post passes for the rest of the members of his headquarters platoon until, as he stated, "All you God damn stump jumpin' country mofuckas learn how ta flush a mofuckin' crapper!"

Except for two company formations each day, at which time he was forced to be civil because either the CO or XO was present, Cowboy and I managed to avoid Staff Sergeant Polk altogether. Now life with *the drum* out at the tech area didn't seem as bad in that it gave us some degree of refuge from Polk's possible retribution. Cowboy on the other hand, lived in constant fear down in the basement arms room at the company barracks where he was forced to work out a warning system with others in the building so he could scram and hide if Staff Sergeant Polk was on the prowl or came anywhere near his work station. It was a short lived situation for all of us, however, because a little over a week after our successful rebellion, Polk got orders for Vietnam and, we thought with great satisfaction, it couldn't have happened to a more deserving guy.

CHAPTER 8

TOP PENIS &
FUSCO'S REVENGE

As they say, life goes on and things begin anew, even in the Army. Stacie and I settled into a sparsely furnished rented duplex and bought a new red VW Bug when my made in Italia Fiat's electrical system fried. About that same time the 17th Ord got a new Top Sergeant who, it turned out, was nicer than anyone could possibly imagine a First Sergeant could be. His name was Fitzpatrick, a tall jolly man of Irish decent who had a wonderfully good-natured wife with a big heart. She was always fixing hot soup and coffee for the boys on night guard duty, iced tea for any unfortunates who pulled a hot outside detail, and brought cool munchies like brownies and cookies out to the tech area for us paranoid drum watchers. It seemed Top Fitz and his wife didn't have any children of their own and so had a history of adopting the boys of each unit at which they were assigned, presenting a side to the Army I didn't think could have existed anywhere.

Needless to say, the morale of the company shot sky high, which was a much welcomed change though it didn't affect the work at all because truth be known, there was hardly any work to affect. Just the same, people actually smiled when the opportunity presented itself and the stress and paranoia formerly imposed by the ever-present threat of unnecessary harassment was lifted. It was a better time. The guard duty roster was handled more fairly, John Lennon was singing "Give Peace a Chance", Elvis made a comeback, Clint Eastwood hit the big time with Spaghetti Westerns, the Pizza Hut invented Cavatini, and life in general got better, felt better, and finally offered up a chance for some domestic newlywed bliss. Then finally the baby dropped, it was a boy, a little junior Fusco, and except for some sleepless nights, which by now were nothing new to me, all seemed right with the world.

For Sims and I, experience led to sly wisdom and we eventually learned, of all things, to volunteer for special opportunities that got us out of guard duty, such as one week long

office administration classes and a three week long speed typing
course. Not that there was any real need for those specialties, there
wasn't even a typewriter in our tech area cubbyhole. Just the same,
I'm proud to say, I learned to be the Army equivalent of a
corporate executive secretary and I successfully completed my
speed typing class with a high rate of 87 words per minute, and
that was on one of those old standard Army manual metal clunker
boat anchors. Sims and I even went as far as to join the newly
formed base soccer team because it placed us on ED (exempt from
duty) status and kept us off the guard roster. The privilege was
short lived, however, because the coach was a demanding ex-pro
and college all-American and we by now were way out of shape,
having spent so many sleepless nights on guard duty and sedentary
days sitting and smoking in the security documents cubby hole
staring at that damn fifty gallon drum, not to mention the
aforementioned stretch in Texas and adventures in Wazoo. We
gave it up but remained optimistic that we could go pro any time
after a brief two-week intensive workout.

Then as suddenly as happiness had arrived, our newfound
nirvana crashed and burned throwing us back into the dark ages of
military hell. It began when I came into work one morning and
found everyone just mulling around aimlessly in the halls. It was
quiet, dead quiet, which is always an indicator of bad news in an
Army unit. I grabbed someone and made inquiry.

"Top's dead," they said.

"What?"

"Dead, man. He shot himself."

The news was a total shock that made no sense whatsoever. I
could hardly believe it. Of all the men I had met and seen in the
military, why this one? I felt downright depressed and bewildered
but like everyone else I had to accept and live with this unforeseen
and unexpected turn of events. Another surprise came when I
discovered this wasn't an uncommon occurrence being First
Sergeant Fitzpatrick was the second Top Sergeant assigned to the
17th Ord to eat a bullet in less than two years. I don't know what
inner turmoil drove him to his demise but somehow the Army must
have felt this second incident of suicide created a pattern that
dictated it was a local problem. It was bewildering to all of us
though we assumed the suicides were the result of previous duty in

Vietnam. Regardless, the repercussions of the incident were about to teach us just what a STRAC unit really was and it wasn't going to be fun.

A new First Sergeant appeared the very next morning. A big Chicano named Penyas who wasted no time informing us he was selected especially to jack this outfit up and straighten it out. I wasn't sure what that meant being the 17th Ord never really did much of anything anyway, which left little or no room for screwing up in the first place. And what the hell could any of us have done to influence Top's suicide? Just the same we were now a marked company and he was supposed to be our deliverance, or as it turned out, our curse.

In his first week on the job he managed to cancel all leaves, issue twenty-seven Article-15's, (non-judicial punishment), I believe I was number nineteen, bust two people for smoking on guard duty, and basically make life miserable for everyone for no apparent reason. My particular Article-15 was punishment for my wife getting a parking ticket in town. The military justice system is kind of fickle that way. Only in the military can you be punished, court-martialed, castrated, or beheaded, for something someone else did. Other such bizarre unwritten rules, though not initiated by the new Top soldier but certainly enforced by him, included the post rule of not being permitted to be seen in any civilian facility or establishment off base wearing your daily fatigue uniform. In a town that only existed because of the Army's presence it seemed to be a more than ridiculous handicap. It meant putting your career in jeopardy if the wife called and asked you to stop and pick up some bread and milk on the way home and you actually did. Word got out of an incident where one young officer actually lost his *hard commission* when he stopped off at the local Sears store in his fatigues and bumped into the Post Commander and his wife.

Another unreasonable post prohibition hit close to home for a great many of us married humble enlisted men who were financially challenged. It seems the Army was uncomfortable with the fact that many of its underpaid heroes were forced to seek second jobs in order to feed their families and therefore declared that anyone wishing to get a second job had to get permission from his Commanding Officer who was instructed to flatly disapprove all such request. This resulted in some enlisted men actually applying for and qualifying for supplemental welfare. When the word of welfare acceptance reached the ranks it was viewed as a Godsend, but when it reached the higher-ups it was so embarrassing to the Army that it was declared a Cardinal Sin and the declaration went out – *Any military personnel known to apply for welfare would get an automatic Article-15 and a demotion.* Such a "Let Them Eat Cake" attitude certainly wasn't conducive to the reenlistment effort and fortunately many COs and Top soldiers ignored the rule, except that is, other than our newly appointed First Sergeant Penyas. I never applied for welfare or had time for a second job and my wife had to stay home with the baby and her soap operas. To make things worse, no one in the Army ever bothered to inform me that I was eligible for a separate housing and rations allowance, leaving us poverty stricken for most of the last two weeks of each month. The ignorance was mine but due to the Army's neglect. Thanks Uncle Sam.

And so the company had to start over once again. From our point of view it was a puzzling state of affairs. How were we responsible for the suicidal death of two First Sergeants and why did the Army feel we needed some wannabe Nazi to make things right? Sims, Cowboy, and I concluded that whatever the official reason, which was never explained to us, it all boiled down to that damn fifty gallon drum of mystery shit at the tech area, and that First Sergeant Penyas was in some mysterious way, a good ole' boy Army conspiracy of revenge for our stellar victory in the Great Okalahoma Crapper Rebellion. First Sergeant Penyas was, we deduced, a KIA Sergeant Polk reincarnate, except with more juice, more determination, more cunning, and more brains.

The real fun began with IG (Inspector General) inspections where the IG would never show up to inspect, a favorite Army trick often imposed by a certain breed of Top Soldiers everywhere. The new Top scheduled such exercises to impress the CO and the brass. Little things like emergency call-ups at 0200 in the morning requiring all off post personnel to pack their entire Army issue and rush to the base. On those call-ups once all the company personnel were assembled we just sat around doing nothing, or had to pack up all the company assets, ordinance and associated equipment, except for *the drum* of course, haul them to the airstrip, load everything on aircraft and take off for points unknown. Not having the opportunity for a proper farewell to your family and carrying that kind of load heading for points unknown had a tendency to mess with your mind. After an hour in the air we were informed it was just a drill and returned home to unload and undo everything we had packed up, following which we still had to make it to work on time in the morning. Once again the constant pressure started to take its toll. After all, we were a stateside unit, the war was 12,000 miles away, and it wasn't likely anyone would be using the weird junk we took care of anyway. We presumed the Army had decided to give the rest of us the opportunity to go the way of First Sergeant Fitzpatrick and was doing all it could to encourage and help us along.

Working in the cubby hole with a lot of time on our hands, staring at the drum, and putting up with Top Sergeant *Penis*, as he had affectionately come to be called, tended to awaken the dark side of our character resulting in Sims and I devising a few diabolical programs to counter the man's accursed agenda. It's not that we were unhappy and vindictive but more that we were, well… unhappy and vindictive.

The first was an impromptu mission we quickly hatched when we were told by Top Penis that he was spearheading a dog and pony show at the tech area for some visiting brass. He rudely informed Sims and I that we were to give up our Sunday off and instead come in early enough to clean the office in the admin building in the tech are then set up coffee and donuts after which we were to go home; meaning he didn't want us around to embarrass anyone or take credit for a job well done. Needless to say, we were a little pissed because time off was now rare, we had little or no notice, and had made plans to go to Oklahoma City and look at the cows and oil wells on the grounds of City Hall. And who the hell puts on a dog and pony show for the brass on a Sunday anyway?

We came in at 0600 hours as instructed, cleaned up the already spotlessly clean area for the upcoming dog and pony show as instructed, then set up the donuts in a way that would make Dunkin himself proud. After that we were to hang out and turn on the oversized coffee machine exactly twenty minutes prior to the arrival of the dogs and ponies and brass entourage to insure it would be freshly perked and peaked to perfection. Completing those task, as instructed, we would… "Get the hell out."

The clock ticked off the minutes, we each ripped off and consumed two brass designated chocolate donuts, then at the proper time plugged in the coffee pot and initiated our diabolical deed. For the enjoyment of all dogs, ponies, and brass monkeys, and to enrich and enhance the flavor of the coffee, we added a generous helping of - liquid laxative.

To Sims and I it was a mission of pure inspired genius, and though it was ever so tempting, we never inquired as to the results of our mischief, fearing we would tilt the odds of discovery against us and suffer retribution. Never was a secret better kept. We did, however, eventually hear a rumor regarding the unfortunate demise of some poor night baker who was responsible for making what First Sergeant Penis often referred to as "those motherfuckin' donuts!" except we had to get Cowboy to translate because Top usually expressed his profanities in a very angry Spanish.

Our second mischievous adventure was more cerebral. As is commonly known, it's customary in the United States Army, in fact, universally in most all military organizations, for all shit to flow down hill. This means not only the bad shit details and the blame for shortcomings and failures, but also the daily labor and duties. In this case it was an assignment delegated to a junior officer, one 2nd Lt. Horace Richards, who in turn dumped the assignment on we two brainiacs in the technical manuals cubbyhole. His reason for doing so being that we looked like we didn't have enough to do, which was true, but not any more truthful than the fact he did just as much nothing as we did, if not more. The assignment was to develop and designate the radio call signs and procedures for each vehicle participating in an upcoming convoy exercise and, being the technical manual page counting geniuses that we were, we accepted the assignment with vigor, imagination, and a shameless desire for vengeance.

The call sign we came up with for the 17th Ord convoy of vehicles was an inspirational piece of word mastery that, and credit is due, only a true intellectual Utah cricket cruncher like Mike Sims could have spawned. The call sign was 'Healthy Fossil', and the simplicity of its application as a subversive weapon was, in both theory and application, a marvelous thing to hear and behold.

For example; the CO in the lead pace jeep would be 'HEALTHY FOSSIL 6', as all Commanding Officers are traditionally referred to as 6, the XO in the rear vehicle would be 5, and all the other officers or NCOs in particular vehicles would be assigned their numbers accordingly. Though this may seem like a simple call sign, it was quite the contrary. Imagine riding down the road in open-top military vehicles, suffering from a case of dry mouth from the heat and continuously talking on the radio in an effort to keep a long line of trucks and other vehicles full of potentially nasty mysterious ordinance all in order and progressive harmony. You're looking back and forward and before each sentence to each vehicle to which you're communicating you have to say your call sign.

"Healthy Fossil Six to Healthy Fossil Five, over."

"Healthy Fossil Five, over."

"Healthy Fossil Five I need you to pull up and get Healthy Fossil Four to close up his group on Healthy Fossil Three's group. Healthy Fossil Four seems to be off air. Over.

"Healthy Fossil Five to close Healthy Fossil Four on Healthy Fossil Three. Roger, Healthy Fossil Six. Over."

Needless to say, after a three-hour convoy everyone was pretty much tripping over their involuntary lisp so much so that the chatter on the 17th Ord's frequency sounded more like a gay rights parade in San Francisco than a military movement. With myself driving the lead jeep and Sims driving the XO in the rear and each of us able to clearly hear and monitor the entire show, it was a monumental feat and pure torture trying to keep from laughing, especially after Captain Sears finally succumbed to the total frustration of his inability to blabber.

"Hellssy Fothal Five. I mean Fellssy Fourthal… I mean… God damnit! Who the hell came up with these fuckin' call signs?" grumbled our usually composed Captain Sears

"Fellthy Foth… I mean Fossily… Shit! I think it was Lt. Richards, sir. Um, over."

"Get that little rat bastard up here!" growled Captain Sears.

"The little rat bas… I mean, Lt Richards isn't with us, sir. I believe he's driving the General. Over."

"General! What fuckin' General?! Over."

"General Hinckley, sir. He decided at the last minute to observe the convoy exercise. Over."

"Observe... Well...where the fuck is he? Over."

"Um, he's um... right behind me, sir. Over."

"Healthy Fossil Six this is Healthy Fossil General. Do you ladies think you could possibly observe the proper radio protocols on this mission? I hate to think I'd have to reprimand an entire company for... uh, inappropriate lisping. Over."

"Uh, roger that, Hellfy...um... Hellthy Fa... Femer... General Fossil, um, sir. God damn it! Over."

It seems the only people who thought the entire episode was hilarious was myself, Sims, and General Fossil of whom it was said was laughing so hard he could hardly spit out the words, "Turn this vehicle around and take me home, Lt. Rat Bastard."

It was also rumored that after that experience General Fossil imposed the same Healthy Fossil call signs on unwary units in subsequent exercises just to get a rise out of his commanders. You gotta' love a guy like that.

Eventually running out of tricks and patience, Sims and I decided to get drastic and do the desperate and unthinkable. We both put in for transfers - to Vietnam. Our reasoning was that a request for transfer to anywhere else was sure to be ignored but being nearly everyone in the Army was trying to stay out of Vietnam, there had to be a great demand for those who wanted to get in and being we weren't grunts it was unlikely we would end up in the boonies. Anything, we thought, was better than living under the heavy anvil of First Sergeant Penis whose reaction to our request was fairly predictable.

"What? You want what!"

"I'd like to put in for a transfer, First Sergeant Pen... uh, Top. To Vietnam."

"Are you fuckin' nuts? I heard you're a jokester. This some kind of a damn joke, Fusco? Because if it is I ain't laughin'."

"No Top. It's not a joke. I'd like to request a transfer to Vietnam."

"Well that's tough shit. You're not requesting anything."

"But..."

"I said forget it, Fusco. I ain't approving any damn transfer request for Vietnam or anywhere else. Just forget it."

"I believe I have a right to make the request and pass it on to the CO even if you don't approve, Top."

I didn't know if that was actually true or not but I had seen the movie Mr. Roberts three times and if it was true in the Navy then I figured it had to be true for the Army as well.

"What are you some kind of shit-house lawyer now?" observed the irritated Top Sergeant Penis.

I stood silent until Top did as he had to do, search out the proper forms and hand them to me.

"Thanks Top."

"Bullshit."

With the paperwork completed Top had no choice but to pass it on to Captain Sears who called me into his office first thing the very next day - before going to the golf course, of course.

"Fusco, you want to explain to me why you want to go to Vietnam?" asked Captain Sears.

I wanted to say, because that cock suckin' hatched from hell heathen grim reaper of a heartless bastard in the outer office is making my life so fuckin' miserable that I'm on the brink of a suicidal breakdown, but... Mama didn't raise me that way and Top would have probably heard me and crashed through the door and split my skull right down the middle with a file cabinet. So I lied.

"Well sir, I just don't feel like I'm contributing here. I mean, I voluntarily enlisted and I'm not afraid to fight and well... I just feel like I'm wasting my time here... sir."

Captain Sears sat in serious thought then said what I hoped he wouldn't say, "I'm sorry. I can't approve this. You have critical MOS's and we need you here."

Critical MOS's, I thought. Shit, all I do is count pages and stare at that damn drum.

"But whether I like it or not I have to pass this on," continued Captain Sears. "I'm going to disapprove it but I have to pass it on. I don't think you'll get anything out of it though so don't get your hopes up. Just the same, I want you to be sure you understand what you're asking for."

"I understand, sir."

He looked at me with serious concern. "Didn't your wife just have a baby a few months ago?"

"Yes sir."

"And you want to go to Vietnam?"

"Yes sir."

"What does your wife think about this?"

"She's fine with it sir," I lied. Actually, Stacie didn't know. I figured I'd blame it on the Army to avoid any domestic conflict.

He looked at me a long moment, shook his head, then I was dismissed. As I exited the CO's office Top stuck his head in the door, "The other one's here, sir."

Sims was waiting at Top's desk when I passed through the orderly room. He looked at me with hopeful anticipation but all I could do was offer a shrug of disappointment.

Both our requests were disapproved at the company level and as far as we knew at every other level. I was forced to resolve myself to a long and miserable continued existence at the 17th Ordinance Company, which became even more miserable when we discovered that due to the shortage of personnel Top had denied all requests for Christmas leave. That's great, I thought, I'm going to spend a cold Christmas night freezing my balls off out there in Lala Land singing *Joy To The World* to some uncultured skunk that may or may not show his appreciation by pissing permanent perfume on my high tech top-secret crypto *missile* toes.

Then, a few weeks later, out of the clear blue sky fell a request through the Red Cross for the presence of my wife and me at a funeral; a fortunate circumstance for me but not the deceased who was a close non-immediate member of my wife's family. Close enough to justify the request. It griped Top's ass, but he reluctantly gave me a twelve-day compassionate leave and off we went. Admittedly, I felt guilty for the circumstances of the opportunity, but must admit I relished the relief from the monotonous tyranny of the Penis parade.

When I checked into the orderly room upon my return from the compassionate leave the company clerk, SP4 Letterer, handed me a tall stack of papers.

"What's this?"

"It's your orders, man. You're going to the Nam," said Letterer.

"What?"

"Yeah man. They came down ten days ago. You know you were the only one on this entire damn base who came down on levy this month?" said Specialist Letterer. "Talk about shitty luck."

"I thought my request was denied."

"You're kiddin', right. I mean everybody and their uncle is trying to stay the hell outa' that damn place," Letterer stated as though it were a new development. "Even the lifers don't want anything to do with it anymore. I talked to a buddy at Battalion and he says the lifers are startin' to bail. Takin' retirement. Pissed off with the politics and all their friends getting' killed and all that shit. You think the Army's really gonna' say no to anybody who's crazy enough to ask for it? Don't bet on it, man."

"What about Sims?" I asked.

"Who?"

"Mike Sims. He requested Vietnam the same time I did, remember."

"Oh yeah. He's gone man. Left six days ago. He's already there."

"Where?"

"Nam, man. Where do you think?"

"I thought you said I was the only one who came down on levy."

"That's right. You're January. He was December."

"Great, so what's that make me, Pinup of the Month?"

"No, but it'll make you AWOL if you don't hurry up and get the hell outa' here."

"What do you mean?"

"Listen man, like I said, these orders came down ten days ago and you only got four days left to clear outa' this place. Three days of that is a Vietnam orientation briefing that starts tomorrow morning."

"Four days!"

"That's right, man. Four days. Three days orientation, one day to clear and report to Tacoma for transport to the shit. You weren't here when these orders came down and you lost time. Tell you the truth, I don't think you can do it."

"Christ man, I got a family. I gotta' pack them up and get them home."

Letterer looked around to make sure no one was within hearing range, then said in a hushed voice, "Listen Fusco, there's a little known reg that says when you're transferring into a combat zone you're supposed to get a thirty day leave. I'm not promising anything cause it's up to Top. But if I were you I'd give it a shot."

"You sure?"

"Yeah," said Specialist Letterer picking up the fat U.S. Army Regulations book. He started flipping through it then just tossed it down on the desk. "Oh hell, it's in there someplace. I read it once."

The thought of facing Top with a leave request was spine chilling but I had to do it. Predictably, Top went ballistic, seriously pissed because I had just come off a twelve-day compassionate leave. Then grumbling all the usual profanities he broke down and gave me, not thirty days but twenty-nine days. The one day difference, I surmised, being a matter of pride and discipline on his part. Army regs or not, nobody was going to get the last word on First Sergeant Penis.

The next day I began the required Vietnam Orientation Program which basically consisted of a day in a classroom being told what not to do while in Vietnam, or as they say *in-country*. It was mostly cultural and social instructions of the following nature;

"If you see two South Vietnamese men or soldiers walking down the street or in the field holding hands or walking with their pinkies interlocked, you do not, I repeat, do not laugh, giggle, point, or make any other gestures, vocal or otherwise, of a disparaging or derogatory nature. This does not mean these men are homosexual. It's the way they express friendship much like we express comradeship by placing our arms on each other's shoulders. Should you make any such remarks or gestures a number of things may occur such as; you may be punished, you will be hindering the United States efforts in Vietnam by fostering bad will, and last of all, those little slope headed bastards may get royally pissed off and blow your shit away. Remember, we are guests in their country and must behave accordingly."

Other advice included things such as the various names not to be used when referring to the Vietnamese people, names such as Dinks, Chinks, Slopes, Slope Heads, Slant Eyes, Slides, Gooks, and Monkey Fuckers. Also recommendations such as; it is not advisable to get hung up on the female of the species to the degree that marriage is considered because it is very likely that the complicated process of immigration approval for the female in question may actually take longer than your tour of duty, etc, etc. And, of course, there were the usual social disease warnings being basically, "If you catch it you ain't coming home with it and will be held indefinitely at a safe and secure medical facility outside of the United States until you are either cured or dead."

And so it went, with little or nothing being said about danger, combat, staying alive, or why we were at war and fighting in Vietnam in the first place. That is until day two when we spent the first hour in a class room viewing captured enemy film depicting just how bad and nasty the VC (Viet Cong gorillas) and the NVA (North Vietnamese Army regulars) really could be. There was captured footage of the enemy performing various atrocities and casually shooting prisoners in the head, and there was one particularly uncomfortable film showing the NVA ambushing and completely wiping out a convoy in less than fifteen seconds. Needless to say, that footage came to mind every time I went anywhere on wheels while in Vietnam.

Following the film follies we were issued weapons with blanks, instructed how to deploy and secure an LZ (landing zone), and flown into the field via a Chinook helicopter to practice what we had learned. This also included assaulting a replica Vietnamese village complete with explosive booby traps, pungy traps, and other harmful devices, one of which was particularly disturbing. In the village hanging over a large pit was a tripod of bamboo poles under which hung a basket containing, for our training purposes, a baby doll. It was a revealing display of one of my future enemy's many inhumane tricks. The baby had been left there knowing it would cry as it starved and also knowing that most all Americans were not so heartless as to ignore it or leave it alone. Of course, it was booby-trapped to explode, baby and all. Though it sounded cruel and heartless to be instructed to think of that baby as a weapon and to ignore it, the point of the exercise was well taken, especially when having a baby of my own just a few miles down the road.

Still undecided about the legitimacy of the war, I couldn't help but think that had such programs as this been available to civilians there might be far less animosity regarding the war, whether folks thought it was our fight or not.

I completed the orientation and cleared the post with my mandatory final stop being First Sergeant Penis.

"You all done clearing post, Fusco?"

"Yes Top."

He glanced over my paperwork, approved and initialed it, handed it back to me without looking up then unceremoniously stated, "Alright then, get the hell outa' here."

As I started for the door he looked up, "Fusco".

I stopped and turned.

"You do what you're told over there and don't trust anybody and you'll be okay", he said in what seemed to be a surprisingly unusual softer kinder fatherly Chicano accent.

Not sure how to respond, I simply smiled and nodded.

"You're a good soldier, Fusco. You're a pain in the ass but you're a good soldier. Now get the hell outa' here and take your damn twenty-nine days", he smiled.

I'll be damned, I thought as I departed the 17th Ord for the last time, the son of a bitch has a heart. I think.

Regardless of the revelation that Top may actually have some semblance of compassion, I was now free of long cold nights at the tech area, preparing for IG inspections that never took place, flying to nowhere in the middle of the night, bumping into fresh Butter Bar Lieutenants who thought they had been crowned king with nothing better to do than harass the lower ranks, and, of course, that damn ever-present fifty gallon bucket of mystery shit, one spoonful of which could wipe out every living thing within five miles of Geronimo Road and beyond.

Halleluiah!

CHAPTER 9

SECOND THOUGHTS

As we packed the U-Haul trailer for our trip to Florida where I would park my wife near her family for the next year, a letter came from Mike Sims who had been assigned to a post somewhere down around the Mekong Delta southwest of Saigon. He wrote of his first impressions of the country, wished us all well, and offered up a kiss for the baby. Although he stated he was happy to be free of the relentless chicken shit harassment of Fort Sill, I could somehow read his anxious concerns and fears between the lines. Especially when I read his MOS had been arbitrarily changed once again. Mike Sims was now an 11B, a grunt. It was something that played on my mind all the way to Maryland where I would say goodbye to my folks, then back to Florida.

On the day before I was to leave from Florida for Tacoma and from there process on to a flight for Southeast Asia, I decided to take a ride to the beach. Growing up on the shores of the Chesapeake, I could usually find a little comfort on, in, or around just about any body of water anywhere, and this was one of those occasions that called for a spiritual return to my roots. The beach was pretty much deserted, characteristic for that time of year in northeast Florida, and as I walked through the dunes to the surf, the cool breeze and evening solitude made it easy to contemplate and possibly regret my decision to transfer. The petty grievances that motivated me to make my choice seemed distant and unimportant now. Suddenly all that mattered was family. I tried to tell myself my decision was justified due to the Army's indifference of the needs and talents of its soldiers, but in all honesty that didn't wash, it was just an excuse. Somewhere in me was a curious gnawing of pride that forced me to face a desire to find out if I had the same stuff as my father and his brothers. I questioned if this was some kind of antiquated right to passage disguised and wrapped in the flag, a thing that infested young men and motivated them to go to war, a trait now easily and outwardly subdued and denied by many of my generation for what appeared to me to be selfish reasons.

Reasons possibly derived from living in a comfortable industrial society dictated by the necessity of luxury, or maybe there had just been too many wars for too many generations, three successive generations, with my generation finally deciding that enough is enough.

As I strolled along the beach, flashes of the day's events unwillingly surfaced and mixed with my current thoughts as though I was afraid I might lose them. It was emotionally confusing. I saw a flash of my baby, Vince Junior, laughing then barfing all over my shirt. At the same time I contemplated whether I was part of a generation engulfed in misguided bullshit rock and roll wisdom or part of some new collective insightfulness or clarity, the result of a life of exposure to mass media and wrong education? Maybe that was the difference between the older generation and mine, I thought. Maybe we were critical because we knew too much or maybe we didn't know enough. Hell, maybe I didn't even know enough to get out of my own way. Fusco Junior didn't care if I got out of the way. He barfed on me big time.

Then came another memory, the baby holding tight to my little fingers as he pulled himself up to stand in my lap with his wonderful innocent smile. I felt frustrated, confused, young, and dumb. Stupid, I thought, as I walked along the now darkening beach, stupid for being me and stupid for having to deal with these issues, the emotions of which seemed more easily understood than the thoughts. What happened to the innocent kid who didn't curse, didn't drink, didn't smoke, had no prejudices, and no excessive ambitions? Who gave them the right to impose changes? Did they do it or did I?

Another flash with Stacie laughing as I was changing a diaper, making faces, and playing the fool, then got pissed on when Vincent Junior decided he wasn't quite finished filling up the first one. The baby was everything now and ironically he knew nothing at all. I was violating everything, I thought, all those values taught me by a well meaning over religious mother. I could also now see and feel the silent concerns and fears of a strong father regarding my safety and well being as I was about to enter into a reality of which he was far too familiar. I felt like shit. I felt I was too young to go through this crap as though anybody is ever old enough, and there wasn't a damn thing I could do about it except fulfill my obligation to serve, knowing all the while that in doing so I could quite possibly screw up my entire life... or lose it. Fusco Junior didn't think about any of this. He thought it was a big joke, pissing right in my face and laughing. Was this a sneak preview of his generation?

As I walked along the beach I came upon a group of five hippy type teenagers circled together, apparently trying to block the wind in order to light a cigarette. They grew paranoid at the sight of my presence and quickly turned away, waving off the smoke. I caught a whiff and quickly deduced it wasn't exactly a Lucky Strike. They in turn quickly but wrongfully deduced that because of my short hair I was some kind of a narc or uncool establishment pig. Hell, I thought, if they only knew. It was no big deal but it reflected my dilemma. Who the hell was I and who the hell was it I was taking to Vietnam?

The questions came as frequently as the breakers on the beach. Could I believe everything I had heard about Vietnam and could I trust myself to deal with it? Would my wife, whom I had just taught to drive, wreck my new car? After all she did run into a gas pump already. Would I ever see her again? Would my son, who hadn't even learned to say my name, have to grow up without me? Would the Pizza Hut still be serving cavatini when I came back? Damn, I thought, why couldn't I just go back to the days when all I had to worry about was the next football game, or algebra test, or coming up with fifty cents to contribute to the gang's gas fund for Saturday night? I remembered someone once saying, "Life's a bitch and then you die," and I wondered what the creator of that philosophy knew that I didn't?

That evening after Stacie had gone to sleep I sat up all night holding the baby and the questions continued to roll around in my mind - unanswered. The baby slept peacefully. He was fragrant, warm, soft, and unaffected by the rest of the world, innocent of everything in life. I tried to imagine what kind of wars and personal conflicts he and his generation would have to face and who the hell would be the bastards responsible. In the quiet darkness of the pre-dawn I silently questioned how any man, great or small, having held a child like this could even think of war, much less start one.

"You're dead," they kept telling Leroy Smith, and although he was actually walking and talking, I wondered if perhaps they might be right.

CHAPTER 10

SHIT CLOUDS,
DRY BONES & FNGs

Cam Rahn Bay was a typical sleepy Vietnamese coastal fishing village until the forces and fortunes of war invaded and brought it into the 20th century by turning it into a thriving air and seaport. It was there many Americans experienced their first impressions of Vietnam and I, like most others, remember departing the commercial airliner and being engulfed by the overwhelming stagnant heat then being impressed by the ever chattering and seeming indifference of the indigenous population of little people. Surprisingly they scurried about freely inside the various military compounds with impunity, which was at first unnerving, at least to me after having been told the enemy flourished within the population and that danger lurked around every corner. This must have still been the case since the olive drab bus we loaded into right off the plane sported caged windows necessary to fend off grenades that were sometimes tossed by the locals.

Nearly everywhere we looked military wood and tin roofed structures sat baking in the sun, a few two storied and most all fortified with sand bags and other precautions. At least that was our first impression if not our full and only impression. In reality and not immediately seen by us, Cam Rahn had become a military metropolis situated like an Asian Manhattan surrounded by water, inclusive of every service; Army, Navy, Air Force, and Marines. Like many other military installations, it was a confusing maze of structures separated only by designating numbers and initials. It was here that not only military personnel shipped into and out of the country but also everything and anything required to support the war, the peace, and the pastimes of the entire U.S. effort in Vietnam. This place that had the potential to be a destination resort paradise was instead a conglomerate of various military services installations, shipping and receiving depots, and massive in-ground munitions storage bunkers. Trying to take it all in was, of course, impossible.

We were ferried directly to in-country processing that included the collection of our orders and filling out another shit pot full of paperwork concerning mostly our disposition as future casualties. Mostly items such as powers of attorney, last will and testaments, verification of insurance beneficiaries, home of record, next of kin, et cetera; all the things necessary to die in an orderly fashion and hopefully avoid becoming another Leroy Smith. Then finally the exchange of our U.S. currency for Military Pay Script, better known as MPC, that little monopoly type of money issued and used by American military personnel.

To us the MPC was small and comical but more highly valued by the Vietnamese than their domestic equivalent, the piaster, and certainly easier to deal with. It had also evolved over the years into the unofficial basic currency of the South Vietnam economy simply because of its wide spread use. When the U.S. Military initiated one of its unannounced periodic MPC changes, which is when all military installations are locked down and personnel exchange their existing MPC for newly designed and newly printed MPC, the entire population of South Vietnam would go into a panic. Among other things, some of the reasons for the change were to thwart the black market and purge the civilian population of all that currency they weren't supposed to have. One of the reasons the change came quickly and without notice was to prevent enterprising G.I.'s from making major amounts of money exchanging currency for desperate civilians. G.I.s were restricted as to how much money they could exchange, leaving some of us having to spread our funds out among friends so as not to take a loss. Not wanting to be caught with tons of worthless money, the panicked Vietnamese, from hookers to fish mongers, would line the fences and gates of the American military installations screaming and pleading and literally throwing huge wads of cash over the fences in an effort to get a sympathetic American to exchange it. Doing so was a serious punishable offense, but no doubt many a GI made a profit even though most exchanges were well regulated and limited. The only currency more valuable than the MPC was the US dollar, which was supposedly illegal but existed nonetheless.

At Cam Rahn none of us new arrivals said much of anything because none of us knew each other. We were pretty much led around by the nose through the entire process by robotic impersonal personnel who appeared not to give a shit simply because in truth they really didn't give a shit. Everything was quick and dirty, probably reminiscent of the old days at Ellis Island in the shadow of Lady Liberty in New York Harbor, though most assuredly less cordial. It was an indication of things to come regarding the in-service social situation in Vietnam, but we failed to see it at the time. We were *FNGs*, (Fucking New Guys*)*, or *Newbies* for short, also known as *Cherries* who had no time in-country, no knowledge of the war or the place, and as such, no status other than just being FNGs. And there was another acronym, STDs, (Soon To Die). It was less known and used more selectively depending on the established troops' impression of the newly arrived individual's ability or lack of same, the real idiots, and whether or not they were in a true combat unit.

With the Cam Rahn portion of our in-country processing eventually completed, we were assigned a temporary billet where we would hurry up and wait for notice of further transport to wherever we were destined, which in the case of three of us, was the the 17th Aviation Group, of the 1st Aviation Brigade, wherever and whatever that was. No one volunteered any info so we were always in the dark about our destination.

The next day we were shuttled up the coast to Nha Trang where we again surrendered copies of our orders and were again instructed to hurry up and wait for more orders to our next and possibly our ultimate destination. It was here we FNGs would be baptized into the irony and attitude of the war in general. We were put up in another transient hooch with about twenty other G.I. travelers and told to just relax and stay put because it could be at least two to three days before our assignments came through. We were further instructed not to leave the hooch or wander off for any reason other than chow and trips to the latrine in case any orders did happen to come down prematurely, leaving us only minutes to catch our ride. Knowing anything ever happening in the Army prematurely was an impossibility we quietly laid back and resolved ourselves to the situation.

The small billet or hooch, as they had come to be called, constructed only of wood and sand bags on a cement slab, was the

standard military fair for tropical Vietnam. It had surrounding
screens and hinged plywood and corrugated metal covered flaps,
which were propped open for circulation. The inside was set up
with nothing more than a line of metal bunk beds on each side and
included what we thought was the considerate placement of two
luxury items in the form of large pole mounted fans blowing the air
in, one at each door on each end of the hooch. As instructed, we
quietly settled in with little or no fanfare or conversation, just a
regiment of sleeping and lying about in our skivvies to take
advantage of the forced air flow of the fans. We were too hot and
too short on sleep to socialize and being none of us knew what the
hell was going on, or where we were going, or how soon we would
be going if we did go, or if we would even see each other again
after the next hour or next day or ever, we just kept to ourselves.
We simply lay around as usual, waiting as fast as we could, as
usual, dwelling on what we hadn't been told, as usual.

Then, in the middle of the second night of our limbo while we
were all slothfully hibernating, we were suddenly awakened by the
sound of the exterior corrugated window flaps crashing shut
followed by a continuous loud popping and banging on the tin
roof. We came to with the dazed impression the noise was the
result of enemy gunfire then quickly discovered we were engulfed
in a swirling cloud of CS gas. As every G.I. learns in basic
training, CS gas, most commonly known as tear gas or what was
sometimes referred to as *the nasty shit cloud*, can more than ruin
your day along with your ability to breathe, speak, see, or even
think in a rational manner. This particularly nasty shit cloud did its
job and in choking unanimity we all opted to face what we thought
was assaulting enemy bullets outside rather than the continued
misery of the chemicals inside. We rushed to and through the
doors, knocking down the big pole mounted fans in search of relief
and fresh air, and in doing so we suddenly found ourselves being
pelted by... rocks. ROCKS!

"What the fuck is...," exclaimed one transient as he partially
regained his vocal cords.

"Shit! Shit!" another attempted to say in a suffering teary-eyed
forced rasp. "Somebody's... somebody's throwing... fuckin'
rocks!"

Eyes and noses drooling, choking and gasping for air, tripping and bumping into each other, we finally came around to realize we were not under attack, at least not by enemy communist forces of North Vietnam or even Viet Cong guerrilla forces.

"God... God damn it! This supposed to be... some kind of... fuckin'... joke?" wheezed and stuttered one transient. "Because... 'cause if it's...," spit, choke, "I'm gonna'... kill the motherfuc... who...," puke, gurgle.

There we stood outside under the stars by our transient hooch in front of God and Vietnam, half naked, confused, bewildered, puking, dripping and drooling from every facial orifice, and wondering, as expressed by one of our unfortunate number, "What the hell just happened?"

There was no one around, no one anywhere to be seen. No one to assist us, no one to offer any kind of explanation, no one to even laugh at us, though I could swear I heard someone laughing in the distance. Recovering from the shit cloud we filed back into the barracks to discover two expended CS canisters that had been strategically placed by each door near the previously highly appreciated pole fans, those same fans that had forced and circulated the nasty shit for maximum effect. We kicked the canisters out the door and reversed the fans to clear the hooch then returned to our individual bunks to clean ourselves up.

"Hey. Hey man, my wallet's gone!" I heard someone say.

"Maybe you lost it outside."

"How the hell would I do that? Don't keep my fuckin' wallet in my fuckin' grundies, man."

"Hey, God damnit! Mine's gone too!" someone else said from across the hooch.

We all quickly checked and discovered our fatigues, which in our panic were left lying or hanging on our bunks, had been rifled though by some gas-masked bandits and all available valuables and wallets had been pilfered. In a group fit of anger and profanities, fatigues and gear were hurled in every direction, eventually culminating with a final expression of exasperation when someone launched an entire bunk bed into one of the still humming pole fans sending both objects to crash in a wrecked heap in front of the doorway. Needless to say, we were pissed off because we had all been chumped, victims of a well planned, obviously well established and often practiced act of conspiratorial thievery. We had just been robbed, raped, and ridiculed by our own troops in a foreign country, a damn combat zone, and no one we complained and mentioned it too, neither officer or NCO anywhere in Nha Trang, did anything about it or even cared it had even happened.

"Don't trust anybody," First Sergeant Penis told me before I left Oklahoma. But hell, who would have guessed he was talking about the good guys. Welcome to Vietnam, FNG Fusco.

By some odd coincidence our orders prematurely came down the morning after our experience with the shit cloud bandits, resulting in myself and a SP4 Randy Colatazzi, a tallish brown haired wop who wore granny glasses and hailed from the Bronx of New York, being loaded onto a C-123 Provider for points unknown - at least unknown to us. Our written orders were for the 52nd Combat Aviation Battalion, Camp Holloway, Pleiku. But as far as we were concerned they may just as well have said the Holiday Inn Motel on the moon because from the time we had stepped off the plane at Cam Rahn Bay we had no idea whatsoever where we were or where we had been. We didn't know Saigon from Singapore, Cam Rahn from canned soup, north from south, I Corps, II Corps, or III Corps from an apple core, and we sure as hell didn't know anything about a place called Camp Holloway. If the C-123 had been shot down or had to crash land and the two of us somehow survived, we probably would have bobbed and weaved and hiked all the way to Hanoi like two lost dorks at Disneyland looking for the Country Bear Jamboree in Tomorrow Land. Not that this really bothered me, after all, the Army always knew where everybody was, right? Okay it bothered me and that same geographic disorientation would be a recurring insecurity all through my tour.

Though I wasn't prone to it, I never liked being geographically disoriented and that aircraft took us belly hopping and dropping or picking up cargo or people all over the central highlands, sometimes stopping at places where you wouldn't think a C-123 could make a stop without sliding in sideways. In addition, each stop made along the way seemed to become more isolated and more ominous than the one before, leading Randy and I to believe that our final destination wasn't exactly going to be a five star resort. One particular stopover left a lasting first impression. Unlike the other stops, the plane rolled to a halt on a short dusty dirt airstrip and cut her engines. The crew chief unbuckled himself, popped up and headed for the rear cargo door.

"They say this strip is secure right now. You guys got time to step out for a smoke and a piss if you want," he said.

The large ramp opened slowly like the yawning mouth of some animated whale and in rushed the sun and heat of the central highlands.

"Where are we?" I asked.

The crew chief looked out the door and busying himself securing tie-down straps said, "Uh, hell, I don't know, man. Some old French air strip or somethin'. Special Forces camp right over there," he said, throwing a thumb over his shoulder.

Randy and I exited the aircraft, lit up a cigarette, and turned to find ourselves facing a group of near naked natives right out of the pages of National Geographic. The men wore nothing but a black loincloth and the women were topless with only a black or patterned sarong. One woman had a breast-feeding baby hung precariously around her neck inside a pouch-like sling. They were all shoeless including the hand full of small children, some of which were buck-ass naked. Unlike the lighter Vietnamese of Chinese decent we had seen elsewhere, these people were dark skinned and full bodied, even muscular, with full-featured faces and thick rich glossy black hair. They simply stood or squatted about with emotionless but cautious eyes regarding the C-123 as though it were just another bus at the station. As primitive as the first impression was, the children had a natural beauty the likes of which I had rarely ever encountered and seemed to have a bit of a curious but reserved glint in their eye. A small girl I guessed to be about five years old offered a slight smile that was quickly redirected and doused by a few critical words from her mother. I couldn't help but think how out of place these people seemed. But it was a perception based on my own ignorance and limited knowledge because we were actually the foreigners who were out of place.

The crew chief joined us for a smoke and noticed our obvious FNG interest.

"Yards," he stated.

"What?" replied Randy.

"Mountainyards. Well, actually it's French or something. Spelled weird like M-O-N-T-A-G-N-A-R-D-S. Mountain tribe people that live in the mountains around the Nam. Different tribes all around with maybe ten, twelve, fifteen thousand in a tribe. Good people if you can get to know 'em. Don't say much though."

"Why not?" I asked.

"Not much for bullshit I guess," he laughed.

"They look lost," observed Randy.

"Lost. Hell no, man, they ain't lost. This is their country, man. Was theirs a long time before the Chinese took it over. According to a guy in my outfit, one of those college history guys ya know, they got here first along the coast from the islands in the Pacific. Island people, ya know, like those cannibals that ate Captain Cook. Like American Indians except instead of white men messin' them over they got pushed into the mountains by the chinks."

"No shit?" said Randy. "Somebody ate Captain Cook? I didn't know that. Must have missed that movie."

"Yeah man. You didn't know that? Cook got cooked," he laughed. "Stewed and cannibalized on some island. Anyway, they're good fuckin' fighters too and loyal as hell. Mostly fight with these Special Forces guys or the Spooks around the highlands. They got whole units of Yards on our side. Don't worry they won't eat ya. I don't think. You can trust 'em. Not like the rest of the fuckin' gooks 'round this damn country. They might all look the same to us maybe but there ain't no love lost between them and the ARVNs."

"Arvans?" I asked.

"Vietnamese Army. Army of the Republic of Vietnam or some kind of shit like that, A-R-V-N. Hell, you put Yards and ARVNs together in a firefight and they'll start killin' each other before they go after Commies. It's a crazy fuckin' war, man," the crew chief said as he brought a cigarette to his lips. "You know, like all that enemy of my enemy is my friend and all that philosophical shit. Yeah, right. Until he kills your ass."

About that time the sound of a Jeep drew his attention, "Here we go," he said as he snubbed out his cigarette with his boot and moved off to meet it.

The jeep bounced up to our aircraft and slid to a stop. Driving it was a Special Forces Sergeant accompanied by a shirtless medic. Sitting silently in the back was a Montagyard soldier in tiger fatigues. The medic hopped out and started helping the Yard soldier to his feet.

"Listen buddy," said the Sergeant to the crew chief. "You keep an eye on this guy or he'll slip off and dee dee mau for home. He doesn't like doctors and all that shit."

"No problem. Our next stop's the air base anyway so he's got no place to go. We'll get him straight into the 71st Evac. What's wrong with him anyway?" the crew chief asked, not noticing any bandages, blood, or obvious injury.

"He's got a broken back," answered the medic.

"Jesus Christ, you're shittin' me. A broken back? And he's sittin' up in the back of a jeep? Must be some kinda' morphed out not to feel that kinda' pain, man."

"No," answered the medic. "Wouldn't take any meds or morphine but he's gotta' be in a hell of a lot of pain."

"No fuckin' kiddin'. He sure ain't showin' it. How'd he do it?" asked the crew chief.

"Got knocked off an APC," answered the SF Sergeant.

"Oh Yeah? Imagine that. Okay, let's get him loaded."

I watched with amazement when after the medic motioned for the Yard soldier to get on the plane the Yard left the jeep and walked without assistance onto the aircraft without so much as a cringe or whimper and then sat upright on one of the uncomfortable nylon cloth seats against the fuselage.

About that time Randy tapped me on the arm and I turned to follow his eyes with my own. The little Montagnard girl had wandered away from the group and was poking around in the dirt with a stick. When I looked closer at what she was poking, I noticed some bones and the partial remains of a human skull. Looking further, I saw other skeletal remains lying scattered about the edge of the small dusty dirt airstrip, some blackened, presumably by fire, some dried and bleached by the seasons and tarnished with the red soil of the Vietnam highlands. I would find out later this was a common sight near many fire support bases and outpost because after attacks the enemy bodies that weren't retrieved by their comrades would be collected and either buried or burned. A beautiful innocent child playing among the dry marred bones of the dead was a scene neither of us were quite prepared to see.

"Shit," was all Randy could say as we viewed the macabre scene. And shit pretty much said it all because I sure as hell couldn't think of anything better.

CHAPTER 11

PEOPLE,
CHICKENS & PIGS

The final stop for us on the C-123 was the Air Force Base just outside of Pleiku. We off-loaded into what appeared to be a small terminal and informed a Corporal at the counter of our destination. He made a call then instructed us to sit tight and wait for a ride to Camp Holloway that was due to arrive in about an hour. There were no seats or benches prompting us to just plop our gear and our asses on the floor. Situated on the floor across the room were three Army grunts also waiting for a flight or ride to somewhere. One, a black guy, was stretched out sleeping with his head propped on the leg of his comrade who was sitting back against the wall. Randy and I couldn't help but stare and knew, in contrast to them, our crispy clean FNG status, or non-status, was extremely obvious. They were unshaven with hair beyond the regulated and accepted G.I. norm. Their fatigues had no name labels, no insignias, and were worn, torn and faded to a near khaki color or lack of color due to extended exposure to the elements and imbedded red dirt. The black leather on their boots was scuffed to a rough raw brown and the upper green nylon was faded with shredded edges. Three M-16's and bandoliers of ammo along with assorted other gear lie in a dormant pile at their feet. These guys looked as though they had been buried twice then exhumed for another go-round, which was reflected in their tired eyes, dead, emotionless, as though they had long ago surrendered their souls to hell and were now just biding time until someone or some thing came to collect. I wanted to ask who they were and where they had been but felt I was somehow unqualified to pry. After a long silence one of them finally spoke up.

"Hey man, got a cigarette?" asked the dark haired dark tanned one.

Randy popped a pack out of his top pocket, rose and took it to them. The two who were awake each accepted and Randy lit them up with his Zippo.

"Here, keep the pack. I got more," he said.

"Thanks. Where you guys headed?"

"Some place called Camp Holloway," answered Randy.

They looked at each other knowingly, then to us. "Shit, that's too bad."

"What do you mean?" I asked.

"That's rocket city, man."

"Rocket city?"

"Yeah. Place gets hit by rockets all the time, man. Sorry."

"Better in da bush. You da major mofucka in da bush," said the stretched out sleeper who apparently wasn't actually sleeping but just resting his tired eyes.

Looking at him and assuming he spent most of his time there, I couldn't imagine how being in the bush, as he said, would be preferable.

"Don't mean nothin', man," said the blond haired smoker who's leg was the sleeper's pillow. There was the inference of a southern accent. "Don't matter. If you're it, you're it. It's the same difference. What's fuckin' difference? It's same difference."

"Difference is day don't have to live wit yo ugly fuckin' cracker ass," replied the black sleeper.

The sleeper's joke lay flat as though it had been said and ignored a hundred times before.

"You guys are new, right?" continued the dark haired smoker. There was a bit of a Boston accent now.

"Yeah," answered Randy. The answer wasn't necessary but it kept up the conversation.

"Where you from?"

"New York," answered Randy.

"Maryland," I said, "Annapolis."

He offered only an apathetic nod, probably because we weren't from his neck of the woods in the states.

"You guys going home?" asked Randy.

"Fuck no," stated the southern blond coldly as he leaned back and closed his eyes.

That was it, no introductions, no handshakes, no who won the Super Bowl or what's going on back in the world? Nothing else was said for nearly half an hour until a ¾ ton truck, the Army's version of a four-wheel drive pick-up, pulled up at the door and in popped its driver.

"Anybody here for Holloway?" he asked.

We gathered our gear and headed for the door.

"Hey," came the voice of the dark haired faded grunt. "Good luck, man, and thanks for the smokes."

"Yeah, you too," answered Randy.

"Don't need it," he smiled, but the smile was only a cursory extension of his lips. His eyes said something else altogether.

I didn't see much of the Air Force Base and didn't know then that I would return there a number of times for a number of reasons, not all good. Without as much as a 'howdy-do' our driver wheeled us off the base and onto Highway 14 toward Pleiku City. After passing through Pleiku we would turn onto Highway 19 that would take us to Camp Holloway. Highway 19 had a history, none of which we were aware at the time. The road was a main artery and ground re-supply route from Qui Nhon on the east coast to Pleiku, a western province capitol and one of the main burgs of the II Corps area. The road then continued on through the Ia Drang Valley and the highlands into Cambodia. It was a lifeline road and, given the particular climate of the war, the whims of the NVA, VC, or the late Ho Chi Min's aggressive attitude at any unforeseen time, had been and could be as dangerous as a Wal-Mart the day after Thanksgiving or safe as a Putt Putt golf course on a Monday morning. It was a blood route that had hosted nearly every kind of hostile action imaginable on every scale. A pipeline, about six inches in diameter, ran beside the highway from Qui Nhon to An Khe, and then from An Khe to Pleiku, which was the main feed of MoGas, JP4 aviation fuel, and Diesel. There were guarded pumping stations about every six miles because NVA or VC sappers blew the pipeline up just about every night at various spots. For that reason, the pumping of POL was usually only done during daylight hours.

Be it the 14 or the 19 road, all I knew was we had left the safety of a perfectly good military base and headed into the unknown, unarmed, and judging by the driver's attitude, unconcerned. I suddenly remembered the captured film where sixty men of a convoy died in less than half a minute in an NVA ambush, and though I didn't show it, I was a bit unnerved. Had I known at the time that the countryside surrounding the small city of Pleiku was littered with military installations, including the 5th Special Forces, an engineering base, artillery base, ARVN bases, and a varied selection of outpost and other base camps, I probably would have been a bit more relaxed. But then that was an FNG mentality. In my ignorance I developed a healthy case of insecurity with no intention of suppressing it for at least 362 more days. Truth was this was hostile country littered with NVA, North Vietnamese Army regulars, in large quantities who filtered into the II Corps AO by the thousands from the Ho Chi Min trail near the tri-border area of Cambodia and Laos. Fortunately, I wasn't aware of any of this so I wasn't sure how to feel and, for now, had to settle for just feeling FNG stupid and paranoid.

Randy and I sat in the back of the truck that was completely naked of its canvas top, taking in as much of the scenery as we could. That is when we weren't rocking back and forth while our driver dodged motor scooters overloaded with people, chickens, and pigs, or bicycles overloaded with people, chickens, and pigs, or lambrettas, a kind of three wheeled mo-ped on steroids with either back seats or a mini truck bed also usually overloaded with people, chickens and pigs. On one occasion he whizzed past a made in Detroit Army jeep driven by an ARVN soldier that was also overloaded with people, chickens, and pigs to such a height that it was Rube Goldberg comical and looked as though it would easily tip over with the slightest nudge or first turn. The driver, obviously ignorant of the physics, seemed impervious to the possibility and flew down the road like he was on a mission from Buddha. As for civilian automobiles, they must have been rare in this neck of the woods because we failed to see any. What we did see was people and as we neared Pleiku the number of people increased.

Small dwellings and one room shacks, and I have to say small and I have to say shacks, were scattered hear and there, appearing to host families too large for their intended purpose. Nearby, the Vietnamese seemed to be busying themselves at menial task, all of which could apparently be performed from a squatting position that would make a Yoga instructor proud but cause the average American a great deal of pain. As we rolled along the road we ran parallel to a large ditch full of water. It apparently doubled as a stream and community water source, as well as a sewer system where squatting people washed clothes or pots and utensils, or themselves. A woman was filling a pitcher, another was bathing a child, nearby other children were jumping and playing in the water, and up stream only a few meters an old man was squatting over the water taking a shit accompanied by a water buffalo that was contentedly situated in the communal tributary right up to his pride and joys. I pointed this tranquil unhealthy suburban scene out to Randy, who being from the Big Apple and used to not much of anything except concrete and asphalt most all his life, was already in a state of environmental distress and disorientation. He stared in disbelief.

"Don't drink the water," I suggested.

"Yeah, you got that right," he said as his focus settled on the water buffalo. "What the hell is that?"

"It's an elephant," I joked, hoping to cash in on the city boy's ignorance of nature. "You never saw an elephant before," I laughed.

"Not with horns and a camel hump. Had a teacher in junior high school once looked like that though. What a bitch."

We continued our A-ticket Disney ride into and through the north side of Pleiku City that at first glance by the unaccustomed eye looked like the Barnum and Bailey Circus run amuck. The smell of nuoc mam sauce and fish heads, incense and garbage, and a myriad of other unrecognizable foreign odors all mixed with the heat of the day creating a sensual overload that only a newborn child crashing onto this planet for the first time could associate, if you get my drift.

"Where are we?" I asked our driver.

"Pleiku," he yelled over the noise of the vehicle. "Holloway's few miles up the road."

"You always drive this road alone?"

"Didn't have any choppers goin' your way so they sent me. It's safe," he said. "Most of the time. As long as you're off the road and on base by five and definitely by dark. That's when the black market sets up and Charlie comes to town for some kicks and to go shopping on the black market for U.S. military supplies. We give the shit to the ARVNs and they sell the shit to the VC, then we kill the VC and give the shit back to the ARVNs. What the fuck, Asian economics I guess."

I sincerely hoped that most of the time was this time and watched the city flash by in a confused blur. There were people everywhere scooting in and out of streets and low altitude buildings and shops, all of which looked to be constructed of whatever material or junk was popular or available at the time or century it was built. Many were some form of masonry structures and the various faded aging colors attacked the senses like an art show featuring the efforts of a kindergarten fingerprinting class on LSD. Occasionally a larger classic old-world Oriental structure stood out among the others, seeming to beg for restoration and relocation to another time. Among the occasional tall pine trees everything reeked of neglect, old age, and overuse, with an overall flavor of an urban slum, yet at the same time it seemed to be a national standard. I'm sure there had to be better places somewhere in Vietnam but I was yet to see any.

The driver slowed to a stop at an intersection waiting for another people, pig, and chicken parade and we were immediately approached by a cluster of excited half naked scroungy Vietnamese kids with outstretched hands.

"G.I. give cigret? G.I. give cigret?" most of them yelled. Others were more ambitious.

"G.I. give dallah! G.I. give empeesee dallah!

Randy and I looked at each other and shrugged, thinking, as we would have in the States, that it was bad form to contribute to the delinquency of a minor. The kids were insistent, if not unrelenting, and growing in number, homing in on us newbies like sharks to an uncooked ship's roast.

"G.I. give cigret! G.I. give dallah!" they begged desperately without shame as they banged on the side of the vehicle and waved their hands. "Give cigret! Give dallah! G.I. give! G.I. give!"

"No. No cigarettes," we told them, secretly wishing we could give them an entire K-mart instead. "Go away. No cigarettes."

We started moving again and as we pulled away the kids turned from cute and pesky to downright belligerent.

"Fuk yu, G.I.! G.I. numba ten! Fuk yu!" they yelled as they shot us the bird and threw at us whatever they could find lying in the street. It was like watching the Dead End Kids revert to character after conning and smoozing a Pat O'Brien Father Flanagan type who just departed and rounded the street corner.

Every society has its little hustlers, I thought, but these guys were downright brazen.

The driver started laughing as he whacked the horn to work his way clear of more people, chickens, pigs, and Lambrettas.

"You shoulda' tossed 'em a couple cigarettes, man," he laughed. "They don't smoke 'em, they use 'em for money. They got better shit to smoke than cigarettes."

He introduced himself as Bunky, just Bunky, and Bunky according to Bunky, was a driver. Bunky could and would drive anything anytime, and anywhere without fear, including a war zone, simply because Bunky just loved to drive. Now on his second enlistment, but still only a PFC, Bunky had set himself a goal to literally become qualified and to drive every land vehicle in the U.S. Army arsenal, and according to Bunky he had just about achieved his goal. There remained only a tracked howitzer with a bunch of impressive letters and numbers before its name remaining on his list. He hadn't driven the tracked howitzer yet because the only one in the II Corps area that he knew of was the personal pride and joy of some jerk sergeant named Dechermann who refused to let Bunky play with his machine. According to Bunky, Dechermann had a bur up his ass because Bunky, in his excitement when coming upon the tracked howitzer, ran over and killed Dechermann's dog.

"Can you imagine that," said Bunky. "I mean it was just some dink dog."

The tracked howitzer's name was Geronimo. In spite of Bunky's attempts at bribery, which included everything from a full month's pay and case of booze to a night with a round eye nurse, there was no way in hell Sergeant Dechermann was going to let Bunky get his hands on Geronimo. So Bunky, figuring he could outlast Sergeant Dechermann and get his chance at Geronimo after Sergeant Dechermann's DEROS, (Date Eligible for Return from Over Seas), reenlisted for another tour in Vietnam. Unknown to Bunky however, Sergeant Dechermann had done the same.

"I'll stay here 'till the damn war's over," declared Bunky. "Cause me and Geronimo got a date with destiny."

Randy and I listened patiently as we continued our journey, wondering how anyone could be so obsessed with driving anything except maybe a '68 Corvette, until Bunky explained how he got in the Army in the first place. It seems Bunky was from Scooptown, Pennsylvania. Scooptown was noted for only two things being; it was the native home of Charles Bronson the famous actor and that it was so obscure that nobody even knew it was the native home of Charles Bronson. Scooptown was nothing more than an isolated hand full of old small coal mine company houses precariously perched on the side of a mountain near another coal town named Nanty Glo, and Scooptown being what it was, offered little in the form of entertainment, leaving the very few teenagers who were unfortunate enough to live there few options other than to occasionally *borrow* someone's car and go joy riding. Bunky, being the natural driver that he was, decided to borrow a neighbor's car and cruise to the nearest city of any size, which was Johnstown, where he was promptly detained by the police and accused of speeding and reckless driving.

"That was bullshit," declared Bunky. "I was just sittin' in a pizza joint eatin' a slice of pizza, with anchovies, and they took me in. Said they recognized the car, a '59 Buick, you know the one with the big wings and two-tone paint job."

To make a long story short, Bunky had a short fuse and when the police ganged up on him in the station accusing him of terrorizing the town he finally said, "Okay, damnit! If yuns are gonna screw me for reckless drivin' then I'm gonna give ya some *real* reckless drivin!"

Bunky ran out of the station, jumped into the first police cruiser he found, switched on the lights and siren, and took off at high speed purposely running into every police vehicle he could find, six in all, then a Dodge pick-up truck loaded with four barrels of used French fry grease from McDonalds that spilled all over the street, a VW bus, two Oldsmobile's, thirteen parking meters, and the front of a Woolworths 5&10 store. When the judge gave Bunky a choice of six months in the Harrisburg penitentiary or a hitch in the Army, Bunky chose the Army thinking if he had to do time he might as well get paid for it and possibly get to drive something while he was at it. To his delight, Bunky discovered a whole new world of wheels in the Army and to Bunky this was like having Christmas every day, and a hell of a lot better than Scoop Town.

Currently Bunky was a self appointed full time driver volunteering for every driving mission that popped up which he always got because nobody ever volunteered for driving missions. They didn't volunteer because when you drove an Army vehicle you had to inspect it, sign it out, fill out the driver's log book, drive it, bring it back, refuel it, fill out the log book, check all the engine stuff, wash it, and sign it back in. If there were any discrepancies, a big ugly burly motor pool sergeant would kill you. That's also why officers never drive military vehicles except in the movies where it looks cool and masculine to do so. And it's also one of the reasons why the U.S. Military needs so many extra enlisted men. They're needed to chauffeur the officers who never drive military vehicles. I suppose Bunky thought it was necessary for us to know all this and I guess it was nice of him to care enough to tell us. It was obvious Bunky was proud of his achievements and also obvious he had a great future in the Army. We came to sincerely hope that Bunky and Geronimo would someday have their date with destiny.

Making our way out of the city, Randy tapped me on the arm and pointed to the right side of the road. I looked over to discover another little shack perched in the middle of another little dusty grassless piece of red clay. This one, however, was you might say, uniquely American. It had been constructed of some form of junk wood and entirely sided and shingled from top to bottom with flattened out Budweiser beer cans, hundreds and hundreds of them. A naked child stood in front of its only opening that was curtained with a U.S. Army issue camouflage poncho liner, no doubt purchased on the black market or simply stolen. The entire city, at least what I saw of it at that time, seemed to me by American standards to spell poverty, but the energy and activity within somehow said otherwise. It wasn't poverty as we knew it or perceived it. It was more a matter of quality, or should I say, an accepted lack of quality of modern life. There was no apparent order, or planning, or governing, or visible pride, just an odd lethargic kind of busy bee existence without social consciousness. At least none I understood at the time.

Further along highway 19 the road continued into a large plateau with the highlands looming up in the distance, then eventually Camp Holloway popped up on the left like some small country town where, before turning to enter the camp, our vehicle slowed and waited for some more mobile people, chickens and pigs to pass. Where all those people were heading with all those chickens and pigs beat the hell out of me, but what I would learn of this country during my visit would lead me to believe that everyone traveled with their chickens and pigs just to make sure they still had their chickens and pigs when they returned home. Theft seemed to be a national past time. We turned left through the gate, past the SPs, and rolled to a halt in front of the Battalion HQ area on the immediate right.

"This is it," Bunky informed us. "Personnel office is right over there."

Before we could say thanks and figure out exactly where *there* was among the cluster of hooches and with our feet barely hitting the ground, Bunky sped off in search of another mission. We were left standing like Dorothy and Toto in the land of Oz in front of the headquarters area of the 52nd Combat Aviation Battalion, but this sure as hell wasn't Oz or Kansas. At first glance and compared to Cam Rahn Bay or Na Trang, and especially compared to home, Camp Holloway looked like a real shit hole. It was dirty and dusty, worn and weary, yet not being one to always see the worst in things, I quickly surmised that whatever it was it certainly impressed me as being safer than where most grunts would end up. Hell, some of it even had sidewalks, and I would discover later, the showers and shitters were constructed of concrete. Being only a couple of enlisted chaps and required to be ignorant and uninformed, we stood there not knowing if we were here for the duration or once again just passing through.

What we didn't know is we were standing in the birthplace of the war. It was from here the real war in Vietnam started for America back in February of '65 when the VC assaulted and nearly destroyed Camp Holloway, resulting in eight dead Americans and over a hundred casualties, most of which were so badly wounded they had to be evacuated. Some were even killed in their beds. That number of casualties represented more than half the total occupants of the camp at the time. Nine helicopters were destroyed and fifteen put out of action. The attack caught the Americans off guard since until that time as advisors no American facilities had been touched. It was that act that transformed the U.S. from an advisory to a full combat status. Twelve hours later President Johnson ordered the bombing of North Vietnam's Army barracks north of the DMZ in retribution, then things escalated with the subsequent Air Cav launching of its troops from Camp Holloway into the nearby Ia Drang Valley and the battle at LZ X-Ray.

Camp Holloway, named in honor of a WO1 Charles Holloway, the installation's first casualty, soon became the hub of the highlands operations and the birthplace of many of the standards of the *Chopper War*. The buzz was that it was built up from a rubber plantation and a small French airstrip and small fort. Camp Holloway was at one time also thought to be the busiest airport on the planet even though its facilities were small and limited. I suppose that claim was based on the number of incoming and outgoing aircraft. An amazing feat considering it's small size. Whether the tally included incoming and outgoing rockets and mortars I don't know. Holloway became a strategic thorn in the side of the bad guys and as such often reaped the rewards in the form of enemy retribution.

Holloway was also a favorite place of ole General "Vinegar Joe" Joseph Stilwell Jr. of WWll fame. The old fart loved flying and loved the pilots and crews at Holloway, and on one occasion even parachuted into the middle of an awards ceremony there. So the old man was a little nuts, who wouldn't be after they'd been fighting Japs and who knows what else in this part of the world since before Pearl Harbor? Why he hung around that long I'd never figure. The mosquitoes alone would make you a basket case. I guess a basket case with a few stars on his shoulders was bound to be a well liked soldier's soldier, especially in this place.

So Stilwell was famous and known to the world, and Camp Holloway was famous and known to the White House, the Pentagon, and Hanoi, and now here we were, Specialist Vincent Fusco and Specialist Randy Collatazzi, two newly arrived enlisted WOP's about as obscure as a flea on this huge historic elephant's ass, reluctantly ready, willing, and able to change the course of the war, - maybe.

The hooches extended in all directions that I could see from our drop-off point with the red dusty road on which we stood continuing down hill toward the maintenance hangers across a large active helipad. Further down were revetments and a runway. It then angled right and out of sight. Most immediately notable in the battalion area was a small well kept courtyard surrounded by a number of various office hooches designated with signs stating they were S-this or S-that or S-something or some kind of HQ something or other. It was a quick and obvious reminder that we were still in the same Army we had left in the states, cursed to live with the same endless string of brevities, codes, confusion, bureaucracy, and autocracy.

"What's all those S offices?" asked Randy.

"They're cubby holes," I explained, drawing on my extensive knowledge and experience acquired during my education at Fort Sill and at the 17th Ord. "Like in a chicken coup or pigeon roost. They're a kind of holding pen for fast rising officers with organizational skills and quick one-liners."

As we grabbed our gear and strolled across the courtyard I clarified my statement to Randy who was fresh out of gunnery school but not so fresh that he naively bought into my sarcasm.

"During my long extensive time in the military," I told him, "no one had ever been able to explain to me what all those S's stood for, leaving me to assume I was always asking the wrong people or that since there was always an officer assigned to the S office it must have stood for *Something to do* or *Some day* I'm gonna' be a CO and not have to piss around in one of these boring S offices. Of course, it doesen't really matter much what it stands for because most of the officers assigned to the S offices are never in the S offices anyway, leaving most of the responsibilities of their particular S to an enlisted man. There are G offices too," I explained, "which were the same thing except higher up at a brigade or division or something. It seems many of the S offices' officers are always out working on special projects, not that any officers actually work on special projects but there are always lots of special projects to be worked on. In the Army just about everything qualifies as a special project, especially if it's above and beyond the call of duty, whatever the call of duty in an S or G office is. That means that where officers' written evaluations are concerned, everything is above and beyond the call of duty and because of that, writing an Officer Eval is an art form all its own."

"Where are we going?" asked Randy.

"Don't know. Personnel office I guess."

"Wow. You knowing all that shit. Impressive"

"It just came to me. Want to know more?"

"Sure, why not. But I think you're full of shit."

"As much as anybody, I guess," I laughed.

As we surveyed the area I continued the lesson, explaining that in the career officer's world all things hinged on the personal proficiency evaluations written by their commanding officer. Hence the special project concept determining how far a career officer could advance. Aside from the perpetual ass kissing and ass covering, and a continuous effort to become overqualified, certified, and degreed for just about everything except making war, it was limited only by their imagination and ability to dream up special projects, sell the idea to a higher up, then after gaining a confidential deniable unofficial approval, getting a senior NCO to get a junior NCO to get a talented Specialist or Private to complete the special project. If the project was a dismal failure the poor enlisted dupe who actually performed the function took all the heat and was promptly court marshalled, shot, or transferred. That's after he was verbally abused by the junior NCO then mentally tortured by the senior NCO and skinned and castrated by the originating officer. If the special project was a gleaming success, however, the low ranking dupe got nothing, the junior NCO got a pat on the back, the senior NCO got a bottle of scotch, and the officer who originated the special project eagerly accepted and humbly received all the glory and accolades for the special project in the form of a special project certificate of achievement or a special project plaque of recognition, and sometimes even a medal for meritorious service.

Most importantly, however, was that almost always the creative officer in question would receive a long drawn out complimentary personal endorsement on what was known as his Officer Evaluation, efficiency, report stating how he could walk on water and how he demonstrated incredible *outstanding professionalism* and *initiative* by being so *proficient* and *talented* and *dependable*. So *professionally proficient, talented,* and *dependable* was he, it would say, that he more than demonstrated *exceptionally outstanding professionalism* and was a credit to his company, the battalion, the United States Army, the United States of America, the entire western hemisphere, and chunky little apple pie moms everywhere. In fact, it would say, he *regularly excels* in such endeavors that require such *outstanding professional initiative, proficiency, talent and dependability.* And again, in fact, the officer in question demonstrated so much *outstanding professional initiative, proficiency, talent,* and *dependable professionalism* that once the CO's signature had been affixed on the professionally written and prepared personal proficiency evaluation, the officer in question could pretty much spend the rest of his tour in the O-club picking his nose, scratching his ass, and whoring around, knowing that no CO on the planet could justify or would suffer the embarrassment of reversing his opinion after penning such a glowing canned *professionally* written *professional* review of such a *professional* officer who was so full of... *professionalism.*

"Are you following me here, Randy?"

"Oh sure. No problem," laughed Randy.

Randy's ability to attentively listen while we strolled among the various S hooches searching for the Personnel Office was encouraging, so I continued the lesson.

Of course, unless the officer was a total moron, the evaluations were usually always favorable being it automatically assumed the officer was efficient in the first place. Therefore, I explained further, the special project was necessary to distinguish one automatically intelligent favored efficient officer from another. It didn't matter that *outstanding* and *professionalism* were the most overused words in officers' personal efficiency proficiency evaluations, as long as they were used in a most outstanding professional original manner. The result I'm sure, of the authoring officer's inability to write without the use of military brevities and numerical codes. Nor did it matter that the special project in question could have been something as simple as planting banana trees outside the battalion HQ or re-writing the manual which regulates the size and color of all the S and G signs in the HQ area, or having all the S and G signs in the HQ area repainted so that everyone would have no problem at all finding the officers who weren't there - because they were all out somewhere else not working on special projects. What mattered was that the officer in question had the personal *initiative,* another favorite word, to initiate such *outstanding professional* endeavors as to have appeared, on paper at least, to have been capable of achieving the entire Normandy invasion single handedly, all the while exercising that *initiative* with great *outstanding proficiency, talent,* and *dependable professionalism* in the tradition of the United States Army.

The writing about such personal initiative was a must and highly valued in an officer's personal efficiency proficiency evaluation even though personal initiative, by definition, went contrary to all Army doctrine and orders, and was pretty much a court martial offense most any other time. Especially in a combat situation where there was zero tolerance for any initiative which might cause confusion, or the perception of confusion, or failure, or the perception of failure. In the military, *having initiative* and *taking the initiative* are two different languages altogether and having a clear understanding of this was critical in covering one's ass. And even though having initiative was necessary and taking the initiative was risky, losing the initiative was a career killer altogether. As such, all initiative was best restricted to officer's special projects where they could remain aloof with deniability until rewarded for the special project's success.

Therefore the S and G offices, I concluded in my sarcastic one-person groupthink session, were a direct extension of the officer liar's test required to obtain a hard or even a soft commission. And seeing so many S offices in one place and in a combat zone was, I predicted, an ominous omen and indication of future fun and games for both Randy and myself.

"How do you know all that?" asked Randy.

"I was volunteered to type some officer efficiency reports once. The rest is off the cuff. I was on the school debate team."

"Am I supposed to believe all that?" asked Randy.

"Not really," I said.

"Oh," said Randy, fully accepting and recognizing my authority on the subject but not really giving a shit either way. He was more focused on finding a place to park his gear and wolf down some chow.

He and I were sure we weren't supposed to go to any of the S offices simply because we didn't know what the hell they were but we did know, due to training and conditioning, that all things begin with the personnel office so we finally stopped a passing soldier and asked directions.

"Right over there," he pointed. "The S-1 Office."

"The S-1 Office," repeated Randy.

"The S-1 Office," I echoed.

"Thanks for the education, Fusco," said Randy. "I'd hate to see what you could do with the rest of the alphabet."

"Give me time. I'll come up with something."

"Come on," said Randy. "Let's go to the… 'S-1' and see who isn't there."

We started in that direction, but not before we inspected the memorial wall that sat in the center of the courtyard. The wall was a simple affair rising nearly head high and spanning about thirty feet in width. It was covered with plaques, hundreds of plaques, each one carrying the name and representing the memory of a single member of the battalion who was killed in action. They were the same kind of names attached to the same kind of young faces we had seen and heard and worked and lived with since our joining the Army, and it quickly impressed on us that in this place we were mortal and vulnerable.

Welcome to Rocket City FNG Fusco, I thought, and may you be fortunate enough not to gain this type of perpetual standing.

CHAPTER 12

WE CAN TYPE
CHICKA-BOOM CHICKA-BOOM

Randy and I made our way to the battalion personnel office, (also known as the S-1), and entered to discover what was most likely the largest office in all of Camp Holloway. It housed about a dozen clerks plus whatever supervising senior NCO and officer who wasn't there because they were out not working on special projects. The dull metal desks, each with a typewriter, were all neatly arranged like eggs in a crate, a few manned by clerks in OD T-shirts who, like other places I had seen in the Army, were doing their damn best to look fast sitting still, except here they did it with pretty much a give-a-shit attitude. Electric fans circulated the air while some clerks circulated the room with no apparent purpose. Like every other office, room, hooch, tent, or bunker in Vietnam, there was a portable radio tuned to the Armed Forces Network that at the time of our entry was playing *Down Town* by Petula Clark. In the back of the room were various office machines surrounded by a myriad of incoming and outgoing circulation boxes and a wall of IN and OUT distribution cubbyholes not unlike those of an old post office. At the front of the room was a desk that faced all the others where sat some sort of a clerk honcho. The entire arrangement somehow reminded me of the slave rowing set up on the Spanish galleon in the movie The Sea Hawk, where a tired sweaty starving Errol Flynn and company of English slaves pulled on their ores while being whipped on the back by some Spanish asshole with an overseer keeping up the beat on a drum with two big wooden mallets. Needless to say, this clerk honcho wasn't swinging a whip and the rest of the staff sure as hell weren't starving or working up a sweat, but in the Army you have to imagine analogies to the outside world or run the risk of getting hopelessly lost in the reality of the military world like a little heavy leadfooted fly that just landed in a bowl of unappetizing soft oatmeal. It was to this clerk honcho we were directed when entering the office.

"Orders," he stated, barely looking up as he stretched out his hand. Obviously he had done this before - many times over.

I pulled the stack of orders from the big brown envelope containing my bulky 201 file and handed them to the clerk honcho who glanced at them, tore off one copy, and handed the other unnecessary forty-nine copies back to me.

The hand extended again, "File."

I passed the clerk honcho my 201 file and he proceeded to go through it. Flipping from one page to another he began to gain interest in its contents. When he came upon a series of attached sealed envelopes and, what some in the military refer to as confidential content or security flags, he looked up to discover that I actually had a face. He then looked back to the file, flipped a few more pages, and again looked to verify I was still there. Once again he doodled with the confidential stuff and security flags. I don't know why because he wasn't permitted to open them but then that's probably why they call them flags. They catch your attention like the red flag of a bull fighter then eat away at your curiosity. He then flipped through the pages with my multiple MOS info and once again looked to confirm I was still there.

I smiled.

"Where the hell did you come from?"

"My mother," I said, trying to maintain a sense of humor as I ventured into the valley of death.

Randy snickered but the clerk honcho maintained an even strain.

"No. Where the hell were you stationed before you came here?"

"Fort Sill," I answered.

"Yeah, that's what it says here but that's artillery. Nothing in your file about artillery, just top-secret missiles and shit. What the hell were you doing at Fort Sill?"

"Drinking Coors and trying to stay out of trouble," I smiled.

He again looked at my file then back to me with complete confusion, possibly even a sense of trepidation thinking that since I was so overqualified for whatever I wasn't doing here that maybe, just maybe, I was here to surreptitiously conduct a Congressional investigation of possible war crimes or even the very common practice of misappropriation of just about everything.

"Your file is full of security flags and top secret crypto shit I can't even look at and you got critical MOS's. What the hell are you doing here?"

"I volunteered," I smiled.

"You what?" he said.

"You what?" echoed Randy.

A couple of nearby clerks overheard, stopped talking, and looked at me as though I was the Elephant Man. I just smiled and shrugged, suddenly feeling like some bony-ass effeminate band geek in a football locker room at half time.

"Man, you shouldn't be here. I don't even know if you should be in-country. How the hell can I assign you if I can't even read your file?"

I was starting to get that sinking feeling as though I was somehow destined for a reunion with Staff Sergeant Polk, and not wanting to dig slit trenches for the duration or enjoy the fate of my buddy Sims down south who had been converted to a grunt, I seized on what appeared to be an opportunity presented by the sight of a few empty desks.

"I can type," I heard myself saying, breaking a promise I had made to myself to never say those three words again as long as I was still in the Army and trusting those same bird-in-hand instincts that misguided me into the 17th Ordinance Company in Oklahoma. "Took an Army speed typing course. Also took the Army admin course. It should all be in my file there," I added for good measure as I viewed the long line of file cabinets.

Not knowing what was ahead, I had decided in that split second that what I saw was pretty damn acceptable and I was more than willing to sacrifice and suffer the obvious boredom of becoming one of clerk honcho's *Remington Raiders* to whatever else lurked out there in the unknown. Hell, if it was good enough for Errol Flynn, it was good enough for me.

"My primary MOS is clerk typist, admin, right?" I asked, encouraging him to explore the file.

"Not what it says here. Says a bunch of missile shit. But, hey, you say you can type? You can type!" lit up the clerk honcho approvingly.

"Eighty-seven words a minute," I smiled, "on a manual. But I thought my primary was changed to clerk typist," I said, not knowing they had restored my primary security MOS in order to keep me a primary candidate for guard duty at Lala Land back at Fort Sill. Top, you crafty bastard.

Randy picked up on my strategy quick smart and jumped right on the bandwagon. "Yeah, so can I," he chimed in. "Guess that's why they sent us here, huh?"

"Far out. You can type too?" said the obviously pleased clerk honcho.

"Yeah, guess that's why the sent us here, huh," Randy repeated.

"Yeah, guess that's why they sent us here," I smiled. "Guess we can work right here with you guys, huh?"

The clerk honcho looked out over his domain, thought a minute, and then said to our disappointment, "No, I got too much help around here already. Tell ya what though. The 189th just lost their awards clerk and their company clerk is short, leaving here in a week or so. How's that sound? You up for company clerk?" he asked me as he snatched Randy's file.

"Yeah, that sounds cool," I said. Then as quickly as I had said it I realized I might have just condemned myself to hell by remembering that each subsequent transfer since Cam Rahn Bay took me further away from civilization and with each move circumstances seemed to worsen. I suddenly envisioned the 189th as being located in some lost little muddy shit hole in the middle of nowhere with sun dried bones and strange natives lining the runway, and since I didn't know where the hell I was at that very moment I sure as hell didn't want to go from one geographic mystery to a totally enigmatic spit on a map full of other little spits and unpronounceable targets of opportunity - ours or theirs.

"The 189th?" asked Randy. "What's that?"

"Assault helicopter company."

"Assault helicopter?" I said, cringing and diving right in for the bad news, "Where is it?"

The clerk honcho sat silent for a moment as he scribbled our assignments on our files. He didn't even bother looking in Randy's 201, which was just fine with Randy being it would have revealed his true MOS. Randy preferred a job as a clerk typist to that of a helicopter air crewman door gunner for which he was trained, and considered clerking was far more suitable taking into account his non-athletic character and deficient funky eyes and granny glasses. Nor had Randy any burning desire to be a hero for any cause whatsoever because the mere thought of being shot down and ending up in a wooded area, especially a hostile foreign tropical enemy held jungle, was an extremely distasteful concept to the city boy from the Big Apple, not so much because of the fear of pain or death or capture or torture, but because he simply could not and would not so much as entertain the idea that he might have to shit in the boonies and wipe his ass with a collection of local foliage. Besides, by his own admittance, even though he had successfully completed gunnery school, he was probably the only door gunner in the entire United States Army who couldn't hit the Queen Mary with an M-60 even if the chopper he was shooting from was sitting on the old girl's deck. How the hell he successfully made it through gunnery school was a true mystery - even to him.

"I need to see your IDs," said the clerk honcho, not looking up, hand extended.

"Don't have one," I said.

"Got gassed and ripped off in Nha Trang," added Randy.

"What, you too?" replied the clerk honcho without surprise. "Like to be around when they catch those fuckers."

"So would I," I said.

"Yeah, me too," agreed Randy.

"So, where'd you say the 189th is?" I asked again.

"Okay, we'll have to make you up some new IDs using the spare mug shot in your files so you guys will have to sit tight for a while. Take about an hour."

"Where can we get some chow?" asked Randy.

"Just around the corner. If you hustle you might make it before they quit serving lunch. Just leave your shit here with me."

"Uh, that assault helicopter company is where again?" I asked.

Just then the clerk honcho's phone rang and as he snatched it up Randy turned away and headed for the door like a hungry dog on the trail of a fast moving juicy pork chop. I quickly followed, realizing I had skipped breakfast, and not knowing where this mysterious assault helicopter company was located, the possibility existed that I may not have a chance to get dinner. That is if they even had a mess hall at the 189th.

We cruised around the corner to find the battalion eatery then entering through a squeaky screen door we found the place nearly empty except for a group of about a dozen black guys occupying two tables in the far corner. We walked to the chow line, grabbed metal trays, and asked if we were in time to get some lunch.

"You just made it," answered the mess Sergeant who rather than serve us by portioning the food out as usual, turned all the serving spoons around so we could reach them. "Here, you guys help yourselves. I'm just gonna' feed the rest of this stuff to the locals anyway."

While loading up our trays the screen door squeaked open and in walked another black brother. At his side he carried a large stereo tape player. A rumble of mumbled recognition rose from the group seated at the tables in the corner resulting in a raised black-power clenched fist in return. The new arrival then switched on his stereo and out poured the Temptations singing *Can't Get Next To You*. When he cranked it up it was as though some electrical shock passed through the group causing the brothers to join in the Temptations rhythmic rhetoric while banging on their trays and tables and twitching in their seats.

> *"Can't get next to you babe, I can't get next to you!"*
> *"Can't get next to you babe, I can't get next to you!"*
> *"Ne-ext to you!"*
> *"Chicka-boom, chicka-boom!"*
> *"Ne-ext to you!"*
> *"Chicka-boom boom boom!"*

As the mobile DJ moved across the mess hall to join the group, his jive walk morphed into a disjointed dance that somehow motivated two others of the group to rise from their seats and join in while the rest became possessed by the overwhelming rhythm and near Shakespearian flow of the Temptations' libretto.

> *"Ne-ext to you!"*
> *"Chicka-boom, chicka-boom."*
> *"Ne-ext to you!"*
> *"Chicka-boom boom boom."*
> *"Wooooooooooo woooo woo."*

"Chicka-boom, chicka-boom."
"Wooooooooooo woo woo woo."
"Chicka-boom boom boom."

It was about that time the mess Sergeant laid down the law.

"Turn that shit off in my mess hall, Jackson," he yelled from the kitchen. "Or I'll come out there and shove it up your chicka-boom boom ass!"

Jackson took the noise censorship order in stride as though it were expected, switched off the music and continued to dance across to the group.

"Yo, Jackson, my main man. You hear dat? Mofuckin' lifer honky mess sergeant wanna' boom boom yo mofuckin' ass. Shiiiit."

"Yeah, don't dat mofucka wish," came Jackson as he approached the group. "Jus' like I mofuckin' boom boomed his mofuckin' mama laz' night."

It was at this time Randy and I were introduced to the greeting ritual of the *brothers blood.* As Jackson came to the table he greeted each and every individual brother with a tapped fist, low five, high five, hand jive that evolved into some kind of slap happy, elbow tapping, chest patting, finger tapping, sliding exchange culminating in a hooked hand shake. The entire process excelled even the most secret of secret society or fraternity greetings and it wasn't hard to recognize this was a black thing. At first glance it was actually kind of cool but likewise it didn't take long to realize it was an extensive greeting with a few negatives. By the time Jackson got through saying hello or *givin' some skin* or *dapping* as it was called, to each and every individual *blood* at the table, Randy and I were nearly finished with our meal. Then, after Jackson went and filled his own tray and returned to the table to eat, he repeated the entire hand jive process once again, leaving his food long enough to get cold, old, and grow fungus. The process repeated itself whenever any brother departed or arrived at a table, having to slip each and every other brother some skin. When two or more brothers were coming and going at the same time it was like watching the Three Stooges trying to discard sticky fly paper, except these guys professed to have a lot more cool and much better timing. It was no wonder they were the only ones left in the mess hall, having little or no opportunity to get any food from their trays to their mouths. In fact, the process was so disruptive that a few months later it prompted a written directive from the battalion CO that stated the hand jive greetings were to cease altogether immediately in all mess halls. This was because *slippin' some skin*, along with its ups and downs and bumps and grinds in the now crowded mess halls was evolving, becoming longer in duration and more and more complicated and inclusive of more and more tricky flicks and flutters and slaps and taps and pats until it included nearly every possible move, save that of an ass wipe, and was taking nearly the entire meal time for just one brother to greet only one other brother.

The lengthy process of greeting all the brothers interrupted and disrupted other soldiers' ability to quickly sit and consume their chow, leading to a major available seating problem, not to mention a few cultural confrontations. It also began to cause a mealtime gridlock that eventually affected officers' ability to get through the line and eat in a timely manner as well, even though they dined in a separate room. This encroachment on the enchanted world of the battalion level hard commissioned was the straw that busted the jive camel and generated the battalion CO's action directive. Being that most mess halls weren't designed to hold the entire unit's consignment of people at one time but to rotate the chow-down crowd in a timely manner, the Colonel finally decided that taking two hours to simply say hello and be seated at a table was a little much and detrimental to the war effort, eventually putting an end to it altogether and leaving the brothers to grudgingly settle for a single fist tap with the man next to him and a short verbal, "Happnin' Bloods" to the rest.

Though this was my first exposure to the brothers' hand jive, it wasn't my initial introduction to the music of the Temptations. In every place where there was a juke box and even some places where there weren't, on every military installation I had been to, it seems the only music the black guys ever listened to was the Temptations. It dominated the barracks, the day rooms, the snack bars, the EM clubs and even the latrines. Before I joined the Army I liked the Temptations. After my first year in the Army I hated the Temptations. I hated the Temptations because all I heard was the Temptations. Even in Mexico I heard the Temptations, although with a Spanish accent. So I began to avoid all those places where all I heard was the Temptations no matter how tempting it was to go to those places where all I heard was the Temptations. Should I ever become a civilian again maybe I'm sure I would like the Temptations again, but until that day I would hate the Temptations, every damn *woo woo* and every damn *chicka-boom*. I'd have preferred to hear some other group like maybe the Beatles or the Beach Boys, who in reality sounded like a bunch of alley cats with their balls in a vice and could be just as irritating were they also presented with the same incessant frequency and repetition, but then that wasn't likely. For some reason I disliked most country music as well, but the country music wasn't as prevalent or recurring and intrusive either since the country boys didn't tend to be prone to a necessity of groupthink melodies.

No matter what some people may say or think, sometimes too much of a good thing can actually be too much of a good thing, but it wasn't just that there was too much of the Temptations, it was also that there always seemed to be a group dialogue that accompanied the Temptations that was usually almost as loud as the usually over-volumed music itself. The music drew the brothers together like kids to a pile of presents on Christmas morning and the ensuing group dialogue always seemed to include one single ear piercing dominant phrase that proceeded and seceded nearly every sentence or utterance or expressed thought.

It was *mother fucker*.

I suppose the phrase 'mother fucker' has been around for some time, indeed the concept of the phrase has been in practice for, well, longer than most historians would like to admit. Certainly as long as the adventures of Oedipus and a few other famous Greek deep thinkers, not to mention a few demented Roman Caesar wannabes. And it came as no surprise to me that the word *mofucka'*, as it had now come to be used in a single utterance and somehow evolved into a single word, was out there. I wasn't that naïve but then having a Christian upbringing and decent background that demanded a little consideration for other folks within earshot, I wasn't that accepting of its use in everyday verbal exchanges. Hell, I was just catching on to the latter part of the phrase being a necessary and common part of the military vocabulary. But who, I thought, could be that unsophisticated and that comfortable always crudely including and involving everybody's mother? Many of the brothers on the other hand, especially those who joined our ranks from the mean streets of Boston, New York, Philly, D.C., Baltimore, Atlanta, L.A., Chicago, and all points urban, certainly had a gift for its inclusion in all expressions great and small, and for them there was no shame and nothing urbane about this urban incursion into the English language.

In point of fact, the word mofucka' had so many uses and connotations as practiced in Vietnam by the brothers that it had become its own science and was almost a language unto itself. If the brass in the Pentagon had been smart they would have taken all the brothers and turned them into radio operators just as the Marines had utilized the Navajo Indians in the Pacific during WWII. Surely the VC and NVA would have gone nuts trying to decipher a code that in reality would have been nothing more than simple urban jive talkin' ebonics, inclusive of a background scramble of the Temptations. *Chicka-boom chicka-boom.*

I entertained the idea that, in theory at least, just about anybody could use the word mofucka' along with an ability to walk with a limp and hold his crotch at the same time, and therefore have no difficulty gaining acceptance into any group of brothers. The only problem being that, if you were white, the spoken phrase *mofucka'* always seemed to express itself as an insult, which of course it originally was. It was a genetic or DNA thing I suppose that was near impossible to overcome or master convincingly for a white guy. For a PHD linguist to study the verbal exchange of a group of brothers such as that overheard by Randy and myself on that day, and subsequent days during our tour, would have been a rare and enlightening experience indeed, right up there with deciphering the famed and mysterious Rosetta Stone of Egypt. For me, it was this experience that fermented the fact I was now in a foreign country. I just wasn't real clear on what country that was.

"Happnin', mofucka'?" said Jackson.

"Yo, mofucka. Cool."

"Skin, mofucka. Yeah."

"Yeah."

"Oh maaaan. Mofuckin' nigga motor pool Sergeant wantin' send my mofuckin' nigga ass to da mofuckin motor pool to wash mofuckin' trucks'n shit. Moooo-fucka!"

"Oh man, mofucka. Dat mofuckin' lame, mofucka."

"Yeah."

"Yeah."

"Yo."

"Daaaaamn mofuckin' right, nigga."

"Yeah."

"Yeah, yeah."

"Yeah, mofucka. You mofuckin' gots dat mofuckin' shit straight, mofucka. Mofuckin' lifer nigga mofuckin' Sergeant sendin' dis mofuckin' nigga to da mofuckin' motor pool and shit. Washin' trucks'n shit. Shiiiiit. I ain't be washin' no mofuckin' trucks'n shit, mofucka."

"Shiiiiit. Oh hell no, mofucka."

"Yeah, hell no."

"Yeah."

"Yeah, mofucka."

"Damn mofuckin' right, nigga.

"Mofuckin' shiiiit."

"Gots dat mofuckin' shit right, mofucka."

"Yeah, Jack."

"Yeah."

"Yo."

"Yeah, yeah."

"Mofuckin' shit ain't mofuckin' right, man."

"Hell mofuckin' no, mofucka.

"Yeah, mofucka."

"Yo."

"Yeah."

"Yeah."

"Yeah, yeah."

"Fuckin' AAAAAA, mofucka. Mofuckin' lifer nigga messin' wit da mofuckin' brotha's and he be a mofuckin' brotha nigga hisself. Shiiiiiit."

"Shiiit yeah, his own self."

"Shiiiiiiiit."

"Yeah."

"Yeah."

"Yeah."

"Yeah, yeah."

"Shiiiiit."

"Yo. Shiiiiiiiit."

"Mofuckin' gots dat mofunkin' shit straight, mofucka. Shiiiiit."

"Shiiiiiit."

"Yo, mofucka."

"Shit yeah, mofucka."

"Oh, shit yeah, mofucka."

"Yeah."

"Oh shit yeah."

"Yeah, yeah."

"Shiiiiit."

"Shiiit."

"Yeah."

"Mofuckin' aks me mofucka, ats a real mofucka. Ain't dat right nigga?"

"Yeah, mofucka."

"Gots dat mofuckin' shit straight, mofucka."

"Shiiiiiiiiiiiiiiiit."

About that time some locally hired Vietnamese started filtering into the mess hall for their free lunch. That seemed to be a cue for the brothers to depart. The bloods rose from the table in ones and twos, all doing the hand jive departure, all 'mofuckin' dis' and 'mofuckin' dat' all the way from the table to the tray dump and out the door. Meanwhile, the influx of Vietnamese began chattering in their *indigenous foreign* language and, between the brothers and the Vietnamese chatter, Randy and I suddenly found ourselves dangling in a world of verbal confusion.

After we unscrambled our brains, we briefly observed the Vietnamese who, for us at this early time of our in-country experience, were still a novelty. We departed the battalion mess hall leaving behind those remaining *mofuckin' bloods* who were still dapping and hand jiving their *mofuckin'* farewells and we returned to the *mofuckin'* battalion personnel clerk honcho to pick up our *mofuckin'* gear, our new *mofuckin'* IDs, and some *mofuckin'* directions to the *mofuckin'* 189th AHC. *Oh yeah.*

CHAPTER 13

A HOOCHO CURSE &
THE ONE-DOUBLE-DEUCE

The hour or so it took to make up our new ID's turned into two and a half hours due to the fact the IDs had to be signed by the battalion S-1 officer who was not there because he was out not working on a special project at the officer's club. Yeah, this place had an O-club, and an EM club, and an NCO club to boot. The true measure of time and endurance, and a sure method of determining when Amrican troops have been in one place too damn long, is when they build officer's clubs followed quickly by NCO clubs and EM clubs. When a PX pops up then it's time to go home, and yep, they had a PX as well. It was tiny, no bigger than a one-car garage, but it was a PX.

"Ghostriders. 189th Assault Helicopter Company. Just down the hill on Hollywood Boulevard across from the runway. Can't miss it," said the clerk honcho as he handed us our new IDs. "Go to the orderly room and ask for Roabley the company clerk. I called. He knows your coming."

"Hollywood Boulevard? Just down the hill?" said Randy.

"You mean it's here?" I asked.

The clerk honcho confirmed his statement with a nod and we confirmed our satisfaction of his confirmation with a smile and a thanks. Just down the hill meant Camp Holloway was our last stop and not some dried up National Geographic bone yard in the boonies. Though Camp Holloway wasn't exactly paradise it appeared to be secure, offering safety in numbers and firepower, not to mention a roof, hard floors, hot food, inside commodes, and running water - sometimes.

We snatched up our gear, departed the S-1 and weaved our way through and out of the clustered battalion area until we came into the clear on a declining dirt road. The road eased to the right and ran just past a small fenced in water tower maintained and occupied by an old bent back local Vietnamese guy and his goats. Past the goat man we found a string of hooches that comprised the company area of the 189th. The narrow dirt road was also known by some as Hollywood Boulevard, referring to the combat fame of the units headquartered along its right side. The first unit along the boulevard was the Ghostriders, the 189th Assault Helicopter Company and the first hooches in the row housed the enlisted platoons that included the 1st Silver Air Lift, 2nd Scarlet Air Lift, and the Avengers Gun Platoon. Next came the orderly room HQ, followed by the supply hooch that doubled as the armory and mailroom, and lastly, on the corner was the enlisted Headquarters Platoon hooch. Between the hooches were dugout bunkers heavily sand bagged up to about roof level. The company officers and senior NCOs, in fact, most all of the battalion's officers, lived in their own neighborhood up the hill in a separate area, probably so they wouldn't be contaminated by us cultureless idiots who couldn't perceive the difference between daylight and dog shit. But it really didn't matter because, be it on the hill or along Hollywood Boulevard, it was still just government housing, which as we all know, regardless of how esthetically impressive it may be when it's originally constructed, inevitably degenerates into a place of questionable repute and lack of appeal. This was no exception.

Behind that line of hooches was another line of hooches and the company mess hall. In the center of it all was a small single goal basketball court that also acted as the company assembly area. All the hooches and bunkers had seen better days. The red dirt and dust of the highlands had long since seared and soaked itself into the wood and just about everything else. The rusting tin roofs and the faded and torn sand bags victimized by season after season of dust, monsoon rains, and beating sun resulted in a dull mix of green and dirty orange patina or hue that created the dingy character of some post-apocalyptic movie. Further along the road were other companies such as The Headhunters and the Gladiators. How this all translated to Hollywood Boulevard I was yet to know. It seemed a name like Death Row or Lethal Lane would have been more fitting.

The 189th rolled into Camp Holloway with their first 31 aircraft and personnel in April of 1967 and set up housekeeping in a group of tents along the runway that was actually outside the camp perimeter. With the arrival of their additional aircraft bringing the number to over a hundred, it forced an expansion of the perimeter that would grow even more with the escalation of the war and subsequent addition of other units. The 52nd Combat Aviation Battalion, or the Flying Dragons as they were known, became the largest aviation battalion ever formed. It also included various satellite units scattered here and there in the II Corps AO (area of operation). It was subordinate to the 17th Combat Aviation Brigade with the 17th being subordinate to the 1st Aviation Division that was in fact, the largest Army Aviation organization formed since World War II. The Ghostriders were initially missioned to support the 4th Infantry Division and various Air Cav units throughout the Central Highlands during which time they became jacks of all trades often finding themselves writing the book of everything from aircraft maintenance to combat methods and strategy. In addition to their usual airlift and 911 services, they were eventually assigned the primary mission of supporting the 5th Special Forces and the mystery shit fun and game excursions across the borders by SOG (Special Operations (or Observation) Group), CIDG (Civilian Irregular Defense Group), and other covert ops.

The Ghostriders suffered their first fatality that May following their arrival and had pretty much been in the middle of the shit ever since, securing a reputation worthy of the lethal implications of their name. Nine months later when they surrendered their tents and rain barrel bathtubs for the high class shack-on-a-slab digs they now enjoyed, the neighborhood enemy welcome wagon was so overjoyed they gifted them with nightly mortar attacks often consisting of as many as 150 rounds per incident. This forced them to forgo their new comfortable abodes and take to the safety of their bunkers, their perimeter defense positions, and to the air to combat the problem. All of which just goes to prove that when it comes to real estate location is everything, even in the Army.

Randy and I approached the opened door of the Ghostrider brain trust as most FNGs would, slow and timid, and found ourselves facing an assortment of four desks and file cabinets with that of the First Sergeant's situated furthest in the rear. A portable radio was crooning somewhere in the room and just as we entered we heard Petula Clark singing, *"Don't sleep in the subway darling..."* We looked at each other, each having the same thought and wondering if this was a fluke or if we would be forced to listen to only Petula Clark and/or The Temptations for the duration of our tour.

"What the hell do *you* want?" barked the Top Sergeant standing behind his desk with a phone in his hand.

Before I could respond he redirected his ire to the individual on the other end of the line, seeming to instantly lose all interest in what I might have to say or even the fact I was standing there.

"I don't want to hear that shit," he spouted angrily into the phone as he danced nervously behind his desk. "That's not what I asked for and not what I need. How many damn times do I gotta' tell you? Get it right or I'll bust your fuckin' ass and find somebody who will."

I learned not to put a lot of store in first impressions since joining the Army, realizing nearly everyone you meet is not always what they seem due to the necessity of maintaining some degree of military fascia, especially the lifers, but my first impression of First Sergeant Strickland was simply too strong to ignore. Immediately noticed was the fact this guy simply didn't fit the usual profile of a company Top Soldier, at least physically, and none I had encountered in the military thus far. Not even the civilian cinema and TV Ward Bond types. He was short and boney with a graying crew cut and appeared to be so damn wired that it would take the full bottle efforts of both Misters Jim Beam and Jack Daniels to bring him down, possibly even requiring a little help from some Wild Turkey. Not having the obvious physical stature most folks would assume was necessary to walk the walk and manage a company of hard core killers, Strickland's management method of choice apparently consisted of carrying a big stick labeled United States Military Code of Justice. It appeared to be management by fear and intimidation, that old *wait until your father gets home* routine many of us were familiar with as children. In addition, Strickland appeared, with his graying crew cut and worry wrinkles, to be from my young perspective anyway, too old, not just older than most soldiers but just too damn old to be in the Army and definitely too old to be in a combat unit and combat zone. Old, wired, and wirey was my first impression of First Sergeant Strickland, and *oh shit, I'm going to have to work for this little pit bull SOB every damn day*, was my first thought. Maybe it was the war, maybe it was the years, or maybe he just had hemorrhoids; all I knew was whatever his problem was it wasn't my fault and I immediately had fearful flashes of yet another Sergeant Polk and the possible necessity of another Great Crapper Rebellion, which by the looks of this guy, I wouldn't have a chance in hell of winning.

In the midst of my fit of anxiety came the voice of Specialist Roabley sitting at the desk to our immediate right, "You Fusco?"

"Yeah," I replied, dropping my gear and moving a few feet closer to his desk, not so much to more easily converse but more to find some secure refuge from the raving top soldier on the phone.

"This is your new company clerk, Top," Roabley announced over Top's animated phone conversation, but not really expecting an answer. Apparently Top could think with two brains at once and Roabley as company clerk was accustomed to the arrangement or just didn't give a shit whether or not he was heard.

I glanced over to offer First Sergeant Strickland a smile but instead found myself staring into the intense eyes of desperation, at least that's how my particular radar picked up on it. It was a strange feeling, possibly even a guilty feeling, as though I were the straw about to break the camels back. In those hard eyes there also seemed to be a hint of paranoia as though he were walking on thin ice or about to get cathorized or something else just as threateningly evil. Whatever it was, I found myself once again beginning to regret my ability to type and my dumb-ass ability to let it be known. He simply grunted and continued reaming the ass of some poor NCO over the phone.

"Okay, you guys give me a copy of your orders and then we'll get you moved in," said Roabley, seemingly indifferent to the First Sergeant's ranting. "We'll get you started on the job tomorrow morning. Getting you bunked in might be a problem though. The headquarters hooch is pretty much full up. Be back in a minute, Top," he stated as he rose and passed through the two of us and out the door. We grabbed our gear and followed as he led us to the headquarters platoon hooch at the end of Ghostrider row. We discovered upon entering that, unlike the other hooches we had stayed in since arriving in-country, this hooch was no longer a barracks set up but instead had over the years been converted by it's occupants to a series of small private rooms, all of which according to Roabley were occupied, requiring us to double up with someone. As Roabley searched for possible roomies, Randy noticed a partially open door and nudged it open further to discover an empty room with a double bunk.

"Hey, what about this one?" he asked.

"Um, you don't want that one," returned Roabley.

"Why, somebody already got it?" I asked.

"No. You just don't want that room."

"We don't? Why not?" asked Randy.

"Well, it's jinxed."

"What?"

"You just don't want that room, man."

"Why not?" insisted Randy as he pushed the door open completely and walked on in.

"Okay, you asked," replied a serious Roabley. "Everybody who stays in that room gets dead."

"What?" I said.

"Dead. The last guy who lived here emptied a clip into his mouth and the guy who lived here before him got fried to death when a lightning bolt hit the hooch. Hit the roof, ran through the electrical lines, came out of the overhead light on the ceiling and zapped him right in the brain."

"Lightning," said Randy, surprised, revealing a touch of his bucolic fears.

"It's happened before," said Roabley. "Man, Vietnam is lightning central or maybe it just seems that way. Mostly down south though, you know, kind of like down there in Florida. You can't imagine how many guys have been zapped in this country. All those guys out there in the boonies are like magnets humping around metal gear and weapons and wearing steel pots. I've even heard a few choppers have been zapped when they were in the air. There's this sergeant up the hill who told me about back when he was a grunt here in '67 in the Delta. They got caught in some shit with the VC. When it was over they realized everybody in his platoon had been wounded except one guy. He said that guy stood up and said, 'I'll be damn, I can't believe I didn't' get one scratch,' and just then the guy gets zapped with lightning right in the helmet. Lifted him right off the ground and blew off his pants and boots and everything. He went from being the only one who wasn't wounded to the only one who got killed. Just like that."

"So this room is supposed to be cursed or something just because two guys died in it?" I asked.

"And the guy last week who was staying here for a couple days. Wasn't even from our company, just hanging out until his chopper got fixed. Got killed when it went down on the way back to Qui Nhon. We think it's a jinxed room."

Randy and I looked at each other and shrugged our shoulders. Maybe it was our collective inherent Italian sense of adventure spurning fate or possibly the simple fact we both preferred the known to the alternative unknown such as the possibility of bunking with an undesirable with peculiar characteristics and body odor, but we quickly decided without speaking to take a chance on the jinxed room. We tossed in our gear and were then pointed toward the company supply hooch where we were issued sheets, blankets, poncho liners, mosquito nets, flack jackets, helmets, and all the other comforts of home. The supply hooch also doubled as the armory and seeing all the weapons reminded me we were in a war zone, not that I needed much reminding now that I was moving into a room with all the appeal of a Vincent Price movie, but not being offered a weapon prompted me to ask, "What about a weapon?"

"You're the new clerks right?" said the supply clerk.

"Yeah," I answered.

"You don't need one."

"Bullshit!" spurted Randy.

"Hey, you guys are pencils. You don't need weapons."

"What?" Randy objected. "Why the hell not?"

"You won't get perimeter duty so you don't need 'em."

"Hey man, this is a combat zone right?" I asked.

"Yeah, right. You noticed."

"And those are bullet holes in that wall over there aren't they?"

"Well, yeah."

"And I bet that's why you just gave us these spiffy helmets and flack jackets, right? So how 'bout a weapon to go with them?"

"Yeah, if we get hit are we supposed to shoot paper clips and throw typewriters or what?" asked Randy.

"No. You come to me and I'll issue you a weapon."

"Who the hell's got time for that shit?" reasoned an excited Randy who may not have been the Audie Murphy type but being from New York had developed enough street smarts to know the value of time in a crisis, meaning you only have time to either fight or run and as best he could see around here there was nowhere to run to.

He began to do what I would eventually come to call his *Randy dance*, which he always did when laughing or getting excited or up tight or sometimes just standing around. The best I could figure is it was a kind of nervous urban thing indigenous to the sidewalks of New York, the urban white boy's equivalent of the black boy's crotch grabbing limp and stroll. Though I didn't join in the Randy dance, we were both in agreement that FNGs or not, neither of us had any intention of spending time under fire standing in line like a bunch of kids waiting to get tickets at a Captain Cody Saturday morning matinee. Waiting for some supply dude to *maybe* show up and methodically dole out weapons and ammo just plain didn't make sense.

"Do you keep a weapon?" I asked.

"Damn right. I sleep with the sucker," he answered.

"Yeah, well. I gotta' live with him and he's ugly as shit," I said, pointing a thumb at Randy. "Not only that, he's from New York. So I need a weapon."

"Hey," objected Randy.

"Yeah, right. That's real funny. I give you guys weapons, you'll probably shoot your foot off or something."

"Are we authorized weapons?"

"Yeah."

"Then give us some damn weapons before we come over the counter and take one and shoot *your* fuckin' foot off... please."

"Okay, okay," he conceded as he turned and pulled two M-16s off the rack, recorded the numbers, and passed them over the counter. "You're supposed to keep them with you at all times. So don't leave 'em layin' around. And don't keep a round in the chamber."

"Yeah thanks," I said. "And in case you haven't noticed, we're in the same Army as you."

"What about some ammo?" asked Randy.

"What, you want ammo too?"

Randy looked to me with a tilt of amazement, "Either that or a few extra boxes of paper clips," he said. "What the hell we 'sposed to shoot, rubber bands?"

"Didn't you just say not to keep a round in the chamber?" I asked. "How the hell are we not gonna' keep a round in the chamber is we don't have any rounds not to keep in the chamber?"

"Shit," replied the supply clerk.

"Yeah, shit," said Randy, looking at me and rolling his eyes.

"You know, ever since that guy blew his head off I'm not supposed to issue ammo to the headquarters platoon."

"Why? Are we all supposed to be retarded or suicidal or something?" asked Randy.

"Yeah, aren't you in the headquarters platoon?" I asked.

"Yep."

"Are you suicidal or retarded?"

"Hell, no."

"Do you have ammo?"

"Hell yeah."

"That figures. So give us some damn ammo and we promise we won't point our weapons at you after we figure out which end the bullets come out of."

"Okay, one bandolier each. You need more when the shit hits, you come see me."

"Oh, right," replied Randy. "Should we make reservations?"

We got our weapons and ammo and a week later when the company scrounge, a PFC Mondo, who would later come to be known to me as the *Tooth Fairy*, heard of our supply clerk encounter and arranged for two more bandoliers each to mysteriously appear on our bunks. We would eventually learn to get whatever we wanted or needed whenever we wanted or needed it, such is the power of the company clerk, but just coming out of the gate as we were and as yet to harness that *clerk power* as we called it, it was comforting to have a few more bandoleers of ammo hanging next to the bunk.

For the most part those were the highlights of our first day at Camp Holloway; having successfully wandered through the S office forest at battalion, the cultural education at the mess hall, obtaining a new bundle of anxiety in the form of a wired and wirey Top Soldier, and discovering that as newly appointed 'pencils' we were not essential enough to the war effort to be targeted by the enemy or issued weapons and ammo in the event we actually were. Having a good dinner and settling into the cursed ghostly room from hell to get a much-needed night of sleep would be the icing on the cake. We thought.

The headquarters hooch in the evening, I suppose much like any other hooch, became a hells kitchen of sounds and music representative of the diversity of its residents. The in and out traffic of friends and residents, beer cans hitting the concrete floor, and the varied choices of entertainment, wasn't exactly conducive to a peaceful slumber, at least not to us fidgety FNGs. Everybody had their separate music preferences such as Roabley's one cassette tape album of Tommy James and the Shondells that he played repeatedly, over and over and over in his corner room.

> *Yeah*
> *My mind's such a sweet thing*
> *I wanna do everything*
> *What a beautiful feeling*
> *Crimson and clover*
> *Over and o-over*

Yeah. Over and over and from another room down the hall came the sound of Jose Faliciano's version of *Light My Fire.*

> *Come on baby, light my fire*
> *Come on baby, light my fire*
> *Try to set the night on… fire*

And in yet another room the sounds of an argument over whether Barbarella had a nicer ass than Goldie Hawn on Laugh In and whether either of them was as hot as Raquel Welch. As best we could tell Raquel Welch was winning out and Randy and I agreed she had our vote, though as much for her tits as her ass. In the room next to ours was someone who by the sound of things must have been a full fledged schizophrenic. Through the thin plywood wall we could here him talking continuously to himself, for his was the only voice we heard. Talking, that is, to himself or with himself, or to and with the little voices in his head.

"It don't mean nothin'," he said to himself.

"Yeah, you got that right," he agreed with himself.

"What the hell, right? I mean what the hell?" said another one of himself.

"Yeah, sure. Shit. Shit! The silver bird! The big PX! Bitch don't care so why not. Get my damn GTO and go. Hit the road, man. Never lookin' back. Cheeseburgers, bad ass bitches." said his other self.

"You did it, man," he told himself. "You did it."

"Damn right I did it. I did it. Now what?" his other self asked himself.

"What the hell?" he answered himself with the question. "What the hell? Don't mean nothin' anyway, right?"

"Yeah, what the fuck?" agreed his other self.

"It's over," he mumbled. "It's over. It's over. It's o-over," one of themselves chimed in with the music.

"Crimson and clo-over. Over and o-over," chimed in another self with his other self and Roabley's Tommy James and the Shondells cassette that intermingled with Jose's Feliciano's *Light My Fire*.

"Fuck it. Fuck it!" another self mumbled.

Then, from our neighbor on the other side in the corner room across from Roabley came the inevitable… Temptations.

Psychedelic shack, that's where it's at
Psychedelic shack, that's where it's at
Psychedelic shack, that's where it's at
Psychedelic shack, that's where it's at

The schizo went into high gear when his other self tried to keep up.

"Psychedelic shack, that's where it's at," he mumbled in rhythm with the Temptations. "Psychedelic Shack, that's where it's at, Psychedelic Shack, that's where it's at. Fuck it. Fuck it. Light my fire over and o-over, that's where it's at. That's the meaning of sooo-oul - crimson and clo-over. Fuck it. Fuck it. One more night. Then it's over and o-over."

It sounded like the guy was a conglomerate of personalities and I had no idea what he looked like but I could somehow visualize him sitting cross-legged in a corner rocking back and forth pulling on his ear and twirling a fuzz ball in his navel.

"Hey Vince," came Randy from the bunk above me. "I'm beginning to get an idea why that guy who lived in this room blew his head off."

"Yeah," I said. "I was thinking the same thing.

"So what if it's like this every night?"

"Then I guess we'll have to flip a coin," I said.

"Flip a coin? What for?"

"To see which one we shoot first, you, me, or the guy next door or the guy next door's other guy next door."

At that very moment, above the noise of the music and the female anatomy argument, and the guy next door, and the guy's other guys next door, came the fast screeching swish and earth shaking WHOMP of an enemy rocket. Immediately all the music stopped as everyone in the hooch killed the lights and hit the floor, including the schizo and himself. The camp siren sounded signaling an attack and soon after, in the distance somewhere outside the perimeter, could be heard the PUMPH of another launched rocket. Even over the siren it could be heard screeching through the sky, and though it sounded like it was about to hit somewhere between my left ass cheek and my right ass cheek, it actually impacted a few hundred yards away on the runway.

As FNGs we had not been oriented or instructed by anyone as to the procedure regarding saving our asses during a rocket or mortar attack, but seeing everyone else quickly gear up with their flack jackets and helmets, and the weapons and ammo they weren't supposed to have, and then scrambling out of the hooch, we didn't have to ask or be told to do the same. We threw our clothes on as fast as possible, shoved on our boots, helmets, and flack jackets, grabbed our weapons and ammo we weren't supposed to have and followed the traffic out of the hooch. This time it was the real deal with no gaseous tear-wrenching CS shit cloud or anyone throwing rocks. Instead there were a lot of fast moving G.I.s, nearly everyone in the company actually, either heading for bunkers or climbing on trucks to be ferried the half mile down the hill to reinforce the perimeter in order to defend against a follow-up ground attack.

In the midst of all this perceived chaos Randy and I probably looked like a couple of five year old T-ballers bouncing off each other around second base while trying to catch a pop fly that was actually hit over the backstop. In other words, we didn't have a damn clue, and while trying our best in the dark of night to find an entrance into the bunker next to our hooch so we could hide and crawl into our skin, we were unfortunate enough to be discovered by First Sergeant Strickland.

"What the hell are you two doing?" yelled First Sergeant Strickland over the siren.

"Um, trying to get into the bunker," I answered, knowing I must have looked as stupid as I felt.

"You're the new guys right?"

We nodded our heads yes and Strickland offered only a cursory smile of frustration. Just then the siren ceased.

"Get in the damn bunker," he ordered. "Stay there until another siren signals an all clear."

With that he turned and headed for the orderly room but not before looking over his shoulder and informing us, "The fuckin' bunker entrance is on the other side."

After Top disappeared into the orderly room we scrambled over the top and into the safe sanctuary of the bunker where we joined three other members of the company. The bunker was dug into the ground a few feet deep with walls two sand bags thick. Its roof was made of PSP (perforated steel plate) with a few layers of sand bags on top. Inside it sported a few old ammo and rocket crates for seats and smelled musty with a hint of Vietnamese fish, oyster sauce, and the additional odor of a few seasons of piss and stale beer. It was pitch black inside but a flashlight came on briefly to guide us as we crossed through the small entrance. The light afforded us a quick glance of the occupants. One was already stretched out and asleep, or as we would come to later know the troops, most likely stoned or drunk and passed out. Another, the one in the dark behind the flashlight beam, sat deep in the corner, a mere dark shadow under a helmet and bulging flack jacket. We grabbed a seat on the opposite side and out went the light. We sat there anxiously listening to the events taking place outside, some distant weapons fire, people running here and there, and trucks pulling out for the perimeter. Then finally the noise subsided and all was quiet.

"I think it's over," said a voice from a dark corner across the bunker.

We sat silent for a long ten minutes. There were no more sounds of incoming rockets and no sounds of weapons fire coming from the bunker line on the perimeter.

"Yep, it's over," declared the voice in the dark again.

"This happen very often?" I asked our unseen bunker companion.

"Not lately," he answered. "Once, twice a week. Sometimes twice a night, sometimes every night. Sometimes one rocket or mortar, sometimes thirty. Who the hell knows? The Man's just fuckin' with us. Keepin' us on our toes. You the new guys? You the new company clerk gonna' take Roabley's place?"

"Yeah."

"Shit man, your looking at almost 365 and a wake up. Jesus Christ man, that's forever. Wow, three hundred and sixty-five days. Shit, that's forever, that's a lifetime. Well you got your cherry popped tonight but you're still a virgin, my man. This was nothin' except for whoever was at the business end of those one-double-deuces."

"Double-deuces?"

"Yeah, one-deuce-deuce's, 122 millimeter rockets. Charlie loves 'em. All he needs to do is stick it in the ground out there somewhere past the perimeter. He can set some kind of timer then he dee dee mows long gone down town for some after-hours fun and snatch before it ever goes back to the hole he climbed out of. We get boomed while he gets boom boomed," he laughed.

"One-double-deuces?" said Randy.

"Yeah, like big bottle rockets on the fourth of July. They're not real accurate but then they don't have to be. Plenty to hit around here for sure. But what they really want to take out is the aircraft. Problem is they're usually short or long and end up hitting our hooches and shit. Bad news to 'cause they're designed to penetrate before they explode so if it hits your hooch you're in deep shit. Through the roof and right up your ass, ya know. And then there's the mortars. They use that little village, Plei Mo Nu, as cover and lob those fuckers in."

About that time Randy started squirming and messing with his feet and his crotch.

"So how long do we stay in here and how do we know what's going on?" I asked, wondering what the hell Randy was doing squirming around in the dark.

"They'll blow an all-clear siren when they think it's safe then you can get out," he answered. "But not me. I'm stayin' in here 'till the sun comes up, man. I'm outa' here tomorrow, headin' home, and I'll be damned if I'm gonna' let some damn dink one-double-deuce ruin my fuckin' DEROS day."

With that declaration he faded silently into the darkness of the bunker until a few minutes later when Randy and I once again heard, "Don't mean nothin'. You did it, man. O-over and o-over. Crimson and clo-over. Over and o-over..." And we realized the voice in the darkness we had been talking with was in fact the one-man group think schizo from the room next door - or possibly his other self or maybe even his other other self. So I sat there for the longest time in the pitch black of the bunker wondering if he was tugging his ear and playing with his navel and also wondering if I would ever come to do the same.

When the siren finally signaled an all clear, we returned to our room and tried to settle in for at least a partial night's sleep. As we did, I decided I would sleep with my pants on for obvious reasons, which I would do on a regular basis, only removing my boots and shirt. On that night, however, I came to realize that in our FNG haste Randy and I had put on each other's clothes and gear, which explained Randy's uneasy squirming while in the bunker. Though he wasn't fat he was two inches taller than I and wider and his feet were a full size and a half bigger.

"I thought those damn boots and all this shit was too damn tight," laughed Randy.

"Yeah, well it's a good thing I was wearing your clothes instead of mine," I told him as we exchanged garments.

"Oh yeah. Why's that?" asked Randy.

"Cause I think I dropped a double-deuce shit in your drawers, man," I laughed. "O-over and o-over."

"Are you shittin' me?" laughed Randy.

"Exactly," I laughed.

Somewhere in the hooch someone turned on the Armed Forces radio station. The DJ on the radio had just taken a request as he did from many G.I.s with access to phones. The request he was now playing came from Camp Holloway.

"This one goes out to all the guys in the 52nd CAB up there at Camp Holloway as requested by PFC Hearnden."

The song that came up turned out to be the Carpenters singing *"We've Only Just Begun"* and the irony of those words certainly weren't lost on Randy and I as we lay back on our bunks contemplating the phrase *365 and a wake up.*

No sooner did the Carpenters' song finished that Petula Clark came on singing,

We choose it...win or lose it
Love is never quite the same
I love you...now I've lost you
Dont feel bad...you're not too blame
So kiss me goodbye
And I'll try not to cry...

"Damn," said Randy. "Somebody out there sure as hell likes Petula Clark."

CHAPTER 14

A POPPED TOP
& BRONZE HEROES

Settling in and learning the job of company clerk was actually no big deal with the exception of the anxious insecurity derived from the knowledge of facing a long working relationship with Top Sergeant Strickland. Roabley's transitional training was fairly cut and dry, boiling down to the following; "This is the Morning Report. You do it first thing in the morning, get it signed by the CO, walk it up to the Battalion S-1. It's pretty much self-explanatory and don't worry about making mistakes because nobody reads these damn things anyway. You keep your files in this cabinet drawer, action files here, and blanks here, and the rest is easy so you shouldn't have any problem."

Other than introducing me to the guys at Battalion S-I who already knew me by sight and reputation as the idiot who volunteered, or a possible congressional spy, there endeth the lesson.

Roabley was one of those high-energy people who could look fast standing still and appear to do a great deal of work when he actually did little. Somehow he generated a great deal of gratitude by everyone for all that work and effort he didn't put out on their behalf, which basically meant he was a damn good ass kisser. In truth, Roabley pretty much worked only for Roabley and the closer he got to his DEROS the harder he worked at less and less except for Roabley. As I slid into the company clerk saddle, Roabley shifted his primary focus to the creation of a homecoming hero by the name of Roabley, something that wasn't likely to happen with the ever-feisty First Sergeant Strickland at the helm, but fate, especially Army fate, once again turned the worm as we all discovered when coming to work a few days later.

As I exited my hooch in the morning and turned for the orderly room I was quick to notice an ambulance backed up to the HQ door. They had just loaded an occupied stretcher, closed the door of the medical truck and sped away up the hill. When I walked into the office everyone was just standing around in silence.

"What's the ambulance for?" I asked.

"Top," answered Randy.

"What?"

"Top had a heart attack," clarified Roabley. "I don't think he'll be back."

"A heart attack?"

"Yeah," explained Roabley. "Somebody tried to frag him."

"But you said he had a heart attack."

"Yep. You'd probably have one too if the same thing happened to you."

Roabley went on to explain that someone had attached a hand grenade to Top's bunk in such a way that when he sat or lay down on it the bedsprings would stretch and pull out the pin, but he said, the grenade was a dud.

I found out later what actually happened was that when Top sat down to hit the hay the previous night the pin popped out but the release handle of the grenade caught on the bedspring failing to fully eject and trip the fuse. Strickland heard the sound, leaned down and glanced under the bunk quickly evaluating his situation and realizing that the unreachable grenade was either a dud or had a faulty timer about to explode. He assumed any further movement would eject the handle completely so he dared not shift his weight. His options were to sit and wait for help or to make a desperate dash for the door in hopes the fuse wasn't defective. As we all learn in the Army, most all six-second grenade fuses only last about three seconds – if you're lucky. Oddly enough he chose to stay, not because he was gutsy or gallant or even stupid. He chose to stay at the risk of his own life because had the grenade gone off it would have killed Top Strickland's pet monkey Gladys, which he affectionately named after his wife.

Top had come across Gladys in a whorehouse in Ben Me Thuot in Darlac Province while he was fornicating instead of attending an NCO leadership course in Nha Trang. He was ordered to attend the course by the CO after a letter from somebody's mother complaining about Top's treatment of her baby soldier got to somebody's Congressmen resulting in a letter that got to some General leading to a letter to the battalion CO that resulted in a call to the 189th CO. Gladys, the monkey not his wife, was acquired for a mere ten dollars and a promise to take his whore-for-a-day home with him to the States after the war. Knowing he would not likely keep his promise but often wishing he could, Gladys and Top returned to Camp Holloway a wiser man for all the sensitivity training he didn't receive in Nha Trang and a better-fed monkey.

Top lived alone in a secluded hooch, as many top soldiers and also COs often preferred, alone with Gladys, possibly the only individual in all of Camp Holloway who offered him unquestionable love, loyalty, and affection. This meant there was no one around to immediately come to his aid and forced him to sit frozen in fear gazing wide eyed at Gladys who every so often would move to hop on the bunk to join him but was quickly halted when Strickland sternly ordered her to freeze. This caused the monkey to experience an entire range of emotions - he loves me he loves me not - while circling and testing varied approaches to gain access to the bunk and her beloved master and sending Strickland into a sweat of fear and dread that she would succeed. This continued until sunrise the next morning when Sergeant First Class Promisel, better known by the troops as Sergeant Popsicle and possibly the only one who even came close to liking Top Strickland, came by early as he did each day to collect the First Sergeant for morning chow.

Now Sergeant Popsicle was a much-liked soldier who gained his rank due to his exceptional ability as an aircraft mechanic despite his communication skills. Sergeant Popsicle, though he could rebuild an aircraft jet turbine engine blindfolded, was cursed with a speech impediment in the form of a mild stutter. It was, however, by no means a debilitating handicap especially when he was performing his duties as an aircraft maintenance supervisor, but it did tend to be a problem on some occasions such as when he was required to use the radio or telephone, when he was trying or about to have or actually was having sex, or when he had to call for assistance when someone was frozen with fear on a frag-rigged booby trapped bunk bed.

Once he discovered Top Strickland perched in an indeterminate state in his Army issue grundies and came to appreciate the Top Sergeant's predicament, Sergeant Popsicle, afraid to stay for fear he would be blown to hell and afraid to leave for fear Top would get royally pissed off at his deserting both him and Gladys, had absolutely no idea what to say and tried repeatedly to say it, not

giving Top an opportunity to get a word in edgewise. Sergeant
Popsicle postulated all manner of emotional hems, huhs, and duh
duh duhs for at least a full ten minutes before Top Strickland
finally yelled in a nervous frustrated whisper, "Will you shut the
fuck up and go get some help!"

About that same time Sergeant Popsicle, in spite of all his
mumbling and stumbling insecurities, finally screwed up enough
courage to take command of the situation and get down on his
hands and knees in an attempt to remove the grenade. This
contributed little to First Sergeant Strickland's sense of safety and
welfare because First Sergeant Strickland had on one occasion
witnessed Sergeant Popsicle's attempt to woo a Vietnamese whore
at which time Popsicle stuttered so intensely that she just threw up
her hands and declared him *beaucoup dien cai dau* and went off to
screw an NCO from the Air Cav. Sergeant Popsicle then entered
into a two week long emotional funk when First Sergeant
Strickland declared that having a whore forgo an elite Ghostrider
and default to the Air Cav was such a discreditable, embarrassing,
and shameful defeat that he may never regain his faith in Sergeant
Popsicle again. Now he certainly had not nearly enough faith in
Popsicle to entrust him with a grenade that could shred both their
asses into a military memory.

As Sergeant Popsicle slid under the bunk he discovered there
was not one grenade but four, one mounted on each bedpost, and
he was immediately intimidated for never had he been faced with
such a difficult challenge - other than trying to impress a foreign
speaking prostitute. Sergeant Popsicle quickly realized someone
wanted to insure that Top Strickland would be sent on his way to
that old soldier's home in the sky but didn't count on the fact that
his tough but slight physical stature was insufficient enough to
weigh down and pull all the pins from the grenades.

"Oh shi shi shi shi shi shit, Ta Ta Ta Ta Top! T,There there
there's fo fo four o-of th-them mo mo mo motherfa fa fa fuckers
u,u,under th,th,there! And and and and they's um um um all all ba
ba 'bout to to pa pa pa pa pop the the their pa pa pins!"

Faced with not one but four deadly grenades, Sergeant Popsicle
was electrified with such fear that suddenly and miraculously he
was purged of his handicapping speech impediment and filled his
lungs and mind with the clear confidence to state more plainly than

he had ever said anything before in his entire life, "FUCK THIS SHIT! MY MAMA DIDN'T RAISE NO FOOL!" After which he promptly departed, leaving First Sergeant Strickland alone and so emotionally stressed that he pissed his OD boxers. I say alone because seeing how quickly Sergeant Popsicle made his exit influenced Gladys to do the same. Popsicle did recruit braver and more adequate help, however, but by the time they arrived at the scene the top soldier's burly hard-corps bust-ass character had degenerated into the equivalent of a sobbing little pile of grandma's bread pudding, as much from the four-way threat of death beneath his ass as the rejection of being abandoned by Gladys and Popsicle, leaving him emotionally useless to the Ghostriders, the Army, and himself. By the time he dragged into the company orderly room for another day of kicking ass and taking names he appeared ten years older and pale as a Japanese Geisha girl. Then five minutes after his arrival the simple sudden ringing sound of the telephone on his desk sent him into cardiac arrest.

I'm sure there must have been a more pleasant side to Top Strickland but during our very brief relationship I wasn't given the opportunity to experience it. And I never did discover what contributed more to raising Strickland's blood pressure to the point of messing up his heart, the all night Mexican stand off with the grenades or Sergeant Popsicles courageous desertion. To his credit, I discovered later that his give-em-hell attitude was necessitated by the fact he had taken over a company with festering drug and racial problems, a questionable work ethic, an alcoholic for a CO, and an XO with avoidance tendencies. All combined, he faced quite a challenge. He had apparently raised enough hell with, or read the riot act to, a few soldiers too many and for his efforts generated a series of death threats and nearly reaped some serious payback. This accounting for the first impressions of paranoia I detected on the day of our arrival. Then again, somewhere in the back of my mind there was also an inkling of an idea that maybe I was somehow a jinx for Top Sergeants because this was the third one that sort of bit the bullet or caught one after our coming together in the same company. But I quickly dismissed the idea. After all, I had what Randy called the hoocho curse to worry about and so decided that Top Soldiers could do their own worrying.

Top's departure created a temporary void in the Ghostrider HQ, a road I had traveled once before and wasn't eager to go down again. I had visions of once again having to endure some new Top Sergeant Penis type arriving with that old scenario of cleaning house. Roabley on the other hand viewed all this as an opportunity and wasted no time at all putting his hero plan of action into action. Within two hours of Top's removal and with the help of the gift of a few cases of beer to someone at battalion, Roabley had managed to get promoted from Specialist-4th Class to Specialist-5th Class even though he didn't have the required time in service or go before a promotion board to qualify. A few hours later he had managed to come by orders giving him a lateral transfer promotion from SP5 to Buck Sergeant even though his MOS didn't qualify for hard stripes, and by the end of the next day, with the help of a donation of a case of T-bone steaks, was promoted to acting Staff Sergeant E-6, all of which was supposedly the will and orders of the ballsy uncompromising little bony-ass dictator now incoherent and near death First Sergeant Strickland along with the signature and endorsement of our recently installed Ghostrider CO, Major Anthony, whom I'm not sure had any knowledge whatsoever of anything regarding Roabley's advancement. Such was the persuasive efficiency of Specialist-4th & 5th Class Buck Sergeant Acting Staff Sergeant Roabley. Why any of this was even worth the effort was beyond me until I discovered that Roabley's ultimate goal and brass ring was the coveted award of a Bronze Star medal, hence becoming a hero in the eyes of the folks back home.

One of the reasons the medal was obtainable was because Vietnam being such an unpopular war, both on the streets of America and within the ranks of its military, it was decided that the war needed lots of heroes. Not to mention the fact there was an entire generation of career commissioned who desperately craved and needed the chest bobbles for advancement. To get lots of heroes the Pentagon took a lesson from the Wizard of Oz, declaring that all personnel in-country with the rank of E-6 and above automatically receive a Bronze Star for Meritorious Service; meritorious service meaning anyone who could chew gum and tie their shoes without tripping over their own ass. Somewhere in the halls of the Pentagon there danced a staff officer singing *Somewhere Over The Rainbow* as he stroked all that extra salad pinned on his chest, earned and obtained through the Cowardly Lion inspired and implemented Oz Reward Program, a *special project* policy which was so well received that damn near every medal short of the Medal Of Honor was freely dished out to upper echilance lifers and the *hard commissioned.* If Vietnam was anything it was certainly medal heavy, handing that career candy out like it was Halloween.

Though deserving medals of all sorts were also awarded to a great many Ghostriders, well-deserved medals for valor, especially among the rank and file not only in the 52nd CAB but all over Vietnam were so often overlooked it was near criminal. And the Air Medal, the aviation equivalent of the infantry CIB (Combat Infantry Badge), that was meant for air crewmen was also handed out to the infantry and just about any ranking officer who took a few flights on a chopper. It was heavy medal mayhem and a state of affairs that would send Specialist-4th & 5th Class Buck Sergeant Acting Staff Sergeant Roabley home as a Bronze Star hero with no one ever questioning how a company clerk of all people managed to reach such heady heights of achievement behind a typewriter. Few civilians actually know the difference between a medal for valor and a meritorious servous medal for *just being there,* and I doubt Roabley was going to volunteer the distinction. Roabley, I decided, was an example and legacy I had no interest in being a part of.

The very next morning I walked into the orderly room to discover an all new face at the top soldier's desk and the first thing that caught my eye was the art work on the man's collar. It was three up and three down with a star in the center, a Sergeant Major, and my morning chow SOS began signaling an SOS of it's own in my gut, as in - Oh Shit! The second thing I noticed is that this guy was one right and tight looking soldier with eyes that quickly signaled that the lights were on and *everybody* was home, and he maintained the physical prowess and demeanor as well. I immediately assumed from here on out there would be no room for error.

He was Sergeant Major Norman Buchinsky, coming right off an assignment as acting Battalion Sergeant Major where the arrival of the new battalion Super Top, Sergeant Major Corklyn, just happened to coincide with the demise of the Ghostriders unfortunate First Sergeant Strickland. This freed up Buchinsky to stroll right onto the mound like Satchel Page on a cool spring morning. Buchinsky's acting Sergeant Major star between his chevrons fell to earth to become instead a First Sergeant's diamond and he quickly settled in with total confidence as though he was born to the task. Combined with a recently appointed new CO and XO, and without hesitation, the new top soldier began changing our universe – for the better.

The first changes were headquarters orderly room esthetics with desks reconfigured in a priority U-formation, Randy and the Admin Officer's desk to the left facing the center as you entered and the company clerk, myself, opposite on the right facing center. The Top Sergeant's desk now sat between the CO's and the XO's office doors and faced all of us and the HQ orderly room front entrance, meaning no one entered without coming under the scrutiny of the Top Soldier. It also left no question as to just who the hell was in charge. Officer or enlisted, to get to the CO all living souls had to pass by the Saint Peter of Ghostrider Central that was now First Sergeant Buchinsky.

Next came varied decorating improvements, functional adjustments, most all of which were common sense necessities or designed to enhance unit pride. Buchinsky was also the first Top Sergeant I'd seen who didn't, either with or without maintaining his dignity, have his head up the COs ass. He was the real deal and his method of management wasn't complicated nor did it depend on a bag of lifer tricks or boisterous persona, though it did pretty much abide by the letter of Army law, and of course, *Buchinsky's Law*. It boiled down to a simple philosophy that all soldiers were equal in the eyes of the Top Soldier, and as long as they did their job and stayed out of trouble they would in turn earn his full support, respect, and loyalty. On the other hand, failing to do so would result in very undesirable consequences doled out in a cold reality of style that only our new Lithuanian lineage First Sergeant could muster.

Top demonstrated this during the first company formation he held on his second day on the job. Prior to that time the company apparently did not have many or any formations on a regular basis, which was not surprising. Not only the Ghostriders but many other units were slack in the area of military protocol partly because of the constant unpredictable demands of the war and partly because they could get away with it. What the hell, it was Vietnam. It was also the only formation I attended. I later self appointed myself to stay in the orderly room during all formations to listen for the phones, plus the fact I was paranoid, remembering my Vietnamese orientation back in Oklahoma where we were advised to avoid daily repetitions such as assembling in the same area at the same time each day for fear the enemy would eventually target the event. Back in Nha Trang I had heard rumors of guys who had been blown away their first day in-country because some dumb ass in processing had a habit of calling his FNGs into a formation at the same time and place each morning. Those poor guys hadn't even had time for their first cup of combat coffee. Regardless of the lore and perceived safety of our aviation unit comforts and stabilities, I wasn't about to forget I was in a combat zone.

It was at this first company formation that Top Buchinsky introduced himself to the Ghostriders and also introduced a morning ritual of handing out or verifying work assignments, a concept heretofore apparently alien to some members of the unit. It's not that work didn't get accomplished at the 189th but that all the members of the unit weren't doing the work that was getting done. Now, with the arrival of Top Buchinsky everyone had to be accounted for and accountable and when a number of the names were called out to actually perform work there immediately rose a few groans of opposition.

"Do we have a problem here?" asked the cool and composed Top Buchinsky.

"Yeah," answered one of the Ghostrider's own mofucka' bothers from the back of the formation.

"What's the problem?" asked Top.

"We don't do dat shit," answered another of the brothers.

"Who is we?" asked Top.

"We," answered the brother pointing to himself and two other brothers. "Us here."

"You're in the service platoon right?" asked Top.

"Yeah, dats right."

"Yeah what?"

"Yeah."

"You mean, 'Yeah, First Sergeant' don't you?" suggested Top.

"Oh, man. You fuckin' wit me now, Top. Why you wanna be fuckin' wit me?"

"Sergeant Webber, are you in charge of the service platoon?"

"Yes, Top."

"You want to tell me what kind of... *shit* it is that these three people do?"

"I don't think they do any kind of... *shit*, Top. I didn't even know they were in my platoon."

"How long have you been in this unit Sergeant Webber?"

"Three months, Top."

"And you don't know these people?"

"They're not on my roster, Top."

Top just shook his head then repeated the assignment, "You men will report to Sergeant Webber immediately after this formation for duty in the motor pool."

"Oh, man, you jus' fuckin' wit us. You jus' doin' dis shit 'cause we black," complained one of the brothers.

"Always fuckin' wit the brothas. Fuckin' wit da black dudes," came another.

"Das right, 'cause we black," chimed in another.

"Sergeant Webber, I want those three men in front of my desk immediately after this formation." With that Top continued his assignments then dismissed the company.

A few minutes later I stood behind my desk and watched as Sergeant Webber paraded the three black soldiers into the orderly room to the front of Top's desk. A minute after that Top Buchinsky came out of the CO's office, stood behind his desk and stated coldly, "For your information I want you men to know that I am color blind. I see only in military colors and in my eyes all soldiers are OD green."

Top allowed time for a possible response or apology but got only a give-a-shit expression and silence.

"You three men are now demoted to Private E-1 and permanently assigned to night guard duty on the perimeter each and every night until your DEROS. In addition you will perform you're regular duties at the motor pool during the day. The very first time you show up late or miss any duty or the Sergeant of the Guard catches you sleeping on duty; I will bring you up on charges of desertion and AWOL for not reporting to work for the past three months. Now get the hell out of my orderly room."

I stood behind my desk waiting for some kind of scene to develop but none occurred. The three slackers simply slithered out of the office, banished to the outer reaches of the perimeter like dissident Russians being shipped off to Siberia, after which Top looked at me, smiled and said, "And how the hell's my company clerk this morning, Fusco?"

"Um, just fine, Top," I smiled in return, not wanting to give him any reason to send me to Siberia but somehow coming to know that from that moment on the Ghostriders and I were in good hands.

Needless to say, the attendance of Top's company formation the next morning and following mornings increased substantially, with no complaints.

CHAPTER 15

HOOCH MAMAS, HOOKERS,
& STINKY BANDITS

As soon as the schizo and his other self departed for home Randy took over his room, giving us both the luxury of a private eight by ten suite. I got rid of the top bunk so I wouldn't have to take in a roommate, pitched my mosquito net, and redecorated with a collection of custom furniture I manufactured from empty rocket crates. It was pretty much the fashion statement of the time and not exactly the Beverly Hills Hilton but then what the hell is? Hooch living wasn't actually all that bad considering the alternative standards of the mud grunts in the boonies, the guys at the FOBs, and some of our sister units elsewhere, and in fact it took no time at all for us to realize we were pretty damn fortunate. Maybe some grunts in the field would have contemptuously considered us to be REMFs (rear echelon mother fuckers) but I figured that was relative. To me the real REMFs were in Na Trang in starched fatigues, working 9 to 5, shit-clouding FNGs and ripping off their wallets.

One of our most appreciated luxuries was discovered after returning to our hooch soon after our arrival where, much like a couple of first time tourists rolling into their hotel room after a day at the Miami Monkey Jungle, we unexpectedly discovered a neat and tidy abode with our bunks made up all nice and tight, our dirty clothes washed, pressed, and on hangers, our clean clothes pressed and on hangers, and our second set of boots shining like a new pair of wing-tips on the rack at JC Penny. We hadn't come by the hooch all day and actually had no idea what had taken place. I was at first irritated, thinking that someone had violated my privacy and come in and messed with my stuff, and I wondered if maybe we had some obsessive-compulsive neat freak Suzy-home-maker platoon sergeant with nothing else to do. However, a few inquiries revealed more favorable facts as it turned out that we had been invaded by a hooch maid, one of many who flooded into Camp Holloway each morning and went to their assigned hooches where they swept, cleaned, tidied up, and basically performed all those wonderful domestic duties you could never get your wife to do back home. That is all the duties except those performed in the kitchen and in bed, which was just fine because their favorite meal seemed to be fish heads and rice, and as far as the sex goes, most of them at age 30 looked 60, had bowed legs, stained black teeth from some kind of junk they chewed on called betel leaf, and they created an incessant chatter that would drive a chicken farmer nuts. If the Army Air Corps, as it existed in Vietnam, was in the least bit spoiled it had to begin with the services of the indigenous hooch maid who, after adopting a handfull of G.I.'s, was often affectionately adopted in return. It was all a surprise to us, having arrived on Friday after the hooch maids had left and discovering this near hotel quality service on the following Monday.

Our particular hooch maid's name was Ba, (Bah). In fact, it seemed like almost every hooch maid's name was Ba, a name I would find out later was more a title than a name, meaning a married woman like Mrs. Your particular Ba either liked you or didn't like you and expressed this by referring to you as *Numba One* or *Numba Ten* or if a G.I. was exceptionally rude, crude, and demanding she would often refer to him as *G.I. numba ten same same shit* or *G.I. numba ten thou* (thousand). On the other hand, if they liked you they would call you by your name or at least their version of your name. Mine some how became *Foo-see-ko* instead of Fusco and usually included a slight giggle leading me to believe there must have been some inside linguistic joke involved in the translation.

The hooch maids were tough enough to fend off any occasional sexual advances by jerk G.I.s and though they spoke a good bit of rudimentary English, they were savvy enough to play dumb and avoid trouble or conflict by saying *no bic,* meaning *don't understand,* when they were asked about anything they chose not to speak about, which was just about everything outside of their immediate chores. For their fifty-cents a day from each adopted soldier they performed their duties with more efficiency than a hive of honey bees, leaving me to assume their work ethic was do to the fact that, unlike the average American house wife, they had no lifestyle distractions such as soap operas, game shows, or telephones. The most surprising fact regarding the hooch maids however, was it was widely known and accepted that one out of every three were married to a VC (Viet Cong) or *were* VC or North Vietnam sympathizers. This uncomfortable revelation was explained to me as a sort of blessing in disguise being these enemy or enemy spouses acted as a barometer of sorts that alerted us to pending peril. If all the hooch maids finished their chores and would *di di mau* (quickly depart) early for the front gate then we knew there was a good chance of some form of enemy attack or enemy action that very evening or night. This knowledge might have rested easy with some soldiers but I had heard the sapper stories such as the time the enemy sent a small child into one of the Camp Holloway hooches with a gift basket of fruit that concealed a satchel charge. The result wasn't pretty with a dozen dead and not the slightest trace of remains of that innocent kid. The kid and the gift basket had to come from somewhere and the most likely source was his mother.

The claim that the VC mama-sans were harmless did prove to be ill perceived on occasion, such as the incident and mystery case of the missing weapons. A number of personal weapons, M-16s, and some ammo when left in hooches during the day managed to disappear. As for who solved 'The Case of the Stinky Bandits' I don't recall but it did reveal the ingenuity of the locals, either for black market profit or the communist cause.

After the disappearance of a number of weapons the natural method derived to solve the case, either devised by some S or G officer who wanted a special project or by some Sherlock Holmes wannabe who took on the challenge, was to set a trap and follow its lead. The inspiration and key to this diabolical solution was actually not the missing weapons but more a case of missing underwear. In Vietnam one of the first wardrobe adjustments made by many American soldiers was the total disregard and elimination of their underwear, especially those graceless obtrusively uncomfortable oversize boxer shorts that ran up your ass and absorbed heat, sweat, and moisture like a doubled baby diaper on night duty. The total elimination of your grundies meant free breathing, freewheeling, blowing in the wind comfort and the ability to get through the monsoon season with a minimal amount of discomfort. Therefore the neglected undesirable inactive boxer shorts that were usually folded and put aside became the critical clue when it turned out that characteristic to each missing weapons incident there was an equally mysterious incident of missing grundies.

Through the powers of deduction or possibly some form of investigative groupthink, the possibility surfaced that these two mysterious elements were connected and setting a trap of opportunity by providing both a few sets of grundies and a neglected weapon revealed the who and the how of the entire operation. The trap was successful and finally exposed that the weapons were being taken by one of those harmless VC mamas-sans who would expertly break-down the M-16, something she obviously learned in the Vietnamese Girl Scouts, wrap it in a pair of boxer shorts, something they don't teach in the Girl Scouts, and stick the entire package in the trash. Putting it in the trash was necessary because she would be unable to get it past the scrutiny of the SPs at the gate. The company trash was collected from behind the mess hall on a daily basis by a locally hired trash man with a beat up old French truck who, after leaving the base, would dig through the smelly garbage to find the smelly grundies and retrieve the now smelly and valuable weapons and ammo. Hence the guilty mama-sans and papa-sans were all busted and the mysterious hooch-mama-drama 'Case of the Stinky Bandits' was solved. The soldiers who lost their neglected grundies and weapons were reprimanded and had to replace them with beaucoup bucks and a visit to the Pleiku black market. That's the weapon not the grundies.

My first adopted hooch maid, Ba, turned out to be a disappointment when a few small things of mine vanished and I then caught her in the act of pilfering more. When the other hooch maids told me she was in fact the wife of a VC, I went to the company individual who oversaw their services and told him she had to go. He laughed, said she was harmless, reassigned her so she could steal someone else's stuff, and I was quickly adopted by a more congenial and much more likable Ba who not only did a great job but had an insatiable interest in all things American.

"My name Ba. You le me clea you clo? Foo-see-ko my G.I. now. I clea all thing fo you," was her eager introduction.

It was more a declaration than a request and since she had already done everything I simply smiled and agreed. Once she grew comfortable with me I would often find her curiously flipping

through my books and magazines, especially the Playboy
Magazines, marveling at the state of the average all-American girl.
Not that I could blame her, I did much the same thing - often. She
had a million questions regarding the American lifestyle, which I
usually tried to answer. I didn't bother to explain that all American
girls didn't look like the girls of Playboy but I did explain that most
American girls kept their clothes on. Ba was also fascinated by the
pictures I kept in my room of my wife and baby, inquiring nearly
every other day about their welfare.

In addition to her usual pay each month I gave her a carton of
Salem menthol filter cigarettes, the preferred brand of the
Vietnamese, not because she smoked, she didn't, but because they
only cost me about a buck-fifty but would bring her around $20 on
the Pleiku black market that for her was a financial windfall and
helped feed her family. I also made the gift of a Sears catalogue I
had sent from home with the original intention of selling. I was
told that in Vietnam the big Sears books sold for a hundred to
three-hundred bucks or more and were used as guide books by
tailors and craftsmen who could just look at the pictures and
duplicate the clothing and merchandise to the last stitch. Watching
my Ba and the other Bas pour over that catalogue with the excited
fascination of a group of kids in a toy store, and rather than allow
the increasing assembly of Bas in my room each day to the point I
would have to start charging admission, I decided to just give her
the catalogue so she could take it home and share the American
dream with her family and the rest of her neighborhood. The
catalogue was like a window to another universe that put them into
a cultural head-spin. It was that gift alone that assured me of her
loyalty and affection throughout my time with the Ghostriders.
Gifts such as silk pajamas for my baby boy and a shopping bag full
of southern style boiled peanuts at a time when I was missing and
lamenting some of the amenities of that South Georgia Jesus
school were my reward.

Regardless of our obvious fundamental human similarities, the
local Vietnamese who worked at Camp Holloway and some of
their accepted culture was indeed odd, not that I delved into it that
thoroughly, after all, I wasn't there to do research for the Lands and
People Encyclopedia. There was that high-speed traveling chickens
and pigs thing, which I never did get a handle on, their tendency to

drag their sandaled feet beneath their bowed legs, the ability to perform all functions while squatting, which I determined accounted for their bowed legs and certainly accounted for all the foot prints on the toilet seats in the latrines, and then there was their willingness to all wear black silk pajamas pants and white or light colored cotton tops, the one factor in all of Vietnam that pretty much guaranteed there would never be a GAP store in down-town Pleiku.

I also came to learn, not being sure if it was rumor or true, that many of the women would have up to ten children each with the tenth and each additional child sold off for sometimes up to the equivalent of $10,000, destined to work the fields or rice paddies or raised into prostitution. Prostitution, especially with the massive presence of a half million American and other foreign military, was a national industry and probably accounted for the circulation of more MPC than any other business source, and the business of prostitution as it existed at Camp Holloway was as simple as a signature.

At Holloway the gates were shut and the camp was closed at around 1700 hours at which time most all civilian workers such as the hooch maids and assorted male labor had to be out. Then arriving at the gate came an assemblage of lovely young local ladies who, with white teeth and little dignity, were ready, willing, and able, and had only to be signed in by a soldier, any soldier - first come first serve. One soldier could sign in only one hooker and it was usually the entrepreneurial type G.I.s up at battalion who arrived first. The rule was one hooker restricted to the one soldier who signed her in. It was bim bam thank you ma'am, or *boom boom* as it was called in Vietnam, then he was to return her to the gate and signed her out. The reality was that one soldier usually got a freebee then turned his girl lose on the masses at five or ten bucks a boom boom, after which he took his cut and escorted her back to the gate and signed her out by the usual cut-off time. The entire process was no big secret since it kept the alternatives to a minimum, those alternatives being G.I.s wanting to head down town to Pleiku where there were all manner of nasty things and possibilities, including the availability of drugs, violence, culture clashes, a black market that rolled out onto the streets the minute the bases closed up for the day, and the fact that the VC and NVA, that's the bad guys, often rolled into town in the evening for their fair share of the joys of life as well. The stories were many of Holloway personnel who had ventured downtown at night and actually partied with the enemy, sharing wine, women, and war stories. Hell, a soldier's a soldier except when he ain't, as they say.

The acceptance of the Holloway hookers was just about the only way to combat that old adage *where there's a will there's a way*, and when it comes to sex, the American G.I., regardless of rank, will nearly always manage to circumvent the system and have his way. In the past when the hookers were disallowed, American ingenuity, driven by a rising sperm count along with native creativity inspired by the lure and rewards of free enterprise, merged to overcome policy. The hookers managed to appear in all manner and methods. Of course the easiest method, though one that would generate the most reprisal if discovered, was to simply fly them in. There was, after all, an abundance of resources to achieve this and a few adventuresome closet pilot crew chiefs and even young officers accepted the challenge, usually under the pretext of performing maintenance check-flights. This succeeded regularly until someone noticed that maintenance flights had increased nearly 200% and investigated, subsequently discovering the flights could not be attributed to actual mechanical problems, or repairs, or even patriotic diligence, not to mention the discovery of a series of in-flight photos of crew members and aircraft mechanics being initiated into the *mile high club*. That's the civilian version of the mile high club, not the combat version that involved individuals involuntarily exiting aircraft while in flight.

In addition Holloway hookers were spirited into camp through the perimeter wire by the infantry types and pathfinders coming off patrols, ambulanced in by the medical detachment, passed off as hooch maids incognito by domestic services personnel, and even held as POWs by S-2 Intelligence where they became perhaps the most interrogated and probably the most cooperative enemy prisoners of the entire war. The most impressive achievement however, at least as measured by single incident volume, came when the members of the Ghostriders Avenger gun ship platoon, noted throughout the highlands for their daring aggressiveness, decided to have a party that required the attendance of a large number of after hours ladies. They had a notion to simply truck them in the back of a deuce-and-a-half through the front gate but that would have been a little obvious therefore obviously required was a more stealthy approach. Their alternative solution was clever if not diabolical, resulting in their confiscating a large water tanker, emptying it and then filling it with 22 fluid floosies. A piece of cake until someone discovered and returned the empty tanker during the party, leaving the gun platoon and 22 hookers high and dry and unable to exit in the manner they had arrived. The situation was remedied when Avenger creativity, inspired by desperation, led to the negotiation of the early morning air transport of the 22 hung-over hookers on a Chinook re-supply mission to somewhere in the Phu Bon Province. From there the girls were to be convoyed back to Pleiku, but not without first generating great quantities of MPC along the way. The convoy was commanded by a soldier named Cosmo Moses, which led to the creation of one of the Vietnam War's greatest legends having something to do with a journey that took Moses and his people 40 days and 40 nights criss-crossing all the outer reaches, camps, and fire bases of the II Corps area before they found their way back to Pleiku. It was even rumored the intrepid Moses lead his people into the promise land of Cambodia where he and General Giap, the Commander of the North Vietnam Army, negotiated a temporary truce for the purpose of... enhancing morale. But then that's a story, if believed, best told by one who was actually there.

Now the Ghostriders had its collection of characters, nearly two-hundred actually, ranging from straight up dutiful types to the just plain insane, but when it came to hookers, girly magazines, booze, and generally tripping the light fantastic, there was a fly in the ointment in the form of a Chief Warrant Officer pilot from southwestern Minnesota by the name of Theodore Thorsen Thigpen. CWO T.T.Thigpen, other than fortunately never developing a lisp because of his name, was a low-key likable guy who, until he was drafted by the United States Army, had never been anywhere his entire life other than a small town in southwestern Minnesota. Nor had CWO T.T.Thigpen ever watched television, viewed any movies other than those created by Disney, or had he ever read any magazines other than the Guideposts and Boys Life. CWO T.T.Thigpen was a narrow gangly guy of about six-feet-five who, oddly enough, closely resembled the animated character Ichabod Crane in one of the few movies he had ever seen, Disney's Sleepy Hollow. Following the social and cultural trauma of the military experience, which included the pure shock of combat and the knowledge that there were people in the world who actually wanted to kill him, coupled with the receipt of a great many care packages from friends and relatives back home, most all of which contained religious material, CWO T.T.Thigpen had become a Born-Again Christian. Now there is, of course, nothing wrong with being a born-again Christian, or any other kind of Christian for that matter, hell the war was full of them, in name at least. The problem arose when the born-again CWO T.T.Thigpen decided to dedicate all his spare time and energy to the moral sanitization of the Vietnam War, and he decided to begin sanitizing the war right there at Camp Holloway. His goal was to cleanse this Asian based Sodom and Gomorra by eliminating the selling of all alcoholic beverages as well as the sale and possession of pornography from the small post PX and in the Officer's Club, as well as the NCO and enlisted clubs. And to also close down the base steam bath massage parlor, better known as the Steam & Cream, and of course, to cease and ban all activities related to the front gate ladies of the evening.

He began his efforts by simply making this request known to the Ghostrider Company Commander, Major Anthony.

"Okay, let me get this straight. You want to ban the selling of pornography in the PX?" asked Major Anthony.

"Yes sir."

"What pornography?"

"Playboy and Penthouse and the like, sir."

"That's pornography?"

"Yes sir."

"Some folks might disagree with you there, Thigpen."

"How sir?"

"Well some folks consider that to be art. You know, like the Ghostrider emblem on the nose of your chopper."

"Really sir?"

"Yes really. And other folks consider Playboy to be informative and educational."

"I don't know how, sir."

"Have you ever read one?"

"One what, sir?"

"Playboy."

"Um, yes… I mean, um, not really, sir."

"And if we actually removed these magazines from the PX what do you suggest we put in their place?"

"Well, there's always Readers Digest and um, Guideposts."

"Uh huh. And you also want to eliminate the practice of allowing prostitutes access to the base?"

"Oh, yes, most definitely, sir. And I'm sure *that* alone would raise morale significantly once our troops discover all the available alternatives."

"Alternatives?"

"Yes sir. Like ping pong and softball."

"And pool. Don't forget pocket pool."

"Yes sir. But I don't think we have a pool table, sir."

"Uh huh, and you want to ban the consumption of all alcoholic beverages?"

"Yes sir. I don't have to explain what a detriment the consumption of alcoholic beverages has been to the war effort, and not to mention the negative social factors and influence it's had on the Vietnamese people. Remember sir, *morale* is just *moral* with an E."

"I can spell Thigpen."

"Yes sir. Of course you can, sir."

"CWO Thigpen, are you actually saying you want this Army, the United States Army, to forgo the consumption of… beer?"

"Yes sir."

Major Anthony, not prone to excitement, thought for a long quiet moment then expressed as diplomatically as possible, "Thigpen, with all due respect for your religious beliefs and your ideals and your puritan values, I have to tell you… I don't think you have an ice cube's chance in hell of ever achieving any of this, bull sh… um… noble… um… Well, hell Thigpen. I couldn't help you even if I wanted to because none of this falls under my purview of authority. It's a battalion level issue and I suppose that's where you'll have to go. I mean, if you want the Army to bow to the wishes of a higher authority why then you'll just have to take your request to a higher authority. Get my drift?"

Having expressed his ambitions outwardly to Major Anthony, CWO T.T.Thigpen's mission seemed to become even more clearly defined than ever, if not inspired, and he now felt empowered to champion his cause further. After somehow managing to gain an audience and bring the issue to the 52nd CAB Commander, Lieutenant Colonel Silas J.J.J.W. Chestnut, he was again met with a long and silent sigh of disbelief until suddenly and surprisingly he was given full support, but only with the proviso that CWO T.T.Thigpen could present Lieutenant Colonel Silas J.J.J.W. Chestnut with a petition containing enough 52nd CAB personnel signatures to clearly represent a majority. CWO T.T.Thigpen had unknowingly just proposed his own *special project* of which Colonel Silas J.J.J.W. Chestnut enthusiastically approved in such a way as to avoid any responsibility whatsoever, and CWO T.T.Thigpen was elated, somehow enthusiastically interpreting the Battalion CO's words as a direct message from Jehovah himself when in fact the crafty battalion CO, Lieutenant Colonel Silas J.J.J.W. Chestnut, was a devout closet agnostic with a fondness for Asian ladies and Appalachian bourbon, and knew damn well that it would be a snowy day in the hell he didn't believe in before that bothersome born again Jesus nut could ever come up with an adequate number of signatures... if any at all.

Lieutenant Colonel Silas J.J.J.W. Chestnut was extremely proud that during his tenure in command of the Flying Dragons no one above or below his rank had ever been able to best him when it came to military political maneuvering, which he attributed to an uncanny insight and the fact he had more damn middle initials than any other officer in the United States Army. Growing up with the classic New England name of Silas Chestnut but having no middle name at all, gave Lieutenant Colonel Silas J.J.J.W. Chestnut such an inferiority complex that he immediately added three other initials as soon as he became legally old enough to do so. Choosing three Js instead of one, none of which stood for any name in particular, was a means he developed to gain a strategic career upper hand. After realizing his success he later added the W just for shits and giggles. The additional insurance of the additional initial created a name few people could forget and everyone hated, which was of great benefit once he enlisted in the Army. It generated fast promotions for no other reason than to facilitate his transfer because the many middle initials, especially the W, made his commanding officers nervous by creating the automatic assumption that anyone with that many names had to be a legacy with a military lineage of high ranking American officers going all the way back to the Revolutionary War and as such would most assuredly have the ear and favor of the most powerful people in government and the Pentagon, meaning they, as his commanding officer, would be under continuous scrutiny exposing all of their shortcomings, deficiencies, insecurities, and indiscretions. Now, being a Lieutenant Colonel on the cusp of becoming one of America's youngest Generals, no one dare ever ask Lieutenant Colonel Silas J.J.J.W. Chestnut what the three Js or the W, which didn't actually stand for anything, actually stood for. In meetings, briefings, and encounters of all kinds, no one could ever adequately focus on the subject or issue at hand because they were so distracted and intrigued and preoccupied trying to guess. This left him, Lieutenant Colonel Silas J.J.J.W. Chestnut, the most focused and proficiently dominant and impressive mind in the room - at least in his opinion.

Therefore there was no way Colonel Silas J.J.J.W. Chestnut was going to be manipulated by a lowly born-again Warrant Officer, especially in the midst of his fast rising stellar career, and especially not by an officer with only three Ts. Not to mention the fact that he, Lieutenant Colonel Silas J.J.J.W. Chestnut, being over the hump of his tour of duty and about to go home, would most likely have scooted out of the country before CWO T.T.Thigpen with his bullshit petition, could reach even a fraction of the 52nd CAB's 1700 battalion personnel, many of them at satilite bases around II Corps.

Out of sight and out of mind, thought Lieutenant Colonel Silas J.J.J.W. Chestnut, leaving his mind free and clear to contemplate and formulate a plan for passing up the eagle and going directly to the star. Little did he realize, however, the spiritual wheels he had just set in motion in the form of CWO T.T.Thigpen.

CHAPTER 16

JESUS CHRIST, JESUS NUTS,
& KILLING FOR JESUS?

Someone once told me that Jesus was everywhere and I politely accepted that belief as a form of metaphor. That is until Vietnam.

There are all kinds of nuts in the world but as far as the Ghostriders were concerned we had more than our fare share of which CWO T.T.Thigpen was just the tip of the iceberg. In fact we had more than our fare share, enough to make for a potluck combat stew so diverse it would put Sigmund Freud in a tailspin. Unfortunately however, Sigmund Freud wasn't the company clerk, I was, and as such I would find myself the de facto everything in everyone's eyes simply because whether or not I knew everything about everything I was expected to, or at least they thought I was supposed to. It didn't take long after Roabley's departure for me to discover this curse or blessing, depending on your point of view, as well as the awesome responsibilities it incurred. Roabley for instance used this position and its acquired information, or perception of information, as a power source from which he often managed to prosper financially, a tradition I should continue he suggested on the day of his departure. The opportunistic Specialist 4th & 5th Class Buck Sergeant Acting Staff Sergeant and Bronze Star hero Roabley handled many of his routine chores with a capitalistic flair that would make a law firm billing clerk blush, for when it came to promotions, R&Rs, or other personnel actions requiring paperwork or orders created somewhere in the mysterious dark hole of the military paperwork universe, his often *can-do* spirit included the *cha ching* of a cash register. It worked because in spite of having a Commanding Officer, Executive Officer, and a First Sergeant, everyone knew that all things began and/or eventually landed in the lap of the Company Clerk therefore perpetuating the theory that anyone needing anything dealing with personal or personnel issues of any kind could circumvent the system and the chain of command and take their case directly to my desk. Formally the letters CC stood for Command and Control and was usually applied to a high ranking officer, but in reality among the ranks the formal definition and initials of CC applied to the company clerk.

"Gee, I know you requested that date for you're R&R in Hawaii Lieutenant Shaffett but it doesn't look like you're going to get it."

"Oh no! I gotta' have that date! My wife's already got reservations and it's the only time she can get there and it's our anniversary. Jesus Christ it's our first anniversary. I just have to have that date."

"Well, um, I'll do the best I can but it doesn't look good but hey, well... tell you what. There's this guy up at battalion who might be able to get it for you. I don't like to do this kind of thing but well... for twenty bucks this guy can probably juggle a few dates and get you the week you wanted."

"Oh wow," smiled Lieutenant Shaffett. "That would be great! Really great! Tell you what Roabley, you do that for me and I'll throw in another twenty bucks for you too. A deal?"

"Oh no," a caring conscientious Roabley would say. "I wouldn't take your money. But I'll pass the twenty on to that battalion guy and see if I can persuade him to come through for you."

After Roabley's disappointed but hopeful clients would depart the orderly room, usually twenty bucks lighter, he would open the locked drawer in his gray steel desk and verify the safety and well being of the already existing R&R orders guaranteeing the desired date in question, or their promotion or whatever else he had just negotiated while knowing they had already come down approved from battalion or the CO. He would proudly present those same orders to his extremely grateful clients a few days later, solidifying his place and reputation as a can-do guy and champion of the people; a method and a reputation he would probably continue cultivating in civilian life, coupled with his status as a reluctant Bronze Star hero to put him on the fast track for a successful political career as a sometimes hawkish sometimes dovish sometimes liberal and sometimes conservative money grubbing closet Republican running on the Democratic ticket.

If Roabley was a hustler, I on the other hand was a consumer advocate trying to serve the masses as honestly as possible, discovering along the way that if information is power it is also a nuisance that drew every lightheaded odd ball to my desk like proverbial moths to a porch light, all of them thinking I was the answer or had the answer or could find the answer to all of their personal ills. Strangely enough it all began with Jesus Christ. Not CWO T.T.Thigpen, but Jesus Christ himself who walked into the orderly room and stood right there in front of my desk.

"Send me home."

"What?" I asked, looking up from my typewriter where I was struggling with five carbon sheet copies of something nobody would ever read.

"Send me home."

"Send you home?"

'"Yes. You have to send me home." he insisted in what I perceived to be an Hispanic accent.

"Who are you?"

"Jesus," he said in the Anglican biblical form of the name.

"What?"

"I am Jesus."

"Um, say again," I asked.

"I am Jesus."

I noticed there was no last name above the pocket of his uniform but I recalled seeing the name Jesus on the morning report and glanced at the personnel roster to indeed discover a Private Jesus Martinez.

"Okay, here it is. Jesus Martinez I said, pronouncing the *Jesus* in the Latin vernacular. Says here you DEROS in um… in about nine months."

"No," he disagreed. "You don't understand. I am Jesus and I must go home."

"Why," I asked.

"Because I am Jesus. I am Jesus Christ."

Upon his declaration that he was Jesus Christ, Randy, First Sergeant Buchinsky and the Admin Officer paused what they were doing and looked across the room with intense curiosity. Randy turned down the radio, either to better here whatever was coming next or in reverence to a potential wartime miracle in the form of a personal appearance by Jesus Christ.

"I am Jesus Christ and you have to send me home."

I looked at Top for assistance. He looked at me and shrugged his shoulders. Top always expected his people to carry their own weight and I could see that he expected me to carry this one, even if it was in the form of a hundred-fifty pound biblical celebrity.

"Um listen, Jesus. I don't have any orders for…"

"No, I an not Jesus. I am *Jesus, Jesus Christ*, the Son of God, and I am not supposed to be here. You have to send me home."

"Okay, so you're Jesus Christ. Why do you have to go home?"

"Because the Holy Father has called for me and given me a mission."

"A mission?"

"A mission to return to my flock. A mission to return home."

"Is that the Holy Father in the Pentagon or is that *the*, um… Holy Father up there?"

"I am Jesus Christ almighty and I must leave the Army and go home."

"Well it's like this," I replied politely, trying not to ruffle any hallowed feathers or trigger any psychological surprises. "I don't have any transfer or discharge orders right now for Jesus Martinez or Jesus Christ but I'll certainly let you know as soon as I get some. Is that alright?"

Jesus looked at me and I could see the disappointment welling up in his eyes then after a time he simply turned and walked out of the orderly room.

I sat there for a moment not really sure how to react then looked to Top for guidance. Top again simply shrugged his shoulders without comment and returned his attention to his paperwork. Randy on the other hand, being a New York City Italian must have also been a devout Catholic for after watching Jesus walk out the door he immediately made the sign of the cross, but ended the ritual with the sign of a nut case, a whirling finger at the side of his head. He then looked to the sky, obviously hoping not to be struck by lightning.

Having Jesus Christ pay a visit wasn't the kind of thing I expected during the course of my usual long day in a combat zone, though I imagine stranger things have happened. Anyway, I simply let the incident go without much thought until Jesus Christ visited again about a week later on a Tuesday, resulting in a similar conversation with similar results with all of us extending similar reverence and curiosity. He wasn't excessively demanding or rude or insistent. He simply made it perfectly clear that he was in fact Jesus Christ and he wanted to go home, which was understandable. I suppose if I were Jesus Christ I wouldn't want to hang around in an Asian combat zone either, especially after all the crap I went through in the Middle East. Naturally Top had no intentions of catering to Jesus Martinez's fantasy or Jesus Christ's demands, and therefore I had no alternative but to continue patiently patronizing and dealing with his issues and visits. I say visits because visits from Jesus Christ became a regular event, though not always predictable. They weren't always on a Tuesday or always in the morning or the afternoon, and sometimes he didn't show up at all for a week, which was a bit disappointing, but life and the war continued, Jesus Christ or no Jesus Christ, and so did my rein as the Information Czar, becoming the facilitator for all things great and small from simple records and finance issues to psychotherapy sessions and confessionals with guys who were emotionally perturbed to guys who were emotionally disturbed. I suppose if I had a fault as a company clerk it was that I was a patient and sympathetic listener, which somehow at the ripe old age of 21 made me some kind of father figure to the numerous kids who, due to the war, were aging faster than they could dispose of their training wheels. They approached me in my hooch, in the mess hall, and at incidental passings everywhere, looking for answers at which time I almost always offered a sympathetic ear. Though most all of them were magnificent in combat in the face of the enemy and maintained an even strain most other times, some of them had the personal and domestic prowess of a cantaloupe, needing only an occasional kind word and the reassurance they were appreciated. Or a bottle of booze that at their age they wouldn't even be permitted to purchase in the States. On a very few selective occasions I did take Roabley's advice and perform a favor or two for money but the money wasn't for me. It actually went to the guy at battalion who could fix things. He thought I was nuts for not taking a cut of the action but like I told him, "I want to be able to look my guys in the eyes every day."

Not long before my encounter with Jesus Christ I had an opportunity to be introduced to another Jesus factor. One that was unique to aviation units such as ours. The Ghostriders, being an aviation unit, had a lot of helicopters, which means of course, that it had pilots and co-pilots and crew chiefs and gunners. It was a company consisting mostly of UH-1H and UH-1C choppers referred to as Hueys or more specifically as Huey Slicks and Huey Cobras that were also known as Gun Ships or Hogs. This is where the serious war part of the war came into play for the Ghostriders. Usually when you combine flight and combat with soldiers going into harms way there develops a great many quirks and superstitions, especially superstitions regarding death.

When I was less than a few weeks on the job there was an announcement regarding the time and place of a memorial service to be held by the battalion chaplain for one of our pilots. I went to the ceremony expecting to see a large group of company personnel attending but was surprised to discover about twenty empty seats set up outside facing a small portable pulpit. I thought I was early then I was even more surprised to find only a half dozen of those seats eventually filled when the Chaplain began his eulogy, and only three of those were Ghostriders being myself, the night baker known as Buns, and of course, CWO T.T.Thigpen. As the Chaplain spoke I leaned over to Buns and whispered, "How did this guy die? Did he get shot down?"

"Jesus nut," said Buns.

"What? No, I mean, how'd he get killed."

"Jesus nut," repeated Buns. "Heard he lost his Jesus nut."

I wasn't quite sure what Buns meant so I assumed that the pilot in question had either lost his nerve, lost his mind, or had a testicle shot off which would certainly explain why he crashed his chopper. Deciding to get clarification after the memorial service, I simply sat back and listened then became enthralled by the words of the chaplain.

"To die in combat is a noble thing," said the chaplain. "As we fight this war we can take great joy and satisfaction in knowing that God is so proud of our actions," said the chaplain. "And we can take great comfort in the knowledge that Jesus is at our side as we fire every bullet and launch every rocket," said the chaplain.

Now having grown up walking through the church doors every time they opened and having heard just about every angle and spin of biblical interpretation that existed, I set my mind into an exploratory mode for any and all references that making war, killing and possibly even dieing for any reason whatsoever was a noble thing blessed by God and accompanied by Jesus. I'm sure something could be found somewhere in the Bible but I'll be damned if I could remember it.

Out rolled more of the Chaplain's twisted platitudes, each and every one expressing God's endorsement of the war, Jesus' participation, and our dead pilot's joyous acceptance of his fate as he "now soars through the skies of heaven as a soldier of fortune for Christ."

"Amen." I heard CWO T.T.Thigpen say behind me.

"Amen." I heard night baker Buns whisper next to me.

Amen? I thought. Ah shit is more like it. Whether I'm here for kicks or corn flakes, and whether I choose to agree with the war or not, there's no way in hell I'm going to buy this line of military religious propaganda. Where do they find these chaplains anyway, I asked myself, briefly remembering Chaplain Captain Quack and his flying circus of domestic wisdom back in Texas. And hearing this entire dribble I began to realize why no one attended the memorial services. There was something about a memorial service that irritated the concerns and superstitions of flight crews as well as company personnel. They were the equivalent, one might say, of rubbing up against the rough abrasive skin of a man-eating shark all the while knowing you might be his next meal and that wasn't exactly their idea of showing a dead comrade their respect. Like true men of valor they instead decided to get drunk on their collective asses and rather than dwell on the fact that Jesus was loading their M-60s and guiding their rockets, preferred instead to laugh and talk about the time our much loved late pilot flew a night firefly mission wearing nothing but his helmet and a pair of Ho Chi Min sandals, an act in which I'm sure Jesus was unlikely to participate.

After further inquiry I discovered that our unfortunate pilot had not lost either his Jesus nut or his mind at all but was in fact shot down on approach to an LZ by an enemy RPG and other hostile fire. The *Jesus Nut,* I learned, was a reference to the single device that holds the main rotary blade securely to the chopper and was called the Jesus Nut because if it ever failed, all aboard the aircraft were soon going to meet Jesus when the chopper dropped from the sky like a loaded cement truck. At least that was the prevalent explanation. They hadn't called it that in flight school, probably because they didn't want to freak us out with the belief it would actually come off but then it goes to sound reasoning that if it hadn't come off sometime somewhere why would they call it the Jesus Nut? Another explanation was that if the Jesus Nut failed the only thing a crewman would have time to say before crashing was "OH JESUS!" I tend to believe more the previous explanation to the latter, however; because as all pilots and air crew come to learn shortly after taking to the sky, both by first hand accounts and by experience, most all pilots and crewmen say pretty much the same thing when they are about to crash, being – "OH SHIT!"

CHAPTER 17

COLD WATER WINGS
& WHERE'S THE WAR?

"OH SHIT! THAT'S COLD!" I yelled as my spine compressed, my gonads shot up to take refuge behind my colon and my dick shrank by two thirds.

Such was the ritual I suffered in the morning simply because I couldn't get up early enough to be the first in line for the showers. First in line meant you were fortunate enough to get hot water that only lasted about three or four minutes then all the showers went the way of the great northern ice pack for the rest of us. And first in line meant getting up long before sunrise, before the Chicken Man on AFVN radio, before the START WAR NOW buzzer went off, before all the rest of civilization, and even before God. I'm not a morning person, never was and never would be, which is not in harmony with the military way of life and sure as hell wasn't in harmony with the Holloway water schedule and pre-dawn water race.

The pre-dawn water race was necessary because the water didn't even flow until 0500 hours when the little old Vietnamese guy with the goats inside the fence under the water tower turned it on, which he promptly turned off two hours later. That was his job – turn it on – turn it off – talk to the goats. During that few hours he was the most powerful man in all of Camp Holloway, for at his bidding the showers flowed, the sinks flowed, and the toilets flushed. This happened only twice a day, meaning if you were left standing soaped up and buck-ass naked in the shower or in the shower line waiting your turn when old papa-san and his goats turned off the water in the morning you were left there shit out of luck until 1700 hours in the evening. And most of the time 1700 hours wasn't really acceptable to most of us because everybody was still working, or eating chow, or still flying missions, or at the club drinking, or laid back in their hooch drinking and listening to the *mofuckin'* Temptations, or laid back with a Holloway Hooker, or otherwise occupied with more important things like trying to decide whether or not you wanted to freeze your gonads off in the shower. Depending on the time of year, it wasn't a decision made lightly.

Occasionally the 1700 schedule was convenient but on most days, like many other guys, I didn't leave the job until chow time so it was the morning frozen follies or no shower at all. Contrary to popular belief all of Vietnam is not a hot tropical paradise. The Central Highlands could get cold at night, and in the central highlands at the crack of dawn in that doorless open-air masonry building cold water was not just cold, it was damn cold! And who the hell was that crazy, I wondered each morning, or that dedicated, or even cared that much what the hell they smelled like anyway in this third-world zoo? A place where people reeked of fish heads and oyster sauce, and bathed in shit water with their pet water buffalo, and left their footprints on the toilet seats. There was a self-consoling psychological approach I occasionally used on myself but as my tour went on I used it less and less. I would think of how fortunate I was compared to the men in the boonies who were struggling through mountain jungles or sloshing through shitty rice paddy water, getting all funky with no showers in sight for extended periods of time. It was that old routine our mothers used to use to get us to eat our spinach. "Think of all the poor children in China who don't have any food," they would say. All that did was play on our collective conscience and give an entire generation a guilt complex as they crammed spinach into their pockets or flushed it down the commode when mom wasn't looking, then grew up to eventually kill those same Chinese. So what's a little cold water? Just think of all the poor grunts in the boonies, I would say to myself. Then I would feel guilty but that didn't prevent my icy decline.

The shower building was a simple affair with a line of half a dozen sinks along one wall and four showers on the other, and that was about four showers and six sinks too few, being it was supposed to serve a number of companies. Most everybody shaved with their little round portable PX mirrors and brushed their teeth in the shower because while you stood there all goose pimply and buck-ass naked, soap-frothed and freezing, with your personal pride shrunk to the point of disgrace, a full complement of hooch maids who began work at the crack of dawn, were busily using all the sinks to wash somebody's clothes, or their fish head pots, or sometimes even their own feet. I don't know when the hooch maids came to retain dominance over the sinks but to me it had evolved into one of those cultural things that took a little getting used to. Bathing wasn't exactly the beautiful harmonious experience depicted in, say, an ancient roman spa or one of those steamy Japanese communal garden bathing scenes you might see in the movies. It was instead just a bunch of naked G.I.s standing around grumbling, cursing, and complaining, waiting their turn while another bunch of naked G.I.s took too long shivering and shaving in the cold showers while a bunch of homely hooch maids chattering like disturbed seagulls were washing their feet or somebody's funky socks, all the while ignoring or pretending that we naked American G.I.s were about as interesting as a rusty old Ford Fairlane on a pay by the week used car lot.

It was certainly demeaning to think that a group of healthy virile young naked American men couldn't generate the least bit of interest from a group of women who seemed to care more about their fish head pots than... well. Sure I would eventually get used to it, no big deal as long as none of the Bas in the bath house happened to be my particular hooch maid Ba who fortunately was quite content using our rain barrel for her chores. How would I look her in the eye each day if she frequented the showers? Quite simply, I wasn't ready to handle that much familiarity or relinquish that much of my American honed civility. What I really couldn't handle, even after the social conditioning of the mandatory group-shit sessions at Fort Bragg, was all those chattering Bas in the latrine when nature called, which it so often did in the morning. The nature calls therefore were pretty much postponed or restricted to those times when the goat man was not in power and the hooch mamas abandoned the throne room because there was no more water coming out of the spigots - or into the toilets.

War is hell.

If there was a drawback to being a company clerk it was the restriction of the job. Regardless of the excitement of the shock of cold showers and a parade of crazies, having to function in the same room with the same faces each day tended to get a little monotonous and generate a form of cabin fever. Walking up to the battalion S-1 each morning helped but didn't offer much of a distraction, nor did the occasional visit to the EM Club, which was a rustic place much like I left behind in Mexico. No matter how you looked at it we lived on the job and that was a downer. One day I must have appeared down or a little agitated or distracted, so after I left for my usual morning trip up the hill to S-1 First Sergeant Buchinsky asked Randy if I had a problem.

"I think he's just bored," Randy told him.

"What makes you say that?" asked Top.

"Well, last night we had a few drinks up at the club and he was talking about how nobody ever tells us anything about the war and how shitty it is to be in an aviation unit and not be able to fly or see any of the country or know what's going on."

"Oh yeah," said Top. "And he thinks that's a bad thing?"

"We were talking about how this isn't what we expected. You know, like in the movies where you got thousands of guys always moving out to take some enemy city or something. The big team kind of thing, you know? I think Fusco's one of those gamer guys, you know, like he was telling me about his football in high school. Said he went both ways and never sat on the bench, and felt like that's what he was doing now, just sitting on the bench, but wasn't sure because he doesn't know what's going on, doesn't get the big picture."

"How 'bout you?" ask Top. "You think you're missing the war?"

"Who me? Shit Top, I'm from New York City. I'm not proud. You can take all this cave man crap and shove it. I'm for whatever gets me home but I think Vince was expecting to be a part of something or expecting to see shit, you know, like the battle of the bulge or something. He says the war is kind of like we're all relief pitchers in the bullpen who can't see the game and don't know what's happening. Then they send you out to toss a few pitches for an inning and when you're done they send you back to the bullpen. He's not a big drinker so I don't know if it was the booze talking or what. Personally I think he's getting cabin fever or something. That plus I think there's something going on with his wife. He thinks she's messing around or something. Jody shit, you know."

Top laughed and about that same time Major Anthony, having overheard the conversation, strolled quietly out of his office.

"First Sergeant don't we have a security dispatch or something that needs to get to MACV. I'm thinking maybe it should be hand carried by um… Fusco. That is if you can spare him."

There was a slight grin exchanged by both men as Top replied, "Yes sir. I'll send him out as soon as he gets back." Top then picked up the phone and called S-1, "This is First Sergeant Buchinsky, 189th. Is my company clerk still up there?"

He listened to the answer on the other end.

"Good. Send him over to the Sergeant Major to pick up the dispatches for MACV."

He then called Sergeant Major Corklyn and arranged for me to go on the courier run.

When I walked through the door of the orderly room twenty minutes later with the battalion security dispatches Top looked at his watch then looked up at me and said, "There's a currier chopper by the Yard shop on the main pad getting ready to leave on the dispatch run in five minutes. Be on it and deliver that package to MACV."

"What?" I said, surprised.

"Five minutes, Fusco. Get a move on."

I looked at Randy who just smiled. After I left the office Randy looked to Top who just grinned and said, "New York my ass."

Major Anthony must have been a travel agent in a previous life because he certainly booked me on an air tour of II Corps that would more than get me off the bench of boredom, more so than he could possibly have imagined. Dispatches were usually sent here and there as the traffic would bare, meaning whatever chopper was heading this way or that would drop off whatever or whoever needed to get there. For some reason, however, MACV was collecting and disseminating a lot of intelligence data lately, more than usual, from all over the highlands II Corps area, including Pleiku and Kontum Provinces, and I had just caught a ride on the air-mail special that was making all the stops.

Our first stop was a one-unit aviation compound near Kontum that was situated along the Ia Drang River about 35 or 40 miles north of Pleiku. It was the new location and current home of one of our sister companies from the battalion, the 170th AHC known as the Bikinis, and their compound had been renamed accordingly as Bikini Beach. We stayed there just long enough to pick up their dispatches and a quick lunch, and for our pilot to look up a friend who it turned out wasn't there. Noticing that Bikini Beach was a small set up where the perimeter wires ran a mere few yards from the hooches, I asked a few of the residents if this was of any concern. I was told with a laugh that it was exactly that which gave the Bikinis a sense of security. "Hell," they told me, "this place is so small that the rockets and mortars pass right on over, and when they do we just pop another cork and laugh." But not all rockets or mortars passed completely over and being the majority of the area around Kontum and Bikini Beach was infested with NVA, I'm not so sure I would have maintained a similar attitude, though I didn't know that at that time.

Next on the tour was the Special Forces camp at Dak To. It was also an OPS base for SOG teams, known as the Special Operations Group if they were SF or the more clandestine Studies and Observation Group with MACV, both of whom ran around the highlands and popping in and out of Cambodia and Laos on a regular basis gathering intelligence and poking the NVA in the ass whenever the opportunity presented. They worked out of Dak To northwest of Kontum along with the Central Intelligence Agency's CIDG (Civilian Irregular Defense Group) outpost because it was a hop skip and jump from the tri-country borders of Cambodia, Laos and Vietnam. Like the A Shau Valley just to the north and the Ia Drang Valley to the south, the mountainous border area was an entry funnel and refuge for the NVA from their supply lines and base camps across the border to the west. Our primary enemy in the central highlands was the North Vietnamese Army as opposed to the indigenous rebels known as the Viet Cong down south. They were straight up troops, uniformed, well trained, and well disciplined. Dak To had a history of a number of big time bloody battles and conflicts starting back in the mid sixties.

As we headed there the crew chief handed me a set of headphones with a mic that allowed me to hear all the chatter aboard the aircraft and through which he acted as my tour guide.

"Kontum to Dak To is pretty much all a freefire zone," he said.

"What's that?" I asked.

"If it moves, kill it," He answered. "You got more ammo for that?" he asked, pointing to my M-16.

"Yeah," I answered, slapping my ammo bandoleer hanging under my flack jacket.

"Good, 'cause it's a freefire zone for the bad guys too," he said. "Lock and load and keep it secure. And keep the damn safety on. Got it?"

I nodded affirmative, did as instructed, then sat back mentally patting myself on the back for deciding to bring my weapon, flack jacket and helmet. At first I thought the crew might think I was a bit too paranoid, just some dumb ass *pencil*. Now I know why it hadn't generated a second glance; they knew better. It was the first time the crew chief had offered any instruction. Prior to that his only advice came somewhere between Holloway and Kontum when he told me to, "Pucker up 'cause we're going through the Kontum Pass." The Kontum pass was a rise of mountains on both sides on route to Kontum. Mountains from which the enemy took frequent pot shots at everything that flew, like choppers. On this particular trip nothing happened that I knew of, but I was well prepared to pucker up if necessary even though I had no friggin' idea what it meant. I would later learn that pucker up referred to the *pucker factor* which was a 1 to 10 scale form of measurement that pilots and crew used to describe the degree of terror they felt during any given incident of danger. A pucker factor of 10 pretty much meant you were in big trouble, so much so that your asshole puckered completely shut and you would be unable to shit for a week.

We were in an area of mountainous terrain that seemed even more ominous to me because I again had no damn idea where I was, north, south or inside out. I had removed the headset and as we approached the camp at Dak To I noticed our pilot and copilot exchanging a few excited words, then the chopper made an abrupt change of direction. When it did I saw two other ships lifting off from the camp heading on a similar course. The crew chief reached around the corner from his gun well and slapped me on the leg to get my attention. He then came around and gave me some quick instructions.

"Listen, there's a hot extraction and they might need some help or some cover. You put on that headset and get your 16 ready to rock and roll. Don't say anything because it's going to get pretty busy and you don't want to junk up the radio with extra chatter. If we have to go in you put your helmet on and keep your shit together and try and help out. Okay? Are we cool?"

He didn't wait for an answer as he turned quickly back to his M-60 and began searching the area in all directions of his side of the aircraft. I did as instructed and through my headset got an ear full of information. The more I heard the higher up shot my pucker factor.

"Bikini Red Lead, this is Ghostrider two-niner at your high six."

"Red Lead, Go Ghostrider."

"Whatcha need and where, Red Lead?"

"Thanks for the offer Ghostrider. How's your fuel?"

"Just topped off at Bikini Beach. We're good. What's up?"

"We got a SOG team stuck on the ground about a dozen miles other side of the line. Under fire and heavy pursuit all night by NVA hunters. They're having difficulty reaching the PZ and there's no other immediate clear ground for pick up. Been tryin' under fire for nearly an hour to get to them but had to break off and refuel. Red Three is currently orbiting their location and Cobras are flying cover. Suggest you orbit when we arrive on site. Cover as you deem necessary and be ready for possible extraction."

"Roger that Red Lead. Can you ID the Red Three AC?"

"Affirmative. It's the Troubadour."

The Troubadour was LT Mickey Fletcher of the 170th Bikinis, an all around likable guy known as the Troubadour for his poetry and musical talents. He was also a good friend and relative by marriage of our pilot, CW2 Fuzzy Lamphere, who first met Fletcher's sister when she visited them at flight school. In fact Fuzzy Lamphere had actually finagled a transfer to the 52nd CAB with the hopes of getting in the same unit but only managed to get in the same battalion. His assignment to the Ghostriders turned out to be nearly as good because for a time the Bikinis were located right next door on Hollywood Boulevard at Holloway. Unfortunately the Bikinis were later moved to Kontum where they replaced the Gladiators, leaving Fuzzy and his brother-in-law to rendezvous whenever their flight missions allowed.

The besieged SOG team leader on the ground was a Lieutenant Brandon Learner and as we approached the site I could hear him on the radio breathlessly updating whoever was listening. The team was tired and spent, having been fighting, running, and ambushing all night, and was currently being closely pursued by a relentless group of NVA. A napalm strike had been called in to give them escape cover and breathing room. It bought them some distance but in the process had started a serious fire that became as much a threat as the NVA who were once again closing in and were even using dogs in the pursuit.

I heard Learner state clearly, "We're taking heavy shit down here and we got wounded. If we're not extracted now we're dead. We're all dead!"

Learner himself was now wounded and the team had become restricted to little or no movement.

"Roger that, ground, but I see no clearance. No possible PZ clearance," answered the Troubadour.

I could see between the pilots through the windshield as we approached the sight a few miles off. The Cobras were making runs through a narrow ravine to spook the NVA and draw fire, then only returning mini-gun fire, not firing their rockets because they were too close to the SOG team. That plus the high canopy dense growth of jungle obscured their ability to target without the chance of hitting friendlies. Below, through increasing enemy fire, Lieutenant Learner somehow maintained his sense of humor as he again came on the radio to the Troubadour, Red Three.

"Red Three, we're piss out'a luck here. If you don't pick us up right now you don't have a hair on your balls."

"Okay, Roger that," replied the Troubadour without hesitation. "There's a ravine about 20 meters to your south. I'm coming in!"

"Copy that. We're on our way."

Red Three shot into the small ravine then hovered and dropped into a patch of tall grass and tall brush that appeared barely large enough to host a jeep much less a single huey chopper and the full spread of its violently rotating blades. He was followed by enemy fire in the form of multiple lines of green tracers from all sides, some hitting his tailboom. His gunners immediately began returning fire from their M-60s in all directions but were unable to strafe the higher areas of the cliffs due to the vertical limit restriction of their mounted weapons, and that was where most of the enemy fire originated. I watched in amazement while in the midst of that beehive of small arms fire the aircraft dropped confidently to the ground.

"We're down! We're down!" I heard the pilot say.

I moved to the side of our aircraft for a better view as we came around. I could see the team making their way out of the jungle and begin climbing on board, helping others do the same while the gunners on both sides of the chopper fired relentlessly. One minute. Two minutes. The ravine offered little room for other aircraft to provide cover leaving Red Three dangerously alone and exposed. It seemed to take forever.

"I've got 'em! I've got 'em! We've got all eight of 'em and we're coming out!" I heard the Troubadour say as he pulled pitch and lifted off through a gauntlet of enemy fire.

I could almost feel the collected exhale of relief from all the aircrews orbiting above. As for myself, I don't think I took a single breath during the imagined eternity it took for Red Three to extract the exhausted team. It all seemed so surreal, so intense, and was magnified even more in my mind knowing that had he failed another chopper, possibly even mine, would attempt the same thing. I watched as Red Three rose triumphantly from the ravine and continued for nearly a dozen yards when suddenly a white streak shot out from midway up the side of the hill. It struck the aircraft dead on and exploded with a tremendous WHOMPF, sending debris and body parts in all directions and the ship into a forward falling ball of fire. My mind froze with shock, somehow slowing and repeating the scene over in my head. All chatter on the radio ceased. Then a large secondary explosion occurred when the JP4 fuel ignited as the aircraft hit the canopy of the dense jungle. A cloud of black smoke rose quickly and billowed above the site.

"Jesus Christ! I don't think… I mean, I didn't see anything bigger than a football hit the ground," said one of the Cobra pilots, finally breaking the silence.

"I'm going down," said Fuzzy as he dropped our chopper toward the ravine.

I had an inexperienced eye but I knew what I saw and knew just as everyone else did that there was no chance in hell of anybody surviving that explosion, but as frightened as I was I somehow felt that our pilot's decision to go down there was the right thing to do, not that I had any choice in the matter. My senses sharpened and I felt helpless with my fate now in the hands of a flight crew I hardly knew and an enemy I had never seen. And I quickly discovered that the pucker factor was the real deal. When we made our high speed pass over the crash site we drew fire from both sides including two white streaks that passed behind us and exploded on the opposite side of the ravine. The crew chief and gunner both opened up with their 60s. I don't know what made me do it but as we passed by the burning crash site I took the risk of moving to the edge of the door to better look out in hopes that maybe I'd see someone who might have actually survived. The downdraft from our blades pushed and spread the black smoke into the trees below revealing a smoldering canopy growth too thick to see much of anything, which was probably just as well. I stared and marveled at how the essence of twelve men and an entire aircraft could vanish so completely in such a short violent flash of time.

Fuzzy pulled out of the ravine and at the direction of Bikini Red Lead, who also made a low pass and came to the same conclusion, we returned to Dak To. After a time, and to his credit, CW2 Fuzzy Lamphere completed the dispatch run returning us safely to Camp Holloway just as a beautiful red sky on the horizon was giving way to dusk.

When I dragged in from the revetment area Randy met me with my mail then joined me in the mess hall where I scrounged up some leftovers. He had already eaten but kept me company as I picked at my food. He laughed when he explained how his conversation with Top had resulted in getting me on the dispatch run so I could have some fun, and then asked, "Well, how was the tour? See anything cool? Did you find the war?"

"Yeah," I said. "I saw a chopper with twelve guys get blown away someplace near Kontum."

"You're shittin' me right?"

"No," I said, then went to my room and sat quietly alone on my bunk for quite a while, a myriad of thoughts and emotions running through my mind, and wondering how I had managed to so quickly grow from watching Crusader Rabbit on Captain Kangaroo to watching guys like myself getting blown to hell in a foreign country. I stared at a letter from home but didn't open it, knowing there was little I could read that would remedy what I was now feeling. I didn't even know those guys and I didn't know what to feel. I just sat there. That is until the loud WHOMPF of a rocket struck somewhere in the camp followed quickly by another, then another. It was the third rocket attack since we had arrived and was just as frightening as the first.

The siren sounded and Randy threw open my door carrying his gear, "Top says we always report to him in the orderly room when we get hit. Get your shit, let's go."

I grabbed my weapon and gear and we rushed to the orderly room. We were the first to arrive, finding it dark and unoccupied except for the lone soldier on night CQ duty. I went for the flashlight I kept in my desk and just as I turned it on Top rushed though the door.

"Get on that field phone to Battalion, Fusco. Crank it up and keep it open. I'll give you the sit-reps and you call 'em in. Got it?"

"Got it, Top," I said. "What the hell's a *sit rep*?"

Top looked at me and laughed, then explained. "Sit reps, son. Situation Reports. You're going to inform battalion of our strength status as we man our area of responsibility on the perimeter and keep it up until we are one hundred percent manned. Then you report on damage and casualties. Got it?"

By then various NCOs were rushing in and out of the orderly room with flashlights flickering in all directions, informing and getting direction from Top Buchinsky. Armed troops rushed from their hooches and other areas and mounted trucks that came out of the darkness and skidded to a halt in front of the hooches. I could hear choppers lifting off across the field and with the departure of each loaded truck Top would turn to me with a status update.

"189th at twenty percent manned, Fusco. Call it in."

I did as instructed and continued to do so with each truckload. Forty per cent, then sixty, then eighty. The siren finally died and in the far distance outside the perimeter I heard the thump of another rocket being launched. The troops who were already on the perimeter opened up on the area where they saw the rocket flash, then the choppers opened up and as the rocket shrieked toward the camp a chorus of personnel yelled, "INCOMING!" and we all dove to the floor. Again it sounded as though it was going to hit right smack in the middle of the orderly room but the actual impact was somewhere up the hill in the battalion area or the BOQ. I could hear the sound of more choppers taking off and the sound of another M-60 opening up from an aircraft that was already flying over the perimeter.

As I witnessed all this I felt somehow privileged to be in the company of these particular soldiers. What I was watching was an instant transformation from what I had begun to consider a collection of odd balls and ding bats into an armed and serious group of men rushing off without hesitation or complaint to meet whatever challenge the enemy had in mind. For the first time I thought of them as *The Ghostriders*, my Ghostriders, not just a bunch of names on the company roster or the morning report. Another thump and as we once again hit the floor I looked out the door just in time to see a bright flash where the rocket struck the far side of the runway. Silhouetted in front of the brief flash was a gun ship as it rose and launched forward. Then all was quiet.

Everyone stayed on station for the better part of the night in anticipation of some form of following enemy ground attack but none occurred. As the hours passed tensions eased and anxiety turned into jokes and stories about everything from Staff Sergeant Wheeler's 800 pound pig in Alabama to Staff Sergeant Satterfield's supposed 800 pound girlfriend in Colorado, which, he claimed, is why he reenlisted for Vietnam. "She was more dangerous," he said, "than the damn NVA." Then in walked night baker Buns carrying a tray full of very large and very fresh aromatic sticky buns right out of the oven, for which I discovered he was becoming famous. While the rest of the company was scurrying to meet the enemy, Buns was laboring undaunted in the darkened kitchen of the mess hall. Talk about courage under fire.

Buns had used his time in the Army to perfect his buns, not just sticky buns but all kinds of buns and bake goods, including the most wonderful yeast rolls you could possibly imagine, and when Buns got out of the Army Buns was going to open a chain of bakeries that he intended to call *BUNZ* with a *Z*. When it came to buns Buns could do no wrong except for the fact that any food prepared in the mess hall that required the use of government issued flour also contained some kind of little tiny weevil bugs. There was no getting around the little weevil bugs in the government issued flour anywhere in Vietnam. It had something to do with the climate I was told, but they were completely harmless if not nutritious and once you came to terms with the ever-present little tiny specks you had to agree that Buns' buns were the best buns in the entire United States Army. In fact, if the 189th was blessed with anything it was a great mess hall crew who regularly cranked out some damn good food. Even though everyone complained about the regularity of roast beef on the menu we had to admit it was a hell of a lot better then a steady diet of C-Rats with canned biscuits. The only black spot on our mess hall record was the time one of the local bridges was blown up and the chow trucks couldn't get through leaving us with a diet of chicken and grapes for nearly a week. Yeah, I know what you're thinking. We could fly anything anywhere anytime but we couldn't fly in our own food. What can I say? Apparently logic wasn't a required course at the Army Command School. The important thing is the beer always got through so the complaints were minimal.

Buns' sticky buns were followed by fresh coffee and the all-clear siren, then on came the lights after which Randy turned on the radio and low and behold there came once again Petula Clark singing.

It's a *sign of the times*
That your love for me is getting so much stronger

"God damnit!" said Randy, starting to do his irritation version of the Randy dance. "God damnit! Shit!"

Top and the rest of us turned and looked to Randy thinking he had lost it while faced with the stress of the rocket attack. Randy picked up the phone and dialed the Armed Forces Radio station. He had the number under the Plexiglas on the top of his desk. We all had the number because we all had our favorite songs that we occasionally called in and requested when we got sick and tired of hearing Petula Clark. Somebody out there or somebody at the station truly loved Petula Clark because you could count on hearing Petula Clark singing on Armed Forces Radio at least three times an hour, twenty-four hours a day.

"Armed Forces Radio. Specialist Evenson speaking." said the voice on the other end of Randy's phone.

"Is this the Armed Forces Radio station?" asked Randy.

"Yeah, Armed Forces Radio. Specialist Evenson speaking."

"Specialist Evenson, you don't know me but I called to tell you that I have a one-five-five howitzer. In fact I have three one-five-five howitzers and I have all three of my one-five-five howitzers targeted on your God damn radio station right now as we speak. And if you don't stop playing Petula Clark songs I'm going to blow the shit out of your God damn radio station."

"Yeah right," said Specialist Evenson. "And I got the U.S.S Forrestal parked in my fuckin' driveway. Smart ass."

I looked at Top, thinking Randy had just dialed his way into some serious disciplinary problems but when I saw him looking at

Randy with a slight smile then take a chomp out of one of Buns' sticky buns I stopped worrying.

At this same time in the dark bush just outside the secure perimeter area near the location of Specialist Evenson and the Armed Forces Vietnam Network radio station, a young Viet Cong gorilla named Anh Dung Phuc fumbled in the dark with a long tube loaded with a one-double-deuce rocket. Anh Dung Phuc was only 13 years old and had joined the Viet Cong communist gorillas because he was about to be drafted by the Army of the Republic of Vietnam, the ARVNs, who were going to make him an officer. They were going to make him an officer because his father was an officer when he was killed in combat at the young age of 21, but not before fathering four children and naming his son Anh Dung that means in Vietnamese, *heroism and strength*. His father was also a realist as was evident by Anh Dung's last name *Phuc* that in Vietnamese means *lucky*. Anh Dung chose to join the VC as opposed to the ARVN because as an ARVN officer his involuntary enlistment was for life, or until death, whichever came first, and in spite of his name he didn't feel much like a lucky hero. And besides, serving with the VC gorillas was easier and only part time, kind of like serving in the U.S. National Guard.

After a crash course on one-double-deuce rockets, *Lucky Hero* set out to deliver havoc to the completely non-strategic installation that housed the Armed Forces Radio facility. Lucky Hero and his family were recently transplanted to Pleiku from the urban clusters of Ton Son Nuit where his mother operated a massage parlor that catered to U.S. Air Force officers, which meant Lucky Hero was a city boy and found it difficult to maneuver and navigate in the boonies, especially at night. As a result of Lucky Hero's bad bush performance he was in the wrong location, placing him and his rocket too close to the perimeter where he squatted setting up his one-double-deuce and its timer that he was supposed to set to launch early the next day. He was just about finished and was in the process of setting the timer when he was stumbled upon by an American security patrol accompanied by three whores they were smuggling into the AFVN compound. Suddenly one of the whores while making her way though the dark tripped over and fell on Lucky Hero, causing him to set off the rocket that shrieked through the sky sounding, to the untrained ear of Specialist Evenson in the radio studio, much like a 155 artillery shell. It overshot the compound altogether but exploded with thunderous chilling affect, convincing Specialist Evenson that Randy meant business.

"HOLY SHIT!" said Specialist Evenson on the phone. "You're fuckin' serious!"

"Uh, damn right I'm serious," replied Randy with all the deliberate verbal inflection of a deranged artilleryman. "We artillery men are always serious. Now I don't ever want to hear Petula Clark on your God damn radio station again. You got that? I want to hear, um… the Rascals."

Randy liked the Rascals because he graduated from the same high school as the Rascals.

"And the Rolling Stones and some Jimi Hendrix and the Beatles and um…"

"And Wayland Jennings," suggested Staff Sergeant Wheeler in honor of his 800 pound pig named Camellia. Wayland Jennings was the music he often used to put Camellia to bed.

"…Wayland Jennings," repeated Randy. "And um…the Cowsills."

When Randy said the Cowsills everybody in the orderly room gave him a questioning look.

"Hey," he defended, "Fusco likes the Cowsills."

Then everybody gave me the weird look and I offered a half-ass smile and shrugged. "…and other stuff," I said.

Then Top said, "Yeah, the Cowsills aren't so bad. I like the Cowsills."

Then one by one everybody came out of their musical closet, risking being labeled a pussy by admitting they liked the Cowsills.

"Yeah, I like the Cowsills," said Buns as he continued passing out his buns.

"Guess they're okay," said Staff Sergeant Wheeler.

"The Cowsills, yeah. That *flowers in her hair* thing. I can dig that," confessed Staff Sergeant Satterfield who actually hated the Cowsills because his 800-pound girlfriend liked the Cowsills, but didn't want to be the odd man out.

"Okay," said Randy into the phone to Specialist Evenson after getting the general consensus about the Cowsills. "I'm going to let you slide this time, Specialist Evenson. But if I hear Petula Clark on the radio one more time I'm going to turn you and that damn radio station into a God damn smokin' memory. Affirmative? Got that?"

"No more Petula Clark. Got it," said a nervous Specialist Evenson.

"Damn right," declared Randy as he slammed down the phone to the appreciative applause around the room from music aficionados with sticky bun sticky fingers. It was Randy's proudest moment of the war to date and he celebrated with a smile and a big bite of one of Buns' big buns.

On the radio we heard the abrupt scratch and slide of a needle as it sped across the recording of Petula Clark's song. The radio went silent and there was a long charged moment around the orderly room as we all waited. Then there came the instrumental intro and finally the words of the Cowsills.

> *I saw her sitting in the rain*
> *Raindrops falling on her*
> *She didn't seem to care*
> *She sat there and smiled at me*
> *Then I knew I knew... I knew... I knew... I knew*
> *She could make me happy... happy... happy...*

Everyone in the room, these fearless Army warriors who only moments earlier were preparing to face death, now with mouths full of Buns' sticky buns and coffee, bobbed their heads and chimed in with, "...happy... happy..."

In the pitch black darkness near the Armed Forces Radio compound, Lucky Hero, just as he was about to be zippered with a full clip of bullets from an anxious M-16, was recognized by one of the Vietnamese whores, who it turned out was his sister. In fact, all three whores turned out to be his sisters who inevitably became whores because their mother owned a massage parlor and their last name was Phuc, which of course, catered to the average American soldier's inept ability to deal with foreign languages. The security grunts, realizing they would get little cooperation from the Phuc sisters if they killed their little brother, decided to let Lucky Hero return to his part time job with the VC as long as he promised not to shoot any more rockets at their particular compound. Lucky Hero eagerly agreed because he didn't want to hurt his sisters who would probably be spending a lot of time selling their wares in the AFVN compound, and naturally because he didn't want to be zippered by an M-16. On that particular night, Lucky Hero Phuc was indeed one lucky fuck - and so were the members of the security patrol.

The next day Fuzzy Lamphere left for the States on a compassionate leave to be with his sister in her grief at the memorial service for her husband Lieutenant Mickey "The Troubadour" Fletcher. The Troubadour appeared in spirit only, being there was no identifiable body parts found when they finally got in to search the crash site.

As Fuzzy left for the States that morning I made a side trip on my daily visit to the battalion S-1, stopping by operations to find out what it would take to qualify for flight status. SP5 Larry Graham, a buddy in the HQ platoon who worked there, set me up on a program to get my air crewman wings. I needed some basic instruction and a pre-requisite amount of flight hours that I would somehow have to squeeze in during my off time as the Ghostrider's CC. He explained that whatever spare time I had he could fill with flight time without a problem. Down time for air crewman was in big demand and some were even willing to pay for it. As a result, Graham pretty much became my booking agent and I soon started subbing for gunners on what they called rat fuck or bullshit missions, being those missions that were uneventful, boring and or non-critical. In other words, if I wanted my air crewman wings I had to fly the shitty end of the stick and did, sometimes even getting paid for it. I was concerned that I might get in some kind of trouble but Graham was quick to point out that hardly anybody in our outfit was working their primary MOS and some often doubled as aircrew, which I confirmed after checking the files. We had gunners working in aircraft maintenance, aircraft maintenance guys flying as crew chiefs and working in the kitchen, motor pool mechanics flying as gunners, a door gunner as an awards clerk in the orderly room, and as I was informed by Graham, "Hell, we got a cook who's a crew chief and crew chiefs who pilot aircraft on the sly, so who's going to give a shit if a Remington Raider wants to get behind a 60?"

It all worked for me because I had now seen why these guys dragged in at the end of a long day over the skies of Vietnam and drowned themselves in beer. And I now understood why, even though they showed us no disrespect, some of them thought of us as just *pencils* or *desk pilots*. Maybe I couldn't fly all the time but neither was I going to sit on the bench all the time. I felt that just being a pencil wasn't good enough and if I was going to be their resident personnel trouble shooter and listen to them cry in their beer about their troubles at home or any other inner demons they possessed, then I needed their respect. In my mind it would take a set of wings to get it, otherwise I felt like I was cheating, sitting on that imaginary bench. And besides, Randy was right. I wasn't a heavy drinker, didn't play cards, and had no taste whatsoever for Holloway hookers who smelled like fish heads bathed in Old Spice. And I was in fact becoming bored shitless, not to mention dangerously curious about a war where I could go from witnessing an incident of wholesale death to sticky buns, coffee, and the Cowsills all in one day. I still had no idea what the hell was going on here and was somehow eager though reluctant to find out. I also couldn't seem to shake the memory of the vibrating thunderous power of that aircraft and the rush I felt while witnessing the events that took place in Cambodia. I felt as if I was again making a decision that would take me in an unwanted or unexpected direction, but for some reason I was somehow compelled to do it.

CHAPTER 18

FIREFLY &
CLUB MILE HIGH

Graham arranged for me to cut my teeth as a gunner on a midnight firefly mission. Firefly was a Huey Slick with the addition of a locally conceived jury-rigged large array of spotlights mounted on one side. So many lights in fact that they could only be turned on for a limited time as needed because they could get hot enough to fry your eyeballs right out of the sockets. The extremely bright light also made one hell of a nighttime target for the enemy. The lights were managed by the crew chief while the chopper flew over Camp Holloway's perimeter. Basically, it was night guard duty in the sky, boring duty for the air crews from various companies who occasionally got stuck with it. But to me it was my first everything and exciting, and I was determined to get everything right.

Prior to nightfall I met crew chief Reggie Dillinger, a slender fair-haired young kid from San Diego. Anticipating the usual question he immediately informed me that he was no relation to the infamous gangster killer of the same name. He then gave me a run down on the chopper and everything I needed to know to get me through the night without making a complete ass of myself, which of course I did, but at least this time I didn't have an instructor banging on my helmet comparing me to his damn pet monkey. That night after about twenty-five minutes in the air the AC gave Dillinger permission to let me fire a few practice burst from my M-60. We flew over a safe area, I fired a few short burst into the darkness below, felt I had just joined the ranks of John Wayne and Audie Murphy, and then sat back into the gunner's well to gloat and relax. Dillinger meanwhile busied himself with the spotlights by popping them on and off on an irregular basis, searching for sappers in the perimeter wires or other little people near the perimeter with mortars or rockets. The uneventful night dragged on.

Some aircraft have fixed ammo boxes by the gun mounts and some don't. This particular slick didn't. Instead it sat on the deck and as I began to feel more comfortable with my station I looked down to notice that the vibration of the chopper had shifted the ammo box back toward my seat so I decided to slide it back next to the gun for a better feed. When I did the chopper banked and out went the box, ammo and all. Suddenly I felt stupid, like I was some dumb-ass clerk trying to pass himself off as a door gunner, which I was. Not knowing what to do and fearing I would come up short if we ran into trouble, I crossed over and informed Dillinger who immediately checked out my gun well.

"No sweat," he told me. "Just stay on your gun and don't tell anybody. We'll be down soon and take care of it then."

When we set down for the night the pilot and co-pilot immediately left us to tie down the main rotor blade and secure the aircraft. It was then Dillinger told me that they usually secured the loose boxes with a utility belt. "Oops, forgot to tell ya, sorry," was all he could say, then decided the important thing now was to replace the ammo so that no one would know we had screwed up. I was all for that and Dillinger's solution was simple, we had to make it someone else's problem by borrowing someone else's ammo from some other aircraft, preferably an aircraft from another company. Slithering around in the dark among the many available choppers, and hoping not to be mistaken for enemy sappers, we just happened to come across two perfect candidates in the form of visiting Air Cav birds that had put in for the night.

Now, from the Ghostriders' point of view there were two enemies in the Vietnam War; one being the communists and the other being the arrogant Air Cav who on many occasions claimed to be winning the war all by themselves. Therefore we had no qualms whatsoever about confiscating ammo from an Air Cav chopper.

"Air Cav. Hate those bastards," said crew chief Dillinger as we lifted the heavy metal case of ammo from their Huey.

"Why's that," I asked, as I quietly as possible slid the Air Cav chopper door closed.

"Shit, you don't know?"

"Know what?"

"About that night. At the club."

"What night?"

Dillinger began telling me the story while we walked the 75 yards or so to our chopper carrying the confiscated ammo.

"The Air Cav. Those bastards think their shit don't stink but I can't tell ya how many times we snatched them right out of the fires of hell. I guess they're just like the rest of us but shit, they're so uppity with those dumb damn cowboy hats and all that shit. Anyway, a whole bunch of 'em, maybe eight, nine choppers rolled in one night. Had to RON, you know, remain overnight because of the weather and they all decided to go to the EM club for drinks. It was one of the nights we had some Dink band from the Philippines playin' and since most everybody was grounded most of us Ghostriders decided to head up and tie one on. Even some of the pilots joined us," he added, looking at me with a smile. "Guess you figured out by now that Pilot Officers aren't normal officers. They don't mind mingling with the hired help, ya know?"

"Yeah, I know," I said. "I almost was one."

"No shit. You were a WOC?"

I offered an embarrassed affirmative with a simple nod.

"Washed outa the program, huh," laughed Dillinger. "Don't sweat it man, you're not the only one. But it don't mean nothin' here. Like Chief Chief says, 'we're all equal in the eyes of the enemy's gun sights'."

"Who's Chief Chief?"

"Pilot named Zamboni. He was there that night. Crazy sum'bitch. You'll meet 'em," explained Dillinger. "Anyway these damn Air Cav cowboys rolled into the club struttin' their shit as usual and started drinkin' and havin' a good time. You know, just like us. No big deal I guess, until it was time for the Dink band to play *The Song*."

"*The Song*?" I asked as I slid the door back on our chopper exposing the gun well.

"*The Song*, man. Our song," said Dillinger as he set the metal ammo box on the deck, reached into a small compartment and pulled out a standard G.I. utility belt then rigged it to the box. "That's how ya do it. Got it?"

"Got it," I said. "So what about this song?"

"Okay, you know about the Animal's song, right? You know, the one the Animal's sing? I mean the *we gotta get outa this place* song?"

"Yeah sure," I answered. "It's like a national anthem around here."

"Yeah well, this is Ghostrider country and no band is ever gonna come play at Holloway if they can't play the Animal's song and the *Ghostriders in the Sky* song. That's *the song*, man, Ghostriders in the Sky, and it's usually played on request maybe two or three times a night, and it's also always the last song of the show."

"I think I'm starting to get the picture," I said. "Like maybe the Cav guys weren't music lovers."

"You got that right," agreed Dillinger. "So we're all drunker than shit right, and the band is singin', 'we gotta get outa this place, if it's the last thing we ever do,' and we're all singing along and laughin' and throwin' beer and pretzels and shit, and so's the Air Cav and that's okay. But then comes the request and the band starts playing Ghostriders in the Sky and the Cav guys start booing and shit, and then they start singing '*You* gotta get outa this place...' over top our song, *The Song*."

I lit up a cigarette and climbed onto the seat in the gunner's well, watching Dillinger's animated delivery of the Air Cav story. I knew it was about to get good but had no idea how good.

"Can you imagine that? Those fuckers messin' up *our song* like that? And in *our place* too. And it wasn't like they insulted just us Ghostriders. I mean there were a lot of guys from other companies from around the battalion, Head Hunters, Gladiators, Panthers and some RON Bikinis and Gators, all 52nd Flyin' Dragons, who didn't like it either. It's like me and my brothers, ya know? We would fight all the time but if anybody else in the neighborhood messed with any of us we'd all get together and kick their ass, ya know? Anyway, these guys start singin' real loud so we start singin' louder and we all start standing up on the tables and on that long bar singin' louder and louder 'till you could hardly even hear the band. Then it happened."

"What," I smiled, soaking up Dillinger's story like some wide-eyed kid watching a Johnny Weissmuller Tarzan movie for the first time, and thinking this had only been the stuff of movies.

"It was Chief Chief. In the middle of all this shit this drunken Cav guy tells Chief Chief, who was just kind of minding his own business and laughing at the whole damn thing, that the Ghostrider song wasn't our song but that it belonged to the Cav, and not only can't the Ghostriders sing but they can't fly for shit either. He tells Chief Chief that we weren't Ghostriders in the sky like the song says but that we were just cows or turkeys in Volkswagen microbuses or some stupid shit like that. Hey man, you don't ever tell a Ghostrider pilot he can't fly for shit. So Chief Chief cold-cocks this dude right in the face with a full can of Pabst Blue Ribbon and all hell breaks loose like we're in some damn John Wayne movie or something. You know, the big Duke, like one of those big bar brawls in his flicks."

"No shit?" I said.

"No shit," said Dillinger. "But that isn't all. I mean, it really got crazy. So bad somebody called the SPs. Those security patrol guys came in like they owned the place but nobody gave a damn and started kicking their asses too. Threw them all right out the door. So then more guys from the security detachment showed up and got their asses kicked and thrown out the door too. So the next thing you know the SPs start tossing in tear gas."

"Oh man," I said, remembering the Nha Trang shit cloud.

"Yeah, you got that right. Nasty shit, but it didn't matter. I mean everybody was pissed and pretty much so damn drunk it didn't matter and they took the CS canisters and tossed them back out the door to keep the SPs away. Crazy right?"

"Yeah," I said, lighting another cigarette.

"Anyway, to make a long story short, there were so many people messed up in that thing that nobody ended up getting in trouble. I mean, there were officers in there, ours and theirs, who weren't supposed to be, and the SPs were all embarrassed 'cause they got their asses kicked, and the Cav guys were all embarrassed and didn't want everybody in Nam knowin' they got their asses kicked, and let's face it, you couldn't lock everybody up because there wouldn't be anybody left to fight the war, right? And then there's that Colonel Chestnut, you know, our battalion CO with all those fuckin' middle initials. He doesn't want any bad shit in his 201 'cause he wants to make General or God or something so it was like nothing ever happened, just another day on the farm. But I tell ya, the Ghostriders sure as hell earned a lot of respect that night, and that wasn't the best part. You can't even guess the best part."

"Don't tell me," I said. "You ripped off the Cav's Stetsons. I've heard about those."

"No. I mean, yeah we did, and we burned 'em in effigy and some of 'em we filled with shit and air dropped over the Cav compound at Radcliff. I think somebody got a medal for that, but that wasn't the best part. The best part was that Dink band. Those little dudes were scared shitless the whole time. You could see it. I mean those slant eyes got seriously big and round but those little bastards just kept on playin'. The whole time they just kept on playin' Ghostriders in the Sky, so we gave them all patches and made them all honorary Ghostriders."

"And that's it?" I asked.

"Hell, isn't that enough?"

"Nobody died?"

"Nah. Just lots of blood and stitches and broken shit."

"Wish I could have been there."

"Hey man, I just put you there. You're the pencil right. So maybe someday you'll write about it."

"Oh yeah, right," I laughed. "As if anybody would believe the shit that's happening here, or even care. Hell, you know what it's like back home. Peace, love and dope. They don't want to hear about this place."

"Yeah. Guess your right."

"So who's this Chief Chief guy?"

"Tomorrow's Sunday. You working the HQ tomorrow? If you can get off I can get you on the gun with me and Chief Chief. Some rat fuck mission flyin' convoy cover for the 4th Infantry out near An Khe. Helping out the 119th Gators who need some wrench time."

"Top usually gives me a free hand on Sundays. But I've got to get the morning report out first."

"We'll lift off early, about 0600."

"Okay, I'll get Randy to cover but aren't you afraid I might lose my ammo?" I laughed as I hopped down and slid the door closed.

Dillinger chuckled as he lit a cigarette. We walked through the darkness toward the company area with the heavy M-60s thrown over our shoulders. "I'd be more concerned about you losing your nerve or your head but you're okay. I can usually tell about guys. Some freeze up and fuck up first time out but you'll do okay.

You'll just piss your pants and keep on shootin'. You'll catch on," he laughed.

"Oh, thanks a lot," I laughed.

We walked across the broad expanse of the PSP main pad and I noticed for the first time how quiet and peaceful it was. The runway was lined with revetments constructed of faded green sand bags and 50-gallon drums full of dirt. In the protective revetments were parked some of the Huey Slicks and Huey Cobra gun ships. Nearby were a few of the new generation AH-1G Cobras belonging to the 361st Pink Panthers, sitting there in the darkness with their narrow profile and staggered tandem cockpit, they looked more like fighter jets than helicopters and appeared threateningly awesome with their mini-guns below the nose and multiple rocket pods under abbreviated wings. Everything about our battalion's arsenal was impressive to me, exciting, like when I freely roamed the halls and grounds of the Naval Academy back home as a boy, marveling at the tradition and history and power of it all, the old heavy cannons, long intimidating torpedoes and other war memorabilia from the past. Here, however, it was yet to become tradition and the history was still being written.

"So, you actually shit in an Air Cav hat?" I asked.

He smiled as he exhaled the smoke from his cigarette into the darkness, "Fuckin' A I did. Twice."

Dillinger filled me in on a few things I should take care of if I was to fly on a more regular basis and the next morning I managed to take care of all of them except one. That is, after I had suffered through an early cold shower.

It was Sunday and there were no mama-sans puttering around the sinks and commodes as usual, which I hardly even noticed. I was too dead on my feet to notice anything, having had less than three hours sleep. Fortunately the CQ got me up on time as requested. It was all I could do to just stand there in that damn cold water while cursing my own ambitions. While my family jewels shrunk with the dropping temperature of the water they seemed to retreat even more as I ran through my mind what Dillinger told me the night before.

"Get you a side arm from the armory when you check out your 60 in the morning," he told me. "They'll probably give you one of those shitty .38 revolvers but don't sweat it 'cause you can trade with a pilot later. Pilots are issued .45 automatics but for some reason most of them like the .38s better and will trade. Don't know why. Guess they all think they're Roy Rogers or somethin'. Also be sure and bring your 16 with ammo. Might need it if we get shot down. You can get a chicken plate if you want one. It's up to you. Actually they're required and they help but they tend to get in the way. And bring your steel pot and flack jacket in case we get stuck on the ground. You can sit on the flack jacket for extra protection. It might keep you from getting' your ass chewed up or your balls shot off. Actually, I prefer to wear the jacket and sit on the chicken plate. And oh yeah, when you get a chance pick up an extra nomex flight shirt and take it up to the tailor shop on the hill and have them sew some Lieutenant's or Warrant bars on the collar. And be sure it's got your name on it to. Either that or get some LT or Warrant collar brass."

"What the hell for?" I asked.

"Two reasons," answered Dillinger. "One is, if we get shot down and you live through the crash and it looks like you're going to get captured, you need to be wearin' officer rank. If you're an officer they take you prisoner because they think you know shit. If you're a crewman they'll just do your ass right there and leave you to rot."

"No shit," I said, surprised.

"No shit. And they're not too nice about it either. We had a chopper go down somewhere over around Happy Valley and when we finally got in to the crash site we found the pilot dead in his seat full of rounds taken in the air and the crew chief killed in the crash. The Peter Pilot was missing."

"What about the gunner," I asked, as Dillinger knew I would.

"We found him about sixty yards away tied to a tree. They had cut off his dick and nuts and shoved 'em in his mouth then stuck his own knife in his chest with a note that said, *G.I. talk too much – fuck too much,* and left him there to bleed to death. Ya see they took the co-pilot, the officer. They took him prisoner. I don't know what they do to the prisoners, but hell, it can't be any worse than what they did to that gunner. So you get a shirt with some bars on it or some bars you can stick on your collar if you're going to fly CAs and shit. And if they're gonna' get your ass you bury your enlisted tags and be wearing those bars."

"What's the second?" I asked.

"What?"

"You said there were two reasons. What's the second reason?"

"Oh yeah. It's to get you in the Officer's Club at the Pleiku Air Force Base. That damn base is like stateside, fat mattresses, outdoor theaters, a big PX, hot damn water all the time, and the O-Club has steak dinners for a buck-twenty-five, double drinks for fifty cents, movies and bands all night long. Hell, you name it and those Air Force bastards got it. They even got camo fatigues. Can you imagine that? Their security guys are wearing camo fatigues like they're gonna go boogie around in the boonies or something. The Army grunts don't get 'em and our pathfinders gotta go buy 'em on the black market. They can't get camo issue but those air force dicks are standing at the gate all spit shined in camo fatigues and berets like they know what this war's all about. Shit. Anyway, every once in a while we just so happen to RON there for weather or mechanical reasons and when we do we head for the O-Club. Nothing like a night at the O-Club to get your chopper up and running again. Know what I mean?"

I got everything on Dillinger's recommended list except the extra nomex flight shirt with the officer's bars that I definitely planned to get as soon as possible. We met on the pad by his aircraft not far from the maintenance hanger. He was busy crawling all over the chopper, checking everything from the engine and the eight-track player he had mounted under his seat to, of course, the Jesus Nut securing the main rotor. As I secured and mounted my M-60 and secured its ammo box I looked up to catch my first glimpse of our pilot, one Chief Warrant Officer Fox Zamboni, as he walked out of the dark shadows of the maintenance hanger into the dim early morning light and across the cool hard PSP. He wasn't much taller than I but moved with a confident stride as though he was at least six foot two. Dark hair, slightly dark complexion, flight helmet on, suited up, ready to fly, and… taking a swig of vodka from a fifth he just pulled from his back pocket.

Crew chief Dillinger climbed down off the chopper and started checking my gun mounting job and other preparations.

"Okay. You're lookin' good here," he said. "Get any sleep?"

"Not really," I said.

"S'okay. You can catch some shuteye in the air. Convoy cover's kind of laid back. Usually not much happening."

"Is that Zamboni?" I asked, nodding toward the pilot walking toward us.

"The great CW2 Chief Chief Zamboni, live and in person," answered Dillinger.

"Um, did I just see him take a swig of vodka at six in the morning?"

"No sweat," said Dillinger. "He doesn't get drunk. There's something wrong with his metabolism or something. He could drink the state of Kentucky dry and still fly better than any pilot in Nam."

"No shit?"

"No shit. Doctors can't figure it out."

"I don't think that's possible," I said.

"It's possible. Believe me, we tried. Poured so much alcohol down his gullet one night woulda drowned a whale and it didn't even faze him. He can drink anything, and I mean anything, and just keep on cruising like he's on mother's milk."

"If he can't get drunk then why the hell does he drink?"

"Some guys smoke or chew gum, he sips a little Smirnoff. Says it's his tolerance medication. Calls it *Put Up* juice. Keeps him just mellow enough to put up with the Army chickenshit and all the bad stuff."

"I thought that was a real serious no no, drinking and flying," I said with concern.

"Not with him. He's one of the best in the Army. Like I said, he's got that condition. But listen, nobody and I mean nobody goes on missions if they're boozin' or dopin'. At least not intentionally. You stay dry in the sky and you go home standing up. You get high in the sky and you die and go home in a box. You remember that. If you got a crewman that's fucked up you kick his ass back on the PSP. You're better off without him."

"So what's with the Chief Chief thing?" I asked.

Dillinger just laughed then climbed in and across the deck to the right side of the chopper, greeting Chief Chief Zamboni who opened the pilot's door and tossed in his bag. I could swear I heard the clank of a bottle or two when it landed on the seat. After glancing at the logbook Chief Chief Zamboni worked his way around the chopper, inspecting the tail boom, tail rotor, then on around until he came to me. I watched his every move as best I could, trying not to be obvious as well as trying not to appear like some inexperienced proletarian idiot.

He stopped right in front of me, looked me dead in the eyes and said, "You don't know shit do you?"

I thought right there that my first scheduled mission just got unscheduled until Chief Chief grew a wide smile, wrapped his arm around my neck, and strolled us both across the PSP about thirty feet away from the chopper. He then turned us back around to face the aircraft and said with great authority, "That is an aircraft, a helicopter to be precise. It flies. I am the aircraft commander, a pilot. A helicopter pilot to be precise. I drive. You are an air crewman, a gunner to be precise. You shoot. If I tell you to fart in the wind, you fart in the wind, and if I tell you to shoot, you shoot. Affirmative?" He turned my neck lose then faced me and extended his large hand. "Chief Chief Zamboni," he introduced himself.

"Got it. Affirmative," I answered as I extended my hand. "Fusco. Vincent Fusco."

"Welcome aboard, Fusco. Don't fuck up," he said with a smile, then walked away and continued his pre-flight.

Dillinger chuckled and seeing that our co-pilot had arrived on the other side of the aircraft said, "Full crew, Chief Chief. Time to fly."

A few minutes later after Chief Chief and the co-pilot whizzed through their check list we lifted up and away, rising above and along the runway, out of the pattern and into the wild blue yonder. Suddenly from nowhere there appeared two gun ships from the Ghostrider Avenger platoon. I sat on the side of the aircraft like some idiot tourist on a paid ride over the Grand Canyon, fascinated by the wind and noise of the turbine, and the powerful throbbing vibration of the blades. I was leaning forward, checking out the landscape and the sight of the gun ships flying in our formation, when Dillinger tapped me on the helmet. I turned to find him holding my COM cord in hand and pointing to my ear. He plugged it in, gave me a thumbs up, then returned to the gun well on his side of the aircraft.

Yeah, I felt stupid.

"How 'bout a COM check there Gunner Fusco?" came Chief Chief Zamboni's voice into my ears.

Not knowing what was expected in a COM check, and at the risk of appearing to be a total fool, I decided to just strike up a conversation. "Chief Chief Zamboni, sir."

"Cut that *sir* shit, Fusco. It makes me feel old," replied Chief Chief.

"Roger, Chief Chief. But I was wondering."

Glancing over to the front of the aircraft as I spoke, I saw Chief Chief look to the co-pilot with a smile and I could swear I saw his lips say, "Here it comes."

"You were wondering what, gunner Fusco?" asked Chief Chief.

"I was wondering, why do they call you Chief Chief, Chief Chief?"

"Because I'm a Chief," said Chief Chief.

"Right, I mean, roger. But why do they call you Chief Chief?"

"Because I'm a Chief," repeated Chief Chief.

"Got it. I mean, roger. Affirmative. You're a Chief Warrant Officer but why do they call you Chief Chief?"

"Because I'm a Chief, gunner Fusco."

I decided that Chief Chief was screwing with me so I simply sat there without comment for a long moment. Hell, I wasn't new to head games and locker room bullshit, and if Chief Chief got his jollies with a weird confusing call sign then okay, I'd let it ride. But I couldn't stand it for long and had to try again.

"Okay, Chief Chief, I give up. Why do they call you Chief Chief?"

"Because I'm a Chief," repeated Chief Chief.

I could see the co-pilot look to Chief Chief and chuckle. Okay, I thought, this guy's a broken record and had one fifth of vodka too many for breakfast, and it's more than just his metabolism that's off. After a few minutes I suppose Chief Chief decided he couldn't leave me dangling there on the side of the chopper in the gun well in ignorance and would finally cut me some slack.

"I am Running Fox Zamboni, Chief of the Turtle Clan People who live on a reservation in the Dakota Bad Lands. I am an Indian Chief who is also a Chief Warrant Officer. I am therefore Chief Chief Zamboni. Got it gunner Fusco?"

"A Chief who's a Chief," I laughed. "I got it, Chief Chief."

As Chief Chief said, he was really a Chief who was a Chief and considered it his duty and honor to serve as a warrior for his country and in doing so was highly respected by his people. As odd as it may sound, Chief Chief would explain to me later during one of our future RONs at the Air Force Base, American Indians (they weren't fashionably called Native Americans as yet) are among the most patriotic of all Americans and consider it a great honor to serve as warriors in the military, and likewise have a great deal of respect for other Americans who do the same, *"Even door gunners who lose their ammo,"* laughed Chief Chief.

"Hard to believe isn't it?" Chief Chief would say. "After getting screwed, blued, and tattooed by the white man, here I am in a foreign country saving his peachy ass on a regular basis."

As for the *Zamboni* part of Chief Chief's name, Chief Chief claims his mother, Princess Sliding Goose, who once had dreams and ambitions of winning a spot on the Olympic ice skating team, and who unlike Chief Chief had a metabolism unfavorable to alcohol, got sidetracked at the Olympic tryouts when she met some guy with an ice fetish who liked to create experimental slushy cocktails. After partaking in some of those experimental cocktails, Chief Chief's mother woke up the next day and realized she had missed her Olympic trials. Her newfound lover was so guilt ridden and repentant that he invented a large ice shaving machine for the sole purpose of improving her chances of making the team the next time around. Though the Zamboni ice machine was extremely successful, Chief Chief's mother never again donned her skates because soon after came the future little Chief Chief.

"But I never met my father," Chief Chief added. "They got married and he died soon after when he fell through the ice on a lake testing his new invention. Then my father's brother stole the design and got rich selling Zamboni ice machines all over the world."

"You mean you never got a dime?" I asked.

"Not a friggin' penny," answered Chief Chief. "But I got something better."

"Better than being rich?" I asked.

"Yep. You see, after years of experimenting with all those frozen cocktails and chemical additives, my old man built up a complete immunity to alcohol and somehow passed that immunity on to me. Do you have any idea what that means to an Indian?" he said, after gulping down a triple scotch.

Being the son of Princess Sliding Goose and possessing the most amazing and impressive drinking prowess of any Indian on the reservation, in fact in the nation, Chief Chief was clearly the most obvious candidate for the position of Chief of his tribe. And being a popular young Chief, Chief Chief was expected by all the members of his tribe to become a warrior and go the way of Elvis who was a big favorite on his reservation because of a rumor he was part Cherokee and because he dyed his hair black after serving as an Army warrior in cold war Germany. Naturally Chief Chief did as expected and went to see one of those car salesman recruiters, took the FAST Test and the Officer Liar's Test, got a Certificate of Guarantee for Fixed Wing Training then successfully completed helicopter flight school, in spite of the yellow pink slips. Chief Chief Zamboni was a true military marvel.

We rendezvoused with the convoy, an element of the 4th Infantry that was heading west on highway 19 from somewhere in the Binh Dinh Province, and were joined by an LOH or Loach scout chopper from the 119th. As Dillinger said it was a fairly boring assignment. The road below wound through a lush jungle in a semi mountainous area and the convoy of trucks just wound along with it. I watched as the small Loach, sometimes referred to as a Little Boy, flew below, bobbing and weaving at low altitude ahead of the convoy, trying to draw fire and looking for signs of a possible ambush. The only other thing to break the monotony was Dillinger's eight-track tape player he had mounted under his seat in the gun well on which he now played Merle Haggard tunes that he somehow piped into the COM system. I wouldn't have thought Merle Haggard would have been the choice of a blond haired boy from California but found out later that Dillinger was actually born and raised in Oklahoma. He had married a Navy brat whose feet were securely planted in the salty seaside turf of the west coast and she planted him there as well. Watching Vietnam go by and listening to Merle Haggard moaning something about his failed love life had almost dulled my senses until one of the pilots in one of the Huey Hogs keyed his mike and addressed Chief Chief.

"Ghostrider Two-Five. Avenger One-Seven."

"Two-Five," acknowledged Chief Chief.

"Hey Chief Chief. Since you're the boss of this here flying fête, what you say we find us a topless go-go joint and drop in for a pint or two?"

"Oh hell, is that you Pully? You back on the farm again?"

"You know damn well it is. In the flesh... and the AC seat as usual."

"What's the matter, Pully," asked Chief Chief, "You don't know what to do when you got both hands occupied? That's typical."

"I'm workin' on it," returned Pully. "But sometimes I get confused. This is a helicopter right? And I know one of these sticks goes up and down and the other one goes round and round, but I'll be damned if I can find the steering wheel anywhere. Why don't you walk over here and help me out."

"I knew it. I knew all those rumors were true," said Chief Chief.

"And what rumors are those, Chief Chief?"

"All those rumors about you learning to fly in the Peoples Republic of Burbank,"

"Not true. not true, my man. It was the Mexican National Air Force. And I have a perfect flying record. I haven't left an aircraft in the sky yet and don't intend to."

"Hey, that's pretty damn impressive there Pully. What's your secret?"

"Well, I always try and stay in the middle of the air, ya know? It's a lot safer that way. There's no trees and things."

Pully Johnson was just plain crazy and everybody knew that Pully Johnson was crazy, but in Vietnam a crazy helicopter pilot was much more highly regarded than any other pilot because a crazy pilot would go anywhere and do anything to get the job done, which usually translated to saving lives. A crazy pilot would fly a chopper where choppers can't be flown and would land a chopper where choppers couldn't be landed, and then in most cases raise that chopper up through hell's own fire like the mythical phoenix. It was that kind of crazy that gained the Ghostriders their reputation and motto of *Anywhere Anytime*. And even though Pully and Chief Chief were both considered to be that good kind of crazy, as were most helicopter pilots, that's not the kind of crazy most people generally thought of when they thought of Pully Johnson.

To begin, Pully Johnson wasn't really Pully Johnson's real name, even though everybody in the 52nd Aviation Battalion knew him as Pully Johnson. In fact they also knew him by a number of other names such as Peter Pan, Peter Piper, and Peter Pecker, but the most familiar and long-lasting label was *Pully Johnson* the *Peter Pilot & Master-Baiter*. Even though Pully Johnson was a true AC and not a peter pilot, a name used to refer to a co-pilot, the name Peter Pilot was probably more aptly used when referring to Pully Johnson than any other pilot. Pully Johnson's real name was Reginald Roosevelt Hightower, which was a perfectly good name. The name Pully Johnson, however, was a title earned by reputation because CW2 Reginald Roosevelt Hightower, better known as Pully Johnson, spent all of his spare time literally pulling on his *Johnson*.

Pully pulled on his Johnson without embarrassment or any inhibitions whatsoever at just about every opportunity and at the most unlikely of places simply because Pully wanted to get out of the Army. Pully had pulled his pud while standing at attention during the raising of the flag at battalion, and Pully had even pulled his pud in the face of the enemy while standing on top of a bunker at an SF base camp during an attack. Unfortunately for Pully, however, all his public pulling ever managed to do was get him transferred out of and into literally every flight company in the 52nd Combat Aviation Battalion, and being a truly crazy and talented pilot who lived to fly, Pully quickly and remarkably became qualified and excelled in flying literally every kind of aircraft in the battalion inventory as well as many that weren't, which was nearly every kind of aircraft known to the Army at the time. Therefore Pully became one of the most accomplished pilots in the history of U.S. Army aviation and as such was considered too valuable an asset to squander away on an early-out discharge or a transfer to the states for psychiatric care. It was said that Pully was so good that he was the only known pilot to actually pull off a barrel roll with a helicopter and that he once actually rolled an AH-1 Cobra full over just to win a bet.

The crème de la crème of Pully's efforts came on the day he received his second Distinguished Flying Cross and the Silver Star.

The awards ceremony took place on a surprisingly clear day during the summer monsoon season and was attended by visiting dignitaries that included none other than Secretary of Defense Melvin Laird who just happened to be touring in the neighborhood. The ceremony was the last event of the day on the Secretary's schedule. Immediately after presenting the awards the sky opened up and down poured the rain. Everyone scattered and scurried, including the Secretary and the accompanying South Vietnamese dignitaries who were hustled up the back ramp of their waiting Chinook helicopter. After everyone was seated and the large rotary blades cranked up and began turning, the crew chief went to close the back ramp only to be suddenly frozen in his tracks at what he saw outside the door. When the wife of one of the Vietnamese dignitaries gasped everyone looked out the back of the Chinook to discover the unflappably determined hero, Chief Warrant Officer Reginald Roosevelt Hightower, alias Pully Johnson, standing there in the rain with his medals glistening, his nomex down around his ankles, and his Johnson at full attention. Needless to say, as the ramp slowly closed everyone noticed that Pully's farewell salute was not quite regulation.

It was later explained by Lieutenant Colonel Silas J.J.J.W. Chestnut to Secretary Laird who wanted to court martial and castrate the offending Warrant Officer, that Pully's actions were the temporary result of the extreme stress experienced during the combat action in which he had won his medals, which Lieutenant Colonel Silas J.J.J.W. Chestnut added that he could personally avow and testify, (even though he wasn't there). The medical term is *Post Traumatic Stress* Lieutenant Colonel Silas J.J.J.W. Chestnut told Secretary Laird, while mentally patting himself on the back for being so creative and quick on his feet as to invent the convincing bogus psychological medical term right there on the spot. The Secretary was so impressed and sympathetically moved by Chestnut's explanation, and so confused and distracted by Lieutenant Colonel Silas J.J.J.W .Chestnut's name and many initials, that he arranged the awarding of a Silver Star to the Colonel as well for being able to personally attest to Pully's combat incident of valor. The Secretary then went back to Washington and suggested to the Medical Corps and Veterans Administration that they start doing something about Post

Traumatic Stress before it becomes rampant and an embarrassment to the entire United States military.

Following that incident Pully was no longer recommended for any more medals because no one was sure how he would behave at the ceremonies, but oddly enough, due to the example of Lieutenant Colonel Silas J.J.J.W. Chestnut's Silver Star, Pully became a medal magnet for higher ranking officers who only flew once a month to fulfill their two hour minimum requirement in order to maintain their flight status and receive flight pay and accumulate Air Medals. To fly with Pully almost always guaranteed they would receive a medal for valor because Pully, even though he hated the Army, was a combat junky and pilot extraordinaire who somehow always managed to accomplish some form of heroic action. Pully was damned if he did and damned if he didn't, and damned if he was going to give up. Pully simply continued to *pound* away at the Army in hopes of securing a Section-8 endorsement and a ride home, all the while inadvertently building a reputation for daring and gallantry and heroism and, of course… *professionalism,* even if it did include some *sleight of hand initiative.*

"Hey, Chief Chief," came Pully's voice through the thin air. "Me and my FNG co-pilot here say you can't set that thar air truck down on that thar empty flatbed truck in the middle of that thar convoy."

"Is that thar right?" answered Chief Chief. "Well, I got me a virgin door gunner over here says that thar cherry peter pilot of yours needs to put some money where his mouth is. Isn't that correct Gunner Fusco?"

"Um… roger that, Chief Chief," I choked, wondering how the hell I suddenly became part of their sky-high tête-à-tête.

"My virgin gunner says fifty bucks," challenged Chief Chief.

I looked down the more than two thousand feet to the convoy. The empty flatbed truck suddenly looked like a postage stamp and was just as suddenly getting smaller as I imagined the possibilities of failure.

"That's affirmative, Ghostrider two-five. Fifty it is," accepted Pully. "Straight patch of road coming up. Avenger one-seven says put up or shut up."

Without another word our Huey Slick dove for the convoy below and all of a sudden I started thinking about the pucker factor and how it needed more numbers. Chief Chief came in behind the flatbed, descending to about 50 feet, lined up and then descended down to a few inches above the trailer. From my perch at what seemed like nearly ground level the roadside scenery flew by faster than I could take it in and I could swear, but wasn't sure, we flew past something that was full of people, chickens, and pigs that ended up spread all over the roadside ditch. I was also occasionally glancing at Chief Chief who I could swear was laughing the entire time. He eased the chopper on up to the middle of the flatbed trailer behind the truck cab and set one skid down on the edge. When I looked down on my side of the aircraft I could see that the chopper was too wide and just wasn't going to fit and hoped that Chief Chief could see the same through the chin bubble. We steadily maintained that position on only one skid as the flatbed cruised down the road until our presence gained the attention of the driver who turned to discover our magnificent flying machine bouncing on the back of his truck. The surprise on his face was priceless. Suddenly the truck began to swerve and Chief Chief wisely pulled pitch and up we went.

As we gained altitude another voice came over the airwaves.

"Ghostrider Two-Five, this is Gator Six."

"Ghostrider Two-Five," acknowledged Chief Chief, glancing over his shoulder to discover a formation of choppers from the 119th Gators. Gator Six was their Commanding Officer.

"Ghostrider did I just observe you dancing with a flatbed truck?"

"Uh, just a little waltz, there, Gator Six."

"Well, I just wanted to thank you, Ghostrider. That *dien cai dau* shit just won me a hundred bucks."

"Oh, you're quite welcome, Gator Six. Anytime." answered Chief Chief.

"I know you kids would like to stay here and play with your trucks but your presence is requested near Plei Me, chop chop," said Gator Six. "Leave the little bird with us but take that pervert Pully Johnson and his hogs with you," he added.

The Gators relieved us from the convoy cover assignment being they were on a re-supply mission with a load of replacements, beans and bullets destined for the same FSB as the trucks. Once relieved we were diverted to assist in an extraction taking place somewhere west of the Plei Me Special Forces camp in the Ia Drang Valley involving an SF team and a few ARVNs. Upon our arrival we joined three other slicks from the 57th Gladiators and were instructed to orbit and wait our turn to make a pick up. Our Avenger gun ships provided cover with some direction from the ground while the first two Gladiator slicks extracted half the ground team that included two wounded, out of the small pickup zone.

"You with me back there, Fusco?" I heard Chief Chief say.

"Roger that, Chief Chief," I said, nervous as hell.

"Good. Now listen up. All our boys are in the PZ and the bad guys are in the tree line. When we go in I want you to cover our asses and spray that tree line and pepper any damn thing that moves or shoots back. Copy?"

"Copy that, Chief Chief."

"But don't shoot the good guys. That tends to piss them off. You copy?"

"Roger that, Chief Chief."

We followed the next Gladiator ship into the small pickup zone, a PZ that was barely large enough for two choppers. Both ships, however, managed to set down at nearly the exact same time and as we did I killed as many trees as I could with a series of short burst, not ceasing fire until an SF sergeant and a Ranger grunt approached with three NVA prisoners in tow. The Ranger quickly loaded the POWs, seating them against the bulkhead, then he settled opposite on the deck behind the co-pilot where he could keep his weapon and an eye on all three. The sergeant on the ground looked over to Chief Chief who had just pulled a fifth of Smirnoff from inside his flight vest.

Spotting the bottle the SF sergeant perked up and yelled over the noise of the chopper, "That you Chief Chief?"

Chief Chief turned, recognized the sergeant and smiled, "How you been doin' Stumper?" He then reached down into his bag and pulled out a new full fifth of Smirnoff and tossed it to the sergeant who caught it with a smile.

"Same-same war, same-same shit, Chief Chief," said Stumper. "Thank you much," he said, holding up and acknowledging the receipt of the bottle, then shoving it in his pocket. He pointed to the POWs and said, "Special delivery for MACV," after which he made a jerking off motion with his hand.

Chief Chief laughed as his SF sergeant friend Stumper backed away from our chopper and ran off to join the rest of his team who had boarded the Gladiator slick. As soon as he climbed onto their bird it rose and pulled out of the small PZ. Before Chief Chief turned back to the cockpit we exchanged a quick glance and he gave me a reassuring wink of confidence. Suddenly above the impatient screaming throb of the engine I heard the sharp repeat of enemy fire then saw a rocket from Pully's Hog above rip up the trees about forty-five yards away. I sent a few brief burst of fire into the same area, then to my surprise there came the AC's voice.

"There are three major rules of survival in this world, Gunner Fusco," Aircraft Commander Chief Chief Zamboni's voice crackled in my headset.

He finished off his fifth of vodka and tossed the empty bottle to the back of the chopper where it struck an NVA prisoner square between the eyes. At the same moment a riff of enemy AK-47 fire splattered across the front of the aircraft punching a few holes in the windscreen, missing the pilots by inches and causing all of us to constrict right off the pucker chart. Chief Chief gripped the controls, pulled pitch and quickly lifted and banked the chopper away from the PZ. Undaunted he continued offering up his words of wisdom.

"You never kiss a rattle snake on the lips. You never play marbles on the freeway. And you never, I repeat, you never take anything serious in the United States Army. Got that Fusco?"

"Roger that. Got it," I told Chief Chief as I again sprayed a few rounds into the bush. I was frightened and my mouth was dry as an uncooked bag of grits, but I managed to continue the conversation just the same, which was probably Chief Chief's intention. Keep the rookie talking so he won't freeze up and fuck up. "Does that include you, Chief Chief?" I asked.

"Especially me, Fusco," said Chief Chief

Just then the NVA prisoner who was struck by Chief Chief's empty Smirnoff bottle keeled over on to the deck. I checked and discovered he was dead.

"Oh shit. I think you killed him," I said, looking at the dead POW at my feet.

"What?"

"With the bottle. You killed a gook prisoner."

"Are you serious?" asked Chief Chief, glancing back over his shoulder.

"No, you just told me not to be. But he's dead."

"Are you serious?"

"No. But he's dead."

"No?"

"Yes!"

"Yes, he's dead! Are you serious?"

"No but yes. Why don't you believe me? He's dead. You killed him."

"I killed him. You're not serious."

"Okay then, maybe he kissed a rattlesnake, but he's still dead!"

"Are you serious?"

"No. What do I do?"

"What?"

"What do I do now?"

"Throw it out."

"Throw what out?"

"Yeah, just throw it out."

"Throw the gook out?"

"The bottle, Fusco, throw out the bottle," ordered Chief Chief. "Then throw out the gook."

"What! Are you serious?"

Not quite sure if I should take the order to toss the dead gook at face value, I decided to get a second opinion. After all, Chief Chief just told me not to take anything serious in the United States Army including him, and being this was my first mission, I really didn't want to be contrary or rock the boat, but then hell, this was serious.

Dillinger, now comfortably perched behind his gun on his side of the chopper, was oblivious to our situation resulting from Chief Chief's lethal vodka bottle. Thinking we were high and dry and safely clear of the PZ and enemy fire, he had wasted no time switching on the eight track player mounted under his seat and was now comfortably kicked back spewing out the lyrics of Merle Haggard's song *Okie From Muskogee* from the top of his lungs as though it was some kind of inspired religious experience. Fortunately for the rest of us, as we passed two thousand feet above the highlands at a hundred miles per hour, his toned-deaf performance was lost in the sound of the turbo engine and rushing wind, and the deep throated whop whop whop of the chopper's main rotor blades.

"We don't smoke marijuana in Muskogee," sang Dillinger and Merle Haggard. *"We don't take no trips on LSD."*

I unplugged myself from behind my gun, stepped over the dead POW, crossed over in front of the other POWs, and tapped Dillinger on the shoulder. "Chief Chief wants me to toss the dead gook off the chopper," I shouted over the noise of the aircraft and Merle Haggard. "What should I do?"

"We don't burn no draft cards down on Main Street. We like livin' right, and bein' free," Dillinger continued singing. Then seeing me, he left Merle to sing alone. "What? Say again? What?" He pulled his helmet away from his ear and leaned to me for better reception.

"I said Chief Chief wants to toss the gook off the chopper."

"What?" he yelled above the noise. "Toss a gook? Are you serious?"

"Yeah."

Dillinger thought a moment, shrugged his shoulders, then reached around and snatched one of the two still living NVA prisoners by the collar, yanked and tossed him out the side.

I couldn't believe what I saw and leaned out the side and watched the little man flail desperately about as he shot through the sky behind us. His free-fall tumbling through the crisp air of the highlands seemed to be an endless horizontal journey of doom. Endless, almost poetic, like some damn spastic ballet dancer in the Nutcracker Suite.

"OH SHIT!" I said.

"What's wrong?" yelled Oakie Dillinger.

"That one," I answered, pointing to the dead NVA on the deck. "He said to toss that one, the dead one, not the other one. The dead one!"

"What?"

"The dead one," I repeated, pointing to the dead gook.

"Hey man, what's wrong with that guy? He sick or somethin'?"

"He's dead."

"He's dead?"

"Yeah, he's dead."

The grunt sitting on the deck behind the co-pilot guarding the three, now only one remaining live prisoner, looked at the dead NVA, poked him in the head with the business end of his weapon and agreed, "Yep, he's dead."

Then together we agreed he was dead.

"He's dead," I said.

"He's dead," agreed Crew Chief Oakie Dillinger.

"Fuckers dead," agreed the grunt.

Dillinger assumed the death was an act of God, I thought it was the act of Chief Chief Zamboni's errant vodka bottle, and the grunt just didn't give a rat's ass either way. For him, another dead gook was just another step closer to home. What we didn't know was the NVA POW had caught one of his own countryman's AK rounds square in the heart at the exact same time he was beaned by Chief Chief's empty bottle, a double whammy that some G.I.s might possibly, in a stretch, consider an act of God but most would likely just call an unfortunate twist of fate. After agreeing he was dead the three of us looked to the remaining NVA prisoner to see if he agreed as well, but instead of joining in to make our prognosis unanimous, his eyes grew large and desperate and he began shaking and mumbling incoherently, and then to our complete surprise, he flung himself right out of the chopper.

"Oh Shit!" I said.

Seeing this, Dillinger just threw up his hands dismissing the entire affair and returned to his gunwell and the soothing comfort of Merle Haggard. As for the grunt, none of this fazed him in the least and taking advantage of his newly created passenger-only status, he settled back to cop a few Z's. Being the new guy on board and not sure what I should do, I simply stepped over the dead POW, returned to my gun seat and plugged back into the chopper's COM system where there came once again the crackling voice of Chief Chief Zamboni.

"Hey Gunner Fusco, you still with us back there?"

"Um, Roger that, Chief Chief."

"You toss out that bottle?"

I reached down and grabbed the guilty vodka bottle and tossing it out of the chopper replied, "Roger that, Chief Chief."

"You know I was just kiddin', right?"

"What?"

"The gook. You didn't actually throw out that dead gook did ya?"

"What?"

Suddenly Merle Haggard was piped into the COM system interrupting the conversation and the entire crew except for myself joined in and started crooning,

"I'm proud to be an Oakie from Muskogee..."

"What?" I said. "What? Just kidding?" I said. "Are you fuckin' serious!"

Looking out over the valleys in the distance I could see some of the multi-terraced fields being burned off in preparation for the new growing season. Viewing the distant drifting columns of smoke while taking in a deep abundance of the high cool air seemed to clear my mind. Then, as though I had become possessed by the space and altitude and the beat of the powerful chopper blades, I started humming along with Merle Haggard, an amazing thing considering how much I disliked country music.

CHAPTER 19

IF THIS IS TUESDAY
I MUST BE IN PLEIKU

"Have you found Jesus?"

"What?" I asked, looking up from typing another five-carbon copy of something that no one would ever read, including Major Anthony who would sign it.

"Have you found Jesus? You need to find Jesus. We all need to find Jesus. That's why I want you to sign my petition."

"Well, actually, I think he's in the service platoon, or maybe it's the motor pool," I said, looking up across my desk to the tall born-again CWO T.T.Thigpen. "Or maybe he's one of those guys who just pulls guard duty all the time. I'm not sure, but if you want to wait around he might show up. He mostly comes around here on Tuesdays and today's Tuesday. Isn't that right Randy, Tuesdays? Jesus usually comes by on Tuesdays?"

"Yeah, Tuesdays," agreed Randy, looking up from trying to look busy behind his desk opposite mine across the room.

"Yeah, mostly Tuesdays," I repeated. "And today's Tuesday."

CWO T.T.Thigpen handed me his petition, which I immediately noticed had no signatures on it except for that of CWO T.T.Thigpen.

"What's this?" I asked.

"A petition for Jesus," he said.

"Sir, I know the guy is a little strange and he could probably use a little mental help, but I don't think a petition will do any good. I mean, Top's not buyin' into his bullshit and I already told him that he doesn't DEROS for quite a while."

"Who?" asked CWO T.T.Thigpen.

"Jesus," I answered.

"Jesus has a DEROS date?" he asked, surprised.

"Well, sure. Doesn't everybody? I mean, we all have to go some time, right?"

"I suppose that's one way of looking at it," agreed CWO T.T.Thigpen.

"So what happens if you get enough signatures?" asked Randy.

"Then everything changes," answered CWO T.T.Thigpen.

"Just like that?" asked Randy.

"Just like that," repeated CWO T.T.Thigpen. "I have the battalion CO's word on it."

"You mean Colonel what's-his-nuts with all the middle names?" asked Randy.

"Yes, of course," answered CWO T.T.Thigpen. "Colonel Silas J.J.J.W. Chestnut, the battalion commander."

"Does Jesus know this?" I asked.

"Of course," said CWO T.T.Thigpen. "Jesus knows everything."

"Well, I really shouldn't sign it," I said, handing the petition back. "I don't think Top would appreciate it, and if I did and if the word got out that I was sympathetic to the cause, then I'd start getting every nut case in the Old and New Testaments rolling in here wanting to go home. Moses, John the Baptist, Barabas, probably even a Mother Mary or two."

CWO T.T.Thigpen took his petition and turned to Randy.

"Sure, I'll sign it," said Randy, reaching out and accepting the petition. "Jesus has got my vote."

"That's wonderful. Thank you," said CWO T.T.Thigpen.

Randy quickly signed the petition and CWO T.T.Thigpen quietly exited the orderly room.

"I can't believe you signed that," I said to Randy.

"Why not," he replied. "If it gets Jesus Martinez out of here then, hell, I'll start my own petition and get my own ass out of here. Besides, I didn't sign my real name."

"You didn't?"

"No. I never sign my real name. Where I come from people are always coming to the door with petitions so to save time I just sign them and send them on their way."

"So what did you sign?"

"Bing Crosby. You know, the singer? My mom likes Bing Crosby. But usually I sign Franklin Pierce because nobody knows who he was."

"Who's Franklin Pierce?"

"See what I mean."

"So, who's Franklin Pierce?"

"A president."

"Of what?"

"The United States."

"Are you sure?"

"Yeah I'm sure because I got it wrong on a test when I was in grade school and caught hell for it, right across the knuckles. I thought he invented something special like penicillin or Absorbine Junior or something. Boy was I wrong and boy I tell ya, those damn Nuns who teach in Catholic school got no tolerance for fuckin' up. That's why I'll never forget Franklin Pierce, and now Franklin Pierce is on every petition in New York. Serves him right for being so damn obscure."

Randy and I were both in the dark about the actual purpose of CWO T.T.Thigpen's petition because we didn't bother to read it and wrongfully assumed it was a petition concerning our usual Tuesday Jesus, but that didn't really matter. What did matter was Randy had just put CWO T.T.Thigpen's petition in motion. By signing Bing Crosby he had set a precedent for all other signatories. Inspired by Randy's bogus endorsement, guys all over Camp Holloway began signing CWO T.T.Thigpen's petition, but they were all signing the names of entertainment celebrities and other famous people. Everyone from Specialist Clark Gable and PFC Boris Karloff to Privates Ricky Nelson, James Brown, Ringo Starr, Sal Mineo, and Yogi Bear appeared on the list. And CWO T.T.Thigpen had no damn idea what was going on because he had led a secluded and sheltered life in the Midwest, absent of all the social influences of the media and cinema. Nevertheless, he was so exuberant about all the signatures he was collecting on his petition that he failed to even notice the one signature that should have immediately gained his attention and given away the entire ball game, that of Staff Sergeant Donald Duck. Hell, even CWO T.T.Thigpen should have known that Donald Duck was in the Navy.

CWO T.T.Thigpen's self-perceived growing success wouldn't have been a problem except for the fact that it resulted in CWO T.T.Thigpen the pilot becoming *persona non grata.* Because his petition threatened to end all extracurricular life as we knew it, everyone declined to fly with him. In the eyes of the Camp Holloway community, eliminating beer, hookers, and Playboy Magazines was the moral equivalent of forcing the Oakland

Raiders to give up football and take up knitting, and it generated such resentment that CWO T.T.Thigpen became known as the Flying Nun, an ironic call sign considering no one would fly with him, thus he never flew except for short lone maintenance test flights. This in turn created a dual dilemma. Not having to fly because no one would fly with him meant CWO T.T.Thigpen had more time to circulate his petition, and having more time to circulate his petition meant more signatures, and the more bogus signatures he collected the more signatures he sought out because he perceived his petition to be that much more accepted. The enthusiastic CWO T.T.Thigpen was on a roll and was popping up everywhere like a contagious disease, and usually just as welcome.

If you worked a support function in Vietnam every day was pretty much just like all other days unless you managed to get a little time off. Sometimes Sunday's were a little more laid back than others but not by much, generating the periodic pick-up game of basketball or football or a stroll to the club. But for the most part it was business as usual from sun up to sun down. Surprisingly, Jesus Christ never came around on Sundays, not even for football or basketball, which both Randy and I thought would have been a little more appropriate for a self-proclaimed religious deity. Tuesdays on the other hand, became known to us as, well, *Tuesday,* because in Vietnam, in the small but sometimes exciting world of our orderly room, it seemed every Tuesday there must have been a full moon, and as we all know a full moon brings out the loonies like CWO T.T.Thigpen and Jesus Christ. It's not that Tuesdays were special or any different than any other day, but all other days were just days on the military *Julian* calendar, a calendar that much like the military twenty-four hour clock, had absolutely no respect for the generally accepted knowledge and method of time keeping of the rest of the world. It just kept on going and going like that damn pink rabbit on TV with a battery up its ass. For some odd reason we could always count on Tuesdays being interesting, and this particular Tuesday, which started with the Jesus-inspired CWO T.T.Thigpen's petition to sanitize the war, promised to be quite normally abnormal when after CWO T.T.Thigpen, in came Fred Blurtz.

"My name is Fred Blurtz."

The voice was somehow familiar but the rest of him, other than being on the short side, was just normal G.I. faded olive drab like a million other guys. The only exception was his homely Army issue black horn rim glasses, often referred to among the ranks as *pussy repellers.*

"Yup, if this is the 189th, I'm in the right place, alright. I'm supposed to report to the 189th," he said with an engaging smile. "Is this the 189th?"

"Sure is," I answered, automatically smiling in response, somehow knowing, feeling deep down in my soul, that Fred Blurtz was a nice guy.

There really are people like that who go through life, even a war, with a smile and an indestructibly pleasant temperament that only the cruelest of indignant jerks would abuse or exploit. It took all of ten seconds to realize that Fred Blurtz was one of those people; kind, honest, and trusting, almost to the point of naïvete and self endangerment, yet somehow still capable. You simply had to like him because he was Fred Blurtz. You had no choice. He was another one of those western Pennsylvania boys whom I suppose could best be described as a cross between a lost puppy and one of Snow White's seven dwarfs, and he had just entered into the world of the Ghostriders by way of the Big Red One.

"Yup, if this is the 189th then this is where I'm supposed to be," said Corporal Fred Blurtz - smiling, always smiling.

It was Fred's *yup* and the slight lisp that gave it away, pegged it for me right off, and I recognized that familiar voice to be none other than that of Mortimer Snerd, friend and confident of the famous TV and radio dummy Charlie McCarthy. Making the connection, I simply smiled and accepted a copy of his orders then noticing his 1st Infantry patch asked, "You were in the Big Red One?"

"Yup, the Big Red One alright."

Fred began nearly every verbal expression with a *Yup.*

"Yup, until that President Nixon sent me here."

"Nixon?" I said, then I remembered what I saw on the Armed Forces TV News at the Air Force Base Officer's Club. "Oh that's right. But I thought all you guys in the Big Red One went home."

"Yup, that's what we thought too," replied Fred. "But that President Nixon…well, phooey."

Up to his eyeballs in anti-war public and political pressure, President Nixon tried to pull another *Checkers the Dog* moment by announcing to the nation that he was fulfilling his campaign pledge and phasing down the war, which he was and he was beginning that phase down by bringing home "Those fine boys of the famous Big Red One," the 1st Infantry Division. As usual, ole Tricky Dick proved to be a man of his word. There they were on network TV, those fine boys of the 1st ID, all smiles and happy as they disembarked the planes and went to their knees and kissed U.S. soil. What the public didn't know, and what the powers that be actually did, was round up all the 1st ID troops who were already scheduled for DEROS within a short time span and sent them all home in a cluster for the benefit of the media and a Kodak moment.

"Yup, the rest of us just got mish mashed all over Vietnam," as Corporal Fred Blurtz put it with his engaging smile. "Yup, and here I am at the 189th."

"Yup, here you are," I smiled; realizing now that the Mortimer Snerd routine was real… and contagious.

Being President Nixon didn't see fit to send me any instructions regarding Fred's placement, I decided he was going to have to hang around until Top returned to decide where we were going to put him. Meanwhile, since Fred Blurtz was naturally sociable and trusting and congenial, he didn't hesitate to entertain us with his exploits and experiences in the infantry. We soon discovered he had quite a history that was even more fascinating when being storied with all that goofy dawdling eloquence. Fred told us of his brief three months in-country during which he had managed to cheat death, save his entire company, lose his virginity, discover an exotic disease, and ascend from village idiot to a decorated hero. Surprisingly, none of this altered in the least Fred's warm personality and wonderful outlook on life - that is except for the disease part, which had a tendency to worry Fred to no end.

"Yup, I got the drip and I think I got the black clap," revealed Fred after telling us of his rendezvous in the boonies with a band of roving Vietnamese whores.

"Yup, they came right out thar where we was by them rice paddy's and they were pretty and gave us some fruit and I got me a roll in the hay for only five dollars, and then I got the clap. Yup, that boom boom gave me the clap right off the bat alrighty."

"Oh man, that's tough," said Randy.

"And that was my first time."

"And that was your first time?"

"Yup," smiled Fred with a slight blush and a chuckle. "And it was my only time and I got that clap, and I got them shots but what if it's that black clap is what I'm worried about. What if it's that incurable black clap drip where your dick turns black and falls off and you never get to go home and have to live on some island some place without a dick. Yup, I heard about that clap, that black clap kind of drip. Do you think my dick will fall off? Do ya? That'd be bad I tell ya. Yup."

"I wouldn't venture to guess, Fred," I said. "What did the doctor say?"

"They don't say nothin'. Yup, they just give me them shots and laugh. But that's pretty bad, huh? I mean to live through all that fightin' and then lose your dick from the black clap. And it was my first time and I ain't even had a second time 'cause I got that clap."

It was rumored that the so-called *rumored* black clap was a rumor started by the Army to discourage promiscuity by the troops. If it were indeed a rumor it was a damn effective one, at least among those of us with some degree of self control and who were serious about going home with all of our body parts.

Fred's fighting experience was impressive, especially the firefight during which, through a combination of skill and luck, resulted in his receiving a Bronze star for Valor. It took place late one night on a small fire support base while his platoon was snoozing. Fred was stationed on the perimeter where he dutifully stayed awake and aware.

"Yup, it was scary out thar in that dark and I kept watchin' and listenin' and I knew thar was gooks out thar in the wire. I kept wakin' all those guys up and sayin', 'thar's gooks out thar in the wire,' but they kept tellin' me I was crazy and goin' back to sleep. 'Thar's gooks out thar in the wire I tell ya,' is what I told 'em. 'I can smell 'em,' I told 'em. But they didn't believe me," smiled Fred. "But I knew thar was gooks out thar in the wire 'cause I could smell 'em."

Randy and I listened with fascination as Fred related his intense story with all the grace and sincerity of Miss Nancy on Romper Room reading The Little Red Chu-Chu That Could.

"Yup, so I crawled out there a little bit and then I could hear 'em good, and so I popped a flare and then I shot 'em. I shot lots of 'em and they were all shootin' at me too, I tell ya, but I shot a bunch of 'em and I just kept shootin' until I used up my whole bandolier and the rest of 'em ran off. Those guys believed me after that, I tell ya," laughed Fred. "Yup, they believed me after that 'cause the next morning they found all them gook bodies I shot and they believed me then, I tell ya. Yup, I can sure shoot okay 'cause I go huntin' all the time back home. I can sure shoot. And I could smell them gooks and I showed them gooks."

It seems Fred's sense of smell and west Pennsylvania determination had aroused his comrades and beaten back the late night ambitions of a large force of VC. In addition, further investigation determined that good ole mild mannered Fred Blurts had single handedly accounted for two thirds of the enemy kills, nearly twenty in all, and for his efforts he was recommended for a Silver Star, which he fully deserved but was, of course, downgraded to a Bronze Star because he was only a PFC at the time and their weren't any high ranking officers present to share the glory. Then there came the clinger to Fred's amazing story.

"Yup, and them gooks shot me too. They got me right in the heart they did, and I was so excited I didn't even know it."

"Wait a minute Fred," I said. "I think you just lost me here. You don't look like you got shot in the heart."

Fred smiled and reached into his pocket and pulled out a souvenir that he now carried everywhere he went. It was an M-16 ammo clip with a hole in it dead center made by the impact of a single round from an AK-47. He wore the actual mangled bullet on a chain around his neck.

"Yup, this is what saved my life." smiled Corporal Fred Blurtz. "I sure was lucky I tell ya."

Fred handed the clip to me for closer inspection then Randy came over and marveled at the clip as well. Very quietly old Papa-san, our resident Vietnamese janitor, nudged his way over and leaned in to see the famous ammo clip as well, offering his one tooth smile and head bobbing approval that for some reason alerted me to Papa-san's ability to understand English, even Fred's version of English, for it was generally accepted that Papa-san, who also just happened to be the spitting image of the late Ho Chi Minh, understood no English at all.

Papa-san was a permanent fixture in the orderly room every day but Sunday. Like the hooch maids and the goat man, he was a local hire and his only job was to clean the HQ offices which for the most part never got dirty except for the ash trays, trash cans, and ever-present red dust. So Papa-san would dust and wipe and sweep and empty the trash cans and the ash trays, and generally piddle around quietly until near the end of his work day when he was outside burning the office trash in an old fifty gallon drum. The only exception to Papa-san's piddling was when someone cued him to do his trick. As far as we knew old Papa-san had been at the Ghostrider HQ longer than anyone in the company, and somewhere during that time someone taught old Papa-san a hip little trick that he would do for anybody at anytime just for the asking. We didn't know when he learned his trick but he never failed to perform on demand and always gave it his best effort. All anyone had to do was say, "Hey, Papa-san. Get short." At which time Papa-san would stop his piddling, light up with his toothless smile and bobbing head and say; "UP TI, OUA SI, FUCKIT, I SHOR!" and then give a middle finger salute with a goofy giggle.

Naturally everyone got a big laugh out of it, especially Papa-san, who would then return to his piddling. It took two performances for me to figure out what hell he was saying, which was *Up tight, outa sight, fuck it I'm short,* and personally, I thought it was a bit demeaning like making your dog roll over for a biscuit or a bone. Eventually, like everyone else, I came to think old Papa-san didn't mind at all because he hadn't any idea what he was saying, leaving me to think he was just eager to please and be one of the guys, and in doing so, hoped to keep his job. It was on this Tuesday, however, that I first began developing my doubts about good old Papa-san.

"Yup, I'd say I was pretty darn lucky but I hope my dick don't fall off 'cause I got the drip. 'Yup, 'cause of that clap, that bad black clap," continued Fred.

"Who's dick fell off," asked Top Buchinsky as he walked in the door.

"Corporal Fred Blurtz, Top," I said. "Just transferred in from the Big Red One."

Top stopped and looked at Blurtz. "Your dick fell off?"

"Oh no, First Sergeant," smiled Fred. "Not yet."

Top returned the smile, as everyone always did with Fred.

"I still have my dick. I got the drip is all."

"You getting the shots?" asked Top.

"Yup," answered Fred.

Top simply nodded approval then went to his desk and started going through his in-box.

Then in through the door wandered a bewildered looking skinny young private who walked slowly to the middle of the room and just stood there looking lost.

"What ya need there troop?" I asked.

"Um, I have a problem," he said timidly as he walked to my desk.

"Okay," I said. "Shoot."

"I need to get paid."

"You have a finance problem?"

"Yeah, I guess so."

"Your pay isn't right?" I asked.

"Well, I didn't get paid."

"What did the Pay Officer say when you reported for pay? Didn't he have a voucher for you?"

"What Pay Officer?"

"When you went to get paid. When you got in line and saluted and reported for pay to the officer who hands out the money. What did he say?"

"Oh, him. Um, he said he didn't have it. He said to talk to you."

"Okay, we'll get you straight," I said, heading for the filing cabinet and pulling out an action form. I stuck it in the typewriter to proceed as usual by asking a few questions. "Have any trouble last time you got paid?" I asked out of curiosity.

"No," he replied. "They always got it right at Fort Ord."

"Fort Ord? Then you just got here?" I asked, not remembering ever seeing him. "Maybe your finance records haven't been processed yet."

"No. I've been here for a while."

"A while? When did you get paid last?"

"At Fort Ord."

I glanced over at Top who was now taking interest in the timid private with the pay problem.

"Come here son," ordered First Sergeant Buchinsky.

The private moved cautiously to the front of Top's desk.

"What's your name?"

"Ziederhold, First Sergeant. Private Clarence Ziederhold."

Private Clarence Ziederhold was one of those people who was permanently psychologically damaged or socially handicapped simply because his name began with one of the last letters in the alphabet. This meant that all of Private Ziederhold's life he was the victim of the English alphabet by which most American institutions are organized. Because of the alphabetical process he was always told to sit in the back of the class room or get in the back of the line, always last, always ignored, and usually overlooked simply because his name started with a Z. As a result of this social conditioning, Private Ziederhold automatically assumed a role of complete anonymity in all things, including the Army. In his Army basic training at Fort Jackson, Private Ziederhold knew he would never participate in any training because there would never be enough time to get to the Zs, just as he knew he would be placed in the fourth squad of the fourth platoon, and that the fourth squad of the fourth platoon would always come in last because they all had names that started with the last letters in the alphabet. Therefore Private Ziederhold had long ago resolved himself to simply not participate, and being his last name began with a Z no one ever even noticed that Private Ziederhold didn't participate. Now Private Ziederhold was in Vietnam - not participating.

The First Sergeant glanced at me and I immediately grabbed the company roster where I could find no Ziederhold. I silently shrugged the negative results to Top who continued his questioning.

"Son, are you a member of this company?"

"Yes, First Sergeant. I think so."

"You think so?"

"Yes, First Sergeant."

"Yes you are or yes you think you are?"

"Yes I am... I think."

"Son, how long have you been in Vietnam?"

"Um, about six months, First Sergeant."

"Six months?"

"Yes First Sergeant."

"And you haven't been paid since you got here?"

"No First Sergeant."

"And when did you come to this company?"

"Um, about six months ago, First Sergeant. When they told me to."

"Six months?"

"Yes First Sergeant."

Top looked at Private Ziederhold for a long moment, hesitant to ask the next question, which he knew he had to ask.

"Private Ziederhold, when you arrived at this company did you report to this office?"

"Um, no I don't think so."

"You don't think so?"

"No, I don't think so."

"Why not?"

"Um, I don't know."

"Private Ziederhold, where do you live?"

"Ypsilanti, Michigan, First Sergeant."

"No Private Ziederhold, I mean where do you live here? Where do you sleep?"

"Um, in the empty hooch down by the showers."

"That's not our company area Private Ziederhold," observed Top. "That's not anybody's company's area."

"It's not?"

"No."

"Nobody told me."

"Did you bother to ask anybody?"

"Um, no, First Sergeant."

"Private Ziederhold, where do you work?"

Private Ziederhold began to squirm and shuffle his feet.

"Um, I helped in the mess hall one night. So I could get some sticky buns."

"Private Ziederhold…" Top paused, trying to determine if this kid was cunning or just plain stupid. He decided on stupid because a cunning Private Ziederhold would not have walked into his orderly room looking to get paid for his non-existence in the Army. "Private Ziederhold, I want you to stay here. Don't go anywhere. Just stay right here. I'll have to talk to the CO about you and he's not here right now so I want you to stay right here until he gets back. Do you understand?"

"Yes, First Sergeant."

"Here. Stay right here."

"Yes, First Sergeant."

"Good," said Top, looking to me and trying not to laugh. His attention was then drawn to the door where in walked Jesus Christ.

"Oh shit," said Top, seeing Jesus and knowing it was Tuesday and deciding that one nut case a day was enough. Looking to me he grabbed his hat and headed for the door. "I'm going to lunch, Fusco, it's all yours. And if Ziederhold here tries to go any place, shoot him."

"Deserter," I mumbled, as Top smiled and made his exit passed Jesus who made his entry and his way to the front of my desk.

"I am Jesus Christ."

"Yeah, I know. How ya doing today, Jesus?"

"I must go home. The Holy Father wants me to go home."

Through the door behind Jesus came Staff Sergeant Promisel.

"Just missed him Sergeant Popsicle," I said. "He went for lunch at the mess hall but sometimes he eats lunch up at battalion."

"That's Promisel, Fusco. Not Popsicle. *Promisel.*"

"Ah come on Pops. You know we all love ya. That's why we call ya Popsicle, Pops," said Randy.

Popsicle managed a smile and once again conceded to being called Popsicle.

"I don't need Top. I need you," said Staff Sergeant Popsicle. "I got a personnel problem and you're the personnel guy."

"Yup, me too," said Fred Blurtz, thinking Sergeant Popsicle meant *personal* instead of *personnel*. "I got the drip. I think I got the black clap."

"What?" asked a surprised Staff Sergeant Popsicle, cautiously edging away from Corporal Blurtz.

"You know. The drip," said Fred. "You got the drip too?"

"Hell no I ain't got the drip. What's he talking about, Fusco?" asked Staff Sergeant Popsicle. "I ain't got the drip. I got a payroll discrepancy. I ain't getting my flight pay."

"I didn't get mine either," said Private Ziederhold. "But the First Sergeant can fix it."

"Can the First Sergeant fix the clap?" asked Fred.

"I want to go home," said Jesus to anybody who would listen. "God has given me a mission. I must tend my flock."

I glanced up and caught a glimpse of old Papa-san who was fixated on Jesus with a most curious expression. Whenever Jesus spoke Papa-san's eyes seemed to grow a little rounder and he got nervous like a pet dog with a sixth sense having a premonition about some impending dangerous or mysterious event. I was really starting to wonder about Papa-san.

"W,W,What the hell is he talking about?" stuttered Staff Sergeant Popsicle.

"Oh, that's just Jesus," I told him.

"What?" said Staff Sergeant Popsicle.

"I am Jesus Christ and God wants me to go home."

"Really?" said Private Ziederhold.

"Are you nuts?" asked Staff Sergeant Popsicle. "Fusco, is he nuts?"

Then, to Randy's displeasure, Petula Clark spewed out of the radio.

"When you're alone and life is making you lonely
You can always go – downtown"

"Oh God! I swear I'm gonna blow that son-of-a-bitch away!" blurted Randy.

Jesus turned to Randy with indignant surprise and Randy immediately likened it with the wrath of the nuns.

"Oh, sorry Jesus. I didn't mean oh God *that* God. You know, *him.* I meant that Specialist Evenson dude at that fuckin' radio station.

"Hey, that's the song that was on when I got screwed and caught the clap," said Fred. "Yup, that's the one I tell ya. I sure hope my dick don't fall off."

"You got the clap?" asked Private Ziederhold.

"I didn't think you were on flight status," I said to Staff Sergeant Popsicle. "You have to fly to get flight pay don't you?"

For some reason the question made Staff Sergeant Popsicle a little nervous, like when he was having sex or about to be killed by hand grenade booby traps - or when he was lying. Everybody knew Staff Sergeant Popsicle hated to fly. Even though he was an expert aircraft technician he absolutely hated and refused to fly.

"Sure I f,f,f,fly all the time. This is a a,av,aviation c,c,company ain't it?"

"I got flight pay. Yup, I got flight pay and I was in the infantry," offered Corporal Fred Blurtz.

"You got paid for catching the clap?" asked Private Ziederhold.

"Yes fly. You must fly me home. I am Jesus Christ and I must fly home."

"J,J,Jesus Christ, F,F,Fusco. What th,th,the hell are these g,g,guys talkin' about?" stuttered Sergeant Popsicle.

"Yes, yes!" said Jesus, throwing his arms around Sergeant Popsicle. "I am Jesus Christ! You must fly me home!"

"Whoa, Jesus is on a roll today, Vince," observed Randy.

"Yup, I got the clap," Corporal Fred Blurtz told Private Ziederhold, "And I was still a virgin."

"Oh yeah? Wow, I was a virgin once but she turned me down," said Private Ziederhold.

Even Corporal Blurtz had to scratch his head on that one.

Then, through the door returned the long and lanky and determined CWO T.T.Thigpen who immediately saw another potential signature in the person of Staff Sergeant Popsicle.

"Sergeant, will you please sign my petition for Jesus Christ?" asked CWO T.T.Thigpen.

"Y,you're d,d,damn right I will. I'll s,s,sign anything that'll get this f,f.fuckin' nut outa here."

"I am Jesus Christ!" said Jesus, hugging Sergeant Popsicle. "Fly me home!"

"Jesus Christ?" said CWO T.T.Thigpen.

"J,J,Jesus f,f,fuckin' Christ!" exclaimed Staff Sergeant Popsicle.

"Yes! Yes! Yes! Jesus Christ!" said an excited Jesus.

"Holy shit," said Randy.

"God almighty," I said, contemplating clearing the orderly room with my M-16.

"Yup," agreed Fred Blurtz.

"UP TI, OUA SI, FUCKIT, I SHOR!" yelled old Papa-san.

Everyone paused and turned to discover Papa-san with his middle finger extended upward, beaming his big one toothed smile, and laughing like the village idiot with his head bobbing like one of those dashboard car things they sell at baseball stadiums.

"Hey, that guy looks just like Ho Chi Minh," said Private Clarence Ziederhold.

"Shit," I said. "Tuesdays."

CHAPTER 20

GENERAL GIAP &
THE KAMIKAZE

The cool clean white sheet slid away as she moved slowly across my body, kissing my chest, my neck, my eyes, and then my lips. She was warm and soft and wonderful, and smelled of Ivory soap and perfume. I laid there, surrendering to this wonderful sensuous moment and the clean safe comfort of home. Her lips were moist and perfect as they tenderly explored my own. Our tongues met and I heard myself expend a slight moan of delight. I would explore her body one more time before we ventured into the wonderful world of sexual ecstasy, and with the expression of another soft moan of delight, I opened my eyes to discover - the biggest fucking rat I had ever seen in my entire life sitting right there on my chest licking my lips. At first I thought the rat was a dream, a nightmare, then suddenly I was back in Vietnam thinking and wishing that being back in Vietnam was the nightmare. Then all too quickly I realized that my wife and the cool clean white sheets and soft bed were the dream. I stared at the rat, that big damn rat that looked even bigger because it was a mere two inches from my nose looking back at me. Then partly in fear and partly with anger for his creating and then ruining my wet dream, I grabbed him and slung him across the room where he bounced off the tits of the Miss April Playboy centerfold pinned to the wall. He recovered quickly, ran to the corner, and finding no exit, scurried back across the room and under my bunk.

"SHIT! SHIT!" I yelled, jumping to the floor, repeatedly spitting and wiping my lips with the back of my hand, chills running up my spine. "SHIT!" I grabbed my M-16 and aimed it at the bunk. "You bastard! You fuckin' rat bastard!"

The door flew open. Randy rushed in and quickly froze when he saw me poised with my weapon, desperately wiping my mouth. Curious onlookers piled up behind him.

"Oh shit!" said Randy. "It's the room. I knew it. He's gone nuts. He shoulda never stayed in this room. Oh damn, he's gonna blow his fuckin' head off! Vince, you don't want to do this, man! It's not you, man. It's the room. It's the hoocho curse, man. It's the war! It's the Army!"

"SHIT!" I repeated, wiping my lips on my sleeve. "What? Don't do what?" I asked Randy.

"Don't do it, man! You don't have to do this. What's wrong?" asked Randy. "What's going on? Whatever it is we can deal with it, buddy. You don't have to kill yourself."

"That bastard. That giant little gook bastard fuckin' rat crawled right in my fuckin' mouth when I was asleep!" I said with a shiver.

"WHAT?" said Randy.

"A rat. A giant damn rat!"

Randy immediately paled and went into his nervous Randy dance, not his usual city boy *I'm happy and cool dance* but his scared shitless and totally nervous kind of bouncing dance, because Randy was from New York City, and being from New York City Randy had an innate fear of rats and rodents, and in his case, a fear unrivaled by any other known phobia. He backed through the small crowd of half a dozen HQ hooch onlookers like he was avoiding the black plague or an elevator full of lepers and immediately took refuge in his own room.

A few of the other guys squeezed bravely into my room but they were more interested in Miss April then my rat.

"Is that Miss April?" some one said.

"Hey look he's got Miss April."

"I thought somebody said it was a rat."

"A rat? Oh hell, that's just General Giap," said Specialist Alvarez as he bent over and looked under my bunk. "Big sucker right? Kind of gray brown and got a little piece missing from his left ear?"

"I didn't notice his ear," I said. "General Giap? You mean it's got a name?"

"Yeah, man. You know that NVA George Washington type general up in Hanoi or someplace who's been running the war since old Ho Chi Minh bought the farm. That's what we named him. Same name 'cause that little bastard's indestructible and just won't go away. We all tried to kill him. Set every kind of trap and poison you can think of but he ain't givin' it up, man. Tough little motha. He go under here?" asked Alvarez, looking under the bunk.

"Yeah, I bounced him off the wall," I said, looking to the wall where the other guys were inspecting and discussing Miss April's tits. "Then he ran under the bunk."

"I like Miss February better," said one.

"Yeah, she had a bodacious ass but April's got better tits," said another.

"Ya think so?"

"Yeah man. Check out those nipples, will ya."

"Yeah, maybe you're right."

"Yep. There's a little hole in the wall down there, see?" said Alvarez. "He chews little holes in the walls and that's how he scoots all around the hooch, through those little holes in the plywood. Must be a VC like those damn tunnel gooks always disappearing under ground and shit. Crawled out of one of my boots once. Gutsy little bastard. Looks a little like my cousin Weasel. We call him Weasel 'cause he looks like a rat, but we also call him Weasel cause we already got a cousin we call Rat."

"You call the rat Weasel?" I said.

"No. My cousin. We call my cousin Weasel. We call the rat Giap, General Giap."

I looked under and saw the little hole.

"Guess he went through there, huh?" speculated Alvarez. "Oh man, you said he got in your mouth? Oh man, that's disgusting, that's some nasty fuckin funky shit."

"Yeah, tell me about it. Hey, Randy," I called out through the plywood wall, knowing Randy could hear us. "You hear that. The rat has a name, General Giap. His name is General Giap. Oh, and it went through a hole in the wall into your room."

Suddenly a series of crashes and bangs came from Randy's room followed by his fast exit and exodus to the assumed safety of mine. He appeared suited up for danger with his helmet, flack jacket, and M-16.

"Yeah, I got a name for that sucker. Dead. That's the name, Dead. I'm not living with any fuckin' rats. I don't give a shit what their rank is. I can't live with rats," said a nervously animated and seriously concerned Randy, who at this time was more into his nervous Randy dance than I had ever seen on any former occasion, including rocket attacks.

Randy went on to explain how the sewer rats in New York are twice as big as cats and have been known to chew their way through cement and up through the walls and basements, and actually kill and eat small pets and even babies in their cribs.

"Everybody in New York is hell bent afraid of rats," Randy told us. "They hate rats. They hate rats more than they hate politicians," he told us. "And in New York that means a lot, because everybody in New York hates politicians. General Giap has to go," declared Randy. "I'm not gonna live with rats and that's all there is to it. No fuckin' rats."

Randy didn't sleep for three nights following my romantic encounter with General Giap. He piled stuff on his bunk and then sat on top of the pile wearing his flack jacket and helmet, cradling his loaded M-16. Each night he made the pile a little higher. When he unwillingly closed his eyes he had paranoid visions of General Giap, a huge ugly scraggly rat with a little pointy straw Vietnamese hat, rubbing his grubby hands together and licking his chops just before chewing Randy's nose off of his face or gnawing out his eyes. The only sleep Randy got was behind his desk in the orderly room, which wasn't anything new because he was prone to cat naps anyway, not having much else to do. Randy's job title was Awards Clerk. He assisted the Admin Officer who also didn't have much to do and was always out flying or working on special projects.

As awards clerk most of Randy's work time was spent hunt-and-peck typing and filling out canned paperwork recommending automatic Bronze Stars for - being there, or Medals of Commendation for – being there. Sure there were some well deserved medals for valor also, but for the most part Randy's job was only critically essential because all officers in the military who hold any type of position in any type of office must always have an enlisted man to assist them, much like those hot looking chicks in high school who always have homely looking girl friends around to make them look even hotter. It was another one of those things that perpetuated the old established military feudal system and social strata, like separate clubs, separate quarters, and separate dining areas, insuring the separation of the perceived lower classes of the enlisted men and upper class commissioned. Sure the Army would argue that the class separation was to maintain respect, discipline, and leadership, based I suppose, on that old axiom *familiarity breeds contempt,* but then how much contempt was bred through the existing class separation? And the higher their rank the more enlisted men the office officer was assigned, even though there wasn't much of anything for those enlisted men to do, in spite of the fact they did most all of it. Therefore it was essential that Randy always be there to assist the Admin Officer who wasn't, even if Randy was asleep. I was always amazed at how well Randy could sleep on the job, sitting up straight as an arrow with his closed eyes hidden behind his John Lennon wire rim glasses. Randy, I always thought, was destined for a very successful career as a civil servant.

What I didn't' know was that behind those sleeping eyes Randy was formulating the plan of destruction of our infamous rodent, General Giap. It came to fruition very late when most everyone at Camp Holloway was asleep. Suddenly the dead of night erupted with the harsh penetrating frightening sound of automatic weapons fire. A full clip of shots sounded loudly and echoed throughout the base, waking and sending everyone in the HQ hooch to the floor. Then just as quickly another clip followed the first and I realized it had come from the other side of the wall in Randy's room. I jumped up and rushed over to find Randy in his OD boxer shorts, standing high on his small mountain of stuff, his helmet banging the wall, staring wide eyed at the corner of the floor across the room. When I looked at the corner I saw a few morsels of food, the remnants of one of Bun's buns, and a place where the wood and concrete floor had been chewed up by two full clips of ammo released on full auto. Before I could speak the attack siren went off and all thousand plus inhabitants of Camp Holloway went into the defense mode. Amazingly, everyone, even the guys in the HQ hooch in their deep slumber or hangover state of confusion, didn't realize where the shots had originated and they all assumed it was small weapons fire somewhere along the perimeter.

"I missed him," said Randy in total amazement while staring at the corner of his room. "How the hell did I miss him?"

A short time later in the orderly room I cranked the field phone and called in twenty percent, then forty, and so on as directed by Top as our trucks were loaded and rushed off to the perimeter. Randy just sort of stood in the dark behind his desk amidst the chaos and urgency of the moment, clutching his M-16, doing his Randy dance, occasionally mumbling to himself, "I missed him. How the hell could I miss him?"

When the first truck reached the 189th area of responsibility at the perimeter it hardly slowed as two guys from the service platoon jumped off the back and into a bunker that sported a roughly made sign that read, *Dawg Town*. That particular bunker was called Dawg Town because it was the domain and usual duty station of a tall straw headed scrawny slow-walking slow-talking South Georgia boy and University of Georgia Bulldog, or *Bulldawg*, fan who's only purpose and existence in Vietnam was to sit there on guard and stare into the darkness through the wire and the free-fire zone of no-mans land - all night long, each and every night, for a year. His name was Andy Puffin, and PFC Andy Puffin both hated and loved his job. He hated it because it was in Vietnam but he loved it because it was better than anything else he had done while in the Army. In fact he had volunteered for full time guard duty on the perimeter, the job everyone else hated and regarded as punishment or a form of exile. There on the perimeter PFC Puffin was independent, a man apart, night after night, each and every night, all night long. Even on his one night a week off he would sometimes end up out there at Dawg Town.

It was there, alone in his sand bag covered hole in the ground with only one other soldier who was usually asleep, that PFC Andy Puffin was king. At Dawg Town nobody messed with him or told him what to do, or insulted his intelligence by telling him how to do it after they told him what to do. There he could smoke his Camels or snuff his snuff, or hum his favorite Glen Campbell songs, or dream of the starry night he nailed Susie Mae Donaway in the back of his father's Dodge pick up truck. And sometimes he would even recall the entire John Wayne production of The Alamo, including the crappy parts with the faggy Colonel Travis. And if that weren't enough, it was there that PFC Andy Puffin could eat, and PFC Andy Puffin could sure as hell eat – a lot. Like Chief Chief Zamboni with his vodka, the tall skinny PFC Puffin had a metabolism that Hollywood starlets would kill for and major drug consortiums would pay a billion bucks to bottle. In fact it was that very thing that almost kept PFC Puffin from enlisting and

being accepted in the Army to get away from Susie Mae
Donaway's six-foot-five hell fire and brimstone minister father.
The doctors were afraid that his eating disorder, or order of eating,
might have been detrimental to his ability to perform his duties. In
the field PFC Puffin required triple rations of C-Rations, which he
declared wasn't a problem because a great many soldiers simply
hated C-Rats, and preferring to starve rather than consume the
canned delights, they would hand them over to PFC Puffin.

PFC Puffin was an eating machine and a junk food junky like
no one you could possibly imagine and to feed his tremendous
appetite and desires he received cases of junk food from home
nearly every other day. Boxes full of cookies and Slim Jims and
candy bars and chips and dips and pork rinds and Twinkies and
Goobers and cans of Brunswick stew, boiled peanuts, Vienna
sausage, and everything you could imagine that wasn't available
from the tiny little Camp Holloway PX. It was no problem at all
for Puffin to get any variety of junk food and as much junk food as
he wanted because his family owned the only grocery store in his
small home town called, of course, Puffin's Market & Feed Store.
And then there was PFC Puffin's precious Yoo-hoos. There was no
way in hell PFC Puffin was going to fight a war without his
chocolate Yoo-hoo drinks. He received a full case of Yoo-hoos in
the mail each week, each bottle wrapped and padded with love and
care as though it were the finest and rarest French champagne. PFC
Puffin guarded his Yoo-hoos with his life, and though on one
occasion he had been offered up to twenty bucks and a free Hustler
magazine for just one, he refused to relinquish so much as a single
delicious refreshing chocolaty sip.

It was for this reason PFC Puffin hated any and all enemy
attacks on Camp Holloway. Not because of the communist enemy,
but because every time the siren sounded, his Dawg Town was
augmented and invaded by at least two additional soldiers. It was
bad enough he thought, that he had to share his bunker and
sometimes his Twinkies with one other guy each night, sometimes
even a damn Yankee, but he all too often had to tolerate two more
soldiers at a time of crisis. As PFC Puffin often argued to the
Sergeant of the Guard, the additional regular body when all was
quiet wasn't necessary based on his own nocturnal habits. But
being forced to accept one, he would often encourage that bunker

mate to just sleep all night. Naturally, for that reason, everybody liked pulling the duty with PFC Puffin at Dawg Town.

Nor was PFC Puffin the least bit worried about the North Vietnamese because he knew damn well he had enough firepower and claymore mines set up to defend his stash of high value Yoo-hoos from anything they could throw at him. And though it wasn't evident by his unhurried laid back southern manner, PFC Puffin was so hyped on sugar and junk food that he had no problem at all staying awake and being ready to counter an attack. His main concern was the overcrowding of Dawg Town, and the possibility that while he was busy killing gooks some damn Yankee carpetbagger might slip his hand into his enormous canvas bag of goodies and rip off a Milky Way or, God forbid, one of his prized Snickers bars.

Unaware of Randy's rodent rampage and determining the small weapons fire was just a harassing joke on the part of our North Vietnamese enemy, battalion security eventually blew the all-clear siren. The trucks rolled back around collecting all the extra troops that were deposited at the perimeter bunkers leaving PFC Puffin alone once again with his sleeping buddy and his goodies. The first thing he did was reach into his big bag of munchies and pull out a Ding Dong. Nothin' like a Ding Dong after an intensive alert along the bunker line, he thought. Then of course, he reached back in for a celebratory Yoo-hoo when all of a sudden something gripped his hand sending an intense sharp pain shooting up through his arm to registered in his brain. When PFC Puffin yanked his hand out of the bag of goodies, attached to it was an enormous rat, no doubt the bigger brother, or cousin, or some other near relative of our headquarters hooch General Giap.

"GAWD DANG!" Puffin yelled, waking his bunker buddy. "GAWD DANG IT! SHOOT! AH SHEEE-IT!"

His bunker buddy startled and woke to find PFC Puffin jumping and twitching and hollering and swinging and flailing his arms around in painful desperation, bouncing off the dirty dusty sand bag walls like an oversized racket ball, striking his steal helmet on the perforated steel plate of the low roof of the bunker.

"OH SHOOT! DANG IT, SHOOOOT!" yelled Puffin as he twirled and jerked the large rat around in an effort to free his hand from the painful jaws of death. "AH SHOOT! GAWD ALMIGHTY! SHOOT!"

On this particular night PFC Puffin's bunker buddy was in fact a northern boy by the name of Bernie Schladecek from up-state Ohio. Schladecek was born of Canadian parents and completely unfamiliar with the peculiarities of the language of South Georgia where "SHOOT" translates into many meanings, none of which actually mean to fire a weapon, which instead was expressed simply by saying "FAR". Schladecek, having earlier conceded that PFC Puffin was the Commander and Chief of Dawg Town so he could have a complimentary Tootsie Roll and sleep all night, was eager to do as ordered and grabbed his M-16, locked and loaded, flipped off the safety, and tried his damn best to take a bead on the huge rat flying around the bunker attached to PFC Puffin's hand.

Upon seeing this and having little faith in Bernie Schladecek's ability to hit a moving target, such as a rat attached to his hand, PFC Puffin freaked out completely yelling, "OH, OH GAWD SHOOT! FUCK! NO! SHOOT! NO! GAWD ALMIGHTY! DANG NO! SHOOT!" and began backing away from Schladecek until he inadvertently knocked over the flat board on which was attached his ingenious jury rigged clothes-pin switches that were attached to the wires that were attached to a dozen claymore mines and a 55 gallon drum of foo gas, a kind of homemade napalm full of rocks and various pieces of lethal junk, planted out on the perimeter. At the same moment the would-be thief of a rat that was previously in Puffins goodie bag consuming a bag of Fritos and now had a toothy death grip on his hand, decided to let go and landed in the middle of the bunker screaming and squealing and jumping and bouncing off the sand bag walls. Schladecek took his best shot, which amounted to letting go with half a clip of ammo, sending Private Puffin back in a panic on his ass and landing hard on the clothes-pin control switches, which set off twelve strategically placed claymore mines and the foo gas. The perimetert lit up the night like Shea Stadium, in turn setting off the alert siren and sending all the personnel of Camp Holloway into a defense mode... again.

When the reinforcement truck pulled up to Dawg Town it found PFC Andy Puffin standing there with his weapon slung over one shoulder and his bag of munchies and Yoo-hoos slung over the other with his hand bleeding profusely like some junior high school shop teacher on a Monday. As soon as the two reinforcements jumped into the Dawg Town bunker more shots rang out and back out of the bunker they came along with Private Bernie Schladecek. All three then regrouped, cocked their weapons and strategically attacked the bunker, opening up on full automatic like a precision team of TV commandos. Fortunately they were all better shots than Randy and as a result General Giap's large cousin, or brother, or uncle, or mother, or whoever, never had a chance, ending up resembling more the filling of a Georgia pecan pie than an oversized furry rodent.

That night after everything had settled down and everyone had gotten their lies straight about what enemy they were firing at and why, Randy went back to his room and his perch atop his pile of stuff atop his bunk. I returned to my room, and being too wired from all of the excitement, decided to take up a paperback and stretch out on my bunk in hopes of reading myself to sleep. Things quieted around the hooch and my book was starting to do the job when suddenly there came something through the air from nowhere that struck me dead in the middle of my forehead, knocking me back against the wall. Nearly unconscious, I immediately grabbed my forehead expecting blood and thinking I had been shot, the victim of an errant bullet from where I couldn't imagine. The lump came fast and big and felt to be the size of a golf ball, but I was immediately relieved, though painfully, that it hadn't been a bullet at all. Then it came at me again, just missing my head when I ducked. It crashed into the wall, flopping down on my poncho liner then shooting all around inside my mosquito net until it found the opening. Out it went, bouncing from wall to wall, over and over, into the window screen, off of Miss April's tits and crashing into Miss March's ass. It sounded hard like a rock but in the dim light of my lamp appeared only as a black streak. Then again it went for my head, always seeming to return to my head, and I decided it was time to fight back. I swung the book and knocked it to the floor then grabbed a boot and went for the kill. One whack and it was down, helpless enough that I could inspect it closer. After I turned on the overhead florescent light Randy came rushing into the room.

"What is it? Is it General Giap? Is he back? Did you get him? Did you kill him?"

"Yeah I got it," I said, tenderly exploring the lump on my head with my fingers.

Randy looked to the floor where my defeated attacker squirmed and waited for me to close in for the kill.

"What the fuck is that?" asked Randy, squatting down for a closer inspection.

"It's a bug. Looks like a roach," I said as I bent closer for a better look. "Biggest damn roach I've ever seen. Biggest damn bug I've ever seen. I didn't think they made 'em that big."

And it was. It was a prehistoric man-eater if there ever was one, more like the size of a bird, a good four inches long and built for combat. It wasn't one of those dim-witted one inch Florida palmetto bugs that get lost and wander into the house, but rather a big serious kamikaze of a roach that was not only fearless and willing to come into the light but it could fly, and not only could it fly, it could go supersonic.

"Shit!" said Randy. "That's a serious God damn roach. Oh man. Rats and roaches the size of tanks. Man this country is the pits."

I decided not to squash the kamikaze roach but instead wrapped it up tight and saved it. The next day I found an olive jar about to be discarded by PFC Puffin at which time I told him of my romantic encounter with General Giap and my near death experience with the commie kamikaze roach. He in turn showed me his bandaged hand and told me about his vicious encounter and the subsequent commando slaughter of General Giap's cousin, or mother, or whoever. We put the kamikaze roach that was now dead in the jar, filled the jar with pickle juice preservative from his kosher dills, then sat and ate all the kosher dills and marveled at my new trophy.

"Gawd almighty," said PFC Puffin. "That's the biggest damn roach I ever saw. Shoot, that's the biggest dang bug I ever saw."

He then went on to tell me how he was going to have to take rabies shots, one a day for ten days.

"I thank I'd rutha take a AK round," said PFC Puffin. "Those dang needles is six inches long and they stick it right in your gut. Shoot, that's worse'n get'n your pecker caught in a cotton gin."

The events of the night before were still swimming in my mind later that day during my trip up the hill to the Battalion S-1, when I decided to stop in their latrine to dump a load. I often did this because their shitters were in stalls offering some degree of privacy. Naturally the first thing I did was search all the stalls for toilet paper. If you catch the latrine at the right time in the morning it will have some available, otherwise it disappears fast because, for the average American soldier in a war zone, a roll of toilet paper is one of the most prized and valuable possessions in the world, second only to his weapon. Certainly something no one wanted to be without. A draw back was that also during the day there's no water running resulting in unflushed dry bowls full of flies and crap, leaving the additional challenge of finding a toilet that hasn't been used, and for that matter, a toilet seat with a minimal amount of native footprints. I assumed the footprints were the result of the locals' determination to perform all functions from a squat position.

Could I be so lucky as to find both some TP and a clean commode, I usually thought as I went through this near daily ritual. While searching I thought of the events of the night before; Randy's rat ambush, my roach assault, and especially Puffins ten six inch needles in the gut, not to mention trying to imagine why or how someone could possibly get their pecker caught in a cotton gin. Then of course, there was that ever-present fear held by every soldier who ever passed through a combat zone, that fear that I would be sitting and shitting when it was my time to go, when the mortar hit or the rocket struck. As part of the experience of war we learn there's not a lot of dignity expressed by the human body after it's dead, but every G.I. has a fear of being found dead and defenseless in the shitter, lying there bare ass, caught with that big cigar in mid release. And no matter how much you tried there was really no way to rush things.

On this day, however, the gods were with me and there it was, a clean toilet, absent of dirty footprints and with a fresh roll of paper. Outstanding, I thought, anticipating a near civilized moment of peace. As I dropped my ODs over my boots and started to mount the throne, for some odd reason, be it instinct or simple curiosity, I decided to look back one more time into the empty bowl. When I did chills ran up my spine, an electric charge of fear crawled through my gonads, visions of six-inch needles shot through my head, and the pucker factor suddenly became so literal as to make a one-double-deuce rocket attack seem like a day at the beach. There in the bowl, just waiting for me to park my ass, was a bigger, badder, nastier looking rat than my friend General Giap, and he was showing teeth, nasty teeth, leaving me to immediately assume that this particular rat wasn't interested in my lips and a romantic encounter but simply wanted to bite my ass or something else much more valuable and painful. I shot up into the air somehow defying the physics of my awkward position and turned. He stared at me and I stared back at him thinking he was about to pounce, when he turned quickly and somehow squirmed his fat nasty body down into the toilet, disappearing into the pipes.

Up came my ODs and out I went, all the while wondering how amazing it was that an animal that big could squeeze through those small pipes, shivering at the very thought of what would have happened had I not taken that fateful final glance back.

I would never again sit on a toilet that wasn't full of water, and I would no longer be concerned about how many uninterested mama-sans were in the peanut gallery. Regarding the native footprints on the seats, well, lets just say all things primitive are not without wisdom.

Randy was finally cured of his paranoia when we convinced him that General Giap had been captured, cooked, and eaten by the hooch maids. We even convinced mama-san Ba to go along and back up the story, though she thought the whole concept was grotesque. It was a lie but it was a good lie, and Randy knew it was a lie but he somehow managed to convince himself it was true. He could then sleep at night, which meant he didn't have to sleep as much during the day, a good thing because Randy didn't like to miss anything, especially on Tuesdays.

CHAPTER 21

DAK SEANG'S
MAGNIFICENT STEPCHILDREN

My freelance agent, SP5 Graham up at OPS, kept me flying on my free time and I quickly earned a set of air crewman wings. They weren't always the most choice of missions but they had their purpose and their moments, and they put wings on my chest and let me hold my head just a little bit higher. They included a few dispatch and personnel transport, or taxi flights, and standard re-supply missions where we ferried beans and bullets, or hash and trash as they called it, meaning food and ammo, to boonie bases, SF camps, and guys in the bush, sometimes a medivac of wounded to the 71st Evac hospital at the Pleiku Air Force Base. And then there were the occasional insertions into LZ's and extractions from PZ's. Fortunately, to date, most were uneventful.

On one particular mission where we hauled an SF team into Cambodia from Doc Co, a 5th Special Forces base camp on the border west of Pleiku, we first staged a phony insertion to draw the NVA away from the true LZ, then dropped the team off a few miles away. It was a two slick flight where one ship would stay at altitude about 2500 feet and guide the other into a very small LZ, necessary because it was extremely hard to see on approach at a hundred knots and tree top level. This flight included a relatively new peter pilot Lieutenant in from the States with the nickname Hickory Grove. The AC had him take the ship into the phony LZ for training. He handled it well and dropped the ship in and just hovered long enough for us gunners and the SF guys to deliver what was called a *mad minute* of fire into the surrounding bush. After the co-pilot took us out the AC took back the controls. About that time I glanced over at the SF team who were seated on the edge of the deck on each side of the aircraft. I was amazed to see, with their soft hats, darkened camouflaged faces, and legs dangling out over the side of the chopper, that they showed no fear or apprehension of any kind about their mission. Then I glanced up at our newbie Hickory Grove who had just turned and was looking intensely at the team members on the opposite side of the ship.

When I looked around the gun well to see what he was looking at I saw one of the SF guys had pulled out a grenade and pulled the pin. He joked with the guy next to him then they both turned with a quick whistle to get the attention of their team members on my side of the chopper. When the guys on my side turned to the sound of the whistle, the smiling white teeth of the dark camo face broadened with laughter as he released the handle and rolled the green baseball size fragmentation grenade across the deck. Just then the AC banked left, the grenade decided to pause midway across the ship and Hickory Grove's eyes widened. Being a new guy he didn't know what to do, of which I could fully associate, and in fact he could do nothing other than nearly break his neck trying to turn against the restriction of his armored seat and safety harness to follow the grenade's progress. I'm not sure, but I think my eyes were about to close in fear when the chopper finally banked again in the opposite direction and the grenade continued on its journey to where it was swiftly snatched up like an infield grounder. By then Hickory Grove was squirming like a worm on a fishhook because he lost sight of the grenade altogether. When I announced, "Grenade out the side!" all the possibilities and hazards that grenade presented ran through our collective minds.

"What the hell…!" I heard the AC declare.

"Oh shit!" exclaimed the crew chief.

While they expressed themselves outwardly, Hickory Grove and I both cringed and puckered up for a worse case scenario, like becoming aerial confetti, or at best hopefully and miraculously surviving a crash and burn. The SF guys weren't rattled in the least and were still laughing when the grenade went off. Fortunately we had been accelerating and gaining altitude all through the episode and there had been no damage to the aircraft. I looked at the SF guys and the one nearest me just smiled reassuringly and patted me on the leg. I smiled in return, shot him a bird and we both laughed.

If the SF guys had respect for anybody in Vietnam it was the chopper crews and they often swore that if we went down they wouldn't hesitate to come after us. We believed it because we wanted to and because we knew it to be true. These guys were real hard-core. They were elite and they knew it and they relished what they did. Basically, they were just damn nuts. That particular insertion went well but I never had occasion to see any of that team again, not that I would have recognized them if I had. The newbie peter pilot Hickory Grove went on to become an AC, make Captain, and win a DFC and Silver Star a few months along in his tour. Such was the crash course school of life for our pilots.

Having met the requirements and flown the required hours, air crewman was added to my long MOS list and my part-time flight status earned me an occasional spot on what you could say was a privileged chopper. We called it 4-Balls simply because its number was 400, but its privileged status was because it was the personal on-call bright and shiny UH-1H ride of General Marra, one of the powers that be at II Corps Pleiku. 4-Balls was always on stand-by and to date I had only flown it at night when the General, as pilot, decided to get in some flight time and practice approaches. We would hop over to II Corps without a co-pilot and pick him up then he would take the stick and fly back and forth between Camp Holloway and the Pleiku Air Force Base practicing approaches and getting in his required airtime. A number of higher ups pulled this routine, taking short crash courses to become qualified chopper pilots, some learning just enough to be dangerous, then puttering around the sky just enough to get the money and the accolades. Meanwhile, the crew chief and I just kicked back and the pilot would tune in some late evening easy listening music that drifted in from somewhere on an FM frequency.

During one of these moonlight air strolls in mid April, while we were counting the stars and nearly asleep, the General must have been flying with a head full of concern because he knew at the time what we EM types certainly didn't know. The NVA were not only moving down the complex Ho Chi Minh trail through Laos and Cambodia in force as usual, but had set up a number of major base camps from which they could and were inserting thousands of troops into South Vietnam's central highlands. In March the Cambodian government was getting a little antsy with their presence and powerful build up and demanded that the North Vietnamese get out, even giving them a two day time limit to do so. Knowing they couldn't withdraw their many divisions within that time limit, and in fact having no desire to do so, the NVA decided they would instead just take over Cambodia. By mid April they were well on their way, having already seized a number of provinces and preparing to overrun the Cambodian Capital. Things were getting busy in the central highlands as well, with major enemy buildups near villages all around the II Corps area, and specifically our strategic base camps of Dak To, Ben Het, Dak Pek, Dak Seang, and others that acted as stop gaps in the main arteries of NVA infiltration from their bases across the border. Units all around the highlands AO were in constant contact with the enemy, and SF and SOG teams were busy as hunt dogs on the opening day of deer season, collecting intel and monitoring movement. It was the intention of the NVA to keep the U.S. and its allied forces defensively occupied to the point we could not interfere or prevent their take over of Cambodia. In addition, intelligence revealed that one of those SF base camps, Dak Seang, was the object of a massive enemy buildup estimated to be of Division strength and there was no doubt they were going to attack.

All of this and more must have been racing around in the General's mind during the night hours of his repeated flying approaches. Maybe flying was his way of coping, mulling the building crisis around in his head, or maybe the flying was a form of therapy to quell a sleepless night. Who the hell knows? As far as the crew chief, and I and probably the pilot, were concerned, well... we didn't have a damn clue. We were jacked back listening to the Ray Conniff Singers and dreaming about raiding the kitchen as soon as we got back to base and tied 4-Balls down for the night. At least that was our agreed plan because Becker the crew chief and I, before we flew off to pick up the General, bumped into Buns the night baker who hinted he might be baking up some more of his big sticky buns. Buns was always sending stuff out to the guys on the perimeter, sometimes hot soup, sometimes coffee, and sometimes his famous sticky buns that were never on the official menu but always in demand. Sometimes I would even drive the jeep for him when he made his rounds. But usually getting some of Buns' famous sticky buns required luck and timing and the nocturnal determination of a raccoon. So there we were, high in the night sky with the General on the stick fretting about a major enemy offensive and us gunners staring into the starry sky, dreaming of coffee and fresh sweet warm sticky buns, while a division of NVA were hiding in the boonies dipping their bullets in piss and working their Budha beads, or whatever they used for praying, in anticipation of a glorious People's Army victory for the cause.

It was getting late and for some reason on this night the General made a few more trips and practice approaches than usual. He usually wrapped it up around 2300. When we finally flew back to II Corps about 0200 he ordered us to shut down and sit tight and we quickly realized our sticky bun ambitions were shattered. We settled instead for small talk and lying flat on our backs on the pad, smoking cigarettes and looking up at the stars. The pilot was a young Warrant officer named Massey who couldn't seem to get over the idea that I could type 87 words a minute without looking at the keys. He confessed he almost failed typing in high school because the young teacher had great legs and a seriously nice ass that made for a bit of a distraction. This blew my mind being it was coming from someone who could deal with the complexities of flying a $300,000 aircraft that through all applications of common sense by the average mind should not even be capable of flying. We laughed as he credited his ability to fly to his sustained fear of the TACs at Fort Rucker and I credited my typing to the fear of a very threatening Army WAC Sergeant at Fort Sill. We then explored the possibilities of what achievements would have been accomplished had the TACs at Rucker had the legs and ass of his typing teaching. It was just friendly chatter until we all three dozed off for an uncomfortable but peaceful and brief sleep that ended abruptly when we were awakened and told to make ready for immediate departure as soon as the General arrived. As we cleared our eyes and minds I looked to the east where I saw the light gray and rust of the distant sun beyond the horizon struggling to begin a new day. I caught the smell of coffee drifting through the dark predawn air. It was tantalizing and I wanted some so badly I could almost taste it.

Soon someone else, a Captain, brought another message to our pilot ordering us to go refuel and then return to the pad ASAP to pick up the General. At the time I was taking a piss near the tail boom and the Captain gave me a disapproving glare. I simply smiled and said, "Morning sir," as I shook it off.

He turned and hustled back to his General.

"Starchy little bastard isn't he," commented our AC Massey with a smile.

"Probably a ring knocker," guessed crew chief Becker.

"Nah, ring knockers are cool," I said. "At least all the ones I've met."

"Probably a ring kisser," said Becker.

"Or an ass kisser," added Massey. "Lots of those around. 'Specially in these parts."

We refueled and returned to II Corps where we found the General and two others, a Special Forces Colonel and a civilian, waiting at the pad. They boarded without a word and we lifted off immediately after the General got situated in the co-pilot's seat. Becker got the two passengers hooked up with two of the many extra radio head sets rigged on the ship for visiting VIPs and media, then came over and instructed me to keep the chatter to a minimum, leaving the COM system free for the brass.

"Where we heading?" I asked him.

He just shrugged and it was apparent we were both out of the loop on this one. For me this was par for the course. As usual I had no idea where we were or where we were going and this time no idea why. I assumed we were just ferrying the brass to a meeting at some other base but I wasn't fully confident with that assumption when I remembered the predawn hour. Actually I didn't really give a damn as I sat quietly, pissed at having to take off with only the memory of a quick whiff of coffee, but, I thought, since when were General officers required to be considerate of the troops? The General knew where we were going, however, and he was hell bent to get us there, instructing our AC Massey to push 4-Balls to the limits. Our destination was Dak Seang, the SF/CIDG camp about 20 miles north of Dak To in Kontum Province. The camp at Dak Seang sat in a valley canyon near Highway 14 between the Dak Vai and the Dak Si, tributaries of the Dak Poko River and was surrounded by high rough mountainous ridges. It was a border surveillance operations base placed there for the purpose of detecting and preventing enemy infiltration from Laos only 14 klicks to the west. Like most such camps, it was home to SF teams, SOG teams and a Montagnard strike force. Now they were under attack. The NVA's 28th Infantry supported by artillery began attacking Dak Seang at the very first hint of light, part of their spring offensive in an attempt to cut off Dak Pek at the closed end of the canyon - and our General wanted a front row seat.

Before our arrival the enemy had already bombarded the camp with mortars, rockets, and artillery, destroyed a number of buildings, and were in the midst of an all-out ground assault, working their way to the wire. A TAC-E (Tactical Emergency) had been called at Camp Holloway and Bikini Beach in Kontum and reinforcements were already being airlifted from Plateau Gi, another SF camp in the Kontum area. We were there now and I was watching it all from high above, hearing the muffled explosions and seeing a spider web exchange of tracers between the attacking NVA and the camp defensive positions through the low morning light across the kill zone around the base, some finding targets, others glancing away into the sky or through the camp, red tracers going out of the camp and green going in.

As the early morning light crawled over the mountains and revealed the siege, the entire scene seemed surreal. Being safely divorced from it all, thousands of feet above, I was seeing it yet somehow at first not believing it. Our gun ships were already working over the NVA, leaving me to feel we should be doing something as well, something other than just observing, and in fact expected that we would. The NVA got closer, then reached the wire, and for the longest time it seemed the security of Dak Seang would be breached, but the repelling firepower from the camp and supporting air assaults continued, even increased, and the NVA were beaten back. Soon after their retreat an airlift with a company of reinforcements arrived and landed outside the wire but they were immediately surrounded before they could move into the camp. Pinned down, firing, and being fired on, it was a battle within the battle for Dak Seang.

We circled and watched the drama on the ground all day except for a brief time when we refueled at Dak To. The refueling break was a welcomed respite. It gave us an opportunity to grab a bite to eat in the form of a can of lima beans and ham from a C-rat pack along with a shared can of beer we scrounged from an SF sergeant who was pumping us for info about what we had seen. It was his last can and he gave it up without hesitation, and with the enemy build up expecting to soon reach Dak To, it quite possibly could have been the last he ever saw. As for the General and his company, they disappeared for a short time into the TOC. The crew chief handled the refueling while I filled in the SF sergeant and thanked him for the beer and C-Rats. Then we gave the aircraft a quick once over after which I just leaned on the chopper and ran everything through my mind, seeing again that relief company outside the wire, surrounded and holding their own just like the guys in the camp. And then there were the choppers, gun ships and slicks from various units of the 52nd CAB, including our Ghostriders and Avengers. They ran the gauntlet of enemy fire without hesitation to assault and provide cover, drop ammo, and supplies and take out the wounded. They went in balls to the wind and came out bullet riddled by enemy fire, their crews and pilots exposed with little or no protection as they returned fire and flew their ships with steely determination. They were selfless, ignoring their own safety beyond any reasonable expectation.

When the Army needed pilots to fill these mass-produced new fangled air machines and to beef up the new air-mobile military they needed them fast, and to fill the seats they waved the standard officer college requirements and decided to let anybody who could pass the test take their shot. And though the six-month training program encompassed the same rituals and standards as the OCS program, the Army was unwilling to award these pilot officers the coveted and long respected *hard commission.* In other words, they were denied membership in the club and instead they were relegated to a position of commissioned limbo and limited advancement, somewhere between the NCOs of the enlisted ranks and the supposedly more valued and respected upper class officer corps. As far as the Army was concerned they were, in a way, the stepchild soldier, a bunch of Cinderellas, and just another piece of equipment. What the Army didn't count on was the fact it was that very status that made these talented men different, independent, rebellious and courageous. Most, some as young as 18, respected their superiors but also respected and accepted the enlisted man as an equal and in doing so gained the same in return. And this attitude at this stage of the war was contagious, affecting regular commissioned officer pilots as well. What the hell, it was a war and one thing war does when the shit hits the fan is generate a lot of honesty born of necessity, trust, fear, and courage.

Could the brain trust of the Army have been so stupid as to assume that a young man who had the intelligence, talent, and courage to fly complicated expensive aircraft into the jaws of hell wasn't capable or deserving of respect and command? What I was witnessing were the actions of the most heroic pilots in aviation history. It was one thing to fly over the shit but it was something else altogether to fly down into it where you could actually see the angry eyes of the enemy, knowing you were their prize target. It was no wonder the NVA had a bounty on the Ghostriders. There was an old American Indian saying that a warrior was only as great as his enemy. To the NVA that philosophy translated to a reward of $20,000 for a Ghostrider patch with a pilot attached and $10,000 for a crewman. The nose panel off a 189th chopper with the Ghostrider or Avenger artwork made for a really big prize. If the Marines could call themselves Magnificent Bastards, then considering all this, I thought, our guys, our Army chopper pilots and their crews, could certainly be labeled *Magnificent Stepchildren*.

The General returned with an addition to his party in the form of a Vietnamese Colonel and I immediately noticed in his hand he carried what looked like a stack of neatly wrapped sandwiches. Typical, I thought, as I turned away and shrugged it off as rank and privilege then watched our passengers climb aboard. Then a tap on my shoulder turned me around to find General Marra putting one of the sandwiches in my hand. I thanked him and watched him toss one to the crew chief and the other to Massey in the left front seat. He patted me on the back with a smile and climbed in the co-pilot's seat. Needless to say, my opinion of the General should have changed but then I was schooled in the art by an older half brother with the same technique. In my early days of elementary school he would talk me out of my lunch money then at the end of the school day when my stomach was grumbling he would charitably give me a nickel for a candy bar and expect me to be forever grateful.

"Let's get back to the war," I heard the General tell our AC Massey while putting on his flight helmet. "What you say I fly us out and give you a chance to chow down on that well-deserved roast beef sandwich, son?"

"Thank you, sir. She's all yours," Massey smiled.

The General busied himself with the switches in the cockpit, the igniters popped, the engine whirred, and when the blades were cranked up the ship rose, tail up, nosed down, and slipped away from the pad with ease. Not that I was one to judge, but it seemed the General had a pretty good touch on the stick.

With our ship and our bodies refueled, we approached Dak Seang in the midst of a maelstrom from hell. The cutoff reinforcements were still surrounded and the NVA were again attacking the base camp. There were layers of aircraft orbiting and alternately attacking from all directions. Huey gun ships and cobras were working the perimeter through a hail of enemy fire, getting as close in as possible with their miniguns and 60s splattering the flesh of the attacking enemy in all directions. They sent rockets into enemy NVA who were now dug in a mere 30 meters from the wire, and into the tree line to take out gun emplacements. The controlled chaos of the aerial defense alone was mind boggling, forcing us to shadow the Command and Control ship in order to stay out of traffic and trouble. At one time when I looked to the C&C ship I locked eyes with one of its passengers. He was decked out for combat in tiger fatigues with a ragtop, a .45 pistol, an M-16, an M-79 grenade launcher, and ammo bandoliers for both. I at first wondered why he was there since the command ship would only orbit at altitude and play quarterback, much as we were doing, then I concluded he must have been added security in case the ship went down, the security blanket of whomever was on that chopper calling the shots. As we grew near he looked straight at me and smiled and I somehow felt a connection or an odd sense that we knew each other, or an uncanny feeling that we someday would. The feeling sped away when my attention was again drawn to the actions on the ground.

A-1E Skyraiders, attack prop planes common to WWII and the Korean War, roared in like ghosts from the past, turning the surrounding multilayered jungle canopy into a huge billowing fiery red and yellow inferno with their napalm drops. In the midst of all this, small LOH hunter/observation choppers, the Loaches, buzzed around the tree tops like pesky bats looking for trouble and drawing fire in order to find and pinpoint the enemy for destruction by dropping smoke or white phosphorus. Green tracers rained down at the various aircraft from the sides of the cliffs and it sometimes appeared the entire valley was in conflict. Incredibly, the North Vietnamese forces didn't seem to be discouraged by the awesome symphony of air support as they continued to send men and sappers against the camp.

Repeating concussive impacts in the distance revealed B-52 bombers were dumping their loads on suspected enemy base locations. Then my attention was drawn to the fast-movers, Air Force F-4 Phantoms, that were napalming the bald peak of a dense jungle covered mountain. The mountaintop was the highest and most advantageous peak in the valley, known as LZ Orange. It had been cleared and previously used as a night defensive position and a fire support base by the 4th Infantry. When they moved out the NVA moved in and was now directing enemy fire support for their own troops against us from the same location. Once again someone somewhere decided LZ Orange was now critical to the defense of Dak Seang and the rest of the valley forming a plan to retake the mountaintop by inserting a SOG Hatchet Force to secure it, then land an ARVN Mike Force to occupy it. Then if necessary, they could move down the mountain to aid and rescue the SF camp. Throughout the day the mountaintop was barbequed with nape runs as were other areas around the Dak Seang base camp where the NVA were repelled again only to attack a third time with the same result.

Even at altitude the impact and sounds of the battle mingled with my heartbeat and the throbbing of the chopper blades as I sat there, clutching my gun, leaning out, observing. I felt as though we should be down there and at the same time felt fortunate that we weren't. I was like a small child taking his first Ferris-wheel ride, excited yet frightened, looking down at all the marvelous lights and sounds and confusion of the rest of the world. I was ignorant of everything I saw, and unlike the General, I had no background and no preview of what was going on or what was going to happen next. I had just shown up, an observer with no purpose, and there was something obscene about watching people die from a safe distance. Hovering while the brass chatted and pointed like Greek gods up in the clouds looking down and placing bets on mortals in conflict.

We toured the valley from above and watched the assault on Dak Seang and the events on the mountain. The only thing that slowed the bloody efforts by both sides was the eventual setting of the sun. As it slid behind the western mountains and darkness fell we pulled away. We were leaving just as safely and securely as when we had arrived, not taking part or so much as firing a single burst. When I looked back I saw a surreal portrait of conflict. Tracers, both green and red, dotted with flashes of explosions, created what looked like a patchwork of electrical charges throughout the valley below. Ground fired flares briefly lit perimeters and bright rocket flares shot from aircraft, sent broader extended balls of light floating through the smoky air on parachutes above the jungle canopy like the bright firey breath of flying dragons, delivered by our own 52nd CAB Flying Dragons. And indeed, the deadly night sky now belonged to those thunderous flying machines with names like Ghostrider and Avenger.

We returned the General and his company to II Corps with instructions to be back on the pad by 0500, predawn, the next morning. I watched them walk away from the chopper like they had just stepped off a commuter train, met by the smiling ass-kisser Captain who, holding his soft hat on against the wash of the rotor blades with his left hand, looked at us, dropped his smile and pointed skyward, twirling his right hand and index finger. Yeah right, I thought, as if we needed his damn permission to lift off. Maybe it made him feel good or look cool in front the General, or maybe he was just a shit, who knows. He had seen them off like some mother hen and now he was meeting them at the threshold after a hard day at the office. The only thing missing was the kiss on the cheek and a cocktail. I wondered how men like him slept at night, how the hell they could discard their dignity in exchange for ambition, that is if they ever had any in the first place.

⚔️

We returned to Holloway where we refueled and scrounged the equivalent of a full meal from the officer's club. We said little, our minds involuntarily dwelling on the men at Dak Seang who we knew would get no rest or sleep at all, and probably not even a chance to eat. The meal came courtesy of PFC Mondo whose only job of consequence was working at the officer's club. Mondo was a long lanky fair-haired southern California draftee who seemed to walk in slow motion. He was determined to go home alive and in one piece, and to achieve this he had somehow turned his former limited bartending and fast food experience into a management position at the O-club. His only other job was to pick up the mail each day and deliver it to the mail clerk in the supply room. To further insure his safety, instead of living in the HQ hooch with us, he had constructed sleeping quarters behind the club, his own little refuge consisting of two adjoining steel conex containers protected by a triple layer of sand bags on the outside. They were completely wired for electricity with carpet and furniture as well. A small sign hung on the door that read *Mondo's Motel, No Vacancy.* Mondo was also the most talented scrounger in the company, if not the battalion, and could somehow come by anything for anybody if he liked them or was convinced it was for a good cause. For the most part he kept to himself but if he did happen to like you he would, without your asking, bring you the least likely of presents at the most unexpected times, usually late at night after the club closed. For this I called him the Tooth Fairy.

I was fortunate enough to make PFC Mondo's short list of friends, probably because I once took the time to listen to him cry in his beer about how his girlfriend wrecked his car while he was here serving his country in the O-club. Mondo worked part time jobs all through high school just to earn the down payment for his dream car, then his father rewarded his diligence by paying it off as a graduation present. Most of the time when the guys were pouring their hearts out and wanted advice I would simply ask them what they wanted to do, leaving them to unwittingly find their own solution, but this time Mondo caught me in a rare mood and when he informed me that also riding in his hard earned paid for dream car baby at the time of the accident was his girlfriend's new boyfriend, and then asked what I thought he should do, I suggested the obvious.

"Dump the bitch," I said. "You can always get another girl but you can't always find a really cherry '64 candy apple red Corvette convertible with black leather bucket seats and a T-shift."

I didn't mention my other thought; that it was pretty damn stupid to leave the car with his girl in the first place, which is what everybody else had told him. So occasionally, the Tooth Fairy with his access to the exclusive goodies at the O-club up on battalion hill that were flown in by the battalion higher ups, would come quietly tapping at my door in the middle of the night with wonderful gifts like T-bone steaks or whatever else was on special that night. Sometimes with a fine wine or beer and once even a steamed lobster freshly stolen from some place in Dha Nang. He and I and sometimes Randy or someone else would munch and shoot the shit about home, or distant school days, or surfing and all-nighters on the beach. They were good quiet moments in contrast to all that surrounded us.

After refueling and securing 4-Balls we decided we would all spend the night at OPS so we could monitor events and be sure we would be up and out, and back at II CORPS by 0500. Massey went to the club to see about getting some chow and when Mondo found out from Massey that I was part of the crew he loaded him up and even helped carry the hot chow to the chopper.

"I heard what's going on," said Mondo as we lounged around the chopper chowing down on beef stew, chocolate cake, and beer. "The guys have been dragging in and out all day. They'd down a beer and shove down a sandwich, some not even that, and head right back out. Some were goin' back against orders and some were goin' off mission, carrying in supplies, ammo, and replacements from here and other SF camps, and haulin' out the wounded. You want some more cake? I can get you some more cake."

We answered with a silent negative and he continued.

"Yeah, well, you won't believe this but one of the hogs, you know, that screwfaced WO from Memphis who says his sister dated Elvis, he came in for a reload and refuel and his damn main rotor blade fell off. Are you believing that? When they shut down and the blades stopped turning, it just snapped and flopped down. It was torn up, shot full of holes and just snapped. They said the centrifugal force must have kept it up and kept it together when they were in the air. Centrifugal force my ass," continued Mondo. "I think the angels brought that bird in. Looked like Swiss cheese, holes in the fuselage, the rocket pods, leakin' fuel, and not a scratch on the crew. Not one damn scratch. Lucky bastards. It's right over there by the hanger if you don't believe me. So when are you guys going back?"

"0430," said Massey.

"Sure you don't want any more cake, Fusco?"

"No thanks," I said, taking a slow swig of the cool beer.

"So what's the count? I hear we lost a few. Were they ours?"

None of us wanted to answer. Massey finally spoke up.

"Yeah, we saw some go down. One outside the wire and one inside. I think the crews made it but don't know for sure."

We sat there silent for a moment and when Massey finished his beer Mondo took that as a queue.

"I'll go get you guys another beer. And some more cake."

We spent the better part of the next day in the air over Dak Seang, a sight and situation no less impressive than it was the day before. The reinforcement company was still surrounded outside the wire until the Air Force cleared them a path to the camp with an impressive hell storm napalm drop. They carried their dead and and wounded and fought their way into the camp, not only becoming relief but relieved as well. The action at LZ Orange however was something I would be hard pressed to forget because located atop a mountain we could fly a little closer for better observation. We watched and could do nothing and when it was over I felt guilty and depressed. I felt there was something unclean or immoral about being able to watch your comrades at war but not participate. After that day, I guess the General had seen enough because we weren't told to return the next day. If 4-Balls was called back it must have went with a different gunner because I had to get back to my main occupation at the Ghostrider HQ.

For the next few days I didn't say much. Upon my return to my duties in the orderly room I was certain I would be in a world of shit with Top or the CO for not showing up for two days but nothing was said. Major Anthony was not a problem because he and other Ghostrider pilots were still rotating their services out at Dak Seang and other hot spots, dealing with the enemy's Spring offensive. Top on the other hand didn't know what I had been doing, that I had been flying during my spare time. I never bothered to ask if it was okay. He had found out when questioning my absence. Randy had covered my ass with the morning reports. Then apparently everyone eventually found out that I wasn't off dicking around when General Mara or someone from his office, maybe the ass kisser, placed a call to the unit citing their appreciation for our services. It kept me out of the doghouse and as a result, all I got from Top was a quiet approval with a simple,

"Next time I want to know," and, "Be careful out there. Don't want to lose my company clerk."

It never dawned on me that Top had seen his share of combat on a previous tour, which was why he occasionally rose from his desk and cringed when he stretched. He never took off his fatigue blouse like the rest of us, even on the hottest of days, because under it he wore a girdle type brace around his mid section to support and hide his condition. Necessary, he one day confessed, to avoid a forced medical discharge resulting from a fractured back he received in a chopper crash during a previous tour in-country.

CHAPTER 22

COMA?

It was evening. The sun had set and a few of us HQ types were gathered at a table in the EM club when Randy finally decided to ask me about Dak Seang. After three beers and a few Scotches I told them what I had seen, about the camp under siege and the relentless attacks, the cut off relief company, the bombings and our gutsy-ass chopper crews. When I started telling them about the action on top of the mountain at LZ Orange I trailed off. They sat there for a quiet moment waiting for me to continue, but I didn't. Then I heard the story continuing without me and at first I thought it was the booze messing with my head or that I was losing it. The story came from behind me, from the next table, and I turned just as the orator rose to join us. From my slumped position in the chair, and through the eyes and influence of the alcohol, he looked to be a giant but when he sat next to me he became more real. I guessed him to be a few inches taller than I, maybe five-eleven and, of course, couldn't help noticing his closely cropped, if not nearly bald head, highly uncommon for the times, even in the Army unless you were a gung ho SF type, a spook, or an Airborne extremist. Then when he smiled and ordered a round of drinks I recalled and placed his eyes. They were the same eyes I had caught in the command ship over Dak Seang, the guy who sat there on that chopper loaded for bear, who smiled at me as though Dak Seang was just another day in the park. Again I got the odd feeling that we were somehow connected. He had a wide muscular physic and features, solid all around, with a deep clear confident voice that sported a touch of a southern accent that somehow pulled it all together. There was a cheerful glint in his eyes that grew slightly as he spoke and remained throughout the seriousness of his oral recollection. He looked quickly around the table then looked at me, studied me, and continued the story of LZ Orange.

"They showed that morning soon after you did," he said looking at me. "A flight of Bikini slicks and Buccaneer gun ships out of Kontum with the first elements of the ARVN 3rd Battalion of the 42nd. They were there to take that mountaintop and hold it, then juke on down and rescue the SF camp. The first bird came in. No problem. Dumped two 52nd Pathfinders to secure the LZ and guide in the other choppers, Bobby Hawkins and Curtis Montgomery, along with six ARVNs. The place had been bombed and fried with napalm by the Air Force the day before and saturated again that morning, so nobody expected any resistance. Montgomery carried the radio and they parked themselves by a big bomb crater and started bringing in the other ships. Montgomery was on the horn and Hawkins was guiding in the second ship with a load of ARVNs when all hell broke lose. Montgomery got hit right off, was the first to go down, but stayed on the radio, then they were hit from three-sixty, all sides, and he sank dead on the spot. Hawkins pitched himself into the crater and returned fire until he ran out of ammo. The ARVNs took cover in another crater but they just laid there. Those little bastards didn't even shoot back."

The new round of drinks arrived at our table and our strange new guest paid the Vietnamese waitress without even looking at her. He downed and finished off his original drink, wrapped his big hand around the fresh one, turned it a half turn and continued.

"All the dink soldiers on that second bird had been chopped up and killed on approach when the NVA first opened fire, and I saw the door gunner get slammed back when he caught a couple rounds. He slumped over and I thought he was dead too but he forced himself back up and got on his gun and started returning fire just like the crew chief on the other side of the ship. Then the bird went out of control, danced and bounced around until it crashed on its side near the edge of the jungle. On its side like that, the wounded door gunner got buried under all those dead ARVNs. The other gunner, the crew chief, climbed out and fell on the ground. The first chopper, the one that dropped off Hawkins and Montgomery, came back, popped up the side of the mountain to get them out but caught so much enemy shit it had to back off. It radioed that they saw the front-seaters in the crashed chopper still alive and struggling to get out through the broken chin bubble. When they did get out Hawkins left his cover in the crater and rushed over to help. The pilot went down when he got shot a few times in the back and the co-pilot dragged him to cover over near the ARVNs. The crew chief made it there too and they laid there catching hell from all sides."

Our guest paused for a gulp of his drink then smiled, not a smile of joy but of amazement, "They were surrounded by fortified positions set up to catch any choppers on approach. It was a meat grinder, but Hawkins, that beautiful bastard, jumped up on that crashed chopper and found the door gunner trying to dig his way out from under all those dead ARVNs. One of the dead soldiers on top of the gunner had his guts blown open and all that shit was running all over the gunners face and in his mouth. Hawkins pulled him out and they huddled in the gun well for a time. Then I saw this wounded gunner jump out of the chopper, covered with blood, shot in the shoulder and the side, carrying a couple grenades, and he ran to the other crew who were layin' by the crater where the six ARVNs were hold up. Hawkins climbed out and ran to Montgomery. I could see him checking the radio but I guess it was shot up so he ran back to the chopper and manned the sixty. That gutsy wounded door gunner wasn't about to cash it in either and he climbed in the crater and took a weapon and ammo from the ARVNs. Then all six of those worthless Dink bastards deserted, took off into the jungle. All six of 'em."

He took another sip of his drink to quell his contempt for the ARVNs, looked at the others and me and continued. "The gun ships started pounding the entire perimeter with rockets and mini-guns. Then two more ships loaded with ARVNs started coming in. Bullets ripped through the windshield of the first one, hit the pilot in the breastplate and set off a smoke grenade on his survival vest. Then the ship caught rounds in the transmission, slid left and dropped for the valley below, spewing yellow smoke like nobody's business. The pilot somehow got control and nursed it over to Dak To for an emergency landing. The second chopper caught the shit too and had to force land with a damaged gear box."

"They turned them back. That 3rd ARVN battalion airlift," I said. "I saw them turn and leave."

"Yeah, but you saw other choppers keep coming, right? You know damn well those guys wouldn't be left there without cover. Like those guys from the Pink Panthers who were coming back to Dak To from a SOG job and heard all the shit on the radio. That wounded pilot on the ground was a high school buddy of one of those Panther pilots or something, and those guys were hot to trot. They went to SOG command and demanded to be released from

standby so they could pick up a Bright Light team to attempt a
rescue. Command approved and included two Cobras for cover.
Then the Air Force in Pleiku ordered them to stand down, said that
the Air Force was taking over the rescue and were sending in fast-
movers. But those guys said fuck it and refueled and went back
anyway, the same as all the other aircraft that had returned to Dak
To. They were all on their own initiative and didn't give a shit what
the Air Force or anybody else said." He looked to me and took a
drink then said, "You want to tell what happened next?"

I took a drink, lit a cigarette, thought a moment then nodded
agreement.

"A plane came in. A C-130."

"C-123," he corrected.

"Yeah, I guess. Anyway, the cargo door opened and it flew
over the LZ and dropped a crate of supplies. I was told it contained
a radio, weapons and ammo. It missed and landed in the jungle on
the side of the hill. Then three ships, I think they were Bikini,
170th, tried to come up the side of the mountain. A slick with a hog
on each side. But halfway up the mountain they were beat back by
heavy fire. It was like the entire mountainside came alive. And
then three little birds, Loaches, showed up. I remember hearing in
all the radio chatter that nobody knew who the hell they were or
where they came from and they didn't bother to say, they just went
in low-leveling across the bottom of the valley then one of them
shot up the side of the mountain for the LZ but had to pull away.
They turned him into Swiss cheese. Then a slick came in, another
Bikini carrying a single SF guy with a radio. I could see him and I
recognized him. He's the one they call Stumper. But less than a
quarter mile out they pulled away with both their gunners and
Stumper all shot up."

"Jesus Christ," said Randy. "It's like they were using those
guys as bait."

"That's right," said our mysterious new drinking buddy.
"They've been known to do that and that's pretty much how it was
this time. After each rescue attempt somebody would fly over the
LZ and the guys would wave at them. They were usually under
fire, sometimes heavy, sometimes light, but between rescue
attempts it slacked off to a series of pot-shots and all those guys
had going for them was that wounded gunner with an M-16 and

Hawkins on the sixty gun of the downed chopper. The co-pilot was wounded and the crew chief was busy caring for his wounded pilot. You could see the dirt popping around them when they came under fire and those bastard gooks kept shooting into Montgomery's body and the radio just for fuckin' kicks. Those damn gooks were only about twenty meters away on all sides. They could have rushed them and ended it. We know that because SOG HQ in Kontum radioed the C&C chopper I was on and said they had confirmation the LZ was the Division Headquarters for the NVA. They were dug in all over the damn mountain top."

He finished off his drink and speaking in Vietnamese to the waitress ordered another. He pointed to our drinks as if to ask if we wanted another and we all declined but he had already ordered the round anyway. We sat silent for a moment as we finished the drinks we had. Then he continued.

"By mid morning the wounded pilot stopped waving. He was dead or dying," he said.

The waitress returned with the drinks. After she distributed them around the table and departed, he reached into his pocket and pulled out a small tin of pills, withdrew two, popped them in his mouth and chased them down with a gulp of his drink. I don't know what the pills were for but I made the drink out to be a straight up tall bourbon. He then looked at me curiously, "It's up your ass isn't it? Churning in your gut. I can see it in your eyes. You didn't like just watching all that shit up there with the weenie brass and not doing anything?"

I didn't answer but he knew he was right. Randy looked at me and pushed my fresh scotch closer to my hand in a silent suggestion that I drown the anger.

"Those Pink Panther guys managed to put together a Bright Light team of SFs and 'Yards and their flight of two slicks and two Cobras arrived just as two Air Force F4s were strafing the hillside," he continued. "Four Spads were dumping napalm. Then two Air Force Jolly Greens that had come down all the way from Da Nang up in I CORPS came in and lined up for approach."

"Yeah," I said. "I heard the Bikinis warn them off. Said the approach was impossible. 'High risk,' they said."

"Right. Well they went in anyway and the lead Jolly started taking fire over a quarter mile out, and at a quarter mile they were in a shit storm, taking it from three-sixty, and then dropped into the jungle and went up in flames. The other Jolly followed them down and they were taking a lot of shit too but they managed to retrieve the downed crew. I heard the pilot was dead and another one died at the 71st Evac. That second Jolly was so shot up they had to scrap it."

"They had to… I mean, well, shit, did they give up then? Wouldn't they give it up by then?" asked Randy.

I looked down into my drink as Randy got his answer.

"That's not the way it works, son," he said with a slightly heavier touch of the southern draw.

I figured the pills and the bourbon were kicking in.

"What if it was you on top of that mountain?"

Randy sat silent, corrected and feeling a little slighted, but recovered quickly as the story continued.

"Another ship came in, another Bikini slick. I heard the crew was wearing full body armor with extra breastplates under their seats and even crammed in the nose bubble, hoping it would provide more protection. They came close but caught so much enemy shit their engine caught fire and they crash-landed a little southeast of the LZ. They came out of it but didn't get those poor guys at Orange."

"The weather," I said.

"That's right," he remembered. "The weather started gettin' funky."

"You could see it coming, rollin' in like drifting smoke through the hills, and there was a lot of chatter on the radio," I added. "People trying to figure out how to get in there before the weather closed them out."

"Those guys with the Bright Light team, the high school buddy, were getting desperate, and the weather didn't help any. I saw them steep dive into the valley, level off at the valley floor then go low and fast up the side of the mountain. They got hit right away from all directions and by the time that first ship reached the LZ the entire Bright Light team inside that chopper was all chopped up, deader'n shit. When it hard-landed in the LZ the co-pilot, crew chief, and gunner from the first crashed chopper ran to board and escape, but a squad of NVA popped out of the jungle behind them firing and chasing them down. Hawkins opened up with the sixty at another squad of NVA who were rushing to attack the rescue chopper. That wounded gunner was hit again in the back and leg but made it to the ship. The crew chief made it too, collapsed in the ship with bullets through his jaw, back and hands. His co-pilot helped him aboard then turned and went back for his pilot's body."

He looked at me, took his glass and tapped mine and said, "You want to finish it?"

"The drink?" I asked.

"No, the story."

I nodded and took a swig of my scotch. After it had burned its way down to my gut I finished the story. "He was trying to drag the pilot's body to the rescue chopper. I think he was screaming for help. I could see it but couldn't hear what he was saying. It was a ways off. The wounded gunner took the weapon of one of the dead Bright Light guys and was firing then started out of the chopper to go help but he was shoved back in by the crew chief who was covering with his sixty, shooting into the NVA who were rushing out of the jungle. The wounded gunner grabbed another weapon and started shooting again. The pilots in the front of the chopper were catching hell. I don't know how anybody could have lived through it. The incoming rounds looked to shatter everything, windshield, chin bubble, and I could see the co-pilot was hit. But the pilot was on the radio and he sounded all calm, like… I don't know, it was unreal. He said he was losing fuel and he was down to 400 pounds and was lifting off. He lifted off and nosed over the mountain then he reported he had lost tail rotor control."

"Damn right he lost tail rotor. He had an unexploded B40 rocket stuck in his tail boom," added our nameless guest.

"The Pathfinder on the sixty, the one you call Hawkins. He covered their extraction but he and the copilot were left behind." I paused for a drink and looked at our bald headed friend.

"Out of the pan…," he said.

"…and into the fire," I said.

"What?" said Randy.

"The rescue ship," I said. "It got out of the LZ but was in trouble, damaged and out of fuel, so the two choppers made their way through the valley to Dak Seang and landed in the middle of a shit storm. They landed nose to nose and when that rescue chopper sat down bodies were falling out of the side doors. And right away it became a bullet magnet with debris and shit flying everywhere. They had set down outside the wire in the middle of an all out ground attack. The NVA were advancing from about a hundred yards away. Everybody stumbled or fell out of the chopper and were struggling to board the other chopper with help from the other crew so when the NVA saw that they changed targets and started on that one. Rounds were hitting all over the ship and I could see the dirt flying up all around them, but somehow they lifted off and got out and headed for Pleiku."

"So, the guys on the mountain?" asked Randy.

"They were still there when we flew off the site. The weather rolled in," I said, looking across the table for a conclusion.

"Flyovers the next day reported seeing only two bodies, the pilot and Montgomery," said our nameless friend. "The co-pilot and Hawkins are gone, MIA. We still can't get into the LZ. Won't be able to until we finish kicking that division of bad guys off that damn hill."

"I gotta take a piss," I said, scooting away from the table and making my way through the neighboring tables to the pisser. The booze had set in just right; just mellow enough to ease the memories freshened by our discussion. When I came back our guest was gone.

"Where'd he go?" I asked as I sat down, looking about the club for his telltale baldhead.

"Just up and left," said Randy. "And you didn't even introduce us. My mother would chew your ass for that."

"How could I introduce him? I don't even know who the hell he is."

"He Coma," said a high-pitched hurried voice.

We all turned to find the Vietnamese waitress cleaning a nearby table.

"What?" I said.

"Him nem *Coma*. Him be here long ti. He pat-fina," she said in her chopped English.

"A Pathfinder?" I said.

"He Coma," she said. "You stay away. Coma beaucoup dien cai dau."

Beaucoup dien cai dau she had said in her mix of French, Vietnamese and English. It meant very crazy, but we didn't know him well enough and weren't in a position to agree or disagree.

The NVA's Spring offensive was wide spread all the way across II CORP, keeping the Ghostriders and the rest of the 52nd CAB busy and in big demand. The siege at Dak Seang lasted a couple more weeks. It was extremely costly for the NVA and it cost our battalion fifteen lives, four of which were Ghostriders. I wanted to know where the war was and I had found it, big time, but it wasn't the kind of war I'd expected and it just didn't seem to make a lot of sense. Something in this war was missing, something very basic, but one thing I came to know for sure was that whatever the war was and whatever it was that was missing, it sure as hell wasn't the courage of the American soldier, at least not those I had seen in action on the ground and in the air.

CHAPTER 23

PIGS ARE BEAUTIFUL

"Ghostriders. Fusco," I said into the phone.

"What?"

"Ghostriders."

"Who is this?"

"Fusco."

"What's your rank?"

"Spec Four. What's yours?"

"Lieutenant. Are you some kind of smart ass?"

"No, not Lieutenant, Specialist. Fourth Class. I'm the company clerk."

"You *are* a smart ass."

"No, a company clerk."

"Is that the way you answer the phone, company clerk Specialist Fusco?"

"Only when it rings. Who is this?"

"This is Lieutenant Lochridge. You stay put, Fusco. I'm coming over there right now, damnit."

"No problem... sir," I said, then hung up the phone and warned Randy. "We're going to have a visitor. Some Lieutenant. Sounds like a real winner with a case of the ass about phone etiquette."

"You know, one of these days your phone jokes are going to get you into big trouble," said Randy. "What if that had been the battalion CO or somebody even higher?"

"Nah, he doesn't bother with that kind of chicken shit. He just grunts and says, 'Gimme your CO' and I just say, 'Yes sir, hold one.' Then two minutes later, when I figure the phone is pretty much sweated and stuck to his ear, I tell him the CO went to the golf course."

"The golf course. Are you nuts?"

"Hey, don't blame me if our CO has a sense of humor and damn near every time he walks out the door he says he's going to the golf course."

"Golf course. What golf course?"

"I don't know. I think those pussies over at the Pleiku Air Force base have a golf course. Chief Chief went and played a few rounds once while Dillinger and I pigged out at their O-Club. I don't fink on the Major though. I usually cover for him."

"You're kiddin'. They got a golf course?"

"Yeah and I'm sure it's a nice one. Typical Air Force."

"And the battalion CO doesn't get pissed when you tell him the Major went to the golf course?"

"Nope. I guess that's par for the course once you get some rank. No pun intended. I had a CO in the states that spent damn near every day, or at least half the day, at the base golf club."

"Yea but this is a war zone."

"Not for the Air Force. They got the best of everything. I'll take you over there some time. You won't believe it. It's just like stateside."

It wasn't the first time I'd caught a little hell for my telephone protocol, or lack thereof, and I'm sure it wasn't to be the last. It had taken me less than two weeks to develop the stylish greeting I now used and I thought it to be quite an achievement considering what had been the standard telephone answering procedure previously. The required wordage was a mouth full by any standard and considering the number of calls I had to field each day, I decided I had to make a choice between spending the better part of the day just answering the calls before I could even answer the calls, or following the spirit of the Army's predilection for brevity. I chose brevity, and began whittling away at the usual company telephone greeting.

"189th Assault Helicopter Company, Ghostriders, 52nd Aviation Battalion, Specialist Vincent Fusco speaking. You are on an unsecure line. Good morning. How may I help you, sir?" is how I was instructed to answer the phone and I had mastered the entire soliloquy to the point to where it rolled swiftly and inaudibly off my tongue like tasteless caviar after you found out it was fish eggs. Not that it mattered much, because most everyone who called on a regular basis was immune to the words or simply interrupted with a quick, "Yeah, yeah, Fusco, this is…"

Randy hated the standard mouth-mangler so much that he rigged his phone line so that it wouldn't ring by slipping a pencil under the receiver and making it appear to be on its cradle when it was actually sending out a busy signal. He then put a triple layer of tape over the little holes of the earpiece to muffle the beeping sound the phone made to tell him it was off the hook. No one ever noticed because hardly anybody ever called him. That meant the only one in the office answering the phone was myself being I was charged with catching and screening most all the calls for Top, the CO and XO. So I began the task of shortening the greeting a little each day, then measuring the response. No one on the other end of the phone calls ever seemed to notice and no one in the office seemed to care. The progression from day one went something like this,

"189th Assault Helicopter Company, Ghostriders, 52nd Aviation Battalion, Specialist Vincent Fusco speaking. You are on an unsecure line. Good morning. How may I help you, sir?"

Then on day two;

"189th Assault Helicopter Company, Ghostriders, Specialist Vincent Fusco speaking. You are on an unsecure line. Good morning. How may I help you, sir?"

Then on day four;

"189th Assault Helicopter Company, Ghostriders, Specialist Vincent Fusco speaking. You are on an unsecure line. How may I help you, sir?"

On day five;

"189th Assault Helicopter Company, Ghostriders, Specialist Vincent Fusco speaking. How may I help you, sir?"

Day six;

"189th Assault Helicopter Company, Ghostriders, Specialist Fusco speaking, sir."

I let that one ride for a while, then on day ten,

"189th Ghostriders, Fusco speaking, sir."

Day eleven;

"Ghostriders, Fusco speaking."

Then finally the evolutionary verbal pearl was cast.

"Ghostriders. Fusco," which I thought pretty much said it all and being everybody knew who the hell they were calling in the first place, and nobody even listened to the quick-lipped formal salutation anyway, then what the hell was the point of delaying the war just to answer the phone. The first and only other complaint I

received was from a Major somebody, who I assumed was the CO of another company.

"Ghostriders. Fusco."

"What?"

"Ghostriders. Fusco." I repeated.

"Is this the company clerk?" he asked.

"Yes," I answered.

"Is that the way you people answer the phone at the 219th?" he asked.

"No," I said.

"What do you mean no? I just heard you. All you said was 'Ghostriders, Fusco'."

"Yes, that's right," I said. *"Ghostriders.* Fusco."

"This is Major Sanford, soldier, and your smart ass is treading on thin ice right now."

"Sir, would you like me to give you the correct number for the 219th?"

"The correct number for the… Oh, um, disregard," he said, just before the line clicked off.

Being an aviation battalion and company, one would think that most military standards and disciplines would be enforced and in a combat operational sense they were, in a lax sort of way. But there was something about the constant threat of death from the enemy and the possible threat of death by a disgruntled friendly that created a great deal of tolerance by field level management. For example, though most of us may have started the day with a full uniform of lightweight jungle fatigues or nomex flight suit, nearly all of us quickly stripped down to T-shirts, and often when outside, no shirts at all. The result was a mixed fashion statement that would have given a stateside CO a heart attack. Some wore T-shirts from their old high schools, some with peace signs or rock and roll references, and some had the simple homemade F.T.A. slogan that everyone knew stood for Fuck The Army. When confronted by a questioning officer or NCO, who most likely knew exactly what it meant, the wearer would explain that it stood for something like Free Ticket to America or Fun, Travel, and Adventure. My personal favorite unauthorized T-shirt was one I'd picked up at a gift shop on our stopover in Hawaii. The shirt was yellow and on the back was the endearing face of a hog and large letters proclaiming, PIGS ARE BEAUTIFUL. At the time both cops and G.I.s were being referred to as establishment pigs by the anti-establishment anti-war counter culture of America, making my shirt to be a kind of anti-anti establishment statement with which hardly anyone in uniform could disagree. But as far as I was concerned it was just a joke and a cool looking pig. Being the T-shirt was yellow it was way out of reg as opposed to the Army issued OD green or white, but I usually got no complaints, only laughs.

Troops with irregular jobs or hours such as flight crews, grunts, perimeter guards, and even over-extended flight mechanics, well, just about everybody except us, often failed to shave or maintain a regulation haircut, resulting in five o-clock shadows and a few ragged heads. And then there was the ever-popular mustache ranging from the trendy non-reg turned down Foo Man Chu and the turned up John L. Sullivan, to the sparse half-ass see-threw that was usually sported by young fuzzy-faced hopefuls, which of course, was the most prevalent. It was one of the few small ways of holding on to your civilian identity from our stateside world where long hair and facial hair had become fashionable, and for some reason, socially relevant. Certain forms of creative jewelry were popular as well, like the T/R Chain Bracelets. These bracelets, made from helicopter tail rotor chains, were pretty much a status symbol prized by air crewmen and flight mechanics, and considering the high cost of the chains due to incompetent military purchasing agents, were probably as valuable as their equivalent weight in gold. Some were even made from choppers that had been shot down and were worn in memorial to the crewmembers that died in the crash. Montagnard beaded necklaces were also popular but mostly among the black brothers who also wore an imaginative assortment of black power bracelets and necklaces made from black nylon bootlaces. These and a host of other minor violations were all signs of the times and our current human condition, and even though a few took it to extreme, most were simply seeking a little self expression in the Army's world of conformity and expected uniformity. Regardless, if it weren't for the mama-sans keeping our clothes clean there's no telling what our state of appearance would have been.

Numerous directives came down from the safe, clean, starchy air conditioned environment of the brigade commander complaining and demanding full compliance with all Army codes of dress and behavior, but it was a wise field commander who conveniently developed dyslexia when they were received, or chose to simply pass the orders along with little enthusiasm. Needless to say, military protocol wasn't high on anybody's list of things to do such as salutes, which weren't exactly common behavior either. *"What are they going to do, send me to Vietnam?"* was the usual retort and attitude of the ranks when a group chastising threat took place. As Chief Chief Zamboni put it, "The only uniformity in the Army that really counts is that we all bleed red."

An unkempt appearance or the failure to salute or wear a hat wasn't going to get you court-martialed, but unfortunately there occasionally arrived the chicken-shit predator who flew in fresh from the States like my soon to visit Lieutenant Lochridge, still so caught up in his OCS experience and rebirth as an Army God that he didn't have a clue and was yet to catch on or be indoctrinated to the true nature of the combat zone beast.

So in he walked, all spit and polish and clean and unblemished in appearance and spirit, and he went straight to Randy's desk and started reaming him a whole new asshole.

"I'm Lieutenant Lochridge. I just spoke to you on the phone," he said, angrily removing his hat. "Don't you know the proper procedure for answering the phone in the military?"

Randy looked at him, looked at me, looked at his taped up pencil-rigged phone, and then looked back at him.

"Well, what do you have to say for yourself? And stand up when I talk to you troop," he demanded.

Randy rose slowly looking to me again for support and rescue. I could see his Randy dance wanting to kick in and I know it was cruel but I simply shrugged my shoulders, smiled and watched the show.

"Do you or do you not know how to answer the phone, soldier?"

"Yes sir," answered Randy.

"Yes sir, you do or yes sir, you don't?"

"I do," answered Randy, putting on his glasses.

"Then why don't you do it, and who the hell said you could wear those non-regulation glasses? Who the hell do you think you are, John Lennon? You look like some damn hippie. And where's your blouse? Why aren't you wearing your blouse? How do you expect people to know your name and rank if you don't wear your blouse?"

Randy retrieved his fatigue shirt from its nail on the wall and began putting it on.

"And don't you people stand at attention when an officer enters the room?" asked Lieutenant Lochridge, scanning the room and seeing myself and the amiable Admin Officer Captain Whitley in his OD T-shirt leaning back in his chair behind his desk, leisurely reading the Army Times. Whitley usually wasn't there because he was usually out flying or working on a special project at the officers club.

About that time Top entered the room from the CO's office where he had just placed some paperwork in the CO's in-box and apparently overheard all of Lieutenant Lochridge's ranting.

"Excuse me Lieutenant, do you have a problem with my clerk, Specialist Colatazzi?" asked Top.

"With who?" the Lieutenant asked, looking to Top then looking back to Randy who was buttoning up his fatigue shirt with the name above the pocket in big letters that clearly read, *Colatazzi.*

Just then the phone rang and I answered, "Ghostriders. Fusco."

The Lieutenant turned and shot me a glare that I thought would bounce my own in-box right off the desk and out the door, but before he could say anything Captain Whitley intervened.

"Standing at attention is required when an officer of a higher rank enters the room, Lieutenant," said Captain Whitley. "But we usually don't bother with that bullshit unless the officer outranks our CO."

"Is that what you call it, bullshit?" said the Lieutenant. "I don't see any officers here and I expect nothing less than full military courtesy."

With the phone cradled between my chin and shoulder, I rose from my chair to retrieve a file from the top drawer of the file cabinet and when I did the Lieutenant caught sight of the back of my yellow pig shirt.

"What the fuck are you wearing, soldier? Do you realize what I could do to you for that breach of uniform protocol?"

I set the file on my desk, finished my phone conversation and hung up the phone. This was getting good, I thought, glancing over to Captain Whitley with a cursory smile.

"Lieutenant, if you would step outside I think the First Sergeant has some advice he'd like to give you and if you would like to discuss it with me later just call Fusco over there and ask for me, Captain Whitley. Fusco's the one with the pig shirt," smiled Captain Whitley.

Lieutenant Lochridge's adam's apple started doing a nervous little bounce as he followed Top out the door to the perceived privacy of the front of the HQ. We all listened intently to hear our First Sergeant politely and respectfully, according to the Lieutenant's rank, tell, or should I say suggest and advise, him to never come into his orderly room or his company area and harass any of his people again unless he was prepared to explain himself to our commanding officer, and also suggested that if he had any intention of surviving in Vietnam for more than two weeks, he should forget the chicken-shit he learned at OCS and just focus on being a good soldier. Top was wonderfully diplomatic and persuasive as usual. In his mind he wasn't defending or excusing my minor insolence but rather helping a young officer become a better leader or at least a lesser asshole.

"The man whose ass you chew up today," said Top, "just might be the man who decides *not* to save your ass tomorrow. In other words, Lieutenant, in this part of the world you don't demand respect, you earn it."

We didn't know where the jerk Lieutenant came from or what he wanted in the first place, or where he went after that, and truthfully we didn't give a shit, but like years and wars past there were more like him coming and going in the Army all the time, and inevitably and unfortunately, some of them had to learn the hard way, the way that didn't always offer second chances. Just as I had quickly learned soon after arriving in-country, these kinds of officers would also have to learn, being this is Vietnam and in Vietnam all things are not what they seem and sometimes all rules do not apply.

"I don't think he liked my shirt," I observed.

"I still think you should sell it to me," suggested Captain Whitley. "Before it gets you in real trouble."

"You left me hanging," laughed Randy. "Thanks a lot, buddy. God's gonna get you for that."

"God will have to get in line behind a few million little yellow people," I said.

"Whose going to cover your ass when I leave here, Fusco?" asked Captain Whitley.

"I should kick your ass, Fusco," laughed Top as he returned to the orderly room.

"Twelve bucks," offered Captain Whitley, raising his original bid of ten for the pig shirt.

"Nope."

"Fifteen."

"Nope."

"Come on, Fusco. I'm out of here in a few weeks. Make it a farewell present."

"Nope."

"Now I got pig shirts to worry about," said Top, as he settled behind his desk and reached for some paperwork in his in-box.

"Twenty."

"Nope."

"I want that shirt, Fusco," said Captain Whitley.

"Nope."

"Okay then, Top, you can bust him," said Captain Whitley. "Send his ass to LBJ."

"No, I can't do that," said Top.

"Why not?" asked Captain Whitley.

"Because I want the shirt," said Top.

"Nope."

CHAPTER 24

GOOOOOOD
MORNIN' CAMBODIA

I had been to Cambodia but didn't know it and it didn't matter that I didn't know it because, actually, I hadn't been there. I know this because President Richard Nixon was always on television saying we have no troops in Cambodia. I'm sure this must have been confusing to everyone who was in the know along the military chain of command and in Washington, considering Nixon had authorized the CIDG, SOG and SF OPS, and cross border incursions in the first place. That plus the bombing of NVA assets in Cambodia, called Operation Menu, meant there was a lot on the plate. But for now, in July of '70, we no longer had troops in Cambodia, and in that manner of speaking, we had no troops or Ghostriders in Cambodia almost everyday. It was the Ghostriders primary mission to support, insert and extract 5th Special Forces, SOG teams, and Spooks all over II Corps and the tri-border area on both sides of the fence, and it was always reassuring for our tired pilots and crews, after a day of dodging rockets and bullets and eliminating the enemy, to come home at the end of the day and watch President Nixon on the AFVN news talking about how we weren't there. For us it was just business as usual, the way it had been for quite a while, because that's where the bad guys were. But ever since that operation back in May where we got really serious about the NVA in Cambodia and dealt with it in a big way, things had changed both politically, and for us, operationally.

In all fairness to Tricky Dick, of whom it could be said certainly had a brass pair when it came to the war, he was pretty much forced into telling that particular prevarication as a matter of necessity when the U.S. Senate lost its pair altogether and passed the Cooper-Church Amendment prohibiting the use of U.S. ground troops in Laos and Cambodia after June 30. The restriction didn't include aircraft, however, so it was perfectly okay for us and the aircraft of all the other branches of service to fly in and do bad things to the enemy and his Ho Chi Minh trail. Only in the political world could killing the enemy be so ridiculously delineated as to view a difference between killing the enemy from the ground or from the air. To a soldier dead is dead, and when it comes to winning a war the death of the enemy, no matter how or where the hell he is or how it's done, is the main objective and as such death is necessary. At least that's the soldier's point of view. So what was the big deal?

The trick was to first find them, then watch them, and then punch their lights out, hence the SOGs and spooks and SF special OPS teams in there that weren't really in there. In affect the Senate was worse than the clowns who had earlier advised President Johnson and who perpetuated the irrationality of the Vietnam War. Those boys were just plain stupid but the Senate on the other hand, as a group and like most all politicians, were cowardly in the face of their duty and got severely weak-kneed in the face of the reaction to the war by a minority of a very vocal and active piss and moan generation that didn't even vote, and were more concerned with not being drafted then the actual purpose, events, and outcome of our war itself. These kids, augmented by the liberal *monkey-see monkey-do don't think it through* crowd, were all up in arms in their supposedly passive but radically violent manner. Was I aware of and hosting opinions about all of this? Hell no. Like most G.I.s my age I was more concerned with the state of my own physical union than that of the country. Politics was something I had yet to grow into.

For the first time, other than the Tet Offensive in which we actually decimated the enemy but were portrayed as losers by Walter Cronkite and his media colleagues, something big took place that actually looked like a war and made strategic sense. It was called Operation Fishhook and in less than two months we successfully invaded Cambodia, ravaged the enemy's sanctuaries and resources, and thwarted or postponed the overthrow of not just one but two, and possibly even three, Asian countries. For this the pissers and moaners marching in the streets of Washington condemned us to hell. It was like the Green Bay Packers winning the Super Bowl and then having the news clowns find the only ten idiot cheese heads out of a full stadium of eighty-thousand who would say, *"Well, gee whiz fella's, winning the Super Bowl was kind of nice but did you have to get so dirty?"* Thanks to television and inept idiot journalists who couldn't differentiate between the battle and the war, we were fighting both the NVA and the flower clowns whose principal argument was '*War is bad for birds and children*'. Well, no shit. Who the hell knew that better than us? But then that's about all we knew.

The Cambodian Offensive began for me when I woke up one morning in late April. As the sun strained over the eastern horizon to spread its first light on the Pleiku plateau and the highlands everything felt and sounded different. The air carried a sense of urgency that my fuzzy early morning radar easily detected the moment I sat up on the edge of my bunk. Usually most choppers would have already gone on missions with others coming and going periodically all through the day, but on this morning when I walked to the door of the hooch and squinted into the new dawn, I discovered the traffic was mostly incoming. It included not only all types of aircraft but trucks full of troops and gear and supplies as well, with convoys rolling in like it was rush hour in LA. Unknown to us, similar activities were taking place at other staging locations as far south as the Mekong Delta in IV Corps.

The urgent sounds, smells, and sights of activity were everywhere. Noisy deuce-and-a-half trucks rolled past leaving a trail of black diesel exhaust fumes forced through the top of the snorkel stacks endured by the unenthusiastic grunts perched uncomfortably on the wooden benches in the back. We exchanged glances without acknowledgement as they passed. I took it all in, the sounds and sights that had invaded enmasse our otherwise relatively stable environment of Camp Holloway. Maintenance and support facilities all over camp were being augmented to accommodate the overload of additional troops and aircraft. They were rolling in and flying in and setting their tents up wherever there was room, including the rarely used softball field down near the ammo dump and bunker line.

It had all started gradually in the middle of the night but I hadn't heard a thing as I slept because I had finally learned to condition my mind to blot out those types of disturbances other than threatening rockets, mortars, and gunfire, not to mention the Temptations. It was a movement, a big one, and I didn't have a clue as to what the hell was going on or why, which was typical. After all, why would I need to know there were huge NVA base camps hidden just across the border with massive amounts of enemy soldiers, divisions of them, training, building, and preparing to come across to kill me? Why would I need to know that the North Vietnamese commies were backing Pol Pot's Khmer Rouge in an attempted take-over of Cambodia? Why would I need to know anything, and for that matter, why would the aircrews need to know anything? After all, they were just the guys who were going to fly in there and get killed.

Like just about every other American enlisted soldier in Vietnam we never got war status briefings, or big picture briefings, or even little picture briefings. What news we got of and from home came with incoming personnel, or in letters, or hometown newspapers. And then there was the watered down and sanitized feel good crap from the AFVN broadcasts. The lifers read Stars & Stripes and the Army Times but mostly just to see who got promoted and who got killed. Those publications weren't really trusted by the rest of us and were generally considered to be in-house military propaganda. I didn't read them either so I wouldn't know for sure but the enemy knew lots of things for sure. The enemy always seemed to get the word before most of us EM types, and too often even before our commanders. This wasn't surprising being they ate, drank, lived, fought, and worked with or for us at every level of the war. The North Vietnamese were plugged in all over the country with the heroes of Uncle Ho's Peoples' Liberation Army and sympathizers serving in nearly every ARVN unit and working as local labor and domestic hires at every American military base. And certainly they sat out there beyond the perimeter wire watching, always watching, as they were right now watching all this new activity at Holloway. And if they couldn't find out what they needed to know in those ways then they got it by getting into the G.I.'s pants. Nothing like a tickle and a wiggle to loosen the tongue and get a tidbit of intel, maybe not the big secrets but enough of those little pieces of info here and there to come together to reveal the big secrets. Collecting intel the average G.I. didn't even know he knew. That old WWII maxim that loose lips sink ships was still very true, except in Vietnam the ships had rotary wings and they didn't sink, they went down in a ball of fire.

It didn't take a diplomat or rocket scientist to figure out what most G.I.s quickly came to know, that the American presence and the American G.I. in Vietnam was nothing more than a national cash cow. For the most part the Vietnamese were an uninformed people who learned a thousand years ago how to go with the flow. The French had treated them like shit and so did the Japanese. Having learned from such role models, those in power in the so-called Republic of South Vietnam, and those in command of their military weren't much different, and certainly no better. In the eyes of the average ignorant Vietnamese with a little info spin by Uncle Ho, coupled with the very simple fact that the war was being fought south of the DMZ, we allied forces were considered nothing more than just another bunch of invading occupiers - but with beaucoup bucks. We didn't take from Vietnam we gave. We built roads and bridges, and schools and entire cities, ports, and airports. And all we asked in return was the opportunity to die for their country, a concept that most cultures simply have a hard time swallowing, including the culture of the enlisted ranks of the U.S. military. Therefore, while enjoying the fruits of our labor, not only did many of the Vietnamese sympathize with what they thought was a simple movement to oust the western foreigners and their own corrupt South Vietnam government, they probably thought we were just plain nuts.

So I would soon discover we were going into Cambodia, as I'm sure the North Vietnamese already knew and the entire world would soon come to know. I'm sure President Nixon knew we would be there because apparently he had gotten a serious case of the ass and decided to send us there. What else could he do in the face of North Vietnam's abuse of the peace talk process, their usual Spring time offensive antics in South Vietnam, and their demonstrated ambitions regarding the transfer of power of Cambodia? But then old Dick was a weird egg and he may just have been expressing once again his dislike for the anti-establishment counter culture, or simply gotten tired of hearing that odd duck Henry Kissinger mumble his suggestion that we start dropping nukes. Hell, how do you guess the motives of somebody like a President who spent millions of dollars to get a part time job that only pays a couple hundred thou' a year and requires that he live in public housing. For whatever reason, militarily or politically, this was the war I hadn't seen, not that I hadn't seen any, but it was the kind of war I'd expected to find when I had arrived in-country, purposeful and aggressive. If there had ever been the historical equivalent of a Normandy D-Day in the Vietnam War, I suppose you could say this Cambodian thing was it, and shit, I thought, I was going to be watching from the sidelines, from behind a typewriter.

"What the hell's going on?" asked Randy as he joined me in the doorway.

"I don't know," I said. "We're either running away from something or getting ready for something else."

"I checked in the orderly room but nobody knows anything. It's just the CQ in there," said Randy. "Top's not in yet. Let's head over to the mess hall and see who knows what."

I rarely got to the mess hall in time for a full breakfast just as I rarely got to the showers in time for hot water but this time I was on time, if not early, and the place should have been full. It was nearly empty. The flight crews, gun crews, and pretty much everyone else were already at work in the hangers and on the flight line. Many were already in the air shuffling troops, ARVNs, and equipment to various staging areas for a quick deployment west across the border.

"What the hell's going on," I asked Sgt. Goetz, one of the cooks who was serving up the morning chow as we grabbed our trays and moved along the line.

"Not sure," he said. "Had some guys in here real early from Qui Nhon and some other guys up from Nah Trang. Big time assault is all I could pick up on. Everything is moving west. All I know is they're bringing in a lot of shit, including extra med people, and we're stocking up to feed a lot of extra swingin' dicks. You get anything from Top or the CO?"

"Haven't seen them yet."

"Me neither," said Goetz. "And Top is a real early bird, ya know? First in first out lifer type. My guess is they're all in a head session somewhere up on the hill. Aircrews were in real early too. Come and gone. This is my second tour and the only time I ever saw activity like this was Tet in '68. I was a cannon cocker back then and was sitting around Tan Son Nuit waiting for my ride home. Just five days from my re-up when the shit hit the fan. They turned me into a grunt for a week. Didn't like that grunt shit. That's when I decided to become a cook," he laughed.

"Cowards taste of death many times before they die, but the brave die only once," quoted Randy.

"What the hell is that supposed to mean?" asked Goetz.

"That's Shakespeare, you uneducated slob," said Randy. "It means maybe you're a chicken shit."

"Yeah, well, what the hell does Shakespeare know about taste, and he never spent a year knee deep in paddy shit and living on C-Rats either. I'd bet you my two Purple Hearts that English faggot wouldn't know the difference between a Hero sandwich and Mighty Mouse. Besides, I don't see your clerk ass out there dodging tracers."

"I hope you were better at arty then you are in the kitchen," laughed Randy.

"Hey asshole, don't give me that shit. I've seen you eat my cookin'. Your mama can't feed you as good as I do."

"Yeah, you're right," laughed Randy. "But with Mama I got a kiss and a hug with every meal."

"You can kiss this," said Goetz, grabbing his crotch.

"You wish," bounced Randy.

We crossed the mess hall and parked our asses at an empty table. Just as Randy was about to insert the first bite of food in his mouth he was struck on the side of the head with a biscuit. We turned to find SGT Goetz twenty-five feet away pointing and smiling from behind the serving line.

"Incoming troop," Goetz laughed. "Right on the mark. This cannon cocker cook just smoked your ass."

"Damn, Randy," I said. "What the hell was that all about?"

"A morning ritual," laughed Randy. "Friendly banter. He's a hometown Bronx boy. We're just having fun. Talking shit. You know."

"Shakespeare? They quote Shakespeare in the Bronx?"

"The nuns," explained Randy.

We soon found out by word of mouth what was going on and were eventually filled in by Top. It was Cambodia and it was big, and it was expected to be bad, and that was about the extent of our knowledge. The particulars were reserved for the flight crews and it was in their eyes and that of the CO that the real story began to unfold. An ominous veil of reality and anxiety became the norm, and the focus of nearly everyone in the company became an effort of preparation. The oddities and the queer little quirks that make up a group of military men suddenly vanished and the mission was everything. Little was said on our part because as desk pilots we were pretty much excluded, but the apprehension was contagious and sat heavy on us as well. Then the Ghostriders, Avengers, and the rest of the 52nd CAB finally went on mission with our own Major Anthony as the Air Mission Commander. It was a massive operation, a repetitious eagle flight, inserting nearly eighty thousand ARVN and US troops across the border north and south, surrounding, pounding, and choking the NVA in his own sanctuaries. At least that was the plan.

What was first encountered in Cambodia was a large serious North Vietnamese military that had hightailed it for places unknown, leaving behind a mass of booby traps and snipers. The original objective was to find their HQ from which they were supposedly running their war effort, but failing that, the strategy changed and we got down to business going after their supply depots and staging areas. Day in and day out our gun ships provided cover and killed the enemy, our slicks carried troops, ammo, and supplies in, and wounded, dead, and prisoners out. It was a revolving door of war and we soon discovered the fight wasn't restricted to just one side of the border.

The North Vietnamese knew Camp Holloway was pivotal to the operation and wasted no time in letting us know we weren't appreciated. Rocket City once again began living up to its name and the multiple mortars and rockets weren't just restricted to being an occasional late night surprise, but became a round the clock concern. Their targets were most likely the aircraft and maintenance facilities, but with the crowded state of affairs and the number of rockets fired, it was rare that the incoming ordnance didn't result in some form of over or under shot leaving impressive damage. PSP was shredded on the runway, some aircraft were hit, and various buildings suffered damage, but the most jarring incident took place at mid day when a single rocket struck a tent on the ball field where there slept a tired fourteen American soldiers. Six were killed and the rest wounded and flown to the 71st Evac at the Pleiku Air Force Base. It would be a long tense month with few on the base getting more than a few hours sleep each night, either from periodic rocket and mortar attacks, or the demands of the job.

Flight crews were especially hard pressed, flying pre-dawn to sunset and often beyond. The Ghostriders and other units of the 52nd were transporting and flying support for elements of the 101st Airborne, the 4th Infantry Division, Rangers, 5th Special Forces, Long Range Recons, CIDG, and Multiple ARVN units. The initial flights were great aerial armadas that soared over the highlands and invaded the enemy with surprising results.

Near the maintenance hanger a day after the incoming incident on the ball field, a young aircraft mechanic named Tony Ostolaza balanced precariously atop a Huey slick as he peeled open the engine cover just aft of the rotary shaft. When he looked over the side to the ground he could see only the legs of the aircraft's crew chief, SP5 Dillinger, who was on his back under the main fuselage counting bullet holes and searching for damage. Specialist Ostolaza, nick named Half Wrench because of his lack of height, hailed from Albuquerque, New Mexico, and was one of those kids that everybody liked. He never complained, was always high spirited, and was always the first to jump in on the job. The bigger the problem or the bigger the challenge the more excited he became. He liked what he did, and for the short time he had been in the Army he had absorbed his training and working knowledge of aviation and aircraft faster than a politician accepts campaign money. His goal was simple, he wasn't going to just fix aircraft when he got out of the Army, he was going to build them, and everyone was convinced he would.

"I count eight. No, nine. Plus the three in the tail boom and one in the chin bubble, makes an unlucky thirteen," came Dillinger's voice from under the chopper.

"And two up here. Small stuff. In and out with no engine damage. Lucky," said Half Wrench. "You know, if you guys would smile when you went into an LZ maybe they probably wouldn't shoot at you so much."

"Smile my ass," said crew chief Dillinger as he slid around on the PSP under the aircraft.

"Now there's an idea. Maybe you should go in showing your ass instead of your gun. Ya see, I got this theory," said Half Wrench as he raised the hood on the other side of the engine. "You guys always go in there with your guns blazing like your looking for trouble, so naturally those dumb ass dinks just start shootin' back. So what if you go in there shootin' a moon and singin' In-a-gatta-da-vita instead? What do you think they're gonna do?"

"They're gonna send an RPG up my ass."

"Well maybe. But think of the possibilities. What if you write peace on one ass cheek and love on the other ass cheek? You gotta write it in Dinkanese though so they can read it. What do you think they're gonna do then?"

"If they're not fuckin' queer, then after they get done laughing they're gonna blast me a whole new asshole and you're gonna be cleanin' my guts off the gun well."

"Nah, never happen," I said as I approached the chopper. I kicked Dillinger's boot and continued, "Your ass is so damn ugly it would scare those bastards all the way back across the DMZ."

"Oh, hey, I know that voice," said Dillinger. "It's the Remington Raider who thinks he's a bomber and drops his ammo box on the bad guys."

"What?" said Half Wrench, turning to discover my presence.

"Just an inside joke, Half Wrench. What's happnin', Fusco? You out slummin'?" asked Dillinger, still sliding around under the chopper.

"Yeah, something like that. Wanted to see how the other half lives," I said as I hopped up in the shade of the chopper and sat on the gunner's bench. "Safe to smoke?" I asked as I pulled out a Raleigh.

"Sure. Got no fuel leaks… that I know of," answered Dillinger, crawling out from under his Huey. "Got another one?"

He climbed onto the deck, accepted and lit a cigarette, then sat and slid back against the pilot's armored seat. He looked tired and his movements were a bit labored. I could see that after only three days into the Cambodia offensive he was on the edge. I was thinking it was the extended hours that weren't just showing on him but on the faces of the other flight crews as well when they dragged into the mess hall or back to their hooches after a full day of border hopping. I was wrong. It was something else.

"So what you doing out of the HQ?"

"Needed some space," I joked. "Thought I'd come by and sniff the gun powder."

"The space is up there," said Dillinger, pointing his thumb to the sky. "But it's been a little crowded lately."

"So I hear."

"Your looking to get on a gun, aren't you?"

I smiled. He read me just right.

"Shouldn't be a problem. Everybody's pretty much ragged out and could use a few beers and an eight-hour stretch in the sack. Why don't you just ask OPS to stick you on a slick so somebody can catch a break?"

"I'm not sure Top would go for it. I kind of pissed him off last time I went out and got weathered in at Dak To."

"No problem. Hey look, everybody's flying and everybody's beat and we need every ship and crew we got. As a matter of fact, my gunner caught a round in his foot so I'm short a crew."

"Yeah, I heard."

"I figured that's why you were here," smiled Dillinger. "I'll get Chief Chief to ask for you. That way it's up to the CO who isn't going to say no 'cause he knows the situation and he usually leaves that shit up to OPS anyway. Then I got a gunner and your ass is covered with Top."

"Works for me," I smiled.

"Get your shit together. My guess is we go in the morning. That's if Half Wrench up there gets that asshole sergeant to sign off on my bird when we're done here."

"What Sergeant?" I asked.

"Some big mean SOB Staff Sergeant they got TDY here to help take up the slack for this Cambodia thing," answered Dillinger as he flicked away his cigarette butt and slid off the chopper. "Fucker doesn't do shit. Doesn't know shit either. Just walks around and chews ass and tells war stories about his Cav days down south like anybody actually gives a shit. Name's Fender. What a prick. And they got that Flyin' Nun Thigpen filling in as Caretaker maintenance officer 'cause Captain Beechem is flying CAs over the border, so this Fender jerk pretty much runs his own show. Our guys are good. We don't need that asshole. Isn't that right, Half Wrench?"

"Got that shit right," laughed Half Wrench as he stood and rested his arms on the main rotor blade. "That fat ass is about as useful as tits on a chicken. Don't know a Huey from a fuckin' Good Humor truck."

I was reaching for another cigarette when suddenly a mortar screamed in and exploded on the far side of the broad pad in front of the hanger. The pack of cigarettes slid from my pocket as Dillinger and I immediately hit the ground. Half Wrench jumped from the top of the chopper and landed hard on the perforated steel plate twisting his ankle, then sprawled flat on the ground next to us. The first mortar was quickly followed by another. It impacted closer to our location fifty yards away then was followed quickly by another impacting fifteen yards closer.

"They're walkin' them into the hanger!" yelled Dillinger as he started getting up. "Get in the bunker!"

He quickly got to his feet and took off running for the bunker about twenty-five yards away. I was reaching for the pack of cigarettes as I rose when a fourth mortar struck thirty yards in from the third. I left the pack, rose and took off running. Some of the maintenance crew had already sought out the sand bag bunker and others were dashing through the small opening as we approached. When Dillinger and I arrived and headed through the entrance I glanced back to see Half Wrench limping as fast as he could toward me. He was only a few yards behind and didn't appear to need any help so I turned and dashed into the safety of the bunker.

It struck with an incredibly loud booming WHOMPH that seemed to suck the air right out of our lungs and stop my heart as we jerked, cringed, and fell back into the dark shelter of the protective steel and sand bag cave. Dirt and torn sand bags shot in from the bunker entrance filling our eyes and fouling our mouths. It filled the bunker with a dark cloud penetrated only by a thin odd shaped streak of light that filtered through the dust from the damaged entrance. Another mortar struck some 15 yards behind us then all grew quiet except for the camp's warning siren. A few of the guys sat, others leaned against the sand bag walls until the siren ceased. No one spoke. A few minutes later we could hear choppers scrambling off the pad and trucks heading for the perimeter.

I stood there in the darkness and watched the dust settle until Dillinger tapped me on the arm, "Hey Fusco, got another cigarette?"

I reached for the pack, forgetting I had dropped them by the chopper.

"I think I lost them. Sorry."

"That's okay. Half Wrench's got some. How 'bout one of those shitty menthols of yours Half Wrench?" asked Dillinger.

There was no response from Ostolaza. I looked from dark face to dark face in the bunker then Dillinger and I both realized the worse and we charged out of the bunker and into the blinding light. When our eyes adjusted to the bright sun we froze in horror. Mixed in with the impact damage from the mortar were the bloody body parts of SP4 Half Wrench Ostolaza. He had obviously made it to the bunker entrance but his body caught the full impact of the mortar. Half Wrench had unintentionally become the shield that prevented the mortar's direct entrance into the bunker opening that would have killed or maimed all of us. Everyone slowly filed out into the light. The nine of us at first turned and looked about for the bulk of Half Wrench's body. It was everywhere and nowhere. We stood quietly, eyeing the bloody remains. There was little to identify yet we knew who it was. After a long quiet time Staff Sergeant Fender walked up to the group and surveyed the scene. He was a tall, big boned and big bellied.

"God damn," he said. "Bet that boy ain't feelin' no pain." He took another glance then turned to one of the flight mechanics and gave him a slight shove on the shoulder saying, "Okay, okay. Let's get this shit cleaned up and then get back to work."

The mechanic shot him an angry look then sent a hard-fisted punch into Fender's mouth, sending blood down his chin and taking out three of his front teeth. Before the surprised Sergeant Fender could bring his hands to his bloody face another punch landed up side his head. Then the others jumped in. Dillinger and I stood and watched as the seven men beat Fender to the ground. It got messy and brutal and I turned away and faced the bunker only to see part of Half Wrench's bloody hand and forearm wedged between a couple of sandbags. The beating was still taking place when Dillinger and I turned and walked away.

The medics who were called to deal with Half Wrench Ostolaza's remains found the heartless smart-ass Staff Sergeant Fender lying unconscious. He was near death from blood loss and had more broken bones than they could treat so he was airlifted to the 71st Evac where it was reported his injuries were the result of a turned over jeep due to personal negligence caused by alcohol consumption. No one ever disputed or questioned the report.

CHAPTER 25

BORDER HOPPING

The sun had barely come over the horizon when we lifted off the next morning as part of a formation of three slicks and two Avenger gun ships. When we crossed the border into Cambodia we were loaded with hash and trash and a single passenger, a curious silent non-military type in tiger fatigues with long hair and a goatee. His gear consisted of only a small pack, one small and one large knife on his belt, and a pistol with a silencer attachment nestled in a shoulder holster. The odd thing was he was oriental but bigger than most, in fact, he was a good two or three inches taller than my own five-eight. Someone later said he was Taiwanese, another speculated he was Chinese, a mercenary. Someone else even said he was a hardcore converted chieu hois now working in the Phoenix program, an assassination program that targeted Viet Cong leaders and organizers. It was hard for me to believe that an enemy soldier could be turned in such a way until I was told that most of them used the job to become one man mafias, stealing and extorting whatever they wanted from the small hamlets and villages where they found their targets. What I noticed most was what he didn't have - an assault rifle, and more importantly a radio, which meant he was rigged for silent running and once we dropped him off he was on his own with no chance of rescue or pick up if he got in trouble, but from the looks of him I didn't think that was likely.

Midway between our destination and the border he tapped Chief Chief on the shoulder and pointed to the ground. While the other choppers orbited above, Chief Chief dove the aircraft to the deck, buzzed along for about half a mile at treetop, then hovered for a few seconds in a small clearing of high grass where our mystery passenger jumped from the ship and quickly disappeared into the jungle. He had never said a word, never even looked us in the eye. He just showed up with the cargo and then disappeared like a breath of steam on a cold morning. Maybe for him it was just another day at the office, but I would always wonder who he was, who or what was his mission, and if he succeeded.

We were no sooner flying back in formation than Chief Chief started to chatter.

"Hey Fusco, Dillinger tells me you guys had a little excitement yesterday. A couple mortars up by the hanger," said Chief Chief.

"Yeah, a close one," I said.

"You won't believe this Fusco, but I slept through the whole damn thing. Slept like a baby," laughed Chief Chief. "Even had a dream about this bodacious busty Cajun chick I met in New Orleans. Said she was from Baton Rouge. You know, at first I could hardly understand a word that girl said but then there's more ways to communicate than just words. Know what I mean? You ever been to New Orleans, Fusco?"

"Not really. Just drove through it once," I answered.

"Well, personally I think New Orleans is a real shit hole. Let me put it this way, if North America's lower forty-eight had an anus it would be New Orleans, at least what I saw of it, but if you're just looking for sin and satisfaction then I guess that's a good place to start."

Just then another voice came over the radio.

"Red Six to Ghostrider leader. Over."

"Ghostrider leader," answered Chief Chief.

"Ghostrider what's your make up and ETA?"

"We are two hogs and three slicks with hash and trash inbound about one-niner miles from your location. ETA about six minutes. Over."

"Be advised Ghostrider, we've got wounded and chieu hois for your back haul."

"Roger Red Six, dust off and POWs, no problem. What's your LZ status? Over."

"LZ secure but suggest you approach from the Southeast to avoid snipers and suspected .51 bunker. Our FAC can direct your hogs on assaulting the bunker. Over."

"Affirmative Red Six," said Chief Chief. "Pop smoke on our visual."

"Roger Ghostrider. See you in six."

"Avenger guns did you copy that?" asked Chief Chief.

The ACs on the gun ships acknowledged and Chief Chief resumed his on-board conversation.

"So you guys never had any Cajun boom boom?"

"I dated a chick from south Alabama once," said Dillinger. "Does that count?"

"Not even close," said Chief Chief. "Gotta be a hot and spicy garoontee swamp queen. Ain't that right Fusco?"

"Guess so," I said, leaning out on my gun and watching the vast Cambodian countryside pass below. In the far distance I could see rising smoke.

Chief Chief glanced back over his shoulder toward my gunwell then back forward as he continued in a more serious manner. "That shit yesterday with Half Wrench is over, Fusco. You couldn't help it and you can't change it so put it out of your head. My guess is you're gonna see worse in a couple minutes. You with me?"

"Affirmative," I answered. "And when we get back I want to here more about that swamp queen," I smiled.

"Oh, I could tell you things that would make your hair curl," laughed Chief Chief. He then kicked in with a melody and the partial lyrics from a song in Elvis Presley's movie King Kreole, *"...with a black eyed baby from the old bayou."*

Chief Chief had a way of putting everyone at ease when he flew. My guess is it was as much for his benefit as ours because no matter what the rank or the training, or the experience, there was no way in hell anybody with half a brain could do this and not think about all the danger and negative possibilities, real possibilities, that we knew occurred somewhere in II Corps and all over Vietnam each day, and were occurring now in Cambodia. It was the down time and the empty fly time at altitude when you had to avoid dwelling on it or it could tie you in knots, and who was more aware of what could happen than the AC. From simple mechanical failures to enemy action, just flying in a chopper over Vietnam was a crapshoot, and the unfamiliar turf of Cambodia was no different. We were kids flying high priced complicated aircraft that were being maintained and fixed by other kids, and we were too young to realize it, just too young and dumb to fully appreciate the danger, yet not so young we didn't feel it. Some of our choppers had already gone down in the Cambodian offensive, including that of a General who was killed along with the entire crew when his ship was hit by enemy fire. Always suspicious of the motives of Generals and other higher ups, we weren't exactly sure how to take the news other than a sincere empathy for our crew. But it wasn't only this I had on my mind, it was as Randy put it, the *hoocho curse*; the room curse that delivered lightning bolts, made a guy stick an M-16 in his mouth, and gave us oversize rats and suicidal roaches, or as Roabley had put it, "…created a spooky unlikelihood of survival."

The day after they kicked off the Cambodia operation I played host to two civilian journalists. They were photographers up from Nah Trang who came in on a hop. We met at the club, had a few drinks, and they ended up spending the night on the floor in my room where we all had a good time talking about the Nah Trang shit cloud, the antics of Pully Johnson, some of the weird things they had seen, Fred Blurtz's black clap, the Flying Nun, and assorted other wartime oddities. They were okay as war zone civilians go, but I got the impression they were more interested in furthering their own careers than understanding the war. They were body shooters, looking for *the shot* that would get them the brass ring. They talked about past assignments on combat assaults like they were recalling an outing between the Orioles and the Yankees in Memorial Stadium. I could see the other guys from the hooch were fascinated by their conversation as was I, but like me I could also see they found it distasteful. Our guests were talking about photographing wounded and hideously mangled dead soldiers, and wrecked and twisted aircraft like it was an art form and a professional challenge. About getting the right angle and light, or catching the fatality at the moment of impact. One even suggested the upcoming Cambodia assignment could make his career – if he was lucky.

The next day they went in with the Ghostriders on one of the large CAs thinking, I'm sure, that this was the day they'd get that Pulitzer Prize winning shot, but instead their chopper was shot down and they, along with the entire crew, came back in body bags. Possibly they're death was photographed by someone else, and I wondered if that someone else thought maybe *he* was taking the lucky shot of his career. Back home their fellow journalist would probably call them heroes, and the anti-war crowd would probably call them seekers of truth, which was far different than what they were calling us. The simple truth was they were here for the jazz and the fame, and maybe a piece of the bank via some damn distasteful coffee table book about *their* war. What they found instead was a severe and final dose of reality.

After that Randy suggested I might want to move out of my room. I asked in return if he wanted to trade and of course I got a quick NFW. But I can't deny that the hoocho curse played on my mind and seeing how casualties were as much a fluke or pure fate as they were the intention of the enemy, I began to see it as a real possibility. Nor could I shake the fact that if I had decided to stop and pick up my cigarettes it might have been me and not Half Wrench who caught that mortar. For some reason, putting my trust in luck or defying fate, I chose to stay in the room. It wasn't much, I thought, but for now it was my damn home and superstitious bullshit wasn't going to chase me out. In addition there was this odd feeling somewhere down in my gut that someone or something was taking care of me, that I would be okay no matter what happened. An unexplainable feeling, as though I were going through preordained motions and events of which I had no control.

"Ghostrider. Red Six. We've got you in sight and are popping smoke. Over."

"Roger Red Six," acknowledged Chief Chief. "I see goofy grape smoke. Confirm?"

"Affirmative Ghostrider. Again I suggest a southwest on a short approach and there's room for the whole family."

"Roger, three on approach, Red Six."

"Be advised, Ghostrider, I have six wounded, two KIA and all the chieu hoi you can carry."

"Roger that, Red Six."

The LZ was in a small valley and of fairly good size, allowing all three of our slicks to come in at the same time. Just over the tops of the trees about a half-mile off I saw a formation of six other choppers rise and fly off for the border. The Avenger gun ships split off and wasted no time eliminating the NVA .51 emplacement to the satisfied cheers of some of the ground troops who stood in small groups and watched the action from afar. Two G.I.s were sitting on a stack of NVA bodies taking a cigarette brake while another was taking their picture with a pocket size instamatic camera.

We made our approach and set down, and I could see we were coming into an action that was just rapping up from earlier that morning, a predawn assault. At the edge of the clearing was a downed medivac chopper. The nose and better part of the cockpit had been blown off, the main blades shredded, and the tail boom twisted and nearly detached. All this was the result of a company size ambush set up to cut off retreating NVA only a few klicks from an assault on a main enemy supply depot by other U.S. troops. It had started at the crack of dawn and in the far distance I could see the smoke rising and hear artillery or bombs still working the area. The ground was littered with NVA bodies and body parts that were being kicked around and picked through for documents, weapons and souvenirs. To my side of the LZ huddled about a dozen POWs, some wounded, most stripped down to their skivvies with their hands tied behind there backs. Nearby were two filled body bags and a group of wounded Americans being treated by medics. When we set the aircraft down the POWs turned away from the blast of the rotor wash of the chopper's blades. American wounded who were capable covered their faces, the medics and assisting troops shielded those that couldn't. Once on the ground we were quickly approached by the ground troops who immediately started unloading the cargo.

No sooner was it off-loaded than others began loading the wounded. I sat at my gun looking at them as they were carried and put aboard our ship. Two of the wounded came to us on stretchers accompanied by a medic who climbed aboard and grabbed and held up both their IVs, IVs he had salvaged from the downed dust-off chopper. One was bandaged heavily from head to waste, and most all of the bandages were blood soaked. It looked as though a portion of his side was missing. I couldn't see if he was conscious because his face was covered with a mess of red gauze. The other stretcher case was stripped to the waist, his left ribs bandaged and his left pants leg had been cut away. His eyes were open but didn't seem to be focused on anything around him. I assumed he was so far gone on morphine that he wasn't even aware of what was happening. His upper left leg was covered with blood soaked bandages, as was the stump of his left arm, detached just above the elbow. Two other walking soldiers, one with a head and left shoulder wound, the other with his arm and neck bandaged, were helped on board and squeezed in wherever they found room. The medic immediately handed one of them the IV of the armless patient and began monitoring and tending the other. I tried to look back and see what was loaded on the other choppers but they were already full.

Everyone on the ground backed away, the blades revved up and we began to lift off when I saw one of the medics on the ground waving frantically for us to set back down.

"Hold on Chief Chief!" I said into the mike. "I think we got another one."

Chief Chief began to set the ship back down but before the skids had even touched the ground a medic ran to the chopper cradling something in his arms. He motioned for me to accept what he was carrying and pointed to the man on the stretcher nearest me. I nodded acknowledgment, thinking it was the wounded man's personal property and reached out and accepted it. The cloth it was wrapped in fell away. Chief Chief watched the exchange, waiting for my okay to lift off. When I looked at what had been put in my hands my mind went blank until Chief Chief's voice came through the headset.

"Talk to me Fusco!"

I turned and looked to Chief Chief who strained against his safety harness to look back and connect with me eye to eye.

"Are we clear, gunner?"

"We're clear," I finally said. "We're out."

I didn't want to but I looked at it, surprised that it felt as heavy as it did and cold to the touch. There was a ring, a high school class ring much like the one I was wearing. As the ship rose, tail up and nosed down, and flew out of the LZ, I slid from my seat and reached over and began to place the severed arm next to the bloody stump of its owner, but before I could he reached up, took possession of it with his good arm and held it to his chest. He looked at me and smiled and I'll be damned if I know why.

"Damnit! Oh God damnit!" I heard the medic shout over the noise of the chopper. When I looked over to the medic he was sitting back away from his other stretcher case. He dropped the IV down on the man's chest then dropped his face into his own bloody hands. The medic, who had probably saved dozens of lives during his tour, now angrily grieved over the one he had just lost. He sat back, brought his knees to his chest, wrapped his arms around them as though he were trying to shrink himself into some place safe, and stared back at me, straight into my eyes, but I felt as though he didn't see me at all. He sat there, the front of him from his face to his boots, covered with the blood of the morning's victims. I turned away and found refuge in the gun well and the wide space of the distant sky.

The rest of the day went much the same, flying re-supply and replacements in, wounded and POWs out. It was during the first month of the operation that most of the action and allied achievement took place, but I would only get a sampling of it all, having only flown for five more days and on different aircraft. The first of those days were SOG drops and extractions, but the third took me into the cratered smoking ruins of a large NVA base camp, estimated to have accommodated at least three battalions, where there was piled a goodly number of enemy bodies being burned near a large cache of weapons and supplies. It was a place where the enemy lived with supply and ammo bunkers, sleeping areas, a medical facility, kitchens and mess areas. Hidden nearby in the trees were trucks and other vehicles, even a tank. The smell and condition of the dead enemy would become an ineffaceable memory and the captured arsenal a surprising revelation. It consisted of everything from the latest Chinese and Russian supplied armaments to WWI era wooden spoke-wheeled artillery. Weapons from nearly every decade of the century, even American Sears & Roebuck mail-order rifles and shotguns still new in their original boxes. Like many other soldiers, I'd never really thought of the enemy as men, but seeing how he lived and realizing they had the same needs and requirements as we, struck a cord. Oddly, I started imagining what the NVA would do or think if they were going through my stuff while cleaning up after overrunning Camp Holloway. What would they think of my books, my pictures from home, of Miss April's tits?

On my last day in Cambodia I was again flying Chief Chief's bird and we had participated in lifting a unit of ARVN into a strategic location from which they were going to be part of a sweep to engulf a large contingent of the enemy. The operation was apparently a bust because the NVA had gotten the word and bugged out. Later that day we went back in to pick them up. Along on our flight was the ARVN's American advisor, a Major, who for some reason was unable to come along on the initial insertion. We flew to what was the prearranged designated pick up zone only to find no one there. It was the rendezvous point in case the mission failed or was aborted. When the Major had called the ARVN unit commander on approach to confirm the pick up he was informed they were waiting as instructed, but we found no one on the ground below. He called again and once again the ARVN CO instructed us to come on in. After circling the area the Major sat back and began to curse profusely.

"Those bastards!" he yelled. "Those worthless fuckin' dink bastards. They did it again. God damn worthless fuckin' ARVN bastards!"

The Major then instructed Chief Chief to fly to the original LZ where we had dropped off the ARVN unit earlier that day. Sure enough there they were, all laid out on the grass in the sun like they were at some mellowed out country picnic. A few had even hung hammocks on nearby trees and were stretched out snoozing. Once again the Major let loose a few choice words.

"God damn dink mother fuckers! They didn't move! Didn't move one mother fuckin' inch! We ought to leave 'em here! We ought to waste every fuckin' one of those dink bastards and just leave 'em here to rot!"

"That can be arranged, Major," said Chief Chief to my surprise. "Pully, you and your hogs good with that?" he asked of the gun ship pilots.

"Just say the word there, Chief Chief," came Pully Johnson's voice over the COM. "Shouldn't take long."

I wasn't sure if everyone was joking or not, though I honestly didn't believe they were. I had seen enough in my limited experience to understand the frustration of fighting with and for an ally that always seemed to be laying back in reserve and then lay on their ass when deployed and expected to contact the enemy. I looked around the gun well to the Major. The anger expressed in his face turned to a more reasonable look of frustration, and though he, if not possibly all of us, wanted to leave the ARVN to fend for themselves, he gave in to his better judgment and ordered us in to the LZ. I'm not sure if I would have contributed to the wholesale slaughter of a group of cowardly allied soldiers, although I certainly wouldn't have felt bad just leaving them behind where possibly the enemy could have achieved the same thing.

As per the U.S. Senate's knee jerk decree, the Cambodian offensive was wrapped up by the end of June, but the resulting tally was impressive nonetheless – that is if you believed the Pentagon's published results. We had captured enough rice to feed 25,000 enemy soldiers for a year, enough ammunition for 52,000 enemy soldiers for a year, enough crew served weapons to arm 33 battalions and enough individual weapons to equip 55 battalions of NVA. We killed nearly 12,000 enemy soldiers and took over 2,300 prisoners. The U.S. suffered nearly 1,900 casualties, only 338 of which were KIA. The ARVN loss was 638 with over 3,000 wounded. Not that any loss is ever acceptable, especially if it's on your side, or by chance it happens to be you, but the kill ratio was undeniably and impressively in our favor, the kind of figures that won wars.

When the NVA tried to mount a counter attack they succeeded in killing only one U.S. soldier. The operation was a success, as were many other operations during the war, but it wasn't reported that way to the public, and in many cases our successes weren't reported at all. Essentially achieving all this in a brief one-month period and spending the better part of the time cleaning up has to make you think twice about the so-called venerable Walter Cronkite's declaration that the war was un-winnable. Cronkite reported our major victory during the '68 Tet Offensive as a set back and his assessment of the Cambodia actions weren't any better. Our fate was in the hands of media talking heads who spent just enough time in Vietnam to shoot just enough footage to pad their highlight films and their resumes and promo spots, and to see and experience just enough war to be dangerous – in the news room. This and other operations during the war proved that if there had been a will to win and a willingness to take the fight north to the source of the problem, it could have been won swiftly and decisively. As young and isolated as we were we weren't that young or that naive that we couldn't figure that out. But as we were all learning, in our new age of mass media and communications, wars were beginning to be won or lost by the man behind the microphone not the man behind the gun, even though the man behind that mic may be dumb as a donut or have some kind of personal agenda. Unfortunately what no one seemed to realize or remember was that wars could also be started in the same fashion. "Remember the Maine!" Our highly valued free press was like an agitated hornet buzzing around in the jock strap of our national leaders and often inept upper level military management, making it difficult for all to see and accept the realities of Vietnam and the war in general.

I suppose I was fortunate in that I didn't have to fly nearly each and every day as others did in our airlift and gun platoons. But for that week the duty took its toll and the almost nightly rocket or mortar attacks at Holloway during what should have been our few available hours of sleep didn't help any. I soon found myself taking the advice of one of the crew chiefs that clued me in on the wafers. The wafers were just what they sounded like, wafers resembling Neco Wafer candy. They were included in our survival packs along with a battery operated strobe rescue beacon, pen flares, and other necessities. Essentially the wafer was a big ass hit of speed and the trick was to take a quarter of a tablet about every four hours to keep yourself awake and on the edge, basically turning you into a regular jungle superman should you be in a survival situation. Many of the air crews, knowing that if they were ever shot down they would most likely be immediately rescued, killed or captured, opted instead to use the tablets to compensate for the lack of sleep and the demanding heavy schedule. I was no different. Flying dawn to dusk and dodging rockets at night didn't afford the opportunity for much rest. A bit of wafer here and there, and by the end of the week I realized I had been awake for nearly three days straight. When I came down I crashed for a solid twenty-four hour stretch. I slept through everything, including another rocket attack, an offer of coffee and sticky buns from Buns, multiple wake up efforts by Randy, and even a visit by PFCs Mondo and Puffin bearing junk food and a T-bone. When I did finally wake up it was in the middle of the night. The only one there to greet me was General Giap the rat, sitting on my improvised rocket crate book shelf, sniffing and twitching his nose and admiring Miss April's tits. Like most Vietnamese, I think that rat was really hooked on America – either that or he was a reincarnated horny G.I.

CHAPTER 26

BUTTERFLIES EAT SHIT

We were here and he wasn't. He was a damn draft dodger and he was going to get his ass kicked, at least we hoped he was, and that's all we knew, all we cared to know, and all we needed to know, for enough cause and justification to roll out the beer and Champagne. He whimped out when he was called up by the Selective Service and so, we hopefully thought on this particular night, he was about to receive some form of poetic justice as we watched his latest spectacle courtesy of AFVN. Until dodging the draft he was everybody's hero, the guy who kicked ass with a wink and a smile and a cool style.

"He could float like a butterfly and sting like a bee, but called by Uncle Sam he buckled at the knees." That was how we paraphrased his boastful famous words.

Everyone knew he wouldn't have been subject to the nasty shit of the Vietnam War. Dead celebrities don't exactly make for good press, especially in a war this unpopular. Hell, they probably would have given him one of those honorary imaginary hard commissions and paraded him around like some kind of hero in the company of a pack of higher-ups and Generals like they did with a lot of the movie stars in WWII. And he most likely would have been allowed to continue boxing – for the honor of the corps, of course. But then in all fairness there were those rare celebrities in the big war, and even a few in Vietnam, who chose to be the real deal, some of whom even paid the ultimate price for doing so. Rumor was that Beaver Cleaver. the famous kid character of the TV show *Leave It To Beaver,* had been drafted and was killed in Vietnam. The rumor was false but we didn't know that and so we thought what the hell made this other guy so damn special? Either way, just putting on the uniform meant a lot and though most of us had no respect for the average draft dodger, we at least had an idea as to why they avoided the draft in the first place, being simply that they were a bunch of selfish pussies hiding behind some convenient religion or phony politics. They just didn't want to interrupt their adolescent love-fest long enough to serve their country. In his case, however, it was a little hard to swallow a man claiming to be a religious pacifist when he was world famous for beating the shit out of other people and making millions of bucks a minute while he was at it. Cassius Clay, now the professed converted Muslim Muhammad Ali, was fighting on this night on an AFVN replay, and win or lose, we were going to revel in every painful punch because, like Cassius Clay, *we* had all become converts as well, but converts of the reality of death while fighting for his right to fight for the big bucks. At least that was the theory. For us there were no excuses, no high priced lawyers, and no money-grabbing phony religious zealots to plead our case. All we asked of Mr. Ali was a simple statement of truth, such as, "I don't want to put on a uniform for two-hundred-sixty bucks a month when I can make more than a million a minute in the boxing ring." Now honesty like that we could swallow and possibly even respect.

On this night our impromptu party came by way of someone's little twelve-inch TV they mounted on top of the sand bags outside the hooch in hopes of getting better reception. We also had to move it outside because inside there wasn't enough room for all of us to gather and watch. But it didn't work very well outside either and all seemed hopeless until one of the guys from the gun platoon came by and ran a wire and a coat hanger to the top of the hooch's tin roof. With our technical difficulties overcome we still had thirty minutes to go until show time, during which the AFVN ran the usual fillers consisting of a news pop, assorted announcements, and the occasional previously recorded song, a kind of music video, the first of which featured Bobby Troop on the piano crooning something that none of us really paid much attention to, probably because none of us knew who Bobby Troop was. Then there was Jimmy Durante on the piano singing *"Smile when your heart is broken..."* There was something about that big old nose and crooked smile of his that seemed to reach and mellow out the guys. Maybe it was because he was so familiar. For most of us he had visited our living rooms on a regular basis via his TV show when we were kids. That made him a visual connection to home and memories of a less complicated time and life. Or maybe it was the feeling that Durante somehow really cared, or maybe it was simply his choice of song. Then again, maybe it was just the booze. For whatever reason, by request or lack of other programming, it seemed to be the most repeatedly played filler on the AFVN single channel tube.

So for the moment we had Durante and for the occasion we had beer in abundance as we did on most other occasions, as well as half a dozen bottles of buck-and-change PX Champagne to be popped in celebration when Muhammad got his ass kicked. Not to mention a couple of pass-around quarts of Jack just for good measure. It seemed to be a well-planned unplanned occasion but in truth, a Cassius "Mohammad" Clay fight that had already taken place wasn't really much cause for celebration. At that time and in that country, however, we often looked for any reason to celebrate. Hell, just being alive was a good enough reason to celebrate. The trick was not to dwell on it, which was why we celebrated, which at the time seemed perfectly logical in an illogical sort of way.

The sun had gone down and we settled in around the small made in Japan Pacific PX mail-order black and white box with a black and white 12 inch screen, passing around the semi-cool beer and sharing a limited number of can openers while bullshitting about everything from the war as we knew it, or didn't know it, to Joey Heatherton's hot lips and sweet ass as we'd like to know it. While waiting for the show to begin the beer began to take its toll and I noticed our number was growing. The word had gotten out and we were being joined by others who weren't in the headquarters platoon but were also eager to see Clay get clobbered. Some brought their own libations and makeshift lawn furniture that consisted of everything from ammo crates and defunct chopper seats, to steel drums and actual well seasoned drugstore lawn chairs held together with duck tape and wire. Also merging into our group of a few dozen were a number of the brothers which led us to believe there would be conflicting sides to our expanding peanut gallery that might possibly result in a little unnecessary tension. To our surprise it was just the opposite.

"Yo Fusco, move yo ass over and le'me hold dat can opener," said big Samson Wheeler as he flopped down next to me on our makeshift park bench. He carried a sack of rusty Budweisers and offered me one. "I wanna' gets me a buzz on befo I see dat nigga get his black ass whooped."

"Are you shittin' me?" asked Randy. "You want your super brother to get his ass kicked."

"You got dat shit right," answered PFC Samson, a re-enlisted draftee from Jackson, Mississippi.

Samson was okay. He had a good disposition and a great smile and was comfortable to be around. Kind of like the big brother you didn't have or the one you wish you did have. By his age you would have thought he'd be a Staff Sergeant or at least an E-5, and most everybody thought he was because he never wore any visible rank, but he was just a PFC.

"I thought all the brothers thought he's a hero for beating the system and the draft," said Randy.

"Dat backwoods Kentucky draft dodgin' mofucka might be a bad ass in the ring but to me he jus 'nother candy ass who don't wanna be in d'shit over here wit us other brothas," said Samson. "Maybe peoples back in the world be buyin' into all dat Cassius Muhammad shit but not dis here nigga. Float like a butterfly, sting like a bee. Yeah right. Come over here mofucka, I'll sting yo black ass."

"Butterflies eat shit," entered PFC Andy Puffin in his usual slow southern drawl. He followed this injected revelation with a deep swig of a Yoo-hoo.

We all turned to find him perched on the sand bags atop the bunker. After talking about tits and ass and listening to Samson's opinion of Cassius Clay, Puffin's declaration was kind of like getting slapped upside the face with a wet mullet. It was his night off and he was present with his ever-present goodie sack and precious Yoo-hoo, joining the group simply out of curiosity just because it was a group and there was nothing else to do. By now we were too laid back to respond, so we just stared and waited for his explanation if indeed there was to be one. That is all except the two guys who were still intensely discussing Joey Heatherton's ass. It was a tough choice to decide which discussion to listen to but for some reason most of us were drawn to Puffin's shit eating butterflies.

"I got this dawg," continued Puffin. "Name's…"

"You got what?" interrupted Randy.

"A *dawg*. You know, like a arf arf dawg. Like a Georgia Bulldawg."

"Oh," replied Randy. "You mean a *dog*."

"Course. What the hell ya think I meant? Anyways, I got this dawg," Puffin continued once again. "Name's Jupiter. Call him Jupiter 'cause… well, I forget. No, I remember. Called him Jupiter after that Jupiter space rocket 'cause he could run fast like a rocket. But Jupiter's this really big dawg and when he shits he shits really really big shits, and all us kids use ta watch him shit. You know, ta see how big a turd it'd be. And sometimes we'd stick firecrackers in 'em. Blow 'em up."

"Oh man, you put fire crackers in your dog's ass." said Randy. "That's cruel, man. That's just plain cruel."

"Well, shit no. I ain't crazy. Not in his ass. Put 'em in the turds. But there's this kid stuck one in a cat's ass once and then tossed it on top of the roof of the feed store. Weren't too pretty and I think that cat went crazy."

PFC Puffin paused to shake up and wrench the top off another Yoo-hoo and to search out a Twinkie from his junk food booty bag. As he did we just sat and stared, most, like myself, probably visualizing a juvenile Puffin squatting behind some big ugly dog watching a slow turd succumb to gravity and wondering what the hell this had to do with anything at all and whether or not his story had reached it's climax. Apparently it hadn't. He continued.

"One time while we's watchin' Jupiter shit and then go and drag his ass in the grass, along comes these butterflies. You know them really pretty ones, them royalty kind called moonarks or somethin'. So them butterflies fly all around and sure 'nuff they land right there on that really big pile of Jupiter shit and start eatin' it like they's just pulled into the Burger Chef or somethin'.''

"So what the hell's your point, Puffin?" asked Randy, while hoping not to get back-sprayed by foam as he struggled to find a rust free spot on his can of Pabst Blue Ribbon with a dull can opener.

"Point is," answered Puffin through a mouth full of Twinkie, "Ya just don't know. Ya know? Ya take a really pretty chick and she's liable to be dumber than a doorknob and frigid as an iceberg. But then a homely chick can ring your chimes till the cows come home at sunrise. Know what I mean? Or a really hot lookin' car that you'd think could tear up the road but might just have some piddlin' ol' grandma six-banger under the hood. I mean, ya just don't know no more. Know what I mean? Like that Cassius Clay Muhammad dude. He might be a bad ass in the ring but just a pussy if he's in this man's Army and over here havin' to deal with incoming and other shit like us. You know what I mean? Like my granddaddy would say, 'The man might just have a pocket full of cotton 'stead of greenbacks.' Like who'd thought that some beautiful butterflies would eat Jupiter shit is what I'm sayin'."

"Is that honky for real?" asked Samson as he handed back the can opener.

"He's a real trooper," I said. "Took a dozen six inch needles in the gut for a rat bite once."

"Damn," said Samson.

"Yeah, that's what I said. Actually, I think what he said is kind of insightful. I mean, how many people would turn shit eating butterflies into a life philosophy?" I slurred after my fourth beer and a swig of Jack. "Sometimes, like in Puffin's case, you have too look beyond the simple to find the wisdom. Like you. I bet inside all that big ugly gorilla of a guy there's a mild mannered intellectual Teddy bear."

"Shiiiit," said Samson.

"I guess you could say we're all wise in our own way. Even Samson Wheeler," I chuckled.

"Shiiit," said Samson.

"Yeah, like them fuckers at the Pentagon in Washington," said Alverez in agreement with Puffin's hypothesis. "All straight, neat, sharp, and pretty. Toy soldiers flutterin' around like Puffin's fucked up butterflies, but they're eatin' political shit and fuckin' up the war and we're over here payin' the price."

"See there," I said. "Given the opportunity the intellectual cream will flow from the most unlikely of places. You just have to be able to appreciate it."

"Shiiit," said Samson.

"Ain't the Pentagon, it's those political assholes that are fuckin' everything up," suggested our TV antenna fixer from the gun platoon.

"What's so fucked up? Ain't the war that's fucked up. It's the Army," entered one of the Joey Heatherton fans. "That's what's all fucked up. Hell, we're winnin' the war except it ain't never over.

That's the problem. I think those damn Generals like this shit. This is their thing right?"

I looked around with a lazy smile, not eager to join in but eagerly anticipating what was evolving into another one of those spontaneous groupthink sessions I so much enjoyed, the kind that occurred when you get just the right mix of culture, intellect, and distilled liquids.

"Yeah. You'd think those idiots would get it right and get it over with. I mean if you want to beat the enemy you got to kill the enemy, right? I mean go after the bastards where they live, like in the big war," offered another. "So what are we doing pissing around down here? Those little fuckers are up there, up north, north of the DMZ. What kind of damn war is it that lets the bad guys come down here and raise hell but we can't go up there because some UN fuckers say we can't? I mean it's like we're in a damn football game except we ain't allowed to go past the fifty-yard line, but they can go all the way to the goal line and score. How we supposed to score? I mean, what the hell? It's like that Cambodia shit, right? We flat ass put a hurt on those peckers over there, big time. I mean, we always know where those commie bastards are but we can't go get 'em 'cause some damn senators and pricks in Washington say we can't. Then those dumb bastards complain cause we're still here. I mean, what the hell do they know, they ain't the ones lookin' down a barrel and getting' stuffed in body bags."

"And they sure as hell ain't likely to be either," chimed in another.

"Got that shit right," agreed Samson, just prior to a heavy belch. "It's the same ol' song, man. A rich man's war and a poor man's fight. 'Cept this time them rich mens can't get their shit together."

"They ain't never got their shit together, ever. And then they blame us. Like we got somethin' to say about it."

"Oh I don't know. Sometimes maybe. Like the big war and shit like that."

"Nuh uh. Not even then. That's just the movies and TV and that kind of shit, where they make it all look good like everbody knows what the hell they're doing. Don't work that way. Never works that way."

You could pretty much say the booze was doing most of the talking by now, which in the case of some of these guys was probably an improvement and even lent credence to the discussion. Like me, most were ignorant or little informed of the whys and what-fors of the war. We simply had to deal with what was in our face and anything else was pretty much speculation. The problem was, right or wrong and for better or worse, they were the choir preaching to the choir.

"Thing is I don't think these gooks over here even give a shit. All they care about is our money, man."

"So if they don't give a shit then why the hell should we give a shit?" asked one of the boys from OPS who worked in the tower.

"I don't know, man. I just don't see it and there isn't exactly anybody in the Army filling in the blanks or volunteering any info. Seems all they want is the money and what they can steal."

"Wow, do butterflies really eat shit?" asked one of the Caretaker guys, putting the conversation back on the sidetrack where Puffin had originally derailed it.

"So how come Jupiter dumps those really big turds?" asked Gas Roberts as he passed out a couple more beers, collecting a quarter in MPC for each.

Gas wasn't into the politics of war. He was into profit. And Gas was the only one in the HQ hooch with a refrigerator from which he sold beer for a quarter and soft drinks for fifteen cents each. The fridge didn't get as cold as it should but for him and us it was cold enough. And to him the fridge was well worth his trade of a captured AK-47 that made its way back from the Cambodian deal. Gas bought the canned drinks by the case when they were available at the small Holloway PX. I usually got mine free because I let him use my ration card to keep up his stock, plus the fact I didn't bother to mention to anybody that he was a ghost soldier, meaning he was rarely around except during mandatory formations and prime merchandising hours such as now.

Gas was a real piece of work who, to my knowledge, never really worked. At least I never saw him work. It seemed he was always playing grab-ass with the mama-sans or just laying around reading magazines, and on occasion would simply disappear altogether for a day or two at a time with none of us knowing where he went. Rumor was he had another life and a going enterprise in a nearby village. He came by the name of Gas for the simple reason he was known to let loose with a series of humongous farts at the most inopportune times on a regular basis. But the most notable thing about Gas was that he had a near religious devotion and dedication and desire to love and live with Marilyn McCoo, a girl member of the well known singing group, The 5th Dimension.

"She's the most beautiful woman to ever exist on the planet Earth," Gas would tell you as he'd turn his eyes in reverence to one of her autographed pictures on the wall near his bunk. He had all her tapes and magazines and any other Marilyn McCoo paraphernalia he could gather via mail order. Marilyn McCoo was his life and his life's ambition, and his refrigerator enterprise, along with some black market wheeling and dealing, was the beginning of his master plan to gain riches and social position so that he could become worthy of her love. It didn't seem to matter to Gas that she was already married, and even if she wasn't she would most likely overlook him because he was only five foot three. In other words, Gas had a reality problem as well as a flatulence problem, but Gas always had cold beer and sodas, which was all any of us really cared about.

"Jupiter don't have giant shits no more," answered Puffin.

"But you said Jupiter makes really big turds."

"Not no more. Jupiter's dead. I ran over him with my daddy's Dodge truck when I was tryin' to get away from Suzy Mae Dunaway's ol' man."

"No, I mean when he was alive, dumb ass."

"Oh yeah, well… don't know for sure. Jupiter was just a who-done-it dawg and he didn't start shittin' them big turds until he was 'bout half grown. Don't know why he shit so big 'cause I fed him the same stuff I eat and I don't shit giant turds. He was specially fond of Twinkies," added Puffin while brandishing his half eaten Twinkie.

"God almighty, no wonder the South lost the war," mumbled Samson.

"Hey Puffin, trade ya some Pabst Blue Ribbons for some of those Yoo-hoos. Two for one," proposed Gas.

"Hell no. No way, man," Puffin responded quickly, protecting his Yoo-hoo.

"Three for one."

"No sir re."

"Four."

"Hell no, man."

Damn," mumbled Gas. "I could get some serious MPC up at the BOQ for those Yoo-hoos."

The conversation seemed to bounce around like a steel marble in a pinball machine, going from the late Jupiter's big turds, to guessing at the constellations in the starry night sky, to various convertible dream cars, and to whether or not the XO had actually pissed his pants the first time he flew a combat assault mission. The general consensus of the latter was based on a well-cultivated rumor claiming that he actually had and as a result had ended up in the same category as CWO T.T.Thigpen as persona non grata. Seeing the XO every day as I did, I wasn't quite ready to believe this to be true, but with the help of a few more swigs of Jack and a few outdated rusty Buds, I toyed with the idea in my head. The XO, Captain Andrew Patrick, by all appearances was a damn sharp guy, on the quiet side and a bit humorless, but sharp nonetheless. In fact he was probably the sharpest looking soldier in all of camp Holloway. He was tall, handsome, athletically built, and physically capable, as well as articulate, neat as a pin, and black. And being black and a Captain in the Army was still a bit of a rarity to a great many soldiers and my guess was it was that half-ass prejudice that germinated and fed the rumor. Samson however, had an entirely different take of the subject.

"He jus another token nigga in the program," said Samson. "We call him HNIC. Means, Head Nigga In Charge. He the man and dat's cool but if the brotha piss his pants when the shit get hot then dat ain't cool."

"I'm not sure I believe it. I'd give him the benefit of the doubt." I said. "The man is STRAC. Could even pass for a ring knocker."

"Dats right. Dats what it take. You aks like the white man and you gets the token slot but dat ain't enough. You gots ta walk the walk and take care of binness. Can't be losin' it and pissin' yo pants and shit like dat. What dat gonna say 'bout all the other brothers? You gots to soldier. You gots to get down baby. You gots to get down and do it right. Dere's lot'sa brothas doin' it right out dere in da boonies. I know, I seen 'em. Ain't no different up in the air fo da HNIC. He ain't nothin' special."

"Hey man, he's not the first dude to lose it in his nomex. That's some scary shit up there," said one of the guys from the Avenger gun platoon. "What kind of shit are you talkin' anyway, Samson? You're a wrench in the motor pool. You don't know shit."

"Dis my second tour, man. I done three years before and I got out in sixty-eight," said Samson. "But I couldn't get no job on the outside. Then my ol' lady left me. Run off to St. Louis with some fast talkin' A-M-E preacher what got caught stealin' all the church moneys. So I come back in. B'fo dat I was a grunt down in the Triangle. I done some shit and I seen some shit, nasty bad shit too. Got a shrapnel scar on my black ass ta prove it too."

"Yeah, right next to the scar where his ol' lady stuck him with a spoon," added one of the brothers.

"It weren't no mofuckin' spoon. Was a butter knife," replied Samson. "How many times I gots ta tell ya dat?"

"Looks like a spoon scar to me. All curvy and shit."

"What the hell you doin' lookin' at my black ass anyway, nigga? You queer or sup'n?"

"Cause it reminds me of yo mama. Now dats a woman can shake and bake some serious…"

Samson rose threateningly from his seat with serious intent but was halted by the group's laughter, then sat back with a smile. It was at that time the fight came on the tube and we all changed our focus to the events on the small screen, all except for the two guys who had resumed their anatomical evaluation of Joey Heatherton.

By the time the first round bell rang we were three-sheets in the wind and the only thing we cared about was cheering and guzzling down a shot each time Muhammad the draft dodger got popped. We no longer cared if he won or lost, and probably wouldn't have known either way. We just wanted blood and apparently Mr. Float Like a Butterfly took enough hits to knock us all out of our senses.

I don't remember how long the fight lasted or how the fight ended but I do remember somewhere along in the evening the clouds and the rain rolled in. And I remember stepping out of the hooch that night to take a piss, then waking up some time later face up in the mud, being pelted by the downpour. The monsoon rains had arrived and so had I, drunk, lying face up in the mud. Was it really me or was I dreaming? How long had I been there being one with the muddy earth? It seemed forever. I opened my eyes and discovered looking down at me was a face as wet as my own, a familiar face but one I had not yet gotten to know. A contented face that was revealed to me by the dim light filtering through the hooch door. A rare face for these parts, I thought, a face that had nothing to hide but offered little information, a perfect poker face. His name was Garnett Buillaume and he worked in one of those S offices up at Battalion. I'd seen him around at times but never had a chance or reason to get to know him, until now that is. He bent down and leaned in further to assess my situation.

"Are you alright?" he asked.

I thought a moment as I came to realize my condition and position, then asked, "Am I dead?"

"Not yet," he smiled.

"Who won?" I managed to say as I sat up slowly, discovering I was covered with mud and water.

"Who won what?"

"The fight. Who won the fight?"

"I don't know. But it looks like you lost."

"It's raining. Shit. What time is it?"

"Somewhere around 0400."

"In the morning?"

He nodded a yes as he helped me sit up.

"Damn. I just came out hear to take a leak, not a swim. I think that was about two hours ago."

"A couple more minutes and you might have drowned," he said as he pointed at the hooch door.

The monsoon rain was heavy and relentless, causing a near river of water to roll on down over the red clay of Hollywood Boulevard and right into our hooch's front door, then, like the Colorado River shooting through the Grand Canyon, it ran through the narrow hall between our self-constructed personal suites and out the other door. Out the door and right over my unconscious face, which is what caused me to wake and look up to discover the curious Garnett staring down at me as though I was some strange exotic fish out of water.

We sat there in the rain and talked a while, and I discovered
Garnett was a true marvel of the military draft system. Prior to his
being drafted he was one of those few straight-A genius students
who actually maxed his SAT scores. It was disgusting. Nobody
maxes their SATs. But Garnett did and he was also one of those
rare, very rare, breed of individual who not only had a brain but
also knew how to use it. I knew people who were supposedly
straight-A geniuses but they would inevitably turn out to be total
duds in other critical areas of life, sometimes having limited or no
common sense, or short just on a few social skills, or being so
physically and athletically deficient as to sometimes appear nearly
retarded. Not so with Garnett. Garnett had it all and hated it. It was
his very genius and total athletic and overall human competence
that, in his eyes, made him a freak and therefore motivated him to
underachieve, or at least appear to.

First impression would lead most individuals to assume that he
simply didn't care, or had a bad attitude. This was a false
impression derived from his usual quiet unenthusiastic posture.
Actually, Garnett thought of himself as a freak much like one of
those knock out gorgeous women who live a lonely miserable life
because they can't get a date due to the fact everyone assumes they
are snobby and untouchable and out of their class. Other women
jealously hate them and intimidated men avoid them. Likewise,
Garnett discovered that when he used all of his natural talents and
abilities he also lost all acceptance among his piers and superiors.
Everyone became either jealous, or looked on him as a threat, or
simply felt belittled in his presence, leaving Garnett in what he
perceived as a no-win social and professional scenario. His
solution was to simply dial it down and appear to be just a stupid
as the rest of us. When the Army asked him if he wanted to attend
the United States Military Academy at West Point he declined.
And when the Army asked if he wanted to attend their Officer's
Candidate School he declined, just as he had declined to attend
their flight schools. In fact Garnett had turned down just about
every golden offer the Army threw at him, most all of which would
have set him up comfortably for his two year enlistment just about
anywhere in the world except Vietnam. He even turned down an
invitation by the CIA, which would have helped him avoid the
Army altogether. But Garnett, like myself, had made one major

mistake when he filled out his shit pot full of paper work; he told the Army he could type and that resulted in his working at the Battalion procurement office where he sat at an old Remington typewriter and filled out procurement forms all day - in triplicate.

I learned all this as we sat there in the mud and rain for another hour and exchanged our life stories. There was really no reason to get up because we were already soaked to the bone and that particular rain felt warm and cleansing. For some reason I trusted him and he mutually trusted me, and we soon discovered we had a great deal in common such as an independent will to be independent of other peoples' will, and an appreciation and fondness for observing military groupthink sessions. And I knew right off the bat that we were intellectually similar, for example; I liked to read books, mostly suspense and adventure novels, and Garnett, a speed reader, liked to read and quote books also, and not just certain books but all kinds of books. In fact Garnett could quote just about every damn book ever written from Homer to Tolstoy to Mark Twain to Shakespeare and the World Book Encyclopedia. He could discuss Einstein's Field Theory as easily as most folks would interpret a Cracker Jacks box, and if that weren't enough, he could juggle three filled bear cans and a banana while doing it, for he was also a master juggler, something he picked up during his off time while stationed in the states. He was a multitalented total recall genius extraordinaire. All that and he was a year younger than I. Who the hell, I thought, reads that many books in such a short lifetime. It was out-and-out unnerving.

And so after meeting Garnett, I concluded that if a mind is a terrible thing to waste, his mind was being terribly wasted, at least for now in the Army and in Vietnam. He was underutilized and intellectually unchallenged, which accounted for his insomnia and wondering around in the rain at 0400. But he was a refreshing change from the usual G.I. and I looked forward to bringing him into my little circle of friends since it appeared he was in no other. As we rose from the mud I thanked him for saving me from drowning and saving me from insanity. We then agreed to get together with the guys at the club that night to put down a few beers and further discuss the perils of Army life. That is if I could make it through the day. It was now Tuesday - again.

CHAPTER 27

THE DEAD LETTER

I was never one to suffer from a hangover, which was surprising, because I was also not one who could deal well with alcohol. I could handle a few beers here and there, maybe a scotch or two, but never anything in quantity. I sure as hell was no Chief Chief Zamboni nor did I have any desire to be. Any booze I consumed while in Vietnam was as much for the purpose of killing time and killing the reality of the war as killing a thirst. So after my drunken night in the rain, I was hoping only for a quiet productive Tuesday unlike the usually unusual Tuesdays usually experienced, but when I strolled into the orderly room I discovered a file on my desk with a note from the CO that read simply; *Write and type this and return to me (Must be perfect).*

In the folder was the outline of a sympathy letter addressed to the parents of one of the company's pilots who had been killed in action. The letter had been roughly composed with various passages and sentences scratched out and rewritten. It amounted to no more than one full typed page and in essence stated that their brave son was killed when his aircraft had been shot down while engaging the enemy. It detailed his heroic actions and made reference to his professionalism and sacrifice, and included most of the other standard canned catch phrases you would find in an average officer evaluation report. Obviously in this case *perfect* meant exactly that, perfectly composed, perfectly typed, and perfectly clean, and naturally the letter had to be typed in triplicate using the technology of the day being the ever smudge creating carbon-copy paper.

I knew right off the letter would prove to be a monumental challenge considering the conditions of messy carbon-copy paper dictating that any typo or mistake meant a complete retype, and the usual dirt smudges due to the inability to keep anything seriously clean in or about Camp Holloway, plus the expected constant interruptions of a Tuesday and any other day. I therefore set it aside until I completed my usual morning chores. Following a brief trip up the hill to the battalion S-1 to deliver the morning report, and after a short visit from Jesus Christ who informed me that I was God's messenger but was highly disappointed that I, as God's messenger, had no message to deliver, I finally opened the file and for the longest time just stared at it.

This was a chore I had never expected I would be charged with doing. To date my only experience with sympathy letters amounted to watching John Wayne or some other notable hardcore Hollywood hero scribble out a significantly heartfelt message on a dirty piece of notebook paper with a chewed up snub-nosed pencil. There were always a few tears while sucking on a well-chewed cigar and ducking bullets and shrapnel in a foxhole. Yeah, a little melodramatic and extreme, but then that's Hollywood where reality is a dirty word. Just the same, 1970 was a time when most people still wrote very personal communications by hand for the simple fact they were personal, and in this particular case I would say this letter was very personal. I suppose that was what caused my hesitance and led to my reading and re-reading the CO's original rough draft until I finally rolled the paper and multiple carbon copies into the typewriter, only to stare a bit longer. Is this what they actually do, I wondered, send impersonal typed letters full of canned jargon. I polished and typed the letter, made typos and retyped it, screwed up again and retyped it, and repeated the process throughout the day until I finally had as perfect a letter as I could produce, then deposited it in the CO's In-Box for his signature and mailing. The following morning I found it in my own In-Box with a few changes that amounted to the inclusion of a few more canned compliments. I repeated the day long routine and once again returned the clean finished product to the CO who approved it and had me send it up to the Battalion CO for his endorsement. This was when the very personal letter began to evolve into a very impersonal object of military bullshit.

For some reason the Battalion CO eliminated some of the true combat facts of the letter and replaced them with a few generic references, then included or excluded some punctuation and even watered down the personal stuff. The letter then made its way back to my CO and subsequently back to me requiring another full day producing another perfectly typed and perfectly clean product. That one somehow gained the approval of both my company CO and the battalion CO, to then be forwarded up the chain of command where it once again fell victim to the red pencil. By the time the letter had made its way back to me it had been stripped of most all of the facts of the actual combat situation, and even most of what little expressed personal feelings could be read between the lines. The time required for the letter to make its rounds then return to me after each instance of approval, all the way up to group HQ, grew significantly and the letter was now weeks into its process of creation. And if that wasn't bad enough, the letter had somehow morphed into something altogether unrecognizable from its original form and content. It now seems that the death of our killed in action by the enemy hero of a pilot, was not the result of combat or the fact he was a soldier who died a soldier's death, but instead *"he was killed while on a standard re-supply mission when his helicopter experienced a mechanical failure and crashed."* It had all the impact of a witness statement describing the plight of a neighborhood milkman getting a flat tire and running into a telephone poll. *Gee folks, we're sorry, but you know, shit happens, even in the Army.* Well, maybe shit does happen but the shit that happened here was in the form of the now impersonal personal letter that had evolved to a total load of crap, the reason for which I simply could not comprehend. I only knew the frustration on the CO's face each time as he returned it to me for revision and now understood his reluctance to personalize the supposedly personal sympathy letter in the first place.

Where did the chain of command get off reviewing a CO's expression of grief to surviving relatives anyway, I thought. And who came up with such a CYA policy in the first place? Our hero's folks should have received the letter, a very personal letter, as originally written directly from the CO soon after the incident of death, I thought. Instead, here I was, well over a month later, once again trying to produce a perfectly clean and perfectly false piece of shit. Though I felt a great deal of sympathy for our pilot's family, for me the letter itself had become an object of disdain. I finally reasoned that it was all about the numbers. Those damn numbers the Pentagon so dearly feared and the media so dearly loves, and at the time loved to use to bash the war. "How many bad guys did you kill today and how many of our boys died in combat today?" I could hear the reporters ask. "Well, actually very very few of our boys were killed *in combat* today," I could hear the

Army say at the five o'clock follies in Saigon, purposely not including the soldiers who supposedly died accidentally when their helicopter had a mechanical failure while on a standard re-supply mission. Though that's indeed what I was putting on paper, I felt I could just as well typed instead,

Dear Folks, Your wonderful, dutiful son whom we all loved and cherished, sustained fatal injuries while frolicking in the sunshine through a field of clover where he was accidentally struck by a falling meteor. We feel your grief and sincerely hope you will find comfort in the knowledge that your brave son's death was a total fluke and a fucking waste of life.

Why not? It would have had the same effect.

The letter finally made its way to someplace other than my desk but then it wasn't the last nor was it the only type of correspondence involving families of deceased Ghostriders. The bullshit letters resulted in inquiries by family members questioning the contradictions of information they received from their son's friends, fellow soldiers, and varied military sources regarding the circumstances of his death. And there were letters inquiring about known personal belongings that never arrived home, letters that landed on my desk with simple instructions; *Answer this.* Those were the letters, or should I say the straws that broke the camel's back and, I thought, would probably land me on the CO's shit list. What was I suppose to say in those responses; *I'm sorry but the reports of your son's death were total bullshit, or, I'm sorry but your son's personal property was stolen by some low life bastard in his hooch or some no good asshole at graves registration.*

Regarding the demands of creating perfectly crafted false letters, in all good conscience I could perform that duty no longer. Taking a dead letter in hand which had been mangled by the higher ups, I walked into the CO's office, placed it on his desk and stated simply, "Sir, I can't do these anymore." I fully expected I would be dressed down, demoted, and stuck out on the perimeter with Puffin and the rats for the duration of my tour, but instead Major Anthony looked at the letter for a quiet moment, showing obvious displeasure, but only nodded his head yes and tossed the letter aside to later make it the responsibility of the Admin Officer. Nothing more was said.

That particular Tuesday when I was given that first dead letter, Jesus had strolled in and informed me I was God's messenger. It was odd if not uncanny that he would say that. I don't know about being *God's* messenger, but surely I had become some kind of a messenger all right and I felt like sending a message home to my own folks saying, *We regret to inform you that your son has become a purveyor of bullshit and is fast on his way to compromising his integrity and his soul. There is also an extreme possibility that he may be struck by a lethal meteor while flying a standard re-supply mission. But what the hell – shit happens.*

CHAPTER 28

TACTICAL QUANDARY

The NVA's spring offensive had been defeated and Cambodia was becoming a memory as most of us settled into a routine dictated by the seasonal monsoon rains. The rains limited everything from flights and missions, to football and morale. For some it was a blessing, for others a curse. One thing was for sure, there wasn't a damn thing we could do about it.

The guys in the HQ hooch, when not working, just seemed to apathetically accept the heavy downpours that created the river-like wash that ran in one door and out the other. This, I supposed, was the result of the ever-present knowledge or philosophy that most all things here were temporary therefore most all things were bearable as long as you stayed focused on your individual DEROS. Their solution to the flooding was to simply bring everything up off the floor of their small abodes and hang them on the walls or set them on the windowsills, but as for me, I wasn't quite fond of splish-splashing in and out of my room like some Bayou wharf rat, especially with the knowledge that one of my predecessors got his brains fried by lightning in the same room. Since I didn't want to be standing in water if lightning decided it wanted to strike in the same place twice, following a number of days of periodic flooding I snatched a few sandbags and stacked them across the hooch's threshold. Just like that the flooding ended and everyone was amazed as though I had achieved some marvel of engineering, and I was amazed that they were amazed, but then it wasn't hard to understand their attitude.

It wasn't that I had equaled the accomplishments of the great Tennessee Valley Authority by creating a dam with a couple of sand bags, but rather it was the influence on them of the monsoon season. It rained, and then it rained some more, and when it stopped raining it stopped raining just long enough for nothing to dry out before it rained again. And it didn't just rain, it poured, and when it poured it flowed and all the dry red dusty clay of the highlands turned to wet red shit. It was nature and Southeast Asia's equivalent of a prolonged water torture on a grand scale that penetrated your soul as well as, in the case of the guys in the field, your feet, your crotch, your armpits and your brain. I honestly felt for those unfortunate grunts that suffered from funky foot and crotch rot, but we suffered as well from an extreme desire to be someplace else. It wasn't that rain and mud didn't exist in the States, of course it did, but in the States we had comfortable 20th century options like paved roads and walkways, drainage and sewer systems, air conditioning and indoor plumbing. Honestly speaking, the rain was at first and on occasion refreshing, but for the most part it could be and often was a spirit dampener, a climatically induced succubus of sorts that invaded your sleep and all other functions. It was just another way of reminding us we were in a foreign country. Regardless, we had to admit it was easier fighting the rain than the NVA, and definitely more preferable.

It seemed the rain wasn't a detriment to the hooch maids, however, who were as determined and busy as ever performing their duties each day regardless of the weather. They simply rolled up their black silk pants and went bare foot as they performed their chores, which I suppose was their manner of coping. And being the 50-gallon catch barrels were newly filled with fresh water off the roof with each new rain, the clothing and sheets the mama-sans were laundering were becoming cleaner than ever. Unable to dry them in the normally hot Vietnamese sun, however, they instead were hung inside the hooches, transforming our quarters into what looked like... a Chinese Laundry. As an alternative to the sun, and to their creative credit, those busy little ladies did their best by trying to dry our clothes with a hot iron. As a result each morning after rising from our damp bunks we always had a set of pressed fatigues offering us the civilized choice of damp and dirty or clean and clammy, which didn't really matter much because whichever we chose to wear made little difference. It was usually only a matter of minutes before we were once again soaked if we spent any time at all outside. A simple stroll to the mess hall or the latrine or the orderly room or anywhere else at Holloway would do it. The Army standard issue ponchos would repel the rain but they were pretty much a pain in the ass to toss on and off every time we stepped in or out a door so few of us actually used them. *Once wet, what the heck.*

If there was a plus to the rain it was that it washed away the urine odor that accrued near the hooch doors where the guys would step out in the middle of the night for a quick wiz rather than walk the long walk to the latrine in the dark of night. Another was that during a rain, if we so chose, we didn't have to walk that same distance to the showers but simply had to step out the door and lather up. What the hell, one cold shower was just as good as another and there was little chance of the rain being shut off by the goat man right after you soaped up your cookies. Such a heavy rain came in handy when on one Sunday during a brief pause in the weather we decided to play a game of football. The rain came back and the game turned into a mud bath. We showered on the spot but it didn't help much and the hooch maids damn near revolted the next morning when they discovered our piles of mud caked boots and uniforms. They simmered down though when we told them we had all been out in the field killing NVA and insisted they take extra care to wash out all that muddy Vietnamese blood.

"What you do, Fu-see-ko? You make bad mess. All mud! Today you numba ten. All G.I. here numba ten today. Too much mud. We need clea too much mud."

"Sorry mama-san," I said. "I was crawling in the mud and killing beaucoup VC last night. Beaucoup blood and guts and mud. You be sure to clean off all VC blood, okay?"

"No. You numba ten today. I no like clea blood."

"But mama-san, it's bad VC blood. I get all bloody when I kill VC and eat their hearts. But I saved you some. You want some for lunch?"

"No! You bullshi me. You beaucoup dien cai dau. Numba ten!" she declared as she waved me off with a half smile.

"Mama-san, you make too damn much rain," Randy said jokingly to another hooch maid.

"I no make rain," she replied, not bothering to look up as she squatted down to begin her chores. "I no make rain. Rain come."

"Mama-san, how you gonna' win the war with all this rain?"

"What you mean, win war? I no do war. G.I. do war."

"You're husband do war, right mama-san? You're husband VC, right mama-san?"

"No bic," came the standard Vietnamese answer. It literally meant *don't understand* but in reality meant *I don't want to talk about it* and signaled they suddenly and conveniently no longer spoke or understood any English.

Randy knew this particular mama-san's husband was a VC, or at least an NVA sympathizer. At least that was the word around the hooch. There were actually many hooch maids at Holloway married to active NVA sympathizers and no doubt some that were VC, but for some reason they weren't considered a threat. It was an uncomfortable reality at first but like much about this odd place it was accepted.

"No bic."

"Mama-san, you VC, right? You're man VC, right?" goaded Randy, his accusation accentuated by the rain pounding on the tin roof.

The other mama-sans pretended not to be listening but their quick glances revealed they're interest. My mama-san gave me a quick glance and a slight nod silently confirming Randy's accusations.

"No bic," repeated Randy's hooch maid.

"Mama-san, why you make it rain so much?" I said with a joking smile to my own Ba.

"I no make rain. Foo-see-ko make rain. You make rain," she joked in return. "You beaucoup dien cai dau."

"Yeah, you're right," entered Randy. "Foo-see-ko makes the rain. Foo-see-ko makes all the rain. Foo-see-ko numba ten. Foo-see-ko beaucoup dien cai dau."

"Foo-see-ko not numba ten. You numba ten," said my Ba in my defense as she inspected my muddy fatigue shirt.

"You tell him, Ba," I said, glancing over to the other Ba who was suspected of being married to the enemy. She looked back and before I could say a word she said,

"No bic."

"No bic my ass," said Randy as we walked out of the hooch and into the rain.

The monsoons lasted for weeks and though it tended to slow the war down it didn't negate it altogether. Various bases were harassed with rockets or motors or both, as were we, and a few of the smaller camps were attacked by the NVA trying to take advantage of the weather and our inability to fly in reinforcements or rapid reaction forces, or provide air cover. In terms of daily work it was a time to catch up or lay back, depending on your particular function within the company. In terms of pastime, some of us withdrew with books, music, imaginations, or memories of home, while others just plain partied. I chose to do a little of each.

On one particular evening the rain had let up so Randy and I gathered a few of the guys, then headed up the hill and collected Garnett for an expected dull average night of booze and loud music at the EM long bar. We were surprised, however, to discover a USO band had arrived, a rarity for sure because Camp Holloway had long been considered too dangerous for touring shows. The famous Bob Hope and others usually stuck close to Saigon or Cam Rahn, the larger secure bases where a few thousand troops would be given the day off and ordered to attend the show. The shows that never came to Holloway were a bit of a slap in the face for the Ghostriders since we had on more than one occasion been the transport of choice for such touring celebrities as Miss America and company. The show we had on this night had already begun and the band was blasting away. It wasn't the usual Asian excuse for a band but real live Americans cranking out real live American rock and roll. A great deal of hooting and whistling could be heard as we approached the building, the kind usually generated by a stripper or really hot round-eyed female singers, which is what we expected. What we found on this night as we entered the club was something else altogether, and admittedly it was a welcomed surprise. The EM Club was filled to near capacity and doing a booming business but still we were fortunate to spot an empty table in a far corner and wormed our way through the crowd and claimed it.

About that same time young Lieutenant Dennis Sosovitch whistled a tune and listened to the echo bounce off the corrugated metal walls and high roof as he walked through the Caretaker maintenance hanger. It was a half-ass rendition of the Turtles' song *Happy Together*, one of his favorites. He wasn't sure he had the melody right but then it really didn't matter because he was tone deaf and he knew it so it wouldn't come out right anyway. He thought the echo was kind of cool though and his whistling helped to fill the long empty silent night hours. He was the Duty Officer of the Day for Camp Holloway, and as such he liked to keep on the move thinking it helped pass the time. He had just come from the Officer's Club where he stopped in for a snack, and while crossing the expansive PSP active pad at the top of the runway and enjoying the rainless break in the weather, something he had observed at the club started making him a little uncomfortable. Though he knew of no special occasion or events taking place other than the entertainment at the EM club, he had noticed there were an added number of Vietnamese bar maids serving up drinks to the more than usual number of weather-grounded and bored pilots. He'd seen the club filled before but had never noticed such an increase in servers. It was just one of those little ticks that nagged at that extra sense many of us seemed to develop after a time in-country, a sense that made you restless when the hooch maids were especially quiet during the day, or left the camp earlier than usual, or when fewer than usual ladies of the evening showed up at the gate to offer their services. Things like that were often a sure sign of a pending action of some kind by the enemy that would take place later in the evening, be it a barrage of mortars, rockets, sappers or an all out attack. But this was just the opposite, more bar maids than usual not less. Odd he thought, but apparently not threatening, and so he dismissed it and strolled over to shoot the bull with a couple of off-duty maintenance guys who had just snuffed out and stashed their shared marijuana joint at the sound of his tone deaf whistling. Sosovitch smelled the weed but reacted with only a smile. After all, they were off duty, and except for the usual missions allowed by the weather, nothing much had happened lately. Everybody deserved a little down time, he thought; his fellow pilots and officers at the club, the air crewmen, and the wrenches on the ground. They all earned it. As long as they didn't smoke that crap when they were tooling on the aircraft there was no problem he concluded, and tonight all was quiet.

"Hey LT," smiled one of the stoned wrenches. "What you got against good music?"

"Funny. Real funny," replied Sosovitch as he turned to the sound of fast approaching footsteps behind him on the PSP outside the hanger.

After entering the club and finding our seats, we quickly discovered she had her audience smiling, rolling with laughter and eating out of her hand, and it was understandable why. She was a well-endowed pleasingly plump bold blond singer with a personality that didn't just fill the stage but filled the entire club from wall to wall. She didn't just sing she talked, communicated, and was engaging and fully entertaining. You could tell she had been a real looker in her day and could easily say that, except for the extra weight, she still was. And it was more than obvious she was a well-seasoned professional entertainer. Every song had a story and she had every trooper's attention. She was here for us and she made sure we knew it. It wasn't difficult to perceive that we were her favorite audience, indeed her life, for she had been entertaining troops since she was 16 and now in her young 60s, with the amount of energy she displayed it was evident she had no intention of quitting any time soon.

"And here I thought we were in for another night with the Temptations," I said as we laid claim to the table and seats in the far corner.

"She's sure as hell not the Temptations," laughed Randy.

She was just finishing a song that had well over a hundred of Camp Holloway's Flying Dragons on their feet with applause and as we were ordering a round from the Vietnamese waitress our USO showgirl entered into a monologue that segued into three more songs.

"I've been doing this for over fifty years," she said as she smiled into the microphone that she wielded as though it were a natural appendage. "And even though the music has changed over the years the faces of the boys I love haven't. The faces of the American G.I.. The best God damn soldiers in the world!"

With that her audience raised their drinks in agreement followed by whistles and applause.

"And the best damn soldiers ever to take to the air are the boys of the 52nd Flying Dragons, right?"

Naturally we all agreed and let our feelings be known. She had won us over as she probably had done with a million other G.I.s before us, but we didn't care. Right now on this night she was ours, she was everything - our sister, mother, grandmother, hell, maybe even the crazy-ass lady down the street who chased you out of her yard when she caught you in her cherry tree. More importantly she was home, regardless of the 60 year old package.

"This is the song we sang for your grandfathers," she said as she strutted the stage. "Those brave doughboys that fought in the sky and the trenches in the first Great War."

The band kicked in and she proceeded to sing *"Over There."* She sang it like she wrote it, like she owned it and was making it a personal gift to each of us. It was that classic song known to most of us only through old movies on the late show but we listened and were transfixed as we suddenly realized *we* were there as well. Like our grandfathers, we were in the trenches and in the sky. The uniforms were different and the slang had been altered over the years but the feelings, fears, and emotions were the same. She had just become our link with the past as well as home, and somehow tied it together with pride.

> *...and the Yanks are coming*
> *The Yanks are coming*
> *The Yanks are coming over there...*

Following that song she quickly jumped to a different time and a different war.

"And this is the song I sang for your fathers and uncles in World War Two," she said as the band changed gears.

I recognized the music and knew what was coming.

> *Don't sit under the apple tree with anyone else but me,*
> *Anyone else but me,*
> *Anyone else but me,*
> *No no no...*

Applause of approval rang out among those of us who knew and appreciated the song, and could visualize our fathers sitting in an audience in front of this same great lady, listening to this same great song while they yearned for home, or even our mothers actually sitting under a tree, or on a stoop or porch with a radio nearby playing the same song, wondering, hoping that her man would come home safely.

"And now here we are," she said after finishing the song. "Here we are in 1970. Here we are again on the other side of the world at Camp Holloway in the highlands of Vietnam." She smiled and panned the room as she paused to emphasize her next statement. "And we're kickin' ass and takin' names, right!"

Whistles and applause rang out in agreement.

"And we have a new song?"

The applause came again, starting slowly as everyone began to realize what that song would be.

"Are you ready!" she said as the band changed gears once again to the repeated throaty six-note guitar introductory tempo. "Are you ready!" she yelled again with a broad smile.

The applause and anticipation grew among the now well-lubricated crowd and then slacked off as the mix of soldiers from nearly every company in the 52nd CAB waited in anticipation of that famous chorus. And she began to sing.

In this dirty old part of the city,
Where the sun refuse to shine,
People tell me there ain't no use in tryin'...

It was an odd song, not so upbeat as the others and not even patriotic, but it was our song and it expressed our feelings because it somehow fit. As she made her way through the lyrics we began to clap to the rhythm, our clapping building as she neared and then finally reached the well known chorus that summed it all up. Everyone, well over two hundred in the house stood on their chairs, tables and on the long bar and joined in.

We gotta get out of this place,
If it's the last thing we ever do.
We gotta get out of this place,
Girl, there's a better life for me and you...

It was the popular song by the band *The Animals* and it had become the American G.I.'s Vietnam anthem and she knew it, just as she knew our hearts and souls. When the song ended she didn't miss a beat and rolled right into another by *Sly And The Family Stone* as she danced about the stage snatching members of her audience from nearby tables, bringing them up on stage and shoving their face into her large breast and giving them a shake, kiss, and hug then sending them back to their tables red faced but happy. She had just taken one young shy soldier and shoved his head right up under her blouse, sending us all into a roar of laughter. Then the announcement came from the sergeant who managed the club.

Stepping up on the stage he silenced the band with a wave of his hand and taking the microphone stated simply, "Ghostriders. TAC-E!"

A Tac-E was the slang for a Tactical Emergency and the Ghostriders were just missioned for one. It meant somebody somewhere was in trouble, possibly an SF camp, a forward operating base, or an artillery fire support base was under attack. We were the on-call company and our choppers were to scramble to provide support.

LT Sosovitch was still in the maintenance area when the first call came in and the CQ runner brought him the message. He then immediately sounded the base alarm for the perimeter at Holloway to be on high alert, for when he had heard the order for the Tac-E he lost no time putting together the pieces. The NVA were attacking fire support base Oasis and in doing so had tried to cover all the bases when they planned the assault, concluded Sosovitch, first by attacking a small fire support base with overwhelming force and second by acting on good intelligence that the artillery guys had moved out their heavy 155's earlier that day, leaving only a few 105's. In addition they knew the air support would come from Camp Holloway and as a safety measure in the O-club that night there were just too many bar maids, more so than normal, pouring doubles with the intention of insuring our pilots were boozed up and well out of kilter in case their biggest trump card failed them. But the NVA's biggest trump card was the weather, which was now in our favor. Sosovitch was smart enough to know there could be a backup plan to the bar maids and the weather's failure to accommodate the NVA, and that backup plan could quite possibly be in the form of an enemy force poised just outside our own perimeter, prepping for an attack on Holloway for the purpose of keeping our aircraft on the ground or worse, to destroy them altogether. After seeing the condition of his fellow pilots at the club he also knew well enough to call the mess hall and order up a large quantity of coffee.

Oasis was a fire support base located right in the middle of the Cateka tea plantation near the hamlet of Thanh Ahn just south and west of Camp Enari and slightly due east of Duc Co. The NVA attacked from the west about 2230 hours that evening, initiating their attack with mortars and RPGs, and throwing satchel charges into the perimeter wire to blow pathways into the base. It was a full frontal ground assault. The Ghostriders were missioned to air lift elements of the 47th ARVN Regiment to blocking positions to the southwest of the fire base just northeast of the Plei Me Special Forces camp. The purpose was to cut off and trap the NVA who would be boogying back to their base area in the Ia Drang Valley, known as 609.

Following the EM club sergeant's announcement of the Tac-E, all the members of the 189th quickly made their way out the door. The announcement causing a good many of them to sober up mentally if not physically, with most knowing the high altitude in-flight cold night air would do the rest. Some started down the hill to retrieve their weapons and gear, others, mostly the crew chiefs headed straight for their aircraft. When the security siren sounded as a result of Sosovitch's orders all of Camp Holloway's residents went into an alert mode. As we headed down the hill to the company area we were intercepted by Mondo who was hastily making his way through the night from the officer's club in search of assistance.

"Hey you guys!" he called out through the darkness. "We got a problem. You better come with me."

As I turned to respond to Mondo, crew chief Dillinger, who had also just left the club and was heading for the runway, turned back and joined us.

"Hey Fusco, I need a gunner," said Dillinger. "My guy is passed out behind the Club. You up for it?"

"Sure, no problem," I answered.

"Ain't none of you guys goin' anywhere if I don't get some damn help," said Mondo.

"What's wrong?" asked Dillinger.

"The pilots," answered Mondo. "At the club. They're all drunk on their asses. And I mean drunker'n shit, man."

"Damn," said Dillinger. "Shit!" He thought a moment then turned quickly to Randy. "You gotta' get down to the crews before they head for the choppers. Tell them to truck up here to the O-Club to get their pilots. And tell the mess hall to get a truck load of coffee and cups over to the Christmas tree, and be pretty damn quick about it," he said, not knowing the coffee had already been ordered and in the works.

The Christmas tree was an area on the far side of the runway and maintenance hangers where we parked many of our choppers. It was called the Christmas tree because from the air the configuration of the many choppers in their revetments appeared to resemble a large pine tree. Most of our choppers that would be involved in this Tac-E were located there and it was there that the beams of light from the vehicles danced off the aircraft and revetments as the pilots and crews arrived. The jeeps and trucks rolled in, being driven by the most sober members of the air crews, with their inebriated pilots hanging over the sides or slung over the hoods like trophy kills on the opening day of deer hunting season. Close behind came night baker Buns and the mess sergeant with tankards of coffee that were quickly snatched up by the gunners who wasted no time pouring it down the gullets of their pilots.

"Man, some of these guys are really out of it," I said to Dillinger as we approached our aircraft.

"Yeah, sure as hell looks that way doesn't it," he replied.

"This is where we separate the men from the commodes," laughed Chief Chief Zamboni as he emerged from the darkness to meet us by the chopper.

Just then another jeep rolled by carrying our CO, Major Anthony, who tried his best to pretend he wasn't seeing what he was seeing. He had been at the O-Club as well but being a conservative man and a conservative drinker, it didn't show. When the jeep slid to a halt next to his chopper and the engine was cut, there came through the sudden silence the sound of an incredible painful retching. We all looked to the source of the sound to discover CW2 Pully Johnson in a nearby revetment hanging onto the tail rotor blade of his Avenger Hog for dear life as he hurled his evening's intake of booze and victuals all over his door gunner's nomex.

"Oh shit! Thanks Pully. Thanks a whole fuckin' lot, man," said the gunner as he offered Pully more coffee. "Now drink this shit quick. We gotta fly."

Chief Chief Zamboni burst into laughter, looked to the CO who simply shook his head then went to his aircraft. "Okay, let's get these birds heated up!" yelled Chief Chief.

I looked around after mounting my gun to see one chopper after another cranking up, and not all with pilots in the saddle. Other than the CO's chopper and ours, many had crew chiefs in the driver's seats while their door gunners were still pouring coffee into their ACs and peter pilots. I began to have my doubts as to whether any of those guys would be able to get three meters off the ground, much less fly a mission without losing their lunch and their bearings, and I was suddenly very grateful for Chief Chief Zamboni's mysterious alcohol immune system.

"Shit," I said. "They're going to turn the Christmas tree into a train wreck and we're all going to die, we're all going to die in a ball of fire."

Looking around I saw gunners shoving pilots into their seats. In some cases the crew chiefs sat in the co-pilot's spot on the controls and cranked their birds to full RPMs, a few were already in a hover. Some copilots and even a few ACs were still on their aircraft's decks near the gun well as the choppers began to hover and edge their way out of the revetments for an orderly takeoff.

"Oh hell no. Piece of cake, Gunner Fusco. These are Ghostriders we're talkin' about here," said Chief Chief Zamboni. "Undefeatable and indestructible. Except maybe for that crazy sum'bitch Pully Johnson over there. I think he tried to set a record tonight. Boiler makers. I think he drank a dozen of 'em, not to mention a gallon of Jack or Jim or some damn shit like that. Wouldn't want to be that boy in the morning."

"If he lives till morning," I said.

Chief Chief laughed, knowing his assessment of the Ghostriders would soon be proven right. By some miracle each aircraft made it into the air safely, and surprisingly all held to formation as we left Camp Holloway's air space. It was as though no one had even been to the O-Club or touched a drop of booze, or drank so much as a Shirley Temple. Looking out I saw Pully Johnson's ship at the head of the other Avenger gun ships formation and in the dim light of their cockpit I watched the once overly inebriated Pully climb inelegantly from the back of the chopper into the front seat. He strapped in and took control without a hitch. After his crew chief vacated the co-pilot's position and climbed over into the back of the aircraft, the co-pilot, a young Warrant Officer named Pinky, not long out of flight school and in-country only two weeks, began to attempt the same maneuver with the assistance of the crew chief and gunner. Halfway over the seat he hesitated then clumsily crawled back to the side of the ship where he attempted unsuccessfully to piss. The results were disastrous for both the crew chief and gunner who suffered the windy wet backwash while desperately trying to keep him from tumbling out into the night sky. Looking back on this comedy of errors, CW2 Pully Johnson broke into uncontrollable laughter then banked his chopper wide of our formation of Slicks. The other Avengers followed.

Our flight of Ghostriders picked up the ARVN Rapid Reaction Force and arrived on site at around 2330. By then the enemy had breached the wire and pungi spikes, and were actually involved in hand-to-hand combat with our troops. The arty guys were down to shooting their 105 howitzers loaded with flachette rounds point blank into the attacking NVA when an Air Force C-130 gunship known as Spooky arrived. Oasis had been overrun and the arty boys and their small security force dove into their bunkers, some unfortunately followed by a fatal NVA satchel charge. Spooky stayed on site for nearly an hour, having been told to shoot inside the perimeter. Spooky was an awesome killing machine with its many mini-guns putting rounds in every square foot of the small base. Our gun ships had already gone into action and had been joined by a few Hogs from the Pink Panthers but they all had to back off their over flights when the C-130 was engaged.

Meanwhile the Silver and Scarlet Lift Platoon Ghostrider ships with the ARVN troops had reached the designated LZ and we quickly discovered it was inadequate and would accommodate only two ships at the most. As if that weren't bad enough, the small LZ was also overgrown with trees and shrubs. From our hogs first arrival at the firebase the radio was full of descriptive chatter that I was taking in like a kid at his first big-screen matinee. Then I heard the concerns over the LZ.

"Ghostrider Six, this damn LZ just isn't gonna get it," I heard Chief Chief Zamboni say.

"Roger that Chief Chief. I think we're going to have to find a different neighborhood."

"Negative Six. Hold one. I got this covered," came the voice of Dirty Joe Hail. Dirty Joe was one of our seasoned pilots and a well known basket case typical of many of our other pilots. When last I saw him he was in a complete stupor and slung over the hood of a jeep at the Christmas tree. Without hesitation his Huey broke formation and dove for the small LZ. It was difficult to see everything but with the aid of his chopper's lights I could certainly see enough to decide that the man was just plain crazy. Dirty Joe took his chopper smack dab into the center of the LZ, the fuselage crushing and spreading the growth and trees under it and the aircraft's blades violently ripping up everything they touched. In the midst of the flying debris the door gunner threw himself back into the corner of the gun well, covering his face with his arms, and most of the ARVN soldiers on board went into a sheer panic. Once down in a low hover, Dirty Joe used his aircraft's main rotor blades like a huge Weed Eater, a Tasmanian Devil slicing through the LZ, risking a crash, his life, and the lives of those aboard, but not without deliberate intent, for Dirty Joe knew his machine and knew well what it could do and what it could take, and he wasn't about to let something like a bunch of small trees get in the way of a good time. Having sheared and opened up the LZ he then hovered into a corner and used his landing lights to guide the rest of the choppers in one at a time. The ARVNs in his aircraft were quick to disembark, eager to leave this crazy-ass pilot behind, many of them cursing him as they went and probably more willing to meet the enemy than to once again fly with Dirty Joe.

We were the third ship in and as we off-loaded our passengers I surveyed the mess and the ARVN soldiers difficult maneuvering through all the debris. I wondered just how the hell Dirty Joe's chopper, especially its rotor blades, were still in tact but then when it came to chopper pilots, I decided, this whole damn war was full of miracles.

The attack ended around 2430 hours. I don't know just how successful our ARVN Reaction Force had been in cutting off the NVA retreat but I did see and get word on FSB Oasis. They had a good many casualties and a few dead but the enemy suffered even worse with an estimated 120 plus killed. Characteristically the NVA had carried off most all of their dead but as we continued flying out the casualties and flying in support, the morning sun revealed a mass of body parts and blood trails, the gruesome remnants of a harrowing night which could have been even more disastrous had the enemy attack been aided by the weather. It was a gruesome scene indeed, but like others in the highlands, it was a scene soon to be washed away by a monsoon rain. Cleansing the soil but not the mind.

⎯⎯⎯⎯⎯⎯

When we finally returned to Holloway we heard they had also been hit with an attack consisting of only a single one-double-deuce rocket. Not bad I thought, just one little harassing rocket that struck the thick nearly indestructible concrete communications bunker up at battalion. That is until Randy told me it had killed someone.

"Garnett," said Randy. "He was at the COM center listening to the radio traffic from that fire support base you were at. He caught a piece of the bunker in his head."

Garnett had stopped by the COM bunker when he heard them monitoring the radio traffic from Oasis. It was about the time when the firebase had been overrun and they were listening to its young radio operator who was beginning to panic. He was describing what was taking place.

"They're on us!" he yelled into his radio. "They're through the wire and they're everywhere!"

As Garnett stood in the doorway and listened to our chopper chatter and that from Oasis, the rocket came screaming in. Upon impact a flying piece of the concrete the size of a golf ball struck Garnett in the temple. The rocket's impact and excitement that followed distracted them from the sound of the radio and neither Garnett or the guys in the bunker heard the Oasis radio operator's last desperate words.

"Oh shit!" he yelled. "They're all around me! They're just… they're just standing there and… they're just standing there and laughing at me! Shit, they're laughing at me! Oh sh…"

Both the oasis radio operator and Garnett died at that moment.

We'd scarcely gotten to know Garnett but knew him well enough to know he didn't deserve to die young. He was a likable guy who got a little goofy after only two beers and then would beat your ass at any number of mind games. He was just doing his time, three more months until his discharge, after which he was going to meet up with his fiancé and cash in on a full scholarship to the University of Oregon, surprisingly not for his genius mind but for gymnastics. He sure as hell didn't deserve to die simply because he just happened to be standing in the wrong place at the wrong time, a fluke of a death that gained nothing or meant nothing other than to remind the rest of us where we were. I wasn't really sure how I should feel that day as I lay on my bunk wondering why it was him and realizing it could just as easily been me had I chosen not to fly. I was glad it wasn't. I then felt like shit for having the thought.

I heard a slight rattle on my make-shift rocket crate book shelf and looked over to discover General Giap the rat sitting there just as calm as you please. He looked at me as though he could feel and understand my emotions. I just stared at him and that was when I realized I was no different, that all of us were no different than that damn rat. We were all just animals who live as we can and then die. Like a rat. I was no different than a fuckin' rat. Suddenly it was clear to me, very clear and very simple. In the great scheme of things none of us really have any control and life is a matter of luck. When you're dead your dead - that's it. If you're lucky they bundle you up and send you home then stick you in the ground. If not they rake you up with the rest of the body parts and stick you in a hole or set you afire with the help of a little diesel. Either way it's all over. Life goes on for the rest and the only life after death exists in the faded memories of those who knew you. Those who you hope care enough to remember. That is if you lived long enough to create any memories.

CHAPTER 29

PAR FOR THE COURSE

The three of them had been in the CO's office for nearly thirty minutes when they finally came out and moved to the front of Top's desk. Major Anthony didn't look any too happy, nor did Top when he turned to me.

"Go check out a side arm," he told me. "I want you to escort Butterfield here up to security so they can transport him to LBJ."

Going to LBJ didn't mean Butterfield was going to have an audience with former President Lyndon Baines Johnson, but rather it was the acronym for the Long Binh Jail, the in-country jail for U.S. military personnel. Still, no matter how you spin it, this was President Johnson's war so the irony - or if you happen to be incarcerated there - the insult of the ellipsis was clear. Never the less, if you were sent to LBJ you were most likely in some serious trouble and in the Army, unlike the civilian world, it meant you were guilty until proven guiltier.

I nodded a yes to Top, sped off to the armory and collected a .45 automatic with ammo, holster, and belt, and quickly returned. When I entered the orderly room the CO was on his way out saying to me, "I'll be at the Golf Course if anybody needs me."

"Yes sir," I replied, but what I thought was, shit, another day on the golf course. I'll be damned if rank doesn't have its privileges.

The golf course in question, I had presumed, was probably restricted to officers only. Not that I gave a rat's ass because the only golf I had ever played was around windmills and dinosaurs. It was just one of those things that got my goat all the way back to Fort Sill where I saw senior NCOs spend half their day at the NCO Club and officers spending part of the work day on their golf course. It wasn't the first time the CO had just up and gone to the Golf Course, and admittedly, I didn't know his flight schedule so I wasn't sure I had a legitimate beef. He had a right to grab whatever personal time he could I suppose, and actually it really didn't matter that much, the fewer officers and NCOs around the better. What did gripe my ass was that it seemed he simply just went at the drop of a hat and though he never said it, I assumed I was expected to cover his butt should any inquiries from battalion come over the line or any brass come walking through the door. Therefore whenever the CO took off for the golf course and I fielded calls or inquiries I would simply make up some kind of bullshit that made me appear to be a complete idiot for not knowing my commanding officer's whereabouts. What I didn't know at the time was that I was way off base.

On this particular day everyone seemed to be on edge or at least in a bad mood, not uncommon for the Army but fairly uncommon for our orderly room. I suppose it was because it was a day full of problems and top sergeants and commanding officers don't necessarily like the type of problems we had that particular day. Yeah, that's right, it was a Tuesday. To begin with we were all wondering where the hell Jesus was. Not that that was a problem or a priority, but it was nearing evening chow time and Jesus Christ had yet to make an appearance. It made no difference in the great scheme of things around the office but it just felt odd going through an entire Tuesday without doing the deity dance. Even old papa-san kept one eye on the door, ready to shrink away to the far side of the room immediately upon Jesus' entrance. People all over the world were waiting for Jesus to return and here we had him nearly every Tuesday like clockwork. For us the exception was when he didn't show, which was rare. My guess was Jesus was busy up on the flight line helping to clean up a mess created when a couple of Ghostrider choppers bumped into each other while maneuvering near the wash rack. Though it only resulted in some minor injuries and damage, I'm sure a few pilots or crewmen wasted no time calling his name.

Another problem that came down the pike that morning was when the 90-degree gearbox and tail rotor failed and separated from one of our slicks while in flight. Part of the assembly struck an indigenous female on the ground and she was injured. The aircraft then landed without further damage and no injury to the crew and passengers. It was one of those freaky things that often happen when operating under the high-use conditions of war, but still it was a pain in the ass to explain to the armchair commanders in the air-conditioned trailers over on the coast. Our choppers were incredible machines but they were machines nonetheless and subject to a few foibles.

The really true pain in the ass problem of the day came when we got a notice that we were now the subjects of a formal Congressional Investigation, of which we were also notified had already concluded. In the Army a Congressional Investigation, regardless of the reason, is the equivalent of someone sticking a grenade up the ass of your career. It was that old washing your laundry in public thing. In this case the congressman who initiated the investigation was dumber than the object of his inquiry, which was saying a lot because it involved Private Clarence Ziederhold. Ziederhold, the low profile idiot who wasn't here but was here for six months before we discovered that he actually was here when he wasn't here, and then got off with only an non-judicial Article 15 and a fine, plus a promise he would never advance past Private E-nothing. In addition he was indefinitely placed on the shit detail list without the possibility of release until his DEROS and ETS where and when he could go on to continue his life of non-participation as a civilian. Understanding that Private Ziederhold was pretty much an idiot who only did what he was told to do - when he could be found - someone decided to assign him to guard five POWs who were being used to cut the high weeds along the camp perimeter. For the same reason he was given the no-brainer assignment in the first place, he was also not issued any ammunition for the M-16 weapon he was using to guard the POW work detail.

Usually the NVA POWs didn't give anyone a hard time because they knew that no matter how long this war would last they would never have it any better than they were having it in the detention facility near Pleiku. They had a roof over their heads, great food and plenty of it, clean clothes, warm beds, rarely had to work, all the outside fun and games and volleyball they could handle on any given day if it didn't rain, and no one was trying to kill them. They were also very much aware they had already survived the most threatening part of their ordeal being the possible lethal retribution of an angry soldier immediately during their capture, the physical interrogation in the field by one of their own race (southern ARVN style), or the possibility of joining the mile-high club during their transport. Avoiding all that, they now simply had to bide their time while doing their time until the end of the war or until they, or someone on our side, concluded they had mended their ways and decided to convert into a Kit Carson Scout. As a Kit Carson Scout they would then work for us, the good guys, helping us in the field in any way they could while fighting their former comrades, the bad guys. That is until their first opportunity to walk away and head back to Hanoi or whatever NVA underground military mountain abode they came from. Knowing all this, the individual NCO charged with putting together the detail decided there was little chance of a threat or a mishap while Private Ziederhold and his empty M-16 were on the job. He was wrong.

Those little guys may have looked short and harmless, and possibly even stupid to your average G.I., but the reality was they were well-trained experienced enemy soldiers who had no trouble at all spotting an idiot with an empty weapon. I know what you're thinking. You're thinking there's an escape in the works right? Well you're wrong. What there was, was five lazy North Vietnamese soldiers who wanted to kick back and light up and the problem was they had nothing to light up, but the idiot with the empty weapon did. In fact he was proud of the full pack of Winstons in his top pocket because young Ziederhold had finally gotten paid and with his newfound riches bought a beer and a Zippo lighter and a carton of Winstons. Time to start smoking and drinking, necessary he thought, if he was to become a real soldier like the rest of us. Then when one of the POWs smiled and joked, in a language Ziederhold couldn't comprehend, only to win favor while pointing and poking and reaching into Ziederhold's top pocket for a desired smoke, Ziederhold wasn't quite sure how to react. So Ziederhold, seeing only a threatening enemy soldier with a sickle in his hand messing with his head and his new Winstons did what any good idiot G.I. would do in those same circumstances, and promptly knocked the guy unconscious with the butt of his empty weapon, putting him into a complete coma. When word of the incident got out it somehow wormed itself all the way to Washington where some anti-war bleeding heart liberal Congressman initiated an investigation. The Congressman, it seemed, just couldn't understand how an enemy soldier with a deadly sickle, backed by four other enemy comrades with deadly sickles, could pose a threat to one confused and emotionally unstable kid with an unloaded weapon. *"Such abuse could not be tolerated,"* was the assertion of the Congressman, *"regardless of the circumstances. And what about the Geneva Convention? What kind of tortuous abuse are we inducing on those poor little people?"* Apparently the congressman hadn't heard the one about the door gunner found tied to a tree or was he aware that the NVA didn't recognize the Geneva Convention. He went on comparing the incident to the cruel treatment of those unfortunate soldiers who were forced to build the famed bridge over the river Kwai, capitalizing on the public's extensive movie knowledge and history according to Hollywood.

Nevertheless the end result was, at least it seemed to me, to be far worse than the incident itself. The POW recovered and went back to playing volleyball and smoking free cigarettes, and not caring one iota about the opinions of some damn American Congressman on the other side of the world. But our young Private idiot Ziederhold, who for most of his life managed to live cleanly while flying under the radar, had no idea how to handle the prospect of being the object of scrutiny by so many people at once, and by Washington no less, and possibly facing a court martial. Even though everything had been handled by the military with one higher-up calling another higher-up who called another higher-up who called a Washington contact who cracked a deal with the Congressman in question who, having already gotten the political PR benefit of a quick but short-lived headline in the New York Times and NBC, CBS and ABC, had already forgotten the entire affair. But Ziederhold went off the deep end and in less than two weeks the kid who had never smoked or taken a drink or spoke a word in anger, became a full-fledged chain-smoking babbling alcoholic who had to be shipped off to an in-country rehab program.

So Ziederhold was off to rehab, the CO was off to the Golf Course, we had no idea where Jesus Christ was off to, and I was heading up the hill to battalion with one of the Ghostrider's mofucka brothas in handcuffs. His name was Charlton Butterfield and PFC Charlton Butterfield, as I understood it, was in a world of hurt because PFC Charlton Butterfield had decided to take a vacation from the war and the Army, and when he did he also decided to take along a great big deuce-and-a-half truck that he sold on the black market for $5,000. Charlton then took his ill-gotten windfall and moved into a whorehouse in Pleiku where he laid low, got laid, and stayed high for two full months. When he ran out of money he came strolling back to us Ghostriders on Hollywood Blvd. fully expecting to receive only a slap on the wrist and an Article 15. Just like stealing the truck, his decision to return showed very poor judgment.

Charlton also returned with an array of stories about his partying and cohabiting with the enemy that he related to me as we strolled through the company area. According to Butterfield, when the military bases in the Pleiku area closed up tight in the evening, the good ol' town of Pleiku morphed into a resort destination for the enemy, and in addition the black market literally rolled out onto the streets. The enemy could buy just about anything they needed, medical supplies, weapons, ammo, tiger fatigues, poncho liners, and just about anything else, including a deuce-and-a-half truck, most all of which was U.S. government issue begged, borrowed, stolen, or squirreled away by those same good people we were fighting with and for. Aside from the benefits of one-stop shopping, our enemy counterparts also thoroughly and openly enjoyed the hospitality of the whorehouses. Oddly enough these same enterprising establishments were, by unofficial declaration, neutral ground, giving sanctuary to all who could pay and abide by this unwritten truce, be it an NVA soldier, VC, or a PFC Charlton Butterfield. Unfortunately Charlton was now heading for a different house, the big house, where he wasn't likely to have nearly as much fun - perhaps.

"Man dis is bullshit," muttered Charlton. "Dis jus mofuckin' bullshit."

"What's bullshit?" I asked as we walked along.

"All dis. Dey fuckin' wit me 'cause I black. Dats all. Dey sendin' my ass to LBJ jus' 'cause I black. Dats what's bullshit."

"You're kidding right?" I asked.

"Fuck no I ain't kiddin'."

"Shit Butterfield, what the hell'd you expect? I mean what the hell did you think would happen when you came back here? You ripped off a truck and pawned it on the black market and went AWOL for two months. AWOL and grand larceny in a combat zone. I'd say you blew it, man. And you only had five months left until your ETS."

"Dats bullshit. Dis ain't my war, dis da fuckin' white man's war. Dats bullshit. Like my man Malcolm say, dey jus' fuckin wit me 'cause I black, das all."

"Malcolm?"

"Yeah, my man Malcolm X."

"Was he in the Army?"

"Hell no he wasn't in no fuckin' Army. He ain't dumb."

"Then how would he know?"

"Because he Malcolm, dats how."

"White man's war? Looks more like a yellow mans war to me. All kinds of yellow. The good guys are yellow, the bad guys are yellow, and," I laughed, "after two months of AWOL they're going to put you in prison for being… yellow. In a combat zone it's called desertion. They can shoot your ass, you know."

"Dat ain't fuckin funny, Fusco."

"You're right. It's not. I feel for you, man. I mean if I were you I'd be scared shitless right about now."

As we reached the end of our company area and started up the open hill toward battalion three of the brothers came strolling out from around the back of the goat man's water tower.

"Yo, Butters. Happnin' here bro?" asked one.

"Mofuckin' dude sendin' my ass ta LBJ, man," answered Charlton, pointing at me.

"Yo Fusco, you sendin' my man here to LBJ?"

"No, I'm just taking him up to battalion. That's all I know," I said.

"Oh hell no, man. You gots ta let my man go, Fusco. Dats what chu knows."

"I don't think so," I replied, taking Charlton by the arm and continuing on our way.

The three started moving to cut us off so I slowly reached to my hip and unsnapped the .45. Frankly I wasn't sure if I would use it or not and was depending more on the threat. It worked. Seeing this they stood down and backed away, much to my relief, for I had no damn idea how I would explain to the Top about losing Butterfield, and I sure as hell didn't want to be the center of some dumb ass Congressional Investigation for shooting a couple of the mofucka brothas.

"I hope you be a light sleeper, mofucka," said one.

"You better gitchu a mofuckin' body bag, white boy," said another as they backed away. "You gonna need it, mofucka. You one dead mofuckin' white boy."

Not much was said between Charlton and myself for the rest of the walk up to battalion security. There was nothing I could say that would make much difference anyway. I didn't know him that well and frankly didn't care to. As far as I was concerned he deserved whatever the Army decided to throw at him and being he didn't bother to dissuade his friends from blaming and threatening me just for being his assigned escort, I decided he wasn't worth the effort of thought or concern or sympathy. What did require some thought on the way back to the orderly room, however, was whether or not I should take the threats of his friends seriously. I kept it to myself until later that evening when I mentioned it to Randy. Needless to say, I experienced a long sleepless night before heading into the orderly room the next morning. When I did Top was already there and after a brief nod good morning I discovered a holstered .45 sitting on my desk. I picked it up and looked to Top.

"Keep it," he said. "Sleep with it... and don't be afraid to use it if you have to."

That was all that was said of the matter. I smiled and nodded and from that day forward I slept with the comforting side iron, hoping I wouldn't have to use it. There were times however that I contemplated its use in my room. It would have been convenient on those many tempting occasions when I could have blown General Giap's head off, but the General must have pegged me for a wildlife pacifist or at least the less threatening of the other guys in the hooch, leading him to take up residence in my room in the late evenings. By now the rat and I, like in Butterfield's whorehouse in Pleiku, had silently reached a gentleman's agreement, a truce you might say. It was a simple agreement. As long as he stayed the hell out of my bed, out of my mouth, and out of my dreams, I would keep corn flakes or other goodies in a little dish on top of my bookrack where he could munch and admire the latest Playboy pin-up. We had become survivors he and I, defying the odds and fate, and defying the hoocho curse while just trying to get through the war one night at a time. But that's not to say it wasn't always easy just as on this night when the enemy nearly did what Butterfield's buddies threatened to do.

I was laying in bed writing a letter home and had just written about how quiet it was for a change when out of the dark of night beyond the perimeter came the thump of a launched rocket followed by its swift in-flight screech. I rolled out of my bunk to the floor and covered my head with my arms just as the rocket exploded. It was another one-double-deuce and it struck the roof of our hooch, but by some miracle it detonated immediately upon impact instead of first penetrating then exploding as it was designed to do. The tin roof and supporting wood was blown down on to our drop ceiling, which in turn came down on top of me. The florescent lights struck me across my arms and shattered followed by the light fixture then parts of the roof and ceiling. I stayed on the floor and braced for a follow up strike but none occurred. As I rose, brushed myself off and started grabbing my gear, Randy shoved open the door and asked if I was all right. I nodded a stunned affirmative and we both grabbed our gear and headed for the orderly room after checking on the other guys who were okay. Again the trucks pulled up and began loading our guys to augment the perimeter, and as usual I was instructed to man the field phone. In my haste leaving the hooch I had forgotten my flashlight, which shouldn't have been a problem except that the on duty CQ had moved the field phones located on the sill behind my desk and replaced them with a cassette tape deck that was currently playing Simon and Garfunkel.

"Somebody moved the damn phones," I said, turning off the music. "I need some light over here."

Beams of light came from both Randy and Top helping me to discover the two field phones that had been placed on the floor. I picked them up and plopped them on the desk then cranked up the hot line to battalion HQ.

"Okay Top, we're connected," I said, holding the phone to my ear.

Top turned his beam of light away but then turned it back and came across the room.

"What happened to you?"

"They got our hooch, Top. But we're okay."

"Okay. Then what's that all over your hand?" he asked as he directed the beam of light over my hand and arm.

When I brought the phone down from my ear and looked at my hand it was covered with blood. The broken glass of the ceiling lights had cut across both arms, not seriously but enough to bleed. Then I noticed my right hand was also bleeding, the result of a piece of metal about an inch long protruding out from between my knuckles. I pulled it out and tossed it on the floor.

"Get up the hill and get that fixed," he said.

"It's okay, Top."

"I said *go*."

I went.

It was only one rocket, as often was the case lately, just another reminder delivered for harassment purposes, not unlike other nights except this time I new exactly where it hit. By the time I reached the battalion first aid station the siren had ceased and some of the lights were starting to come back on. To my surprise there were a number of soldiers being treated by our medics, about half a dozen in all. I walked in and was quickly met by a medic who looked at my arms and sat me down.

"Got a lot of blood there buddy," he commented.

"Worse than it looks," I said. "Rocket brought the roof down and I got some glass cuts and a piece of metal in my hand. What happened to those guys?"

"Who knows," he answered. "They start bouncin' around in the dark when we get hit and anything can happen. Had a guy got run over by a truck once. He was drunk. One time some guy got nervous and shot somebody in the ass."

About that time a young FNG butter bar Lieutenant showed up. It was obvious he was a little looped, probably a few beers too many. His pants were torn at the knee revealing a trace of blood about which he acted seriously concerned. My medic paused from cleaning my arms and hand, tour open the Lieutenant's pants leg, gave it a quick look, then told him to sit tight until he was finished with me.

"I guess this will get me a purple heart won't it?" asked the butter bar.

"How'd you get hurt?" my medic asked of the him as he continued working on me.

"I fell. I mean, I think its shrapnel from when I dove in a ditch," answered the butter bar. "That's a purple heart, right."

The medic looked at me and laughed, "Not in this lifetime, Lieutenant."

"Oh, hey man. I got to get me a purple heart for this, right."

Just then another medic came up to me and started asking questions and filling out a red card with my answers. "What's your name and serial number? What's your unit? What's your religion? What's your hometown, next of kin?"

"Hey man. What do you need all that shit for?' I asked after answering the questions. "My religion? Hell, I'm not dying here."

"Describe the event of you injury," he said.

"Rocket hit the hooch, I hit the floor and the ceiling and lights hit me."

"Shrapnel," added my attending medic. "In the right hand."

"The man's a hero," said the medic filling out the red card.

"I'm sewing it up now. Looks like it'll take about six or eight stitches."

"Okay," said the red card inquisitor as he walked away.

"Hey, what about me? Don't you want my religion?" asked the butter bar.

There was no response.

My medic finished the stitches and bandaged me up. "Okay, that's it. All done," he said. "What do you do?"

"I'm a clerk."

"You right handed?"

"Yeah."

"Well then this is your lucky day," he laughed. "I'm giving you light duty. Don't strain the hand for at least four days. Don't want to pull those stitches out. That means no typing, no jerking off, and lifting your beer with your left hand. Think you can handle that? You're all done here."

"Thanks," I smiled. "If I see you at the club I'll buy you a beer."

"Bet your ass you will. Come back here in a week and we'll see about taking those stitches out," he said as he turned and began inspecting the butter bar's knee.

"It's a purple heart, right?" the butter bar asked once again.

"Shit, Lieutenant, you're joshing me, right?"

"No."

"Yeah, right. Here's a band-aid, Lieutenant. Now get the hell outa my first aid station. You're taking up space."

Top thought my light duty status was funny as did I and so I managed to type even with the bandage on my hand. As for lifting the beer and the other thing, well…

A few weeks later Top told me to report outside with a number of other Ghostriders for an awards ceremony. To my surprise I received a Purple Heart, which explained the red card questionnaire at the first aid station. After the ceremony Top sometimes referred to me jokingly as his clerk hero but more importantly, however, was the declaration by Randy that I had finally defeated the *hoocho curse* as he called it. What I didn't tell Randy was that not only did I survive the one-double-deuce but so did General Giap the rat who reappeared shortly after the reconstruction.

CHAPTER 30

THE DAY
THE WAR STOOD STILL

I woke up to a ghost town. At least that's what I thought. There were a few guys around when I got up and got dressed, but when I walked out the door of my hooch and into the orderly room there was a peculiar absence of just about everything, an absence of sound, an absence of people, an absence of everything, as though I had entered some strange vacuum. There were no choppers beating on the runway or in the air, no radios playing, no phones ringing, and no one to answer even if they were. I stepped back out and visually panned the revetments and the runway, and up and down Hollywood Blvd, and noticed there was not even a breeze or a bird in the sky. It was in that quick moment it came to me that there were never any birds, at least not at Holloway. No birds, I thought, a fleeting observation that soon became the least of my concerns.

On most mornings I was usually the last one up and the last one in, a personal character flaw that was never received well in the Army. Often shooting in just under the gun, I could usually count on hitting my desk running each morning and this was one of those days. On other days I would manage a quick trip to the mess hall to grab a coffee and something I could munch while I watched Top's morning formation from the back door of the HQ and listen for the phones. Today, mysteriously, there was no company formation, hell, there was no company, and it was damn spooky. No people, not even the usual influx of hooch maids and papa-sans dragging their sandaled feet below their short bowled legs. Where were they and why hadn't they been let into the camp? I wasn't sure if I had screwed up and was missing something or the war had ended and no one bothered to let me know about it. That wouldn't have surprised me. Did we win or lose? Was I dreaming? It was like an episode of Rod Serling's Twilight Zone, queer to say the least. So I decided to just park my ass behind my desk until someone or something happened. After all, I'd seen the Twilight Zone many times and knew that if I started running around looking for answers things would just get even stranger, so why look for trouble. I took my position behind my desk; pulled out a blank morning report, stared at it, and like that blank form in my hand my mind pulled a blank as well. Okay, I thought, I'm filling out a morning report that's going to say there's no one left on earth except me, and then I'm going to take it to *who* to get signed and then I'm going to deliver it to *who* to be read? I sat there for what seemed to be the longest time doing nothing, not even thinking to turn on the radio, the silence interrupted only by the occasional squeak of my desk chair. Then finally Randy strolled quietly through the door and simply stood there sucking on a cigarette.

"Thought I'd find you here," he said.

"Where is everybody?" I asked.

"Gone."

"Gone? What do you mean, gone?"

"I don't know. I think all the honchos are up at Battalion or someplace. And everybody else… I don't know. I think they all just quit."

"Quit? What do you mean quit? We can't quit. Nobody quits the Army… except maybe those guys in the movies who resign their commissions because they had guilt flashes for screwing up or something," I laughed. "And that's just movie shit. You know, like those guys in the movies who always keep their service revolvers. '*He killed himself with his service revolver,*'" I joked as though quoting a line from some obscure movie or TV show. "Ever notice they always say revolver but they always show a .45 auto," I laughed. "You ever notice that?"

But Randy wasn't laughing.

"Nobody gets to keep a weapon. That's just bullshit, right?" I continued.

"Yeah right, that's movie shit I guess. But hey man, don't ask me," said Randy. "All I know is everybody is pissed off and they're just gone."

"Why? Where?"

"They arrested Calley and his guys and they're going to prosecute them. It was on the news."

Randy didn't have to say much more. I could fill in the rest for myself. Lt. William L. Calley Jr., along with his band of merry men, had killed 102 South Vietnamese villagers around Song My back in March of 1968. It became very big news more commonly known in the press as the *My Lai Massacre* and a very bad black mark on the war. Truth is, it wasn't an uncommon experience, though not on that scale and not commonly known. The peaceniks and liberal political doves pounced all over the incident to further their cause, subsequently categorizing the rest of us who served in the war as maniacal baby killers. There wasn't a soldier with half a brain that wasn't aware of what Calley did and aware of most of the known facts regarding the event. In Vietnam there probably wasn't one American G.I. who didn't sympathize or at least understand the motivation behind the act, not to mention a great number of us who, given the right mood and the same circumstances would probably do the same thing, at least on those occasions when you attributed all of your current problems to our presence in the war. Such was the contradiction that was Vietnam, a country ugly and beautiful, a people crude and cruel yet appealing, a culture simple yet intricately complex, a contradiction of sights and emotions compounded by violence and the constant stress and threat of death that could drive you outside yourself to be and do who the hell knows what, a monster or a hero.

I doubt that most of us actually condoned the killings but we certainly understood the circumstances and frustration that spawned them. In our minds we were all there fighting for those people who, for the most part, looked at us as nothing more than a source of revenue as they puttered through the day pretending the war didn't exist. Then there were those who treated us as though we created the war in the first place, not to mention the many South Vietnamese who actually sympathized with the communists cause simply because it had an Asian face as opposed to our Western face that they associated with the arrogant French bastards who belittled and suppressed them for generations. Understanding Calley's actions isn't the same as excusing them but then we, more than anyone, knew that war was indeed hell and had a way of turning boys into killers on both sides.

Calley and his boys were on the ragged edge after being in the field for quite a while, had witnessed the cruel deaths of their combat brothers and were seriously ripe for some payback. Did they do the wrong thing? Yes, and in doing so the young Calley demonstrated he was an incompetent fool, incapable of leading men in combat, but on the other hand, he was following orders and that's the factor that ruffled our feathers. Maybe Calley should have said no to those orders but he didn't. And quite honestly, who of us would have in those circumstances. Did Calley actually want to defy those orders? Who the hell knows, and what would have happened to him if he had? In a way it was a no-win scenario and that was the character of military service. We all faced the no-win option each and every day simply because we have no option other than to follow orders for better or worse, right or wrong. Only those in uniform seem to understand that. From the time you raise your hand to the day of your discharge you no longer have any options. The Army, as they say, *ain't no democracy* and if you buck the system it can seriously mess up your life.

What really pissed off many of us who had the view from the other side of the fence was, however, that only Calley and some of his men were to be prosecuted. It was typical Army bullshit that always somehow left those compliant to the orders holding the bag. The equally guilty higher-ups who gave the orders stroll off into the sunset, leaving those who were most critical of the war, civilians, media, and politicians, to relish the entire process and situation like hungry feeding piglets on a fat sow. And so for that moment, with the news of the prosecution of Lt. William Calley Jr., we in Vietnam suddenly lost our last inkling of optimism and dedication to the cause, vague as it may have been, wondering if maybe we would be the next sacrificial lamb who had just followed orders. Fighting for a people who didn't understand why was something we could write off to the apparent national ignorance of a largely primitive agricultural society, and fighting to derail the communist cancer that was spreading across the globe was also something we could comprehend, if indeed that was why we were there, but being sacrificed by those who ordered us into the hell of combat while the boisterous anti-war media and minority populous at home rejoiced was pretty much the ultimate factor that killed the enthusiasm and broke the collective emotional back of a generation of American soldiers. It simply left us numb, and with no avenue or outlet to express our disappointment, it resulted in this momentary pause throughout the ranks that was so silent and subtle that it was deafening. For that day it stopped the war.

"So what are we supposed to do?" I asked.

"Hell if I know," shrugged Randy as he walked away. "I'll be in my room if you need me."

Hell if I know was all Randy could say and I guess that pretty much captured it right there. A million American soldiers just said *hell if I know* and took a pause from the cause, sending, I'm sure, a chill of fear and apprehension up the spines of Command and those in Washington and the Pentagon. So I just sat there in our empty orderly room watching the war not happen all around me and somehow found it intriguing if not a little frightening, at the same time thinking wouldn't it be interesting if every soldier in the world just quit. Just stood up and said, "That's it, I quit."

I remember very little else from that day except that I tried to write a letter home and couldn't. Suddenly everything was ugly. The war was ugly, the country was ugly, I was ugly, and the people and faces of Vietnam were becoming less interesting or less the fascinating objects I desired to help and befriend. Had I looked into a mirror that day I would have seen eyes beginning to dim, surrendering their youth to disillusionment and the reality of life, death and… questionable justice.

CHAPTER 31

STEAK & EGGS
& MOUNTAIN DEW

I could hardly believe my ears as I sat across the round table in the Pleiku Air Force Base officer's club and listened to Chief Chief's announcement.

"Are you out of your fuckin' mind?" came Dillinger's instant response.

Chief Chief just smiled as he peeled another five-cent hard-boiled egg, dumped the pieces of shell in the center of the table, doused the egg with salt and pepper, and shoved the entire thing into his mouth. His bulging cheeks somehow managed to maintain his smile as he chewed.

"He's out of his mind, right Fusco?"

"Of course he's out of his mind," I agreed. "He's a pilot."

Chief Chief gulped down the egg then followed it with a big swig of his fifty-cent double screwdriver.

The screwdriver was our chosen drink of the night, constructed of a double shot of Chief Chief's favorite vodka in orange juice. We sat around the table, each of us facing no less than three of the double drinks at a time, and all pulling from a large bowl of hard-boiled eggs that were being replenished at a nickel a piece about as fast as we could eat them, which was about as fast as the mama-san in the kitchen could make them. Covered with MPC, booze, eggs and eggshells, the table looked like some goofy ass game of garbage dump Monopoly.

Chief Chief had managed to bullshit our way into an overnight at the Pleiku Air Force Base by claiming a mechanical problem for this very purpose of partaking in a gluttonous all-nighter at the club. We had already spent well over two hours there, consumed a steak dinner and were following it up with an overdose of protein and vitamin C in the form of the eggs and juicy vodkas, when Chief Chief finally told us what it was we were celebrating, that he had extended his tour for another year.

Dillinger repeated his disapproval. "You're out of your fuckin' mind. I think all that damn Smirnoff finally caught up with you and burned out your brain cells. Tell him Fusco."

"He's right," I said. "You're out of your mind. But you already know that right? I mean that's not anything new is it?"

Randy laughed and nearly choked on an egg. He hadn't mixed with as many Warrant Officers as I had and he wasn't used to such a casual dialogue with the commissioned. He was here with us at the round table because I had mentioned our plans for a fun Saturday night and because neither of us had to show up in the orderly room the following day. Free Sundays for us were infrequent and highly valued so naturally I figured out how to create more of them. I had learned to cheat and make the Sunday Morning Report the day before, complete with Major Anthony's signature which I had long since mastered, in fact, I could probably sign Major Anthony's signature better than Major Anthony. We left the phone coverage to the CQ, making it unnecessary for Randy to cover for me as he often did when I was flying. But now being free himself, he insisted on tagging along. The problem was we had a mission the next day and would have to leave him to find his own way home but he didn't seem to care. Another of our party, our co-pilot WO1 Dearing, had slid out after the steak dinner to rendezvous with an Air Force buddy from back home who had lined up an evening with a couple of nurses from the 71st Evac, leaving Chief Chief and the three of us officer *impersonators* to our own devices.

"If I can get around New York," Randy told us, "I can sure as hell get around this damn place. Don't worry about me. I'll catch a hop back to camp with somebody."

"Yeah right," I said. "Like that ride you and I almost caught on that Shrimpboat last week."

The ride I was referring to was in reference to Top having sent the two of us to a signal battalion base for a one-day course to become certified movie projectionists. Only in the Army would you have to get certified to run a simple movie projector, but in this case, without the company having someone on record as being certified we couldn't requisition a projector or the movies to show on it. The assignment was my own fault, however, because when Top was searching out ideas for activities to raise morale during the depressing monsoons I suggested showing movies in the mess hall or a day room accompanied by a sampling of beer and Buns buns. He went for the idea but dumped it in my lap. The problem was we didn't have a day room so the first part of the mission was to build one. This was made possible by myself and the supply sergeant taking a deuce-and-a-half truck for a ride to engineer hill, a base on the other side of Pleiku, where we stole a full load of pre-fab structural lumber. It was sweet and easy, a truly slick operation where we simply backed the truck up to the stack of lumber and a squad of FNGs who were sitting on the stack taking a break jumped up and volunteered to load us up. I left the actual construction phase up to a couple of carpenter types from the company and the next day Top sent Randy and I off on a quest for technical enlightenment and certification at the hands of the Signal Corps.

The guys up at OPS arranged a ride on an outbound CH47 Chinook from a 52nd CAB unit known as the 179th Shrimpboats. We boarded, then just as the duel engine big bird cranked up its huge blades and was about to lift off the Crew Chief came to us with a proposition. He informed us they had just received orders to make a side trip to pick up a platoon of Marines and that it would make things a little tight and probably put us behind schedule by maybe an hour or more. If that was okay with us we could stay on board, and if not, there was a Huey we could catch that was leaving in about fifteen or twenty minutes. I lobbied to stay on board wanting to catch an up close view of the Marine soldier species, but since we had to make the scheduled projectionist class on time or spend the night with the Signal Corps to attend the next class the next day, Randy wisely insisted we catch the Huey. I conceded and we disembarked from the Chinook and watched the big mother take off for points unknown.

We made the class in time. It consisted of some SP4 showing us how to thread the film into the projector and flip the ON/OFF switch. There was some stuff about fixing things if they broke and not burning the film by leaving the light on when it wasn't turning, but we really didn't pay much attention nor did our instructor care if we paid much attention because he had no intention of teaching us for the required full three hours or administering a test. He did spend some time bitching about his wife who just sold his motorcycle so she could help her mother buy a new washing machine. He considered that act grounds for a divorce and vowed to take a sledgehammer to the damn washing machine as soon as he got home. The three hour class was over in twenty minutes and the rest of our day consisted of wandering around while waiting for an Officer, who was out not working on a special project, to return and fill out and sign some impressive certificate stating we were now certified projectionists.

As a result of all this we had time to kill and searched out and found the on-base massage parlor better known as the Steam & Cream. A place highly recommended by our not so highly motivated instructor and being we had hours to wait for our return ride home to Holloway on that same Chinook that we didn't come in on, we decided to explore the possibilities of some nice clean fun. The Vietnamese ladies in the massage parlor were friendly and talented, and very curious to say the least, which wasn't surprising, after all, what better place to glean information than from the unsuspecting troops of the Signal Corps. We showered with hot water that in itself was well worth the money, dried off, then flopped our clean towel-wrapped tired government issue bodies on separate tables in separate rooms where we were rubbed and tugged, all the while being interrogated for military intelligence as though we were total morons just bursting to unload every bit of military intel we knew to the first pair of warm hands that came along. It was a fun game with my mama-san masseuse insisting I was an important high-ranking officer and I agreeing and revealing everything I knew, from the Normandy invasion to the eventual assault on Hanoi by flying monkeys under the command of a General Witch West. I could hear Randy through the partition. To his credit he held out a bit longer than I but finally caved in to his mama-san's persuasive torture and spilled the beans on his plan to assassinate General Giap with a poison donut. He was talking about the rat and not the real North Vietnamese General, of course, but she didn't know that and absorbed each word with intense fascination, thinking she had scored a major coup. He wasn't entirely sure she bought the story, however, because it seems he had a hard time concentrating on the conversation, not to mention explaining why donuts had holes in the middle.

After being bent, twisted, pulled, and pounded at the Steam and Cream we proceeded to grab some chow then went to the helipad to wait for our ride. The Chinook didn't show, and after a number of inquiries resulting in no explanation, we eventually gave up waiting and caught a last minute Huey slick from the Gators that went out of its way to drop us at Holloway before heading back to An Khe. The next day we got the word on the status of our Chinook. It had gone down or was shot down, somehow disappearing on route along with the thirty plus Marines, and was the subject of a wide continuing search. The last I heard it hadn't been found and I never did hear if it had ever been found, or if their had been any survivors. Truth is, being that close to being a part of the mystery, I'm not sure I wanted to know.

"It's all a matter of fate," said Chief Chief after hearing of our close call on the Chinook. "You got to tell yourself that… everyday. You say, maybe today's the day and maybe it's not. Maybe today I'll fall out of the sky. Or maybe a one-double-deuce will fly up my ass when I'm on the shitter."

"Yeah, so what do *you* do? You shoot fate the bird and extend for another year," said Dillinger. "Everybody can't wait to get out of this shit hole and go home and you extend for another year."

"You haven't seen the Badlands have you?" said Chief Chief. "Not much to go home to."

"I'm in the Badlands right now, replied Dillinger after gulping down a double screwdriver. "At least in your Badlands they don't shoot at you."

"Not lately," laughed Chief Chief.

"You haven't seen New York City," said Randy. "And they do shoot at you."

"You said you were short. Twenty-two days," I said to Chief Chief, equally confused about his decision to extend his tour. "You even had me check the records and confirm it for you. And it's likely you'll probably get a drop that will maybe get you home two or three weeks early. Hell, they'd probably discharge you if you wanted. Now that their phasing down the war and turning everything over to the dinks they're giving early outs to flight Warrants. Some of those guys haven't even been in-country two months yet and they're getting out. There's an excess of pilots.

Hell some of those guys haven't even been in the Army for a full year and they're getting discharged. So why'd you extend?"

Chief Chief downed another screwdriver and reached for another egg. The pile of shells in the center of the table was growing as we all peeled and ate and drank and talked. He looked across the table to Dillinger and his face grew abnormally dim. "That village. Three days ago. The SF team. I can't go home as long as those guys are still here doing what they do. So I figure I'm good for another year."

"What village?" asked Randy.

Dillinger took a deep breath then a long swig of another screwdriver. "Fusco didn't tell you?"

"No," answered Randy. "Tell me what?"

He then filled Randy in on the events that took place at a small village in the hills near the Cambodian border.

"About twelve days ago we lifted an SF medical team to a village. It was one of those mercy missions. Seems a lot of the women in the village were getting infections. You know."

"No," said Randy. "What kind of…"

"Down under. You know. Pussy infections."

"Oh."

"Well, the SF med team went in and figured out the problem and gave them all shots and stuff. Turns out all the native women were wiping their ass the wrong way. You know, back to front or north instead of south or something like that. And it was messing things up and they were gettin' infections."

"You're kidding. It was that simple, huh?" said Randy.

"Yeah, weird, huh?" said Dillinger, taking another drink then continuing. "Well, we hauled the team back in there three days ago for a medical follow up. Eight of 'em. Two medics, a Yard and the others, back in for a follow up medical check. Some of 'em carried goodies for the village kids. You know, the usual hearts and minds thing. So we dropped 'em in and took off and we weren't ten miles away when we heard the call for air support and an emergency extraction. Turns out the NVA found out about the first visit and, knowing we'd be back, had the place staked out. They let us go in there just as sweet as you please and drop those guys off. Then when the team entered the village those bastards opened up. When we turned around and flew back there we came under fire. Guess they figured they'd get us too when we came back but two Buccaneer hogs from the 170th showed up about the same time and pretty much wiped them out. Another SF team was inserted to get to the village and help out, also some ARVN React Forces, but it was too late. When we were finally called in for the extraction of the original team all we carried out were bodies. The entire team and all the people in the village had been wasted. It wasn't pretty."

"Ironic isn't it?" observed Chief Chief. "Eight good soldiers and a village full of innocent people all killed just because some Asian hillbillies didn't know how to wipe their own ass. Now that's one for the books. Typical, just fuckin' typical," he said as he shoved in another egg. Chief Chief held his drink up over the now one-foot high pile of eggshells. "Here's to the ass-wipes who start the wars," he mumbled through his chewed up egg. "May they all some day have to eat the shit they shovel and choke on every fuckin' bite."

We all raised and touched our glasses, downed our double screwdrivers, then ordered another round. When we finally departed the club in the wee hours of the night the eggshell pile covered half the table. Surprisingly after a multitude of double screwdrivers we all still had control of our senses, our bladders, and our bodies, with none of us having to barf. Maybe it was the steak, or the egg protein overdose, or the orange juice and vodka, or possibly even the combination of all three, or maybe Chief Chief's amazing genetic immunity was somehow contagious. Whatever the reason, we survived the binge and took to the sky in the predawn with little enthusiasm and no sleep, leaving Randy to fend for himself.

Our mission that morning was a simple one. We were to make ourselves available for a possible insertion of a SOG team somewhere just across the border near a known NVA infiltration route off the Ho Chi Min trail, then if no longer needed, we were to return to Holloway for some overdue scheduled maintenance on the aircraft. We flew into Dak Pek, waited until the mission was cleared to go, then loaded the team and headed for the border. The sun began to rise behind us revealing the higher western mountains in front with an incredible array of greens and grays, with strands of mist rising out of the shadows of the low valleys. It was in one of those misty valleys where we dropped our passengers. Everything took place without a hitch when we slid into the small grassy LZ. Pulling up and away I watched the team quickly disappeared into the darkness below the trees.

As we flew back east I sat back and remembered the letter in my pocket that I had received the day before from Stacie. It wasn't one of those infamous Dear John letters but just as well could have been. It was a mere one page letter written out of duty not love, and actually included a brief weather report to help fill space. It answered none of the many questions I often asked in my own letters but, in fact, through its meager context did answer a very important question. Though I had long accepted the fact that Stacie wasn't the brightest candle on the cake, I knew she was at least capable of writing with some degree of emotion. She was also the worst liar in the world who most often lied by omission. At other times she would simply say, "I don't want to talk about it," or claim total ignorance of the subject and walk away. This letter, like the letters before that were becoming fewer and less frequent with less and less information, was nothing but omission. The between the lines message was clear. I pulled the letter out of my pocket, read it one more time, then crumbled it up and let it fly.

Our back flight took us into a quick change of weather. It rolled in and wrapped around the mountains leaving the peaks protruding like islands in a surreal sea of lingering white smoke. It was mystic or fantastic, like something out of a spooky movie except on a grand scale. As we approached and were about to pass above it we picked up on a call for an emergency medical evacuation. Chief Chief being Chief Chief was, of course, the first to respond and down into the soup we went.

The call came from somewhere in the western mountains a little north of our location near the border. Aware of the unpredictable winds, rain, and the terrain we faced as we entered the area, my pucker factor was again beginning to increase big time. Just flying through these mountains on a good day was a risk and now with Chief Chief somehow swimming the aircraft through the clouds and rain among seven thousand foot cliffs it was damn near suicidal by any standard of aviation safety. Suddenly the enemy was no longer the NVA but the environment. We dodged protruding cliffs that lurched out of the clouds and hundred foot trees projected up through the mist. I was beginning to feel lost and helpless, a haphazard child of chance, searching my mind for some prior life experience or memory that I could reference to guide and stabilize my emotions. Ridiculously, the only thing that came to mind was a previous near death experience on a rickety old Wild Mouse ride I had once taken at a state fair. It wasn't comforting. Following that brief memory flash I pulled a blank but somehow managed to settle my nerves with the simple knowledge that my pilot had no more intention or desire to die than did the rest of us and, as such, would see us through this ordeal safely. That worked for a moment until I remembered the pilot was Chief Chief Zamboni and began to wonder if indeed he was suicidal. I then mentally scolded myself, telling myself to quit over thinking the situation and just go with the flow, with the rationalization that I was here and there wasn't a damn thing I could do about it.

We were searching for a SOG team that had run into trouble with the NVA. They managed to escape and evade by way of the fateful weather and some well-placed artillery, but their problem now was they had two wounded comrades who couldn't be moved further and needed an immediate dust-off. As we neared their location somewhere in a small valley the visibility through the heavy rain worsened and at the low altitude we were flying it seemed like Chief Chief was depending entirely on luck. The ground team on the radio guided us by sound, which was iffy at best considering the way the sound carried in the weather and bounced off the hills. We were forced into a slow roaming mode of flight in search of their yellow smoke until finally Chief Chief caught a glimpse of it barely rising through the trees before it dissipated in the wind and rain. As we carefully approached over the treetops and confirmed the smoke to the team on the ground the hazard of our task suddenly doubled when we saw their situation. They were in a hover hole, a crater created by a five-hundred pound bomb that had ripped out a portion of the sloping mountainside jungle of hundred-fifty foot canopy, leaving a small clearing barely big enough for a single chopper. The clearing, however, was littered with twenty and thirty foot tree stumps and there was no way we could land or even hover low enough to take on passengers.

"Shit!" I heard Chief Chief say into my head set. "Looks like we gotta' go fishing. Hook 'em up Dillinger."

"Roger that," answered Dillinger who immediately showed up at my side and motioned for me to follow his lead. "We're going to drop a line," he yelled to me over the noise of the chopper. "They'll have to tie their man on and then we lift him out."

"Pull him up?" I questioned. "How the hell we gonna' do that? He's dead weight against the rotor blade's down draft."

"No. We'll airlift him to a place where we can set down then bring him on board."

"There's two," said Dillinger, showing me two fingers. "Two wounded. Two trips. You ready?"

I nodded a yes and we proceeded to rig a long length of half-inch nylon line that Dillinger kept stored on board. We doubled it and once it was secured we dropped it down where the guys on the ground attached it to a utility belt and rigged it around one of the wounded. Chief Chief then lifted us up slowly, all the while listening to the voice of Dillinger who scrambled crablike back and forth from one side of the aircraft to the other carefully directing him up through the trees. I slid out onto the skids, standing with one hand holding the gun post and the other on the lift line so I could monitor the progress of our wounded passenger. When he was safely above the trees I signaled to Dillinger who in turn told Chief Chief. He carefully maneuvered us about a mile and a half away to a bend in a small river at the bottom of the valley. The river was rising quickly due to the rain and due to the trees along the riverbank we had no choice but to hover above what looked to be the shallowest part of a submerged sand bar. Our wounded passenger was able enough to sit up in the rolling water until Dillinger hopped out to assist him. When we brought him aboard he informed us that his wounded comrade was heavily morphed and unconscious, and would need assistance.

"That means you gotta go down and get him," Dillinger told me.

"What!" I replied. "What about one of those guys on the ground?"

"No," said our wounded passenger. "Another chopper is fifteen or twenty minutes out and this place is loaded with bad guys. They got to run for a better extraction point and need each other for cover and support."

"You want to repel down or you want to hook up here and drop in?" Dillinger asked me. "I can't do it 'cause I got to help guide Chief Chief during the lift."

"Shit!" I said. I'd done some recreational repelling just for kicks during my fun and games at Fort Sill and right away knew that without a D-ring and heavy gloves I couldn't do it here, so I opted for the joy ride. "Shit," I said again. "Guess I gotta hang."

Dillinger laughed then informed Chief Chief of the plan.

"Put the bait on the hook," I heard Chief Chief say. "And make it quick before the gooks zero in."

Dillinger smiled and handed me the makeshift utility belt harness attached to the line. "Up up and away Superman," he laughed.

I rigged the belt around my back and under my arms and hopped out of the chopper. No sooner had I dropped and plopped on my ass in the cold water did Chief Chief begin his lift, leaving me no time to ponder the situation or have a change of heart. My only concern was keeping the line untangled as it snaked out of the water to eventually jerk me up. Once airborne, I thought things would only be a matter of a tight grip and a prayer but what I didn't count on was my spinning uncontrollably to such a degree that by the time we reached the hover hole I was about ready to lose the steak, eggs, screwdrivers, and everything else I had eaten the night before, something I'm sure the SF guys who reached up and steadied my descent wouldn't have appreciated. In addition, I was quick to regret my placement of the rope around my back and under my arms. Though it was secure, it cut painfully into my back and armpits. The trooper to be lifted had sustained a head wound and serious leg wounds. He was unconscious so the members of his team used their utility belts to secure him to me and secure both of us to the lift line. And they did it all with amazing speed.

"Okay, you're good!" one of them yelled as he patted me on the helmet and gave me a thumbs up.

I offered only a nervous smile in return, lowered my helmet visor, then looked up to Dillinger. With a thumbs up of my own we began to rise. The dead weight of the wounded soldier along with my own strained the double nylon line and the utility belts. Even though the harness formed a seat under my ass, it again cut painfully into my body as we were slowly lifted above the trees. The downdraft of the main rotor blades redirected the rain straight down until we eased over the trees and headed for the river. The rain had increased since the beginning of our rescue and now, in horizontal flight, began pelting us like road gravel so I pulled the wounded soldier's head to my chest and covered his face as best I could. Closing my eyes, I held him like that until we finally swayed just above the river under Chief Chief's careful hover. When the swaying subsided to a slow spin he lowered the aircraft until we met the water. It was deeper now, swifter, nearly hip high. I forced myself to roll under the wounded man to keep his head above water and fought the current of the river until the chopper was only a few feet above us. Dillinger jumped out and quickly rushed to begin undoing the makeshift harnesses. Once free we both struggled to shove the man onboard and lay him safely on the deck then quickly boarded behind him. I pulled in the line and Dillinger tapped Chief Chief on the shoulder and we were away. The first team member we retrieved secured and held his buddy and I returned to my gun well. Chief Chief flew us along a short portion of the river, skirted some trees and a protrusion of rocks, then banked and rose up through the mist and above the clouds. With the worst of the weather below us and eventually behind us as we emerged from the mountains we wasted no time getting our passengers to the 71st Evac Hospital at the Pleiku Air Force Base.

As soon as the medics rolled our unconscious man into the building from the helipad Dillinger began checking me over and inspecting my wet nomex.

"What the hell are you doing?" I asked, removing my helmet.

"You need to go in there?" he asked.

"What?"

"Are you okay?" You need medical?"

"No," I said. "Why?"

"You sure?" he asked, continuing his inspection.

"What the hell are you looking for?"

"Holes."

"Holes?"

"I thought maybe you got hit."

"Oh, yeah. You mean the rain and I think maybe some flying tree shit. That hurt some."

"No, I'm talkin' about bullet holes, dumbass."

"What?"

"Man, they were poppin' off at you all the way down the side of that mountain. When we hit that river I thought you'd be holier than Swiss cheese."

"What! Are you serious? All I heard was rain and chopper."

"Somebody up there is covering your ass," laughed Chief Chief as he dismounted the chopper and slammed the door shut. "That or you're just damn lucky."

"Lucky," agreed Dillinger. "Just damn lucky."

"I could use some coffee," said Chief Chief.

"Yeah," I agreed. "Or something stronger."

CHAPTER 32

HOT ROKS & COWBOYS

After checking the aircraft for damage, refueling, some coffee and a pause for the cause, we were once again saddling up to take to the air when the discussion somehow got around to Major Anthony's fondness for golf. Upon my mentioning it, Dillinger, Chief Chief and Dearing all laughed but wouldn't let me in on the joke.

"So you think the Major plays a lot of golf?" asked Chief Chief.

"Seems that way," I said. "Couple times a week he heads for the golf course and I cover his ass."

They laughed again.

"Well, he probably does spend some time at the golf course but not the one you think."

"There's another one?" I asked. "Besides what those spoiled Air Force weenies got here?"

"Yeah, a really big one. Want to see it?"

Before I could answer he put the question to the rest of the crew. "I think he should see it. You guys want to go to the golf course? Think Fusco here needs to shoot a round of golf?"

They nodded agreement with a sly smile, still refusing to let me in on the joke, and the next thing I knew we were in the air heading east under the guise, according to what Chief Chief called into OPS, of getting in some training time for our new peter pilot. We were skirting over the north side of Pleiku when there came through my headset the sound of Steppenwolf singing *Magic Carpet Ride* that I immediately considered an improvement over Dillinger's usual country bill of fare. I kicked back to let my nomex and boots dry in the free wind of flight as we gained altitude over Highway 19, then shot south to avoid bumping into any aircraft entering or exiting the pattern at Camp Holloway. Chief Chief took it easy, flying due east, first on one side of the road then the other, then up to about 1200 feet as we flew over the famously dangerous Mang Yang Pass through the Dak Pihao Mountains. He then turned the controls over to Dearing.

Coming out of the pass and into the beginnings of flatter rolling terrain, Highway 19 meandered on southeast but we veered off to the northeast. When I asked where we were headed Chief Chief said he wanted to stop off and pick a little fruit. I didn't even want to touch that one so I let it lay. A few Steppenwolf songs later Chief Chief spotted a heavily armed convoy headed north on a small dirt road running from the 19 and motioned for Dearing to fly in that direction. He thought it odd that the convoy was heading into the boonies on a secondary road with no air support until we came close enough for him to recognize who they were.

"We got us some ROKs down there," said Chief Chief. "And it looks like they've wandered a few klicks off their reservation."

"Looks like they're out cruisin' for a bruisin'," came Dillinger. "But I think we're the ones who're wandering."

"Rocks. What the hell are Rocks?" I asked of anyone who would answer. "Bad guys?"

"No, they're on our side," answered Chief Chief. "Allies from Korea. R-O-K. Republic Of Korea Army. Their turf is the northeast section of II Corps. Pretty much restricted to the Bhin Dhin province. And from all I've heard they do a pretty damn good job. What say we go down and say hello?"

Dearing nodded affirmative and banked us over and slowed at an altitude of about 300 feet parallel with the ROK convoy. There were about eight vehicles in all, each sporting heavy guns varying from mounted .50 cals and .60s to what looked like small cannons and 7.62 mini guns. Spaced evenly in the midst of the convoy were two deuce-and-a-half trucks with a platoon of Korean soldiers leisurely spread out in each. They looked up at us with smiles and casual salutes as we flew from one side of the winding dirt road to the other. It was all fun and games as we approached a tree-lined curve in the road that led past a small Bahnar tribesmen Montagnard village. The village was nestled among another cluster of trees about three hundred yards to the left. As the ROKs rounded the curve away from the trees and into the open they began receiving small arms fire that could easily be seen by the tracers as coming from the village. The fire continued, coming from only one location on the village perimeter. Within mere seconds the ROKs reacted with counter fire. Simultaneously all of their vehicles turned left off the road and headed straight for the village. A hundred yards out from the stilted huts the two troop carrying trucks halted and the ROK soldiers poured out in a spread formation behind their attack vehicles. Every gun on every vehicle threw a merciless broadcast of lethal response against the small hamlet. Then suddenly mortars, originating from somewhere in the center of the village, began striking near the ROK soldiers. Chief Chief took over the stick and quickly maneuvered our chopper for a run.

"Coming around on your side Fusco," said Chief Chief. "Mortar set behind that big hooch. Give 'em hell!"

Making our pass, I could see armed Vietnamese, not Bahnar tribesmen, scrambling from the hooches and making for the cover of the nearby trees. I could also see an increase of tracers being fired at the ROK troops from various locations among the other structures and others now being fired at us. It was difficult to stay focused on one target with so much taking place at once until the three man mortar crew came in view. I opened up with short bursts, at first missing by ten or twelve yards, then adjusting until I was right on, then held for two good twelve-round bursts. I could hear Dillinger firing from the other side and Chief Chief saying something, but it was all a mental blur. All I could think was that I didn't want to fuck up. The fear and adrenaline rush did the rest.

Two of the VC mortar crew went down immediately, one actually losing his leg before my other rounds tore apart his head and shoulder. The third man ran for cover under the village's large communal hooch. I followed him with my 60 trying to cut him off, letting go with another burst but the angle and movement of our flight took the rounds directly into the big hooch itself. From inside came a sudden WHOMPH, then an explosion ripped out the side and corner of the structure. Chief Chief quickly pulled the aircraft away to avoid our getting hit with debris or shrapnel and brought us around at a higher altitude behind the ROKs who, firing continuously, were now about to overrun the village. They paused, however, when a huge secondary explosion tore the main hooch to shreds, sending fiery wood, bamboo, and thatch in a black cloud hundreds of feet in the air. Even at our safe distance the explosion seemed to suck the air right out of my lungs. We could see and hear the remaining munitions flashing and cooking off as the ROKs resumed their assault. They were merciless and thorough, rolling over the entire village with the least bit of hesitation, a tsunami of gunfire and explosions from their entire arsenal and force of men. Everything in the village was destroyed and reduced to flames and ashes within, what seemed to be only a matter of minutes, yet it somehow processed through my mind in some form of slow motion. It was an incredible thing to witness and was testimony as to why the ROK's area of operations had the least problems of all of South Vietnam.

We orbited the scene for a short while until Chief Chief gained radio contact with the ground force, asking if they needed medivac for their wounded. A ROK Major was quick to respond with a thank you and a laugh saying they had no friendly casualties and that *all* of the enemy were KIA and would not need medical assistance either. It was an interesting statement considering I could see ROK soldiers on the ground rounding up live bad guys. I would learn later that the ROKs weren't fond of taking prisoners and were very effective and uncompromising at immediate on-site interrogations. They regularly gained excellent intelligence and acted on it swiftly. It wasn't difficult to understand why.

As we pulled away and headed back towards Highway 19, I stretched out over my gun for a final look back at the scene below. The gun was still hot enough that it seared my hand. Likewise the scene below was seared in my memory. The pillar of smoke rose from the center of the village, emanating from a crater that was once the main hooch. Everything else that once formed the small village, all the fragile structures made of wood, bamboo, and thatch common to the Vietnamese countryside, all the property and many of the enemy, smoked and smoldered dead under the hot mid day sun. It was clearly an enemy village most likely seized from the tribesmen to be used as a staging area and weapons cache for an upcoming assault, possibly somewhere along the fuel line on highway 19, or against a convoy. The enemy had probably assumed the ROKs were coming to pay them a visit. They were wrong. The ROKs were just passing by just as we happened to be passing by. Fortunately for us they were *dead* wrong. As a result, the Koreans, who certainly and understandably had absolutely no love for the communist, dealt with them without hesitation.

The ROKs had a reputation for being fearless and ruthless but they got results and they maintained tight control over their AO in the war to such a point that the NVA were instructed to avoid contact with them at all cost simply because contact with them was too costly, usually resulting in an average 10 to 1 kill ratio. With fewer men and less equipment, and definitely less politics, but with a far clearer understanding of what it takes to win a war, the ROKs were undoubtedly kick-ass effective. The first Korean troops arrived in Vietnam in '65 and were assigned to non-combat duty. Those first 200 came under fire that same year and after that they never looked back. Their number grew to nearly 45,000, the second largest allied force in-country, most of which were with us in II Corps in the Binh Dihn Province.

The Koreans were just another surprise and contradiction of the war that I would mull around in my mind as I drew in the cleansing air a few thousand feet above a beautiful landscape of death. I wondered if that was really me who had just done that thing, or was I dreaming. It certainly seemed like a dream, so fast and so intense that there was hardly enough time to absorb the experience or be truly conscious of the fear. Then suddenly, oddly, I became conscious of hearing music again and realized that in all the excitement Dillinger had failed to turn off his eight-track player. It had been spewing out Steppenwolf while I was spewing out bullets. It was a strange association, my first killing experience put to the sound of *Born To Be Wild.* One of the most intense moments of my life imbedded, carved forever in my mind and soul to the beat of some half-ass rock and roll ditty. It was indicative of our existence here, our generation, fighting a war wrapped in our rock and roll culture while refusing to adjust to theirs. Then it got even more bizarre if not complicated.

"Well gunner Fusco. How's it feel to be the hero of the day?" came Chief Chief's voice.

"Ask me when I wake up," I answered.

"I hate to be the one to tell you this Fusco but I'm afraid you can't wake up."

"What?"

"Like the old song says, it was just a dream," explained Chief Chief. "Because it never happened. I mean it happened for the ROKs and it happened for those damn VC but it didn't happen for us."

"I don't get it. You mean because we're off-mission or aren't supposed to be here or something," I speculated.

"Oh no. That's all fine. It's because we fired off a few hundred rounds and wiped out a mortar crew and destroyed an arms cache without asking permission first," said Chief Chief.

"What?"

"That's right kiddies. A new directive from on high. We must now first ask permission to fire before we can shoot at the bad guys, even if they're poppin' off rounds at us. Now ain't that a hoot? Typical, just fuckin' typical."

"Well that's just ripe as a dead dogs ass," said Dillinger. "What genius shit for brains came up with that one?"

"Beats the hell outa me. Something to do with phasing down the war I guess," replied Chief Chief. "Obviously dreampt up by some dumbass who's never been in the shit. There's a way around it though, Fusco. I'll do it if you want. Probably get you a medal."

"What's that?" I asked.

"I can call for permission now and if they authorize the shoot then I'll report the results, that you took out a major arms cache. If they don't… well then, it just never happened. That's my new policy to deal with their new policy. Get it? But then we run the risk of some higher-up wanting to fly in and check out the action and finding out he's just a little late. So whatcha say there gunner?"

I thought a moment then answered. "I don't really give a shit. Maybe next time."

"Oh, he's the modest type. Okay, I can dig it. No medals today for this guy, just slap him on the back and buy him another round."

"Sounds good to me," I laughed.

"You got it Gunner Fusco and I know just the place. Lay your eyes on yon horizon up ahead there my man and you will see a small mountain surrounded by what appears to be a city. You will notice on the side of that mountain is the all-uninspiring shoulder patch insignias of both the 1st Cav and the 173rd Airborne. Impressive to say the least but such false pride is enough to make a missionary cry," declared Chief Chief. "Welcome to Camp Radcliff at An Khe," gunner Fusco. "Also known as…"

All three of our crew said simultaneously, "…*The Golf Course.*"

Chief Chief approached from the south to afford us a view of the mentioned unit artwork cut in on the side of Hon Cong Mountain. There it was, several stories high in yellow and black, the shoulder crest of the 1st Cav. Though it wasn't quite Mount Rushmore or equal even to the famous HOLLYWOOD sign near Los Angeles, it was impressive in its bold excess. Fortunately for the personnel stationed there, the North Vietnamese weren't into bombing runs because it would have made one hell of a convenient target reference, even at night. Above the two massive shoulder patches a portion of the top of the mountain had been cut back and flattened like an Appalachian strip mine, leaving bare red earth where a small number of buildings and a full array of all manner of communication towers and radar protruded skyward.

Camp Radcliff was constructed in early '66 and was named in honor of Major Donald Radcliff who was the first man from the 1st Cav to die in the war. Someone somewhere said "If you control the central highlands, you control South Vietnam," and Camp Radcliff was supposed to be the centrally located answer from which it would be done. It was always a part of the NVA startegy to cut South Vietnam in two with the line of demarkation being the highway between Pleiku and Qui Nhon, Camp Radcliff was center of that axis. This was Ho Chi Minh's original stragtegy because his father had been a regional administrator in Qui Nhon when old Ho was just a kid.

The complex grew and now sprawled from the inner elbow of Highway 19, where it crossed the An Khe River, and extended on and around the mountain. It was also unique in that it was the only military installation that was often attacked from both the outside and inside due to a population of enemy that actually lived in and on Hon Cong Mountain, which was located inside the base perimeter. The shithouse rumor was that the Cav tolerated the pesky commies on the mountain, and even left food and provisions out to sustain them, so they could use them as targets while training their FNGs. The rumor was most likely true with the practice eventually resulting in the mountain's total depopulation.

Aside from the 1st Cav it was also home to the 173rd Airborne, a number of engineer units and support units, and MACV. The *Golf Course* was the name given to the chopper landing and aviation area when an Assistant Division Commander of the 1st

Cav, General Jack Wright, insisted the landing area be cleared by hand instead of heavy equipment to avoid turning it into a dust bowl in the dry season or a mud hole during the monsoons. The wise General said clearing the area by hand and saving the surface growth would leave it as "clean as a golf course" and apparently the name stuck. Easy for him to say. It seems those Generals always say the right thing, which often makes history even if it's the wrong thing. I suppose it all depends on who's listening, an entourage of ass-kissers or some poor mud grunt about to get his ass shot off. I wondered what the place would have been called if it had been named by an enlisted man or even a Sergeant Major. How about clean as a "Fuzzy Navel" or smooth as a "Hooker's Ass"? Tasteless maybe, but then how many enlisted men are thinking about a golf course in the middle of a war. At least if Major Anthony walked out of the office saying he was heading for the Hooker's Ass I wouldn't get pissed thinking he was having fun pushing around a little white ball while the rest of us were putting up with guys who think they're Jesus Christ, or dodging one-double-deuces. And then there would have been the dilemma of writing home to mom or the wife and telling her how dangerous it is flying into the Fuzzy Navel or lifting off from the Hooker's Ass every day.

Part of the complex also included the An Khe Army Airfield that was originally built by the French. Their occupancy pretty much ended in June of 1954 when they sent out Groupement Mobile 100 early one morning only to see it wiped out by the Viet Minh 22 klicks west near the Mang Yang Pass. The French were valiant fighting men and it was a sad state of affairs, but then the French have pretty much been unlucky that way ever since Waterloo. The old airstrip was upgraded and largely expanded into a full-fledged airbase by its current tenants to accommodate large fixed wing aircraft such as C-130s. As I learned all this I wondered of the possibility that I may have been stationed there or anywhere else had my enlistment *fixed wing guarantee* been honored and I managed to get through the training program without collecting any yellow pink slips or crunching any landing gear.

So there I was at the Golf Course and the joke was on me. I suppose I deserved it and I suppose I owed Major Anthony an apology but being he was unaware of my disapproval of his frequent golfing in the first place, I let it slide. We were walking in full gear, including our personal weapons, with me wondering where we were going next and again the guys were snickering and keeping me in the dark about our destination.

"Okay," I said. "What was all that about picking up some fruit?"

"Oh, maybe we'll take care of that on the way back," said Chief Chief. "Right now we have more important things to do."

Out the gate and down the road a piece we finally arrived at our destination.

"Welcome to Dodge City," said Chief Chief.

"Dodge City?" I said.

"That's what they call it," said Dillinger. "Dodge City. Or Sin City."

"Why?" I asked. But no sooner had I asked then I could see the reason. Dodge City was a collection of whorehouses, massage parlors, and bars that had sprouted up in tandem to the growth of the Radcliff military complex. The New York Bar, the San Francisco Bar, the Dallas Bar, cat houses set in structures that were loosely copied from American western movies and TV westerns, the only visual references available at the time to those Vietnamese who built them, leading them to think it would make all us G.I.s feel right at home while we were splashing around all that MPC. Dodge City ran along a dirt road with a few raised covered sidewalks made of wood. The reason we were in full gear and loaded was that both the NVA and VC were known to frequent the place as well, which made for a little confusion resulting in drunken American G.I.s shooting it out in the street with drunken ARVNs whom they thought were NVA. And then there were those few incidents where drunken G.I.s shot it out with drunken G.I.s and ARVNs with ARVNs. Hence the name Dodge City. War is hell.

There we were, strolling up the street like the Earp brothers heading for the OK corral, all loaded for bear and all visiting for the first time except for Chief Chief. He paused, drew long on a bottle of vodka he pulled out of his pocket, then handed me his weapon. When the bottle emptied he tossed it and reached into his little canvas bag and pulled out another, then adjusting the .38 on his belt, started for a whorehouse with a large sign above the door that read, MISS KITTY'S.

"Gentlemen, I will meet you in the street at high noon," he laughed, looking over his shoulder as he was met at the door by an attractive smiling Vietnamese hooker.

"It's already 1300," noted Dillinger.

"Oh. Okay then, I'll meet you back at the ship in two hours," we heard Chief Chief say as he passed through the colored beads that hung in the doorway.

We looked at each other, each silently expressing the same question; what the hell are we going to do for two hours?

"We gettin' laid or what?" asked Dillinger.

"Not my thing," I answered.

"Me neither, actually," replied Dillinger.

"I'm up for a cold one," said Dearing.

On that the three of us agreed and turned for the nearest saloon. We cautiously stepped up on the walk and into a poorly lit bar that was basically an eclectic mix of Vietnamese and discarded or stolen American military furnishings, highlighted with hanging beads, colorful fabrics, and woven mats. A bamboo and plywood bar and serving counter lined one wall. Behind it was an elderly mama-san who sat in front of a small TV mesmerized by the sight of Jimmy Durante at his piano singing S*mile*. Over the sound of the TV from out of a speaker on a wall came the music of Credence Clearwater Revival singing *Keep On Chooglin'* to which a topless Vietnamese girl on a small stage across the room tried unenthusiastically to dance. Only three of the dozen or so tables were occupied, one by American soldiers who were sitting close to the stage. Another was occupied by what were obviously ARVNs and at a third table were two Vietnamese in civilian attire but with weapons. It was to them that Dillinger nodded with some slight concern, most likely because one of them, the one with one eye, carried an AK-47. Dillinger then led us to a corner table by the wall that allowed us to see everyone else in the place.

It was obvious this wasn't exactly the happy hour and I'm sure the establishment did a booming business nearer the end of the day, never the less it impressed me in an odd way. Perhaps I had an overly active imagination or possibly it was due to my state of mind at the time following the incident with the ROKs, but as I lifted off my helmet and set it on the table the feeling and the scene at hand struck me as so dramatically corny I nearly cracked up laughing until I thought of just how absurd, not just this place but my entire day had been. At the crack of dawn I had flown a team into a dark mountainous kill zone, then rescued two wounded soldiers in the midst of enemy fire and a rain storm, then in the clear beautiful sunshine I helped destroy a village full of enemy soldiers. Now I had just strolled into a bar in the middle of a phony 19th century American western Oriental town with a steel pot on my head, with an M-16 and a .45 on my hip, and giving the hairy eyeball to some suspicious one-eyed character at another table. Needing only a change of wardrobe from another century it would have been the stuff of a hokey spaghetti western. And the day was only half over.

We ordered a round of beer and sat quietly taking in the music and staring at the topless dancer who apparently suffered from a slight lack of rhythm and who's forced smile was often distracted when she glanced, with just the slightest touch of concern, over to a dark corner where a small near-naked baby sat playing on the floor. Our attention was then drawn to a couple of hookers who entered the bar from the back and began making their rounds. Admittedly they were attractive with long dark hair, white teeth, and well proportioned with small waists, straight backs and shoulders, good legs, and full lips. One wore a classic Vietnamese silk dress slit up the side to the waist pronounced 'ao yai', meaning long dress, under which most Vietnamese women also wore pants. The long sleeved high-necked dresses were typical of women who didn't do physical work and the colors of the dresses were indicative of the wearer's age and status. Young girls wore pure white fully lined outfits symbolizing their purity. When they grew older but were still unmarried they graduated to softer pastel shades. The married women wore richer colors, usually over white or black pants. This girl prostitute however went bare legged under a mixed blue and red floral patterned version of the dress with a revealing lower cut open neckline and short sleeves. The other simply wore black hot pants and an angel blouse. Both managed to walk semi gracefully in high heels. They were as different from your average Vietnamese mama-san as a Corvette was from an old Ford pickup, forming an attractive package that had most likely been cultivated from a very young age. To be sure there were many *non-soliciting* women in Vietnam that were just as or more attractive, even beautiful, but in my personal zone of the war that resulted in a minimum of circulation among the locals, they went pretty much unseen.

The girls settled at the table near the stage with the four G.I.s from Radcliff, which was fine with us. Unlike Chief Chief, we weren't really in the mood for fun and games. Dearing had his fill with the nurses and the full night without sleep was probably catching up with us so we just sat there saying little, listening to the music and sipping the cool beer. I looked at the baby on the floor and occasionally looked over to the old mama-san glued to the tube, oblivious of everything around her. A conflicting scene when judged by the average American moral standard. The old woman was the boss lady, the owner, and probably an over the hill hooker forced into prostitution when she was about 12 years old. Age on these people was deceptive. They all looked like children until the mileage caught up with them and suddenly aged them beyond their years and before their time. Depending on their role in life, a thirty year old could look sixty and a sixty year old could look young. My guess was this old woman had practiced her trade with the French and possibly even the Japanese, a survivor who rolled with the punches and now just sat there absorbing American culture via AFVN. She probably watched everything from Jimmy Durante to the Chicago Bears being beamed in from another universe, knowing all the while there wasn't a chance in hell she would ever see it first hand.

I wondered what made people accept such rolls in life and whether that's what the fundamental difference was between we Americans and the rest of the world. Most Americans, at least in my world, knowing there is always something better will go for the brass ring and not accept the worst life has to offer. Maybe that's what this war was all about, giving these people choices. But most of the time it seemed all they were concerned with was today, the choices that brought in the MPC and not those that brought a better future. I came to conclude that they had a few thousand years to get it right and haven't yet and wondered, were they too damn stupid to realize it or just too damn busy to care? And, I thought, as I looked at the baby on the floor, if they don't care then why the

hell should I? Then I reasoned it out. There were these people and
other people like them, and there was Ba who took care of her
family, took care of me, cared to ask about my own baby and
somehow saw hope and a better world in a Sears catalog. To me
the perpetuation of poverty, even if it wasn't realized, made no
sense. All I knew was it wasn't my world and one way or the other
I would leave it behind. I wasn't thinking straight. It had already
been a long day and I was looking forward to it being over.

We were heading back to the ship and nearly out of Dodge
City when we heard the shots. At first it was a series of single pops
then there came a string of automatic weapon fire, easily
recognizable as coming from an AK-47. Looking back into the
town we saw a number of soldiers and other people scurrying for
cover. Turning back around we had just enough time to jump out
of the way of an oncoming jeep occupied by two MPs speedily
heading into town toward the sound of the shots. The jeep sped by
throwing a cloud of red dust into the air that nearly filled the entire
street as it went along, then out of the red cloud came Chief Chief
Zamboni running full out wide eyed and buck-ass naked except for
his boots and helmet. In one hand he carried his pistol and in the
other flapped a bundle of clothes and his gear bag.

"GO GO GO!" he yelled as he passed us by. "THAT CRAZY
SON OF A BITCH IS TRYIN' TO KILL ME?

"What?" I said.

"RUN DAMNIT! RUN!"

Bewildered, we started to follow at a fast route step, looking
over our shoulder trying to figure out what the hell was happening
when suddenly there came another burst of fire in our direction.
Then there was M-16 and .45 fire in response, most likely from the
MPs. This increased our pace to a full sprint behind Chief Chief
that we all maintained until eventually seeing the gate to Radcliff.
That was when Chief Chief stopped cold in the middle of the road
finally realizing he was running naked in front of God, Vietnam
and the U.S. Army, not to mention the laughing SP gate guards.
We stopped and stared with a chuckle. Another jeep passed us on
its way to Dodge City, its MPs nearly breaking their necks for a
second look at Chief Chief. But nothing set us off more then when
Chief Chief realized that in his haste to avoid being shot he had

snatched up the whores clothes instead of his own. We laughed until it hurt, thinking our fearless leader would now be forced to walk across Camp Radcliff to the Golf Course somehow squeezed into a pastel silk dress. We were disappointed, however, when we discovered Chief Chief was, as usual, prepared for all contingencies. From his little satchel he withdrew a fifth of Smirnoff, cracked it open and downed a third of it in one guzzle. Then out came a pair of cut-off blue jeans followed by a faded old gray sweatshirt with cut off sleeves, on the front of which was spray painted in florescent orange a large round peace symbol. He claimed it was his beachwear that he kept handy in anticipation of a flight to the coast. He never got to the coast but never regretted being ready for the day when he might have.

Safely inside the gate and on our way back to our chopper Chief Chief told us that the shooting had started when those same two mysterious Vietnamese who were sitting across from us in the old mama-san's saloon had wandered into Miss Kitty's whorehouse across the street. As it turned out, the one-eyed character with the AK-47 was actually an NVA Captain on a quest to find his wife who had left home in search of greener pastures. When he discovered her and another whore rolling in the hay with Chief Chief he went ballistic and started shooting up the place then reloaded with the intention of shooting Chief Chief.

"I don't think I ever moved so fast in my entire life," said Chief Chief. "I ran flat over that son-of-a-bitch and his woman. It's a good thing he only had one eye and couldn't shoot straight or my ass would be in the dirt. Can you imagine that? Crazy bastard. Typical damn Vietnam. Just fuckin' typical. Crazy stuff, huh?"

"Oh, I don't know," laughed Dillinger. "Doesn't sound so crazy to me. Nothin' strange about an Indian gettin' his ass shot at in Dodge City. Think I saw that in a movie once."

CHAPTER 33

CHIEF CHIEF'S FLYING CIRCUS

When Chief Chief said he wanted to pick up some fruit he actually meant he wanted to pick up some fruit. But I was under the impression we were going to put down somewhere and purchase some fruit, which was actually far from his method of shopping. It seemed Chief Chief had a taste for this local small but delicious variety of Mandarin orange that my mother referred to as Clementines, and when the opportunity presented itself Chief Chief would go a-pickin', or should I say, a member of his crew would do the picking. On our way back to Holloway the opportunity did present itself as Chief Chief knew it would, in that we were heading in the direction of a known orchard that was just full of those little tasty orange things. In Chief Chief's mind, since we still had the drop line we had rigged earlier that day to pull the wounded grunts out of the jungle there was no reason not to take advantage. This particular orchard was one of the few niceties created during the Japanese occupation of WWII, a growth of Satsuma Mandarins, or as I thought at the time, little Clementines for little people.

"It's real simple Fusco," said Chief Chief. "Just hook up like you did this morning and we'll hover over the trees while you pick, oh say? About a dozen of those tasty little boogers should do it."

"So why don't we just put down and go get some?" I asked.

"No, much easier this way," insisted Chief Chief.

"Chief, if you want oranges I can get you some damn oranges from the mess hall," I argued.

"Nope, nope. Just not the same," said Chief Chief. "These tasty little suckers make one mean screwdriver."

"So why not just land and buy some?"

"Nope. No can do. Can't be grocery shopping on government time," he laughed.

A tap on my shoulder turned me around to find Dillinger with a broad smile and the rope rig and I realized that nothing I said was going to make any difference so I hooked up. About five minutes later Chief Chief set us down in a small clearing where I hopped out only to be raised and dangled at the end of the line as he slowly raised the chopper up. After hanging me out like a soap-on-a-rope for a brief dangling tour Chief Chief came to an easy hover over a small orchard of about thirty trees fully loaded with fruit. He then carefully maneuvered the aircraft until I slammed into a cluster of branches, the movement of the chopper plunging me in and out like a chimney sweep's brush. Tree branches were poking and exploring nearly every part of my body and with every poke I cursed and yelled up at my AC, not that he could hear me. Looking up, the only one I could see was Dillinger sitting on the edge of the deck laughing and motioning for me to start picking, which I did knowing that until I did this torturous ordeal wasn't going to end.

"You crazy son of a bitch!" I yelled up to Chief Chief as I plucked those little orange bastards and shoved them wherever I could - in my pockets, in my T-shirt under my nomex, and even one in my mouth and, of course, I dropped a few. Then, oddly, the ones I dropped came right back at me. When it dawned on me that gravity didn't work in reverse, not even in Vietnam, I looked down to discover an irate old Vietnamese papa-san getting tossed around in the choppers rotorwash, cursing and waving a stick and throwing the grounded fruit back up in my direction. Obviously, this papa-san was the owner or caretaker of the orchard and he wasn't any too happy about my picking his profits or about the way our Huey was wafting his fruit off the trees. Not only that, he had a pretty damn good arm and a right-on pitch, practiced and perfected I assumed during a misspent youth throwing hand grenades at foreigners. Being the soldier that I was, I followed my survival instincts and tossed a few little fruit bombs of my own down on the enemy, which only served to increase the intensity of the situation even more.

"DU MA! YOU MOFUCK! YOU G.I. NUMBA TEN-THOU! YOU SAME SAME SHIT DOG! DU MA! I KILL YOU G.I.! I KILL YOU!"

His English wasn't quite perfect but it was good enough to get the message across, especially the *kill you* part that was more than easily understood, even over the thundering noise and rotorwash of the chopper above. The crazed papa-san started yelling instructions to someone I couldn't see under some nearby trees at the side of the orchard, which I immediately deduced meant an increase in enemy strength and translating to more flying fruit then I could counter. I looked up to Dillinger and signaled for an emergency lift. He passed my request on to Chief Chief who obliged by not just popping me out of the tangle of the tree branches but lowering and dangling me directly over the outraged papa-san who began an assault with his long stick as though I were a Mexican piñata. Then, instead of pulling up and away, Chief Chief flew slowly down the alley between the many trees where I was pursued by not only the irate papa-san but his mama-san as well, both throwing fruit, swinging their ugly sticks and yelling Vietnamese obscenities. All I could do was cover my head with my arms and hope for the best. Then through the space between my arms I caught a quick glimpse of a group of men casually sprawled out under the trees. About that time I was suddenly struck square in the gonads by one of papa-san's flying fruit grenades just as my ass bounced to the ground. I instinctively grabbed my family jewels, looked up to my pursuers who were closing fast with only about ten yards to go then looked over to the group of men resting in the shade of the trees. They were uniformed NVA, about a dozen or so, complete with AK-47s and other assorted weaponry, and amazingly, instead of taking a sure shot at me and downing our chopper, they just sat there laughing, watching me suffer the wrath of the fruit man and his mama-san. About the time when I fully grasped the situation Chief Chief yanked the stick and up I went spinning like a whirligig with my heart in my throat, and hoping like hell those NVA didn't lose their sense of humor.

I sailed along until Chief Chief put me down on the ground somewhere near Highway 19 at which time I didn't hesitate to inform him that the orchard not only had Clementines and crazy old papa-sans and mama-sans but some fruity NVA as well. We all agreed, however, that by now they surely would have beat feet into the hills and there was little chance of catching them. Not to mention the fact we didn't want to have to explain why we were there in the first place. We had a good laugh, my gonads recovered, and Chief Chief would have his home squeezed Satsuma Mandarin screwdrivers.

Chief Chief Zamboni could handle a chopper like Mario Andretti could handle a race car and this was never more evident than when he buzzed a bird into the pit at Holloway. When he brought an aircraft to roost in a revetment he nearly always did it with flair, not hovering carefully and easily gliding his bird in as most pilots would but instead shooting that $300,000 air truck right into the slot like a mad baseball player sliding into home plate. This day was no exception. Chief Chief, apparently feeling his oats, brought that bird in like it was a hungry dog after a summer sausage. Unfortunately, at that same time our new battalion CO, Lt. Col. Markette, was out for a stroll looking over his new kingdom. Markette had only weeks earlier replaced the ever-ambitious Lt. Col. Silas J.J.J.W. Chestnut who had rotated home to a promotion to full bird and a new posting as staff at the Pentagon where he supervised 28 civilians charged with the responsibility of researching and analyzing the newly discovered psychological phenomenon known as Post Traumatic Stress Disorder or PTSD. The research group under Col. Chestnut, none of which were medically qualified for anything, but all of which possessed Masters Degrees and Doctorate Degrees in something, would eventually decide that PTSD was somehow not caused by the stress of combat as most folks assumed but rather a severe trauma caused by the sudden and extended absence of Western culture, compounded by an overdose of Eastern subculture coupled with the deprivation of sex, entertainment, and a lack of civilized bathroom facilities - a psychologically lethal combination indeed. The recommendation of the group was that American G.I.s while in a combat zone should watch at least one wholesome Hollywood movie a week – Disney movies preferred - and that each trooper should be given a free subscription of Playboy magazine and a booklet on the etiquette and emotional acceptance of shitting in public.

Naturally no one at the Pentagon bought into the Chestnut group's findings, knowing that as civilians not one of them had a fucking clue as to the combat experience and had never even bothered to talk to real soldiers with real PTSD who had actually experienced real combat. That plus the fact that Bambi topped the recommended list of movies. They also knew that Col. Silas J.J.J.W. Chestnut was a total flake, but then even armed with this knowledge no one ever challenged his work because of the fear that Col. Silas J.J.J.W. Chestnut's many initials actually stood for something or signified he was related to, or descended from, someone special. To compensate for and in spite of the incongruous results and recommendations of *Chestnuts Nuts,* as his study group was called, the Pentagon established a multimillion-dollar program through the Veterans Administration to create treatment centers around the country and in VA hospitals, a program that removed the cowardly stigma of what used to be known as *shellshock* and developed treatment techniques for returning combat vets who suffered the symptoms. All this reflected greatly on Col. Silas J.J.J.W. Chestnut who headed up the study and in fact had coined the name of the psychological disorder in the first place during the Pully Johnson affair. For this he received an accelerated promotion to General and was subsequently assigned a highly classified and heavily funded research and development program in which the Army charged him with the chore of researching and exploring the possibility of turning the Frisbee into a lethal weapon.

Chestnut's replacement at the 52nd CAB at Camp Holloway, Lt. Col. Markette, on the other hand, was a capable and serious officer. A tall, broad-chested muscular man with dark serious eyes and Popeye-like hairy forearms who, it was rumored, had once been a professional ball player. Whether or not that qualified him for command I'm not sure. He was tight lipped and tight minded but as far as most of the enlisted men and junior officers were concerned, he was just another tight-ass figurehead who had spent much of the first week or so of his command in small spurts of fury as he frequently passed or came upon soldiers who failed to salute or weren't wearing hats or shirts, or just didn't measure up to his stateside standards of soldiering, whatever that was. He finally slacked off after realizing his stateside haranguing was getting nowhere and especially after receiving an anonymous note of warning about retribution from the ranks if he continued in his wayward ways. For the most part, however, he was a STRAC soldier who like most higher ups at this stage of the war was only looking to get his ticket punched and gain an eagle. Then again he was also a pilot and on this particular day our pilot CO Lt. Col. Markette just happened to be standing within sight of the revetment where Chief Chief pulled off his usual suicide-parking job.

As the big main rotor blades slowed to a crawl and Dillinger and I exited the aircraft we were more than surprised to see our large new battalion CO steaming and stomping his way across the PSP, obviously intent on doing some serious ass reaming. Chief Chief and Dearing were still in the cockpit when the Colonel let lose.

"God damnit! God damnit! Where the fuck did you learn to fly? God damnit!"

For some reason the Colonel was looking at me and I wasn't quite sure why until I realized I was still wearing the lieutenant bars I had put on to get in the Air Force O-club the night before, and he had obviously thought I was the AC. That is until Chief Chief appeared from the cockpit of the chopper. It was then that I thought our new Battalion CO was going to fully blow a gasket when he turned to discover our aircraft commander and super pilot.

"God damnit! God damn…" The Colonel's words froze in his throat at the sight, for there stood Chief Chief Zamboni in unlaced jungle boots, cut off blue jean shorts, and a faded old sweatshirt with cut off sleeves and a peace symbol across the chest, topped with a shoulder holstered .38. At the sight of this the Colonel was surely fast approaching a boiling point, evident by his crimson face, but beyond even that, nothing could have prepared him for the topper of seeing Chief Chief pull that flat bottle of Vodka from his back pocket, twist it open and take a swig, then recap and shove it in his bag. I used that advantageous moment of distraction to quickly remove the gold bars from my collar and shove them in my pocket. When I did a Satsuma Mandarin Clementine fell out of my shirt and rolled across the PSP to settle in one of the steel perforations at Lt. Col. Markette's feet. He picked up the fruit, looked at it then looked at me as though I were some kind of freak in a sideshow, then returned his attention and threatening glare to our sideshow freak pilot, Chief Chief.

"Jesus fuckin' Christ! What the fuck is this some kind of fuckin' flying fuckin' circus? God damnit! God damnit! What the hell makes you think you can fly an aircraft like that? And what the hell makes you think you can wear that kind of shit in my Army? God damnit!"

As he ranted and raved he inched his way closer to Chief Chief until they were face to face only a few feet abart. I started to remove my flight helmet but then changed my mind, ridiculously thinking that if I kept it on it might make it harder for the Colonel to pick me out of a lineup. I slowly slid the tinted visor down over my eyes and began to wonder if I could somehow manage to slip off during the Colonel's onslaught. I caught a slight movement in the cockpit in the corner of my eye and glancing over saw our co-pilot, Dearing, trying to get small by sliding down in his seat also hoping to go unnoticed. I nearly cracked up and had to put my hand to my mouth with the pretense of scratching my nose to prevent it and in doing so caused another little Clementine to dribble out of my shirt. When I tried to catch it, two more popped out, bounced then rolled and settled into the holes of the PSP. The Colonel once again drilled me with his eyes and for some reason I was thankful he wasn't packing a sidearm. Then he again directed his wrath at Chief Chief.

"I have never seen such disregard for safety in flight in my entire career! You flew in here like a fuckin' maniac! A fuckin' maniac! God damnit! You're a fuckin' maniac, a disgrace to the profession! A disgrace to the uniform! Look at you! Just look at you! God damnit! God damnit!"

Wow, I thought, if he could see how our pilots flew on missions he would really freak out, definitely add a few more *God damnits* to his vocabulary. This guy must be a combat novice. Where had he been during all the years this war was going on anyway and how the hell did he end up running the show?

The Colonel seemed to be so upset as to be unable to bring his fury to a conclusion of which I'm sure we all expected to end with a threat or promise of a court martial, but Chief Chief being Chief Chief decided on the best course of action when he removed his flight helmet, stepped up nose to nose with our irate battalion commander, casually took possession of the Clementine, stared him dead in the eyes and said with all sincerity, "Then why don't you just fire my ass."

When Chief Chief drew down in a serious mode something magic took place, a deep penetrating earthy no-nonsense don't fuck with me kind of lightning flash that could only have been attributed to some mystic native American roots and usually only manifested itself in the face of danger or the enemy. It was downright uncanny. Whether it was the anonymous note or the sincerity of Chief Chief's words, I'll never know. All I know is our FNG Colonel decided that retreat was the better part of valor and stomped off into the sunset, leaving us wide eyed and speechless, except for Chief Chief, of course, who simply shrugged and said, "I don't know about you boys but I'm as hungry as a coyote in a snow storm."

CHAPTER 34

DOING TIME

My occasional forays into the war outside of Camp Holloway only served to diminish the challenge of the daily grind that was life at the Ghostrider HQ. Not that it was truly laborious or demanding, but rather it began to seem increasingly uneventful and sometimes meaningless. Though I managed to pick up an accelerated promotion to E-5, which was encouraging, still the small things that once seemed important began to lose their priority and more and more I began to dwell on home.

Except for sporadic harassing attacks Camp Holloway somehow seemed insolated from the war and the existing general attitude of Vietnam's population. At least it often seemed that way. Perhaps it was the perceived growing attitude of indifference of those around me or perhaps it had always been like that and I just hadn't noticed or didn't want to notice. Or perhaps, as was most likely, I was beginning to change, beginning to see things through different eyes, the eyes of reality, the eyes that let the true world in to steal away my youth and optimism. The rockets came and went and the high and low times came and went just as the rains had come and gone while we all trudged on, coping, tolerating, functioning, and counting down the days until our individual DEROS. I began to think a lot about the war itself and why it was the way it was. It wasn't an occupation and it wasn't an all out push to defeat the enemy. If it were we would have rolled over Hanoi a long time ago. The DEROS, maybe that was the problem, I sometimes thought. Nobody gave a damn about winning the war because everybody, including the brass, knew that they were just passing through and as such not responsible or required to produce a final outcome. The pros were there to kiss ass and get their ticket punched but the rest of us, drafted and enlisted alike, who were smart enough to admit the truth at least to ourselves, were simply doing time. Tell all the higher ups that nobody goes home until it's over, I thought, and I bet those steak and lobster boys in their air conditioned trailers would soon figure out how to win the war fast instead of how to line their chests with more career enhancing non-valorous ribbon candy. Unless, as many of us thought, they were just plain incompetent, void of common sense and the common decency to think of the shit their idiocy brings down on the boys in the trenches.

I had always been a bit of an insomniac which tended to make many of the quiet nights seem even longer, slow times that books and beer didn't fill, often leaving me to play mind games like remembering every pair of shoes I ever owned or every movie I had ever seen. On some late evenings when it was just me and the rat my mind would wander to things I knew I couldn't have like a real pizza, my mothers potato candy, or my grandmothers pasta. One night I was so fixated on a soft serve ice cream cone that I could see it, feel it, taste it, and I swear I would have killed to get one. It was on nights like that I almost wished for a rocket attack or even a ground attack because I felt like kicking someone's ass.

Though our crews flew their missions and risked their lives almost daily they returned each day with a silent reserve and demeanor as though everyone had finally accepted the fact that our life here, though temporary, was just an existence of chance. Still, the beer flowed and we managed to laugh while personnel came and went, some unnoticed and unjustly unheralded, some deservedly decorated, some to be discharged, some transferred to other companies in the 52nd or in the states. And some, believe it or not, actually reenlisted and extended their tour for another year, though their reasons weren't always as noble as those of Chief Chief.

There were two categories of the latter that became a problem for the Army. One was the hardcore gore type who really got off on the war, meaning they actually enjoyed it, relished it to such an extent they couldn't get enough of it. The rush and exhilaration of combat, the death and destruction and the power over life itself became a form of addiction to such a point they probably wouldn't or couldn't function again back home even if they did leave. In essence they gave up or gave in to the war and what it had made them. There wasn't anything left at home for these guys, it was all here. The second group was the junkies. These were the white heads, the guys who got hooked on heroin, which was extremely cheap and readily available from the locals. Cheap, pure, and uncut, a bad combination for anybody who ventured into that realm of drug experimentation. Facing the act of returning to the States after getting hooked on coke must have been intimidating, especially knowing they would be switching from a $5 a day habit for the powerful pure stuff to a $100 a day or more for cut down street junk. Some of these guys from both categories were on their second or even third go around and the opportunity to reenlist and extend for rank and pay bonuses just fueled the fire.

The Army's answer to the problem was to create a policy limiting the number of consecutive in-country tours any one soldier could serve. One extension and one only was supposed to be the new cure for the combat gore corps and the coke heads alike. But also for the cokers there was implemented a forgive and forget program to deal with the Army's embarrassment of sending so many junkies back home to mama. It was a countrywide voluntary drug addiction program and was introduced at Camp Holloway in the form of a small hell house that sat all alone in a field midway between the BOQ on the hill and the Ghostrider company area. A small 12 by 12 foot wooden shed with one bunk and one door and no windows. It was a prison with no doctors or nurses or soothing drug substitutes. The volunteer would be locked inside to purge his cocaine demons the hard way, cold turkey, and though we all understood what could bring a soldier to drug use and an eventual visit to the cold turkey house there wasn't a whole hell of a lot of sympathy for those who ended up there. Once you entered the hell shack you were on your own and the rest of us really didn't want to think about the agony you were going to go through.

A bright moment came when I was up on the hill at our small PX purchasing some cigarettes where I bumped into an old friend from Annapolis who had arrived at Holloway only a few weeks prior. Pat Lovington and I were best friends back in the sixth grade, a time that now seemed a hundred years in the past. Back then we were just wide-eyed kids with no problems who had the run of the town, the Naval Academy, and the surrounding waterfront. The closest thing we experienced to human conflict in those days was a tough game of little league baseball. That was back in a different universe when time ran slowly and we ran fast, and a single day lasted forever. He was a Warrant Officer now, which didn't surprise me because he was always dutiful and smart as a whip academically. Briefly catching up with each other's lives was a good feeling, like a visit home, even though neither of us had been home for some time. Remembering this and that and asking was that place or this place still around, and remember that little sandwich shop near the Governor's mansion where they sold root beer in tall frosted mugs for a dime? The encounter was a flashback of civility and it felt good.

He told me he voluntarily enlisted and had been stationed in Turkey as an EM when he decided to apply for flight school. Now he was flying Loaches, those little bird choppers that buzzed around at treetop level looking for trouble and drawing more enemy fire than any rational pilot or crewman would care to experience. Time that day was short and we both had to get back to work so we agreed to get together the next evening at his quarters to kick back a few beers and get reacquainted. Running into Pat was uplifting and I anxiously looked forward to the next day and additional days when I would see him again. I even started to conjure up a plan to maybe crew a few of his missions. One pilot and one gunner with a free sixty was a full load with the little birds and it would be a hell of an experience, especially with an old friend, a trusted childhood friend. He wasn't a Ghostrider but I had already managed to crew once on a slick from another company for the hefty sum of $50 and didn't see any problem pulling it off again, even if this time I had to pay – as long as I didn't get caught or killed while I was at it.

The next evening after chow I copped a few beers from Gas and headed up the hill to the officer's quarters, sought out Pat's hooch, walked in and looked around. Most of the rooms showed evidence of occupancy though no one was around. I didn't know which one belonged to Pat until I found a pilot stretched out on his bunk reading.

"I'm looking for Pat Lovington."

He looked up from his book but hesitated to answer. Just then another young Warrant Officer entered the hooch.

"Looking for who?" he asked as he walked toward me.

"Pat Lovington. This his hooch?"

"Yeah. Whatcha need?"

"We're old friends from back home. Supposed to get together tonight. He gone to chow or something? You know when he'll be back?"

"That's his room there," he said, pointing to a cubical somewhat smaller than mine. "But he won't be back."

I looked at the room. It was sparse with only a bunk and a few personal items and some uniforms hanging on nails on the wall. There were no pin ups, accumulated memorabilia, or souvenirs. He hadn't been there long enough to personalize his cave, I thought.

"Oh. Got a late mission or something, huh? Okay, well, if you see him tell him Vince was here and I'll catch him later. Thanks," I said, and started for the door.

"He won't be back," he repeated.

I paused. For some reason I new what he meant and wasn't eager for an explanation.

"Is he alright?" I asked.

"Afraid not," he said. "Shot down this morning. Confirmed. Sorry man."

I simply walked out and down the hill. All the way to my hooch I pulled a blank, confused, not feeling anything yet everything, wanting to cry but knowing I couldn't, not there, and not even knowing why because until one day ago I hadn't seen Pat Lovington in nearly eight years. I wondered if I really knew him at all. I also wondered why he was even in the Army in the first place and not in college. He was too damn smart. Even in the sixth grade he had a goal that I often kidded him about. He was going to major in Political Science. How would any kid in the 6th grade know what the hell he's going to do in college but he did. Hell, I didn't even know what political science was. He was fascinated by politics and wanted to be President and it wasn't only a kid's fantasy because he knew government, told me all about it with a gleam in his eye and excitement in his voice. But not only that, he was the only son of a single mother and was not likely to have been drafted at all. Like me, he voluntarily enlisted. Pat Lovington, I thought, was truly one of the good guys with a good future.

I remembered the day we became friends. I was returning to class after lunch when I discovered the class bully giving him a hard time, pushing him around. Pat was unsuccessfully trying to negotiate a peace when I walked in the room. I could see it was obvious this mean ass kid was not open to any verbal reasoning so I told him to lay off and when the overbearing clown came after me instead I sent him flying over a desk with one punch. It was that simple. Pat and I buddied up for the rest of the year, he the diplomat and me the curious adventurer, until he moved across town the next fall and we lost touch. His death was a tough pill to swallow, leaving me to feel as though this damn war was now managing to somehow reach out and consume my memories, my past and my home, to eat at me like a cancer, and for what? I was reaching a point where Vietnam was no longer a giving experience to be absorbed by an adventuresome young man but instead it had changed its face and began to collect, to take more than it gave, and for the first time I wondered how much of me, the original me, would be left if and when I ever managed to return home.

Other new faces appeared but they became fewer and fewer as we progressed further into the Vietnamization program and the so-called phasing down of the American involvement in the war. The Ghostriders were the first aviation company to participate in the program which involved our not only performing our primary mission of flying support for the 5th Special Forces and spook teams but also training VNAF (Vietnam Air Force) flight crews to eventually take over our existence as our final replacements. Our responsibility was simple, train them to fly right and safe in combat then hold a feel-good dog and pony graduation show at the end of their training. It wasn't brain surgery but then it wasn't always easy. The Vietnamese fly-guys had their own concept of aviation and weren't always accepting of the rules. After all we were asking them to progress from bicycles loaded with pigs and chickens to conquering the sky with incredible flying machines. One example was a Vietnamese pilot who decided he didn't need to enter the flight pattern when arriving at Camp Holloway and would just dart right in, risking lives and aircraft.

"Me Vietnamese. This Vietnam. I land now!" he blurted over the radio to the tower as he defied their instructions.

"I swear to the almighty if we didn't have some of our own guys on those aircraft I'd crash the bastards," said my buddy Graham up at OPS who worked the tower. "I'd fly 'em right into the dirt. Shit, sometimes it's like trying to train monkeys."

Another problem was when things got hot and antsy some of the Vietnamese pilots had a penchant for lifting off and departing a PZ or LZ before the troops were completely on board or off-loaded from the aircraft. They were also hesitant to respond to emergency calls. I'm sure there were Vietnamese pilots who managed to have their shit together but it didn't help our confidence any knowing, as we were told before we started the program, that it would be very likely one out of every ten of the Vietnamese we would be training were the enemy. That was the official figure. Our numbers, based on instinct, were higher. Like every other military vehicle we turned over to them, I fully expected to begin seeing choppers loaded with pigs and chickens instead of troops.

Of the few new arrivals assigned to our unit some proved to be interesting and others challenging. Just as I had learned to be cautious about first impressions, I learned that one could rarely judge a soldier by his appearance or initial behavior, at least not in Vietnam and at this stage of the war. One such case was SP4 Cleveland Dooley. After my last two-day adventure with Chief Chief and Dillinger I returned to find a new resident in the HQ hooch, a quiet black guy of medium height and pleasant bearing. Randy informed me he had transferred in from a grunt unit somewhere and since he hadn't really talked to anyone since his arrival there wasn't much known about him. When Randy and I invited him to chow with us I discovered he had simply transferred down the hill from the battalion pathfinder detachment. He didn't say much about what he had been doing up there and we didn't actually know much about those guys other than they were like a recon unit and secured LZs. Their SOP had pretty much been established by a former Ghostrider CO a few years prior to our arrival. In a way Dooley was more white than black in nature, at least in Army terms. He was intelligent, articulate, courteous, informed, and very well spoken, even more so than the average white guy, and with none of the street characteristics of the average black guys in our battalion. And he seemed to be exceptionally solid and stable. Not that there weren't other black guys who were as well. It's just that in my experience and in the ranks of our largely conscript Army I didn't come by that many. For Dooley, his exceptional character almost seemed to be a curse.

He informed us he had been drafted soon after graduating from college, felt compelled to go airborne after basic training, and ended up as a Pathfinder, first with the 173rd at Radcliff until they were shipped back to the states, then to Holloway with the 52nd CAB. Rather than shipping home with the 173rd he got the Army shuffle the same as Fred Blurtz when the Big Red One bugged out. As for his polished personality, it was attributed to the fact he was raised by very proper and demanding parents, both of which were doctors. He was eventually transferred to the Ghostriders simply because he was less than two months from his DEROS and it was a place to kill time. Or so he said. I got the impression there was more to it but it wouldn't be until a few weeks later when the real reason for his transfer manifested itself. Meanwhile he pulled easy occasional day shifts on the perimeter and pretty much kept to himself the rest of the time, often borrowing one of my books of which I had a large collection thanks to the Tooth Fairy who always gave me first choice of all the paperbacks shipped in from the USO.

It was on a day when we were walking back from the mess hall that I first noticed any obvious symptoms of stress in Dooley. As we walked past the hooch where most of the *mofucka brothas* resided and often hung out on their stoop I was surprised to see some of them perk up and give us notice.

"Dere he go," I heard one say.

Remembering the Butterfield incident lent me to think he was talking about me so I just smiled and kept walking, as did Randy. Dooley tried to do the same but it became difficult.

"Hey, I'm talkin' to you nigga," said one.

"Uncle Tom mofucka," another of them said.

"You too good a nigga to hang wit da brothas ain't dat right mofucka? Yeah, dere he go, the house nigga hangin' wit the white boys."

"Uncle Tom mofucka."

The trash talk rained down on Dooly like a monsoon and I could see him tense up but he ignored them and we walked on.

"Why you hang out wit dat white honky sum'bitch. He a dead honky anyhow, you know dat? Dat honky mofucka a dead man. Dat's right Fusco. I talkin' 'bout chu, mofucka."

"You hang out wit dat fuck you gon be a dead sucka too, Dooley. Uncle Tom mofucka."

I stopped and started to turn to confront them but Dooley took my arm and insisted we keep walking.

"Hey. I'm talkin' to you Tom. You hearin' me mofucka? Honky lovin' Tom nigga mofucka."

As we walked away I looked at Cleveland Dooley and saw little emotion other than a tightened jaw. Apparently this had been going on for a while, possibly even before his Army days, and I couldn't help but admire his restraint.

That evening he said nothing, just sat on the edge of his bunk. The next day he pulled his guard shift on the perimeter then came back and continued to keep his own company. When I left for the orderly room the following morning Dooley was outside our hooch smoking a cigarette, just standing and watching the hooch maids as they busied themselves around the rain barrel chattering and washing clothes as usual. He didn't seem any different other than his silence but then he wasn't much of a talker to begin with. Later when I returned from my usual stroll up to battalion S-1 to deliver the morning report I passed a medical truck throwing red dust as it rushed along Hollywood Boulevard up the hill. Upon my arrival in the company area I saw two SPs putting a handcuffed Cleveland Dooley in the back of a jeep.

"He just went nuts," Randy told me. "He just lost it and went off his rocker and started beating on a hooch maid. Not saying a thing, just started whacking on her with her yelling 'Dung lai! Dung lai!' And he never said a word. Just went nuts and damn near killed her. You know, that mama-san they all say is a VC. Beat her up pretty bad."

Dooley was hauled off to some medical joint for psycho soldiers but oddly enough was returned to us a week later, released by the psych doctors who declared he was now clear of head and heart. Indeed he seemed a little brighter, more talkative and open like he had somehow purged his system. That night we had a few beers and he filled me in on his problem, telling me that not long before he came to the Ghostriders he was on a pathfinder job where he and a team went out to observe an LZ overnight then clear it for an upcoming troop insertion the next morning. He said they set up around the LZ where, alone, he dug in and camouflaged his position with a cover of brush. Sometime during the night a platoon size unit of NVA showed up and decided to pick that very spot to hold up until the pre-dawn. They were all around him, talking, joking, taking in some chow, an unnerving situation to say the least. But then it got worse when the very spot where he lay curled up in his dark little hole, hidden only by a thin layer of brush, was where the NVA soldiers chose to piss. One then another and another and another, for five full hours Dooley had to lay there motionless while getting pissed on by a platoon of North Vietnamese soldiers. He nearly went out of his mind, he said, and when the other pathfinders found him the next day he couldn't move or speak. They found him curled up in his shallow hole with the business end of a .45 pistol in his mouth.

"So they sent me here," said Dooley. "After a week in the hospital they said I'd get over it, to just take it easy until my DEROS and sent me here. Yeah right. What the hell do they know?"

I had no idea what to say or do. What do you tell someone who went through something like that. And I almost felt guilty for not seeing it coming the day he lost it and started banging on a hooch maid.

He welled up and started to cry then quickly got a grip, wiped away the tears and doctored the emotion with a long swig of beer.

"I hate 'em," he told me. "I hate all of them and I hate their entire fucking country. I just want to go home, you know? I just want to go home."

Another newcomer I misjudged had arrived from the states and just happened to catch me at what I suppose could be regarded as a vulnerable moment. At the time I didn't know our company was actually going to disband at the completion of the Vietnamization deal and I was thinking of possibly requesting a permanent change to flight crew status as a gunner when into the orderly room walked some new meat and what I thought was an opportunity to do so. He was a blond California beach boy type, the quiet friendly type, or so it seemed. Top, who normally would assign him somewhere wasn't around at the time and in fact the only ones in the HQ were the XO back in his office, Randy who was doing a little hunt and peck on his typewriter, and myself. As I checked him in I noticed he had some college so I asked him if he could type. He said yes and that he'd attended UC at Berkley. Okay, I thought. Maybe this is the guy that could take my place.

"Lets see here," I said. "Anderson, Jason Edward, PFC, right?"

He nodded his head in confirmation.

"So what's your MOS," I asked as I looked over his orders.

"Air crewman," he replied. "But I don't want to fly."

"Something else you want to do?"

"Not really."

"But you can type? You said you can type, right? Well, how would you like to work around here, maybe take my place?"

"Doesn't matter where you put me," he said. "Won't make any difference."

"What do you mean, it won't make a difference?"

"I'm not going to do anything," his pleasant but expressionless manner became one of contempt.

"What do you mean? I don't understand," I said.

"I mean I'm not going to do anything. I'm not going to fight in this damn war. I'm not going to be a part of it in any way. So it doesn't matter where you put me."

Randy looked up from his hunt and peck two-finger typing job. Like myself he wasn't sure of what he had just heard.

"Did I just hear you straight?" I asked.

"Yeah, you heard me. I'm not going to do anything. I'm not going to work in your fuckin' office and I'm not going to be a part of your fuckin' war."

We were all aware of the growing peace, love, and get high movement at home, and the fiasco at Kent State University where protesting students were gunned down by a bunch of nervous draft dodging weekend warriors, and of course, the anti-war drug and sex fest in '69 at Woodstock, but it wasn't something we dwelled on and I certainly didn't expect it to walk in and stand in front of my desk in a uniform, so naturally my first thought was how the hell did this guy manage to get this far through the system and land here in the first place.

"Listen, you're going to have to do something. I mean you're here just like the rest of us and there's no going back so why not just take a gig in this office. I mean it's not like you'll be killing people or anything."

"Hey man, don't lay that bullshit non-participation rap on me. It's all the same. You're all fuckin' murderers so fuck you and your office and your fuckin' war. I'm not doing shit for anybody." With that final declaration he simply turned and walked out the door. For some reason I just snapped. Maybe it was the dead letters or maybe it was the valor and deaths of my fellow soldiers I'd witnessed during my time in-country, or maybe I was just a little old fashioned. For whatever reason I couldn't let him walk away and I quickly rose from behind my desk and followed him out and around the side of the hooch.

"Hey, Anderson," I called as I trotted to catch up with him. He ignored me completely so I grabbed his shoulder. He stopped and turned. Having his attention I tried again to reason with him. "Look, it's not all that bad and the time will go faster than you might think. I mean, I've been here seven months now and believe me it goes faster if you stay busy. You can't just refuse to do anything. You'll get a dishonorable or end up behind bars."

He offered up only a half-ass loathsome smile then said, "Fuck you," and started to walk away.

This time I really did snap. There were few times in my life that I can recall becoming so angry so quickly. I grabbed and spun him around, throwing him against the hooch. Pinned there against the sand bags he still failed to show any emotion.

"Listen asshole, in case you haven't figured it out, none of us really want to be here but we are so we just do our jobs, get along, maybe help take care of each other, and hopefully go home," I told him. "If you can't handle something that simple then you're in for some hard times. Not from me but from the Army. So what the hell is your fuckin' problem?"

He said nothing, maintaining his sneer. I pushed him even further against the hooch, surprised at my own anger and that he failed to fight or even push back since he had a good two inches in height on me. His arrogant passive nature made me even angrier. It was an invitation to smash his face and I honestly considered doing just that.

"Oh, so now you're going to kick my ass, right?" he laughed. Offering up his peacenik passive resistance. "Go ahead."

I let him go and backed off. As he stepped away from the wall he continued to smile, again said, "Fuck you," and turned to walk away.

The rest was just pure emotion, anger expressed on behalf of all those guys at Dak Seang, and for Half Wrench, Garnett, Lovington, the team and crew lost on the Troubadour's chopper, and all those names on the memorial wall at battalion up on the hill, and for me as well, unconsciously wanting to vent my own anger and frustrations on someone or something. I turned him around and as hard as I could I shot a punch in his gut that threw him back against the hooch. I wanted to do more, I really did, but left it at that. He doubled over and slid down to settle on the ground, breathless, clutching his mid section, and yeah, he finally lost that damn cynical smile.

"Welcome to Vietnam asshole," I said as I turned and walked away.

The more I thought about what I had done to Anderson the angrier I became because it wasn't me, at least not the me I thought I was, not the me that walked into that recruiter's office two years prior. Something was missing and changes were stewing inside of me and I wasn't really sure if I liked it, or if I could prevent it.

When Top returned I gave him a copy of Anderson's orders and filled him in on his non-participation declaration. Top's response was simply, "Is that right. Well, I'll deal with that."

I suppose Top dealt with it but I have no idea how. I never saw Anderson again and didn't care to.

Every new face I came across wasn't an Army Sad Sack. Soon after the Anderson incident I had the honor of escorting some honest to God American round eye women, as they were often referred distinguishing them from the locals. They had shuffled in on a chopper the day before, supposedly just to hand out donuts and play board games with us homesick G.I.s. They set up in the mess halls and even though Top made the announcement at the morning formation regarding their presence, when I went over to check them out I was surprised to find only three off duty Ghostriders in attendance. There they sat next to a pile of unopened board games, the Parcheesi box on top sitting next to some of Buns donuts and coffee, chatting with some new guy who gun ship's starboard pod, crossed the landing pad and struck the other aircraft, exploding and destroying both the chopper and the mechanic. Small chopper parts and schrapnel shot past me as I jerked back in the seat. People rushed out from everywhere, some fighting the flames, others watching in awed silence. I was dumbstruck, still sitting in the jeep, the engine idling, forced to see that freak split second of destruction and death recycled repeatedly through my mind. Did I really see that? Did that really just happen, I asked myself as I watched the excitement and confusion.

Normally when rockets got hung up in the pod the gunner or crew chief would hang out and kick it until the hung rocket launched. It was armed and simply too dangerous to land with a hot rocket for the very reason I had just witnessed. What happened in this case, I'm not sure. It was like I was there but I wasn't. I'd probably said less than ten words since arriving and I didn't know any of these guys. I felt detached as though I were outside of it all, some sick voyeur, and I knew I was probably the only one who witnessed the entire split second fluke of a death. It was Half Wrench all over again.

When the fire died down and the crowd tightened around the remains of the damaged aircraft I came out of my shocked daze enough to guide the jeep slowly out of the compound and back on the road. A short time later I once again crossed the small bridge and noticed the detail of grunts were gone. As I continued along the road about a quarter mile I came across them sorting out the remains of a blown up half ton truck lying on its side. I slowed then stopped and one of them came to the side of the jeep.

"What happened?" I asked.

"Mine in the road. Killed both of 'em"

I had first focused on the truck but then noticed the two bodies laid out on the shoulder of the road covered with ponchos.

"Hey, didn't you just come through here a little while ago?" he asked.

"Yeah, I did."

"Thought that was you. Ya know you're one lucky son of a bitch. You must of drove right over that damn mine. Just missed it."

"Um, yeah," I said. "So it's okay to keep going?" I asked.

was pretty much making a fool of himself. One of the girls was a tall well built blond about thirty, or at most a very well preserved thirty-five. The other was shorter, younger, dark haired, and a bit plump but attractive.

"Hi. I'm Vince," I said, nearly tripping over my tongue. Let's face it, they were American women and after seven months of hearing "no bic" and seeing mostly short little bow-legged mama-sans with black teeth, they looked like angels from another world. They smiled.

"I'm supposed to drive you over to the Air Force Base when you're finished. Have any idea when that will be?" I asked, thinking it wouldn't be long since no one showed up to play Parcheesi or down some of Buns' sinkers. Then again it wasn't like the Ghostriders were a bunch of grunts sitting around waiting for a mission. Most everyone in the company had jobs either on the ground or in the air, which meant there were few left available to hobnob with our exceptional guests.

"Hi, I'm Susan and this is Kristy with a K," answered the tall blond with a smile. "Actually, it looks like we'll be finished here in about an hour. Is that okay?"

"Sure. No problem," I said. "I'll check out a jeep and be in the orderly room when you're ready." I smiled, grabbed a couple of donuts and headed for the motor pool.

Fourty minutes later the girls showed up and we were off. I explained there were no flights heading their way and since there were some dispatches to drop off at the 5th Special Forces compound near the air base I was elected to kill both birds with one stone. I grabbed my weapon and off we went, Susan the tall blond who seemed to take the lead in all things sat in the front seat and Kristy in the back with their small overnight bags. They said little, actually they said nothing at all until I chose to break the ice as we sped threw the gate, on to the road and past multiple vehicles loaded with people, pigs and chickens.

"So, how long have you been doing this?" I asked.

"Over two years" Susan answered tersely.

"Oh really," I said, for lack of any other response. "Seems like a long time I bet."

"Not really," said Kristy.

"Not really two years, or not really a long time?"

She laughed, "Doesn't seem that long."

"So where are you from?" I asked as I maneuvered the jeep around a slow puttering overloaded lambretta.

"Susan is from Denver and I'm from Gainesville, Florida."

"That right?" I perked up. "I went to school with a couple girls from Gainesville. You know a girl named Deloris Connelly?"

Without hesitation Kristy said yes just as I remembered that Deloris was actually from Lakeland, Florida, not Gainesville, leaving me to assume that Kristy's quick response was conditioned. Something she did with all the guys while handing out donuts and playing Parcheesi, something to give them a sense of connection to home. Kristy with a K was probably from a thousand different cities and just happened to know a thousand folks that a thousand G.I.s also happened to know. I got the picture and just let the lie lay.

"Two years. Wow. So why? I mean why would you volunteer to come here?" I asked. I knew they were Red Cross volunteers and not being nurses I put them in the category of candy stripers and I was seriously interested in what would bring them to a combat zone just to serve donuts and drop comforting untruths on homesick G.I.s.

"I need the money," answered Susan. "I have a daughter in college. It's expensive."

I was about to say *Yeah, but you don't get paid...* when it hit me, so I didn't, narrowly avoiding the embarrassment of letting my naiveté show by sticking my foot in my mouth. I quickly switched the conversation back to Kristy. "So you're a Florida Gator?"

"A what?" she answered.

With that the conversation pretty much went downhill. If the Red Cross *donut dollies*, as they were called, were here to cheer up us G.I.s I can't say they did much for me. They didn't even try to hit me up, or should I say roll me over, for some of that so-called much needed college fund. I would later find out why when I mentioned my discovery to one of my pilot friends. It seems the hole in their donut routine, he explained, was that the dollies only bedded officers because for the most part the officers were supposedly cleaner, free of social disease, and the only ones who could afford the $100 a pop for their round eye company. So once again the military social strata showed its ugly face with the

commissioned receiving round eye affection and the rank and getting only Parcheesi and bullshit. But what the hell, I thoug maybe in this place just seeing an American woman was wo suffering through a Parcheesi game.

I dropped the girls off at the gate of the Pleiku AF Base continued on to the 5th SF compound up the road where I wa and out in a matter of minutes. It was kind of nice driving aro by myself, away from all the usual people and events of the da gave me time to think, time for my mind to wonder and pon alone time that for some reason was hard to come by in the A1 Even when you were alone it didn't feel that way, but that d was different. And it also gave me a false sense of security.

A few days later I had cause to carry a dispatch over to 170th Bikinis at Kontum and decided to do it by jeep. I did tak M-16, helmet and vest, but unwisely left my ever-present para behind. It was a longer drive than just scooting across Pleiku t AF Base and for the most part it was all open country. Alon way I passed a large garbage dump that spread for a mile alon side of the road. It smelled horrible as most dumps and landfil but what impressed me most was that it was awash with pe The trash was American from various bases in the area, v meant the pickens were good, a regular fire sale at K-Mart s speak, with the locals hot to shop and turning over every piece of junk, filling their arms with what, I can't imagine.

Further down the road I crossed a small bridge guarded few American grunts that just waved me past. I then continu to Bikini Beach, as the 170th compound at Kontum was c where I dropped off the package, asked if there was anyth return and then ambled into their mess hall in search of a c coffee. One thing I knew you could count on was that all mess halls always had a large pot of coffee going. I talked one, just wandered in, had a cup, and wandered out.

As I strolled over to my jeep a Bikini Buccaneer gu came in and set down about forty yards away. Across the front of the gunship there was a young mechanic workin; Huey slick. I climbed in behind the wheel of the jeep an cigarette while watching the crew of the aircraft tie down an away. Then just as I cranked up the jeep a rocket shot out

"What can I tell ya? Shit man, it's the Nam, right? But ya gotta get where you're goin', right? I wouldn't sweat it too much. They come in at night and set these things and they sure as hell don't want to hang around when they go off. Those little bastards ain't stupid. Where you headed?"

"Holloway."

"Yeah, well, keep your shit sharp. Good luck man."

I scooted off and headed for home, lost in thought, hearing nothing but the whirring sound of the jeep's wheels and the strain of the engine along the cool breeze that whipped across the topless vehicle past my face, oblivious of everything except the memories of the exploding chopper and destroyed truck on the side of the road that could have or should have been me. When I again passed the garbage dump the smell seemed more intense, almost nauseating, and in my state of mind I would somehow always come to associate it with death.

Upon arriving at Camp Holloway I immediately returned the jeep to the motor pool, filled out the logbook and tossed it on the seat. I then grabbed my gear and headed for the orderly room. The workday was over and the office was occupied only by the duty CQ and his friend so I strolled over to the mess hall where I found Randy, Graham, and a few others having dinner. I grabbed a tray, it was the usual, roast beef, mashed potatoes, some veggies and some of Buns' buggy yeast rolls. I had no sooner sat down than Staff Sergeant Braunsberg, the ruling honcho of the motor pool, came in and headed straight over to our table. Braunsberg was a big guy with big oversized hands, one of which landed heavily on my shoulder.

"What the hell did you do to my jeep, Fusco?" he blurted.

"Your jeep?" I replied. "Nothing. I just drove it."

"No shit you drove it. Where the hell'd you go, Hanoi?"

"Kontum. Why?" I asked, puzzled by his questioning.

"Why! You're shittin' me right."

"Hey Braunsberg, I didn't mess up your jeep."

"You drove all the way to Kontum?"

"Yeah."

"Alone? Through the Kontum pass?"

"Yeah. And I didn't fuck up your jeep."

"Oh no. You just got it shot full of holes that's all, and the windshield's cracked, and there's some bloody shit in the grill. Now come on, what the hell really happened? You run into some gook's pig and piss him off or somethin'?"

The guys at the table stared, waiting for me to drop some juicy adventure story of a roadside shootout but I wasn't in the mood to invent one or play along, especially having just been informed that part of that Bikini mechanic ended up in the grill of the jeep. I hadn't taken the time to wash it or even check the engine as required when I turned it in. If I had I would have seen what Braunsberg was talking about. Hell, I didn't even notice the crack in the windshield.

"They must have been there when I checked it out," I suggested. "I'm telling you, all I did was drive to Kontum and back."

"Nope. I ain't buyin' it. This is my prize jeep, Fusco. The one I reserve for the CO and you guys in the HQ brain trust. Yesterday it didn't have a scratch, today it's a bloody casualty."

"I don't know what to tell you Sarge. All I did was drive it. I swear. Didn't hear a thing. No shots or anything."

I didn't bother to tell him that I was in a daydreaming funk on the road, my mind drifting, lost to or from where I don't know. Maybe even in shock.

"Okay, I'll give ya this one, Fusco. But three bullet holes down the side six inches from the driver's ass. All I can say is you're one lucky sum'bitch," he concluded as he slapped me on the back and walked away.

Bullet holes! He said. Shit. One lucky son of a bitch, he said. It was the second time that day I had been told that. One lucky son of a bitch, but that kid who caught that hot rocket wasn't so lucky, I thought as I toyed with a piece of roast beef, nor were the two guys who caught that mine on the road. They were gone - forever - and I was still here eating roast beef, watching guys pick little bugs out of their dinner rolls and converse as though outside, beyond the bunker line, there was nothing going on. I looked around the mess hall at tired young faces. Tomorrow they would fly out there again and maybe, hopefully like me, each one would be a lucky son of a bitch.

CHAPTER 35

A BLUE HAWAII

The daily grind rolled on toward early December without much happening other than the dwindling of our numbers, and it was done in such a way that it was barely noticeable - by me at least. Assorted personnel were being transferred with so little formality that even myself as the company clerk wasn't aware. There were no orders, not even a mention to allow me to amend the morning reports, which I'm sure must have driven the guys at the far off finance office crazy when pay day rolled around. The Ghostriders who still had the majority of their tour ahead of them, pilots and crew alike, were suddenly shuffled over to sister companies around Holloway. A number of them shipped out to the 170th in Kontum, others to the Gladiators, and some to battalion HQ company.

It was about this time that my R&R orders came down. I had taken the chance of putting in for Hawaii during the week of Christmas and damn if I didn't get it. I chose December not because of the Christmas holiday but because I wanted to be sure and have less time left of my tour to finish than I had already served when I returned. I don't know if it was luck or somebody somewhere just wanted to do me a favor, but I got it just the same and I wasn't complaining. The former company clerk, Roabley, had clued me in on a special phone number, a Pentagon access line was how he described it, a direct line for use by upper brass only. The trick, he said, was to get an operator when the call got through stateside then reroute the call by giving her the number you want. He also said it didn't always work and not to try it too often for running the risk of having the charge traced back to the source. Whatever the risk it was a lot better than trying to find the time and a hop over to the Signal Corps and standing in line for an hour just for a five-minute squawk over the MARS line. That was a real frustrating bitch if you got a busy signal or no answer. Randy and I tried it when we were there for our movie projector training. I struck out with a busy signal and the entire experience reminded me of the third day anal rush back in basic at Fort Bragg with a lot of impatient guys lined up and waiting. So now I waited for a time when there was no one in the orderly room except myself to call Stacie via courtesy of the Pentagon and fill her in so she could make arrangements to meet me in Honolulu.

I put the call through and was holding for the connection when it happened – incoming! One rocket then another and all the usual took place. On came the base siren. Troops started rushing around everywhere. But in spite of it all there was no damn way I was going to give up my connection that had already taken about twenty minutes to achieve. In came the First Sergeant and the usual scramble team wielding their weapons and directing their troops. As the response progressed I could finally hear the phone at home begin to ring. At the same time I cranked the field phone and relayed the sit-reps to battalion, all the while holding the desk phone with the call stateside to my other ear. After what seemed like forever she finally answered and by the sound of her voice she had been asleep, which reminded me that she was on the other side of the world where it was the middle of the night.

As my conversation with Stacie began someone yelled INCOMING and we all hit the floor. In came another rocket impacting somewhere on the runway but sounding as though it were just outside the door. I slid under my ugly steel desk and continued the call.

"Why are you calling so late? Are you okay?"

"Oh yeah, I'm fine. It's not late here. I just wanted to let you know…

"INCOMING!" someone yelled.

WHOMPF!

"…um, just wanted to let you know that I got my R&R for Hawaii and…"

BOOM!

"We're really not interested in your R&R right now, Ghostrider," came a masculine voice on the field phone.

"Oh, sorry. I wasn't talking to you, battalion."

"You're not talking to me? Who's Battalion?" asked Stacie on the other phone.

"Sit-rep, perimeter eighty percent. Call it in, Fusco," ordered Top over the sound of the siren.

"Sit-rep. 189th, eighty percent manned, eighty percent," I repeated into the field phone as I remained huddled under the desk with a phone in each ear.

"INCOMING!"

BOOM!

"What? Who's coming? Eighty percent what?" asked Stacie.

"What?" I said.

"What? Say again," came the voice on the field phone.

"I said eighty percent manned," I repeated.

"What did you say?" asked Stacie.

"You said that already Ghostrider," said battalion.

"What? Oh, nothing," I said. "I was on the other phone. We're kind of busy here."

"No shit," said battalion.

"Busy? Doing what?" asked Stacie.

"Oh nothing really," I said to Stacy.

"Nothing," said the battalion voice on the field phone. "You said eighty percent, Ghostrider. Now nothing. What the hell's going on down there? Are you fully manned or what?"

"Hundred percent," called out Top.

"Um, roger that. We are fully manned, one hundred percent."

"Oh. So you got a hundred percent of what in Hawaii?" asked Stacie.

"My R&R. Christmas week."

"Christmas. It's Christmas there? What's all that noise?"

"What noise?"

BOOM!

"Oh that. Um, that's rockets. Somebody's shooting rockets. How's the baby?"

"We know they're rockets, Ghostrider. And I'm not your fuckin' baby."

I shoved the field phone back in its cradle.

"At night? You mean like the Fourth of July or like moon rockets? Does the Army do moon rockets like the Navy in Florida. Why would they do that?"

"What? No, it's daytime here. How's the baby?"

"It is? Well, who's shooting rockets? Why are they shooting rockets in the daytime? Because it's Christmas? Is Christmas the same time there?"

"It's the bad guys, Stacie."

"Really? They shoot rockets? Why are they shooting rockets?"

"Listen, I think I better go. I'll send you a letter about Hawaii, okay?"

"Oh, okay."

I'm not sure what was worse, the incoming or the conversation with Stacie, but both ended about the same time.

When I came out from under the desk and hung up the phone Top looked over and smiled. "Great timing, Fusco," he said. "How's everything at the Pentagon?"

I simply smiled in return, realizing that apparently I wasn't the only one privy to Roabley's secret Pentagon access line. But the real joke was on Roabley who, thinking the calls were free, told me he called home about twice a month. When he arrived home he must have found one hell of a phone bill because the charge on my call was automatically reversed and my single short conversation with Stacie cost $127. Even though I was now making a whopping $850 a month with hazardous duty and flight pay as an E-5 that was still a big chunk of change. An amount equal to a month's rent on the one bedroom apartment I set Stacie up in before I left the states, or should I say, the apartment *I thought* she was still living in.

The events of the few weeks leading up to my R&R pretty much fell into the category of routine with only a few exceptions, and naturally some of those just happened to happen on a Tuesday. On one particular Tuesday I was going over some newly received DEROS orders that finally included Private Jesus Martinez.

"Hey, Jesus is finally going to get to go home and meet God or somebody back in the States," I announced.

"Oh, too bad," said Randy. "I'm going to miss him. Kind of felt good knowing Jesus was on our side."

Naturally we were all eager to see Jesus' reaction when he came to discover his good fortune and being this was a Tuesday we expected him to drop by. To make sure he did I sent a notice to his platoon for him to report to the orderly room, which is exactly what he did less then an hour later except when he did it created a bit of confusion. In walked the trooper we all knew as Chili Bean.

"You sent for me?"

"No, I sent for Jesus Martinez," I said.

"Yeah, that's right."

"I've got orders for Jesus Martinez."

"Yeah man, okay. So let me have 'em."

"No. I've got DEROS orders and I have to make sure he gets them."

"No shit. So hand 'em over," insisted Chili.

"Just go tell Jesus to come and get his orders, will ya." I told him.

"Hey, come on Fusco, quit fuckin' with me and give me my orders."

"I told you Chili, I have to make sure he gets them. Especially Jesus. I mean, you know how whacked out that guy is, right?"

"What the hell are you talkin' about, Fusco? I'm Jesus Martinez. You got orders for me or what?"

"No, I got orders for…"

Randy perked up and came across the room. Chili was only wearing an OD T-shirt as usual, which meant no nametag that would have given us a clue. He stood bewildered as both Randy and I stared with perplexed interest.

"But you're Chili Bean, the bad ass Avenger ball buster from the gun platoon right?" asked Randy. "The one that nobody can beat at cards?"

"Yeah."

"So how can you be Jesus Christ?" I asked.

"Jesus Christ? What the hell are you talkin' about, Fusco?"

"Jesus Christ."

"Jesus Christ. Hey man, if you got religion that's fine with me. But I just want my orders."

"But what about Jesus Christ?" asked Randy.

"No. I don't know nothin' about any Jesus Christ shit. I'm Jesus Martinez. That's Jesus like in *Hey Soos*, ya know. Jesus. What the hell you guys been smokin'?"

Randy and I just stared.

"You guys are fuckin' with me, right? You do this to everybody or what?"

Just then Top walked into the orderly room and right away picked up on our vibes of confusion.

"What's going on? What's the problem?" he asked as he slid behind his desk.

"Chili here says he's Jesus Martinez," I said.

"Jesus. You mean *our* Jesus," said Top.

"Yeah."

"There's only one Jesus in the company, right?" asked Top.

"Yeah," I answered. "According to the roster."

"You're the one they call Chili, right?" asked Top.

"That's right Top. Chili Bean. But my name is Jesus Martinez. Jesus Gonzalez Avelino Martinez. So what's goin' on man? I got orders or what?"

"Chili Bean. 'Cause you're Mexican?" asked Top.

"Not really. My folks are Puerto Rican from Chicago. But that's okay. Don't mean nothin', you know."

"Got your ID?" I asked. "I mean, I believe you and all but…"

"But what?" asked Chili as he whipped out his ID.

"There's this other guy and…"

"Hey man, if there was another Jesus in our company I would know it. It's not like it's an easy name to live with. Believe me, I know."

"Yeah, so would I," I said, wondering if I actually would.

Everything on the ID matched up and I gave him his orders, which made him a happy man, especially since he was getting a two week drop that meant he was heading home two weeks earlier than his original DEROS. After he departed the orderly room we all sat silent, each wondering the same thing; if Jesus Martinez was indeed Jesus Martinez then just who the hell was the Jesus Martinez or Jesus Christ that had been holy rolling into our office nearly every week for the past eight months?

Is it Tuesday? I thought. Does it even matter? I sat there staring out the door and across the runway for a long quiet moment, wondering if it were the Army, the war, or me that just didn't fit in the picture. It didn't really register in my mind when I saw the chopper rise and move forward down the runway as many do each day, until I was suddenly slapped back to consciousness by a thunderous fireball explosion and rising black smoke mushroom. My first instinct was to hit the floor, but having seen it, I instead rose and went outside where I was joined by the others. It happened up on the runway just beyond some revetments. Graham, who was in the tower at the time, revealed the particulars to me later that evening.

"The Kid was flying," he told me. "You know, that young pilot who just got here. Been with us for a week or so."

Jimmy Baird was his name but they quickly began calling him the Kid because he was vertically challenged, on the short side with a baby face that in spite of his age of 19 on arrival and 20 five days later, gave him an appearance he was all of 14. There was no one else in the aircraft. It was supposed to be a simple maintenance test flight, just once around the park. But soon after lift off the Kid radioed that the stick was frozen. It was that simple. The stick froze and the chopper rolled over and exploded on impact. The explosion and fire resulting from a full tank of the highly flammable JP4 fuel was so intense that he was actually cremated on the spot. They found only a piece of his jaw bone leading to his being carried on the records as MIA for a matter of weeks until, I surmised, they could finish playing their games with the dead letter. It was another fluke death that by this time shouldn't have bothered me at all, especially since I hardly knew the guy. What did bother me was the knowledge that his wife had given birth to their son the very day before his departure for Vietnam. One day, barely long enough for the Kid's kid to open his eyes and see his father for the first and only time, a sight never to be remembered.

Another Tuesday rolled around, a fairly quiet Tuesday as Tuesdays go. At least it started out that way. There was a line of hooches behind ours that had been standing empty for some time but suddenly overnight they had become occupied with none of us having a clue as to when and for that matter who. The occupants slowly filtered out of the hooches while the Ghostriders were standing their morning formation and being addressed by First Sergeant Buchinsky. They were a disheveled bunch and immediately started in with some catcalls and a few comments about our being pretty toy soldiers and chump G.I.s. From my perch at the back door of the orderly room I could see over the top of our group of men and noticed that all of those emerging from the hooches were black. I also noticed that Top was beginning to get a little irritated.

"You people hold it down over there," he ordered. "We've got a formation going on here."

"Yeah, mofucka. We hold it," one of them responded as he grabbed his crotch. "And you can hold dis."

The rest of the members of his company, a dozen or so, burst into laughter and the hoots and catcalls began again. When a few members of our company turned to confront them Top ordered them to hold in formation then once again he advised our new neighbors to keep it down, only to get a similar response.

"Yo, lifer mofucka. Why don't you come over here and make us keep it down. You da big bad fuckin' lifer, right? Whatchu got fo me sucka?"

About that time our mystery boys own First Sergeant strolled out of a hooch. He was a tall confident well-built black man and apparently just as confrontational as his subordinates. It didn't take a rocket scientist to see there was a clear case of racial discrimination involved with this man's company. Not the type of exclusionary racism usually implied, but the reverse. This top sergeant had somehow selected and collected all black troops and then become their mother hen.

"What's the problem here?" he demanded.

"Are these your people?" asked Top.

"Yeah."

"You need to keep them in line. They're disrupting my formation."

"You don't worry about my people, First Sergeant. You let me worry about my people and you mind your own fuckin' business. You got a problem wit my people then you deal wit me. You deal wit me or shut the fuck up."

Top, like the rest of us, was certainly taken aback by their Top soldier's response, unexpected to say the least, and we could all see that he had absorbed just about all the abusive rhetoric he could stand. Their top soldier started removing his shirt and the other members of his company, with even more of them emerging out of the hooches, started strutting and talking trash, causing all the Ghostriders to turn and face them, fully anticipating a physical clash. Then suddenly from above there came the clank and clash of metal on metal, the sound of an M-60 being cocked and locked. Everyone looked up to discover Specialist Georgie Rojero straddling the peak of the roof of the Avenger hooch cradling the weapon at the ready. Georgie, an Avenger gun ship door gunner, was a quiet mix of Mexican and Navajo who had just returned from two weeks in rehab because he had a serious drinking problem. Now he was on a milk diet and a little edgy, which made us all a little edgy as well considering the situation. When top turned and looked up he was as surprised as everyone else but quickly adjusted to take advantage of the situation. He offered a quick glance with a slight smile in my direction then turned back to our new neighbors.

"First Sergeant, I expect you and your people to maintain military standards while you are housed in our area. Is that understood?" said Top. "Or are we going to have a problem?"

Their top soldier offered no response as he and his company shrank back into their hooches. Top called the Ghostriders to attention then dismissed them. When he turned back to the roof Georgie had already vanished.

I discovered later that our mystery neighbors were a company in transit. As for what kind of company and from and to where, no one seemed to know. They remained for the rest of the week doing nothing at all except sleeping and eating and, of course, drinking and getting high. They did however have an interesting ritual that usually took place after late chow. They had all apparently taken their R&Rs in Hong Kong, a favorite destination of a lot of the brothers where for seriously cheap money anyone could have a suit tailored in a single day. Simply show the Hong Kong tailor a picture of what you wanted, he would measure you with a string and in a day or two you had a brand new custom-tailored 100 per cent silk three-piece suit - $25. It was such suits that showed up in front of the hooches after evening chow and even sometimes in mid day, accompanied of course, by the music of the Temptations. Pink suits, yellow suits, baby blue suits, even all white suits with matching hats and snake skin shoes. They would line up and mimic the Temptations. The sight of them, the visual impression considering the environment, was at variance to say the least. During their brief stay their only demonstrated attitude was total spiteful nonparticipation sanctioned and somehow protected by their First Sergeant.

It was that same day when Randy shut off the radio at the onset of another Petula Clark song that I noticed old Papa-san puttering around with his fan broom and dust rag. After so many years old Papa-san had probably taken for granted that we had taken him for granted to such a degree that we ignored him completely as he quietly drifted around our workplace - and he was right. He soft-shoed in and out all day long, sweeping, cleaning, and carrying out the trash, generating about as much interest from us as a stop sign does in California. To us he just wasn't there even when he was there because we just didn't care. If, on the other hand, you did happen to look up and catch his eye it inevitably resulted in his perking up and offering his one-toothed bobbing head smile. And so Papa-san became the piddling invisible man.

For some reason when Randy killed the radio Papa-san's slight little shuffle drew my attention and I casually observed him from behind my tall file cabinet. It took a minute to sink in but when it hit me it hit me like a ton of bricks. Our feeble old one-toothed Ho Chi Min look-a-like village idiot Papa-san... could read! And not only could he read, he could read English. and he was reading everything that happened to be laying face up on every desk. When he emptied ashtrays or dusted a desktop he would, with amazing slight of hand, flip and glance at papers that were face down. His routine was as slick as goose shit and he was as cool as a cucumber but then why not, he was without a doubt the longest incumbent Ghostrider of all time with many years practice.

Papa-san's routine was to piddle around during the workday with occasional breaks for socializing with the mama-sans and copping a free lunch in the mess hall. Near the end of his workday, usually around 1500 hours, he would carry the office trash out to a fifty-gallon drum on the other side of Hollywood Boulevard in front of our HQ and burn it. Having raised my curiosity, I had been observing him throughout the latter half of the day and so decided to also observe him as he burned the trash. Again old Papa-san's moves were slick. He read each piece of paper with extreme interest before he burned it and occasionally saved and stashed a few pages in his pants. For me that was the capper and at the end of his sneaky burn ritual I snatched him and his loaded pants and led him into the office. Top and the CO were out at the time so I marched old Papa-san into the XO's office and presented my case.

"I've been watching him, sir. He reads everything in the office as he cleans and also reads everything from the office that's supposed to be burned. He stashed these in his pants when he was burning the office trash."

"What are they?" asked Captain Patrick.

"Intelligence reports, sir."

The XO took a brief look at the papers then handed them back to me.

"Oh, that's no big deal. Don't worry about it."

"Don't worry about it?"

"Yeah. Don't worry, he's okay."

"Sir, these are intelligence reports."

"Yeah well, don't worry about it. Let the old man go."

"But sir, there's no telling how long he's been doing this."

"Those are dated reports, Fusco. Days old. So don't worry about it."

By now I had accepted the fact that we weren't going out of our way to win the war but giving away intel reports showing what we knew about enemy activities didn't quite set well with my paranoid "stupid enlisted man" instincts. As a result my *give-a-shit bucket*, a means we used to reference measuring our evolving dedication to the war and the Army in general, was beginning to fill, which wasn't a good thing because mine, like the buckets of most everyone else, was nearly half full with Army bullshit upon arriving in Vietnam in the first place. Throw in some near death experiences and encounters with unappreciative locals and then the bucket filled and began to overflow, which was when some soldiers just lost it like Cleveland Dooley, or shut down completely and failed to function. Others began to use phrases like, "ask me if I give a damn", or, "don't mean nothin'." Some buckets filled quickly, others, like mine, took a little longer but once filled, few if any, could be emptied. Letting old Papa-san off the hook was just another drop in my give-a-shit bucket and the dripping seemed to continue, and for the first time I began to notice it getting a little heavy.

Old papa-san would return to work the next day but I wouldn't be there because the next day I departed Holloway for the Pleiku Air Force Base via a three-wheeled lambretta that I caught just outside the gate, shared with a few mama-sans and their chickens. From the Air Force base I caught a hop to Tan Sun Nhut air base near Saigon and from there a commercial airliner to Honolulu, Hawaii.

I didn't necessarily care where we stayed in Hawaii as long as it was clean and American and civilized, so I left making the reservations up to Stacie. We met at Schofield Army base where a courtesy bus full of R&R soldiers' families rolled in from the Honolulu Airport. Surprisingly my 18-month-old son immediately burst into tears because he had absolutely no idea who the hell I was. Stacie burst into tears as well, not because she was glad to see me but because she was still upset after losing our son on the flight over. She had fallen asleep and when she awoke he was gone, sending her into a panic thinking he had somehow gotten off the aircraft. It was a 747 and after her initial panic and an extensive search he was finally discovered in the upstairs lounge drinking a Shirley Temple and banging the piano to the delight of a small audience.

Checking in at the base revealed a few unexpected surprises as well. It seems my week of R&R was going to only be a short five days, requiring me to report back to my unit on Christmas Day – a real bummer. But at least our military R&R advisor was on the ball enough to give us a heads up on Stacie's reservation efforts. With all the great hotels along the shoreline of Waikiki she had somehow managed to make reservations at the Holiday Inn at the airport. One quick phone call and he instead got us an eighth floor room on the shore side in the Holiday Inn on the beach in the shadow of Diamond Head.

After checking into the hotel the first thing I did was take a hot shower then a long hot bath and another long hot shower, leaving the tub in the hotel room coated with the residue of the reddish brown clay of the Vietnam highlands. I didn't know what the maid was going to think when she discovered the mess and really didn't care. All I had my mind on at the time was a clean roll in the hay and a trip to the hotel buffet, all the while getting reacquainted with Junior. Just the simple things to remind me that I was back in the world - my world – and that I wasn't dreaming.

"Yeah, I know what you mean," said Randy as I briefed him on the events of my Hawaiian rendezvous. "That was the first thing I did on my R&R in Australia. A long hot bath and shower."

Randy had taken his R&R a month prior and gone to Australia where he was snatched up right off the plane by a local family and told he wouldn't need any money or a place to stay. They made him a guest at their ranch and even supplied him with a car. This was not an uncommon story coming from American soldiers who went there. The Aussies truly love Americans. Maybe I should have gone to Australia as well. My story was a little different.

"Did you straighten things out with your wife?" asked Randy.

"Might say that," I told him. "I used a little cop psychology. Told her I knew all about everything from a letter I got from a friend so she fessed up right off. Said she'd been messing around. The weird thing is I really didn't care. Strange right? I mean sure it hurt but for some reason I just didn't give a shit and just wanted to be with the kid. That was the best of the R&R, being with the kid."

"Yeah," said Randy. "Kids have a way of changing your perspective don't they? My sister's kids, they're like that."

"Did you boink her?" asked Gas.

"What? Boink her?" I asked as I accepted a beer from Gas who had just entered my room. "What the hell does that mean?"

"Yeah, man," said Gas. "She's your ol' lady, right? I mean you had to boink her, right? After nine months in this shit hole I sure as hell would boink her. Get all the boom boom I could. So, did ya? Did ya boink her? First thing I bet. I sure as shit would. Even if she didn't look like Marilyn McCoo. Does she look like Marilyn McCoo?"

"Damn Gas, it's his wife. Cut the guy some slack will ya," said Randy.

"Yeah Gas, she looks just like Marilyn McCoo," I said. "Except with red hair. And shorter. And white."

"Oh wow. No shit?"

"No shit."

"Wow. Marilyn McCoo. So, did you boink her?"

"Anyway," I continued, trying to ignore Gas. "Because I only got five days and had to report back sooner than I thought, I had to fly out on the morning of Christmas Eve, and you know what? She decided to stay an extra day. There was this Romeo type lounge singer at the hotel that crooned over her during his show. He's singing '*Knock Three Times...*' and she's sending out come-on signals like some bitch dog in heat. Then they were making goo goo eyes at each other when we bumped into him on the elevator after breakfast the day I left. Hell, I can't blame the guy for trying because she is pretty hot but can you believe that? Right in front of me the air-headed bitch silently starts striking up a one-nighter with some fuckin' whimpy Tom Jones wannabe lounge singer."

"Damn, man," said Randy. "You should have decked the guy. Tell me you kicked his ass."

"Yeah, he kicked his ass," echoed Gas as he passed gas while handing Randy a beer.

"Like I said, I just didn't give a shit. Just wanted to be with the kid, you know? Maybe she knew that or maybe she's just too stupid to know anything. What the hell, the damage is done. She's not worth fighting over but the kid, well, I'll have to deal with that situation when I get home I guess. Anyway, I got back to Ton Son Nhut and found out I couldn't get back here, that nothing was flying because it was Christmas Eve and that nothing would be flying on Christmas Day either. So I spent Christmas Eve and Christmas Day stretched out on a wooden bench in an empty deserted hanger except when I was wandering around to find a mess hall, all the time thinking I was going to catch hell for reporting back late. Then when I get back and report in the XO tells me it wasn't important and I should have stayed the extra days in Hawaii. Does that bite the big one or what? I could have had two more days with my kid."

"Shit, you're a better man than me, Fusco," said Randy. "I'd have kicked that singing bastards ass all over the lounge. A little New York justice ya know."

"Yeah well, the jokes on him. She's not that great in bed anyway. If you know what I mean."

"Now how the hell am I supposed to know what you mean?"

"Yeah, how's he s'pose to know what you mean. He never boinked your wife," said Gas as he left my room to retrieve more beer.

"What, you mean you didn't screw any kangaroos when you were in Australia?"

"Hell no," said Randy with a laugh. "But there was this really hot blond koala bear I almost made it with until I found out she was only interested in my money."

"Money. What money?

"Exactly. That's why I struck out."

"You are one lame dago, Collatazi. Couldn't even score with a damn koala. You're a disgrace to your Italian heritage."

"Koala? You boinked a koala? Oh man, that's funky," observed the returning Gas, accentuating his comment with an exceptionally boisterous fart. Where was that? In Bangkok? I heard about weird shit like that in Bangkok. I took my R&R in Bangkok. Didn't see any koalas though."

"Gas, if you're gonna participate you need to keep up with the conversation," I said.

"It's okay, Gas. It looked a lot like Marilyn McCoo," said Randy.

"Really?" said Gas. "A koala? Imagine that."

"No thanks," said Randy. "I'd rather not."

"Hey, what is a koala anyway?" asked Gas.

"An Australian hooker," said Randy.

"Oh wow. Just like Marilyn McCoo. Cool. Maybe I shoulda took my R&R in Australia, huh?"

Our CO, Major Anthony, also left town in December but his departure wasn't due to a violent fiery death as was that of the new young pilot, Kid, and it didn't go unnoticed like the Ghostriders who were shuffled around the battalion. Our commanding officer, Ghostrider-6, completed his one year tour and we sent him off with a bash of a party inclusive of beer, champagne, steaks, a few gifts and speeches, and a striptease show. Somebody somehow managed to fly in a class-A stripper and band from Korea just for the occasion. It was a fun time but seemed to leave a void in our ever-shrinking number because due to our scheduled deactivation he was not replaced.

Not long before he left he called me into his office and gave me a re-up speech suggesting I attend Officer Candidate School. "You could make a difference that way," he told me. It was as though my quiet mild mannered CO had been reading my mind all these months as I silently watched and evaluated the Army and the war. I had always been like that, able to find a better or more efficient way of doing things and sometimes a little too critical. I simply considered it a gift of common horse sense and logic and was always surprised at how many people lacked the same ability. But in the Army you had to bite your tongue, living and sometimes dying without explanations or the opportunity to contribute to the process. It was that old parental *because I said so* routine which gave too many Army idiots power and credence. I was flattered at the CO's suggestion and even gave it a quick turn of serious concern then I asked if it were likely I would end up serving another tour in Vietnam. He said yes - so I said no.

Following his departure battalion simply turned the reins over to the XO, Captain Patrick, who was a nice guy but pretty much a total enigma, at least to the enlisted ranks, and unlike the CO, it seemed he was nearly always in his office which would prove unfortunate for me.

CHAPTER 36

BIKINI BEACH BINGO

The R&R in Hawaii didn't do much for my morale partly because it reminded me of what I was missing back home and partly because the situation with my wife became a real bur under the saddle, a frustration born of my inability to remedy the state of affairs from 12,000 miles away. I found myself blaming it on the Army, the war, even the Vietnamese for being such fools as to be unable to defend their own country. I began to feel contempt for most all of them with the exeption of Ba my hooch maid who seemed to be the only Vietnamese in the country who wasn't a hustler or a thief. I'm sure there must have been many others like her out there somewhere who were by nature basically just simple decent people and the true victims in this political fiasco. But, I would sometimes think, didn't their complacency or acceptance of their condition make them just as guilty? More and more I came to think these people just didn't give a shit. After two thousand years of subjugation I didn't think they gave a damn what kind of government they had or who was in charge because they had little to be taken from them other than their lives, and in this part of the world even that went cheap. It seemed they just wanted their chickens and pigs and rice paddies, and their bug-like existence. The human condition in Vietnam was such that you could glean an entirely different philosophy about it each day and still not get it right. Trying to make sense of it all was in itself an exercise in futility and after a few days back in the world, especially a paradise like Hawaii, then suddenly being thrust back into Vietnam was a bit of a psychological overload. Within days of my return my attitude began to slip, not necessarily outwardly but measurably within, a smoldering contempt for the war and even myself for being there, for actually volunteering to be there.

Another one of the guys I knew in the company was heading home and as was often the custom when guys packed out, there was the ritual of bequeathing accumulated possessions to friends. Things like fans, refrigerators, and anything else they didn't want to bother to ship home. It was a final act of purging that confirmed you were actually leaving. David Kelly was a gunner in the Scarlet lift platoon for whom I had subbed on a few flights so he could spend some time with a young Vietnamese girl he wanted to take back to the states and marry. From the photo he carried she was cute as a button, not a working class girl or a hooker like most of the locals we were exposed to, and she had his head spinning. How and where he found her I don't know. Maybe it was at the orphanage our company supported somewhere near Pleiku or maybe he just bumped into her somehow. He never really explained. He was young and seemingly naïve so we all tried to dissuade him but our attempts were fruitless and the bureaucratic process was in the works. I never found out if his efforts to bring her home to meet mama were successful.

His departing legacy to me included a captured AK-47 rifle, a captured classic WWII grease gun, a Montagnard bracelet that he swore was good luck and said he no longer needed, and a full quart bottle of Jack Daniels he had been holding in reserve for over 6 months. I accepted graciously but only on the condition that we crack the bottle to celebrate his leaving. He, Randy, Graham, and I spent the better part of the night passing the bottle and bullshitting about what we missed in the states. About how we would damn near kill for a cold creamy soft ice cream cone or a good slice of pizza, and about the future and dissecting the war. That is until the bottle got the better of us and we passed out. It was one of those silly stupid drunks directly resulting from the fact none of us could really hold our hard liquor in the first place.

I woke up the next morning with just enough time to scoot into the orderly room a few minutes late as usual, though a bit hungover, unshaved, and not quite motoring at full speed. As I entered I was met by a displeased new CO. Captain Patrick had always been cordial and friendly as the XO and had once even offered to arrange an emergency leave for me to scoot home and rectify my domestic problem, which he had discovered existed when my good friend and mother hen Randy revealed it to him. I declined but always appreciated the offer and his caring. "Don't worry about the kid," he said, trying to reassure me. "Kids are resilient and they have a way of surviving."

I took his words to be sincere and even comforting but on this day his tone had changed. He wasn't caring or trying to sooth my pain. He was instead flaunting his authority.

"Your late," he declared.

"Yes sir," I said. "We had a bit of a party last night."

"That's no damn excuse."

His attitude surprised me completely and my first thought was, okay, he's the CO now so he's going to come on like king shit and let everybody know it. But why, I thought. In all the time I'd been there I never heard him mutter one cross word. So now he's the lord of a dwindling company, a lame duck leader. So what's the point? This isn't the time for stateside spit shine chicken shit. He knows me and he knows I'm not a fuck up. I'm just having a rare bad morning in a shitty war in a shitty country. So I'm a few minutes late. For what, another ten hour day broken up with maybe two or three hours of real work or some gooks trying to kill us? Suddenly it felt like I was experiencing another pointless Staff Sergeant Polk moment back at Fort Sill, and I just wasn't in the mood.

"No sir," I replied. "That's not a fuckin' excuse that's just what happened."

Had Randy not been sitting there I might have gotten away with just getting my ass chewed or maybe a friendly morale propping speech, or a little worse. But I had definitely stepped on the man's pride and authority in front of someone and within seconds reaped the rewards.

"I'm sending you out to the 170th at Kontum to keep you out of trouble," he said. "You can help them close out their HQ just like you've been doing here. Colletazzi can handle your work here."

With that said he retired to his office.

Had Top been there I'm sure I wouldn't have said what I said and, for that matter, had he been there the XO probably would not have said anything about my late entrance in the first place. The entire situation hit me hard. I was a Ghostrider, maybe not much of one by our slick and gun ship crewmen's combat standards, but a Ghostrider just the same. And the expected timing of the company's closing nearly timed out with my own DEROS, a situation I had anticipated and was comfortable with. And as for his statement of doing at the 170th what I was doing here meant what? What I was doing here was the morning report and the usual stuff, which to date had nothing to do with closing out the company. Not long ago when I had asked the XO what I was to do with the company files when we did eventually close up shop his reply was simply to burn them. Burn them, I thought. What the hell? Years of records from the day the Ghostriders came into existence.

"Burn them?" I said, obviously questioning the statement and wondering why the hell we had even bothered to create them in the first place. Sure there were always multiple copies of everything going everywhere but where else would there have been a consolidated file such as ours. Between that and the incident with old papa-san I actually began to question the XO's judgment. Maybe that's what got his goat. But for better or worse his judgment was now law and he just ordered me to Siberia, to the 170th AHC Bikini Beach camp in Kontum. Maybe he thought he was doing me a favor, something that was in my best interest. I don't know. He certainly seemed like a nice enough guy to do that. All I know is I didn't want to go. I knew the Ghostriders wouldn't fall apart without me, hell, I was just a pencil, but with my personal life turning to shit I wondered if I could get along without them, without the reassuring comfort of the known as opposed to the unknown in Kontum.

I had accumulated too much stuff to pack it up and haul to Kontum on such short notice so I packed only a few personal basics, grabbed my weapons and gear, pad locked my room, and left it in the care of Randy.

"Man, I'm really sorry about this," said Randy as he walked me up the hill to the pad. "Wish there was something I could do."

"It's okay," I said. "Guess I had it coming. But I wanted to be here when we closed out, you know? I wanted to be the last Ghostrider of record on that last morning report. I don't know, just seems there'd be something special about that. I don't know what but... Anyway, take care of my shit. I'll get back when I can. Okay?"

"You got it. Just stay out of trouble. Know what I mean?"

"Trouble? What the hell kind of trouble can anybody get into in Vietnam," I laughed. Then as an afterthought, "Oh yeah. And if you see General Giap don't be too hard on him. He's just looking for a little companionship and corn flakes."

"What? The rat! That fuckin' rat's still alive? But you said..."

"He likes corn flakes," I laughed.

"Shit. Hell with that," said Randy. "I ain't feeding that fuckin' thing."

I caught a Bikini chopper to Kontum and was the only passenger aboard, flying with a crew I didn't know. I sat there looking out the door at the hills and valleys of the highlands but in my mind I saw nothing. I was apprehensive about having to start all over again with all new faces and personalities, anxious as hell, and suddenly finding myself emotionally spent. I wanted to convince myself that I just didn't give a shit. Why should I even care, I thought, and if I didn't care what could they do - send me to Vietnam? It wasn't in my nature to not care even with extra effort but I was coming around and getting real close.

It was mid day when we set down at the 170th Bikini camp near Kontum. When I hopped off the chopper I instinctively looked over to the area where I had seen the errant rocket strike the mechanic a month earlier. There was just empty space, nothing there as though it had never happened. That's it, I thought, that's how it works. One day you're here and the next you're not and the beat goes on, and nobody gives a shit, or at least pretends not to because they know the next time it could be them and they don't want to think about it. On my previous visits to Bikini Beach I had noticed how small the place was compared to Holloway but never really concerned myself with it until now. Now I was here to stay and suddenly size was everything. After eight months of existence within the apparent secure confines of Camp Holloway, growing comfortable with and convincing myself of the safety in numbers, I would now have to adjust to the idea of being in a truly vulnerable abode. As I made my way across the pad to the Bikini orderly room I looked in each direction and it seemed no matter where I looked I could see perimeter fence or wire, and visualized a determined NVA force just on the other side. Perhaps like the one I had seen at Dak Seang, relentless and lethal, determined to overrun and kill us. It was again a paranoia born of ignorance like a small child afraid of the water simply because they can't see what's in it.

I made my way to the orderly room and found it much smaller than what I had with the Ghostriders and there was no one in attendance other than the company clerk. He was a high-energy SP4 from Terre Haute, Indiana, named Jimmy Mueller, drafted into the Army soon after he graduated from Indiana State. My first impression was that this clerk was much like Roabley, the Indiana guy I had replaced at the 189th, and for that matter much like the other company clerks I'd met during my time in the service. I began to wonder if there was a certain type of person or personality who naturally migrated to that position, and if that were so, then why didn't I fit the mold. The inner caution alarm sounded in my head simply because my instincts told me I might be facing another self serving Roabley but although Mueller was certainly the type of guy who took care of number one and covered his own ass first, his smile and immediate acceptance quickly disarmed and put me at ease.

"What do we have here, another crewman from the 189th," he said after observing the Ghostrider patch and the wings above my pocket.

"No," I answered. "I'm the Ghostrider company clerk. They sent me here to help you close out your company.

"Oh hell, we don't need any help. I damn near got it all done. Nothing for you to do here. Hell, man, there's hardly anything for me to do here. Tell ya what. Just have a seat. I'm done here in a minute then we'll get you some stuff from supply and set you up with a bunk. I'll show you around then we'll grab some chow. But I don't know what the hell you're gonna' do here, man. We sure as hell don't need another clerk. But then, who gives a shit, right?" he laughed. "What the hell. That's the Army."

I found a small closet of a room in the corner of the HQ hooch containing nothing but a single bunk where I parked my gear. Soon after there arose the growing sounds and shouts of excitement followed by a sudden brief burst of gunfire followed by yet a few more shots. I grabbed my weapon and helmet and darted outside to find some of the guys running around the hooch toward the mess hall so I followed. A crowd was gathering around the back of a paneled food supply truck that had just arrived with a delivery. My first thought was that a sapper had been found in or under the vehicle trying to sneak into the compound and was summarily shot. To my complete surprise as I walked around to the back of the truck I discovered the mess Sergeant and a few others extracting a very large and very long python snake from inside. Out it came and out it continued to come, never seeming to end until finally stretched out in front of us was a very impressive snake. It was thick and long, and it was frightening as hell just knowing that something like that existed. Needless to say, I would never again look upon snakes as pesky little critters to be avoided but now as monsters to be seriously feared.

"Is this somebody's idea of a fuckin' joke?" asked the mess Sergeant.

"I swear that sum'bitch wasn't in the truck when we left Pleiku," said the truck's driver. "I don't know where the hell it came from but that big sum'bitch wasn't in there when we loaded. Hell no. I'd a seen it. I mean how the hell can you miss it. Must be fifteen feet long."

"Eighteen," said one of the guys who had just finished stepping off the distance from its bullit-ridden head to its now dormant tail. "Eighteen and a half actually."

Another tried picking up the snake from its midsection then dropped it. "Damn, that suckers heavy."

I'm not sure how accurate the original measurement was because soon a series of photos were taken with fifteen of us lined up side by side behind the monster which in my mind made it even longer. Then someone suggested that the mess Sergeant cut and cook the thing and stretch the hide out on the wall of the mess hall. But the mess Sergeant was a two-timer who knew a little more about Vietnamese cuisine than did we and quickly looked upon our dead reptilian guest as a business opportunity.

"Hell no," he said. "You're lookin' at some serious prime steak here. The gooks will pay some big bucks for this baby."

And he was right. The snake was sold off to a nearby unit of ARVN soldiers for $600 and they considered it one hell of a deal for such a highly prized delicacy. To them it was the equivalent of prime rib, a lot of prime rib, or not unlike us copping a great deal on a six or eight hundred pound steer for a big time holiday barbecue. The proceeds went into the company slush fund to pay for yet another of its famous parties. The Bikinis, I would discover, weren't shy and truly liked to party.

I hadn't thought much about it but I had arrived at Bikini Beach on New Years Eve and as the sun began to set and I lay on my bare mattress bunk staring at nothing, in popped SP4 Jimmy Mueller with his ever-present smile and an invitation to join *the group in the round* outside.

In the round meant a group of guys who regularly settled in a circle around a sawed off fifty-gallon drum. The sun was just setting when we joined in and they had just started up a fire in the drum. The chairs had obviously been confiscated from the mess hall and though there were at first only a half-dozen guys, the number increased steadily as the sky darkened. I sat next to Jimmy who had described the gathering as *just a nightly ritual*. As others arrived I lit up a cigarette and gratefully accepted a beer then sat silent as the events of the day evolved into fireside chats and laughter. The big snake seemed to emerge as the subject of choice along with who recently screwed up and made the First Sergeant's shit list. Though I hadn't met him, the general consensus was that he was pretty much an asshole but tolerable if you managed to avoid him. I was told he lived in a well protected bunker with the company of a full time mama-san concubine, both of which, according to Jimmy, enjoyed doing it doggy style, which also explains, according to Jimmy, why the top soldier spends most of his time there, that plus the fact he was a short timer and had an acute fear of dying.

As the circle began to fill in I couldn't help but notice that it was a mix of both enlisted men and officers, the latter were discernible mostly by the conversation when an occasional *sir* would pop up, more as a familiar joke than out of true military courtesy. Few were wearing a shirt that revealed any rank. I was introduced by Jimmy and automatically accepted.

"Hey, Fusco. What the hell are you doing here, man?" came a voice from a few seats over.

I turned to find a familiar face from the Ghostriders. It was one of the guys from one of the airlift platoons but I couldn't place his name.

"Banished," I said. "I pissed off the XO."

"Yeah, a lot of that shit going around lately," he laughed. "I got here four days ago. Just like that. They said, 'Pack your shit. You're going to Kontum.' Just like that. Don't make sense though.

These guys are closing out before the Ghostriders and I got six more months. But that's okay. These guys here are uglier than shit, but they're cool."

"Who the hell you callin' ugly, man?" said one of the guys in the circle.

"Yeah," piped in another. "I fucked your sister last night and talk about ugly, oh man, I had to put a bag over both our heads."

"That wasn't my sister, man. What the hell was you smokin'? That was your mother, shit head," replied the former Ghostrider. The locker room diatribe wasn't elegant but at least it was cordial and I felt right at home.

About that time I was handed another beer having tossed my original empty. Then I was handed a joint. I hadn't really paid much attention at first, focusing mostly on the fire and not noticing the pot that was going around the circle. It was pretty much a first for me. I had tried it once at Holloway on the sly while up near the runway with Dillinger after a late flight but it didn't impress me or do much for me so I left it at that. This time, being part of the circle was a whole new ball game. I took a hit, then passed it on only to have another handed to me from the other side. Another hit and a swig of beer and I could already feel it's affect. The next thing I knew the joints were coming from both directions and I was sitting there with one in each hand. It was at that same time the Bikini XO, Captain Fairgood, strolled up and I damn near panicked. He looked right at me sitting there with a beer propped between my legs and a joint in each hand and he smiled. That's it, I thought, my ass is grassed and we're all busted.

"What kind of half-ass New Years party is this?" he said to Mueller sitting next to me. "Somebody better tell me they scored some rice whisky to go with that shit I smell."

"Nope. Nothing but good old American brew," replied Mueller as he handed the XO a joint.

"No problem," laughed Fairgood. "I brought my own. You guys wouldn't know good whisky if I poured it up your ass."

"That's okay," laughed Mueller. "Cause you're the only one who drinks that shit anyway."

Needless to say I was more than surprised as the XO took a toke and pulled up a chair. He was about to say something when he was interrupted by a distant voice from above. It was the guard in a nearby perimeter tower yelling down for someone to toss him a beer. When I turned to look up at the tower I also noticed that, not only the tower, but the perimeter wire itself sat only a few short yards from our hooch and where we were sitting. Once again a twinge of insecurity ran through my consciousness, but only briefly as it was quickly subdued by the affects of the beer and marijuana. Someone tossed a couple of cans up to the guard who I then noticed had apparently already had a few and had mounted one of the empties on the end of the barrel of his M-60.

"As I was about to say," continued the XO. "What the hell kind of New Years shindig is this without any fireworks?"

"I got some pen flares," someone volunteered.

The mention of pen flares quickly reminded me of the impromptu 4th of July celebration we had at Holloway where we had all taken the pen flares out of our survival kits and shot them up the hill into the BOQ hooches. The resident officers began to shoot back. It was a colorful exchange until one of our flares set one of their hooches on fire, sending Randy into a near panic being he was the one who shot it.

"Flares my ass," said the XO. "We need some serious hoopla here. We need to light up the sky."

All kinds of ideas were put forth from M-70 thumper flares to the big rocket tube flares kept in the ammo dump. Someone even suggested calling in some artillery rounds and flares on the ARVN bunker that sat a half klick somewhere outside the perimeter, but all the ideas were deemed too ambitious requiring too much effort, meaning in our current physical state no one wanted to leave the circle. Then Mueller hit on the winning idea.

"Tracers," said Mueller. "Why don't we just fill the sky with tracers?"

"Oh yeah, man. Bodacious idea." Agreed the *high* knights of the circle and out came our M-16s and bandoleers of ammo. Somehow in our limited state of adroitness we manage to continue passing beer and joints while unloading ammo clips, picking out the marked tracer rounds and reloading the clips. We continued this until we each had two or three clips each full of nothing but tracers. The remaining nontracer rounds went back into the other clips and back into the bandoleers.

It was my first real experience with pot and it wasn't difficult to recognize its attraction, especially in Vietnam where with the simple lighting and inhaling of a joint all the bullshit of the Army and misery of the war could momentarily be put aside. To say it mellowed out the war would be more than appropriate and to say, on this occasion, it mellowed out my apprehensions regarding a new place and new faces was also more than appropriate. And how I managed to actually fill three ammo clips with tracer rounds while in that state of influence beats the hell out of me. I felt like a retard taking a motor skills test.

"How much time?" someone asked.

"Bout fifteen minutes," someone answered.

"Fifteen minutes," repeated the XO. "Fifteen minutes and then it'll be 1971. Shit, I feel like I been here fifteen fuckin' years," he said as he played with one of his straight round clips. Then for some crazy reason he tossed it into the fire.

"Oh shit," said Mueller, laughing.

Oddly enough when the rounds started cooking off we all just sat there hooting and cooing and marveling at the sparks and embers that flew out of the burn barrel in all directions. It was like a string of firecrackers except with more lethality and amazingly none of us were hurt, not even the two who fell out of their chairs. Soon after someone else let loose with a yelp and a full clip of tracers into the sky and we all watched as they disappeared into the night like fast moving stars. Then suddenly a jeep came flying around the corner of the hooch driven by a very animated and pissed off First Sergeant. I couldn't see him that well behind the glare of the jeep's lights, but from what I could see coupled with what I had been told I concluded he was pretty much a weasel and for some reason I tried to imagine this scrawny unattractive man and his hooch mama getting it on doggy style. It was an appalling thought.

"What the hell's going on here? Who's firing off those rounds?" he yelled as the jeep slid to a dusty halt, its headlights beaming through us and out through the perimeter wire.

We all sat in silence. As I looked around the circle I was amazed at the total lack of concern by anyone there. The joints continued to be passed with care and an empty beer can was flipped into the fire.

"Did you people hear me? I want some fuckin' answers!"

Just as the top soldier was about to dismount his jeep the tower guard decided to speak for the group.

"Shut the fuck up and go back to your skanky ass hooch whore you lifer bastard!" he said and then, incredibly, he laid a short burst of M-60 fire in the dirt in front of the jeep.

The First Sergeant, wide eyed and freaked, quickly threw the jeep into reverse and spun out and away. It was at that moment I began to tell myself I was dreaming and it was time to wake up, but there was no response. I even found myself calling on General Giap the rat to come to my rescue, but still no response.

"What an asshole," I heard someone say. Zeroing in through the fog of my mind to the source of the comment, I realized it came from their XO.

"Three more minutes."

"Hey, anybody know the words to that song? The one they always sing when the ball comes down."

"What ball?"

"You know. That big fuckin' ball in New York that drops at midnight."

"Screw that ball, man. I'm from California. It isn't new years until midnight in Cali."

"It's already midnight in California dumb ass."

"It's already midnight in New York."

"So what is it here?" asked another as he struggled to talk while holding in a toke of smoke.

"They don't have New Years here, man. This damn country is so far behind they don't even know what damn century it is."

"Twilight Zone," said someone, laughing. "We're in the Twilight Zone."

"Old Ank Zine or somethin' like that," answered someone from the far side of the circle. "The song, it's Old… somethin'"

"That song doesn't make any sense."

"Yeah, you got that right."

"Hey, you know if you sing it you gotta kiss somebody when you're done. At midnight."

"You try and kiss me and I'll frag your ass motherfucker."

"How 'bout if he just kisses your ass?"

"How 'bout *you* just kiss my ass, faggot?"

The conversation came from all around the circle and though the humor was sharp the words flowed slowly due to the weed's affect on their delivery - and my delayed perception.

"Yeah, I think we need a better song. Something like, um… like that one… um."

"No no I got it. Um… yeah. You know…"

The conversation was about to evolve into a slur of grunts and mental telepathy when someone, rather than say the title of the song decided to just sing it.

"In this dirty old part of the city.
Where the sun refuse to shine
People tell me there ain't no use in tryin'"

Someone else picked up on the next phrase and after a few lines everybody joined in, creating a loud mumble of uncertain lyrics until, of course, when they hit the chorus and sang loud and clear with enthusiasm.

"We gotta get out of this place
If it's the last thing we ever do
We gotta get out of this place
Girl, there's a better life for me and you"

Just as we all started kicking in with a repeat of the chorus a quick burst of fire shot out of the tower, then again from somewhere along the perimeter. From down the line there came the shout of "GOOKS IN THE WIRE!"

Then came another burst of fire followed by two bright flares lighting the night sky, rocking back and forth as they drifted and descended, creating spooky shadowy movement where there was none. We all grabbed our weapons and ammo and during the immediate confusion I heard one member of our circle begin the countdown to the New Year from ten seconds while still another continued to sing the chorus of our newly accepted New Year song. I was stoned and disoriented with sudden visions of facing death in the form of hundreds of NVA, and for some reason I didn't care, a contagious feeling I'm sure I must have contracted from the guys in the circle as they rose in what appeared to be cool determination to deal with this latest interruption. Actually we were all stoned shitless and probably would have appeared cool, calm, and cavalier in the face of an oncoming stampede of wild elephants.

"SAPPER! SAPPER IN THE WIRE!" yelled the tower guard.

Two more flares ignited in the sky.

"There he is!" pointed a member of our circle looking out into the perimeter. "There, about thirty yards out!"

The low profile figure of the enemy was barely visible but visible just the same as he froze under the surreal light amidst the concertina wire. A single sapper with the intention of satchel charging a chopper or a hooch full of sleeping soldiers.

We, the *high* and mighty Bikinis of the round order migrated to the edge of the perimeter wire and stood abreast to the sound of twenty-odd M-16s being locked and loaded in near concurrent harmony. As though in response to some prearranged cadence in the form of the continued new year count down – *"5, 4, 3, 2, 1"* - there came simultaneously another bright flare, the outbreak of fire from the M-60 in the tower, and our collective super loads of tracers. The entire impressive bright barrage culminating in a single point of death and destruction from which no creature great or small could possibly hide or survive. It continued until all our newly packed tracer clips were emptied. A mad minute in which over a thousand bright rounds were delivered as much to kill that single enemy as for our own glorious delight to ring in the new year. In the long silence that followed there finally came only a single voice and comment.

"Wow."

CHAPTER 37

INCOGNITO

As the sun rose over the Bikini Beach base the next morning I awakened to a verbal ruckus just outside the window of my small corner room. Dragging myself out the door of the hootch I discovered a group of guys embroiled in a conversation with their First Sergeant.

"You heard me. I want you men to get out there and clean that mess up."

"No way Top. I ain't touching that shit."

"You got that right, man. I'm not messing with that crap either," confirmed another. "No fuckin' way. Call Graves or the ARVNs or somebody. I ain't doin' it."

"You can bust my ass down to Private if you want to Top, but like I said, you're not getting me out there in that shit. Oh hell no. That fuckin' gook can rot."

"God damnit. All you gotta do is dig a hole and shove the shit in it," explained the Top Sergeant.

They all looked down or away, refusing to submit to the order.

The First Sergeant, who didn't look much better in the daylight than he did the previous night, was in the midst of a mutinous dilemma. It seemed he couldn't get any of his men in the unit to go out and clean up the remains of the ill-fated enemy sapper from the night before. Not that there was much to clean up. The poor son of a bitch had been so intensely obliterated with our excessive fire that he now resembled more a large squashed bug or exploded uncooked meatloaf than a man, no more than a large lumpy splotch on the ground that included a few recognizable parts, inclusive of a few vertical strands of meat and clothing dangling from the wire. Hardly enough to be concerned about except for the fact he would probably begin to stink up the entire compound as soon as the wind changed.

I would have thought the sight of him wouldn't have done much for my appetite but surprisingly after a night of indulging the weed in the *high* circle I was craving a substantially large hot breakfast so I left the top soldier with his defiant troops and hit the mess hall for some chow. In the mess while enjoying my breakfast I had an unquenchable thirst for orange juice and put down three glasses. During my morning pig out, maybe as a result of the vitamin C rush, an uncommon clarification of thought led to the oddest realization that I no longer had any purpose. I felt as though I had been tossed onto an obscure island that was somehow divorced from the rest of the war and the chain of command, with a First Sergeant who didn't know or care if I was there or not, and with a group of men and officers who apparently somehow managed to shove all the formal Army bullshit aside and fight the war like a bunch of freelance gunslingers. In a way it was liberating but my status wasn't fully clear to me until I'd spent a few hours sitting in the orderly room with Mueller. It was then I realized I had indeed been made a free agent.

Mueller had little or nothing to do and I had absolutely nothing at all to do except watch him do it. The situation chewed on my nerves until I decided I sure as hell wasn't going to just sit there forever while we both did nothing. It was making for a very long day with the assured realization there were more such days to come. It was during that long day that I realized I had not been given any written transfer orders meaning, I was in affect, a soldier without a home, unassigned and without a purpose. And, I might add, without the desire to bring this to anyone's attention. I came to realize the 170th AHC Bikinis thought I was on loan, an informal TDY, and the Ghostriders thought I had been transferred, exiled. The reason was simple; Capt. Patrick had transferred the guy who writes the transfers, me, which resulted in no transfer being written, therefore I had somehow unintentionally and circumstantially become another Private Clarence Ziederhold, but with full authority to not participate simply because I had no written authority to do so. So I decided to do just that, at least for a while.

"I've got to get back to Holloway for a few days," I told Mueller.

"Sure. No problem," said Mueller "See ya when you get back."

I would have told the First Sergeant, who didn't know I was there in the first place, that I was leaving except he wasn't there, which from what I could tell was par for the course. He had popped in just briefly that morning, asked Mueller if anything was going on to which Mueller gave his standard smiling reply, "Everything's copasetic, Top," to which the top soldier just nodded and bugged out, I presume back to his doggie-son in his short-timer's bunker abode.

I grabbed my stuff and hopped the first chopper out. I was free and though I felt relieved I was already feeling a bit guilty like the time I played hooky for two weeks in seventh grade, but then what the hell, it wasn't like I ripped off a truck, sold it on the black market and then went AWOL living off the proceeds with the enemy in a whorehouse somewhere. I simply thought that if I had to do nothing I could do it much better in familiar circumstances than I could in the foreign confines of the Bikini *Hightimes* Hotel where I could possibly be consumed by an extremely large snake or explosively dissected by some lucky sapper who managed not to get chopped up in the wire.

I had less than a week before the 170th bugged out of Kontum and disbanded, which meant I had that much time to kill before having to return, so I slid back into my old digs on Hollywood Boulevard and laid low for a few days, then to fill the following days picked up a couple of flights as a gunner with the lift platoons. When I returned to Bikini Beach I was surprised to find they had pretty much packed up the entire company and were ready to vacate the very next morning. I was not surprised to discover that no one even noticed I was gone. Again there was nothing for me to do except endure one more night with the smokers around the fire, and what a night it was as damn near every *head* in the unit showed up for a final farewell blowout inclusive of music, food, booze, mass quantities of cannabis, and a continuous parade of hookers. The 170th Bikinis were not passing quietly into the night but instead were taking a psychedelic trip all the way through to the dawn. War is hell.

The sun had barely come over the hills the next morning when the convoy of grumbling trucks started forming up outside the small base. As Mueller and I walked through the compound for the last time and boarded the last deuce-and-a-half heading for the gate I was amazed at how much material was being left behind. The Bikinis had packed up only the essentials relative to the choppers, weapons, primary functions, etc., and left the rest. I figured some

ARVN unit was slated to walk right in and take occupancy but I was wrong. Bunks and mattresses, furniture, phones, filing cabinets, mess equipment, were all now declared useless relics of a departing fighting force and became welcomed fortunes of war by the locals. When the last of us passed through the gate hundreds of Vietnamese poured into the compound like water through a breached damn, spreading out in all directions desperately grabbing and claiming ownership of nearly every piece of junk, furnishings, and equipment that wasn't nailed down and even some that was.

While our convoy sat poised and idling on the road for those last few minutes outside the front gate of Bikini Beach, the now deserted American haven that over the years had served as the satellite domicile of various 52nd CAB chopper units, we watched the Vietnamese shamelessly scramble for our castoffs. Watching first in entertaining amazement then in quiet remorse, somehow realizing that to these people our shed blood meant far less than our possessions, and questioning if it was actually worth it. They didn't line the road to wave farewell with appreciative sorrow or even apprehensive despair about what might happen to them in our absence. Nor did they even acknowledge our presence as we pulled away except to confirm our departure or to weave through our vehicles as they rushed for the open gate. I saw it to be a demonstration of the essence of the national character of Vietnam and as I watched the Bikini Beach sign being knocked off into the dirt from above the gate then tossed in the back of a truck without any expressed interest by the locals, it just might have been the final spurt that filled my give-a-shit bucket to the point of overflowing.

As we pulled away I looked down by the road and watched a group of young boys scramble for cigarettes that some of the guys were tossing from the side of the truck. Then remembering my jeep ride to Holloway as well as that captured film I had watched a lifetime ago at Fort Sill where a similar convoy had been decimated by the enemy, I pulled a clip from my bandoleer and locked it in my M-16. Seeing this, someone chuckled, then Mueller passed me a joint. I accepted the joint, relaxed my weapon, laughed and surrendered my paranoia to fate. I took a hit and passed it on. Our convoy accelerated and rumbled down the road and I leaned back and closed my eyes, letting the weed do its deed. When I exhaled and opened my eyes to the sky there suddenly appeared above us our airborne escort in the form of two Buccaneer hogs and a little boy Loach. They washed over us in a slow low-altitude thunderous roar of throbbing rotor blades and when they did, one of the guys in the truck extended both hands with a peace sign. He was quickly acknowledged with a middle finger salute and a smile by the hog's crew chief as the gun ship peeled off for altitude. The second hog, with its ominous skull and bones nose art, delayed its departure in a dusty hover just long enough for its gunner to drop his drawers and shoot us a moon.

And so this day marked the end of the 170th Assault Helicopter Company Bikinis and Buccaneers. They exited bare ass and flying high, both physically and metaphorically, and the moment pretty much marked the end of my dedication to the Army and the war. My view of the war was now seen through the flowing sands of an imaginary hourglass and it seemed those sands just couldn't flow fast enough.

Shortly after arriving back at Camp Holloway with the men of the 170th I bumped into First Sergeant Buchinsky who was quick to ask me where I was heading now that the 170th had closed out. I told him I hadn't been assigned as yet so he told me to report to the battalion Headquarters Company and that he would be taking over that company as soon as he closed out the Ghostriders. It was then I put in a good word for Mueller, recommending him to Top as his new company clerk because he still had about six months to his DEROS. Mueller got the job. As for myself, all I wanted to do was fly but it wasn't in the cards.

When I checked into the battalion HQ it was another one of those casual paperless orderless walk-ins and they just as casually assigned me to the S-2. Worse than that however was the HQ hooch I was to live in. Unlike my digs with the Ghostriders, it had not been converted to separate rooms though each individuals area had been separated with a wall. That was no big deal except for the fact that it was open to anybody who cared to wander in with the inclination to permanently borrow your goodies. In fact, the area of the hooch I settled in was right next to the door and had been dressed up with bamboo all around, appearing like some sort of

South Pacific beach bar, leaving me to think that some former resident surely had too much time on their hands. The real problem was the cold reception and total indifference I received there. Out of the dozen or more residents of the hooch I received not one introduction or handshake in the first three days I was there. Granted, I wasn't the friendliest guy in the world but to be treated as though I was some kind of NARC or just plain invisible was not quite what I had expected, especially after the many casual months with the Ghostriders and the short lived but overwhelming acceptance by the Bikinis. In a nutshell, there seemed to be a preferred anonymity at the battalion level and living and working in the battalion area felt just like being back in the states, and it pretty much sucked.

To compound my situation my new job at the battalion S-2 Intelligence Office was a total farce. When I walked into the office that first morning I discovered two desks that, except for an old issue of Mad Magazine, were empty of any indication of work in progress, including the In and Out boxes and phones. The office itself was sparse and dull and occupied by only a SP4 who looked up from behind his desk and with as little interest as possible said simply, "What ya need?"

"How ya doing? They told me to come over here and help you out," I said.

My statement seemed to lighten him up and bring him out of his morning stupor. He rose and snatched up his hat then said quickly, "Good. Well, have a seat. If anybody is looking for me tell them I'm out and if anybody calls for the Lieutenant just take a message."

And that was it. He was out the door quicker than I could say 'shitstick'. Leaving me to sit there the entire day doing absolutely nothing. I didn't know who the hell he was or who his Lieutenant was but it didn't matter because no one called, no one entered, and apparently no one cared. I didn't see the SP4 again until the next morning and the next day was the same. As soon as I walked in that morning he walked out. He had never even bothered to introduce himself or explain the functions of the office, or even ask my name. It didn't take any genius on my part to figure out he was using me for an extended vacation and as for the officer assigned to the S-2, whoever he was, well, I just assumed my farcical explanation of the S-offices to Randy on the day we arrived at Holloway was apparently right on the money. On day three when the SP4 at S-2 danced out the door I decided to dance on out the same way. I had no intention of being chumped by a SP4. I had only a few months left in-country and I sure as hell wasn't going to spend it sitting in a nothing office staring at empty desks and waiting for no one to call people I didn't even know, while those same people I didn't know shammed for the duration of their tour. Screw that. Besides, I was still a nonexistent soldier having yet to receive any orders sending me from or to anywhere, which meant I wasn't on anybody's books. And quite frankly, I pretty much just didn't care anymore.

In my exodus from the S-2 I came across Jimmy Mueller and filled him in on my hooch situation only to be answered with his usual smile and a remedy.

"Man I got a whole damn hooch all to myself," he laughed. "Just down the hill from the mess hall across from the BOQ. There's empty hooches all over the place now since they started phasing down. All you gotta do is move into one. Hell, why don't you just move in with me?"

It didn't take much persuasion. I transferred into his hooch in as short a time as it took to move my gear and Mueller and I started setting up housekeeping. With the number of troops that were shipping out we had no trouble scrounging, buying, or confiscating comfort items such as a TV, stereo and tape player, a full size refrigerator, fans, hammocks, extra mattresses, hotplates and skillets, and a fully stocked bar. For décor we came by wall art in the form of psychedelic posters, a parachute we hung from the ceiling, survival kit strobe lights for affect, and even a lava lamp. We had settled in with all the comforts of home, ready to fight the war if for no other reason now than to defend our luxury crib. We called it the Holriday Inn, mocking the oriental language. As for the HQ Company and S-2, I was out of sight and out of mind, an anonymous ghost soldier much like my old pal Gas at the 189th, or as they say, incognito. Teaming up with Jimmy Mueller, however, would prove to be a social change I had not anticipated, for Jimmy Boy had brought with him from Kontum or Indiana the traditions of the *High Circle* and the party had just begun.

Jimmy was one of those guys who could somehow sniff out all the angles, short cuts, or anything else that would make his life easier and more enjoyable, especially when it came to obtaining his much loved weed. Soon after setting up house he obtained a shopping bag full of primo pot at the going rate of $5. To me it looked like overkill, enough stuff to last two wars, but Mueller had an angle that justified the quantity. It seemed he rolled, flattened and inserted two joints each day into letters he mailed home and sometimes to friends back in Indiana. He'd been doing this since he arrived in-country and according to his wife had already accumulated quite a stash that awaited his return. What didn't get rolled and mailed he separated into three leaf sizes, some for rolling, some for pipes, and the smallest of which, being nothing more than a fine powder, was used while cooking our hot plate gulasch, a popular pig out cuisine that usually consisted of a mix of C-Rations, Lurps, canned goodies from home, and whatever we scarfed or pilfered from the mess hall or purchased from a PX somewhere. Our creative gulasch, often laced with Mueller's magic powder, meant that those occasional evening meals were quite a treat, always making it necessary to cook a lot because the more you ate the more you wanted to eat.

Between the two of us and visiting former Ghostriders and Bikinis, it seemed nearly each night became a party. For those nights when there actually was only the two of us under the influence of food or smoke, after surviving an uncontrollable case of the giggles followed by a heavy conversation dealing with the philosophies and wonders of the universe, we would lay back in a mild stupor listening to long mellow or heavy rock albums such as Hot Buttered Soul by Isaac Hayes, Santana or something just as mind bending, and always seeming to end with the Chambers Brothers long recording of Time Has Come Today. For those special times Mueller had made another purchase. It was when I accompanied him on a long jeep ride into the boonies where we came upon a little old mama-san standing on the side of the road. Mueller whipped out five bucks in MPC and mama-san reached down into the crotch of her black silk pants and pulled out what appeared to be a regular pack of Salem menthol filter cigarettes still in the original cellophane wrapping as though they had just popped out of a machine.

"Tell me we didn't risk our asses coming out here just for a damn pack of cigarettes," I said. "Especially a pack of smokes that cost five bucks. You know you can get a carton of those things for a buck and a half at the PX."

Mueller laughed as he opened the pack and withdrew one of the smokes that was in appearance just the same as any other Salem filter cigarette except, as he pointed out, for a few small splotches of brown on the paper.

"No sweat, Fusco. Everything's copasetic. What we have here is a pack of OJs,' he laughed. "Pot rolled in opium, and it's the sweetest natural high in the Nam."

"That's it?" I questioned. "Five bucks for that. You got a shopping bag full of that shit for the same money."

"Just keep an open mind, my man. You'll see."

Mueller lit up and after a few totes we started driving casually down the road. A few more and we were exceptionally high and happy. He was right about the OJs. It seemed just one or two hits were like smoking an entire joint of normal pot except seriously more mellow. I'm sure that if a few of these had been passed around the table at the Paris Peace Talks the war would have ended long ago. Soon everything seemed to be funny, from the bumps in the road and the people, chickens and pigs, to our attempts to harmonize old Beatles songs without tripping over our lips. Then after driving for what seemed to be forever, it finally dawned on me that we were in unfamiliar surroundings, not that any surroundings would have seemed familiar after the consumption of an OJ.

"Hey man, you know where you're going?" I asked.

"Oh, hell yeah. Um... No, not really. Isn't this the road to Pleiku?"

"I don't know. Is it?" I replied.

"I don't know. Is it?"

"You know it's gonna get dark. I really don't want to be out here in the dark."

"I think it's up that way," said Mueller, though not with a great deal of confidence.

"You sure?"

"Yeah. No."

Driving out of a gradual curve we came upon two Vietnamese men standing near the shoulder of the road. One had just finished taking a piss as Mueller brought the jeep to a stop at their side.

"Hey, how ya doin," he smiled. "Is this the road to Pleiku?"

It may have been the effects of the OJ, but it seemed they were extremely slow in responding and for the longest time they seemed perplexed. When they did finally speak it was to each other in Vietnamese. Then another Vietnamese man came out from behind some brush. He carried a long brown canvas sack and extended a laser like stare of contempt at Mueller as he approached.

"Pleiku?" repeated Mueller with a broad stoner smile. "Where is Pleiku? Holloway. Camp Holloway?"

One of the men nodded his head yes then addressed the man who had just approached from the bush. We had no idea what he was saying but it seemed he was surprised that we had stopped and asked directions.

"Hey man, if you can't help us just say so, okay. We don't have all day here, ya know," said Mueller with his usual charming smile and chuckle.

The man with the bag frowned, saying something to the other. The two men were obviously in disagreement about something and while we waited the third man slowly worked his way around to my side of the jeep. He motioned with his fingers to his lips while saying, "G.I. smoke? G.I. smoke?"

I smiled and withdrew my cigarettes from my pocket and popped one up for him. I offered him a light but he refused and slid the cigarette into his shirt pocket, then slowly backed away from the jeep and turned his attention to the animated conversation taking place on Mueller's side of the road. In the midst of the exchange the one man lowered the sack from his back to the ground and out of the top could be seen the barrels of two AK-47 riffles.

"Wooo shit," said Mueller. "You see what I see?"

"Yeah," I answered.

"Man, this ain't exactly copasetic."

About that time one of the Vietnamese men grabbed for the bag only to have it pulled away and even though we were slow-witted due to the OJ, we weren't so out of it that we couldn't figure out what was taking place. Obviously these guys weren't your average local yokels and they most likely didn't want to draw attention to the fact, especially in front of Americans. It was also obvious that one of those guys didn't like us very much and wanted to do something about it. Fortunately he wasn't the one with the guns. It all seemed to happen at once yet due to Mueller's newly purchased Salem Menthols it happened in slow motion as though it were some outer body experience. The argumentative Vietnamese pulled at the bag and this time he won and out came one of the AK-47s. Seeing this I turned to find the man on my right reaching for a knife. I reached for my M-16 that was resting on the floor between the seats but before I could bring it up Mueller threw the jeep into gear, popped the clutch, and we shot away like a spooked horse.

"Are they gonna shoot?! Are they gonna shoot?!" yelled Mueller as he swerved down the road.

I flipped the safety off my weapon, turned and aimed back at the small roadside gang only to hold back my fire at what I saw.

"Shoot! You gotta shoot!" yelled Mueller.

"No. Look," I replied.

Mueller looked over his shoulder then brought the jeep to an idling halt. We sat and watched as the three Vietnamese men rolled around in the dirt at the side of the road. It was a chicken fight, full of constant high-pitched chatter, legs and limbs flailing, and AK-47s flying in all directions. It was cartoonesque, eventually bringing both of us to laughter. When Mueller turned for a better view his foot slipped off the clutch and the jeep jumped and stalled out causing us to laugh even harder, but at the sound of our laughter the three Vietnamese stooges broke apart and now having whipped up their anger among themselves, they decided to redirect it in our direction. They retrieved their weapons, got to their feet and started our way.

"Wooo shit!" exclaimed Mueller as he quickly turned back to the wheel.

"I think we better go," I said, still laughing.

The jeep churned then churned again but wouldn't start.

"Woooo shit!"

Churn. Churn.

"Wooo shit!" repeated Mueller with a nervous laugh.

Churn. Churn.

"That's not funny," I laughed. "Start the damn thing."

Churn. Churn.

"WOOO SHIT!"

"They're gonna shoot," I said nervously, and for some reason still laughing. "They're raising their weapons. They're coming. Start the fuckin' jeep."

"WOOO SHIT! Do something Fusco! Shoot 'em!"

The men were now running up the road, quickly closing the fifty yards between us. I rose and turned in my seat, brought my weapon to bear, aimed and pulled the trigger and... nothing happened.

"Wooo shit," I said, realizing I forgot to put a round in the chamber, and for some reason even that seemed comical. I laughed again, yanked back and released the bolt injecting a round and just as I was about to pull the trigger the jeep cranked up and lurched backward, slamming me into the windshield. Then just as abruptly Mueller jammed it into a forward gear and it lurched forward. I rolled over the back of my seat and nearly flipped out onto the road. Each time Mueller slammed the stick into one of its three gears he jammed the gas pedal to the floor.

"WOOO SHIT!" I heard him say between each brief burst of AK fire that whizzed over our heads. When we were clear and away I climbed back into my seat and for a long moment neither of us said anything. Then came one of Mueller's signature chuckles. Then another. Then we both laughed uncontrollably until one of us, and under the influence I wasn't sure who, said, "I'm hungry."

<hr />

It was near evening when we finally found our way back to Camp Holloway, turned in the jeep, and made our way back to the Holriday Inn. After we ate Mueller was quick to light up another OJ that led to Isaac Hayes music and our retreating to the top of the tin roof of our hooch to take advantage of a current breeze and cool off. It was near dusk and turned into a time of reflection as we laid back and took in the sunset. We talked about the prominence of luck and fate in war, decided we had neither, then resolved to depend on it just the same. Occasionally we checked to see if either of us still had a pulse. Like Mueller said, those OJs were a serious natural high, leaving its consumer in an extremely near comatose mellow.

In the far distance we could just make out the silhouette of a mountain where we saw some flashes followed by the muffled sound of explosions. On closer inspection we saw it was the Vietnamese Air Corps Skyraiders diving in and dumping their arsenal on whatever bad guys decided to make that particular hill their new home. It was Dragon Mountain situated to the south of Holloway, a single massive protrusion reaching alone into the sky amid the miles of flat land surrounding us. I had flown near it a number of times and I could see along its slopes the carcases of many aircraft, going back to the French when a DC-3 plowed into it trying to get to Pleiku. There were also the remnants of a few helicopters that had their altimeters set wrong and their pilots thought they were above the mountain while returning to Pleiku. Dragon Mountain was our own Bermuda Triagle that acted as both a landmark to guide our aircraft and sometimes a magnet to destroy them. The mountain supposedly got its name because it was often engulfed by a mist referred to as the *fire of the Dragons,* and it was from that mountain and that myth that the 52nd CAB's name, the Flying Dragons, was taken in 1967.

"I hear those guys are pretty good," I said.

"Yeah, I've heard that. Also heard they were pretty stupid."

"You mean stupid like driving around in the boonies while you're stoned stupid?"

"No. More like gung ho kind of stupid. Like that guy right there going down on the mountain. Watch."

I watched and noticed that each time those John Wayne Special prop jobs dove on the mountainside they waited a little longer to pull out of the dive, as though they were teasing or challenging the physics of flight. Then the temporary glare of a napalm drop lit up the side of the mountain and highlighted the approach of yet another Spad as it dove down for a drop. The Skyraider closed the distance then, without the slightest hint or attempt at a pull out, it just slammed into the side of the dragon in a bright ball mix of napalm and aviation fuel.

"Wooo, far out!" said Mueller with a laugh and applause. "See, told you they were stupid. Right on, dude."

"Right on? Um, is that for the good guys or for the bad guys?"

"Does it matter?" asked Mueller, handing me the OJ. "They're all Gooks."

"Guess not," I said as I took another toke.

After things settled down on the distant mountain we stretched back to take in the stars and ponder the universe, speaking intelligently, we thought, of the dichotomy of the existence of such beauty in the midst of the ugliness of war. Then just as the discussion slowed and slid into the consequences of both our shotgun marriages, there came across the sky a shooting star followed quickly by another.

"Two... two that close together. Got to mean good luck or something," said Mueller.

"Maybe," I said.

"Hey look, there's another one," said Mueller.

The third star wasn't a star at all but a rocket that impacted with a frightening WHOMPH slap dab in the center of the big PSP active helipad in front of the main hanger, followed quickly by another that struck further down the runway. BOOM! On came the base siren as various sections of the perimeters opened fire. Mueller and I just sat there and took it all in from our perch high on the roof, the tracers going out and the occasional flashing distant thump of a rocket being launched to stream in overhead and culminate in a brief lethal flash and explosion. Choppers scrambled, men scrambled, and trucks rolled for the perimeter bunker line while we just laid back, divorced from the war, watching as though we were kicked back in the balcony of the Circle Theater in Annapolis, chewing on a box of cool Junior Mints and sipping a nickel coke.

"Wow, man. You see that?"

"Yeah."

"Think we ought to get in a bunker or something?"

"Nah. Can hear the music better up here."

"Yeah."

"Besides, I don't think I can move."

"Yeah. Me neither."

BOOM!

"Wow."

"I'm hungry. You hungry? I'm hungry."

CHAPTER 38

THE COMA CURE

I was kicked back in my hammock, eyes closed, absorbing some music on my newly acquired used reel-to-reel recorder, when Coma appeared over me like a silent ghost in a dream. In fact, I thought at first it was a dream because I had just seen him the night before at the club and for some reason he had stuck in my mind. He was sitting near the far wall a few tables away within earshot, alone with his bourbon and beer, watching the others and me with interest. A few of us former Ghostriders had come together to celebrate Dillinger's upcoming DEROS. Dillinger was now officially grounded with less than a week to go but somewhere around our fourth round of beer he finally confessed that he had decided to extend and finish out his enlistment here instead of in the states. He said he didn't want to put up with the stateside crap and needed the flight and combat pay anyway. But I didn't buy that.

"You sure Chief Chief hasn't been messing with your head?" I asked him.

"Hell no," he said. "Not Chief Chief. He wouldn't do that. In fact, he chewed my ass for it. I just... well, you know. And besides, how bad can it be? Everything's winding down. The gooks are taking over. Piece of cake, right?"

"No, I don't know," I said.

"Besides, I'm going to college when I get out and I'll need the extra money for the old lady and the kid until my VA kicks in."

"Makes sense to me," said Randy.

"Are you going to extend?" I asked Randy.

"Hell no. I ain't crazy."

"My point exactly."

I knew Dillinger's motives weren't as he stated. He was cut from the same cloth as Chief Chief, and like some others of us, had mixed feelings about heading home. Few of us liked it in Vietnam and even fewer liked the war, but for many of us who possessed the awareness to think about what we were suppose to be doing, there existed that little inner nudge reminding us that we were not quite finished, a feeling that leaving friends behind to try and complete the job was somehow troubling. Some, like Dillinger and Chief Chief, gave in to the nudge.

"You and I are going to be short soon," Randy reminded me. "Hell, as far as I'm concerned, we're short right now. Just over five more weeks, Vince. Do you realize that? We've just got five plus weeks to go, man. That's short, right?"

"Yeah, I guess it is," I agreed. "Especially if you started counting down on day one."

"Yeah, from day 365. Day one of your tour. Seems like a long time ago."

"No. I mean way back, day one."

"What do you mean?" asked Dillinger.

"I mean being short is what it's all about. You know. Surviving."

"I'm not gettin' ya," said Dillinger. "What the hell does short have to do with survival?"

"Short? It's all about the short. That's how you survive this man's Army, by understanding the short of it all. You start being short from the day they swear you in, and between that day and your last day you get shorted ten ways from Sunday; shorted on respect and dignity, patience and time, information, training, understanding, tolerance, women, hot water, short arm inspections, short-changed on payday, a shortened life expectancy, and lots of short sighted, short minded, short little bastards with short person complexes telling you what the hell you can and can't do. Shit, even the enemy is short. Hell, the short shit runs so deep in the United States Army you can hardly keep your head above it to breathe. That is unless… unless you stay focused on the most important short of them all."

"Meaning what?" asked Randy.

"Life… and death," I said. "Life's just too damn short. Too short to make mistakes. Too short to be really happy and too short for honest misery. Everything is temporary. In that way it screws you over, makes everything too damn fast. And then you throw in a war and it's just too fuckin' short altogether. Especially if you get dead."

"You're starting to sound like an angry man," said Dillinger.

I was pretty much feeling the influence of the beer now, not to mention the few hits of pot I shared with Mueller before the guys collected me and we headed for the club. I glanced over to find Coma was still in attendance and was focused intently on our conversation. He offered a knowing smile, finished his bourbon, then departed the club.

So now Coma was where I lay in a half sleep in my hammock. I opened my eyes to discover him hovering above me, staring down curiously, an extended version of that quick assessing look you might get from a new coach on try-out day. I lay there letting my eyes focus and my mind distinguish the real from the imagined. When he decided my mind had cleared up enough he began to dump gear on my chest, my weapons, ammo, boots… and a set of strange tiger fatigues.

"You got thirty minutes to report to the Pathfinder ready hooch," he said. "Take a cold shower with these duds on. Don't use any soap or shampoo. Don't brush your teeth with toothpaste. Don't shave. Don't eat anything you have here or anything from the mess hall. That's thirty minutes as per the battalion CO. You copy that?"

I half nodded a foggy yes and he turned and exited as quietly as he had entered. No soap, no food. A shower with my cloths on? What the hell was he talking about? Battalion CO's orders?

What it was was a fast and furious induction into the world of the grunt, catching me about as unaware as anyone could possibly be. I noticed the tiger fatigues he left me were used and obviously worn. I put them on and as instructed took a shower - no soap, no shave. It woke me up and cleared my head even more than the shock of the order. I began to wonder just what the hell was really going on. Had I been found out and transferred to the Pathfinders as punishment or what? And what the hell did they think would qualify me for duty with the Pathfinders in the first place. Those guys were all gung ho Airborne types.

When I arrived, damp but cleansed, there were only three others in the ready hooch being, Coma, a guy named Farmer, and a Montagnard squatting on the floor in the corner cooking some kind of stinky gook stuff in a hot plate. The hooch itself was void of any creature comforts except for a few bunks and a small table. It was located in an area intentionally isolated from the rest of the battalion. Coma seemed to be the one in charge though neither of them wore any rank.

"Okay, get this," he told me as I strolled in with my gear. "This is an isolation ready hooch. You don't so much as shit, piss, fart, or even finger fuck, outside this hooch for the next 24 hours. You don't wash or introduce any foreign hygienic substance to your body or clothing. You do not smoke. You can eat whenever you're hungry but you can eat only what this Yard here fixes, which is a choice between Vietnamese rice and shit or Vietnamese rice and shit. And you drink only water. You're watch and rings get left behind or secured in your pocket, or taped and subdued. In other words, nothing shines and nothing chimes. You will dark-tape all loose metal on your weapons and gear, including your dog tags, one of which you will secure on and behind the lace of your right boot. His instructions continued until they led to the complete breakdown and cleaning of my weapons in the midst of which I finally popped the question.

"Okay, damnit, what the hell is going on? Is this some kind of a joke or training thing or what? Is this permanent? Because if it is, you got the wrong boy. I'm just a damn clerk."

"You're an air crewman. A gunner. Right?" said Coma.

"Yeah."

"And you're trained and qualified in ED. Explosives. Right?"

I hesitated, "Yeah, but…"

"You shot expert and graduated third in your battalion at Bragg. Right?"

"Yeah, so?"

"That puts you on the backup list. When the Pathfinders are short we pull from the list. We got a big op and we're short and you're on the list."

"List my ass. I'm still just a clerk. What about all the SPs in this battalion? They're all grunts aren't they and I'm just a clerk."

"Not today you're not. Today you're a Pathfinder and your ass is mine," he laughed. "Don't worry. It's only a one shot deal."

"Yeah, well, it only takes one shot and it's that one shot I'm worried about."

"You got more worries than that," said Sid Farmer, comfortably stretched out on his bunk.

"What? What worries?" I asked.

"Tell him, Coma," said Farmer.

Coma leaned back against the wall and smiled then sat and while inspecting and reassembling my freshly cleaned .45, he lowered the hammer - that's the psychological hammer not the .45.

"You're a marked man, Fusco," he informed me. "Seems there's a few brothers who have decided you're not going to go home upright. They're out to get your ass and the talk is soon. Something about some guy you sent to LBJ. Do you know a big bear of a black guy named Samson Wheeler?"

"Samson? Sure I know Samson. But why the hell would Samson want to get me. I mean we're okay, we're friends."

"No. It's Samson who's covering your ass. Him and the Sergeant Major go way back and the Sergeant Major is Buchinsky's roommate. Seems you got friends in high places. Starting to get the picture. Anyway, Samson mentioned he heard you were on a hit list so we cooked up this little job here to get you off campus for a bit."

"So what good is that going to do? They'll be here when I get back."

"It takes you out of range while Samson deals with the problem," said Farmer.

"What's he going to do?"

"He didn't say and I didn't ask," said Coma. "There's some things better not known. Just think of him as your guardian angel. Oh, and he said something about you owing him a case of beer. If he takes care of this little problem I'd suggest you give him a little more than a case of beer. Actually, I think he's partial to Jimmy Beam."

"I don't get it. Why would he do this for me?"

"He says you're the guru, a righteous dude. That you take care of your own, and something about butterflies that eat shit. I didn't quite get all that but what the hell."

Coma went on to explain that I would be out of circulation for at least three days if things went well, or possibly forever if they didn't, then after kicking the Yard out of the hootch he explained the mission. In his words it was simple. The three of us were to be deposited a safe distance from an area designated as an LZ for an upcoming troop drop in Kontum province. We were to make our way to the LZ, set ourselves up in an observatory formation, then wait and watch for 24 hours. If it was determined the LZ was safe, then we would clear it by blowing any trees or obstructions that would interfere with the chopper landings and then guide them in, a quick company size insertion. There would be no mad minute or leading artillery barrage to give away the troop drop, which was one of three other concurrent drops of company size ARVN units intended to encircle and surprise a newly discovered cluster of NVA who had moved in from the west and set up housekeeping. A quick and dirty three company ambush, if there was such a thing.

"We'll be the first in, last out," said Coma. "Just business as usual."

"It's Army PR bullshit," injected Farmer. "Instead of just blowing the hell out of the bastards some dumb shit decided it was a good chance for the ARVNs to prove their incompetence - again. Nothin' like getting people killed for the hell of it."

"Walk in the park," laughed Coma. "Just another day at the office, right Fusco? A clerk with a few extra talents like yours shouldn't have any problems."

It's amazing how much you can learn about a person when you're locked up in a hooch together for 24 hours. The isolation period was required for mission security and preparation, and the purging of all the everyday odors that permeate the average American soldier, those simple things that we long ago learned to ignore and dismiss from our immediate senses like soap, shaving cream and after shave, smokes, the milk or coffee you had with breakfast, the chewing gum you had after a meal, or any other non-indigenous food you've had during the past few days.

"When you're in one spot for too long the bad guys can smell you a mile away and they'll be on you like flies on shit," said Coma.

Farmer spoke little and it seemed Coma was mysterious and guarded, particularly when it came to exposing himself personally, including his real name or how he came by the handle Coma. Rumor around camp was he had died in combat but luckily while his body was being moved to graves registration to be processed and shipped home it was discovered he was actually in a coma from which he recovered a few days later. Someone else said simply that he was a walking dead man, pushing his luck by extending for a third tour. He wanted to go a fourth round but the

Army turned him down. Most discussion originated by him was instructional, almost fatherly, direct and to the point, but sincere and caring. After 24 hours our relationship was comfortable and I felt I had known him all my life, yet, I actually knew very little about him other than what I had heard through the grape vine.

Okay it's true, the guy was a little on the strange side. No, check that, he was just friggin' spooky sometimes, but that didn't seem to matter because I somehow knew I could trust him, and after all he was a legend, and he was that kind of guy, the kind that was always there for anybody anytime. Hell, the war was full of guys like that. They came and went and they came in all shapes and sizes, and they came with varied idiosyncrasies and mentalities, the guys you least expected to come through but somehow always did. Guys like Dillon who didn't even look like a soldier. They didn't blow their own horn or beat their own drum, they just took it all in stride and rolled along with everything the war and the Army could throw at them. Back in the world Coma would have been the kind of guy who put out fires and saved babies, or repaired downed power lines in the middle of a storm, or had no qualms at all about stopping on a dark deserted road in the middle of the night to help a stranger. He was just plain capable and dependable and fearless, one of the good guys that made you feel safe and secure just knowing he was around. And he was a quiet guy, uncomplicated as most folks go. Yet, somehow in addition to all that he had become a combat zone philosophical psycho - if that were at all possible - meaning the reality of the war had done its deed just enough to leave him dealing with Vietnam in a way most of us wouldn't or couldn't understand. Yeah, I know all that sounds conflicting. Hell, we were all conflicted, more than conflicted actually. Not that any of us would admit it. That was the character of the war and it's influence on us. It's just that some of us dealt with it differently, perceived it differently, and wore it differently than others. In fact you could say a lot of us were just plain fucked up and didn't even know it.

For Coma this damn war wasn't political or ideological, or religious or even vengeful. He didn't give a damn about communism versus democracy or even the prospect that the entire Vietnam show had become a giant political circle jerk and just plain pointless mismanaged insanity. Instead, he boiled it all down to its lowest denominator, determining his entire dogma to be somehow completely encapsulated and expressed in two simple little words being, "fuck it," a phrase he used sparingly. And an occasional shorter version still, being simply, "shit," that he used more frequently. And then there was that thing with the Cheerios. I heard about that. What the hell was that? I mean, who sees their destiny and their future in a bowl of Cheerios. Okay, so at least he eats the Cheerios after he reads them and that's more than you can say about some mystic doodah with tealeaves or a bag of voodoo bones. But who the hell would even think to look for wisdom and fate in the tiny little bubbles inside the tiny little holes in the middle of tiny little oatsy donuts floating around in a bowl of milk.

But that was Coma. Yeah, what can I say? He was the village shaman and the village idiot and a combat Albert Einstein all wrapped in one. And though you'd expect someone with a handle like that to be weird, he was instead so damn focused and proficient in the face of the enemy that those simple give-a-shit words of his seemed to ring hollow and insincere, just so much spurious bullshit like the perpetual smile on a politician or a pasty faced preacher, and like them, somehow captivating if for no other reason than simple curiosity. Depending on the occasion, his one or two word utterances could imply something sensible or nothing at all, or on the other hand, something so profound as to mean just about everything - to him at least. Confusing right? Hence the enigma of his very existence and his name, *Coma*. So what if everybody thought he was fugazi, it didn't make any difference to him. Even the Vietnamese waitress at the club said he was "beaucoup dien cai dau", meaning he was crazy, but he just didn't give a shit what anybody thought and it worked. It kept everybody, and I mean everybody off his case, giving him complete autonomy. He was a necessary evil and a necessary blessing, and he was in their Army and he was in their war, but he was in on his own terms, sort of one of those non-problem-problems that the higher-ups never want to admit to. Coma *was* Vietnam and he was the envy of all who knew him, which is why everybody avoided him.

After a complete final refresher course on explosives procedures, we packed up, each of us humping about 40 pounds of det cord, C-4, and caps, along with a full compliment of ammo, flares, and grenades. Coma carried the only radio along with his

M-16 and M-79 thumper. With no helmets or flak jackets we were "Going Hollywood,'" as Farmer put it. "So don't try stopping any bullets,"

Sporting boonie hats, camo faced, and loaded to the hilt, we were then jeeped over to the Christmas tree where we hopped an awaiting chopper. Looking at the two of them I had difficulty visualizing myself as part of the trio, as something even resembling the special ops guys we often dumped in the middle of nowhere, and I wasn't sure I was comfortable with it, though, admittedly there was a tinge of excitement in my gut. We were off and once we were in the air I was surprised that I hadn't thought about the time. I then noticed evening was approaching and I thought it an odd time to begin a mission but it turns out, as requested by Coma, the timing was just right. He was familiar with the turf and had timed everything out.

Once we had been inserted we were quick to make our way to the proposed landing zone nearly thirty minutes away on foot, during which time that 40 pounds-plus began to feel like a hundred. "Stay with me," were my only instructions from Coma as we swiftly, quietly, and carefully made our way through the bush, he taking the lead and Farmer the rear. The target LZ was an odd shape, much like that of an eggplant, sloping and narrowing to a broad neck at one end. Coma picked my spot in the shadows on the east side at the edge of the jungle canopy that offered me a full view of the entire perimeter, a near hundred-yard area. Farmer would dig in among some lower bush opposite me on the other side of the LZ, and Coma was to take the higher ground among some small trees at the narrow end of the upper neck.

After I dug my hole Coma helped cover and camouflage my location then quickly departed, leaving me alone with my thoughts and fears, both of which increased as the sun set behind the mountains. Wait, watch, and listen were my instructions. "Don't move, don't do anything until I come back for you," said Coma. "If any one of us comes under fire the other two go and help. Then we aid and evade to an extraction point. Copy?"

"Sure, no problem," I told him. How bad could it be? I thought. What are the chances of running into anybody out here in the middle of nowhere? As the hours passed I thought of Samson and the brothers who wanted me dead, and for what, just because I was white and happened to be Butterfield's escort? The entire thing was ridiculous but real nonetheless. I also thought about my marriage that shouldn't be, the child I shouldn't have but loved, and of course, the war that maybe I should or shouldn't be in. I thought about it all, the right and wrong decisions, volunteering for Vietnam, the people I missed and loved, and the people I hated.

It was dark, damn dark, black as the Devil's own soul and without a star in the sky - not that I could even see any sky. Then I heard it, then silence, and then I heard it again. Voices. NVA voices. I'm dead, I thought to myself as I huddled alone in the dark. Sure as shit I'm a dead man. Stupid and dead and I probably deserve it because I'm a damn fool, I thought.

"Think of it as a woman," he told me back at the hooch. "Ease right into her until you're ready to get your rocks off. Then you know you're in control, that you own the night and it's working for you."

A woman? Shit!

He warned me. He said it would be freaky, to not dwell on it, to just embrace it. But I honestly didn't think the night could get so dark and I sure as hell didn't think something as harmless as the absence of light could be so damn unnerving. I put my hand in front of my face and brought it in until it touched my nose and still I couldn't see it. Okay Fusco, so it's dark, so what? You've spent nights alone in the woods and hills hunting and messing around when you were a kid and it was no big deal. Yeah, that's what I told myself but it wasn't comforting because this was different, these hills and mountains were full of death. So maybe I was a little hypersensitive. Who the hell wouldn't be?

But... embrace it? Shit!

Maybe Coma could embrace it. As for me, well hell, I wasn't him. I was too far removed from his universe to accept his soul-searching character crash course and I was getting too damned short to even want to try. Twenty-nine days and a wake-up, just twenty-nine more days and I would be on the freedom bird heading home, away from the Abbot and Costello world of the Army and the primordial ignorance of Vietnam. So how and why the hell he dragged my ass out here I'll never know. Was it really Samson's idea or was he messing with my psyche, brain fucking me for some unknown reason like I was his personal lab rat or rhesus monkey.

Me, the resident Ghostrider psychotherapist and Godfather of conscience and comfort, had somehow become the orphaned patient. I had seen him there in the club that night and I saw the wheels turning in his head but it didn't sink in... until now. I couldn't have expected something like this.

I could imagine him over there somewhere, crouched in his camouflaged hole, laughing to himself as he visualized me quivering in the dark alone, wide eyed and scared shitless, experiencing some kind of life revealing epiphany. Hell, I didn't want that crap. I was just a pencil, a damn clerk and de facto door gunner. Sure I'd seen my share of shit and I had to deal with it like everybody else, but for some reason this gun-toting guru thought I needed an introspective adjustment, a spiritual tune-up. The weird thing is he was probably right. With all the recent events of my life, I had reached a point to where I didn't know if I was coming or going. There in the pitch-black night of the central highlands of Vietnam my mind had no problem at all wondering or wandering or even running wild, racing in every direction including the past. Racing so damn fast I could hardly keep up. It was like the household cat parked its ass on the selector button of the family slide projector sending a hundred flashing memories into non-stop auto. And above it all I could hear things, all kinds of things. I could hear the NVA and the bastards were getting closer. It was spooky as hell. And I could hear other things that weren't even there. I could even hear my own blood rushing through my brain right along side the hundred family slides flashing from the past. It was a hell of a reality rush, bizarre, fast and furious, yet slow, surreal, and frightening, like running a sixty-yard punt return in front of a screaming crowd that you can't hear for the sound of your own heartbeat and heavy breathing. Suddenly each second seemed like a minute and each minute like an hour. It was frightening yet wonderfully exhilarating, giving me some kind of sick twisted satisfaction in knowing I was going against every natural instinct of well-being and survival, defying fate and a violent death. It was a rush.

Shit! Sure as hell, we're dead.

So there I huddled, hidden in a dirty little hole, wrapped in 40 pounds of explosives, hugging an M 16, embracing the harsh whore of darkness, and wondering just how the hell I had gotten there in the first place. Not there in a dark covered hole scoping out an LZ, but there in that damn country, in that life, in that dark hole of my soul. Suddenly I was thinking about who I was, what I was, and where I was, not to mention just how much longer I would survive to be whomever or whatever or wherever I was. And it all seemed unfair, like I hadn't lived long enough to experience or know any of these things in the first place, as though I was too unqualified to die. And I knew I shouldn't be thinking that shit because it wasn't the time and certainly wasn't the place. Maybe Coma was right. Maybe I did need a reality fix if for no other reason than to learn to turn everything on and off at will and live in the moment, focusing on nothing but life and death... on survival. What was it he said; "You either can or you can't - so fuck the rest and move on."

Then just as suddenly I remembered Leroy. For me Vietnam had all begun with Leroy. How was Leroy? Where was Leroy? Had there ever even been a Leroy? Shit, I was losing it! And I didn't even know what it was I was losing. Typical, just fuckin' typical, as Chief Chief would say.

I hadn't thought of Leroy since my first day in the Army. In fact, I hadn't thought much about anything other than myself and what appeared in front of me. That's what the Army does to you, especially in a combat zone - if you care, that is. If you actually give a shit it makes all things, emotions and actions, immediate, and though you occasionally think about family, friends, and home, they remain distant in your mind because you know they're safe in another world, another universe. Leroy? Hell, no matter how screwed up Leroy was at least he was in that other universe, safe and sound except maybe in his own mind.

My immediate problem was the voices. The little voices in my head and the North Vietnamese voices coming out of the bush, coming ever closer which now included the sounds of footsteps and the rustle and thump of weapons and gear. Shit! They were all around me!

It was a patrol. An NVA patrol, I thought, and they were damn near standing on top of me. How many I couldn't even guess but judging from the spread of their presence I thought it had to be a dozen or more. At first I didn't breathe, I couldn't. Not because I was being stealthy but because I was intensely frightened with desperate defensive options and possibilities running through my mind faster than I could evaluate them. Stay put, he said. Rescue and evade, he said. He didn't say shit about being so closely encircled by enemy gooks that they could shit in your ear. What do I do? If I run I'm dead. If I shoot I'm dead. If I so much as fart or sniffle, I'm dead. I leaned ever so slowly and quietly back against my hole, rested my M-16 against my shoulder, gently removed a grenade from my webbing, and very very slowly and quietly drew my .45 from its holster. That was it. That was all I could do to be ready for whatever was going to happen next. Other than that, it was just a matter of waiting, but for what? Waiting for them to leave or for Coma and Farmer to return? That's assuming they were still alive. But I hadn't heard any shots so they must be alive. That means I stay put. Shit Fusco, I told myself, you think too damn much. Just shut it off. Just shut it the hell off and sit tight.

The NVA spoke among themselves for a while with one voice of authority dominating most of the conversation. Naturally I didn't have a clue as to what they were saying but apparently they were dividing and spreading out as I heard some of them tread away in various directions. They were us, the same as us, I thought. They were doing the same thing, spreading out to observe the LZ. Or were they setting up an ambush? Were there more of them, I wondered. More of them parked right on top of Coma and Farmer? Were they surrounding the LZ? If so then they knew about the drop and we were sitting right in the middle of another intelligence breach. For a second I flashed back to old papa-son stuffing intel reports into his drawers at the burn barrel. How many like him were there throughout the system? Secretaries, hooch maids, even ARVN soldiers and officers, and janitors like old Papa-son. Then just as quickly I remembered Cleveland Dooley. Wasn't this what happened to him, what screwed with his mind and sent him over the edge? I can't be Dooley, I thought. I won't be Dooley. If these bastards piss on me I'll blow their shit away. Nobody is going to piss on me, especially some damn gook. Then suddenly a comical thread ran through my mind and I imagined Randy curled up in this hole instead of me. Randy, with his nervous little Randy dance and fear of all things non-human and non-urban, and it brought a nervous smile to the corner of my mouth. Ironically it was somehow comforting. Then there was

Dillon and Chief Chief and Top and even folks from home. It was
an imaginary parade that gave me an odd feeling of security, as
though they were all there surrounding me, protecting me. Once
again something told me I would be okay, that no matter what
happened I would come out of it okay. I closed my eyes and
waited.

Through the night I dozed off a few times and though each
time it seemed longer, in reality it wasn't but only a brief few
seconds. Each time I was awakened but not by the NVA, they were
as quiet as mice. It was the damned mosquitoes and other invisible
critters, and my own paranoia and imagination that would wake
me, that and the occasional far off sounds of someone else's war.
The distant booms of conflict, maybe mortars, rockets or artillery,
resonating softly through the dark mountains and valleys.
Somewhere out there someone was dying but not here, not yet, not
me. I looked to the sky directly above me through my covering
brush and I could finally see a hint of deep gray light telling me it
was nearly dawn. I was at last relieved until the reality of my
situation sunk in once again. I was still in a hole surrounded by
NVA and with the coming light there was a damn good chance I
would be compromised. I tried to see through the bush to assess
their number but there was insufficient light. Were they still there
and if so, how many? Then a minute later I caught a glimpse of
some movement, very slow and deliberate. He came closer and
closer still, and with each movement his head turned and looked in
my direction. He knows, I thought. The bastard's coming to kill
me! I curled my arms over the .45 against my gut to muffle the
sound of the click as I slowly pulled back the hammer then lifted
the gun and pointed it directly at the shadowy dark figure making
his way to my hole. My sweaty nervous finger tightened on the
trigger and just as I was about to squeeze I heard the whisper.

"Fusco."

At first I didn't answer. Not sure of what I heard.

"Fusco."

It was Coma.

"Here," I whispered in relief.

He moved quietly to my hole and began quietly removing the
camouflage cover. "You okay?" he whispered.

Before I could answer he brought his fingers to his mouth demanding silence, then motioned for me to follow. I replaced the .45 and grenade, grabbed my gear and M-16, quietly crawled out of the hole and moved out behind him. After having gone about fifteen yards we met up with Farmer who was waiting near the body of a dead NVA soldier. I stared at the body then at Farmer.

"This dumb shit was asleep," Farmer whispered to me with a slight smile, then said to Coma, "We've got a clear exit out of this nest if we move out directly to the east. Then we can circle around to the north for extract. I'm pretty sure that's a safe AO."

Coma agreed and we moved off quietly. As we did he looked at me and I saw a rare brief smile of approval come through the green and black camo face. He patted me on the shoulder then shoved me forward to follow Farmer. I didn't care where the hell we were going. I only knew I felt a hell of a lot safer in their company.

When we were a good distance away from the NVA at the LZ Coma got on the radio and called for an emergency extraction. Twenty minutes later we were at the extraction point, popped smoke, and were picked up by a wayward Gladiator Huey who responded to our call with a Cobra flying cover. Once we were safely on board, Coma called in the sit rep on the proposed LZ, stating it was hot and surrounded by NVA. Before we were even home at Holloway the LZ and immediate perimeter area had been saturated with artillery and fried with napalm. The ARVN insertion was cancelled. It was considered a blown mission.

After the debriefing and turning in the explosives, it occurred to me that what was really blown on that mission was my mind, and of course, any semblance of operational security and intel confidence. Coma said little to me other than to advise a hot shower and a hot meal. I guess he figured the lesson had been taught and learned, so in his typical fashion he found it unnecessary to waste words. I tried to take his advice but the shower was cold and the meal was only a mix of canned C-rats heated up in Mueller's electric fry pan. As for Coma's lesson, I did learn something. I learned you are never more aware of life until you are near death. If there was more to learn then maybe, like Coma, I would look for it in a bowl of Cheerios some day, but for now I would file that newly procured wisdom away for future reference because at the moment, not having slept in two days, I was drained and too damn tired to care. I got stoned and laid back wondering if Samson had taken care of my newly discovered personal problem as I was told he would. I had complete faith in Samson even though I didn't know him that well. He was the kind of guy who does what he says he's going to do, a decent guy who didn't play mind games or give in to the social bullshit. Knowing that, I gave him my full faith and trust and fell asleep reminding myself to buy him a bottle or two – if I ever woke up.

CHAPTER 39

GHOSTRIDER DOWN & OUT

By now most of the remaining Ghostriders had been distributed among the various companies of the 52nd with only a handful remaining to perform the final task of closing out the company. Like Randy said, we were getting short, but as each day passed and I grew closer to my departure date I found it difficult to think about much else. On my occasional visits to the Ghostrider company area it seemed as though I was watching the death and dissection of a once great formidable beast. Hooches were empty, the choppers, like the men, had been farmed out or adopted by who knows who and to who knows where. It was a slow death that would probably culminate with only a brief pointless ceremony retiring the company colors, then nothing, as though we, as a proud unit, had never existed.

It was difficult filling the time, even in our makeshift luxury hooch, so I started catching rides just for the hell of it. I would jump a chopper heading for anywhere, the Pleiku Air Force base, Artillery Hill, Camp Enari, An Khe, the engineer base, then turn right around and catch a ride back. Anywhere just to get in the air. It was easy because nobody cared. As always, when I flew I had no damn idea where I was, having never even seen a map of II Corps or even Vietnam but that didn't seem to matter. There was something about being in the air, about being on the move, even if it had no real purpose. Maybe I could have pursued a permanent assignment as a gunner but then I didn't know where that would have taken me or whom it would have made me answerable to. I decided instead to stick with my ghost soldier status and just wing it.

Graham was still at Ops and at my request he started selling my services as a substitute gunner. It wasn't a bad arrangement. Twenty-five bucks here, fifty there, just to fly junk missions. I had become a flight whore, getting paid to give guys ground time or safe time as they grew short. On those flights there was never much said except on those occasions when I bumped into a former Ghostrider pilot or crewman, or maybe one of the guys I'd met briefly at the 170th. It seemed we were all lost children now, just counting down the days. But even that petered out when Graham went home. Then oddly enough, during the predawn of what I thought would be an uneventful Sunday morning, a loud knock on the hooch door rolled me out of my hammock to find Okie Dillinger standing there in the dark with a grin and two M-60s.

"Oh, gee. I didn't wake you did I?" he said sarcastically with a laugh.

"Shit yeah," I groaned. "What the hell time is it?"

"Let's put it this way," said Dillinger, "even the roosters are still in the barn coppin' Zs."

"What the hell are you doing here?" I asked, falling back in my hammock after opening the door. "You just getting in?"

"What? Who's here?" moaned Mueller from the comfort of his triple layer mattress bunk across the hooch.

"It's nobody," I answered.

"Nobody. Oh, thanks a lot, buddy. Never thought of myself as a nobody," said Dillinger.

"Oh man, I think I just went to sleep an hour ago so this better be good," I grumbled.

"Oh it is," answered Dillinger with a laugh. "You have been summoned Sergeant Fusco. By the Chief himself."

"I don't want to be summoned by the Chief. It's too damn early and I'm on vacation."

"Vacation my ass. You're in the Army boy. Get your ass up and into your nomex. And if you can do that in less than two minutes we might even have time to grab some of that traditional early mission morning chow."

"Now why would I want to do that?" I asked, covering my head with my silky nylon camo poncho liner.

"Because we got to fly a mission. And after that mission we got a diabolical plan to spend two days in Ban Me Thuot to celebrate Chief Chief's promotion."

"You mean they were dumb enough to promote Chief Chief?" I asked as I sat up slowly, balancing and trying not to roll off the hammock. "So what do we call him now, Chief Chief Chief?"

"Hey, that's funny. That's real funny. I gotta tell him that one. Now get your stoner ass outta that native basket and get crackin' son. I'm hungry and we got beaucoup dinks to deliver someplace in the hills of this beautiful tropical circus."

"Jesus Christ, Dillinger. Isn't it against the law to be that chipper in the wee hours of the morning? If not it should be. Shit. Just because your country-ass likes to get up before God doesn't mean the rest of us do."

"Hey man, didn't you hear what I said? I said Ban Me Thuot. You know, that little Frenchie Shangri-La town in the hills down south a ways. I hear it's got French architecture and French speaking half French Vietnamese girls and all that other cool shit."

"Other cool shit. Sounds fascinating. Probably just another Dodge City," I said as I pulled off my lightweight jungle fatigues and dragged on my nomex and boots. "Okay. But I'm only doing this because… well shit. I don't know. But you're gonna owe me, Okie."

Dillinger shoved a cold heavy M-60 in my arms, hung my flight helmet over the barrel and we headed out of the hooch for the mess hall. I could see immediately that he was right, the roosters weren't even thinking about waking up, and according to my watch that hadn't quite come into full focus yet it was coming up on 0400.

"It's pretty damn early. We either got a long ways to go or it's a big mission. Or, once again your ass is up and crackin' too damn early. Which is it?" I asked.

"So what's wrong with being an early bird?"

"I repeat, which is it?"

"Yeah, my ass is up early. But according to Chief Chief it's just a little CA. Dumping a bunch of dinks someplace in the Ia Drang, then we peel off for a hash and trash run to some FOB, then Chief Chief weasels us two days in Shangri La."

"An ARVN CA in the Ia Drang. Typical. Probably another FNG advisor looking for brownie points by showing off his pet gooks. And for this you thought of me. At 0400 no less. Should I be honored?"

"Damn right, troop. Now step it up 'cause I'm hungry."

"Shit, man. Your skinny ass is always hungry. And why are you so happy? We're in Nam. You're not supposed to be happy here unless you're drunk, stoned, stupid, gettin' laid, or going home. So what the hell's with you, man? Are you sick or something?"

"You guessed it."

"Guessed what?"

"Home. Well, not quite home, but just as good," corrected Dillinger as he slung the heavy M-60 over his shoulder. "Remember I extended for the rest of my enlistment? You know, the nine months I have left?"

"Yeah, I remember. Stupid. Real stupid. So?"

"Yeah, so I found out yesterday that I got me a little leave time for my troubles. I'm meeting' my wife and kid in Hawaii. Leaving in a week and a half. You know I didn't realize how much I missed them until… well, you know."

"And that makes you happy? Dumbass, just think how happy you'd be right now if you had gone home weeks ago like you were supposed to."

"Are you always this hard to get along with in the morning?"

"Only if I'm awake," I yawned.

"Ah," said Dillinger as we entered the mess hall. "This will fix you up. Some of that dark heavy sludge the Army calls coffee. A shot of this and some SOS will give you a whole new perspective."

Dillinger was right but I wouldn't admit it. The coffee did smell good, as did whatever else was cooking in the mess. There was something about the combined odor of various breakfast items floating through the cool pre-dawn air that was enticing if not comforting, civilized, and reassuring. "When we get back I'm going to kill you," I told him.

"See, you're thinking clearer already," he laughed.

The Okie was a lot smarter than he put on and his early bird theory affording us a leisurely breakfast was a good one. Not being rushed as I usually was in the morning let the food and drink go down a little easier, and after the first few bites I could actually taste it. It also gave me more time to prepare mentally for what was most likely going to be a long day. I snatched some fruit and a couple of the small individual cereal packs, Cheerios, as we left the mess. Those items along with a couple of Cokes from the hooch fridge, a canteen of water, and some C-Rats, were all stuffed in my flight bag and secured under my seat in the gun well as we began our pre-flight.

Dillinger was pulling off the air intake filters when he suddenly burst into laughter.

"What's so damn funny?" I asked as I secured my gun.

"Half Wrench," he said. "Every time I do a pre-flight for some reason it reminds me of that day Half Wrench got killed."

"Jesus Christ, Okie, there's nothing funny about that."

"No. I mean before the mortars, before you showed up. Half Wrench was telling me how we should fly into LZs showing our bare ass to freak out the gooks. He had this theory that we should fly in there shootin' a moon and singin' In-a-gatta-da-vita instead of shooting our 60s. Said we should write peace on one cheek and love on the other."

It was good for a laugh but the memory of what happened to Half Wrench played with the emotions in both of us. We rested the beams of our flashlights on the PSP, sat silently on the edge of the deck and lit a cigarette. Fifteen minutes later the pilots showed and twenty minutes after that we were cleared and in the air, along with five Gator slicks from the 119th. We picked up a load of ARVNs someplace on the other side of Pleiku, rendezvoused with three cobras as escorts, then headed southwest for the Ia Drang. Flying with Chief Chief was business as usual, lighthearted and lively, but still serious business. And of course, he still flew by the seat of his pants, pants that included his ever-present small flat silver flask in the pocket and a spare bottle in his bag.

"Hey Fusco, did you hear about Pully Johnson?" asked Chief Chief over the COM as we cruised through the dark morning sky.

"Negative. Haven't heard anything. You're not going to tell me some bad news are you?" I answered as I sucked in the cool morning air that came with the altitude.

"With Pully the news is always good. Even when it's bad," said Chief Chief.

"Okay, I'll bite. What's he done this time?"

"He got out. A civilian now. Went to New York and was flying luxury shuttle choppers from the top of skyscrapers to LaGuardia Airport. Was making some pretty sweet change too."

"Was?" I asked. Just then something cracked and I turned to see the ARVN soldier sitting nearest me had dropped his M-16 on the deck. He quickly retrieved it then looked back at me embarrassed and nervous. I was surprised to discover he was young, very young. Just how young was difficult to tell, but certainly too damn young to be wearing a uniform. I guessed around 14. Just as he turned away from me he was slapped up side the face by his squad leader. Physical discipline was common with those guys. I thought of tossing the mean bastard out the side but quickly dismissed the idea knowing the action would be impossible to defend in a military court.

"Yeah. I got a letter from him," continued Chief Chief. "Said they pulled his license."

"They yanked his pilot's ticket?" I asked, surprised, knowing that if there was one individual on the planet who couldn't stay on the ground it was Pully Johnson.

"Yep. He said in the letter he heard about an anti-war demonstration down on the street in Manhattan so he decided to go down for a look see, then got pissed off and low level dusted the whole damn bunch of protesters right there in the middle of Manhattan. Then he buzzed the entire length of Broadway and back, including a few side trips. Said most of his passengers freaked out and lost their cookies. But he had one hell of a good time. Wouldn't trade it for anything."

"Damn, they pulled his ticket," I said. "That's like chopping the wings off an eagle. Is he in jail?"

"Oh hell no. You know Pully. Always in the shit and comin' out smellin' like roses. Somebody intervened and scooted him out of the country. I think it was the CIA. Sent him off along with a shipload of AH-1G Cobras as a flight instructor. Now he's flying for the Israelis."

"No shit?"

"No shit. Pully Johnson is now buzzing Ahabs and singing Hava Nagila. Typical, right? Just fuckin' typical."

The thought of Pully Johnson raising hell in the Middle East was comical, and the thought of what he might do if and when he was ready to break his contract was even more entertaining. Where would he end up then, I wondered.

"Who's Pully Johnson?" I heard our peter-pilot ask.

"A legend of exceptional achievement," laughed Chief Chief. "I'll fill you in on him later."

I didn't have much of a chance to meet our co-pilot because most of our preflight conversation was taken up with our plans for Ban Me Thuot. I think his name was Harris or Howard or something like that. But I did notice that he too was a little on the young side and obviously inexperienced. I wasn't concerned, however, because if that were true then he was pretty much just along for the ride and we were in good hands as usual with Chief Chief at the stick. Stupid, I thought, as I looked out over the dark hills and valleys that were just now feeling the first warm streams of the light of dawn, imagine me sizing up a pilot as though I was some kind of seasoned veteran. Had I come that far, I asked myself. In less than a year had I lost myself and become someone else that I don't even know? Was I competent enough or did I just quit caring like so many others?

"Okay folks, listen up," Chief Chief's voice crackled again over the COM. "It's a small LZ so we're dropping in sets of three. Gator 6 will take in the first drop and we'll lead in the second. Get your heads and guns ready ladies. ETA to the LZ five minutes."

The LZ. It didn't even have a name. Not for me anyway because I never asked. I'd gotten to where I didn't even bother with the details any more. Not that I ever did or could. In that way I hadn't changed at all, much like a lot of other guys I supposed. Muddling through a war knowing little but possibly giving a lot, maybe giving up everything, maybe dying without knowing where or why.

Our daisy chain of choppers dropped down just after passing over a high saddle between two medium size mountains and as we flew through a gradually declining pass I could now see the LZ in the distance. It wasn't easy to distinguish in the low light but having just been saturated with artillery fire the resulting smoke rising slowly and mixing with the morning mist was a give-away.

The cobras peeled off and dropped down to prep the LZ with a mad minute of suppressing fire. Then I saw the COC chopper for the first time, above as usual, high and dry and calling the shots, the gods making the decisions as to who lives and who dies. Down below, except for a few fresh craters from the arty barrage, the LZ appeared to be fairly level, a manageable piece of ground covered with tall grass and few, if any, obstructing small trees or brush. Still it was uneven enough that we would not touch down but instead just hover at a few feet. It was situated near a slope which led to a mountainside that pitched ever more drastically as it grew in height. The opposite side of the LZ was bordered by jungle canopy that became thicker and higher the further away it grew from the clearing.

It was a textbook action. An arty barrage followed by a mad minute of cobra gunship suppression, and then the spray of bullets into the perimeter from the M-60s of the first three choppers as they made their approach. They quickly off loaded their ARVN troops and lifted away. As the ARVNs exited the choppers they spread to the edge of the LZ to secure the perimeter and no sooner had the first three aircraft cleared did we drop out of our orbit to treetop and into the LZ as well. Chief Chief led the way and as his hover brought us to a halt just above the ground, I looked about the waving flattened grass feeling relieved to discover it was a cold drop, a safe LZ. Chief Chief gave the okay and Okie and I both directed the ARVNs to exit. It was a practiced choreography necessary to prevent too much uneven shift in the load that would rock the aircraft and possibly blow the hover.

The young ARVN next to me was the first to begin his exit but as he was about to jump to the ground a round of enemy AK fire struck him square in the chest and threw him back onto the deck clutching his wound. Witnessing that, the other ARVNs on our chopper froze and refused to dismount. The chatter in my headset quickly increased but became nothing more than a confusing buzz when my mind focused instead on the many weapons flashes popping off just inside the dark shadows of the tree line. Suddenly a continuous hale storm of plinks and planks of enemy rounds hit and penetrated the aircraft. I opened up with my 60 but it seemed they were everywhere and the more I peppered the area the more there seemed to be. I fired and kept firing, wondering why we were still on the ground, not realizing that only seconds had past.

The ARVNs who had landed in the first drop began retreating, using the cover of my fire in a desperate attempt to sprint for our chopper. In their hot panic some were shot down in stride, others even tossed their weapons as they desperately jumped or climbed aboard on both sides, pulling and shoving each other in an effort to find refuge from the intense fire, even using each other for cover. The jumbled mess only provided a better target for the rain of fire from the dark perimeter of the LZ. The enemy must have rushed into established positions immediately after the artillery barrage, then set up and waited, as they often do, for the first flight to offload their troops. If we were performing a textbook CA, they were performing a textbook ambush.

"Shit!" I heard myself saying. "Shit! Shit!"

The sound of my own voice seemed to beat out that of my gun and the noise of the chopper, but gave way to the reception of Chief Chief's orders over the COM as he tried to get us off the ground.

"We're heavy!" he yelled. "We're too damn heavy! Keep em off! Kick 'em off! I can't pull enough torgue!"

At first I didn't understand, then it came to me as I noticed how the ship bounced then dragged its skids, rose and bounced again. The ARVNs, instead of firing and fighting back, ran and piled on board in an effort to escape. The result was we were overloaded with the desperate and dead, and couldn't get off the ground. And even more started to climb aboard. I kicked one in the shoulder and he fell into another sending both to the ground. I resumed firing until another, an ARVN Captain, showed up suddenly from under the tail boom and tried to climb into my gun well. I yelled and protested but he continued, grabbing at my arm, pulling it away from the gun. I finally just kicked him in the face, sending him to the ground. Just as I was about to resume firing on the tree line, the ARVN Captain, still on his back on the ground, pulled his .38 side arm and pointed it at me. I quickly brought the 60 down to fire in defense but before I could, he jerked back and went limp, having lost most of his head and face from a heavy round that penetrated his helmet.

The chopper bounced and skidded once again in a failed effort to lift off. Again I opened fire on the many flashes emanating from the tree line but in the heat of the moment I forgot what I had been taught about the M-60, to fire in controlled burst, not to fire continuously, not to run the gun hot. Instead I fired a continuous spread. As I did the ARVNs on board who were still alive finally got the message and were now tossing off their dead comrades and even their wounded. The effort lightened the load noticeably but not enough. When Chief Chief finally got us off the ground I was still firing. The big bird strained, gained another few feet, and then just as we began to move forward my hot gun caused a round to explode in the chamber. Something struck my helmet and the explosive hot powder flash swept across my face like a quick broad sweep of a blowtorch. I could feel the chamber explosion had seared my hands as well. I jerked back against the bulkhead and brought them to my helmet and quickly realized the visor had saved my eyes but I had little time to assess the rest or to dwell on the pain because at the same moment something impacted the chopper. A heavy round or two of an NVA .51 cal had penetrated the engine causing it to seize up. The aircraft dove and twisted sending the right skid and nose into the dirt, then cart wheeling the entire fuselage and sending the large main rotor blades into the ground where they shattered into pieces, dangerous shards whipping violently through the air in all directions. One ARVN attempted to jump from the starboard side but was crushed and nearly sliced in two by the heavy cargo door that came unlatched and forcefully slid forward when we nosed into the ground. The twisting crash ejected other ARVN soldiers from the port side and threw me out as well with my leg catching the gun mount and whipping me around into an uncontrolled flight of about twenty-five feet, to eventually land and roll into a disoriented heap in the tall grass. At the same time the chopper came down hard on its side, crushing and killing Dillinger under a mass of metal and crushing both of Chief Chief's legs, though he likely felt no pain because either during or immediately after the crash, he caught two rounds in his chest and one through the side of his helmet. Our co-pilot was still alive and still strapped in his seat but losing blood profusely from a wound to his face where a bullet had entered under his chin and exited just under his eye.

I laid there surrounded by the tall grass and the sound of constant fire. Dazed I rolled over and tore off my helmet just in time to see our other two choppers rise and escape above me, their violent rotor wash tossing our chopper's debris and flattening my grassy cover. Suddenly I was exposed, alone in the middle of an LZ without a name, in a country that wasn't mine. An odd thought flashed through my mind - would I have time to cry before I die? Would I have time... Then, I don't know where I am, I thought. If I get out of this where will I go? Am I going to die here tied to a tree with a note and a knife through my heart? I reached for my .45 but it was gone, apparently ripped out of its holster when I was ejected from the aircraft. I fell back, dizzy, and looked to the sky, to the east as the sun shown over the mountains and the morning mist was rising to become clouds. Then something came over me, seized me and told me to relax, that all would be well, that I wasn't supposed to die. Everything became surreal and quiet. I didn't hear the mini-guns from the cobra as it opened up on the NVA who were approaching my position just as I didn't hear the rockets tearing into the enemy entrenched around the LZ. I was no longer aware and no longer worried about anything. I heard only the grass that surrounded me as it began to wave from a distant rotorwash. It was as though I was once again walking in a salty breeze among the sea oats and dunes at the beach. Now, oddly enough, I wanted to stay. It was quiet and peaceful, and somehow I had made this place my own and I wanted to just lay back and stay awhile.

Suddenly there came another explosion and my mind clicked and I looked up to discover a chopper hovering just above the ground about twenty-five yards away. I struggled to see the pilot through the smoke and confusion. He turned his head and looked at me and smiled. Thigpen, it was Thigpen! Of all the pilots in Vietnam, CWO T.T.Thigpen, the man who would make war a pure and sanitary, noble and morally acceptable endeavor was rescuing me. I sat up and saw Thigpen's gunner waving for me to come to the chopper. I rose and started running only to fall flat on my gut when my leg gave way. What was that? What the hell is wrong with you Fusco? Get up and run! I rose again and fell again. There was something wrong with my leg, with my knee, and my face. What is that shit on my face? I wiped my hand across my face and when I brought it away it was red and wet. I looked again to the gunner and he continued to wave me on, beckoning, telling me to try again. I rose once more and hobbled along until I reached the chopper where the gunner extended his hand to help me aboard. When I took hold I looked up into his face. Jesus Christ! It was Jesus; sure as hell it was our come-Tuesday Jesus. His strong hand pulled me aboard in a single effort. I felt strange, light, as though I were floating. Then I fell to the deck. The chopper rose, nosed forward and slid away. I was rising on a thunderous bird, soaring to safety and into unconsciousness.

"That one's alright," I heard a muffled voice say. "Just keep him juiced up and let him rest. And get these bodies over to Graves."

At the mention of bodies I tried to look around but it was difficult. My eyes moved and my mind told my head to move but it wouldn't. I simply laid there as though I had consumed two of Mueller's OJs and a skillet full of his goulash. I was out of it completely, obviously drugged with something more legal. When one of the bodies in question rolled by I managed to get a quick but foggy glimpse just as they covered the face. He looked familiar but I was too far under the influence to make a connection. The next thing I saw was the face of a woman. I thought it to be hours later but I came to learn it had been nearly a day and a half. Her hands were gently applying something to my face, something that smelled familiar but I couldn't place it. Something that smelled like home.

"Sorry. Didn't mean to wake you," she said in a businesslike manner. "But since you're awake we might as well take care of a few things and get you something to eat. Does that sound good? Do you feel like eating?"

"Where... um where am..."

"You're at the 71st Evac. Pleiku. Do you know where that is?"

"Yeah."

"Good. And do you know who you are?"

"Yeah. I'm... lucky. Real lucky."

"Ah, a sense of humor. That's a good sign. Sounds like your head injury was just superficial but I need a real name."

"Fusco. Sergeant Vincent Fusco. Head… What head injury?"

"What head? The one on your shoulders. You only have one, right? Have you always been a comedian or do you just do shows when you're in the hospital?" she snickered. "Is you're head clear enough to hear the verdict?"

"Verdict?"

"Your injuries."

"Oh. Okay."

"Lets go top to bottom. Apparently a bullet penetrated your flight helmet and grazed your skull causing a concussion but judging from the Ghostrider patch on your uniform you're probably too hard headed for it to cause a serious injury. You also have what appears to be a little too much sun, a hell of a sunburn actually, on your lower face and hands. You want to tell me how that happened?"

"Um… powder flash. A round cooked off in my gun."

"Uh huh. And no damage to the eyes. You *are* lucky aren't you," she said while taking my blood pressure. "Well, don't worry about that. This jell will help and there'll be no scarring. Couple more days and you'll be looking like a movie star again. Now, about your leg."

"Leg?"

"Yeah, you know, that thing down below your ass."

I managed an easy laugh. "What's with the leg?"

"You wrenched it."

"I what?"

"You wrenched it. That means you dislocated your leg at the knee joint and then relocated it or re-set it."

"You mean I broke it and fixed it all at once?"

"Something like that," she said as she checked my pulse. "There was a lot of swelling and we had to drain it a few times. It'll be a little sore for a while but it should heal up fine providing you don't try running any touchdowns any time soon. Do you play football?"

"I did… in another life."

"Thought so," she smiled. "I've got three brothers and they all played. I can usually pick out the jocks when they roll in here."

"So, I guess the verdict is all good news," I said.

"Yep. Now you want the bad news?"

"Bad... You mean there's something else?"

"Other injuries? No. The bad news is the injuries you have aren't bad enough to send you home," she said apologetically.

I sighed in relief after having jumped to the conclusion they might have chopped off a toe or my left nut or some other vital thing. "That's okay," I said. "I DEROS in three weeks anyway."

"Well you are lucky then short timer. Okay, Mr. Lucky, I guess that means you belong to us for a while," she said as she gathered her things. "I'll see you around."

After she left to attend to another soldier patient it occurred to me that I had not gotten her name. I watched her across the ward as she made her rounds. She was right in calling me Mr. Lucky, for I was far luckier than most of the guys there. At least I had all of my parts and hadn't been shredded, torn, or punctured. She moved among them just as she had done with me, caring, yet remaining a bit aloof, an attitude that most assuredly evolved out of the necessity to block the painful emotions of watching too many young soldiers suffer and die. For some there was little she could do other than touch their hand and offer comfort. It takes a special breed of people to do a job like that, I thought. It's a job I could never do.

A few days later Randy showed up and bounced his way to the side of my bed. I could see that the sight of most of the patients in the ward made him uncomfortable so I got up and we strolled outside. The sun felt warm and wonderful, and reassuring. Randy handed me a cigarette and we both lit up. He stood there silent but all the while smiling like the Cheshire cat.

"Okay, what's up?" I asked. "The only time I've seen you smile like that was when you came out of the steam and cream. And don't tell me you re-upped or I'll kick your ass."

"I did it," he smiled. "You asked for it and I did it."

"I asked...? What did I ask for?"

"We closed out the company. You know I never dropped you from the company roster. Never transferred you. So that made it easy."

"Made what easy?'

"You said you wanted to be the last Ghostrider so I did it. I made you the last entry on the last morning report. You are the last Ghostrider of record after me and Captain Patrick."

"No shit?"

"No shit."

"I'll be damned. Thanks man."

"No biggy. You know, I thought Captain Patrick would have caught it, and I think he did, but after the other day I guess he decided to just let it slide. Maybe he thought you deserved the honor. Besides, he had no choice, you had to be dumped off the roster like everybody else, right?" said Randy as he took a drag of his cigarette and checked out the butt of a 71st nurse as she and a medic exited the building. "By the way, you might want to stop by and see him when you get a chance. Just to say thanks. Maybe even buy him a bottle or something."

"Thanks. Thanks for what? He exiled me to the boonies remember."

"You're kiddin' right? I mean shit man the guy saved your fuckin' life."

"What? What the hell are you talking about?"

"Who do you think flew into that hot LZ and pulled your ass out?"

"Thigpen and Jesus."

"Thigpen? Are you serious? Thigpen and Jesus? Oh hell no. No way, man. Thigpen went home seven weeks ago and who the hell knows about that Jesus guy. I never saw him after you left. I don't think he belonged to us anyway, just some nut case wandering loose around Holloway. Nope, you were pulled out of there by Captain Patrick and that Coma dude."

"Coma?"

"Yeah, sorry."

"Sorry?"

"Man, didn't they tell you anything?"

"Well, no, not really. Only what happened to my crew, to Dillon and Chief Chief."

"Yeah, sorry about them too. I liked those guys. But it was Coma and Captain Patrick. Patrick was flying the COC chopper and Coma was along for the ride like he sometimes does, you know? Well, Captain Patrick says Coma insisted they go down and get you so they did. Didn't hesitate a bit, didn't even ask the man in command or anything. Just shot down into that LZ like a New York cabbie. Don't you remember?"

"No. I…"

"Captain Patrick said you tried to get up and fell down so Coma jumped off the chopper and got you. Carried you to the chopper and…"

"And what?"

"He took two rounds doing it. And then just after he put you on the chopper he took another round in the back and one in the neck. Died right there on the spot. Sorry."

I wasn't sure how I should feel. I was confused. The story didn't match anything I remembered after the crash, but I knew Randy was telling the truth. I sat down and leaned back against the sandbags that surrounded the building. After a long silent moment I remembered the familiar face that was being rolled out to graves registration. It was Coma and this time he wasn't going to come out of it - because of me. Dillon, Chief Chief, and Coma. Except for Randy and Mueller that was pretty much the end of my small circle of friends. The rest had all DEROSed or been transferred, or died. My war was over, I thought. I had nothing left to give.

"Sorry if I messed up your day, man. I thought you knew all that stuff."

"No, it's okay."

"But I can make it up to you real quick,' Randy said with a smile and a bit of his Randy dance. "You ready for some good news my fellow pizon?"

"I could use some."

"We got our orders."

"Oh yeah."

"Yeah man. And not only that, we got a two week drop. We're going home two weeks early, my man. Two fuckin' whole weeks!

Actually they had me leaving three days before you but I got mine set back so we can leave together just like when we came in... together. How 'bout that Vince? Two weeks man. That means we're out of here in four days! So pack your shit and let's go. I'm here to bust you out of this joint."

It was indeed good news but really didn't buffer my remorse.

"I have to be released first and I don't think they're going to let me go. They said yesterday they were going to keep me for another week or so just to make sure I was good in the head."

"Head? What the hell's wrong with your head? I mean other than the fact that you're a dien cai dau ugly fuckin' wop."

He finally got a laugh out of me and I could see it made him feel better about the bad news he had dropped earlier.

"I got shot in the head," I laughed. "Not bad. See that little scar up there."

"Oh okay, a hole in your head," said Randy, inspecting the small gash in my skull. "That explains a lot. Was that before or after you joined the Army?"

"Oh that's good. You can do comedy on Laugh In or the Ed Sullivan Show when you get out."

"All I know is I'm not leaving without you so you just sit tight. Like they say in New York, it's not what you know but who you know, and you and I are not without friends."

"What's that mean?"

A chopper cranked up nearby, catching Randy's attention.

"Patience my man. Tomorrow will prove the myth," Randy said as he turned and started for the nearby helipad and the waiting aircraft. "Gotta go. That's my cab. Later man."

I had no idea what Randy had up his sleeve until the next day when a heated conference took place around my bed between my doctor and my personal lobbyist from Camp Holloway. I suppose Captain Wieseman was good as doctors go. I wouldn't know how to judge, other than to assess his bedside manner, which seemed to be pretty much nonexistent. There was a touch of anger there somewhere, although it didn't seem to be directed to or originate from his patients. I wrote it off just as I did with the nurses. The staff was caring but drained, strained, and some even appeared to be strung out. Hell, who wouldn't be after living with that shit day

in and day out? Wieseman might have had a little more reason than
the others, however, since his tour in Vietnam was a sentence
received for injudicious discretions that took place at his last duty
station in the States.

According to one of the medics, our Captain Wieseman was
one of those slick doctor wannabes who tried to beat the system
and the bank by letting the Army pay for his medical training and
then doing an about face. It was a pretty slick deal, no tuition, no
burdensome student loans, and all just for the promise of giving
Uncle Sam a few years service in return, inclusive of a hard
commission while practicing his newly acquired profession. The
trick, especially among many of the young Jewish doctors, was to
suddenly develop religion after they began to serve out their
obligation. As doctors and born again Hebrews, they would stroll
into a JAG office where they would proceed to file a request for a
change of status as a Conscientious Objector. In most cases it
worked like a charm and many of these guys stepped right out of
their boots and into the lucrative profession of a practicing civilian
medical doctor. Many, except Captain Wieseman that is, whom it
seems, while waiting and eagerly anticipating his status change and
discharge, was discovered in an examination room giving more
than just the usual medical treatment to the base Commander's
wife. Needless to say his request for separation was side railed and
subsequently denied. He instead received a transfer to the
highlands of Vietnam where his could conscientiously object all
day long while being up to his ass in blood and guts, and dodging
rockets for a year.

All I know is I wanted out of the Evac more than an inmate
wanted out of death row, and to achieve this I answered all his
questions in the positive, being sure not to give any impression of
ill health. Nevertheless he still insisted on my staying at least
another week for observation, concerned about the possible
residual affects of my head injury. He was a Captain and a
physician, and it was entirely his call, but he was up against the
most powerful force in the U.S. Army, he was up against a
Sergeant Major who was determined to gain my freedom.

Sergeant Major Corklyn was a long experienced soldier's
soldier, a species that was fading fast from the ranks of the Army.

In fact, he was more than that because he had previously served in the U.S. Navy, which accounted for the anchor tattoo on his forearm. The older true soldiers were disappearing fast, mostly because of the policy metamorphosis the Army had been experiencing since before the Korean War, as well as Robert McNamara's frustrating politically oriented corporate type micro-management of the war in Vietnam. During the Korean War politics showed it's ugly and ignorant face to the military and during Vietnam it showed again, but reared up and bit everybody on the ass, causing most of the rank and file and wiser officers to focus more on survival than victory. To Sergeant Major Corklyn that meant taking care of his people, and taking care of his people in this case meant getting my ass on a plane home. It also didn't hurt that he was my former First Sergeant's hooch roomy. Randy had set the wheels in motion by talking to Top Buchinsky who in turn sicked the Sergeant Major on the system at the 71st Evac.

"He's going home," Sergeant Major Corklyn stated forcefully.

"This soldier's not going anywhere," declared Captain Wieseman.

"He's got orders, sir. Got to be out of here in two days," argued the Sergeant Major.

"I don't give a shit what he's got. He's my patient and as long as he's my patient, he stays here until I release him. Got that Sergeant Major?"

"Yes sir. Got it. But I'd like to point out to the Captain that if this man misses his scheduled DEROS... well sir, you can't imagine the hassles that would cause all through the chain of command and all the way back to the States. You know Army paperwork, sir. By the time they figured out he was still here, why you'd be turning him lose, and then where would he be? Then they'd lose him in the system, maybe even show him as AWOL, or MIA, or shit-be-gone, sir, possibly even KIA. Can you imagine trying to fix all that, sir? It would delay his DEROS and possibly even his discharge, and poor Fusco here would be stuck in limbo in Vietnam for who the hell knows how long. Now you wouldn't want that to happen would you sir? And you know eventually they're going to want to know who's responsible for all this shit and confusion in the first place. And then I'd have to tell them it was the doctor's orders. I mean, it is the doctor's orders, right sir? And then... well hell, sir... you know what the Army is capable of when it gets a case of the ass. I heard about this Captain once that was just about to be discharged but got caught boom boomin' a base Commander's wife. You know what they did to that guy? They sent his sorry ass..."

"That's enough, Sergeant Major. You've made your point. I'll release this soldier today. But damnit, if he has any medical complications it'll be on your head. Is that understood?"

"Yes sir. Understood."

"Good," said Captain Wieseman, who then turned to me. "Sergeant Fusco, get the fuck out of my hospital and be quick about it," he ordered, then stomped off.

"Yes sir," I replied with a smile.

"Let's get the hell out of here, Fusco, before that bastard changes his mind," laughed the Sergeant Major.

"Good as done, Top," I agreed.

On the ride back to Holloway Sergeant Major Corklyn educated me on the secret of a long and successful career in the Army. "You see, it's all about respect," said Corklyn. "You can say anything to just about any officer as long as you put a 'sir' in front of it or behind it. I once told a light Colonel in Korea that he was one dumb-ass motherfucker. But I said it with respect by adding a 'sir'."

"And he let you slide?" I asked.

"Didn't have much choice. I didn't leave him any wiggle room. It's not insubordination if you're right. And I was right, he was a dumbass and went home in a box because of it, but only after he caused the death of nearly a hundred good men. We have to salute them and we have to sir them, and the book says we're supposed to respect them just because of their rank, but you and I know better. Takes more than rank to earn a soldier's respect."

He went on to try and convince me that I could do worse than a career in the Army. I appreciated the effort but I couldn't buy it, not then.

Randy and I cleared the base and said our farewells but just before we departed I searched out Ba, my former hooch maid from the 189th and gifted her with three cartons of Salems and thirty bucks. She was the only Vietnamese I came close to knowing and respecting, and leaving her to her fate, meaning the ass-backwards reality of her own country, wasn't a great feeling. I'm sure she would continue working for American G.I.s for as long as they were there, but after that who knows? I was also sure she would continue to browse through that Sears catalogue and dream of another world, our world, that she most likely would never see but there was nothing I could do about it.

The out-processing from Vietnam at Cam Ranh wasn't much different than when we had arrived; the attitudes of the soldiers who were assigned there were the same, the pace was the same, and the heat was the same. If there was a difference it was in those of us being processed out. The change could be seen in our motions, our eyes... our age. We were billeted for a day on the second floor of a classic '40s style transient barracks and in typical nonsensical military fashion they issued us each a set of class-B khakis just for the flight home. Apparently the Army didn't want the embarrassment of any ragged G.I.s stepping off the plane in our stopover in Japan or in the States. The khakis were being fazed out they said, and we would exchange them for class-A uniforms at Fort Lewis, Washington. Stupid, I thought, since the new khakis couldn't be reissued. Money down the drain, or should I say, on the plane, on every plane going out. It was typically wasteful but none of us were going to argue the point. We would have worn clown suits if it meant going home. Hell, we would have gone in our birthday suits. So we cleaned up and put on our new duds and tossed the old ones out a back door that led nowhere except into empty space, but to my surprise, that space was filled with a literal mountain two stories high of dirty worn boots, hats, and boonie fatigues. I hesitated, looking at the Ghostrider patch on the pocket of my old fatigue blouse, then like the others I tossed it into the pile, never thinking that I should keep it, that I might some day want it. I thought only of going home and dumping the uniform was part of the ritual.

Randy and I boarded the plane, settled in and waited while others did the same. When the plane was nearly full a few passengers grew impatient and demanded the crew close the door and take off. It was rude, but in all honestly we all felt the same way. Just get the damn thing off the ground, we thought, imagining all the possibilities, all the things that could happen that would prevent us from departing, from leaving this hell forever. Almost a year prior, when we were flying to Vietnam from the States, the stewardesses were kind and polite and treated us the same as they would any other passenger on any other commercial airline. On this flight, however, we were treated more like cargo and the stewardesses were short tempered and to the point, not offering so much as a smile. Perhaps it was a preview of things to come or maybe the commercial crews were just picking up on the vibes of their passengers. We were all hot, tense, tired, and anxious, and none of us breathed comfortably until the big bird finally lifted safely off the ground, climbed out over the ocean and the pilot kicked on the air conditioning. Many of those on the plane let out a cheer or a few words of joy, others closed their eyes and sagged back heavily into their seats in relief. A handful even shed a few quiet tears.

TYPICAL

Our two-week drop wasn't the only surprise Randy and I enjoyed after we departed Vietnam. As it turned out, we soon discovered the rumors about early-out discharges were true. Anyone arriving back in the States with less than six months remaining in their enlistment was given a discharge. That is unless you chose to re-up, which very few of us did. The entire process took only one day in terms of hours, a day that began with all the steak and trimmings you could eat, a restless night in the rack, and then a day for a debriefing. Then came the receipt of separation pay and a set of class-A's. For the guys coming out of the boonies who had been living on cold C-rats, the steak dinners must have been a real treat, but for them as well as us not even a steak dinner was appealing if it was perceived to be a delay in our discharge process. Be it a day or an hour, it seemed forever until that final bus ride to the Tacoma Airport.

Randy was heading for New York and I for Florida, but we were booked on the same flight as far as Chicago where we would split up. When we checked in for our flight we discovered we had a two-hour wait until our departure so we decided to cruise the airport and find a bar. Our little tour began with a stop in the rest room where I was surprised to discover the trash can in the corner had been stuffed with newly issued class-A uniforms, shoes, and hats. So many in fact, that the can was full and the overflow literally filled the entire end of the room and piled on to the sinks. Randy was a draftee and I was a volunteer but neither of us could bring ourselves to accept such a disdain for the uniform, or to hate it so much as to discard it at the very first opportunity in a public place. Given the social climate of the times and in the eyes of some, we may have been fools for serving in the military but whatever we thought of the war, we were both proud of our service and what the uniform stood for.

As we headed for the bar we walked past a group of half a dozen young people inclusive of a few very attractive young girls.

Two of the girls approached us with a warm smile, each holding a small brown bag.

"Hi there, Army," they smiled.

We slowed our pace and smiled in return.

"We have a welcome home gift for you," they said as they handed us each a small brown bag.

"Thanks," I said, accepting the gift.

"Don't eat it all at once," giggled one of the girls as they rejoined their group.

We thanked them and continued on. As we did Randy opened the bag and looked inside, expecting to find some home made cookies or something similar. "Oh fuck!" he said, stopping in his tracks.

Seeing his reaction I opened and looked in my bag. The odor quickly signaled its contents. It contained human shit. I stopped and turned to face the girls who gave it to us. They stood there laughing and smiling. One of the boys with them shot us the bird, another a peace sign, then one of the girls said with disdain, "Welcome home baby killers."

"Eat shit, soldier boys," said another, laughing.

"Warmongers. Bloodmongers. Baby killers. How's it feel to kill God's children, asshole?" said the prettiest girl, her fair features suddenly becoming ugly.

Their young eyes were full of hate and anger. I started to move toward them with the intent of rubbing the contents of the bag in their faces but Randy grabbed my arm. The group walked off quickly in the face of the threat while he reminded me of our separation briefing and the fact that we were still accountable to the Army for the next forty-eight hours.

"Those assholes aren't worth it, buddy," said Randy.

He was right, but it was a painful reality.

We dumped the bags of shit into a nearby trashcan and found our way to the airport bar where we both ordered up a good strong drink. After a few minutes a soldier who claimed to have also just arrived from Vietnam joined us but it took only a brief minute to peg him as a phony. His hair wasn't regulation, he had a one-day growth on his face, his uniform didn't fit well and wasn't worn properly, and his attempt at military chitchat and acronyms was way off base. This guy was no soldier, not even a reluctant one, and my suspicions were confirmed when he exposed his real intent for joining us by appealing to us to buy him a drink and loan him money so he could get home.

"Didn't they give you a plane ticket?" I asked.

"Yeah," he said. "But I lost it. It was in my bag and somebody ripped it off."

"You mean, somebody took it the same way you took that uniform out of the restroom," I said.

"Hey man, I don't know what you're talkin' about."

"Yes you do, and if you don't get the hell out of that uniform and out of this damn airport in two minutes I'm going to take you back to that restroom and shove your head in the fuckin' shitter."

He slid quietly out of the bar and, I assume, continued out of the airport. We put him out of our minds just as we tried to put the brown bags of shit out of our minds and by the time we had reached Chicago, having continued our consumption on the plane, we were on our way to a fairly good celebratory alcoholic buzz. Randy was to continue on the same flight so we said our farewells on the plane. With his departure I suddenly found myself alone and facing a five-hour layover in the big box that was O'Hare International. I wandered the entire airport, rounding the first floor then the second then repeating the rounds in a mollified culture shock, surrounded by clean people who's only concern seemed to be getting somewhere on time. Everything reached my senses, the smell of the concessions, the footsteps emanating from the base of clean attractive legs, their perfume, and I even overheard conversations expressing serious concerns over matters that, to me, seemed trite and inconsequential after a year of living with the daily possibility of death. I wandered for hours, not once being acknowledged by another person, and so my thoughts wandered as well. For a while I considered not going home at all and even seriously considered disappearing altogether to some unknown corner of the world, but my thoughts always came back to my son who made the decision for me. Then I thought of Chief Chief and Dillinger. I knew little about Chief Chief's people but I did know about Dillinger and even had his address. Like me, he had a wife and young child. If the chopper had flipped on the opposite side then mine would be the ones left behind, I thought. Then what?

The thought motivated me to change my airline ticket and arrange a side trip to San Diego where upon arrival I called Dillinger's wife, Jennie. She and her little girl met me at the airport and we went to a restaurant nearby where we had dinner and discussed my friendship with her late husband and what I knew of his tour in Vietnam, both the good and the bad. And I told her, though not graphically, how he died, knowing that whatever official correspondence she would receive from the Army would likely be sanitized bullshit. We laughed and she cried and more than once spoke of how they were to meet in Hawaii and would have been there now. I asked if the Army had taken care of business and she said that some things such as insurance and other financial matters were still unsettled. When I was processed out at Fort Lewis I received a final pay, inclusive of unused leave time of nearly eleven hundred dollars. I gave her eight hundred of it. I could only have hoped that someone else would have done the same if it had been me.

Following my brief stopover in San Diego it was back to Chicago and then on to Florida. All the while I was conflicted with the decision of whether or not to stay married and each time the decision came down to my son. When I deplaned that morning in Florida I sat in the airport for nearly a full hour. I hadn't told anyone of my early arrival so I wasn't expected. The very day before I left Camp Holloway I received a letter telling me she had moved in with her mother but there was no explanation as to why. I would discover later it was to purge all of her friends who were living off my paycheck before I arrived home, and that the bank account I thought would be full was actually overdrawn. Not even knowing that at the time, however, I still had every reason for a divorce but remained undecided. In a way it all seem trivial now that I was alive and well and back in the world, a world away from the war. I eventually decided to try and make it work and finally grabbed a cab.

When the cab pulled up in front of the house that morning and I offered the driver the cash for the fare, he refused to take it.

"You just get back from Nam?" he asked.

"Yeah."

"Me too. Six months ago," he said as he shook my hand. "Welcome home, man. And good luck. But don't expect any parades."

For many years he would remain the first and only person to offer a sincere welcome home or to acknowledge any other form of appreciation or recognition for my service.

No one answered when I approached the house and wrang the doorbell. We had lived there at her mother's briefly before I left for Vietnam and I knew where to find the spare key so I let myself in, dropped my bags, and just stood there finally feeling safe, secure, and somewhat relaxed. A few minutes later, after a quiet tour through the house, I heard a car pull into the driveway. I looked out the front window expecting, or at least hoping, to see my shiny new red VW and my curly headed kid. It was instead a car and a driver I didn't recognize, but I did recognize my wife as she slid across the front seat to give the driver a long passionate kiss. For some reason I wasn't surprised.

Welcome home Fusco, I thought.

"Typical. Just fuckin' typical," I could hear Chief Chief say.

11,827 U.S. helicopters served in Vietnam, almost all were U.S. Army. They logged more combat flight time during the Vietnam War than any other aircraft in the history of warfare. Over 7,000 were Hueys and Huey Cobras such as those flown by the 189th Assault Helicopter Company.

5,086 were destroyed, killing 4,906 pilots and crew.

189th AHC Ghostrider's Anthem

Their brands were still on fire and
*   their hooves were made of steel,*
Their horns were black and shiny and
*   their hot breath he could feel,*
A bolt of fear shot through him as
*   he looked up in the sky,*
For he saw the riders comin' hard
*   and he heard their mournful cry:*

Yippee-yi-ya, yippee-yi-yo,
*   Ghost riders in the sky.*

Taken from;
2nd verse of the song,
Ghost Riders In The Sky,
by Stan Jones

American G.I.'s Vietnam Anthem

We gotta get out of this place,
If it's the last thing we ever do.
We gotta get out of this place,
Girl, there's a better life for me and you.

Taken from;
Chorus of the song,
We Gotta Get Out Of This Place,
by Barry Mann & Cynthia Weil

ABOUT THE AUTHOR

As portrayed by the principal character in this novel, through the slight of hand of his good friend, the author Frank Mosco was in fact the last Ghostrider of record when the famed 189th Assault Helicopter Company was deactivated in Vietnam in March, 1971. A few years following his discharge from the regular Army he enlisted and served as a member of the very first National Guard Special Forces unit.

Frank began collecting awards for writing while still in high school and as a journalist while in college where he majored in Broadcast Management & Media. He went on to produce material for all forms of media as a reporter, columnist, producer, director, and a photographer. His writing, coupled with his business management and retail experience, led him to form his own advertising & promotions agency but preferring the life of an independent freelancer he eventually returned to writing and photography.

He is a native of Annapolis, Maryland, who after many years enjoying the beaches of Florida now resides and writes near the waters of the Chesapeake Bay in Virginia where he produces mostly fictional novels, of which he says, *"...can be just as strange as reality but far more convenient and definitely more fun."*

As for his post war life he says, *"I've always lived with one foot in the ocean and one in the clouds, all the while hoping like hell the pelicans in between have good vision."*